SHADOW
STITCH

Also by Cari Thomas

Threadneedle
The Hedge Witch

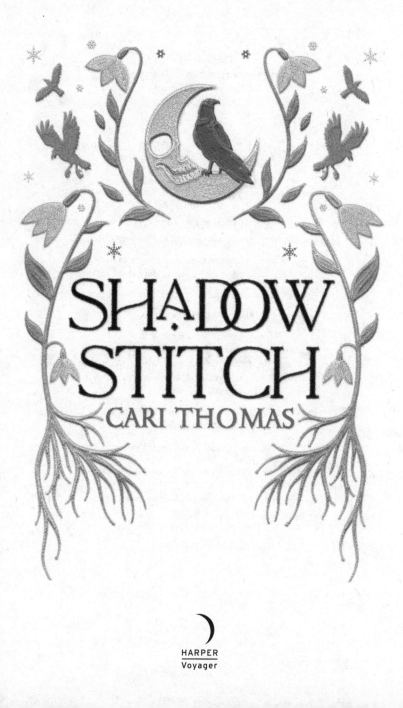

SHADOW STITCH

CARI THOMAS

HARPER
Voyager

Harper*Voyager*
An imprint of HarperCollins*Publishers* Ltd
1 London Bridge Street
London SE1 9GF

www.harpercollins.co.uk

HarperCollins*Publishers*
Macken House, 39/40 Mayor Street Upper,
Dublin 1, D01 C9W8, Ireland

First published by HarperCollins*Publishers* Ltd 2024
24 25 26 27 28 LBC 5 4 3 2 1

A catalogue record for this book is available from the British Library.

ISBN: 978-0-00-866691-0

This novel is entirely a work of fiction.
The names, characters and incidents portrayed in it are
the work of the author's imagination. Any resemblance to
actual persons, living or dead, events or localities is
entirely coincidental.

Set in Adobe Caslon Pro by Palimpsest Book Production Ltd,
Falkirk, Stirlingshire

Printed and bound in the United States

To my husband, James Williams,
for walking through the shadows with me and always seeing my light

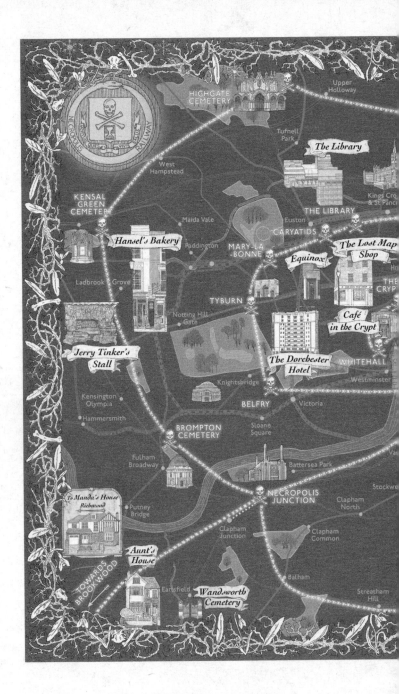

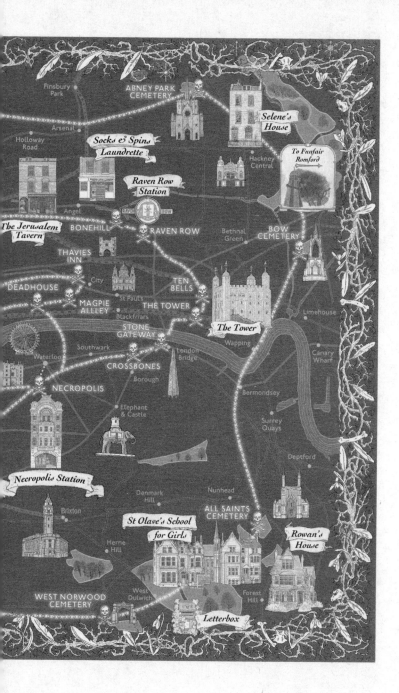

Hel unthreads.

Hel Witch Proverb

One to fall,
Two to get lost,
Three to remember,
Four to distrust,
Five for the heart,
Six for the dark,
Seven to die,
Or learn how to fly!

'*Rhyme of the Ravens*',
Mother Holle Nursery Rhymes

THE KEY PLAYERS

Anna Everdell – Our lead witch, who's grown up under the shadow of her Aunt. Not allowed to practise magic, she's been trained to suppress her emotions, tying them away in her Knotted Cord.

Vivienne Everdell – Anna's cruel Aunt belongs to a grove of witches known as the Binders, who believe magic is sinful and dangerous.

Marie Everdell & Dominic Cruickshank – Anna's mother, a witch, and father, a cowan, who died in tragic, violent circumstances when she was a baby.

Selene Fawkes – An old family friend who went to school with Vivienne and Marie; a hedonistic seductress who specialises in love potions.

Effie Fawkes – Raised by Selene, Effie is rebellious, wild and the self-appointed leader of their coven. Her one weakness is…

Attis Lockerby – Effie's best friend and not-so-secret lover. An insatiable flirt and ladies' man who can often be found in his forge.

Rowan Greenfinch – A wise-cracking, boy-obsessed, self-deprecating member of their coven; hails from a family of Wort Cunning witches who practise botanical magic.

Miranda Richardson – A highly strung, highly driven member of their coven, who comes from a non-magical family.

The Juicers – Darcey, Olivia and Corinne – the ruthless mean girls of their year, named after the green juices they sip each morning.

Peter Nowell – Anna's popular and dashing long-time school crush.

Bertie Greenfinch – Rowan's mum and all round legend in the field of Wort Cunning magic. Gives excellent hugs.

Pesachya – A man with skin covered with words who lives in the magical library buried beneath the British Library. He helped Marie when she came seeking answers to the curse.

Nana Yaganov – An ancient, if somewhat deranged, curse witch with a flair for creating nightmarish visions and a penchant for riddles.

The Seven – The most powerful witches and protectors of the magical world.

The Hunters – Some believe a sect of five members known as the Hunters were behind the witch hunts of the past. However, most witches believe them nothing more than legend.

THREADNEEDLE RECAP

Six women with the same face have been found hanging in the windows of Big Ben. The mystery of the 'Faceless Women' has unsettled the ordinary 'cowan' world, while the magical world knows they are the Seven, protectors of all witches – six found hanging, one disappeared – but who killed them?

Anna's Aunt fears magical exposure, warning Anna that such a thing could lead to witches being hunted once more. Anna must soon follow in her Aunt's footsteps and become a Binder, facing a Knotting ceremony that will leave her magic bound for good.

That is until old family friend Selene arrives at their door with her daughter, Effie, and Effie's partner-in-crime, Attis. On joining Anna's school, Effie and Attis lure Anna into a coven, convincing her to practise magic. But when Anna's spells begin to reveal the seven-circled mark of a curse, 'The Eye', Anna is forced to question the truth of her parents' deaths. They died when she was a baby – her father strangling her mother and killing himself after she accused him of having an affair.

Anna discovers her parents died in the house she lives in, in the room on the third floor that Aunt has sealed off from her. Her search for answers sends her deep into the hidden magical world of London. But suspicions of magic are creeping into the news more and more, while a mysterious organisation has begun to investigate the deaths of the 'Faceless Women', suggesting occult links.

Torn between her Aunt's fears and magic's allure, Anna's magic is spiralling. As she and Attis grow closer and the coven casts a vicious rumour spell at school, tensions and jealousies bubble between Anna and Effie. Tensions that culminate in Effie betraying Anna when she sleeps with her date, Peter, at the summer ball.

Anna is driven back to her Aunt for her ceremony, but that night, breaks into the third floor room discovering her 'father' – although it is actually a replica 'Golem' version of him created by Aunt for her own pleasure. Aunt is forced to reveal that Anna and Effie are twins, cursed to fall in love with the same man; one of them to kill the other over it. The curse goes back through the generations – Aunt and Anna's mother both fell for Anna's father. Aunt claims Marie betrayed her just like Effie betrayed Anna and that the curse must be bound during the ceremony. She warns that it goes beyond them . . . that curses are powerful magic and, with everything going on, will only attract attention.

Anna faces her ceremony. She must sacrifice Effie and Attis to complete the ritual and bind the curse. However, Anna releases her Knotted Cord, unleashing her held-back power and overcoming the Binders. Attis still attempts to sacrifice himself but Anna and Effie unite their magic and save him. Anna turns the Golem on her Aunt, strangling her . . . but when she can't go through with it, Binder Lyanna Withering takes over, killing Aunt.

Selene reveals the truth: that Marie and Vivienne were driven apart over their love for Anna's father, Dominic – Aunt turning to the Binders; Marie and Dominic ending up together. When Marie fell pregnant, she searched for a way to end the curse. But after Anna and Effie were born, Vivienne returned to exact her revenge, binding Dominic's will and forcing him to kill Marie and himself. She blackmailed Selene into helping her frame Dominic and into raising Anna and Effie apart. They would bring them back together aged sixteen to set off the curse so it could be bound.

But Aunt didn't know that Marie had found a solution to the curse – a living spell whose blood could break it: *Attis*. Selene was the one who gave birth to him. Attis and Selene had planned for him to sacrifice himself during the ceremony to end the curse forever. Anna vows she will not let him try to kill himself again.

The book ends with rumours that the Seven have returned but are claiming they are being hunted . . . Meanwhile, the organisation investigating their deaths have rebranded themselves the 'Witchcraft Inquisitorial and Prevention Services' and are publicly stating that the Faceless Women were witches and that magic is a real and growing threat for all. Magic must be kept under wraps but, after the coven's antics at school end up on the news, have they landed themselves right in the centre of the growing storm – *curse and all?*

* * *

They met in secret. They met in darkness. Light was not welcome. The stars pulsed weakly above. They were not welcome either. The walls rose thick and ancient around them – walls of stone; walls woven with bone and magic; walls built not to keep things out, but to keep things in. Beyond, London roiled, restless by night, blaring and bellicose, but within, silence reigned. Silence prickled. The Tower of London had never truly belonged to the city.

One robed figure in the centre, four around the outside. The moon was dark above – the Dark Moon made for the darkest of deeds. They raised their heads but the night recoiled from what lay within their hoods – for they could hardly be called faces at all. Half flesh; half skull. Half living; half dead. One half reflecting the light; the other sucking it into their dark caverns – the voids of their faces where eyes and noses and lips had once been, and now, only rot and bone and hollows deep as death.

They opened their mouths – one side, cheek, lip and tongue flexing; the other, skull, teeth and chasm – and they spoke, but the words were too terrible to comprehend. Words that could have shrivelled the night; plucked the stars from their orbits; stopped London in its tracks; turned everyone within it mad with fear. Words more dead than alive. They echoed like a trapped thing, their echo rebounding between the walls, climbing higher and higher, desperate and hungry, clawing for life, for death, and then, over the walls, escaped—

Flying off into the night, black as the feathers of Hel.

BURIED

Do not bury your dead for they live among us. While their spirits remain active in Hel, their earthly bodies should be regularly bathed, fed and honoured with offerings; their death days celebrated and their altars attended to.

Tending the Dead, Hel Witch Initiation Stage One

I won't look down.
   I won't look down.
   I won't look down.

Anna pulled the cord between her fingers. It was habit more than anything. It offered no comfort now, no knots left in it to hold her together – only rough, bristled cord beginning to fray, like a memory. It had once contained so much of her: her joys, her fears, her silenced griefs, her buried longings, her rage and hate; her love, perhaps. Her life with Aunt ordered into tight bindings of everything she had not been allowed to feel. But the knots were gone now – *why can I still not feel?*

The sky was the emptiest sort of grey, ravens scoring its colourless murk as they moved between the trees, their shrill, indifferent calls the only music in the mute air. The funeral guests huddled around the open grave, their coats black and slick as the birds, their faces grey and bleary too, as if they'd been carved out of the drizzle. There weren't many in attendance – some of Aunt's work colleagues, a few neighbours, a handful of old acquaintances. No Binders. Selene stood out among them in a purple outfit that bordered on inappropriate. Her hair, brighter than anything for miles, tumbled beneath a wide-brimmed hat. No one else seemed to notice that she was entirely dry beneath her umbrella although the rain was coming in sideways. She tried to catch Anna's eye but Anna could not meet it. Instead, Anna looked out over the vast, modern cemetery. Aunt would have approved of its efficiency and organization – endless rows of polished graves, as faceless as death itself. Some had flowers tucked beneath them, wilting in the rain; faded offerings. No one would leave Aunt flowers. No one would visit her grave. It would soon be forgotten, lost among the masses.

I won't look down.
I won't look down.
I won't look down.

Anna clutched the limp and lifeless cord, the world warping and bending around her. Was she really here, at Aunt's funeral? Aunt. *My aunt.* Was Aunt really dead? It didn't feel possible. Aunt had always seemed invincible. An inescapable force. Anna tried to imagine what freedom might feel like but all she could see was grave after grave after grave. How could she live when Aunt was the one who had always given her life shape and meaning? How could she live when Aunt's death was her fault? *All my fault.*

I won't look down.
I won't look down.
I won't look down.

But the cold of the ground began to rise up – over her feet, climbing up her legs like stiff roots, wrapping around her – squeezing – darkness swallowing Anna's mind as she remembered. The day she had undone her knots came back to her in a devastating blur of images: the Binding ceremony, vines tightening, rose petals flying, Attis's blood erupting, her hand in Effie's, their magic uniting, the ragged sound of Attis's breath returning – the most wonderful sound she'd ever heard; the golem's fingers around Aunt's neck as she gasped for air – the worst sound she'd ever heard. The world had turned to magic that day and Anna at the centre of it, sewing its threads into something powerful and terrible.

'Earth to earth, ashes to ashes, dust to dust: in sure and certain hope of the resurrection to eternal life through our Lord Jesus Christ.' The priest bowed his head and the guests followed suit.

I won't look down—
I won't look—
I won't—
I—

Anna looked to the sky. To the leaves dragged from the trees. To the desperate emptiness inside of her. And then – she looked down.

There it was. Aunt's coffin gleaming at the bottom of the grave. Aunt down with the dirt and the worms and decay – everything she'd always hated. Anna tried to look away but she couldn't. The darkness had taken over now – swallowed her. She was down there too. She couldn't see, couldn't breathe – falling and falling with nothing to hold onto—

A scream tore through the air.

Another. Another. Screams erupting all around her. Anna struggled against the darkness – her head jerking back up – trying to understand what was happening, but what she saw did not make it any more comprehensible . . .

The guests were screaming. All of them. Eyes flared wide, mouths gaping, features carved with terror, hollow screams rising from deep within. Mrs Chapman, their neighbour, gripping her face and shrieking; another guest stumbling backwards as they erupted; the priest dropping to his knees and howling to the heavens, as if they held none of the answers he'd promised. The ravens in the trees screeched along, a wretched choir, the noise unbearable, shredding the sky to pieces, so loud it seemed it would wake all the numb and silent dead.

Selene was the only one not overcome. She looked at Anna aghast and then raised her hands to the air and called out: 'Alsamt!'

The screaming stopped abruptly.

Slowly, the funeral attendees began to return to their senses – shutting their mouths, shaking their heads, adjusting hats and coats and clasping hands together once more, as if nothing had happened. As if they hadn't just lost their minds.

The priest clambered back to his feet, continuing. 'Now, let us say the Lord's prayer—'

The guests cast their eyes back down to the grave, and the service trudged along through the rain to its bitter end.

Anna did not look down again.

They held the reception at Aunt's house on Cressey Square. The place had never been so lively – guests nibbling at sandwiches and sipping on sour wine as they offered Anna limp, insincere smiles – *so sorry for your loss*. Anna nodded her way through the room like a hollow wind-up toy, saying the right things, feeling nothing, Selene playing the gracious host – *yes, we were old friends. I know, so terrible, a heart attack at such a young age. We'll miss her terribly.* Anna suspected most of the guests had only come so they could snoop around – to judge and sneer at the house of the woman who had judged and sneered at them.

No one stayed long. After an hour, the whole thing was done and dusted – Aunt's life wiped clean like an accidental spill no one would remember. *Love is all that is left of us and you had little of that, Aunt.* Anna and Selene sat in the kitchen, Selene trying to chase away the silence with chatter, making her way through a bottle of wine.

'Thank the Goddess that's over! Some man had me cornered for half an hour talking me through his fly fishing collection. I do hate cowan funerals. So sombre, so much black. Black is for seduction, not for mourning. I want my funeral to be bursting with colour and men falling to their knees. Champagne fountains. Dancing all night. Wild rituals beneath the moon. It's not a funeral worth attending if there's not *some* nudity—' She tried to catch Anna's eyes with a smile, but, giving up, tipped back her glass. 'Are you sure you don't want some? It might help take the edge off things.'

Anna shook her head faintly.

'It's not the funeral wine if that's what you're worried about. I filched it from the drinks cabinet. One of Vivienne's best, I hope. Makes it taste better knowing it would piss her off.' Selene cackled but Anna didn't respond. Selene bit her red lips and put down the glass. 'Matchstick, what happened at the service . . .'

Anna tensed. She could still hear the screams, she'd been hearing them all afternoon. She lowered her eyes, shrinking into her seat. 'I didn't do anything . . .'

'I know you didn't do it on purpose,' Selene said softly. *Too softly.* 'But I'm worried, darling. Your emotions . . . your magic – they broke free. You have to allow yourself to grieve. It's OK to cry—'

Selene reached a hand towards her. Anna looked at it, not knowing how to take it, not knowing how to cry.

She stood up from the table, gathering the plates. 'I better clear up.'

Selene sighed behind her. 'Don't worry, darling, I've got cleaners coming any minute. Are you sure you don't want me to arrange removal men too? We can get this place all cleared out—'

'Not yet,' Anna replied abruptly.

'OK.' Selene sounded unsure. 'Well, why don't you check there's nothing else you want to bring back with you before we leave?'

Anna looked around the kitchen. Aunt's tea towels. Aunt's glasses. Aunt's weighing scales. Aunt's shopping list, half-written on the fridge. The scent of her still in the air – magnolia perfume, garden soap, the sharp oil of her hair. Anna didn't want to pick through it all, to pack it up, she just wanted to shut tight the doors of the house and leave it all to rot.

'It's all yours now,' Selene muttered inauspiciously.

It was. Anna had learnt the full truth of it all now. Her mother, Marie, had bought the house quickly and quietly with family money left to her after her father had died. After Marie's death, Anna had inherited it, not that she'd ever known. As Anna's guardian, Aunt had simply taken control of proceedings and had chosen to move them in. *Why? Why live in the house where you killed her?* It was a fine house, a respectable neighbourhood – Aunt would have liked all that, but no, that was not the reason. Anna knew Aunt would have wanted to be close, to soak in the blood of her sins, to live beneath the shadow of the curse, to keep a dead-eyed golem-version of Anna's father in the third-floor room where she'd killed Anna's parents. *Punishment and pleasure. Pleasure and punishment.* They'd been one and the same to Aunt.

Anna wondered why her mother had chosen this unassuming house on this unassuming street in Earlsfield. Perhaps its inconspicuousness was exactly what she'd been looking for – somewhere to hide, to disappear so Aunt and the Binders wouldn't find her. But they had. Once Anna was eighteen and could legally sell the place, she would, but until then, she just wanted to lock its terrible memories away.

The doorbell rang.

'The cleaners!' Selene jumped up from her seat, clearly glad for the distraction. 'Go on, have a quick look around, see if there's anything you want to keep. Or burn. I'm a dab hand at sacrificial bonfires.'

Anna managed her first smile of the day. She went through the other door into the quiet of the living room and it died on her lips. She could see it all before her – the Binders lost in their magic, thorns piercing flesh, Attis and Effie bound in the centre, Aunt beckoning Anna to *kill them, kill them, kill them* . . .

The room before her was chilled and bare now. Everything as it had always been – the photographs of her and Aunt along the mantlepiece,

Aunt's books on the shelves, the roses still in their pot, withering now. Anna walked past Aunt's armchair, still moulded to the shape of her head. She drifted a finger over Aunt's Bible on the table beside it – Aunt had used it to select their embroidery verses from. *Stitch in, stitch back* . . .

Anna turned to the piano last. It tugged at her from somewhere deep but she snipped the thread. It had never been her piano. All the music she'd ever played, all the moments of joy in her life . . . all of it had belonged to Aunt. Aunt had been conducting the whole damn thing. Anna could almost hear the sound of the metronome ticking with Aunt's judgement even now. The feeling of Aunt over her shoulder ready to tell her she wasn't doing it right – to play faster, slower, different, better; to be more than she was. *Never enough.* Blood began to well up through the cracks in the keys, onto the floor—

Anna blinked and it was gone.

She stumbled from the room and into one of the cleaners. 'I'm – sorry, sorry—'

The woman smiled. 'Want me to start in there, love?'

'Sure – I – yes—'

Anna made for the stairs, wondering if she was going mad. *Will I ever be free of Aunt? Will I ever breathe again?* She looked up the stairway and could feel it already. The darkness of the third-floor room pouring down from above – a flood that would drown her. She hadn't been up there since that night but it had filled up her dreams ever since. She would go there now and face it. Lock it shut and be done with it forever. *No way out but through.* Aunt had used to say that. She'd never believed in giving up easily, Anna had to give her that much credit.

Anna started upstairs. On the first floor, she walked past her old bedroom, the shadow of her and Aunt flickering in the corner of her eye – Aunt combing her hair in the mirror as they had done every night of Anna's life. She passed Aunt's room, still as meticulously ordered as ever. She stopped at the bottom of the next staircase. Her legs felt suddenly like stone, the stairway above her narrowing and stretching out as if it would go on forever. As if she'd never reach the top. *One step at a time. I can do this.* She began her ascent. Each step harder than the last. The air seemed to thin, a dizziness took over her, her feet growing heavier, like anchors trailing through sludge. The darkness pushed down on her, squeezing the breath from her. She gripped the bannister, pulling herself upwards . . . *one more step . . . one more step . . .* Her vision began to cloud at the edges. She leant forwards, feeling as if she might faint. *One more step . . .* It took every last scrap of her effort in her, and then—

She rounded the corner at the top and scrabbled for the light switch. The light came on but the shadows did not dissipate. The silence slipped itself around her.

The door ahead was open.

It felt wrong to see it that way. Its secrets released. The room in which Aunt had killed her parents. The room that had contained their family curse for sixteen years. *Open.* The curse was out there now. *Inside of me now.*

Anna propelled herself towards the door. Once inside, she twisted around, expecting something to jump out at her. But there was nothing – no ghouls or golems or Aunts waiting to get her. Nothing but a room. Someone had opened the curtains and made the bed. Light streamed in. And yet, Anna could feel the violence as if it were written into the walls, a language made of blood and screams and terror; as if, somewhere, what had happened here was still echoing over and over . . .

She spotted her mirror on the dressing table. The mirror she'd made out of magic and moonlight, the mirror that had helped her get into the room, cracked into pieces now in its case, a shard fallen loose beside it. She picked up the broken slice of glass and placed it back into the missing space. She gasped. The pieces of glass began to melt together, turning briefly mesmerizingly liquid like the surface of a lake finding stillness after a storm. And then – the mirror was whole again. Anna tapped the glass and found it solid, only the smallest whisper of a hair-line crack at the bottom where the large shard had rejoined. But when Anna picked it up – she almost dropped it again.

Aunt's face stared back at her. For a split second, Anna had thought it her own face – the same high cheekbones, red hair, green eyes. But it was Aunt. Anna moved her head to the side and Aunt's moved too. Anna's insides turned to worms, writhing and twisting with horror. She felt her own face drain of colour, but the face in the mirror did not. It flushed with life. The eyes gleamed. A smile played dreadfully along the lips. Aunt tipped her head back and began to laugh. It was Aunt's laugh too, like vinegar poured on a laugh so that it was puckered and sour and bitter and taunting. Blood dripped down the walls behind her—

'Matchstick—'

Anna spun around to find Selene in the doorway.

'Darling, are you OK?'

Anna held the mirror to her chest, her heart hammering against the glass. 'I – yes, I'm fine.'

Selene's frown deepened. 'You shouldn't have come in here.'

'I just wanted to . . .'

'I know, but places like this are better left shut. No point opening old wounds. Come on, it's miserable in here, let's go.'

Anna noticed that Selene had not crossed the threshold of the door. The room held dark memories for her too. Selene turned and Anna quickly wrapped the mirror in an old sheet – around and around like a shroud. She tucked it under her arm and followed Selene down the stairs.

Selene slowed on the landing and swivelled back to Anna, fluttering her fingers. 'Actually, darling, there was something I'm looking for. Perhaps you could help?' Her voice was light but there was tension beneath.

Anna took a moment to answer. Aunt's face was still in her mind. 'Er – yes, sure. What?'

'Oh, it's nothing really. Just a ring. A trinket. It used to be mine. I already checked Vivienne's jewellery box but it wasn't there. Anywhere else she might have put it?'

'There was another box in her room . . . I can check.'

They entered Aunt's room, Anna doing her best to ignore the scent of Aunt's perfume still souring the air; the uneasy feeling, as she reached into Aunt's bedside cabinet, that she might be caught in the act. She pulled out a small wooden box – she'd come across it when she'd searched Aunt's room the year before. It had been full of all sorts of bits and pieces.

Selene took it hungrily and began rifling through the contents, discarding old tickets and receipts, trinkets, a white key – *Attis's skeleton key!* – Anna picked it up off the floor and put it in her pocket as Selene's breath caught. She was holding a thick, plain band between her fingers. It was exceptionally ugly – its thickness uneven, its metal dark and tarnished.

'Is that it?' said Anna, doubtfully.

Selene slipped it onto her finger. It looked out of place next to the vivid, twinkling colours of her other rings.

'Why did Aunt have a ring of yours?'

'Oh, I lent it to her once . . .' Selene stared down at it, looking both relieved and burdened. Anna knew there was more to the story but she didn't have the energy left to question it now.

She stood up. 'I'm going to get some fresh air. I won't be long.'

'I'll just have to open another bottle of Viv's wine in the meantime.' Selene winked. 'When you're ready, we'll go home.'

Home. The word rose up, adrift. Anna didn't know where home was any more. It wasn't here in this empty, besieged house. It wasn't there either – in Selene's house in Hackney. *Effie's and Attis's house.* It did not belong to her. *They* didn't belong to her.

Anna made her way to the gated garden in the middle of Cressey Square. She took out Attis's skeleton key and put it in the lock. It opened with an easy click. That afternoon he had visited her here came back to her like sudden colour, a vivid flare burning the grey film of the day away.

No. She would not remember it.

She'd become good at that – closing the doors in her mind and keeping the keys hidden where even she couldn't find them. She'd tried to shut them out – *Effie and Attis; Attis and Effie.* Where they were. What they were doing. They'd gone away together. *Together.*

She traced her old route down through the garden, the wind pale and still, the plants around her threadbare, clutching onto life. She made it to the oak tree and slid to the ground, its trunk so familiar that somewhere, deep down, her heart began to ache. The rain had stopped but the earth was soft and damp, droplets falling from the leaves like the tears that would not come. It was as if when Aunt died, she'd tied a Choke Knot around Anna's life, cutting her off from it, from herself. A final punishment.

Anna's eyes wandered over the grass, to where she and Attis had lain in the garden and not in the garden at all. A magical world he'd created for her and then taken away. The boy she and Effie were cursed to love.

Effie. My twin. My sister.

The thought still felt too big to comprehend. She'd spent her life believing she was all alone in the world except for Aunt and now Aunt was dead and Effie was her family. Aunt snickered in her head . . . *out of the frying pan and into the fire . . .*

The curse rose up around Anna like black smoke – uncontainable, uncontrollable, overpowering.

One womb, one breath, sisters of blood, bound by love, so bound by death.

How far did it go back? How many lives taken? Sister after sister fated to love the same man and to tear themselves apart over it – one to kill the other. Anna would hardly have believed it if she hadn't seen it, hadn't lived through its destruction.

Aunt killed my parents. My mother.

And I killed you, Aunt. Oh Goddess, I killed you . . .

Anna fell to her knees.

She raised her head to the sky and screamed – but no sound came out. She watched as every leaf on the oak tree fell one by one. She didn't look away until the last leaf had fallen, the branches left bare as bone.

What's happening to me?

She couldn't trust herself and she couldn't trust her magic. She'd seen what it could do; *felt it.* Anna took the cord out of her pocket and tore her fingers through the earth. Once the hole was deep enough she dropped it in. *Earth to earth. Ashes to ashes. Dust to dust.* She pushed the soil back over it and covered it with the fallen leaves.

Buried.

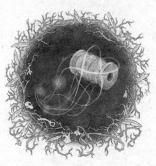

DARKNESS

Seven kinds of dark there are,
can you withstand them all?
Twilight, starlight, midnight-shimmer;
moonlight, shadowlight, candle-flicker;
the darkness of earth's places deep,
where light can't strive nor reach.
And yet, beyond, there lies another,
a darkness far above the others.
Not of this earth, not of this realm,
may none withstand:
The True Darkness of Hel!

'True Darkness', Folk Song, Source Unknown

The train clattered into darkness, the darkness of being buried beneath London, and Anna was dragged back into her dreams. The night before it had come again. It always started the same: lost in darkness . . .

She'd reached out – but her hands had met something unyielding and soft, slyly silken. She'd tried to push herself up but arms were wrapped around her. Not arms – *bones*. She'd known then with dizzying horror where she was. Down with the worms and the rot. Locked in Aunt's coffin – with Aunt, their red hair entwining, the stench of death rising up . . .

Her screams had been soundless but she'd begun to hammer and thrash against the walls containing her, pounding and pounding, until her knuckles tore and her hand broke through – earth pouring in. Then clawing and clawing her way up – up – up – through the dense night of soil until a hand had grabbed hers.

A shock of warmth.

It had dragged her out. Attis standing before her, saying her name over and over . . . *Anna . . . Anna . . . Anna* . . . A voice like music made of smoke. So real. He'd been so real. He'd wrapped her into him, enfolding her in the fire of his arms, his lips threatening to melt her entirely . . . *Anna . . . Anna . . . Anna* . . .

But his voice had begun to change – its softness stripped away, warping into something hard and serrated. A cold caw. A raven's shriek. The tip of a knife had appeared through his chest and he'd exploded into black feathers. Effie standing behind with a smile that gave nothing away. She'd put out her hand. Anna had taken it. *Why had I taken it?*

They'd followed the feathers up a spiralling staircase before them – the feathers condensing into ravens, leading them up – up – up – Attis calling behind them, snow falling on Anna's skin like ice-kisses – up – up – up – no end to the darkness before them, below them, gathering around them – making it impossible to see, to breathe, to remember who she'd once been . . .

A darkness like Anna had never known.

The train shuddered into the next tube stop, flooding the carriage with light and shaking Anna from the clutches of her dream. She tried to shake the darkness away too but it clung to her, as if it was always there, living somewhere inside of her. Facing the third-floor room had not released her. Ever since Aunt had died the staircase had been waiting for her, her nightmares caught on a punishing loop she didn't know how to escape.

The train launched off again and Aunt's laughter seemed to echo around her. She looked about the carriage in quiet desperation, at the blank faces around her. She wanted to run back home and lock the door. Hide away like she'd been hiding all summer, avoiding everything and everyone – *even myself* – the days passing by like drifting snow, never quite settling. Nothing feeling quite real. But there was no escaping now . . .

Attis and Effie were arriving back *tonight*.

Suddenly the darkness was too much, pressing against the windows as if the carriage would crumple – she would crumple. Anna stood up and moved to the door, something threatening to break through her layers of numbness. She didn't want to see them. She couldn't see them. She wasn't ready.

She could still see the Attis of her dreams so clearly. His skin honey and flame, a horseshoe tattoo glinting dangerously on his chest, eyes full of invitations no one could say no to; more real than the real Attis, who believed he was not real at all. Nothing but a *living spell*. And Effie, with her unreadable smile, leading her into the darkness. How could she face them? *Would they want to see me?* Anna had half expected them not to return at all, to disappear into the magical world, leaving her behind for good. It would be the best thing for all of them.

Aunt laughed again. *Love and magic. They destroy everything in the end. And it isn't even the end yet . . .*

The train arrived at Notting Hill and Anna rushed out and up the stairs, temporarily blinded by the daylight like a creature resurfacing after years underground. She looked around for Selene but there was no sign of her yet. Fashionably late, as always. Anna dropped onto a bench outside the station wondering how Selene had managed to lure her out of the house. Selene had been trying all summer but Anna had resisted her attempts until today. Perhaps, because Effie and Attis were arriving back and Anna would rather be out than in. Or perhaps, because Selene had told her she wanted to give Anna her birthday gift.

It was one of their oldest traditions. Whenever Selene had been around on her birthday she'd brought Anna a gift . . . a magical gift that had always filled her with wonder.

Anna knew now that magic was no wonder, but it had stirred some leftover remnant of intrigue in her. And here she was, in Notting Hill, with no idea what they were doing or where they were going—

Her phone buzzed. A text from Rowan.

Hey. Just checking in again. What's going down in Anna town? Still pouring here!!! My hair looks officially like marshland.

Anna moved her fingers to reply but she didn't know what to say. Rowan had been trying all summer too. She'd come over plenty at the start, sometimes with her mum, Bertie, and other times bearing offerings from Bertie instead – baked goods and herbal tisanes, *to help alleviate grief; to lift the spirits*. Rowan's whole family belonged to a motley grove of witches known as the Wort Cunnings who practised botanical magic.

Manda had managed to escape her parents and sneak over a few times as well. She and Rowan had tried to get her to talk, to draw her out, to encourage Anna and Effie to speak . . . but their efforts had been futile. Anna had wanted to tell her friends she was distraught, to fall on their shoulders and wail and cry, but she couldn't. How could she explain to them there was something wrong with her? That she felt nothing at all? Since then, they'd both gone away – Manda sent to church camp against her will and Rowan camping with her family in the Lake District. Not that the distance had stopped her many daily texts.

'I hope you're not reading the news again, darling . . .'

Anna lifted her head to find Selene haloed by sunlight, looking Goddess-levels of ravishing in a curvaceous white dress.

'No.' Anna shut her phone off.

Not able to face school work or anything productive, Anna had developed a new habit – checking the news for any discussion of magic or witchcraft online – scanning tabloids, social media, threadboards . . . It was like picking at a scab – the more Anna dug the more her fear festered. But there was always something new, some new suspicion or accusation – remnants of a ritual discovered in a London forest; someone claiming their neighbour had killed their dog with spells; gang violence being linked to occult activity; a recent murder shadowed by questions of witchcraft and sacrifice. And their school, of course, had been mentioned too— *In these unstable times, are teenagers turning to satanism?*

The whispers are spreading, my child . . .

'Good.' Selene's lips curved. 'I bought you that phone to take selfies, text your friends, sext lovers . . . not to scare yourself.'

'Sorry if I haven't been arranging more *dates*.' Anna hadn't meant to sound irritable but it had come out that way. She stood up, mumbling, 'I was just texting Rowan . . .'

'That's fine then,' said Selene, looping their arms together and pulling Anna through the crowds. 'Thanks for meeting me here, I had a break-fast appointment.' Selene smirked. Anna knew what that meant – an overnight stay with one of her lovers.

Selene slowed as they approached Portobello Market, breathing in the air as if all of London only existed to delight her. 'Isn't it wonderful out here?'

Anna had barely noticed the world around her. She looked up. The sun was streaming, the trees were still holding onto their golden leaves, the road was thronged with people and lined with colourful stalls spilling their wares into the street like sprung-open jack-in-the-boxes. The houses behind were painted a whimsical spectrum of pastel shades. People pushed past, the silence of the house Anna had stewed in all summer replaced by a graffitied wall of noise – the babble of the flowing crowd, market traders shouting out their offers, a group of teenage girls chattering and squealing, careless and carefree.

The row of houses behind began to switch their colours like a flashing carnival ride.

Anna gasped, taking a few steps back, until she heard Selene's tinkling laugh and realized Selene was creating the illusion. Anna stepped towards her. 'Selene! What are you doing? People might see. Magic can't be seen! Especially right now!'

Selene winced imperceptibly and Anna knew why. Because she sounded like Aunt.

'Oh, darling,' Selene waved a hand. 'Cowans don't notice these things. Their heads would quite simply explode.'

Anna scanned the street – everyone was still absorbed in the hubbub of the market; even a man taking a picture of the street appeared not to have spotted the magical display.

'You see? I've been telling you, you've simply been cooped up in the house too long. Out here everything is normal. People are getting on with their lives and don't seem in the least bit worried about accusations of magic made by lunatics on the internet. Come on.'

Selene ushered her onwards. They stopped outside a door that Anna hadn't noticed until they were right in front of it. Its existence was improbable – it sat between two of the painted buildings, in the seam where they joined, squeezed between a souvenir shop and a nail salon. The entrance was made of rich dark wood stamped with golden lettering that read: HANSELS.

Selene smiled at her, violet eyes twinkling like a storm in space. 'Your birthday gift.'

Anna followed her tentatively through the door. The smell hit her first, curling around her – the scent of pastries and caramel and . . . magic, sweet and light as powdered sugar. A bakery. From the outside, it had been cramped between its neighbouring buildings, but inside the room had large windows looking out onto the street. The sunlight that flowed through was softened, thickened, warmed as if it had been churned into butter. Everything gleamed – the marble floor, the polished counters, the glass cabinets and brass fixtures, the icing on the many cakes and treats on display. The ceiling was illustrated ornately – a cloud-strewn sky with little painted birds flitting across it.

It was too bright, too beautiful, and yet, Anna could not feel its brightness, its beauty. Not the way she had done before. This world was no longer for her.

'Every girl deserves cake on her birthday.' Selene winked, making for the counter. 'Especially from Hansels.'

A scattering of people were sitting at the tables. Anna followed Selene through them and joined her at one of the high seats in front of the counter. A burly man built like a bulldozer in an apron placed two ham-sized fists on the counter and leant towards them. 'What can I get yous?' His Scottish accent was as thick as the ruddy beard it had to struggle through. 'Be quick, I've got a batch of madeleines in the oven.'

'You know such decisions can't be rushed, Donnie.' Selene perused the stands on the counter.

The man grumbled beneath his breath and turned his head to Anna. 'She'll deliberate for an eon but she always gets the same thing in the end.'

'What's that?' Anna asked.

'A cappuccino and a brownie. Cannae say I blame her.'

'Today isn't about me, Donnie,' said Selene.

'Makes a change . . .'

Selene pouted at him. 'It's Anna's birthday tomorrow. She needs spoiling and we'll be picking up cakes for a celebration tonight too.'

'Celebration?' Anna gave Selene a troubled look.

Selene's smile ignored it. 'Well, we have to have a little party, all of us back together again.'

Anna turned back to the cakes. She wasn't sure *celebrating* would capture the spirit of their reunion. She tried to push Effie and Attis from the edges of her thoughts but couldn't help remembering how Attis had looked at her before they left. Awkward. Apologetic. Pitying. He'd been looking at her the same since the Binders' ceremony. That day, Anna and Effie had united their blood and their magic in a way that felt infinitely powerful. They'd brought Attis back from the brink of death. But then, reality had returned like a bucket of water thrown over a fire, the hurts and pains washing the magic away, the lies and betrayals hardening to a cold, unbreakable silence between them all.

Effie had spent the weeks following hardly speaking to anyone. She'd stormed about the house, banging every cupboard and door, glaring at anyone who looked in her direction. She'd gone out all night long, returning in the early hours, drunk and laughing or drunk and screaming, sometimes with a boy or girl who she'd made sure to parade in front of Attis the next morning. Selene had seemed afraid to attempt speaking to her. Anna had thought about it but decided it would only make things worse. She was the root of Effie's problems after all, and Anna wasn't sure she had anything to say. Effie had lied to her, betrayed her . . . had broken what they'd had.

It had been left to Attis. He'd tried several times – Anna had heard them shouting at one another, had seen Effie throwing things at him. Then one day they'd disappeared into her room for several torturous hours. When they emerged they'd announced that Attis needed to go back to his old house in West Wales and Effie was going to go with him. Selene had been livid, but what could she do that wouldn't push Effie further away? Attis had tried to explain to Anna that he just needed to go back to his dad's old place to sort a few things out and that it would be good for Effie to have some time to cool off . . . But Anna couldn't help imagining them there together – in the house they'd spent so many summers growing up in – whiling away the cosy evenings, finding solace in one another again . . .

'What can I get yous then?' The deep rumble of Donnie's voice brought Anna back into the room.

She looked over the treats, not sure where to start. There were so many and they all vied for attention: sugar-crusted doughnuts with the fillings still oozing out of them; tarts with bright liquid centres and fruits bobbing along their surface; tiny pastries of such intricate detail it was hard to imagine the owner's large hands making them; jars containing floating macaroons or cookies in a swirling storm of sprinkles; cakes melting through different colours, or stacking themselves higher, and a large volcanic showpiece in the centre with chocolate erupting from its top.

Donnie picked out a cupcake and placed it in front of her. It had glossy orange icing. He reached for a candle on one of the shelves behind and stuck it in. It lit itself. The candle burned brightly, sparkling and crackling. 'A wishing cupcake.' He nodded.

Selene clapped. 'Go on! Cast a wish.'

Cast. Anna pulled back. She'd barely touched magic all summer. Whenever she felt for it . . . it was as if it wasn't there inside her any more – only an empty space that hurt to touch; a numb pain that felt raw and restless and writhing but too deep to reach, like a dark well she couldn't see to the bottom of. Didn't want to see to the bottom of. How could she trust her magic to make a wish? Even the smallest of wishes could spiral out of control and come back a whirlwind. And what she wanted was impossible – for things to go back to how they had been with Effie and Attis when they were all just friends and not sisters, enemies . . . whatever Attis was to Anna now. *What power did a wish have against a curse?*

Selene nodded encouragingly. Anna leant forwards and blew the candle out, a single word coming into her mind instead . . . *freedom* . . . *I just want to be free* . . .

The flame lifted off into the air, circling around their heads and flying away to somewhere. But it was the smoke that drew Anna's attention – dense and inky, swirling with shapes and patterns that unfurled like the darkness of her dreams . . .

Selene's cheer broke her trance. 'Now where's my brownie and cappuccino?'

Donnie shook his head and placed a brownie on a plate before her, then poured her a cappuccino. Its froth displayed a heart which grew bigger before being shot by an arrow.

'You big softie,' Selene chuckled.

'Don't know what yer talking about.' He disappeared through the door behind, wafting fresh scents of baking into the café.

'Try to pick up this plate.' Selene indicated the brownie in front of her.

Anna gave her a puzzled look and reached for the plate but was surprised to find she could barely lift it. The brownie weighed as much as a brick.

'The densest, most decadent brownies you'll find in all of London. They'll weigh your soul down with the sin of them.' With some effort Selene pulled the fork free from it and took a bite. She made a loud, inappropriate sound, rolling her head back.

Anna snorted at the looks they were getting. She dug her fork into her own cupcake. She had to admit, it was the best sponge she'd ever tasted – rich but light, delectable but not too sweet, filling her stomach with a tingling, sparkling sensation that made her feel oddly hopeful.

Selene smiled. 'You see, darling? Whatever is going on in the real world, the magical world will always be here, it can't truly be touched.'

Anna took another bite, wanting to believe in Selene's words, wanting to be transported back into the world Selene had used to create for her. But she couldn't. 'I just don't think we should be ignoring everything going on.' Anna kept her voice steady, not showing the fear that churned and cinched her insides, the fear Aunt had fed her for so many years. 'There are fresh suspicions of magic all the time. Just yesterday—'

Selene waved her fork. 'This is why I don't go on the internet, darling. It's like a party with too many people invited – overcrowded, everybody has an opinion you don't want to hear, someone always ends up hysterical and you simply have to get drunk to survive it.'

Anna didn't know whether to laugh or bang her head on the counter. Selene cheerfully dismissed her every time she brought up the increase in magical suspicion within the normal, or what witches called the cowan, world. Aunt had warned against the whispers, had said they'd be sharpened and pointed back at them, their kind. Aunt had always liked to be right. *What if she had been?*

'Our own school is caught up in this, Selene.'

Anna flinched at the memory. She and her coven – her friends – had ruined lives and beckoned whispers of magic right to their own door . . .

'What happened last year isn't your fault.' Selene tried to catch her eyes. 'Things got out of hand.'

Guilt and blame were not concepts Selene dealt in. They ran off her like water over oil. But Anna would have to return to school in just over a week and face it all. Whatever lay in store.

'I know things are more unsettled right now, darling, but I promise, once the Seven return fully and restore the Balance, everything will go back to normal or marvellously abnormal, which is the preferred state of the magical world.' Selene flashed a smile, but Anna didn't buy it; there was tension hiding at the corners of her lips. Selene preferred distraction over discussion.

'Where are they then?' Anna met Selene's eyes now.

The Seven, the most powerful witch grove in existence, had been killed the year before while carrying out an annual ritual in Big Ben to cast protection over the country. Six of them had been found hanging in Big Ben's windows the next morning; one of them vanished. The event had been witnessed by all – the magical and cowan world alike. It had been the start of all the rumours, the whispers . . . cowans confounded over the inexplicable mystery of their deaths, referring to them as the 'Faceless Women' on account of the women all bearing the same eerie face. The situation not helped by the fact that an organization – who'd recently rebranded themselves the Witchcraft Inquisitorial and Prevention Services – had launched their own investigation and decried the women as witches.

'They are—' Selene's smile froze. 'Coming. It's just a matter of time.'

Her answer was as slippery as always. It was said the Seven couldn't truly be killed and that they'd already reformed but Selene never seemed to be able to tell Anna why they weren't here already.

'The Binders are still out there . . .' Anna reminded Selene, looking out of the window, at the passing crowds, imagining the face of Mrs Withering among them, her wriggling, ridiculing smile, pink as a worm. She'd never truly known if it had been Aunt or Mrs Withering who'd been in charge of her aunt's coven of Binders. Not until the end. Then it had been clear. Anna had turned the golem on her aunt, but at Anna's moment of hesitation, Mrs Withering had taken over. Anna remembered her words as she'd finished Aunt off.

A war is coming, we can't let you live now . . .

The Binders would have killed her and Effie then, and still would. They'd relish it like a sip of Earl Grey tea.

Selene stabbed the brownie a little too violently. 'They're being dealt with. You know that.' Anna had been told that a team of Wort Cunnings and Warders – a grove dedicated to protection – were tracking down each of the Binders in Aunt's circle, aiming to keep them contained, to let them know they were being watched, making it clear their actions would be reported to the Seven in good time. Anna wasn't convinced it would be enough.

'They don't give up easily.'

'The Binders are gone, Anna,' Selene said firmly. 'It's over. You don't have to worry any more. About any of this. You're young, you're free—'

Free. Anna wanted to laugh. 'The curse isn't over,' she whispered.

The bakery disappeared. The warmth of the cake fizzled away inside of her. Anna's world turned small, suffocated by darkness. There it was – the fear at the centre of all the other fears, constricting, confining her. Selene had stiffened. They'd moved carefully around all mention of the curse over the summer but they couldn't avoid it any more – it would be arriving back that evening, a shadow trailing Effie and Attis to their door.

'They shouldn't come back,' Anna muttered, looking down at the broken crumbs of her cake. 'There's no way to stop it. A curse can only be broken by the person who cast it – and that person is long dead – or a spell more powerful – and Attis is that spell and I'm not going to let him kill himself again.'

No way out.

Anna could hear Selene taking a deep breath beside her, searching perhaps for answers she didn't have. She hadn't been able to save Anna's mother and Aunt either. 'You and Effie are sisters,' she said at last. 'You belong in each other's lives.'

'Do we?' Anna replied. They'd been kept apart their whole life. They didn't have years of shared memories and moments to hold onto. Their threads had been severed from the start. And the fact they were now sisters didn't suddenly undo what Effie had done.

'Darling.' Selene's voice shook with sudden emotion. 'I can't bear to see you like this. I've forgotten how your smile looks.'

'I smile,' said Anna, attempting one.

'Calling that a smile is like calling soda water champagne. Your match has been blown right out, my sweet.'

Anna pulled away, ashamed of her pain.

'You will feel better again, matchstick, I promise. I know it hurts right now. I know your heart feels broken but—'

Anna put her fork down, her chest constricting. 'I'm not heartbroken.'

Selene's eyebrows gathered like a bow. 'Heartbreak takes many forms, my sweet – love, loss, losing yourself sometimes—'

Anna tried not to hear her words, the tightness in her chest painful now, the feeling of too much trying to come up and out of her at once.

'My mum used to say a heart must be broken to let the light in, not that I was ever much good at heartbreak myself . . . but you'll do better, I think. You have your mother's heart after all. You know, your birthday gift isn't just the cake. I brought you here because this café was one of your mother's favourites.'

Anna stilled at the mention of her mother. Ever since Anna had found out the truth about her death, Marie had felt more real than she ever had before, which made it even harder to think about her. She glanced up at Selene. 'Really?'

'I took Marie here the first time. She was studying in London and I was sleeping with a rock star who lived in Notting Hill, naturally. I'd discovered this place and knew Marie would love it, and she did. Do you know what she ordered?'

'What?'

'A cappuccino and a brownie.' Selene gave Anna a wry smile, wistfulness at its edges. 'It's why I always order it. I remember Marie smothering her teeth with it and grinning at me stupidly. We hadn't seen each other for months. We laughed and chatted for hours, eating far too much.' Selene chuckled to herself. 'Marie went home with a free box of cupcakes too, of course. That sort of thing happened to her everywhere we went. I don't know if it was her charm, her magic, or a bit of both, but she only had to smile at someone and they were hers.'

'Sounds like you.'

'No, no. I entice, I enchant.' Selene raised a sculpted eyebrow over eyes the colour of enchantment itself. 'But Marie – she captured hearts. You'll be the same.'

'I doubt that.'

'Well, I don't! And I know everything!' Selene took a final triumphant bite of brownie, smiling at Anna with chocolate all over her teeth.

Anna began to giggle – and as Selene ran her tongue over her chocolatey teeth, it changed into a laugh.

'There you go! It was worth dragging you all the way here to hear that.'

'There's hope for me yet.'

Selene shook her head, her eyes shining. 'Hope is too small a word for the world waiting for you, matchstick. All might feel dark right now but I still see your light . . .' Donnie came back through and Selene shook away her moment of earnestness. 'Now! Just wait until you try Donnie's cheesecake. You'll forget your own name.'

'Don't worry, it comes back after about five minutes or so,' said Donnie, quite seriously.

He started to prepare their cakes, Anna smiling at his and Selene's bickering—

'More of that one, please! And a bigger slice of that!'

Donnie waved the tongs about in the air. 'Why don't you just do it yer bloody self!'

Eventually, a box was placed on the counter in front of them. 'It's deeper than it looks.' Donnie nodded to Anna as Selene settled the bill. 'And I've put in a free box of those cupcakes for you.'

'Oh,' said Anna, surprised. 'Thank you.'

'No bother. Happy Birthday.'

Selene winked at Anna knowingly and they waved goodbye to Donnie, heading out onto the street. Anna glanced back – thinking of her mother there among the bakery's golden warmth – finding it suddenly hard to leave. 'Thank you, Selene, for taking me there.'

Selene smiled widely. 'Marie would have taken you, if she could have.'

Anna looked away, something threatening to burst in her again, a hard lump of resistance forming in her throat.

'Come on. Let's walk to the main road – hail a taxi from there. I need to buy some erogenous candles from the market.'

That distracted Anna. 'Some . . . *what?*'

'Light them to light up all your favourite parts . . . you get the idea. Very popular with my clients.'

Anna looked around the market. 'You can buy magical candles here?'

'Darling, there's magic everywhere for those who know how to find it. Portobello's packed with little secrets. See that glass shop over there?' Selene pointed to a shop behind the stalls that was filled with a twinkling window display of delicate glassware. 'It's got a whole magical section full of beautiful pieces – spells cast in glass, glass lamps lit by moonlight . . . I bought a beautiful vase there once – changed shape and colour depending on what flowers you put in it, quite marvellous. There's some fabulous magical vintage fashion about as well. Go and have a look. Meet you at the main street in five.'

Anna watched Selene go, a white dress disappearing into the crowd. Part of her wanted to run after her, to have Selene fill her with more wonder, to make her feel like the girl she'd once been. Isn't it what she'd always wanted? To live with Selene? To be free with Selene? But she wasn't that girl any more and Selene wasn't the person Anna had believed her to be, had believed in. For Selene had always been a kind of belief – a bright, fleeting vision shooting through the dark skies of her life, promising answers . . . escape. But she'd been keeping the truth of Attis and Effie and the curse from her the whole time. There *was* no escape and Selene remained just as fleeting. She'd spent most of the summer disappearing – seeing friends, leaving for days at a time, flitting in and out of Anna's life like a reflection of sunlight on the wall you can't quite catch; dazzling and then gone—

Anna wandered slowly down the street, the thought of magic woven among it all making her feel constricted, exposed, the world darkening around her. *Too busy, too loud.* The crowds too close now, pushing against her. Aunt's laughter tangled in the noise of it all. Anna wanted to go home, to wrap herself back up in the cold blanket of her fears.

The fire never dies. Beware, oh beware, smoke on the wind . . .

Perhaps she *was* going mad. Perhaps she was slowly turning into Aunt – paranoid and unhinged. Perhaps the curse had already begun to seep into her thoughts, spilling the darkness inside her into the world, making everything appear warped and sinister—

'Hellooo . . .'

A voice called out from somewhere.

'Hellooo!'

Anna heard it again. Ignored it. Surely it wasn't aimed at her.

'Helloooooo! Can I interest you in anything?'

She flicked her head to the side, realizing it was coming from the owner of the stall beside her. A short man bobbing up and down on his feet and smiling fervently at her.

'Er – no, I'm OK, thanks.'

Anna nodded and walked on but a few stalls later she heard his voice again.

'Helloooooooo—' The sound a high and insistent squeak like air being released from a balloon. 'Are you sure you're sure?'

Anna glanced to the side again. He was still there behind his stall, which was impossible . . . unless his stall was somehow . . . following her. She walked more quickly, passing several further stalls, but then – his voice again . . .

'I have a new range of floorwashes which I'm sure you'd be most tempted by—'

Anna stopped and turned to him, unsettled and exasperated.

'Ah!' He raised a snappy finger. 'Got your attention now, haven't I?' He held a bottle up. 'How about my new banishing floorwash? It'll clean your floor and kick out those negative energies to boot! Or mop-up-an-argument floorwash – especially good for shouting matches!'

Anna knew she should have kept on walking, should have tried to outrun him, but she stepped towards his stall, her eyes running over it. It appeared to be selling various items of homeware. The stall didn't look too outwardly magical . . . until a knife started chopping along a chopping board of its own accord. She looked up and down the street anxiously but everyone seemed to be walking past quite oblivious.

'Or change-the-colour-of-your-floor floorwash—'

'I'm really not interested in any floorwashes,' Anna replied through gritted teeth. 'Who *are* you?'

He smiled and it was a slippery thing, like something sinking into a swamp. He put a hand to his chest. 'I'm Jerry Tinker, salesman of magical household wares.' His squat head was hairless. His flat nose and wide, moist lips reminded Anna of a toad. 'What's your name, little Cindermaid?'

'Anna,' she replied reluctantly.

'Anna.' He smacked her name between his lips in a way that made her even more uncomfortable. 'Let's see, let's see. Ah! How about my new set of kitchen knives?' He presented them with a flourish. 'Sharpen as they cut – you'll never have to deal with a blunt knife again! Or how about this self-bake bread tin? Pop it in the oven empty and it'll come out with the perfect loaf. Keeps the home happy and the husband at home!'

Anna pulled a face. 'I don't have a husband!'

'Well then, sounds like you need this iron to iron out your love life! Or this apron – it'll slim you down and plump you up in all the right places—'

A toaster suddenly popped with a bang beside her, two enveloped letters flying out of it. Anna jumped away.

'A toaster for your post?' he zipped.

'I don't want anything, thank you very much,' said Anna with finality, trying to walk away but the stall extended alongside her as if it was unfolding, new items appearing – pots and pans, kettles and cups, cloths and towels, needles and thimbles and spools of thread . . .

One spool glinted, catching her eye, but she carried on walking.

'A seamstress, are you?' She heard his squeak in her ear. 'I've got self-threading needles, singing spindles, bottomless thimbles—' He picked a small, silver thimble up and pulled out a rose from inside of it, holding it towards Anna.

She couldn't help the slide of her eyes back to the spool of thread that shone brighter than all the others. It was brighter than the sunshine itself but made of a different quality altogether – a softer, subtler kind of light, as if it did not belong to the colours of the day. Anna went to touch it but Jerry's hand clamped around her wrist.

'No touching. I see the little Cindermaid has expensive tastes.'

Anna pulled her arm away and he picked up the spool, unravelling a little of its thread. 'Moonthread,' he declared. It shimmered against his grubby fingers. 'Never runs out! Never tangles! Never breaks!' He yanked it hard and the thread gave a little tug but did not snap. 'It'll always shine bright, no matter how dark things get . . . I'll knock off twenty and do it for three hundred for you.'

'Three hundred pounds!' Anna almost laughed.

Jerry's smile soured, greened at the edges, but he held it in place. 'It's not exactly a run-of-the-mill product . . .'

'I'm OK, thanks,' said Anna, dragging her eyes from it.

'I can offer it for free, of course . . . in return for something from you.'

It was Anna's turn to narrow her eyes now. 'What?'

'A secret.'

'A secret . . .'

'Oh, I deal in secrets too. Juicy ones.' Jerry's voice squelched. 'And I think you might have one, little Cindermaid . . .' The slits of his nose flared as if he were sniffing her out. 'And don't worry – I'm extremely discreet. Your secret will be safe as a toad in a hole with me.'

Anna stepped back, suddenly afraid, repulsed by the man before her and what he could see in her. 'I don't want anything from you.'

He began to dance on the spot, reciting a little ditty. 'When the tinker comes to call, share your secrets, warts and all! Heed his offers, friend or foe, or else he'll sing: I told you so!'

'Stop it!' Anna barked, remembering they were on a street in the middle of London.

Jerry ceased his jig. 'I'm only trying to help, Cindermaid. Here – if you ever change your mind.' He reached into his pocket and handed her a card. It read: JERRY TINKER. TRADER OF MAGICAL HOUSEHOLD WARES, FOR THE WITCH WITH TOO MUCH ON HER PLATE!

Anna took it, mainly in the hope it would make him go away.

'Unless—'

'No!' she snapped before he could begin again.

He shrugged, his smile sinking back into its foetid depths. 'Your loss,' he said, but as she walked away all she could hear was—

You're lost. You're lost. You're lost.

When she looked back his stall was no longer there among the others.

SHADOWS

It's not what you are made of, but what your shadows are made of that matters.

Garven MacInnes, Hel Witch and Guardian Spirit,
1636–1691–1704

Attis was downstairs. Anna could hear his voice, a low rumble. They were back.

She paced her bedroom, her heart beating too fast. She stumbled on a box – she hadn't unpacked everything yet. She didn't know why. She liked her room here – it was on the top floor of the house, with wooden floors and white walls and a view over the irregular rooftops of East London. She just couldn't get used to the idea that this was her home now.

She checked herself in the mirror again. She'd put on one of the new outfits Selene had bought her over the summer – a black jumper tucked into a suede skirt. She'd teased out her hair into smooth waves with Selene's golden comb. Despite not practising her magic, her hair was brighter than ever, burning gold. She tilted her chin and tried out a smile. She didn't want to look as if she'd done nothing except mope while they'd been gone.

She paced the room several more times before stopping at the door, knowing that, at some point, she had to go downstairs. Either that or the window. *Tempting . . .*

She shook her head, took a deep breath and made her way down to the kitchen, surprised to hear Effie's laughter climbing up the stairway. Anna would know that laugh anywhere – low, vivid, derisive. A laugh that never settled for too long; that pulled you in while holding you hostage so you weren't quite sure if you were in on the joke or if the joke was on you.

'—so I told them to go to hell!' Effie was telling a story. 'They drove off and we're still stuck on this mountain in the middle of nowhere. Everyone's driving past us, then Attis does this magnet spell, halts a huge truck right in its tracks. Driver couldn't understand what was happening. I knocked on his window and—'

Anna stepped into the room and Effie stopped. There they were: Effie at the counter, feet in heavy, black boots up on the stool next to her; Selene swirling a glass of wine as she listened with an eager expression; Attis at the back, his powerful presence leaning casually against the hob, arms folded. A surprisingly, unnervingly friendly scene.

'Hey.' Anna waved. The most awkward wave she'd ever executed. Her eyes passed quickly over Attis without really looking at him and landed on Effie. They locked eyes for a few loaded seconds. *Friend. Enemy. Sister. My curse.* Anna could feel her walls beginning to crumble, not knowing what to feel, how to feel in the face of so much. Anger broke through as she reminded herself what Effie had done: luring her into a coven and turning it into a spectacle of entertainment and revenge; sleeping with her date to the school ball just for the hell of it; leaving her to deal with it all alone . . .

Before Anna could say anything, Effie walked over and gave her an uncharacteristic hug, brief and forceful. 'Darling sister,' she said, and Anna was sure she wasn't in on *that* joke. Effie smiled and it was her indecipherable, half-moon smile of Anna's dreams. Her words were more directly cutting. 'Have you been out in the sun at all while we've been gone? You look pale.'

Anna was still in shock from the hug. 'I always look pale.'

Effie snorted. 'True.'

Effie in contrast looked refreshed, renewed, but harder too. She'd bleached her hair peroxide blonde, the roots abruptly dark. She'd pierced her nose with a ring and her eyes gleamed like a mirror, letting no light through, reflecting outwards, as if they intended to see the world only the way they wanted to see it.

'Not all of us have been off on holiday,' Anna added, sounding more bitter than biting. 'Welcome back.' She tried to inject some cheerfulness into her voice.

'Good to be back.' Effie's dimples popped with sarcasm.

Selene raised her glass. 'All of us together again.' She didn't look at Attis. 'I couldn't be more thrilled – and for Anna's birthday—'

'It's my birthday too.' Effie tilted her head to Selene. 'Is it not?'

Selene appeared flustered. 'Well – I didn't think you'd want to change your birthday . . .'

'But today is my *real* birthday, no? The day my mother gave birth to me, not the one you made up for me?'

Everyone tensed.

'Yes.' Selene threw her hands up. 'Double celebration then! I thought we could head to the roof like old times.'

'Sounds swell,' Effie smiled widely, unnervingly.

Attis pushed himself away from the counter. 'Can I get anyone a drink?' Anna was caught off guard by the sound of his voice, transporting her back to her dreams of him too. Deep and melodic, that accent of his she could never place, like a map with too many pathways to count.

'There's plenty of champagne up there already,' said Selene. 'But you can bring up the soft drinks. Now, come on!' She pulled Anna under one arm and Effie under the other and led them upstairs and onto the roof as if they were all the oldest of friends. *So this is how it's going to be*, Anna thought, *make-believe and fairy tales*. As if a party and some champagne could paper over the cracks.

Even so, Selene had outdone herself. The roof looked ravishing – the walls were waterfalls of twinkling lights, moon lanterns floated in the air above them, blankets and cushions were strewn across the chairs and the table in the centre was stacked high with cakes and treats from Hansels and fancy-looking shopping bags. London twinkled behind as if it were part of the decor. The sky above hung low and overcast, thick grey clouds blurring into the night above – the only thing that Selene couldn't control, couldn't make spectacular.

'The night sky in Wales was so beautiful,' said Effie, trailing her fingers along the table.

'Forget the stars, tonight I have sparkling champagne.' Selene clicked her fingers and three glasses and a bottle floated towards them. As it was poured, the champagne sparkled, quite literally. 'To family!' Selene cheered. They clinked glasses, a brittle sound.

'To family,' Effie responded, downing her drink in one and throwing Anna a smile.

Anna realized her hands were gripping her glass too tightly. 'To family,' she forced out.

Effie collapsed into one of the deck chairs. 'Goddess, I'm tired. I don't feel like I've slept all summer.'

'Well, you're not sleeping now!' Selene chirped. 'We have cake and gifts and lots of catching up to do.'

Selene started handing out the cakes and Attis arrived with more drinks. 'Can I get you anything?' he asked Anna politely.

'No thank – thank you – I have—' She held up the champagne glass, looking at it instead of him, wondering why she was struggling to string a sentence together.

'And, of course, our evening would not be complete without—' Selene clapped her hands and the inside-out candles lining the edge of the roof sparked to life, but there were still no stars above. The clouds remained stubbornly present. Attis drew a symbol in the air and the fire roared, flames snapping.

'So good to be back together!' Selene persisted with her enthusiasm. 'Isn't this wonderful? How was the *trip*?'

'Fun.' Effie raised an arched eyebrow at Attis, crushing a strawberry between her lips. 'Not much in the way of night-life around there but we had the beach all to ourselves.'

Anna felt the fizz of the champagne turn to needles in her stomach, trying not to imagine them alone on a beach together, sunkissed and glistening . . .

'We made some friends who had a boat.'

'Effie stole the boat,' said Attis, taking the seat next to Effie.

'Only for a day. Or two.'

'Until I made you take it back.'

'That's why I keep you around, you stop me from doing bad things, like stealing people's boats.' She nudged his arm. It was a small movement – hardly anything at all – yet it was the casualness of it that was so powerful. They were back to their old selves, one whole again, communicating through their private language of shared jokes and little intimacies.

'How was the summer here?' Attis asked.

'Oh, we've had a wonderful time,' Selene replied. 'We've been out exploring London, throwing fabulous dinner parties—'

Anna was suddenly tired of all the pretence. 'Aunt's funeral was swell too.'

They fell silent.

Attis turned to Anna, his voice gentle. 'I'm sorry we missed it—'

'I'm not.' Effie folded her arms. 'Good riddance.'

'Effie!' Selene chided.

'What? She was a monster. She tried to kill us all. I'm glad she's six feet under.'

'She was still Anna's aunt – your aunt and—'

Anna raised her glass. 'Here's to six feet under.'

She and Effie locked eyes again, a sudden charge travelling between them as they drank. Anna was angry at herself now, for letting herself feel it – the pull of Effie, the draw that had always been there between them; the craving to be seen by her, to be part of her spectacle. She could hear Aunt tutting in her ear and imagined her watching the proceedings with disapproval, bony fingers clasped, throwing them looks of ire. She would have hated the flagrant waste – *indulgence is just a kind of fear, Anna, a way of filling up the empty.*

'Time for presents!' Selene declared, her exuberance still pedalling madly.

Now Effie had demanded they celebrate her birthday too, Selene split the gifts between them. There were plenty to go around. Clothes. Shoes. Bags. Perfume. Jewellery. Effie seemed nonplussed but Anna had never received so many presents in her life. Feeling bad for her earlier outburst, she feigned enthusiasm, praising each one in turn. They tried out all the treats – some sort of syrup cake that locked Anna's teeth together, macaroons with odd flavours that tasted nonetheless strangely accurate: *lost at sea, a dance with the fey, sweet revenge, midnight's shadows.* Anna cut into a rainbow cake which released a plume of colourful iced butterflies that flapped about her head.

Selene plucked one from the air and threw it in her mouth. She was growing determinedly more drunk. She filled up the silences with stories, telling them about the time she and their mother had ended up being arrested on Marie's seventeenth birthday after breaking into the local swimming pool after-hours. 'We just wanted a late-night swim – probably shouldn't have tried to put armbands on the police—'

Effie laughed along but Anna found herself distracted as Attis leant forwards to stoke the fire. She hadn't yet been able to look at him but his hands drew her attention, the way they moved – fluid as a song, yet precise and articulate, beckoning the flames this way and that with long, strong fingers. In her dreams, she'd felt those hands make music on her skin.

'Time for the main event!' Selene swept her arms towards the centre-piece cake – the volcanic creation from Donnie's. She went to get up but Effie jumped to her feet first.

'I'll do the honours,' she said, moving over to the table. She picked up the knife.

Then, without warning, she moved behind Attis and held it to his throat.

Anna leapt to her feet, startled. 'What are you doing?'

Effie laughed, the sound glinting like the blade in her hand. 'I'm marking the start of a new part of the evening's celebrations called – let's get fucking real.' The knife pressed against his skin but Attis didn't move. He did not appear concerned. Anna stood tensely, trying to comprehend what was happening—

Effie laughed again, lowering the knife. 'You really think I'd kill him?'

'Effie,' said Selene tersely. 'What's this all about?'

Effie spun to Selene. 'Surely you'd be happy if I killed him? Finished the job you started?'

Selene stared at her, her glass tipping sideways though the champagne did not spill out. 'Darling, come on, let's not spoil the evening—'

'Oh, the evening,' Effie repeated with a sarcastic flourish. 'I'd hate to spoil the *evening*, only, you did, kind of, spoil our entire lives, so . . .' Selene flinched and Anna realized that Effie's faux friendliness had been a ruse; an opening act before the show started. Effie turned back to Attis. 'I'm simply trying to ascertain how dispensable Attis is to each of us. I think it might be a good place to start before we discuss the curse, don't you?'

Selene took in a sharp breath. There it was. The thing they'd been desperately trying to avoid all night – making sure not to step on the all too real cracks – and now Effie had blown the ground beneath them wide open.

'Effie—' Selene began.

'No, I'm sorry, let's carry on with the cake and the candles and the fucking butterflies and forget about it. Or shall I turn the knife on Anna and get it over with? Isn't that how it goes? Our curse.'

'Effie.' Selene's voice hardened. 'Stop provoking. There's no rush to talk about this all now.'

'That's what you said at the start of the summer and now we're almost at the end. I mean, sure, we can wait it out.' Effie twirled the knife in her hand. 'But that didn't work out so well for our mother and aunt, did it? The curse has begun. We need to deal with it.'

Anna was suddenly struck by just how much she'd missed Effie.

'Do I get a say in this?' Attis piped up. 'Because I'd probably rate me around an eight out of ten on the dispensability scale. Let's say seven if it's a good hair day.'

Effie pointed the knife back at him. 'You do not get a say in this.'

He shook his head and carried on eating his cake. 'Fair enough.'

Selene grated out a sigh, grabbing the bottle of champagne. 'What is the point in all this?'

Effie walked back to her seat. 'The point is, we have a plan. Attis has agreed not to sacrifice himself again while we find another way to break the curse. Haven't you, Attis?' She elbowed him.

'I'm on a sacrifice sabbatical.' He saluted. 'No more sacrifices for me. For now,' he added with a tone that Anna didn't like.

Selene glared at them. 'This isn't a joke.'

'No one is laughing,' Effie replied, her smile lacking any attempt at warmth now.

Selene threw her hands in the air, leaving the champagne bottle hovering. 'This is a curse! It isn't going to wait!'

'So, we *are* in a rush?'

'I never said we shouldn't deal with the curse, I just thought your first night back might not be the moment!' Selene snapped.

'All's going well so far. Neither Anna nor I have attempted to stab one another this evening,' said Effie flippantly. 'I don't particularly feel like doing that. Do you, Anna?'

Anna didn't hesitate long enough for any of them to notice but in her head it was there, it had been there all summer, torturing her – a space between who she thought she was and who she feared she might be. *I killed Aunt.* She might not have finished the job but she'd started it. *Could I kill Effie too?* It felt impossible, but she'd seen what the curse did to people, and too many parts of her were missing now to trust who she really was. 'No,' she said, praying it was true.

'There you go.' Effie displayed a hand towards her. 'The curse is under control.'

'Under control!' Selene laughed. It was rare for one of her laughs to sound so empty. 'Curses are no ordinary spell, they can't be controlled. They don't follow plans. They don't work to deadlines. It's not simply a contract we can sign and file away. It's a curse! It will burn any contract to cinders! It will twist apart your promises and disintegrate your words. It wants to complete its purpose – it will do anything to complete its purpose. It may feel as if you are in control but that's what it wants you to believe, all the while laying out a maze and luring you into its centre.' She took a breath, her lip trembling. Anna gripped her chair, feeling the chaos of Selene's words inside of her. Selene glanced at Attis briefly, her final words low and hushed. 'He's the only answer we have . . . and if we don't use it, he will be the reason you are both destroyed.'

Anna saw Attis wince, a crack in his bravado.

'Well, of course, there's a secondary clause to the agreement,' said Effie, steely as a lawyer. 'While we're finding another way to end the curse, neither Anna nor I can be with Attis. If neither of us can be with him then we can't fight over him and we won't end up, you know . . .' She made a stabbing motion. 'Killing each other over love.'

The darkness of the night sky felt suddenly like the roof of a coffin. *Love.* Effie spoke the word as if it were of little consequence but Anna felt herself buried beneath the weight of it. She'd been taught her whole life to fear and despise love but it had been unloosed now – she'd opened all its knots and let it out and now she had no way to control it. She couldn't love him. She wouldn't. It was presumptuous to assume she'd want to be with him at all. Her fear mingled with humiliation and anger. Had they discussed her this way? As if her love for him was a fact? It hadn't been fair. He'd tricked her into it. A kiss in exchange for a curse.

She looked at him then, at last. He was staring out over the edge of the roof, entirely real and as much of an illusion as the Attis of her dreams.

The vision came back to her, ripping her open: Attis driving his knife through his heart.

A living spell. A sacrifice. Both their curse and the answer to it; the poison and the antidote.

How could he believe he was no more than a sacrifice? It made no sense to her, *he* made no sense to her. Had the boy she'd known ever existed? Had she ever really known him at all?

His contours were carved by the light into shadow but she knew its lines – the deep eyes, the straight nose, the soft curve of his lips. His hair was longer and lighter, the fire catching it where the sunlight had brightened it over the summer, the flames playing across his face so that she didn't know if he was frowning or smiling. He turned to her and her stomach tightened. Their eyes met – his still but dancing, young but old, real but unreal, neither one thing or another; as grey and intangible as smoke—

Their kiss came back to her, ripping her open. That night, after the ball.

Your betrayal . . . Aunt whispered in Anna's ear.

It was true. Effie might have betrayed her, but she'd betrayed Effie too. *Would I do it again?*

'So,' said Effie, and Anna took a moment to meet her eyes. 'Are we all agreed?'

'If not,' Attis declared, 'there's a cake knife here and I'm not afraid to use it. I guess this fork could work but it'll be more painful.'

Anna glowered at him.

'Anna?' Effie prompted.

'No!' Anna cried.

'What?'

Anna's cheeks reddened further. She wished she'd thought through her response. 'I mean – yes. Yes, I agree not to . . . we can't be with Attis. Either of us. However.' She outlined the word firmly. 'I don't think that Attis dying should *ever* be an option. That's just a life for a life.'

'Possibly.' He shrugged. 'Or two lives for a life. The curse could end up hurting you both. Besides, I'm not really a life as I'm not technically human. I'm just a spell.'

'That's ridiculous,' Anna snapped, forgetting her reserve. 'Just because magic was involved in your creation doesn't mean you aren't real. I've seen you bleed – looked pretty real to me.'

Attis looked taken aback.

'Well, obviously no one wants Attis to die,' said Effie, impatiently. 'Least of all me. Which is why we have to find another way.'

'He is the only way!' Selene cried, her voice breaking. Anna hated the way she didn't look at him, the way she could talk about him like he was nothing but a solution. 'It's why he was made . . .'

Effie turned to Selene slowly. 'Only you don't actually know that, do you, Selene?'

Selene recoiled from Effie's unrelenting stare.

'From what I can gather from Attis.' Effie's voice was serrated with hard-edged accusation. 'We only know half the story. You never saw the spell Marie had found – the spell of his creation. All Marie ever told you is that his blood would be needed and you interpreted the rest . . .'

Selene looked out to the horizon as if searching for a way out. When she obviously couldn't find one, she started to speak. 'I begged Marie to leave Dominic, but it was too late by then. They were too in love and she'd fallen pregnant. Your aunt had already been driven into the cult of the Binders, seeking catharsis, revenge . . . Marie was determined to break the curse, just like you. Determined, stubborn, naive—' Selene put her fingers to her lips and Anna saw how they shook. 'I put her in touch with a friend of mine – a divinatory witch – and he helped her trace her family tree back to when the curse began. I didn't know all the details, we were speaking over the phone and Marie was paranoid the Binders were on her tail so she didn't share much. I was away – I should have been there—' Selene took a gulp of champagne. 'We didn't talk again until she came to me to say her search had led her to a written spell – a spell formed at the same time as the curse. It detailed the creation of a living antidote who would have the power to break the curse. You're right . . . I never saw the spell, but Marie told me how it referred to a stone that she believed to be on an old family necklace, an heirloom passed down through the generations, though Marie had not known of its existence until she started digging into the curse. She found it among her mother's belongings when she went to visit her. Vivienne had packed Mrs Everdell off to a care home after she was diagnosed with Alzheimer's. Marie wanted to take care of her but she couldn't without Vivienne discovering her whereabouts. We don't know for sure that – that Vivienne didn't have something to do with your grandmother's sudden illness.' Selene looked between them sadly. 'We suspected she knew Marie was searching for answers and would have wanted to make it hard for her – to shut down all family contact. Your grandfather died suddenly and then your grandmother was diagnosed with advanced Alzheimer's out of nowhere. She wasn't particularly old. It all seemed a little too convenient.'

Anna felt suddenly dizzy. *Did you kill them too, Aunt?* The woman who'd raised her, who'd made her a cake every year for her birthday, who'd put plasters on her knees when she fell, who'd sewn into her skin, who'd combed her hair each night while poisoning her. *Probably.* She was sure there were many secrets buried with Vivienne.

Selene continued, 'Marie gave me the stone from the necklace and told me I had to swallow it and then – have sex with a man and I would fall pregnant.' Anna had never seen Selene look flustered before, especially not with regard to sex. She fiddled with the dull ring on her finger.

'She said that the boy created would be the one you'd fall in love with and that his blood would break the curse. That's all I know. We thought we had more time. Marie and Dominic had made plans to move abroad, to hide until you were grown up, and I would join them—'

Selene didn't need to finish her story; they all knew how it ended.

'So you just decided that blood meant *death*?' Effie spat.

Selene wriggled in her seat. 'It was the understanding I'd been given. A drop of blood is hardly enough to end a curse! It implies—'

'Sacrifice.' Attis finished her sentence. 'Blood sacrifice.' Ending his life was the only thing Anna had ever seen him and Selene agree on.

'When Vivienne told me about the Binders' ceremony it all seemed to fall into place,' said Selene. 'They were going to raise power, channel it into the curse and sacrifice the boy you loved. It felt like it had already been mapped out.'

'How convenient,' Effie retorted. 'I bet you wish it *had* all worked out. That they'd bound me and Anna, and Attis had died.'

'Yes!' Selene yelled. 'I wish it! And you wouldn't have been bound – they can't bind a curse that no longer exists. You'd have been free. Free to love who you choose. Free to live, like I promised Marie.'

Attis turned away with a low sound in his throat, but Effie shook her head. 'Hardly free if you decided it all for us.'

'What you're forgetting is that *he* was on board with the whole thing!'

Effie laughed abrasively. 'He was fourteen when you took him away! When you told him his *purpose*. You manipulated him from the start. Your hands were on that blade too.' Effie pushed her chair away and stalked to the edge of the roof.

'My darling, please—' All the fight had gone from Selene's voice. 'I did what I did to save you . . .'

'She's right, Effie. It was the only viable option,' said Attis.

Effie spun around. 'Don't you start. You both lied to me – to us! Our whole lives were a lie!'

Anna could feel the ice of Effie's anger now. No matter what they'd done to each other, they'd both faced a bigger betrayal by everyone around them.

Effie's eyes narrowed on Selene. 'You've spent your whole life telling me a witch should be in charge of her own life, but you didn't give me the same courtesy. You could have let us be part of the plan. Our real mother would have told us the truth. She would have done more.'

Selene closed her eyes. 'Marie was always better than me,' she muttered.

The look of rage on Effie's face faltered slightly.

'We have to find out what our mother discovered, what Attis's spell was – who created it,' said Anna, breaking the tension. 'What did the stone look like?'

Selene's eyes flickered to Anna as if returning from her memories back to reality. 'Er – the stone . . . it was small enough to swallow, but vivid. Dark red. Warm to the touch. Not like any stone I've ever seen.'

'You don't know any more about it?'

Selene shook her head.

'Well, we have several leads already,' Anna continued. 'We know Marie went to the Library and met Pesaycha and then went on to visit Nana the curse witch. And we need you to find your divinatory friend, Selene, if that's where Marie started.'

Selene was silent, her eyes passing over the table of cakes and presents forlornly, her lips sealed into a hard line; the butterflies flapped about the air around her with futility. 'OK,' she said eventually, her body slackening, the fight going out of her. 'We'll try to find another way but you stick to your terms.' She cast a recriminatory look at Attis. 'No charms, no flirtations, no . . . *anything else*.'

'I'll get the chastity belts out later.' He nodded, earning him a fresh glare from Selene.

'Well, I'm glad that's sorted,' said Effie, forcefully, as if daring anyone to challenge her. She pushed away from the edge of the roof. 'And, as this little *party* is over – I'm going to go to bed. Happy Birthday, sis,' she said as she passed Anna, a tail flick of laughter at the end. She did not look at Selene.

They were left sitting in the wake of her presence, like the sea settling after a storm; still choppy, still uneasy, and Anna still caught in its waves – things moving and shifting inside of her that hadn't stirred all summer. Effie might have besieged them, shouted and cast blame, but she'd given Anna something too – a thread breaking its way through her despair . . . a plan . . .

'So,' said Attis, after several long beats of silence. 'I have a birth father. That's news.'

'What?' Selene snapped.

'You said that you had to have sex with a man after you swallowed the stone. You've never mentioned that part before. Who is he? It wasn't . . . one of my dads, was it?' He said it with a faint smirk but Anna could see the tension in his jaw, the vulnerability in his eyes. Selene had left him to be raised by one of her old friends and his partner. Attis had always spoken of his dads fondly.

'No. The person I . . . selected was not your father. You existed inside the spell; he was required for purely biological reasons.'

'And here I was thinking you were the Virgin Mary, Immaculate Conception . . .'

Selene glared at him disparagingly. 'He was an old flame, that's all. He never knew about any of it. He isn't even a witch. I don't know where he is now.'

Attis shook his head, wearily. 'Whatever. I'm going to hit the sack.' He gathered up some of the empty plates and glasses, pushing the moon lanterns out of his way. He stopped before Anna – no longer hidden in shadow but captured momentarily in moonlight, if anything could ever capture him. 'Happy Birthday, Anna.'

She didn't have time to reply before he was gone. She was left thinking about the way he'd said her name – so warm and sad, like an ember slowly fizzling out.

And then there were two. The clouds had finally begun to clear above, the stars peeking between them like flowers through cracks in a wall.

Selene tried to laugh but it came out all pulled out of shape. 'Well, that didn't go to plan.' She poured herself more to drink. 'I just wanted you to enjoy your birthday – birthdays . . .'

'Believe it or not, it's been one of my better birthdays,' said Anna.

'I don't know if that makes it worse.' Selene laughed bleakly. 'Do you think Effie intends to punish me forever?'

'Not *forever* . . .' said Anna, unconvincingly. Effie did like to follow things through.

'I'm not sure I was ever cut out for being a mother.'

Anna knew she could twist the knife that Effie had dug in. That she could ask Selene, *why? Why didn't you tell us? Why not let us all work together against Aunt?* But Selene looked too broken already, so instead, she said, 'A mother and her teenage daughter arguing, I'd say it's fairly normal.'

'I suppose so.' Selene attempted a smile, then looked up at Anna, eyes strained, wired with pain. 'I just – oh, Goddess, Anna, I just don't want it to happen again. I don't think I could take it.'

'It won't,' said Anna, though she didn't know if she believed her own words.

'Effie is so headstrong, just like Marie . . .'

Like Marie. That struck hard. Effie was just like Marie – both black-haired and dimpled, both wilful and powerful. *And me? Who am I like?* Anna didn't want to know the answer.

Selene leant forwards, eyes burning into hers. 'Please, matchstick, promise me you'll stay away from him.'

'I have no intention—'

'Ah.' Selene raised a finger. 'But love does not care for intentions. Love who laughs at locksmiths, remember? It cannot always be contained.' She gave Anna a gentle look. 'I saw how you were looking at him.'

Anna stuttered. 'What? No. I— he's in love with Effie, anyway. It's her he sacrificed himself for.'

'He's always been in love with Effie, but love does not play by the rules. It's why curses love it so.'

'I don't think I'm the one you should be concerned about. If love laughs at locksmiths, Effie laughs harder and she's melted all the keys for fun.'

Selene exhaled a laugh. 'I shall worry about both of you. As always. The curse of the mother.'

'Well, then you should worry about Attis too. He isn't just a spell. You said it yourself, you had to biologically create him, give birth to him—'

'Anna! Please.' Selene put up a hand. 'I'm sorry, I just— I can't . . . can we leave this be? This evening has been stressful enough.'

Anna didn't want to leave it but she relented.

'Shall we drown our woes in chocolate cake?' Selene suggested.

'I'm not sure I can eat any more cake.'

'Me neither but I'm willing to give it a try.'

Selene cut them both a slice with the knife Effie had left on the table. Anna remembered with a shudder the point of it against Attis's neck.

'So,' said Anna. 'Did you get out of jail?'

'What?'

'You never said what happened after you and Marie got arrested for breaking into the swimming pool.'

Selene chuckled to herself. 'No. Marie invited the policemen into our cell. They were only a few years older than us and, like I said, no one could resist her. We ended up partying with them all night. We crept out in the morning and left them locked inside.'

They snorted over their pieces of cake.

'Though,' Selene added. 'If I'm telling the *whole* story – Vivienne was with us too. After all, it was also her birthday. She was worried at first that we'd get in trouble but she soon gave in to the fun of it. She could party just as hard as the rest of us back then. I know it's difficult to imagine but she was a very different person once . . .'

Anna left the roof with Selene's words haunting her all the way back to her room. If Aunt had once been different, how had she become who she was? Had the curse twisted her into a monster or had Aunt let the curse twist her? Had her hatred grown from the curse or had Aunt poisoned the soils from the start? How could they separate themselves from the curse that controlled them? Her mother had tried to unthread it, Aunt had tried to tie it in knots but it had got them both no matter what they did. And now, it had threaded Anna, Effie and Attis through the eye of its needle and was waiting to sew the next chapter in its dark embroidery. Could they really find a way to unstitch it altogether?

The dark thoughts began to tangle around Anna, dragging her under, but she tried to keep her head above the waters, determined not to fall back into the listlessness she'd been drowning in all summer. The night had been a disaster but at least they'd faced it – Effie had forced them to face it. There was some kind of plan now. The smallest trace of hope. Anna didn't know if she wanted it. Hope hurt. Hope killed you slowly. But the curse would kill them quickly. They had to do *something*. Follow their mother's footsteps into the darkest of woods. They would need to tread softly, carefully, to not leave the path at any cost. *Would it be enough?* Could you change the course of a curse or were all pathways doomed?

Aunt's laughter began to rise up—

Anna ignored the shivers of it, her eyes travelling to the book of fairy tales amid a stack of books on her floor. Selene's birthday gift last year – a collection of the most prominent fairy tales of the magical world. Aunt had sometimes recited them and various other stories to Anna when she was young. Anna remembered being terrified during one reading when Aunt had formed shadows on the walls with her hands. Then, as she'd told the tale, she'd given them life – the shadows rotating around Anna's room – webs of branches, outlines of dark shapes, twisted forms, mouths and fangs—

'Are you scared, my child?' Aunt had asked at the end. 'You should be. For our shadows know us better than we know ourselves . . .'

Anna walked over and pulled the book of fairy tales from the pile. She took it back to her bed but hesitated before opening it – the book had given her the spell for the moon mirror that had led her into the third-floor room; the mirror that had shown her the truth of the curse she'd always wanted to know until she knew it. *Did it help me? Or did it begin everything?* It didn't look menacing. Its cover was pale and worn, threadbare and threaded with a golden title:

East of the Sun and West of the Moon. Beneath was an engraving of a mirrored tree – one above ground and one below, roots tangled. Seven apples on each. Seven tales within.

Anna opened it gently, then screamed—

A shadow flew out at her. She heard Aunt's laugh again as she slapped her hands over her mouth and watched the shadow dance about in the air. *Not a shadow.* A black feather. The kind of black so dark it shines white. She caught it, cold travelling up her arm. *How had it got in there?* She twisted it between her fingers – its shape was sharp, a spine of fear, the fronds thick and strong. She pulled her thumb along its edge, a whisper of sound; the strum of a shadow. She thought of the ravens of her dreams uncomfortably and grew even more agitated when she saw the page the book was open on – the fourth tale: 'The Seven Ravens'.

She knew the feathered omen was no coincidence, that the book had its own intentions, but could she trust it? Was there any choice?

She took a breath and began to read.

In a place neither here nor there, where stones were not yet formed and words flowed like water, there was a girl whose eyes could not see. The blind maiden feared her stepmother's wrath and so followed her orders no matter what they were. Every day, she was sent to sit by the well at the edge of the garden and spin until her fingers bled.

One day, a raven swept down from the dark woods beyond, snatching the maiden's spindle from her hands and dropping it down the well. When the girl told her stepmother what had happened, the stepmother was outraged and demanded the maiden go down the well after it.

The girl went to her room, where she bathed in clear waters and dressed in white. She returned to the well, sensing its darkness, not knowing how deep it went. She was scared but a stronger fear drove her on – and so she jumped in.

She fell and fell until she thought she would never stop and the world seemed to turn inside out. When she landed, it was dark all around but for the first time in her life – she could see. It was snowing. She was in a forest, only the trees were white and the leaves made of shadow and the apples were blacker than a moonless sky. She began to wander through the forest but quickly lost her way, walking in circles as the shadows thickened about her and the trees tore at her clothing and scratched at her face.

Despairing, she looked up to the sky and saw a raven flying above the trees. She followed its path and it led her to a clearing in the forest. Within rose a great castle surrounded by a dark moat. The girl was desperately thirsty and decided to stop and drink of the waters, but before she could dip her hands into the moat a raven landed beside her. It began to drink but seemed unable to stop and then fell in and disappeared altogether. Startled, the girl drew back and moved quickly away to the castle door.

She pushed it open and slipped inside. The castle was empty but there were sounds coming from a doorway ahead. She discovered a great feasting hall – the scene was jubilant, with food and drink aplenty and brightly dressed people all dancing about her. A handsome prince extended his hand and they danced and danced until she felt she would never stop. No one else was stopping either. As they whirled and twirled a fire roared and threw shadows onto the wall which revealed the people in their true monstrous forms. The maiden ran free of the prince and followed the shadow of a raven to a tiny door at the side of the room. On hands and knees she crept through it.

She found herself in the castle courtyard. The maiden's true mother was sitting beside a tree. She ran to her and they hugged and wept and spoke until the maiden forgot the world existed. It was only when a raven cawed and cawed in the tree above her that she remembered she had to leave. With a heavy heart she kissed her mother goodbye and carried on, walking up to the next floor of the castle.

Here, the cold and the dark seemed to chase each other and she was met by an old woman with large teeth and a face so frightful it was all you could do not to run from it. The woman laughed viciously. 'I am Mother Holle and these are my lands! If you wish to ever leave you must come and work for me!'

In her terror, the girl could only nod. The days passed by and time lost its way as the girl worked tirelessly for the old woman, cleaning her rooms, washing her clothes, preparing her food and drink and making her bed each day.

Mother Holle would wag her claw-like finger and say: 'Make sure you shake out my bed so thoroughly its feathers fly! For when they do it snows across my lands!'

One day, when the girl shook out the bed, a black feather appeared among the white ones. It transformed into a raven.

'You have freed me!' it cawed. 'Now I shall free you. Tonight. I'll show you the way.'

The maiden hid the raven until that night, when it flew into Mother Holle's room. She followed and the raven revealed a door behind a tapestry. She was about to open it when a shadow loomed over her. She turned to find a ferocious Mother Holle. But the raven flew at the old woman, pecking and tearing at her with its sharp beak and claws.

The maiden ran. Through the doorway. Up a staircase to the highest tower.

A raven was sitting at the window. It flew out. The girl ran to the window and looked down . . . it was so high but she knew there was no other way out. She climbed up but just as she was about to jump she heard someone call her name.

She looked back.

'Ha!' Mother Holle grasped at her.

The girl threw herself from the window but Mother Holle tore her shadow from her, shrieking: 'Now part of you shall never leave. I shall keep your shadow here to roam in darkness forever!'

The girl fell upwards, back through the well, landing in her garden. The spindle was in her hand and she could still see – the world around her was bright and beautiful. She walked away from her stepmother's house, into the woods.

Anna finished the tale and closed the book but its words kept moving around her like Aunt's shadows on the walls. She waited for something to click, a jolt of understanding to seize her, but she felt nothing and the shadows moved faster – faster – closer – closer—

She picked up the feather and ran to the window, opening it a crack. She let it go. A gust of wind took it away and she watched it take flight – escape . . .

RAVENS

Many superstitions surround that of the corvus corax, the common raven. In the past, those who could understand their song were disparagingly known as 'the raving' or 'ravers', believed to be inflicted by a madness for which there was no cure.

Call of the Raven, Books of the Dead: Tome 10,465

When Anna woke, the night before came crashing back into her consciousness. The roof. The cakes. The presents. Effie holding a knife to Attis's throat. The curse proposal. The flames of the fire dancing in Attis's eyes.

He'd invaded Anna's dreams again. His lips close enough to kiss but he'd dissolved into smoke, leaving only the broken cries of ravens and the cold staircase ahead of her.

That kiss . . . that night, after the ball, it haunted her like the sweetest of ghosts. An echo of a moment in which she'd felt entirely alive. It hadn't been real. *It hadn't been real.*

Anna picked up the book of fairy tales still on her bed but her hand hovered in shock. A black feather lay beside it, caught in the white clouds of her duvet as if a raven had flown straight out of her dreams. *How?* She'd let the feather go last night . . . she'd watched it fly away. *Was it a new one? Or the same one returned?* She placed it inside the book and snapped it shut, not knowing, or perhaps not wanting to know, what it was trying to tell her.

Her phone showed two messages from Rowan from the night before:

How are things? I've just spent the last four hours obsessing over Daniel
Serkis's holiday photos online. Do I have a problem?

Another hour. Problem confirmed. How. Are. You. Text me back!

Downstairs, the kitchen was still caught in the crossfire of last night's
celebrations – champagne glasses, used plates, sparklers still sparking
and the chocolate volcano cake oozing all over the counter. Behind,
Selene's shelves of colourful magical ingredients glinted and winked
provocatively, as if to say *what are you going to do about it now?*

After Effie and Attis had gone away, Anna had spent the first few
days furiously cleaning the house – scrubbing, dusting, tidying and
polishing her way through the rooms; reordering Selene's shelves of
ingredients by colour, type and use. Old habits died hard. But chores
had brought her no peace. She hadn't been able to scrub herself away
and the house had seemed to take delight in undoing her work, the
shelves of ingredients throwing themselves out of order with relish.

She knew there was no point trying to instil order now. Effie and
Attis were back and their arrival had ruptured everything. The plan
they'd made didn't feel quite so robust by the light of day . . . Another
way to end the curse. Was it possible? They needed to uncover everything
their mother had learnt. How had the curse started? Who had cast it?
Why? Who had created the spell for Attis? How had he been created?
Was there more to it? The questions buoyed her up, taking flight around
her, but then, fell quickly back to earth. What did they really have? A
spell that might no longer exist, a divinatory witch whose whereabouts
were unknown and Pesaycha and Nana – two witches who would only
be found if they wanted to be.

She swung open the back door to the garden. The clouds were low
and motionless in the sky. She put out some fresh hay for Attis's goat,
Mr Ramsden – the school mascot Attis had stolen the year before and
named after his least favourite teacher. The goat came over to her and
nuzzled at her hands. Anna leant her head against his and breathed in
the musky smell of his black coat. She could scent smoke too, coming
from Attis's forge – its fires relit.

She closed her eyes. What if it was still a lie? Attis had hardly seemed
convinced by the plan. What if he was only agreeing to it all while he
waited for the right moment to sacrifice himself again?

'No!' Anna cried. To a goat.

Mr Ramsden bleated in response.

Surely Attis wouldn't be so stupid again. But then . . . he'd done it before. He was mad enough to do it again. Or were they mad for believing there could be another way? *Or am I mad for believing them at all?* Perhaps the plan was only a distraction to delude her, Effie and Attis pretending they weren't together when they were. Perhaps they were together right now, in Effie's room, in Effie's bed . . .

They will make a fool of you, my child, Aunt's laugh cackled in the wind—

'Thanks for feeding Mr Ramsden while I was away.'

Anna spun around to find Attis.

His forge opened onto the garden and she hadn't heard him come up the steps. She tried to collect herself, embarrassed by the suspicious spiral of her thoughts and by the way his eyes were moving with amusement over her pyjamas. They were tartan. Aunt had bought them for her. She put her arms around herself. She really hoped he hadn't seen her talking to a goat.

'I didn't think anyone would be up yet,' she said, flustered, turning back to Mr Ramsden.

'You know me, I don't sleep.' He was already dressed in his uniform: dark jeans, white T-shirt.

Do I know you? Anna wanted to reply but bit her tongue. Mr Ramsden nuzzled at her hand again.

'It seems Mr Ramsden has taken to you.' He reached out and patted the goat's nose.

'He did tell me that I'm his favourite now.'

Attis laughed. A rich, ringing sound. 'It's fair enough.'

Anna turned to leave. 'I better get back . . . get ready . . .'

'I wouldn't. Tartan suits you.' The amusement was in his voice now but Anna didn't want it. She didn't want him coming out here, catching her off guard, making jokes as if . . . as if . . . they hadn't kissed. He hadn't lied. He hadn't left.

Perhaps he sensed her reticence because his smile dropped. She went to move past him but he stepped towards her. 'Anna.' He wrenched a hand through his mess of hair. 'I just—' He cleared his throat. 'I wanted to say sorry if last night was kind of a lot. I didn't know Effie was going to do that then . . .'

'You know Effie,' Anna replied, speaking too fast, too high. 'Straight to the point. I'm fine though. I think it's a good idea. Get things sorted.'

Get things sorted. As if they could just pop their curse back into the pot it had exploded out of. Out here, in the light of day, Attis looked more real, his edges clearer. And yet, there *was* something about him that wasn't quite human. A vividness that set him apart from the rest of the world. As if he wasn't less alive than everyone else, *but more.* Perhaps it was part of his spell, designed to glint, to lure and distract. Those eyes of his; one light as a spell, one dark as a trap.

His lips drew her attention, moving as if he wanted to say more but didn't know where to start. The silence between them felt insurmountable, charged, made of so many things they couldn't speak of and couldn't undo. Anna couldn't bear the burgeoning look of pity on his face.

'I've got to go,' she said, fleeing from the garden. She didn't need his pity. She didn't need anything from him, she *couldn't* need anything from him.

By the time she reached her room she wished she'd made a smoother exit. She was still flustered as she opened up her bedside drawer and rifled about for Attis's skeleton key. She lifted it up, knowing she ought to give it back to him, but for some reason she couldn't. Not quite yet. She held it for a few moments then dropped it back in the drawer and turned to unpack a few more boxes. Keeping busy. She came across the photograph that Selene had given her last year: her parents sitting out in the garden at Cressey Square, her mother holding two sleeping babies in her arms. *Effie and I.* Happy and content, before everything had been torn apart.

Anna touched her mother's face, wishing she could see it in motion. Wondering what colours her eyes had been in the light. Before she began to crack, Anna hardened her resolve. She had to try. Not only to break the curse but to find a way to be sisters with Effie. For their mother's sake. She couldn't have died for nothing. Anna unearthed a frame for the picture and put it on her bedside table.

When she arrived back downstairs, Attis and Effie were both in the kitchen.

Attis had the fridge open. 'This house has no food in it except cake.' He turned to Anna. 'Is this all you and Selene have been living off?'

'Basically.'

He shook his head. 'I need to go shopping.'

'I'm content with cake for breakfast,' said Effie, sitting at the counter, taking bites out of the leftovers while flicking through her phone.

'You're always content so long as someone else is providing the food . . .' Attis pointed out.

'Correct.'

Anna sat down next to Effie, offering up a morning smile, but Effie didn't look up from her phone. Anna went through the post – there was a letter from St Olave's. She opened it with a sense of foreboding but it was just the usual start of term administrative information and a welcome back letter from their new headmaster: Mr Ramsden.

'What's that?' said Effie, but then screwed up her face. 'Eugh. School. Do we have to go back?'

'Not legally,' Attis replied. 'But Selene might cut you off financially if you don't.'

Effie rolled her eyes.

'Mr Ramsden's our new headmaster,' Anna stated. 'Which bodes well, seeing as he hates all of us. Well, Attis mainly.'

Attis pretended to look hurt. 'Hate is a strong word. We have a complicated relationship. I think he's fond of me beneath all the glaring and threats.'

'I'm sure we can have some fun with him . . .' said Effie, apparently warming up to the idea of returning to school.

'Effie.' Anna gave her a serious look. 'We leave headmasters alone this year. You know Headmaster Connaughty is facing charges over his relationship with Darcey?'

At least Effie managed to look guilty at that, turning her head back down to the plate.

'And Darcey isn't letting her allegations go . . .'

Effie huffed. 'Her bullshit allegations.'

'The best lies contain the truth,' said Anna, the guilt she'd been stewing in all summer curdling in her stomach. Darcey Dulacey, the most popular if not cruellest girl in their year, had been caught on camera, by Effie, with their previous headmaster. Effie had released the footage at the school ball in front of everyone, ruining Darcey's reputation in an instant. Darcey had since claimed she'd been brainwashed and coerced into the affair by *a satanic cult of witches* within the school. The guilt squeezed tighter, wringing Anna out. They weren't what Darcey was saying but they *were* witches and they *had* cast the rumour spell that had spiralled out of control and led to the affair.

'Darcey's made it clear we're the ones behind her claims,' Anna muttered. 'All eyes will be on us.'

'I'm counting on it.' Effie licked some icing from her finger.

Anna tried to maintain a pretence of cool. 'Do you not remember last year? We started a coven, set off horrific rumours, caused a headmaster–student relationship, ended up on TV—'

'I know.' Effie frowned. 'We need to be much more ambitious this year.'

Anna didn't want to laugh, she really didn't, but she couldn't help it. There was nothing left to do. 'I should move schools now, shouldn't I?'

'You'd only be giving Effie a new target,' said Attis.

'He's right,' Effie agreed, looking back down at her phone.

'I am serious though—' Anna began but Effie's face had twisted.

'Ravens . . .' she said.

Anna's heart jolted. 'What?'

'They're on the news.' Effie turned her phone around so Anna and Attis could read the headline.

RAVENS EXHIBITING CONCERNING BEHAVIOUR ABOVE THE TOWER OF LONDON

Anna had the strange sensation of the world slowing and stretching around her. She wondered if she was still dreaming . . .

Effie pulled her phone back and Attis moved around to read it. Anna stumbled out into the living room and grabbed her laptop, bringing it back into the kitchen and placing it on the counter. She opened up the news and clicked on the story, which had live video coverage. They drew around the screen. The footage displayed the Tower of London and in the sky above it a ring of ravens was flying around and around and around . . . like a nursery rhyme.

A news reporter was speaking over the footage, Anna turned the volume up:

'*—the ravens have been circling above London's infamous Tower of London for several hours now. In keeping with ancient tradition, the Tower is home to seven resident ravens but never before have they displayed such atypical behaviour. According to reports the ravens took to the skies when they were* *released from their cages at six o'clock this morning and have not ceased their strange flight path since—'*

Anna couldn't take her eyes off the birds – black serrated wings slicing silently through the grey clouds, high above the infamous spires, as if the spires were spindles and the ravens spinning invisible threads. Around and around and around . . .

'This doesn't seem normal . . .' she whispered, her body frozen by the vision. It was too close to the bone and her bones had turned cold. Dreaming of ravens, the feather in the book . . . and now there they were . . . above London for all to see as if her dreams had splintered into reality. *Or had they been a warning?*

'Not entirely normal,' Attis agreed.

The footage switched – displaying an old video of the ravens parading themselves around the Tower, strutting along the walls next to tourists. They were magnificent beasts, the apex of their species: large and formidable, oil slick feathers, colossal, hooked beaks sharpened to carnivorous points.

'Large crowds have gathered below to watch the spectacle, although the Tower has been closed and will not be open to visitors today. It has been noted that this strange occurrence comes one year on from the death of the women widely known as the Faceless Women of Big Ben—'

The footage returned to live, the birds spinning dizzily around and around and around. *Were they going faster?*

Effie leant in closer to the screen, narrowing her eyes, taking it all in, then she sat back. 'Huh,' she said, returning to eating cake.

'Huh!' Anna repeated, staring at her in disbelief. 'What do you mean – huh? This is magic! This is blatant magic on the news for all to see!'

'Maybe,' Effie shrugged, nonplussed.

'It's not necessarily magic,' said Attis. 'We can't jump to conclusions yet.'

Anna looked between them. 'A year since the Faceless Women were found hanging! That feels a little more than coincidence, doesn't it? Since when did birds just take to the sky and start flying around and around? This is some sort of magic and you both know it.' She clicked through several other news sites but it was the main story across all of them. 'It's everywhere . . .'

'Well, it *is* pretty weird,' said Effie.

Anna threw her hands up. 'So you admit it – it's weird.'

'I never said it wasn't weird. But it's also just . . . birds flying in a circle. It's not going to keep me up at night.'

Anna breathed out with audible frustration, not knowing how to explain that ravens *were* keeping her up at night, not wanting them to see the extent of her fear. 'But why is it happening? Who's behind it?'

'Could be a prank,' Effie suggested. She smirked at Attis. 'Remember that time in New York that rogue witch turned all the traffic lights into disco lights for the night? Cowans found a way to explain it away. They always come up with something suitably boring.'

Anna looked back to the video. The reporter was now interviewing one of the Tower of London's famous guards, a Yeoman Warder, dressed in their recognizable and bombastic Tudoresque uniform – black with red stripes and emblazoned with the royal initials. A black bonnet perched upon his head. He looked perplexed and disturbed as he answered the reporter's questions, trying to explain that the birds were tame and highly intelligent, that there was no reason for them to be acting in such a way.

Anna was transported to her one and only visit to the Tower of London on a school trip years ago. She recalled the high stone walls, the mighty gates, the way the Tower had felt like a stranded island of old medieval London still standing in the middle of the modern city. Where the River Thames had used to encircle it, it was now surrounded by roads and cars and queues of tourists. A Tower Guard in the same dress had taken them around, teaching them about the Tower's piecemeal history as a fortress, a palace, a prison, a haunting ground of ghosts and ghouls. They'd seen the Crown Jewels, the armoury, the dungeons, walked through Traitors' Gate where prisoners had been brought to be tortured and executed. Anna remembered hearing about how some of them had been suspected witches and she had shrunk into the shadows as if someone might lock her up in the Tower there and then and throw away the key.

Her eyes shifted back to the footage. The ravens were definitely flying faster than before. Tearing through the air in their relentless, silent flight, their wings so black against the white clouds it was as if they didn't exist at all, as if they were merely shapes cut into the sky revealing some incomprehensible darkness beneath. The crowds below were watching mesmerized, with their necks craned, phones pointed to the sky – the birds reflected on hundreds of tiny screens. Hundreds of tiny circles. *Getting faster—*

Anna felt suddenly dizzy, as if she were the one spinning.

I won't look down.

I won't look down.

'Are you OK?' Attis's eyes had narrowed on her.

Anna tried to breathe through her swelling panic. 'Yes, I'm just—'

Effie's head tilted. 'Why is this getting to you so much?'

'Because—' Anna stopped. What could she say that wouldn't make her sound crazy? That wouldn't make her sound like Aunt?

Because Aunt taught me to fear any acts of magical exposure.

Because what if my nightmares are coming true?

Because I may well be losing my mind.

'Because.' Anna steadied her voice. 'The last thing the magical world needs right now is more exposure. It's not just me. Selene's been acting off, Rowan said Bertie's worried too. Talk of magic has been growing in the news, spilling over—' Anna pointed back at the screen. 'This is the last thing we need. A magical act for everyone to see! It just feels like—' She bit her lip.

'Like?' Effie prompted.

'Like – like – it's all connected, like the things Aunt warned about are coming true . . .'

Effie's stare hardened. 'Your aunt said a lot of things.'

She said you'd betray me. She was right about that.

Effie seemed to sense Anna's hesitation. 'She's dead, Anna. Let her die.'

Anna shrank into herself. She knew how she sounded and she hated it more than anyone. 'I'm aware she's dead,' Anna replied coldly, hearing Aunt's laughter even as she said it. 'And I know she was mad but what if she wasn't wrong about it all?'

'The Binders thought magic was the downfall of all. They bound young witches' magic for fun,' said Effie with a knife-flash of hatred. 'All in the name of protecting us against some great and vague conspiracy that witches would be hunted again. Is that what you want me to believe?'

The Dark Times rising again . . .

'Yes. No—' Anna stuttered. 'I'm not saying they were right about all of it. I don't know what's going on but something killed the Seven and the magical world is clearly unsettled.'

'What are you saying then?'

'That we need to keep open minds – keep our eyes open. We need to be careful at school, we need to be careful everywhere, especially considering you and I are . . . cursed.'

Effie narrowed her eyes. 'How is that relevant?'

'Aunt said that curses are powerful magic and would attract attention . . .' Before Effie could jump in, Anna added, 'Nana said the same too.'

Anna could see the ravens on the screen in the background – scoring the sky around and around. *Faster. Faster.*

'Another highly reliable witch,' Effie scoffed.

'OK, not reliable, but powerful – an ancient witch who deals in the language of curses. She ought to know something of what she's talking about.'

Anna thought of the prophecy Nana had spoken of. It had crossed her mind often over the summer, leaving dark ripples in its wake: *The Hunters will rise again when a curse is born – a curse that will bring the downfall of the whole world.* Aunt had known of it too. How much power did this prophecy have in the magical world? Anna had brought it up with Selene but she'd brushed it off as nothing.

Anna decided not to mention it now for fear of sounding even more mad. 'We have to make sure our curse remains a secret.'

'Well, I'm hardly shouting about it from the rooftops. It's not exactly a great chat-up line. *Hey – fancy hooking up? By the way I'm also in a weird, cursed love triangle with my sister and this guy.*' Effie jerked her thumb at Attis.

Anna felt colour flood her face. Attis coughed and looked out of the window.

'But as far as I'm aware.' Effie wiggled a finger towards Anna. 'People already know about our curse – Rowan, Manda, a bunch of Wort Cunnings, Nana, Pesaycha and the Binders.'

'Our friends won't say anything and neither will the Binders, their entire life purpose is to keep magic from being discovered . . . but Nana and Pesaycha – I have no idea. We need to track them down anyway.'

Attis gritted his teeth, as if he were not happy at the proposal of speaking with Nana again.

Effie dipped her finger into the scarlet filling of one of the fruit tarts from the night before. She looked between them. 'Remember our blood pact?'

Anna nodded. Of course she remembered it. The night after their trip to Equinox, when they'd bound their blood together. A declaration of everlasting unity. A silly, drunken game. She remembered how it had felt . . . the pulse and pull of their blood, a feeling of something bigger than them, of power.

'Together, forever.' Effie's words danced somewhere between threat and teasing, but her eyes gleamed as if she were remembering that feeling too. 'With the fun hindsight of our situation, I didn't realize that it was going to be quite so . . . on the money, but it still stands. The curse is ours and ours alone. We keep it between us.'

They looked back and forth between one another, their bindings no longer ones of choice, but inescapable now, twisted and secured in place. Anna wondered if a curse could even be contained. *Or does it always find a way out?*

Cries rose up from the screen. They turned back to it. The ravens were going so fast now they'd blurred into a circle. *Too fast. Impossibly fast.* They leant in to the screen. The reporter had stopped talking, the crowd had turned silent, the circle drawing everybody into its depths.

Then, it began to break apart – splinter – pull out of shape in a frenzy of wings as if the pressure were too much—

The ravens erupted into sudden piercing shrieks, diving towards the ground. The crowd screamed and scattered. The birds hurtled downwards, their caws tearing behind them like broken nails across a chalkboard. For a moment, Anna feared they were going to attack the people below, but instead, the birds flew straight into the ground—

Anna was falling too.

I won't look down.

I won't look down.

I won't—

Something erupted behind them. The sound of a hundred glass bottles shattering.

They spun from the screen towards the noise. Tiny pieces of glass filled the kitchen – not falling but suspended, trapped like the snow inside a snow globe. Bright powders dusted the air around the cold glints of glass, liquids and oils dripped down the shelves.

Selene's collection of ingredients had exploded.

Aunt's laughter was everywhere.

AVE SATANA

Sticks and stones may break your bones,
But Hel will strip them clean.

Translation from Spiritual Communions,
Books of the Dead: Tome 12,890

'Sorry – I'll just – OK, you go that way, and I'll go—' Anna backed into the wall, while Attis passed her on the stairs, a white towel around his lean waist, water dripping down the metal threads of the horseshoe tattoo on his chest.

'Sorry.' He ran a hand through his hair, scattering droplets. 'Thought I'd get up early, get out of the way.'

Anna pulled her robe tighter around her, keeping her eyes trained on his face, wishing there were more bathrooms. 'Couldn't sleep.'

'Worried about the first day back?'

'Something like that.'

He grinned. 'Well, we should discuss shower times. Avoid further stair incidents.'

Anna nodded.

'Right. Breakfast.' Attis walked up the stairs and then stopped. He turned and pointed a finger down. 'Which is this way—'

Anna smiled at that. Perhaps he was more flustered than he let on.

She let herself into the bathroom and leant her head back against the door, breathing slowly. It was proving a nightmare living with him. Awkward meetings. Stilted conversations. The air between them tense and strained, as if they no longer knew how to act around each other.

At least they were communicating, if it could be called that, whereas Anna had barely seen Effie who'd been busy going out or sleeping or going out again. Anna didn't know what she'd expected . . . that after discussing the curse, getting everything out in the open, maybe . . . they could try . . . *what?* She laughed at herself. *Try to be sisters? Pretend like everything was back to normal?*

Nothing was normal.

Today, they had to go back to school and face rumours of witchcraft while Anna's magic was still erupting erratically. She turned on the shower, the first blast of cold driving away distracting visions of Attis's half-towelled body, but in the splash of the water all Anna could hear was the glass of Selene's potion ingredients shattering in the kitchen. Aunt's laughter. The silence that had come after, her fear retreating back into its shell.

After the incident, Selene had come downstairs aghast and no one had been able to explain it. Attis and Effie had kept giving Anna strange looks but Anna had acted as clueless as them, insisting she didn't know what had happened either. Selene had known. Just like the funeral – Anna's magic exploding, breaking everything around it. Anna already felt crazy enough without trying to explain it all to Effie and Attis – the numbness, the darkness she could sense, like something trying to claw out of her . . .

Anna thought of the ravens spiralling in circles, their wings outstretched, feathers fanned, as if they wanted to break free but some dark gravity held them in place; the staggering shadow of the Tower of London below.

Around and around – falling – dying.

Around and around – falling – dying.

Why . . .?

She turned off the shower. She couldn't get lost in thoughts of it today. She couldn't afford any more explosions. *I'm a nobody*, she tried to tell herself, but it didn't ring true. She wasn't a nobody any more, she was a witch with secrets to hide.

An hour later, she bundled herself into Attis's small Peugeot 206. Aunt would have been displeased with the state of her uniform – there were creases down her shirt, her blazer was crumpled from being boxed up all summer. She tried to smooth her hair in the mirror but no matter what she did, she couldn't make it any less bright. Unnaturally bright. She tied it back.

'EFFIE!' Attis called from outside the front door. 'I WILL CARRY YOU DOWN IF I HAVE TO!'

Effie appeared in her own unique take on the uniform. She was half dressed, her shirt hanging open, lacey bra on show, yesterday's mascara under her eyes. Attis handed her a coffee and ushered her towards the car.

Effie slumped into the front seat. 'Does school really start this early? Isn't this some kind of human rights abuse?'

'I'm not sure your case is going to stand up in court considering you went out last night,' said Attis, getting into the driver's seat.

'Oh yeah.' Effie laughed. 'It's coming back to me now.'

'We should go.' Anna tried not to sound tense. 'Probably not a good idea to be late today.'

'You're right.' Effie winked at her in the mirror. 'We need to make an entrance.'

'That's not what I meant . . .'

Attis flicked on the radio. The news blared out: '*A representative from the Tower of London has confirmed that the ravens of the Tower of London are not due to be replaced for the foreseeable future. "We would like to understand more about the cause behind the deaths of our ravens before we consider any kind of replacement. We are working with different experts to determine the exact cause—"*'

Effie changed the channel over to music. Anna fiddled with the buttons on her blazer sleeve and looked out of the window, the sky clear today, the kind of blue only autumn could dream up. 'Did you guys see that the WIPS have released a statement about the raven incident?'

'Who are they again?' said Effie, feigning boredom.

'They were called the Institute for Research into Organized and Ritual Violence before, but rebranded to the Witchcraft Inquisitorial and Prevention Services, remember?'

'Oh. Yeah. They can fuck off.'

'Unfortunately, I don't think they're going to do that. They've only been growing more vocal, lending their weight to all these stories in the news, and now their supposed "Lead Researcher", Marcus Hopkins, has come out saying what happened to the ravens was a *blatant act of male-fice* – the term they use for magic. That they've been trying to caution everyone that something like this would happen, that they suspect it's only the beginning . . .'

Attis's eyebrows met in the mirror. 'The main theory out there is that the ravens were suffering from zoochosis.'

Effie looked at him. 'What's zoochosis?'

'When animals in captivity express abnormal, repetitive or sometimes aggressive behaviours. Like you in an educational institution.'

Effie elbowed him. She turned to Anna. 'See? Cowans already have a suitably boring explanation.'

Anna already knew that zoochosis was the prevailing theory but it was easy to pick holes in. The ravens had hardly been kept in captivity. They were let out every day and had never displayed those kind of behaviours before. Zoochosis didn't simply happen overnight. 'That might be what the official channels are saying,' she mumbled. 'But plenty of people aren't buying it . . .'

She thought of just some of the comments she'd read online:

Ravens are birds of death. Is this a warning to us all?

Those Faceless Witches are blatantly behind this! The WIPS have been trying to tell us . . .

Poisoning. No way. Those birds are displaying clear signs of demonic possession.

It's said if the ravens ever leave the Tower – London will fall. The city is surely cursed . . .

Anna had looked the last one up. It was true. There was an ancient suspicion surrounding the ravens of the Tower, declaring that if the ravens ever left it that London, perhaps even the Kingdom of Britain, would fall . . .

She was about to tell the others when Attis drove through the gates of St Olave's and Anna's mouth went dry. The lawns spread out around them, idyllic in the morning sunshine – the flowerbeds trimmed, the poplar trees lining the driveway polished to bronze by the wind. The school drew itself upright before them, as grand and dour as ever, providing a dark contrast to the surroundings. With its thick red brick walls, small windows and sharply pointed towers and turrets, it offered little comfort.

Anna's hopes of arriving inconspicuously were dashed as Attis manoeuvred the car with expert recklessness into a small space in the busy car park, the exhaust going off like a firework and the radio still blasting as Effie threw open the door and stepped out.

Eyes turned in her direction, eyes that quickly widened and looked away. Students muttered, parents pursed their lips, a mother nearby steered her daughter away from them. Anna stepped out with her head down, wishing she could stay in the car. Attis waved and drove off towards St Olave's Boys' School down the road. The schools were separate but linked, especially in sixth form, where lessons and social areas were all mixed.

Anna took a breath and followed Effie up the wide school steps. Inside, the foyer had never looked so immaculate – the floors gleaming, the wood-panelled walls polished as a chestnut, a WELCOME BACK sign embossed in gold, as if the school administration had spent the summer trying to cleanse away the residues of last year, to present a new and composed face to the world: St Olave's ready to live up to its impeccable reputation once more. But they couldn't conceal the foetid scent of rumour which lingered still . . .

The muttering spread as they walked down the corridors; an edge of something new behind the frenzied chatter, a whiff of darkness, of the unknown, fear bubbling beneath the excitement. Effie cut a path through it all, her very presence already disturbing the school's veneer of presentability, like an ink spill down a freshly painted wall. She stopped at her locker and turned to assess the crowds. 'It feels good to be back, doesn't it?'

Anna gave her a look. She'd done everything she could for years to stay out of the rumour mill.

'There's no hiding in the shadows any more, *sis*. Don't you see? We are the shadows.' Effie laughed thickly.

At that moment, heads began to turn, the crowd hushing. Effie's laughter fizzled and her eyes turned to slits. The Juicers were making their way down the corridor. It was the name given to Darcey and her acolytes: Olivia and Corinne. Darcey's head was lowered, dark sunglasses on, her glossy caramel hair tied back. Olivia and Corinne gently ushered her forwards through the crowd. Pupils stood back, holding their breath, turning phones towards her – capturing Darcey's brave return. As she drew close, she dipped her glasses just a little and took a quick, fearful glance in Anna and Effie's direction. She made a small gasping sound and twitched away. Corinne took hold of Darcey's arm and steered her onwards as if they might at any moment leap out and attack, which, from the look on Effie's face, was entirely possible.

Once Darcey had passed, Effie began to clap loudly. 'And the Oscar for best actress goes to . . .' She flicked a scathing look back to Darcey, clearly annoyed that the stares had turned from them, towards her.

'It might not be an act,' said Anna, the guilt that was always there writhing inside of her again. 'After what we did . . .'

'Of course it's an act.' Effie slammed her locker shut. 'Mark my words. Darcey is loving every moment of this.'

'I'm not sure she's *loving* this. The whole school saw that footage of her with Headmaster Connaughty!'

'And since then she's spread lies about us. If you succumb to her act, she will crush you. We can't give Darcey an inch.'

Anna was about to reply when a loud voice outstripped the babble of the corridor. 'Effie! Anna!' Rowan was pushing her way through the crowd. 'Excuse me – coming through – sorry—' She made an apologetic face at a girl. 'Didn't see your foot there. Or the other one. Hi guys.' She threw her arms around them. 'Am I glad to see you both.' She drew back, her thick eyebrows raised high, her dark hair wilder than ever. 'Is it just me or is everyone looking at us? Talking about us? I'm not ready for this level of attention. My hair is not ready! Weeks of drizzle and wind and it's wild as knotweed. I was hoping this whole thing might have blown over but apparently teacher–student relationships and brainwashing cults are very much still capturing everyone's imagination.' She fell against the wall with a sigh. 'I'd planned on being famous one day but I hoped it would be because I went viral, or was finally dating actor Leonardo Vincent, not because I'm an accused satanist. Am I acting strangely?'

'No more than usual,' said Effie.

'Sorry.' Rowan took a breath. 'I'm not used to being talked about beyond, you know, being "the fat girl". I almost miss those days right now. Almost. It's just—'

'Rowan.' Effie threw an arm around her. 'It's OK. Relax. Sticks and stones may break our bones, but we know words of power.' She winked.

Rowan looked troubled by Effie's words but before she could say anything the bell for assembly rang above them.

Rowan cringed. 'Yay,' she said with monotone sarcasm. 'Time to face the entire school all in one room. Do you think they'll put us in the stocks? Oh, there's Manda!'

Effie grabbed hold of a lost-looking Manda walking with the crowd towards the main school hall known as the Athenaeum. Manda clutched Effie back. 'I wondered where you guys were!' she said, looking half relieved, half distressed to see them. 'Not that I'm sure we should all be seen hanging out together any more. It's not going to look good considering we're supposedly Satan's little gang. Oh Lord, I can't believe I'm a gang member.'

'Manda, you're about as far from a *gang member* as it's possible to be,' said Effie, pulling her down the corridor.

'Why don't I just get 666 tattooed on my forehead and be done with it!'

Rowan chuckled and slotted her arm through Anna's, following behind them. 'At least seeing how stressed Manda is makes me feel calmer.'

Anna forced a laugh, trying not to show she was more stressed than all of them put together.

Rowan squeezed her arm and gave her a look. 'How are you? You stopped replying to my texts.'

'Sorry. There *were* a lot . . . I'm fine.'

'*Fine* is how you replied to the texts you did reply to. *Fine* is not a reassuring word.'

Anna swallowed. 'I'm – things are—' She nodded towards Effie ahead. 'We're at least speaking again. Sort of.'

Rowan smiled encouragingly. 'Well, that's something. And, er – how's Attis?'

'Well, Attis is still . . . Attis.'

Rowan nodded as if she understood. 'There sure is only one Attis. Shame really. It would be great if there were more of him to go around.'

Their laughter fell away as they entered the Athenaeum. It was an imposing room at the best of times, but today its grandeur felt threatening – the ceiling too high, the rows of seats like judgement, the large stained-glass window cold and pale with morning light. Anna had spent the whole summer hiding from everyone, even herself, and now . . . there was nowhere to hide.

They took their seats amid the scrutinizing chatter. On the stage, Darcey, who was now, of course, head prefect, had taken up her position at the front, only she wasn't looking out with her usual air of command. Her head was bowed, hands clasped as if in prayer. If it was an act, it was a good one.

Mr Ramsden stomped up the stairs onto the stage but his presence had little impact on the noise of the room. 'Quiet. Quiet, all. SILENCE!' he yelled, banging a fist on the lectern. He stood taller and gloomier behind it than Headmaster Connaughty had. His eyebrows and cheeks were heavy as a bulldog's; his downturned mouth managed to look both displeased and smug at the same time, as if becoming the new headmaster was a burden he intended to take out on the rest of them with grim relish. He'd always managed to exercise his small amount of power as deputy head with unpleasant efficiency and Anna was sure he'd exploit the opportunities granted by his new role. 'SILENCE!' He tapped the microphone aggressively. 'Is this on? Right, well. Let's get on with it. Welcome back to St Olave's School for Girls. Summer is over. I am sure there's plenty to look forward to in what will no doubt be a bright and shining year,' he said in a voice that was far from bright or shiny. He droned on, taking them through the school updates and news and making sure to remind them all of the school's long list of rules. Then, he came to a pause.

'Now,' he said, livening up a little. 'Following the events at the end of last year—'

Whispers rushed through the crowd. Anna reached for a Knotted Cord that wasn't there. *Keep it together.*

'SILENCE! The matter is being handled by the police and will not be discussed any further. Headmaster Connaughty will not be returning and I will be taking over as your new headmaster for the foreseeable.' He pulled his shoulders back, raising his chin. 'In my new role, my primary concern is the troubling allegations that have arisen in the wake of these events. Allegations of bullying and cult activity on school grounds.'

A fresh wave of unrest broke out. Darcey raised a handkerchief to her eye, dabbing at it with her head still trained to the floor. Anna gripped her chair as the guilt and fear began to drag her down again, her heart pounding distantly.

'I SAID SILENCE!' Ramsden scoured the crowd, his expression like a metal bristle. 'I can reassure you all that we are taking these allegations seriously. As a result, the decision has been made to allow an independent inspection into St Olave's to carry out a full assessment of the situation and a review into our internal anti-bullying procedures to ensure the safety of every single pupil—'

The noise bubbled over. Manda squeaked, Rowan gasped. Anna could feel Effie looking at her but she could not move, fearing what might erupt from her.

'THIS IS THE PROBLEM WITH THIS SCHOOL!' Ramsden exploded. 'Gossip! Gossip! Gossip! I will not tolerate gossip and hearsay under my rule!' He turned an uncomfortable purple colour as he tried to rein in his rage. 'Any discussion of these allegations will be met with severe punishment. If you have any concerns then you bring them to me!' It was not an encouraging invitation. 'The inspection is due to begin immediately and with minimal disruption to everyday life. I expect you all to cooperate duly.' He forced a threatening smile. 'And now, I'd like to briefly introduce you to the man leading the inspection. Please welcome Mr E—'

Mr Ramsden stopped abruptly as if the word had lodged in his throat. He coughed sharply and began again. 'Mr E—'

He released a hostile, irritated laugh. 'Mr E—' He tried again to force the name between enraged lips but the sound merely drew itself out into a long 'Eeeeeeeee'.

Laughter spilt from the crowd now, but Anna didn't join in. Her hands gripped together. *What is happening? Magic! My magic? Is it me?* Then she saw the look on Effie's face beside her. A look of such innocence that she knew at once Effie was guilty. Effie snorted under her breath and Anna nudged her, hard.

'MR EAMES!' Ramsden yelled suddenly at the top of his lungs. He breathed out, shaking his head with irate confusion.

The attention shifted from him to movement along the front row of the audience, where the teachers were sitting. A man stood up and turned to face them. He nodded briefly, abruptly. He was not remarkable. He looked to be in his thirties, lean and dressed in a black suit with a thin red tie. His hair was dark and combed with a hint of grease about it. His face was narrow, tapering to a weak chin balanced on a long neck. The kind of face you'd forget instantly if you passed it on the street – and yet – there was something about it that made Anna squirm. The starkness of his expression or the hollowness of his eyes, which ticked slowly over the crowd. Clinical, cold, empty. The laughter of the pupils evaporated, the man achieving the silence that Mr Ramsden hadn't managed the entire assembly.

He sat back down.

A now dishevelled-looking Mr Ramsden clutched the lectern. 'Thank you – thank you, Mr Eames.' He glared viciously at the rest of them. 'I am sure you will all treat our inspector with the utmost respect as he carries out his work here. And then, St Olave's can put all of this behind it.'

Anna left assembly somewhere between dazed and acutely shocked. She was desperately glad she hadn't lost it, but . . . *an inspection! An inspection into Darcey's allegations!* Mr Ramsden hadn't mentioned anything magical – the school wouldn't want to associate itself with Darcey's more outlandish claims – but even so, it would only draw more attention onto them right at the moment they needed to disappear . . .

Whispers. Whispers. Anna could feel the tickle of Aunt's laugh against her ear.

For a moment, she had the overwhelming urge to run to Headmaster Ramsden's office and confess to it all; to scream the truth from St Olave's spired rooftops. *We did it! We did it! I confess! Then you wouldn't be able to say anything, would you, Aunt? I'd have punished myself once and for all.* But Anna caught Rowan's eyes, which were a mirror of her own alarm and concern, and she knew she couldn't. If she told the truth of what had happened last year, she wouldn't just be exposing magic to the world . . . she'd be turning her friends in too.

The bell rang with urgency above them.

'Let's talk at lunch,' said Effie, giving them all a meaningful if exhilarated look. She appeared to be revelling in the action of their first day back.

Anna kept her head firmly down during her morning's lessons, not that anyone appeared to be interested in speaking to her. Only about her. Assembly kept going around her head – the face of Inspector Eames splicing into her thoughts. She couldn't stop thinking of that stare of his, not knowing if there'd been anything unsettling about it or if it had simply been her own paranoia; her own guilt staring her back in the face.

As she made her way to the sixth-form canteen at lunchtime, she was relieved to hear Manda's voice behind her.

'Hey! Wait for me! I don't want to go into the lion's den alone.'

Anna didn't want to go in alone either. The whole of their year would be there as well as boys from the Boys' School. They linked arms tightly and went through the door. The room reverberated with the noise of a hundred different conversations taking place at once. *Or perhaps all the same conversation* . . . Eyes snapped their way and the chatter oscillated with excitement. Anna saw a group at a table nearby looking up at them and then down at something on one of their phones.

'I feel like I'm having one of those dreams where I'm naked and everyone's looking at me,' Manda whimpered.

'My favourite dream.' Effie laughed, coming into the room behind them with Rowan in tow. 'Soak it up, sisters. This is what popularity feels like.'

'We're not popular, we're the freaks of the school!'

'Even better.'

'Wait.' Manda spun back to the others, eyes frantic. 'Is that Karim over there? Is he – is he looking at me?'

'Yes,' Effie confirmed. 'But not in a good way.'

Manda groaned.

'Come on. There's a spare table at the back,' said Rowan, moving onwards. But someone blocked their path.

> *Witches! Witches!*
> *What a bunch of bitches.*
> *They'll tittle, they'll tattle,*
> *They'll mutter their spells,*
> *They'll fuck with the devil*
> *And send you to hell!*

Tom Kellman completed his song, looking entirely pleased with himself.

'Wow, you're finally learning how to put whole sentences together,' said Effie. 'You've come on so well over the summer.'

Tom laughed boisterously and leant back against the high table he'd been standing at. It was surrounded by the boys Anna had least wanted to come across – the highest-ranking in the school's hierarchy: Tom, Andrew, Hutton, Digby and . . . Peter. He was staring at her intently. Anna looked away, trying not to remember the last time she'd seen him – he'd been unconscious, slumped in a chair in Aunt's living room, about to be sacrificed in the name of her curse. At least he'd never have any recollection of it. Anna wondered how she could ever have thought she *loved* him. She'd believed he wasn't like the others but he'd proved to be exactly the same in the end.

He looked different – his blond hair sheared shorter, his face leaner, sculpted by a summer tan. His eyes had a new intensity to them, as if something had been peeled away. The blue beneath was arresting. Anna couldn't believe how many daydreams she'd wasted on that specific shade of blue. *Fuckwit*, she heard Attis say in her head, and hid the smile that rose to her lips.

Tom looked Effie up and down with relish, as if she was dressed in his favourite sauce. 'Did you miss me, witchy?' He bit his smug, full lips and ran a hand through his impeccably sculptured black hair. He was the kind of handsome that was entirely too sure of itself; the kind of handsome that was entirely undone by his brash and buffoonish personality.

'Who are you again?'

'Come on, nobody ever forgets my name after calling it out all night. Tom! Oh, Tom! Ohhhhh, Tom!' He flung his head back and cried out loudly, not helping the stares in their direction.

'I think you'll find you're calling your own name out there,' Effie replied. 'Which I presume means that you spent the summer masturbating. Alone.'

'Care to help me next time?' Tom heehawed, not realizing he had remained the butt of her joke.

Andrew slapped a hand on his shoulder. 'I wouldn't get too close. You might catch something.' His eyes slid over Effie and then the rest of them. With his twitchy nose and prominent front teeth Andrew had always reminded Anna of a mouse – a mouse that liked to creep out of its hole sporadically to deliver vicious, snide attacks on those he considered below him, which was just about everyone. 'Plus—' Andrew looked back to Effie. 'She's sloppy seconds.' He nodded his head to Peter, laughing.

'Shut it, Andrew,' said Peter, coldly.

Andrew put his hands up. 'Just saying.'

'Actually, Effie and I hooked up first, didn't we?' said Tom.

'In your wet dreams.' Effie rolled her eyes. 'I wouldn't touch you if I was paid to.'

Tom's flirtatious expression soured. 'Too busy with every other boy in this school . . . did they pay?'

Andrew snorted, high-fiving Tom.

'Anna.' Peter cut through them with a voice that didn't need to raise itself to be commanding. 'Could we talk?'

'No, I'm good,' said Anna, realizing her reply sounded mildly sarcastic though she hadn't meant it to. Andrew seemed to find that funny too, turning to her. He'd never paid her any notice but he took her in now and she didn't like the sensation of his eyes roving over her.

'Anna, please—' Peter began again.

'She said no, Peter,' Effie barked. 'But you don't like taking no for an answer, do you?'

Peter's head repositioned to Effie, his pained expression twisting into a tight grimace. 'I'm speaking to Anna.'

'And I'm telling you to fuck off.'

'Effie, leave it,' Anna muttered.

'Yes and please leave.' Digby made a gesture for them to move on. 'Why are we even talking to them? They're fucking weirdos.'

'You bet we are,' Effie bit as Anna dragged her away.

Anna could feel Peter's gaze following her. Why did he want to talk to her? She'd presumed he would have moved on over the summer, found someone more popular, somebody who wouldn't refuse him when he asked them to go back to his room . . .

'Maiden, mother and bloody crone, I hate those guys.' Rowan sat at a table that was as far away from everyone else as possible. 'Have they got worse? I feel like they're worse.'

'They've always been that bad,' Manda grumbled.

'Tom called us witches.' Anna dropped down into a seat. 'To our faces.'

Effie waved a hand. 'It was just a dumb song.'

'That song is the tip of the iceberg we're currently buried under.' Rowan shook her head, taking out her phone. '*Someone* anonymously uploaded this video this morning and everyone's been sharing it.'

Rowan turned the screen to the rest of them. The footage that started playing was black and white, distant and smudged – almost dreamlike: five blurred, unidentifiable figures moving around a fire, flames leaping and looping bright shapes in the darkness. Four of them in white dresses, flying behind them like white-tailed birds; one of them standing tall and mighty with horns upon his head. It was them on the school grounds on last year's May Day. Caught live . . . caught full of life – bursting with it. The CCTV footage that had ended up on the news alongside Darcey's allegations, lending credence to the idea that there were rituals and *cult practices* going on in the school.

Anna's heart quickened as the giddy freedom of that night rose around her, pushing the confines of the room away – hawthorn brandy on her lips, Attis's fivefold kisses on her body, wind shaking, trees quaking, the light of the fire painting wild shapes on their skin. The Coven of the Dark Moon drunk on delirium and delight. It was not what it would look like to everyone else; not the silly jubilations of teenagers but unknown, shadowy figures playing far too close to the fire, crazed and demented, the shape of the devil among them.

'The video title is *Ave Satana*,' Rowan stated wanly. 'It means Hail Satan.'

'Darcey blatantly put this up,' Manda hissed. 'To stir everything up first day back.'

'Of course,' Effie concurred as if she would have done the same in Darcey's position.

'It's not like it needed stirring,' said Rowan. 'Darcey's spent the summer elaborating on her claims, posting personal videos, sharing her story, drip-feeding everyone the drama.'

Anna had watched some of the videos but hadn't been able to face them all.

'What's she said altogether?' Effie sat back as if she was looking forward to hearing it all.

Rowan leant in. 'She doesn't name us. Probably not allowed to, but it's so obvious she's talking about us . . . She said everything started when the *new pupil* joined. She's not wrong there.' Rowan gave Effie a pointed look.

Effie put her hands up. 'My bad.'

'She said that we harassed her, shamed her, taunted her; spread slanderous things about her, pitted everyone against her. Then, it gets darker – that we muttered threats in her ear, cast spells against her, leaving her with migraines and nightmares. That she still has them – seeing our faces in the darkness. That it all culminated when we lured her into an old classroom after-hours and carried out a ritual around her. She really went big on that, apparently we encircled her, chanted Latin, wrote our names in a book, conjuring up dark forces until she passed out and, after that night, she no longer had control over herself; her own mind.'

Effie laughed. 'Latin incantations, blood signatures, pacts with the devil. She's lifted it all from a movie. Cowans have such limited imaginations.'

'Oh, I don't know.' Rowan glanced at the room behind them. 'Their imaginations seem pretty active to me. They've been eating it all up and adding their own tasty twists – there are rumours we drank Darcey's blood, that we raised the dead, had an orgy with Satan . . . I think at one point we're meant to have sacrificed a goat.'

Effie snorted.

'No one's actually buying this?' Manda spluttered. 'I tried to get people to believe in God for years with no one ever turning up to Bible study, but oh, they're perfectly happy to believe I'm offering a dead goat to the devil?!'

'Of course people don't really *believe* it,' said Rowan. 'But they don't care. Fake news is more fun than real news, especially if it involves orgies.'

Effie put a hand up. 'Amen to that.'

'And now we have this inspection to deal with.' Rowan slumped in her chair.

Anna's stomach twisted as the inspector came back into her mind.

'Darcey's blatantly behind that too. Her parents are on the governors' board and Mum's always said it's the parents on the board that really run our school. They've probably pushed for the inspection to make her claims seem somehow legitimate.'

'There was no mention of witchcraft,' Effie retorted to Rowan. 'Even if they find us guilty of bullying or being in some kind of *cult*. What are they going to do? Students aren't expelled for that kind of thing any more, they're made to talk about their feelings.' She looked disgusted at the thought.

'It might go on our records, damage our chances of getting into a top university,' said Manda.

Effie clicked her fingers. 'Oh no, you mean Oxbridge are going to reject me now?'

Manda gave her a flat look. 'You don't get it. My parents are going to find out about this inspection and things are bad enough already. Since the allegations, they've gone into a full restore-the-Richardson-family-image campaign, which seems to mainly comprise of watching my every move. Mum looks at me like she doesn't even know me—' Manda shut her eyes and took a breath. 'I wasn't even sure I'd be coming back; they'd been talking about moving me out of St Olave's but I think they were worried it would interrupt my final year and draw more attention to the whole thing. The only way I can get through all of this is to convince them I'm normal while being exceptional – secure top marks in all my coursework, nail my exams, get into the country's top law schools and get Karim back. I'm sure my parents would prefer a Christian boy but once they find out Karim's going to be a dentist, they'll come around. It's a highly respected profession.'

Rowan shook her head dizzily. 'That's a lot of pressure, Manda. I haven't even got as far as looking up where my next class is, let alone applications . . .'

Anna tried to think about her previous plans but they felt a lifetime away. She'd been intending to apply for medical school but was it even what she wanted? She couldn't remember if it had been her idea or Aunt's. It didn't feel like it mattered any more. She found it strangely hard to imagine any future . . . as if that day Aunt had died, she'd died too.

'If we're caught, it's penance, isn't it?' Manda's eyes widened. 'The rumours are back for us now. The rule of three: *Whatever ye send forth, comes back to thee.*'

Effie waved a hand. 'There's no such thing as the rule of three. Magic doesn't work that way.'

'Well, how does it work?'

'Chaos.' Effie's eyes lit up with the word, like orbs of static.

'Balance,' Rowan countered.

'Either way,' Anna spoke up at last, 'we *are* guilty. We did cast a spell on Darcey.'

'We didn't know it was going to get so out of hand,' said Effie.

Didn't you? Anna held in her reply. She would probably never know the truth – if Effie had truly known how dark the spell would get, the destruction it would cause.

'And we didn't do any of the things Darcey's claiming,' Manda added. 'Well, mostly . . .'

'True.' Effie grinned. 'We never sacrificed a goat.'

They began to giggle – the desperate, uncontrolled laughter that can only be shared by outsiders with the rest of the world at their backs. They looked between one another and despite all of it, despite what they'd done, what they were meant to have done, the threads of the year before pulled at them – magic filled with moments as bright as the moon, as dark as its shadow, the kind of magic Darcey could never dream up.

Effie raised her drinking cup. 'Ave Satana!'

'Shhh, Effie!' Rowan swatted at her. 'Let's not add more flames to the sacrificial fires, OK? It was you in assembly, wasn't it? When Ramsden couldn't say the inspector's name.'

Effie attempted to look virtuous but gave in with a snigger. 'It was barely a spell. A tiny cantrip.'

Rowan narrowed her eyes. 'We just have to make it through one year.'

'Maybe it's a good thing Karim and I split up,' said Manda woefully. 'This way I can keep my focus. But I can't focus because I miss him and now he thinks I'm a whore of Satan.' She dropped her head into her arms.

Effie looked down at her incredulously. 'You guys went out for, like, twelve minutes.'

Manda's head shot back up. 'Three months and fifteen days actually. I had it all planned – power couple, house in Richmond, two kids, a golden labradoodle.'

Rowan threw an arm around her. 'Manda, why don't you join me? This year I've decided I'm over boys. I'm going to concentrate on my studies, my future, not looking at pictures of Daniel Serkis topless on the beach . . .'

Manda frowned. 'Who's that?'

'You know, in our year – tall, auburn hair, rippling six-pack . . .'

Manda shrugged.

'There you go,' Rowan concluded, 'I'm going to become more like Manda, too busy with my head in books to notice the male form. Any boyfriends I have will be entirely imaginary. Easier that way – all of the fantasy, none of the rejection.'

'But, I don't want an imaginary boyfriend. I *want* Karim. I still can't believe he broke up with me. We loved each other, we'd had SEX—' Manda mouthed the word.

'We know, Manda, you've told us. A lot.'

'Then he ends it all and gets back with his ex-girlfriend. Apparently, I was too intense. Well, I intend to get him back whatever it takes. Nobody breaks up with Miranda Richardson.'

Effie stared at them both, astounded. 'What's wrong with you two?'

'We can't all be like you.' Rowan sighed. 'Just talking to men like it's nothing. How it must feel to be Effie for the day.'

Effie smiled and flourished a hand like Selene would. 'Like I can have anyone in this room.'

They glanced behind them, and at that moment – Attis entered. He spotted them and waved. They turned back to one another, an awkward silence settling. They couldn't exactly talk about Anna and Effie's love lives when they were tangled – caught in the net of the boy who had just walked through the door.

Attis, broad-shouldered and hair awry, strode through the room, bending it to his will – people turning and smiling at him. S*miling!* How was he getting smiles and they were basically getting spat at? He stopped to chat to one table and fist bumped someone else before reaching them.

'OK. How come everyone still likes Attis?' Manda asked, mirroring Anna's thoughts.

'Because.' He took a seat. 'I'm the frontman of the group. The devil in disguise. Sex god and purveyor of orgies. Also, I think I'm just more approachable. You guys are kind of scary.' He smiled and the tension of the table dissipated.

'It's true. Witches are more terrifying than any devil.' Effie's lips quirked.

'The things people are saying today.' Attis blew air from his lips. 'I heard Manda can drain a man's entire body of his blood with nothing more than the power of one of her highlighter pens.'

Manda tried to glare at him through her laughter.

But the humour had drained from Rowan's voice. 'Thirteen black moons,' she murmured.

The Juicers were approaching their table, the green juices they were named after in hand. Anna hadn't even noticed them enter but now they were drawing everyone's attention in their direction. Darcey's expression was fragile, as if she might shatter at any moment. Anna wanted to hate her with her old surety, but it was no longer clear who was the real enemy: Darcey or them.

'Darcey, you don't have to,' said Corinne, tossing her dyed red hair.

'I do.' Darcey moved nobly forwards. 'I need to say this.'

'And we can't wait to hear it.' Effie leant back in her chair, tilting her head.

Olivia held her phone up towards them. Darcey discarded her empty juice cup on their table and began to speak, slowly and audibly so everyone nearby could hear. 'I just want to say that—' She stopped, closed her eyes and steadied herself. 'In spite of everything that's happened and what I've been through – what you all did to me – I want you to know that . . . I forgive you.' She said the words like an offering they did not deserve, like a queen reluctantly giving her starving subjects food to eat. 'I know that living in anger and shame won't get me anywhere. I want to move forwards with my life. All I ask of you is that you let go of your bitterness and jealousies and move on too. I don't want you to do to anyone else here what you did to me. I—' She put a hand to her mouth, her nails freshly manicured. 'I couldn't bear anyone to suffer like I have.'

It was convincing, she was entirely convincing, dipping her head to brush her hair behind her ear, Corinne putting a hand of solidarity on her arm. Olivia scowled at them over her phone as if they were unworthy of Darcey's very presence, let alone her forgiveness.

Anna could feel Effie stirring beside her. *Don't do anything rash, please, Effie.*

But Effie placed a hand on her heart. 'Thank you, Darcey. That's very sweet of you. We know you've been through a lot. We've all been very concerned about your mental health.' Effie pulled a face. 'But we're so glad you're moving on and letting your delusions go.'

Darcey's mouth twitched as if she were restraining a snarl. 'I am not delusional. You all know what it is you did to me, what you're capable of . . .'

It was hard to tell if Darcey was performing any more. Anna could see something like fear in her eyes, but her rage was more powerful, propelling her. The whole room had turned silent, craning their necks to see the action play out live. More phones had popped up to film it all.

'Darcey,' Effie sympathized. 'We all just want you to get better, to stop peddling these fantasies. They're making you look kind of . . . crazy.'

'You can try and twist my words, Effie, you can try and humiliate me all over again, but the truth will out. Everyone can feel that you're not *normal*, none of you, and soon they will all see what you truly are.'

Anna could feel the eyes of everyone around her, trapping her in the room; she could hear Aunt's accusations in her ear. *You're rotten, rotten through—*

Effie cocked her head. 'And what is that, Darcey?'

Darcey raised her chin. 'Evil. Powerful. Witches.'

There was an intake of breath around them but Anna's breath had disappeared, locked in her chest, *too tight.*

I won't look down—

Effie's sudden laughter shocked her before she could lose it entirely. Effie threw her hands up. 'You've got us! I confess!' She snorted another laugh. 'It's true. Watch out!' She pointed a finger at Darcey. 'Supercalifragilisticexpialidocious!'

More laughter. People joining in.

'Step back, Darcey,' Attis warned, cracking a smile. 'She's turned a lot of people into frogs that way. Frogs. Rats. Piglets if she's in the mood.'

That set everyone off even more, but Darcey's face was no joke. She leant forwards, placing two hands on the table, her mask slipping and finally revealing the snarl beneath. Her voice was a hissed whisper, for their ears only. 'I will see you punished for what you did if it destroys me.'

Darcey's eyes raked over them, stopping at Anna as if she could see it – *the rot*. Anna could feel it, spilling out of her.

'We can only hope,' Effie replied with a smile formed of threat.

Darcey pushed away from the table, her face fracturing again for the crowd. 'I tried . . .' she said, plaintively. 'They are beyond help.'

'You've done more than they deserve,' Olivia spat. They wrapped their arms around her and ushered her away. The rest of the room parted for them, whispering voraciously, hungrier than they'd ever been.

'Allowing the likes of you into this school was the worst thing Headmaster Connaughty ever did!' Ramsden growled.

'I think he might have done something worse . . .' Effie muttered.

Mr Ramsden's face flushed, the broken veins around his nose flaring. They were lined up in his office: Anna, Effie, Attis, Manda and Rowan; Ramsden pacing and fuming before them like a rhinoceros forced into a suit. 'How dare you! How dare you cause a scene on the first day back at school!'

'Don't see why we're being told off,' Effie spat. 'Darcey was the one who approached us.'

'You had the crowd laughing at her, whipping them up against her, after what she's been through . . .'

'You mean, after how much money Darcey's parents have paid you to instigate an inspection . . .'

Ramsden stopped and stared at Effie as if he wished corporal punishment was still allowed in schools. He narrowed his bloodshot eyes. 'You ought to all step very carefully with the accusations levelled against you.

All summer we've had parents up in arms, the press sniffing around . . . and I have done everything in my power to keep the situation under control. I will not let you make a mockery of me, *or* this inspection.'

'I agree.' Attis nodded firmly. 'I'm sure you're quite capable of doing that yourself, Mr Ramsden.'

Effie snorted but before Ramsden could strangle him, Anna jumped in. 'It won't happen again, Mr Ramsden.'

He pulled himself up. 'You bet it won't. You will not speak to Darcey. You will not break a single rule this year. You will allow this inspection to run smoothly until it is over. And if you are found responsible, I will ensure you face the full repercussions.'

Manda squeaked.

'That's right, Miss Richardson. I hold your future in my hands.'

Anna wondered how their first day back could be going so badly.

'I'd just like to take this moment,' Attis announced, 'to offer my huge congratulations, Mr Ramsden, on your promotion to the position of headmaster. You're doing a fine job already, very commanding, just the right level of intimidation. Not that you're letting the power go to your head.'

It tipped Ramsden over the edge. 'OUT! OUT ALL OF YOU! DON'T THINK YOU'RE GETTING AWAY WITHOUT A DETENTION, LOCKERBY!'

'My perfect future!' Manda wailed as they walked down the corridor from his office. 'Everything I've worked my whole life for – Ramsden's going to ruin it all.'

'Ramsden's just making empty threats,' said Effie. 'They can't prove a damn thing.' She cut down a sudden corner, into a quiet dead-end corridor, an alcove window at the end. She turned to face them all. 'I think we're all forgetting something – we *are* the witches here. The power is ours, not theirs. We can discuss further at our coven-meet.'

Manda shifted from foot to foot. 'We're not . . . reforming the coven here . . . are we?'

'We're not reforming anything,' Effie replied, a hard line in her voice. 'We are a coven. We shall continue to be one. Is there some confusion?'

'Is this really the best time to start doing magic again on school grounds?' said Rowan. 'Olivia was filming our whole interaction back then. Darcey wants to catch us out. One wrong move . . .'

Effie stirred the dust in the light from the window with her fingers, her eyes stilling. 'The Dark Moon is at its greatest power in the dark, not the light, is it not? They are trying to threaten us, intimidate us. Are we going to let them? Are we going to roll over and cower? Or are we going to rise again, greater than ever?'

Rowan did not look convinced by Effie's speech. She put her hands on her hips, looking entirely like her mum, Bertie. 'If we're going to be a coven, it has to be for the right reasons. Not for more revenge.'

'What about mostly the right reasons and a sprinkling of revenge?' Effie smiled, showing sharp incisors. 'Jooooking.' She made eyes at Rowan. 'I'm just talking about keeping our magic alive, growing our powers, staying in control of the situation – not letting it control us.'

Rowan shook her head. 'It's too risky.'

'I agree,' said Attis. 'Which is why I'm appointing myself health and safety officer of this coven. There's going to be all kinds of precautions and new security measures. Box-ticking and unnecessary traffic cones. I might wear a uniform.'

Rowan snorted. 'Unfair tactic, Attis . . .'

Anna had spent all summer running from magic but there was nowhere to run now. She had to face it – to face Effie. 'I don't think we should reform the coven,' she said from behind the others. 'I'm not practising magic right now and don't intend to any time soon.'

After everything that had happened that day, Anna hadn't expected to see them appear at their most shocked *now*. All of them turned to her with expressions of surprise and confusion.

'What?' said Attis, a flare of anger in his voice. 'What do you mean, you're not practising magic?'

'I'm just taking a break,' Anna replied plainly. 'After the whole curse discovery . . .'

An incredulous noise burst from Effie's lips. 'I'm cursed too! You don't see me running away from my magic.'

Anna bristled. 'I'm not running away. I'm trying to do the right thing.'

'By repressing your magic?' Effie lashed out. 'That sounds more like a Binders' tactic . . .'

'Aunt wanted the curse to destroy everything! I'm doing everything in my power to stop that.'

'By giving up your greatest power? You're just afraid.'

'I'm not afraid,' Anna cried, hating the weakness in her voice. 'I'm just making sense. You and I shouldn't be casting together, the consequences are too unknown, too dangerous.'

Effie stared at her, looking somehow betrayed and livid at the same time. She blinked and it was gone, her eyes black and blank, a hard wall of threat. Anna steadied herself against the force of Effie's anger but when Effie spoke her words were measured, formed of compacted ice. 'Deny your magic and you deny yourself. We will reform the coven or I'll personally go to Mr Ramsden myself and confess to everything – bullying, brainwashing, satanic worship, goat sacrifice – *whatever*. Enough to explode all our futures to smithereens.'

'Effie, you wouldn't!' Manda shrieked.

'Wouldn't I?' The look on Effie's face was not something to gamble on. 'We're all in or I'm taking you all down with me.' She pushed past them all and disappeared around the corner, leaving a brittle silence behind her.

Rowan sighed. 'I don't think she understands how a team works.' She turned to Anna, her eyebrows meeting. 'Anna, I know you've been through so much, but you can't give up—'

But Anna didn't want to hear it, she was still too tangled up in Effie's rage, her own. 'Why does everyone think I'm giving up?' she snapped.

'Because you are,' said Attis, his voice rough. 'Join the coven, don't join the coven, I don't care – but, Effie's right, being a witch is not a choice.'

Of course he didn't care what she did. 'What a surprise, you think Effie's right! Let's do everything she says, as always, hey?' She looked between them all. 'Apparently, *I'm* the one who's scared but you're all too scared to ever say no to her! It'll all go back – it'll all just go back to how it was before.'

They shifted uneasily at her words. Attis looked away, releasing a fuming breath.

'You still can't give up your magic,' said Rowan. '*A witch who turns from the moon ends up lost or a loon,*' she incanted quietly. 'An old saying but a true warning—'

'Better than dead!' Anna hissed, swivelling on her heels and storming off, without the composure of Effie but fuelled by just as much indignation.

She fled down the corridors, knowing she needed to go to class, but finding herself running to the music room instead. The place she'd always come to escape. She rushed inside and leant against the door, breathing hard, wanting to scream or cry but finding nothing inside to carry either out of her.

'Fuck!' she settled for instead.

The room met her with its usual hush – the shadowy outlines of instruments, the silence of music waiting to be formed. Slowly, her breathing calmed, the rush and rabble of her thoughts diminishing. She felt bad for losing her temper. She hadn't meant to snap but she couldn't stand the way they'd been looking at her. Couldn't stand to see who she was reflected in their eyes.

Afraid.

Yes, she was afraid. These days it felt as if there was nothing left of her but fear. But didn't she have reason to be? After the things she'd done . . . all the things the curse wanted her to do . . .

They are the ones who should be afraid.

She collapsed onto the piano stool, thinking of Effie. Had she meant what she said? Would she really turn them all in? Anna didn't know. That was the worrying thing; she had no idea what Effie would do, how far she would go.

She put her hands on the piano, remembering with a painful tug the freedom of the night they'd danced around the fire, the feeling of magic that ran between her and Effie, always there, always pushing and pulling. Why couldn't Effie see that she was just trying to protect her? Protect all of them.

Anna pressed the key down an imperceptible amount, not enough to make a sound. How easy it would be to play . . . how impossible it felt . . . as if the piano was a mountain before her, its keys full of obstacles, rocks and overhangs from which she could fall, crevasses she would never get out of, trapped in the darkness between the notes, the silence on the edge of becoming – but never quite there.

I won't look down.

The bell rang and Anna's hand leapt up from the keys. For a moment, she feared the bell would not stop ringing. That it would set the whole school screaming.

What's happening to me?

Rowan's words came back to her, chiming over and over: *A witch who turns from the moon ends up lost or a loon.*

BELLS

It's said that many of London's church bells are tuned to the frequencies of the spirit world, designed to help the souls of London's dead pass on and to ward off spirits who would do us harm.

Excerpt from 'City of Death', London Lore (Published 1908)

'The Tower of London is a British institution. The ruthless killing of its ravens is an attack on our city – our country. In response, we will be setting up an official investigation into the events which will focus on uncovering the source of this flagrant and sinister act of malefice.'

Another statement from the WIPS. Anna's stilled at the words while her heart skittered and sped. *How was this happening? How had the WIPS inveigled their way in again?*

Her eyes moved over the comments.

Thank you! About time too. People who know what they're actually doing.
Those birds didnt have zoochosis, they were being fuckin mind controlled.
Our police force not up to the job then . . .?
Investigating birds, really?! Is the world going mad?

The door to the toilets opened and, even though she was in a cubicle, Anna shut off her phone. She'd spent several lunchtimes in here, avoiding the coven, Effie especially. They weren't speaking again. *So much for sisters . . .*

Whoever had just entered the bathroom was mid-conversation and Anna was not surprised to hear Effie's name—

'She swears she heard Effie muttering Ave Satana beneath her breath in class yesterday . . .'

'Really?'

'I reckon she's a satanist, she's always had that dark vibe, hasn't she?'

'Yeah, but do you really think she did a full-on ritual on Darcey? I reckon Darcey was in on their whole cult. Getting with Connaughty was probably like a dare.'

The other girl made a puking noise and they both laughed. 'I don't know . . . I reckon there was more to it. Did you hear Anna's aunt, like, dropped dead over the summer? Totally out of the blue.'

Anna held her breath at the sound of her name.

'Creepy.'

'There's always been something off about her . . .'

They carried on their discussion as they left but Anna couldn't make out what they were saying any more. The cubicle felt suddenly suffocating, its walls pressing in around her, threatening collapse. She pushed open the door and went over to the sink, splashing water on her face. When she looked up, Aunt was smiling back at her in the mirror.

Anna blinked and she was gone.

She gripped the sink. *Get it together.*

She couldn't lose it today. It had been announced that morning that every sixth-form pupil would have to meet with Inspector Eames for a private 'informal chat'. Rowan had been freaking out about it over text. *No big deal*, Anna tried to tell herself in the mirror, wiping the water from her face. *Just a chat. Just a formality.* She'd spoken to Selene about the inspection but she hadn't been worried: *Cowans love ticking boxes, darling. It delights their small minds. If you want, I'll go and give your new headmaster a piece of my mind . . .*

Anna had shut that down quickly. She straightened herself up, tying her hair back, trying to hide its colour. She didn't want to have to face Eames. She didn't want to have to lie. What if she crumbled? *Just get it over and done with.* But Aunt's laughter rang out, chasing her from the room.

She was halfway through her next class when it was time to go. Her teacher looked displeased, not with Anna, but with a second disturbance to his lesson – another pupil had already had to leave for their meeting.

'Anna,' a voice behind her called. She turned around, knowing already it was Peter who'd been sitting a few rows behind her.

'Yes?' she replied irritably.

'I'll email you any notes you miss from class.'

His thoughtful gesture caught her off guard. 'Er – OK. Thanks . . .' She gave him a brief nod and shrugged her bag over her shoulder.

Mr Archer gave her a smile of solidarity on the way out. It was the only positive thing that had come out of Mr Ramsden becoming head-master – Mr Archer had taken over her English lessons. He was a good teacher and they'd always got along well.

Anna made her way out of the door, trying to ignore the thump of her heart, the sweat collecting in her palms. The meetings were taking place in the Ebury wing, where Mr Eames was stationed. The wing was positioned at the front, east side of the school, one of its oldest parts, with its highest room occupying one of the towers. It was said to have been the original headmaster's office when the school had first opened. When Anna arrived, she started up the stairs, a sign guiding her past the first floor, to a central room on the second floor, which held a desk. A girl in her year was sitting in one of the chairs lined up against the wall. She gave Anna a wary look and turned away. A fairly standard reaction these days. Anna took a seat several spaces away from hers.

After a little while, a woman came through a door on the other side, releasing a pupil. She sat down at the desk which was cluttered with stacks of folders and papers and cups of tea. She typed a few notes into the computer, then stood up and called the next girl through, escorting her through the door.

Anna waited, trying to steady the beat of her heart, but it would not comply. She could hear it in her ears, *too loud*, could feel it fluttering beneath the pulse of her neck, *too fast*. She'd spent her whole life learning how to hide her feelings but her feelings would no longer do as they were told, betraying her in alliance with her magic. She wondered what everyone else was saying about them during their meetings with Mr Eames.

Did you hear Anna's aunt, like, dropped dead over the summer?

There's always been something off about her . . .

The door reopened, making Anna jump.

'Sorry, didn't mean to scare you.' It was the woman again. She let the other girl go then turned back to Anna. 'Anna Everdell, is it? Good to meet you. I'm Laura Seymour, Eames's personal secretary.' She checked the clock. 'We can go in in just a moment.' She smiled at Anna, then went back to typing some notes on the computer. She wasn't young or old, but somewhere in the middle, with a soft, droopy sort of face, bulging eyes, a frizz of dark hair and a busy demeanour, as if she had several things running through her mind at once. She slurped at a cup of tea then checked the clock again. 'OK. It's time.' She seemed on edge as she turned back towards the door but she gave Anna an encouraging look, which Anna clung onto as she followed her through into the next office.

The inspector was sitting behind the desk.

'Please, take a seat.' The secretary gestured to one of three chairs set up in the middle of the room.

Anna took one and the secretary sat down beside her. She smiled at Anna, her upper lip curling above her teeth so that her gums showed. Her voice was soothing and pragmatic. 'We want you to know that this is a completely safe space, Anna. We're speaking to everybody, it's nothing to worry about – just an informal chat about your time at school last year, how you're feeling, any concerns you might have, that sort of thing, OK?'

Mr Eames's dark form stood up from his desk and joined them, a notepad and pen in his hand. Anna kept her focus on the secretary.

'Now, for starters could you confirm your name?'

'Er – yes – it's Anna Everdell.'

She heard Eames make a note, the sharp scrawl of his pen disquieting.

'And you joined St Olave's when you were thirteen?'

'Yes. I was home schooled before that.'

Another note was taken and then Inspector Eames shifted in his chair, clearing his throat with a tight cough. He spoke. 'And how has your time been at St Olave's?'

Anna turned to him. He was taller and thinner than he'd appeared from far away, his long neck hung with a heavy Adam's apple, which pressed against the collar of his tightly buttoned shirt. He was wearing the same black suit as before, his thin red tie too much like a line of blood. Anna stared at it. He coughed again and she looked up into his dull, dark eyes, their blank depths penetrating her right through. They moved to her hair and back again like a dial recalibrating.

Anna found her voice. 'Good,' she stammered. 'I've always enjoyed learning.' She wanted to keep her answers as vague as possible.

'How about last year?' He tried to sound light but his parched voice lacked any true expression, drying the air around it.

'The first year of sixth form, so it was more pressured but much the same as always.'

'It's been noted you had very few friends up until last year. Then you began spending time with Ms Fawkes, Ms Greenfinch, Ms Richardson and Mr Lockerby?' The names rolled off his tongue.

Her throat tightened but Anna forced the words out. 'I did, yes.'

He stopped to write something – her words captured in mid-air, pinned down in black and white, shed of any shades of grey.

Eames blinked. 'From descriptions given by several teachers, you and Ms Fawkes seem very different characters. What drew you to her?'

The question tripped Anna up, her mouth moving but no words coming out. She was still asking herself the same thing. *Because Effie's everything I'm not. Because we're bound together by magic and a curse. Because she's my sister and I love her despite everything.* None of them seemed to capture it.

'Don't rush.' The secretary gave her another gummy smile. 'Take your time to think it through.'

'She's the daughter of my godmother so it was natural we would become friends,' Anna replied finally.

'Selene Fawkes?'

'Yes.'

'Who you are now living with alongside Ms Fawkes and Mr Lockerby?'

'Yes.'

'Unusual living circumstances,' Inspector Eames commented.

'I haven't had a lot of choice,' Anna retorted, perhaps too snippily.

He wrote something down. 'Did you socialize with your friends outside of school?'

'Perhaps a few times.'

'What kind of things did you all like doing?'

Casting spells. Jumping through fire. Dancing in magical clubs. 'The usual kind of things – hanging out, chatting, studying, watching movies.'

'Anything else?' His pupils did not move, but they seemed to pulse with distant intrigue as if he were studying her through a microscope.

'No.'

'You and your friends were witnessed having a handful of public altercations with Ms Dulacey last year.'

Anna shut her mouth, scrabbling to think of an explanation. 'She spoke with us a few times. I'm not sure I would call the instances altercations.'

'It must have been nice to have a friend like Ms Fawkes, who was so much more outspoken than yourself, who could come to your defence.'

Anna didn't reply. It was not a question but an assumption he already seemed to have formed.

'Were you aware of the rumours about Ms Dulacey circulating towards the end of last year?'

Anna shook her head, afraid now to speak. *Our fault. All our fault. Your fault, my child . . .*

His eyes narrowed. 'Did Ms Fawkes or any of your friends ever pressure you into doing things you didn't want to do, Ms Everdell?'

'It's OK to tell us the truth, anything you say in this room will go no further,' said the secretary on her other side, gentle and beckoning.

Yes.

'No.'

'What about Mr Lockerby?' said Eames. 'Has he ever taken advantage of you?'

The questions were coming too fast. She was caught between them. 'No. Never. Never anything like that.'

'Did you and your friends ever stay late at school after-hours?' His questioning swerved and Anna lost her balance. What if she'd been seen then too?

'I – er – I sometimes stayed to work in the library.'

'You don't remember where you were the night of the first May last year?' The secretary jumped in.

May Day. Anna's heart was hammering so loud she was sure they could hear it.

'Try to think back.'

'I would have been at home with – with my aunt. She didn't let me go out at night.'

'Were you often not allowed to do things you wanted to do?' The inspector's pupils expanded.

'I don't see what that has to do with anything.' Anna tried to hold his gaze but Aunt's laughter tickled at her ear and she dropped her head. His black shoes shone as if they'd been freshly polished.

'Your aunt passed away over the summer.' He said it without empathy, crunched down into a hard statement of fact.

Anna dug a nail into her hand, but it wasn't helping, her body felt as if it were floating away from her, the world around her suddenly less solid, fracturing—

'We're very sorry for your loss,' said the secretary, brow dimpling with pity.

That made it worse. Darkness flooded in through the cracks. *No. No. Keep it together.*

Eames leant forwards. 'Your life has been marred by loss, Ms Everdell. Past trauma can make someone more vulnerable to coercion, cult mindset—'

'We're just trying to make sure you haven't been a target.' The secretary tried to catch her eye.

'It is better to be honest with us now . . .' Eames's statement carried the hint of a threat. *Or else.* 'Now is the time to share any concerns you might have with us – any troubles, admissions, confessions . . .'

Confess. Confess your sins, my child.

Suddenly Anna couldn't breathe. Couldn't see. Couldn't escape.

She would never escape.

I won't look down.

That was when every bell in the school went off.

The noise of hundreds of pupils gathering together on the school grounds was not enough to diminish the clanging of the bells – the main school bell, the fire alarm and the distant chapel bells were all going off, high and shrill; a mad chorus.

Even once they'd been switched off, they still rang in Anna's head, tremoring her insides. A teacher came out to report that it had been some kind of electrical malfunction but Anna knew that it was not. She knew she was losing it. She could still feel the inspector's eyes on her, needling into the softest, rawest parts of her. It had set her off again. Set the bells off. *My magic.* Just like the other eruptions. *Would he suspect something? How could he suspect?* There was no reason to link it to her, no *logical* reason . . .

It had been too close. What if she'd exploded all the windows in the room? Or set the inspector and the secretary off screaming? Anna looked down the school driveway, wondering if she ought to just leave now – go home and tell Selene she couldn't go to school any more. That she was going to expose magic and that with everything going on it was all far too risky . . .

'Anna.'

Anna gasped and spun around. 'Rowan.'

'Sorry.'

'It's OK. Apparently, I'm very jumpy at the moment.'

'Understandable.'

Rowan didn't know the half of it. Teachers were beginning to call the pupils back inside.

'I've got a free period, do you have a minute?' Rowan gave Anna a hopeful look.

Anna did not want to go back inside and the secretary had told her hurriedly that she wasn't required back. Her session was done. 'Sure.'

They wiggled through the crowd and around the side of the main building. They walked a little way until they were at the back of the school, overlooking the playing fields. The sun had already begun to dip in the sky, making a distant haze of the clouds. The wind was fresh and cold but not enough to drive the tension from Anna.

They sat down at a bench and Rowan turned to her. 'Did you have your session already? Mine was this morning.'

Anna nodded.

'I've never understood the phrase sweating from every pore, but in that half an hour . . . I was like a sponge being squeezed. Sorry. TMI. It was weird, wasn't it?'

'It felt as if they knew so much already.'

'Yeah, well, I guess Darcey's been splurging about us all summer and I imagine the rest of the school hasn't had much positive to say. It'll be highly ironic if I end up being reprimanded for being a bully when I spent literally all of Year Eight changing for PE in the toilets so Darcey couldn't count – out loud – the number of fat rolls around my bra.' Rowan snorted, but Anna could still see the buried hurt. 'I'm hoping my band friends will put in a good word for us and if we all stick to our stories they can't prove anything concrete. Let's just hope Manda kept it together, that girl is bad at lying. And Effie hasn't done something, you know, Effie-like . . . come through on her threat and confessed for the lot of us.' Rowan chewed her cheek nervously. 'Which I'm sure she wouldn't have . . . would she? Why can't I answer that?'

'Because it's impossible to know what Effie is going to do one moment to the next . . .' Anna replied irritably, but her head dropped down to her fidgeting hands. The bells were still ringing in her mind. She was the one who'd almost given them all away.

'I'm sorry, Anna,' said Rowan.

'For what?'

'The other day, all of us ganging up on you like that.'

Anna shook her head. 'No, I'm sorry for losing my temper.'

'If you think that was losing your temper you should see me when my sisters have stolen chocolate from my snack drawer.'

A laugh broke through Anna's state of despair.

Rowan caught her eyes. 'You know, you can talk to me. You've been so quiet lately . . .'

'I've always been quiet.'

'This is a different sort of quiet. It's OK if you're not OK. I can't imagine how you must be feeling after everything.'

Anna dragged a nail across her finger. 'I'm not really feeling much of anything. I guess I must be as cold as my aunt after all . . .' She turned the statement into a faint laugh.

Rowan looked at her, aghast. 'Anna, that's not true. You're one of the least cold people I know. You're composed, sure, but—'

'Composed!' Anna erupted, her own voice ringing like a too-high bell. 'I've never felt less composed in my life! I'm barely keeping it together . . .'

'You're doing really well considering—'

'Rowan, I set off the bells! It was me. Just then. Me.'

Rowan took a moment to process her words. 'You did?'

Anna nodded. 'I'm sure of it. It's not the first time. At Aunt's funeral I made all the guests scream, I shattered a shelf of bottles the other day. Now this. I'm not doing anything, I can't even feel my magic when it happens, it's like—' Anna tried to articulate the darkness but she had no language for it. 'Like something takes over me, like I can't breathe or think straight or find my way back. Like I'm suddenly lost and I can't control it and I don't know what to do. I feel like I'm losing it.' She hung her head in her hands, her fingers pulling at her hair, wishing she could drag her magic out of her for good.

Rowan was rarely silent but for a few moments she let Anna's words settle between them. When she spoke she sounded surprisingly calm. 'There's nothing wrong with you. I know what this is.'

Anna frowned. 'You do?'

'I think it's a hyper-magical episode. It's like a magical panic attack. During the Binders' ceremony you unleashed a lot of magical power that you've held back for so many years – and that's not just gone away. It's still inside you but you said you haven't been practising your magic, right?'

Anna nodded.

'So it's building up, it's uncontrolled, it's overspilling. It's like – like – you know when guys are going through puberty and they're not really in control of their . . .' Rowan whistled and looked down. 'Any minute, anywhere, things might get out of hand.'

Anna burst into laughter. Rowan's analogy was so absurd after her dark admission. 'So you're saying I just hit magical puberty?'

'Basically.' Rowan chuckled. 'It's because you never had any proper training and you've been through so much trauma and you haven't really—'

'Got my shit together?'

'I was going to say processed it all, but sure. *And* you're pushing it all down . . .'

'I'm not pushing anything down,' Anna argued. 'It's just not there, Rowan. I can't feel my magic, I can't feel myself. And I'm trying to be practical. You said it yourself, my magic is out of control. I can't trust it, especially not when I'm randomly hyper-episoding at school. I'm going to ruin everything for all of us. What am I meant to do?'

'Well . . . magic, for starters,' Rowan replied.

'Magic is the entire problem!'

'No, not practising your magic is the entire problem. You're a witch, Anna. Magic is not something you can choose – it's already chosen you. You can't put a lid on a boiling cauldron, it's going to explode – better to cook something up.'

'The only thing I'm going to cook up is a big fat curse.' Anna tried to sound nonchalant but her words came out desolate. 'The risks are too high. You saw for yourself what it's capable of, what it's done to my family . . .'

What am I capable of? Anna turned her face to the wind, the Binders' ceremony flashing before her eyes again, slicing the view to pieces.

'Mum always says we get to choose what we believe in,' said Rowan gently. 'Now, she might choose to believe in a lot of weird stuff, but that's beside the point.'

'But the curse isn't made up.'

'I'm not saying it's made up, I'm just saying maybe you can choose how much power you give it. Right now, you're giving it everything, you're letting it consume you.'

Rowan's words sounded sensible, they sounded convincing, but it didn't feel that way inside, like Anna could just draw a line between the curse and her magic. They were a tangle – roses and brambles and thorns that could not be separated, each feeding off the other.

'You won't grow stronger against it by weakening yourself, and Effie was right. We're a coven. You don't have to do this all alone, we're all here.'

Anna's hands would not stop moving, searching for a long-lost Knotted Cord. She'd spent her whole life trying to keep everything contained and now her magic wouldn't let her. But the thought of just . . . giving in to it . . . made her feel desperately afraid.

Rowan took one of her hands. 'It's not going to be easy, but we can do this together.'

Anna looked into Rowan's bright, generous eyes and tried to believe in them if nothing else. 'I thought you and Manda weren't sure about reforming the coven anyway?'

'We weren't until we found out you were giving up on your magic. It reminded me that we all need each other, more than ever now. Plus, Effie probably will come through on her threat out of spite. Unless . . .' Rowan nudged her. 'There's some other reason you don't want to join the coven. A certain tall, ruggedly handsome reason?'

Anna gave Rowan a sideways glance. 'If you're referring to Attis—'

'Attis, no, who said Attis?'

Anna tried to sound casual. 'There's no denying that he's caught up in this, he *is* our curse after all.'

'Curses sure are sexy these days . . .'

'Rowan.'

'Sorry.'

'But, no, it's not – we can't – it's not like that. And he never felt that way about me anyway, so . . .'

'OK.' Rowan put her hands up. 'I'm not getting involved, but if you do ever want to talk about it, I'm here.'

'There's nothing to talk about.'

Rowan looked entirely unconvinced.

'You really think practising magic will help?' asked Anna. 'Effie didn't just set you up to this?'

'I'm serious, Anna.' Rowan's eyes stilled and Anna could see a depth in them that was normally hidden. 'I don't think you have a choice.'

'You know, you're pretty wise sometimes, Rowan.'

'You mean I'm not just a pretty face and a sensational body?'

Anna smiled. 'OK,' she said. What choice did she have? Magic had her trapped, had forced her hand. She couldn't risk hyper-episoding again no matter what. 'I'll join the coven but things have to be different. Effie has to be different.'

'I agree. You should talk to her.'

'Me?'

'You are her sister.' Rowan grinned. 'You know, I'm starting to see the similarity; you're both stubborn as a yarrow plant.'

Anna spent the rest of the day stewing on Rowan's words, and when they arrived back to the house that evening, she didn't let Effie pull her usual disappearing act. If she was going to face magic, she had to be brave enough to face Effie first. 'Effie.'

Effie stopped, hand on the doorframe. 'What?'

'I wanted to talk.'

Effie looked about the kitchen. 'Are you sure it's safe for our magic to be in the same room together?'

Anna breathed out. 'Effie, I'm sorry how the whole thing might have come across, but you have to understand where I'm coming from.'

'Not really.' Effie shrugged, still in the doorway.

'Our curse has got a fairly destructive history.'

'Which is why we decided to break it, not let it run our lives.'

'It's not just that,' said Anna. 'My magic's been . . . unpredictable, acting out. Remember Selene's ingredients?'

'I do . . .' Effie shifted with interest.

'That was me, my magic. Rowan says I'm suffering from something called hyper-magical episodes and that casting again is the only way to stop them.'

Effie drummed her fingers on the doorframe. 'What are you going to do about it then?'

Anna lifted an apple from the fruit bowl, rolling it in her palm. 'I'm going to listen.'

Effie took a few steps into the room, raising her chin. 'Oh, really.'

Anna held the apple up. 'On a few conditions.'

'Go on.'

'Things have to change. We have to do things differently this year. We work together as a coven. No one person in charge. No one person calling the shots. That means you, by the way.'

Effie stopped at the other side of the counter, an inscrutable smile forming.

'No more threats, blackmails, bribes. No revenge spells or spells of dark intent.'

'You can't separate out the light from the dark when it comes to magic. All spells have the capacity for both.'

'You know what I mean.'

'I still get to have my surprises. You know how I like my surprises.'

Anna narrowed her eyes. 'Harmless surprises.'

'And the odd cantrip.'

'*Subtle* cantrips.'

Anna rolled the apple towards her and Effie caught it under a finger. 'Agreed. But I have a condition of my own.' She rolled the apple back to Anna. 'You stop hiding behind the curse.'

'I'm not hiding—'

'Tell me this then.' It was Effie's eyes that narrowed now. 'If we break the curse, would you embrace magic then?'

Anna stood silently, not knowing what the answer was. The two were one in her mind now. She couldn't see past the darkness of the curse.

'You see,' said Effie. 'Is it really the curse you're afraid of . . . or yourself? Your power? *Our* power.'

Anna looked down at the apple. 'I'm not interested in power.'

When she looked back up, Effie was watching her with a rippling smirk, as if she did not believe her. She reached for the apple and picked it up. 'You'll be glad to hear Selene has tracked down her old divinatory friend. Demdike's his name but apparently he's known in the magical world as the Blood Singer. He's agreed to see us.'

'The Blood Singer . . .' Anna repeated, excitement and fear squeezing her stomach simultaneously.

Effie made towards the door again. 'Our quest begins.'

'Effie.'

'Yeah?'

'Would you really have turned us all in?'

Effie stared at her, then raised the apple to her lips. 'Of course not.'

Just as she was about to crunch into it, Anna lifted her hand and the apple shot out of Effie's palm and flew through the room into hers.

'Good.' Anna took a bite.

Effie raised an arched eyebrow and laughed. 'Touché, sis.'

SMOKE

I, of the flesh, know that all must rot,
All must become death.
I fear not its darkness, I welcome the Crone.
I trust in my training and abide by the Codes.
I cross now my heart and live to die,
By my Hira of Snow and Bone.

Pledge of the Initiate Hel Witch

On Friday, Anna's locker held two items: a rose on the outside and an apple within.

Both red, both dangerous. *Love and magic.*

The rose was from Peter. He'd been leaving them there every morning with notes asking if they could talk. Anna had spent years wishing he'd utter a single word to her and now apparently all he wanted in the world was to speak to her. She pulled the rose away, its crisp, delicate scent climbing up her nose, as dark and rippling as the whirlwind of its petals. She threw it in the bin and turned to the apple with a knowing look. It was their coven's secret code – an invitation to the coven-meet that evening. She prodded at it, just in case it did something magical or unexpected. It appeared to be dormant.

She picked it up, her smile dropping at the weight of it – heavier than it should be. Should she really be practising magic again? Should she be giving in to its temptations now she knew what darkness lay within? But magic had given her no choice. No way back. No way forwards except to look it straight in the eye while the Eye of the curse stared back at her.

She felt the apple in her bag all day and by her final lesson it was drag-ging her downwards. She hurried to the toilets and waited for Attis to message them with the all clear as they'd planned. It was strange not to have to worry about getting home on time, not having Aunt waiting for her back at the house. Anna couldn't get used to the feeling of freedom. She could go wherever she wanted to go, do whatever she wanted to do, so why did she still feel guilty? So scared?

Because I'm not gone . . .

Anna ran from Aunt's voice, hurrying down the dark school corridors. Her fear only swelled as she descended into the deepest, oldest clutches of the school – the floor below ground – windowless, the air cloying and damp, the shadows clinging to her. She imagined the inspector lurking around every corner, his blank eyes in the darkness. If they were caught running around after-hours, it would confirm every worst suspicion about them. *Witches conjuring up the devil in the bowels of the school . . .*

She turned the corner and walked into someone. 'Ahhhhhhh—' She realized what the hard form before her was. 'Aaaaaattis.'

'People normally just say Attis,' he replied. 'But I'll take Ahhhhhhhaaaattis.'

She pulled away from him, collecting herself. 'Sorry—' They hadn't spoken much since Anna had declared she was no longer doing magic.

'No need to apologize. Technically, we bumped into each other. Don't worry, no one is around, all teachers, headmasters, inspectors have gone home. I watched Eames drive away, though he'll probably only make it a few miles before his car breaks down.'

'You didn't . . .'

'Didn't what?' Attis's smile kinked with mischief. 'If he's going to make our lives difficult, I'm going to make sure his doesn't run smoothly – nor his car.'

Another cantrip. Anna shook her head, smiling back. She was both glad for his presence in the dark corridor and unsettled by it.

He put an arm up against the wall, tapping his finger. 'I'm – er – glad you decided to come in the end.'

'Yeah, well, I figure someone has to keep Effie under control seeing as you're not up to the job.'

He chuckled. 'You're right there. Come on, it's just around the corner.'

He put out his hand towards her. Anna hesitated to take it. He dropped it as if he had never offered it at all. The whole interaction was over in seconds but it changed the feeling of the air between them. It tensed. Hardened.

Attis coughed and turned. 'This way,' he said, and she followed him, wishing he didn't smell so damn good.

'Thank Mother Holle you guys are here!' Rowan was already standing outside door 13B ahead – the old sewing room in which they'd practised magic the year before. 'Why do we meet down here again? Is it because Effie likes to torture us? I can't remember. GAH!' She twisted the handle. 'Except this bloody door won't budge! It's holding tight as a taproot.'

'Let me have a go.' Attis stepped forwards. He pushed down the handle and gave the door a hard shove with his shoulder. Then another. It sprang open with a pop – a belch of acrid air mushroomed out towards them.

'Thirteen dark moons . . .' Rowan wheezed as they took in the devastation in front of them.

Anna hadn't expected the room to be fresh after they'd abandoned it the year before, but, left to putrefy over the summer, it had rotted from the inside out. The walls were glazed with grime, the altar was a wreckage, the plants dry husks, the juice cups still upended, spilling black gunk that looked half alive. The goat skull on the wall had grown out of control, its horns spiralling, its eyes staring back at them accusingly. There were no flies but there was the feeling of flies, of infestation. And the floor, when they stepped inside, stuck to their feet.

'Perhaps we could meet somewhere more pleasant,' Rowan suggested. 'Like a graveyard, a swamp, a plague pit . . .'

'There's no place like home,' said Effie, from behind them.

They turned to find her and Manda, whose eyes were fixed on the room beyond, her nose rising with offence. 'I'm not going in there! It smells like death.'

Effie pushed her in. 'We can get this place cleaned up in no time.'

Manda kept her hands clutched to her chest as if she were afraid to touch anything. 'That would take a year and I've only got an hour. I'm meant to be studying in the library right now. My mum even made the librarian call her to prove I'm there.'

'But you're here,' Rowan pointed out.

'Well, the librarian already spoke to Mum, and then Effie put her to sleep.'

'Isn't your teacher in detention asleep too, Effie?' said Rowan. 'Should we be leaving a trail of unconscious teachers across the school?'

Effie rolled her eyes. 'Are you trying to put *me* to sleep? Can we do something already? Did you bring the smoke sticks?'

Rowan nodded and reached into her bag. She pulled out five chunky herb bundles tied with string. 'I see now why you wanted them . . . they should do the trick, though this room might be their toughest challenge yet.'

'What are they?' Anna asked.

'Smoke sticks. Mum's little army of cleansing plants – sage, balsam fir, rosemary, lavender, bay leaves and sweetgrass. She's refined them for decades, fine-tuning them for their efficient, but extremely friendly, cleansing properties.'

Rowan handed a bundle out to each of them. Anna breathed it in and the stench of the room was suddenly scattered, conquered by the symphony of scents beneath her nose – as fresh as if the herbs were still growing, their individual aromas weaving together to create something sweet and verdant and wild and wise and . . . *friendly*, Anna thought, trying to understand how a bundle of herbs could feel friendly.

Attis brought his smoke stick to his lips. He blew gently and it began to crackle, sparking currents running up and down the leaves. It simmered down into a slow, smoky burn, indistinct from his eyes.

'Show-off.' Effie stuck her tongue out. She stared at her bundle and it burst into flame. She looked triumphant as it burned rapidly for a few moments before calming.

Anna looked down at her bundle, remembering what she'd come here to do. *Magic.* Her throat clenched. She'd performed the apple trick in the kitchen with Effie, but it had been spur-of-the-moment. It had surprised her as much as it had surprised Effie. This evening would require more. More than it felt like she had to give.

Rowan sidled over and, with a click of her fingers, lit up both of their sticks. Anna gave her a grateful smile, blowing on hers to slow it to a gentle smoke. It smelt even more sublime now, the fire lighting the potency of the herbs. The smoke unravelled slowly, rising up and moving this way and that like the head of a snake scenting the air out. The stick trembled in Anna's hand and the smoke dived suddenly forwards, pulling her with it. It dropped to the floor and slithered along it, clearing away the dirt and leaving a trail of polished wood where it had touched. Anna barely had time to stop and marvel before the stick yanked her forwards again, the smoke leaping towards the wall, then climbing up it and scouring away the film of grime. As it reached the ceiling it fanned itself out wide and waterfalled down the next stretch of wall.

Anna grabbed the stick with both hands, trying to administer some control as it began feeding hungrily at the altar, licking at the rotten smoothie cups, curling through the statues and trinkets and churning the old plant stems back to fresh soil. Another trail of smoke met hers and the two wound around one another with playful delight, swirling around the snow globe and whirring the snow inside of it into a storm – then rising up through the goat's skull, untwisting the tight knots of its horns and polishing it back to white. Anna looked up to find Effie on the other side of the altar table, a dimpled smile on her face. Anna grinned back . . . but then, the smoke turned and stared at her. She froze. Without warning, it darted forwards and wrapped around her in a tight coil all the way from her feet to her head. Before she could cry out, it leapt into her mouth. She couldn't breathe. Her throat was thick with smoke.

'Don't worry,' she heard Rowan call. 'It does that sometimes if it thinks you need a bit of a clean-out.'

Anna spluttered and coughed, the smoke pouring back out of her in a sudden, unsteadying rush. Her head felt light and her body lighter still, as if it had been scoured out. The world was suddenly brighter and clearer and she felt strangely like laughing and crying at the same time.

'Feel better?' Rowan asked, holding onto her stick for dear life as it dragged her forwards.

'Yeah, actually . . .' Her smoke stick rumbled with contentment.

She looked around at the room and could hardly believe the transformation. It was cleaner than it had ever been, the walls buffed back to their original cream, the blackboard gleaming, the wooden floorboards stripped and glossed. The old desks stood to attention, the headless mannequins in the corner still wearing their needles and rags but fresh and clean, as if they'd taken a bath. Manda was trying to order her smoke around but it wasn't listening to her, while Attis had turned his into the shape of an aeroplane, which was gliding along the ceiling.

'All right, enough playing,' Effie called out. 'Let's bring our smoke together in the centre!'

They faced her, sticks in hand like smoking guns. Effie stepped into the middle of the room, her smoke moving before her. It spiralled like a whirlwind. 'Draw on the power of the smoke! Join with mine!'

Anna could avoid it no longer. She needed her magic to join forces with the smoke. The lightness she'd been feeling dropped away and kept falling. Fear dampened the smoke stick in her hand. She imagined her innards blackened, the smoke trying to clean away what couldn't be cleaned. What couldn't be saved.

Come on.

She berated herself, gripping the herbs tighter, trying to pull threads of magic forth: the scent of the herbs, the motion of the smoke, the snap of the flame; the magic of the room steeped in the memories of their previous spells. It was all there, she was aware of it, but she couldn't *feel* it, like reading the words of a song but not hearing its music. She yanked the threads towards her by force.

She moved forwards, coercing her smoke ahead of her, but before she got there it snaked off in the other direction. She was glad to see the others weren't faring much better – Attis had managed to weave his smoke with Effie's but Rowan's was crawling along the ground and Manda's was leaping forwards in little darts, refusing to respond to her commands. Effie thrust hers forwards as if to wrap them all together but it shot through the different trails of smoke, sending them scattering in different directions. Anna tried to compel hers again but the threads of magic felt as if they'd grown too thin – just beyond her grasp—

'By the power of the dark moon we stand! Weave together the smoke in our hands!' Effie commanded. 'By the power of the dark moon we stand! Weave together the smoke in our hands!'

Her chanting grew more aggressive – but it was pointless. Their smoke was dispersed, chaotic, unruly. They could not come together.

Effie threw her stick to the floor and roared in frustration. 'Well, this is a complete shit show!' She stalked away from the circle.

'Come on, Effie.' Attis attempted to assuage her. 'It was only a small spell.'

'Exactly! We can't even manage that.'

'We've lost our mojo . . .' said Manda, looking bereft.

Rowan shook her head. 'Nothing is ever lost that can't be found again. It's just gone into a bit of a funk is all.'

Effie spun around. 'We don't have time for a funk! This is our year! Our final year here together – we're meant to be more powerful than ever and we can't even—' She made a disgusted noise.

Anna looked down at the stick in her hands. It had gone out, while

Effie was burning, always wanting everything around her to be burning too.

'I'm out of practice,' Anna admitted apologetically. 'I probably slowed things down . . .'

'It's not you, Anna,' said Rowan. 'It's all of us. We can't just expect everything to go back to normal after everything that happened last year.' She raised her head to Effie. 'A coven's magic is not just about power, it's about trust, communication, connection. Things you can't simply *force*.'

Effie stared back, looking restless, but reviewing Rowan's words. She threw her hands up. 'Well, what do you suggest we do then?'

'I don't know.' Rowan shrugged. 'Hang out for a bit? We haven't had much time with school being so full-on and all of Manda's extra-curricular activities . . .'

'Hey,' Manda protested. 'You're in band club.'

'That's one club. You're in, like, all of them.'

'I'm trying to bolster my applications! I don't just attend clubs to meet boys . . .'

'That was last year,' Rowan said. 'And I only lasted one session; apparently the debate team didn't appreciate me whooping and hollering from the sidelines. It wasn't "respectful" debating.'

Effie moved back to the centre of the room. 'So, when you said hang out, you meant bicker inanely?'

'Of course.' Rowan grinned.

They all dropped onto the floor in their usual circle, the smoke and shadows settling around them.

'I have a question,' said Attis seriously. 'What do you think would happen if you combined colonic irrigation with the magic of a smoke stick?'

They all laughed, except Manda, who looked as if she were genuinely trying to work out the effects of such a combination.

'We could try it out on the inspector . . .' Effie suggested.

Anna laughed at the thought but then gave Effie a look. 'You agreed – no vengeful magic.'

'Maybe he'd enjoy it?'

'Effie . . .' Rowan warned.

She rolled her eyes. 'Fine, no fun.'

'We can have fun,' said Rowan. 'Just no casting on cowans, not with all the stuff going on at the moment. People are still freaked out by the ravens. And—' Rowan stopped.

Anna looked at her. 'What is it?'

'I don't know – probably nothing. I just spotted something online yesterday.' Rowan leant in. 'Do you remember last year there was that construction site in Whitechapel where workers discovered animal entrails in the shape of the curse symbol? It got posted on a few sensationalist news sites . . . people claiming the site was cursed.'

Anna nodded. She remembered.

'Well, a few days ago, some of the construction vehicles there went haywire. They started knocking down the new luxury flats being built there – smashing into them, tearing the building up. All the people on the ground had to run.'

'So, what, construction vehicles are cursed now?' Effie started to laugh but Rowan spoke over her.

'It wasn't the vehicles that lost control . . . but the drivers. The people in them stopped responding to instruction, they just started driving into walls, destroying everything, and they wouldn't stop. It was like they *couldn't* stop. Apparently, they have no memory of it either. I wouldn't have noticed the story, only I remembered reading about that place last year, the magical rumours around it – and now this.'

'That's so weird . . .' Anna muttered.

'I know. It's stirred up all the suspicion around the site again. Marcus Hopkins, the Lead Researcher of the WIPS, reposted the news report on his channels.'

Effie blew out an irritable breath. 'Why do I keep hearing about this Hopkins man? He's started getting on my nerves.'

'His following is growing. Fast,' said Anna. Anna had followed his anti-malefice commentary over the summer and had watched his brief interview with the MailOnline discussing the WIPS' findings on the Faceless Women. His image was still scored into her mind like a black and white afterimage: dark, groomed hair and light, florid skin; a wide-boned, muscled and menacing face. A voice that reverberated like the deep notes on the piano declaring the women guilty of witchcraft.

'Come on,' Effie scoffed. 'Everybody has a following these days. There are enough weirdos out there looking for their saviour. I saw this guy the other day who posts videos of himself cleaning his own bathroom wearing scuba equipment. He has, like, a million followers.'

'Damn it.' Attis clicked his fingers. 'There's always someone who beats you to it.'

Rowan snorted but pushed on. 'Hopkins is leading the investigation at the Tower of London.' She shook her head, a frown brewing. 'With the Faceless Women hangings last year it seemed like the WIPS were on the outside, carrying out their research themselves, but with this . . . they seem to be actively involved. They must have connections in the police or government, otherwise I can't fathom how they are being given access . . .'

'Maybe the government are using it,' Manda suggested. 'There's an election next year and with the state of the economy – as my dad keeps saying – they need all the distraction they can get.'

'Well, let's hope they don't let it go any further. Hopkins has stated he wants every incident of malefice investigated.'

Attis leant back, his arms outstretched behind him, considering her words. 'For that the WIPS would need money, manpower and proper backing. Even then, they can present all the findings they want but they don't have any real power. The Witchcraft Act was repealed in 1951. Admittedly, surprisingly recently, but it means the law no longer recognizes witchcraft or magic.'

'Exactly,' Effie agreed. 'What can they do?'

'What do they want?' said Anna. That felt like the more pressing question to her.

'I think that's the whole problem. Nobody knows. Over the summer, I've heard Mum talking to various Wort Cunnings about it all . . . but I couldn't glean much.' Rowan typed into her phone and turned it around for them to see the screen. 'This is the WIPS' website.'

Anna had seen it before. The page was black with a stark white symbol in its centre – a circle with a cross inside. Beneath were the words:

The Witchcraft Inquisitorial and Prevention Services

Shining a light into the dark.

Experts in the occult, ritualistic practices, witchcraft and malefice.

Stop the spread.

'That's it!' Rowan cried. 'Nothing else. Nothing to explain who they really are or how they function. The only ones I know of are Hopkins and Halden Kramer, their "Head of Communications". They're a black hole.'

'Can't the Seven take care of them?' Manda blurted, looking panicked. 'They've returned, haven't they?'

Rowan bit her cheek. 'From what I've been able to gather – and by gather I mean heavily eavesdropped on – the Seven aren't exactly back.'

'What do you mean?' Anna leant closer.

'It was the Ogham witches who passed on the information that the Seven had returned.' Rowan saw Anna and Manda's puzzled faces and explained. 'The Ogham witches work with the language of trees . . . don't worry, just basically a very old, very revered grove. Apparently, they'd been given the message indirectly from the Seven, but since then, no one has actually heard from or seen them. I think their silence is what's worrying my mum the most.'

'Selene's acted strangely every time I've brought up the Seven too,' said Anna.

'I think the magical world has just always been used to having them there, like a magical safety net and then – BAM.' Rowan clapped her hands together. 'They're murdered by . . . we don't know . . . and while they might have risen from the metaphorical ashes, they're still not actually . . . here.'

'They said they were hunted,' Anna stated, wary she was beginning to edge into Aunt territory again.

Rowan looked uncomfortable. 'No one seems to know what to make of that, whether the Seven meant it literally or just that someone is after them.'

Anna decided to say it. She was tired of trying to tiptoe around it. 'How do we know they're not referring to . . . *the* Hunters?'

The Ones Who Know Our Secrets. Aunt's voice was waiting. Exultant.

Manda's eyes expanded. 'The Hunters . . . the Wolves. I thought they were only legend.'

'They are,' Effie rebutted firmly.

Anna lowered her gaze, crumbling at the look Effie was giving her – at the sound of Aunt's voice in her head. Was Aunt somehow still winning? *Am I letting her?*

'Witches *have* been persecuted plenty in the past,' said Rowan. 'But the idea that there's a group of people behind it, coordinating it all, returning again and again across the centuries, seems a stretch . . .' She nodded, as if to convince herself, but her voice faltered. 'But, then . . . someone did brutally murder the Seven, and this is the magical world, so anything could be possible. What do I know?'

'You know a lot,' said Attis, giving her a sincere look.

Rowan shrugged. 'I've wasted years of my life following all the school gossip online. May as well transfer my skills to something more helpful.' She looked at Anna. 'Honestly, I don't know what's going on but I know I don't want to look away right now.'

Anna smiled. 'Thanks, Rowan. Me neither.' She clutched her knees. 'But . . . I'm the liability here. As you've all heard, my magic is randomly outbursting, hyper-episoding, whatever you want to call it. I could give us all away . . .'

'It won't erupt again.' Rowan tried to sound confident. 'You're practising magic now.'

Barely, Anna thought. 'We don't know that. If anything happens, I just want you all to know that I'll find a way to take the blame. I'll confess. I'm not dragging you all down with me.'

'Don't be stupid, Anna,' said Effie, unexpectedly sharp. 'We're a coven. We stick together, no matter what. To the very end. You confess – we all confess. You drag us to hell and we're going with you. That's how this works.' She looked between them all with her fierce, dark eyes. 'Right, everyone? Come bane or boon – all in.'

Rowan nodded. 'Come bane or boon – all in.'

Attis's eyes moved to Anna's. 'All in.'

'I really don't want to be expelled . . .' Manda began, then shrank beneath Effie's glare. 'Fine! Bane, boon, my future ruined – all in!'

They turned to Anna and she felt a lump rise in her throat, a warmth spreading to some of the cold and aching places inside of her. 'All in,' she agreed, although she still had no intention of letting any of them take the fall for her.

'Coven of the Dark Moon,' Effie declared triumphantly. 'We're back, bitches.'

'Look . . .' Rowan pointed.

The smoke still left in the room had started to swirl around them, dark and potent.

Effie clapped her hands together, her mood lifting. 'You see, our mojo is returning already. It better . . . we've got a lot to accomplish this year. Magical languages to discover.'

'Really?' Manda's eyes bulged. 'There's already so much to do this year . . . I'm not sure I can fit in finding a magical language.'

'Well, we have to because we're behind. Most witches find theirs at sixteen. We're already a year late.'

'It doesn't necessarily happen at sixteen,' said Attis. 'There's no exact time.'

'Easy for you to say.' Effie rolled her head to him. 'You've always known yours: fire and iron.'

He made a face back at her. 'Well, I'm not technically a witch so I don't follow the rules.'

'I've always known what mine will be too,' said Rowan, turning the herb bundle in her hands. 'Botanical. I just don't know exactly what kind of plant magic. I keep thinking I'll suddenly connect to something but it's not happened yet. Oh Goddess, I hope it's not moss. We've got a Wort Cunning neighbour who spends all day muttering to moss-covered walls and I really don't want that to be me. It's going to be me, isn't it?'

Attis put a comforting hand on her shoulder.

'Hey, don't limit yourself.' Effie smirked. 'There are many languages out there – infinite, in fact. Selene always says, a witch's magic is only limited by her imagination . . .' Effie dipped her hand into the surrounding smoke and wound some around her fingers. 'You *could* be Botanical.' The smoke rose up from her hand – a little shoot – but as it grew taller it became a tree in her palm. 'Or trees perhaps . . .' The tree blew away into fragments. 'Or rain, or storms, or waves of the sea.' The smoke whirlpooled and flew about, crashing like waves and then settling into a floating cloud. 'Or dreams or nightmares . . .' She laughed as the cloud blackened and then broke up into letters that trailed away. 'Or words, or song, or dance.' It outlined the wispy figure of a dancer, which spiralled into the centre of their circle. 'Or shadow or spirits.' The dancer became the face of a screaming phantom, which grew bigger and bigger then shot back into Effie's palm, condensing into a little dark moon. 'You see? No limits.'

Anna watched the dark moon spin uneasily. Growing up she'd imagined other languages for herself, but they'd been dreams, glimmers of hope that could slip through Aunt's knots. It was those knots that had been her reality, constricting her world and path to one choice: the Binders. But now . . . every knot had come undone, and what was left?

She could feel no glimmers in the darkness any more; Effie's words did not fill her with the exhilaration they might have once. They made her feel desperately untethered.

'I even met a witch over the summer who casts spells while she orgasms,' said Effie.

Manda spluttered. 'That sounds inconvenient.'

'I reckon I've done it before . . .'

Anna tried to ignore the way Effie flashed a look at Attis.

'But how do we find our language?' Manda asked, looking troubled. 'Isn't there some kind of test we can take?'

'No, Manda.' Effie's mouth flatlined. 'You can't take a bloody exam for this.'

'It's more like . . . it finds you,' said Rowan.

'But how do you know when it's found you?' Manda badgered, the concern in her voice growing.

'Apparently you *just know*.' Rowan shrugged as if she didn't understand it either. 'They call it soul settling.'

A horrible thought needled its way into Anna's mind. *What if my language is still knots and cords?* What if, after everything she'd been through, she'd never really escaped her fate? Was that why she still knew the shape of every knot? Why she missed the feeling of the Knotted Cord in her pocket? *Why I feel so lost now?*

'There isn't some kind of system we can use to work through them?' Manda asked hopefully.

'No,' Effie scoffed. 'There are no systems. The only vague structure to the languages of magic is that originally there were seven – the first ever created by the Goddess out of which all the others grew. They're said to be the most powerful.'

'Planetary, Elemental, Botanical, Verbal, Imagic, Symbolic and Emotional,' Manda recited diligently, as if this was one test she could pass.

'They're not necessarily the most powerful,' said Rowan. 'Although Emotional probably tops the lot.'

'How come?' Manda asked.

'Well, it's at the heart of it all, isn't it? Languages are really only a way of tapping into your emotions, so if you can draw straight from them then you can reach places most other witches can't. But Emotional is also the hardest, so I'm perfectly happy with my plants thank you very much.'

'I think I'd like mine to be poetry,' Manda declared loftily. 'I read about a grove over the summer whose poetry was said to be so beautiful that its magic was released when the reader washed the words away with their tears.'

'I've heard of mud witches,' Effie mused. 'Cast spells in mud with sticks. Maybe that'll be you.'

Manda grimaced. 'I am not a mud witch!'

'Or spitting witches,' Attis joined in. 'They cast spells with their saliva. Do you have an adequate amount of saliva, Manda?'

Manda began to protest again but froze. 'What if I *am* a language I don't like? Can you change language?'

'It happens but it's rare,' said Rowan. 'There are cases of witches not wanting to be the language they're meant to be, denying it and choosing another. I guess anyone can force themselves to be something they're not.'

Rowan's words opened up a new avenue in Anna's thoughts. *Had Aunt's language even been knots and cords?* She'd joined the Binders later. Perhaps before it went all wrong . . . there'd been some other language, buried away like the other parts of Aunt. *What had my mother's language been . . .?* Anna couldn't remember if she'd ever asked Selene or what the answer had been. Selene had always talked about her mother's magic in general, if dazzling, terms and had tended to become evasive when Anna's questions had become too detailed. Perhaps Anna hadn't wanted to know . . . the thought of her mother's language too painful when Anna's own future had been decided. But it wasn't any more. Now, it was terrifyingly open.

'Apparently, there are some witches who never find their language,' said Rowan morosely. 'Spend their whole lives searching. I can't imagine anything worse.'

'I didn't know that was a possibility,' Manda responded with fresh apprehension. 'Oh, I wish there was a test. I'm not entirely sure I am a poetry witch . . .' she admitted. 'All the love letters I sent to Karim over the summer didn't work.'

Effie put a hand up. 'Sorry, what? You've been sending love letters to Karim?'

'Just a few since we broke up . . .'

Rowan narrowed her eyes. 'How many?'

Manda bit a nail. 'I don't know – maybe three – or five – or nine . . .'

'NINE LETTERS?'

Effie burst into laughter. 'No wonder he's running away from you.'

'A love letter is a pure expression of feeling. You'd respond to a girl if she sent you one wouldn't you, Attis?'

Effie's laughter grew louder. 'Attis responds to the words *let's get out of here.*'

He pretended to look hurt, putting a gallant hand on his chest. 'I would reply to any letter sent by someone as lovely as you.'

Manda's momentary blush gave way to a frown. 'So what you're saying is I should send him another?'

Attis tried to keep a straight face. 'Perhaps Karim might not be a letter kind of guy.'

'Perhaps Karim is considering witness protection.' Effie snorted.

They sank into further fits of laughter. Manda began to laugh too, putting a hand over her face. 'I should have stopped at five, shouldn't I?'

No one was able to reply for several minutes.

Effie lay back on the floor, content in her restlessness. 'It's going to be a big year. I can feel it.'

For a moment, Anna could feel it too – a sudden match in the darkness – and then out again.

They made their way back out of the sewing room. It lay clean and fresh behind them, and yet, as Attis pulled the door to, the room beyond seemed as full of shadows as ever, the mannequins standing like headless guards over their umbral kingdom, armoured with pins.

He assessed the door.

'What are you doing?' Anna asked.

'As the coven's health and safety officer, I can't leave this room open to exposure. I'm not sure how an altar and a framed picture of Leonardo Vincent can be explained in an abandoned sewing room on the lowest floor of the school.'

Attis took a few steps back and focused on the door before him. It happened slowly, so slowly it was hard to pinpoint exactly when the door disappeared and the blank wall took over, indistinguishable from the yellowed walls of the corridors.

'A chimera.' Anna smiled faintly. 'Will it last?'

'You doubt my skills?' Attis pretended to look affronted though his own smile remained teasing. He pulled a hammer and nail from his inner pocket – how many items did he keep in his pockets at any one time? He began to hammer the nail into the doorframe, then, without pause, pulled out another nail and did the same several inches on. He continued with quiet efficiency until the frame was studded all the way around. Anna could see a symbol carved into the flat ends of the nails.

'Charging nails,' Attis explained. 'I've charged them up with my magic to sustain the chimera. Should do the job.'

'Number twelve, number fourteen . . .' Manda counted the doors on either side. 'Number thirteen is clearly missing.'

'Luckily for us the number thirteen is often left out of buildings,' said Attis. 'A magical number. A feared number.'

'Good.' Effie patted the wall menacingly. 'The sooner cowans learn that we should be feared – the better.'

BLOOD

In Hel, time loses all meaning. No longer something we can measure ourselves by but something that measures us – swirling and trapped within the dark wells of our being.

Reflections on Hel, Books of the Dead: Tome 9637

'It's taken a lot of work to track Demdike down,' said Selene, throwing a red scarf across her shoulders and admiring herself in the hall mirror, jawline gracefully raised. Her hair tumbled loose, like curls of golden butter.

'I thought you were friends,' Effie replied moodily, shoving her feet into her black boots.

'I wouldn't say *friends*. Anyway, I haven't seen him for lunar years and he's been living off-grid. Goddess knows what's he up to these days; he was always . . . unusual.'

Anna had already concluded that anyone known as the Blood Singer was likely to be *unusual*. His name unsettled her . . . *what did it mean? What would he do?* Selene had vaguely explained that he drew on the power of blood to trace the past and future, but *how?*

Anna held the Everdell family tree book tightly – the book the Library had given her last year, the book that was entirely blank inside. She'd decided to bring it on an impulse. After all, the book *was* their past, even if its contents had been stripped. Anna still had no idea who had removed the words within, who had wanted the secrets of their family buried.

'If he's living off-grid,' said Effie, as they made their way down the path towards the taxi Selene had called, 'then where are we going?'

'A funfair in Romford,' Selene replied as if this made complete sense.

They got into the taxi, Selene taking the front seat beside the driver. As they sped off, she chatted away to him, the driver glancing at her as if an angel had fallen into his cab. Anna hadn't noticed it before, how alike Selene and Attis were – their easy charm, their magnetism, their way of making people feel as if they were the only other person on earth.

Anna and Effie sat silently in the back, looking out of their respective windows. They might have reformed the coven and were even talking in whole sentences, but the distance between them still felt unnavigable. It wasn't just everything that had happened, it was the weight of what they were meant to be to each other now: *sisters*. The word felt alien to Anna. How did you become sisters? The curse, which was meant to tear them apart, was currently the only thing bringing them together. *Where my mother began . . .*

Our mother.

Anna had to get used to the fact Marie no longer belonged to her alone. She felt a prickle of resentment. Effie had grown up with Selene and Attis – she already had a family, still did, but Anna had only ever had Aunt. Imagining her mother over the years had been everything to her, even though Aunt had always tried to take Marie from her – dictating her story, tearing her down, reminding her constantly of how rotten her mother had been, *weak to magic and love*. Anna had hungrily gathered scraps of Marie for herself – from photographs, Selene's stories, snippets she'd heard from other people – drawing them together and trying to form some sense of who her mother had been. Deep down, she knew her version of Marie was no more real than Aunt's, only glimpses of a stranger reflected in a mirror . . . so many details unknown. What had her smile been like? What had her laughter sounded like? What had been her favourite book? Food? Season? What had she wanted to do with her life? *Had she been afraid when she went to meet the Blood Singer? Like me? Or had she been as bold as Effie?*

The city centre slowly dislocated beyond the window into sprawling suburbs, grey streets beneath grey clouds, heavy with rain that had not yet fallen. Anna traced a circle in her breath on the window, thinking of the seven concentric circles of the curse symbol – the Eye – wondering, if Marie had known how her journey would end . . . would she still have begun it? Perhaps even if she'd run away, ignored her past, the curse would still have caught up with her. *After all, how do you escape a circle?*

The taxi crawled down a road where boarded-up shops punctuated cafés and kebab houses and salons, a street market being taken down in the distance. Anna's mind flashed to Jerry Tinker and his *magical wares*. The impossible brightness of his moonthread. They wove down several back streets and pulled up outside a large swathe of scrubland, upon which, without ceremony, a funfair sat, sinking slowly into the mud.

Anna had never been taken to a funfair but she knew they weren't meant to look like this – a few shoddy tents flapping in the wind, a handful of rickety rides, lights flashing feebly against the darkening sky behind. The whole effect was lonely and faded and as sad as the sound of a party horn deflating.

'It looks like somewhere you come to get murdered, not to go on the fucking waltzers,' Effie muttered.

'It's an . . . interesting choice of establishment,' said Selene delicately. 'But Demdike never was predictable.'

'Was he here when our mother went to see him?' Anna asked.

'Oh no. He was at the Theatre of Fortune then, where the most famed and reputable divinatory witches reside.' She looked back at them, smiling. 'It's the most magical place, where the ceiling seems to rise forever and the very air tastes like time itself. Of course, it's hard to explain what time tastes like until you experience it . . .'

The driver was giving them very strange looks. 'Er – are you ladies sure you want to get out here?'

'Yes, this is our stop, but could you keep the clock running? We'd rather not be left stranded.'

'Of course, doll. I'll wait here for you.'

'You're a wonder, Travis. We shan't be long.' Selene stepped out and Anna was sure Travis would wait all night for her to return.

They made their way towards the entrance. The grass underfoot was clumped with mud. Selene gave her high heels a tap and the heels shrank away to flats. She strode onwards, looking entirely unperturbed by what lay ahead.

There was something not right about the funfair. It was not particularly busy and there was a feeling in the air. A creeping feeling. Most of the rides appeared to be shut or looked on the verge of breaking . . . *no* . . . one *was* breaking . . . Anna watched in horror as the swings on a gargantuan swing ride disconnected from the centre, and flew suspended through the air, one lone rider screaming, before they reattached again. A rollercoaster flashed in the background, but its swooping rail fell abruptly away to nothing. Anna hoped it wasn't running. She walked past a stall selling black candyfloss floating like storm clouds. A ghost with flashing eyes popped out at her from a ghost train titled: THE NEVER-ENDING RIDE.

'Fancy a go, love?' A man opposite pointed a gun at her. Anna screamed and stumbled back before realizing he was standing in front of a shooting gallery lined with stuffed animals that had seen better days. 'Shoot the target and win a prize, miss at your own risk . . .'

Effie grabbed her hand and pulled her away. 'I have the feeling we might die here.'

They moved past the rides to a set of caravans, one of which was purple and had a sign outside declaring:

MERYL THE MEDIUM.
CONNECT WITH THE SPIRITUAL REALM INSIDE.

'Ah, there it is.' Selene gestured to a small tent sitting alone at the very back of the funfair. Its sign showed only the image of a hand with a drop of red in the centre of the palm.

'*This* is it?' said Effie, looking unimpressed.

Selene approached the flimsy-looking structure and called through the closed curtains. 'Demdike, are you here? It's Selene.' Nothing happened. 'You know how I don't like to be kept waiting.'

The curtains fluttered and then a hovering head appeared between them – lean, vulpine face, scruffy black hair, eyes dark and wild as an animal's den; a scowl so deeply scored it was as if he'd forgotten any other expression existed. It softened just a little on seeing Selene. 'Well, well, well, thought I'd never see the day – Selene Fawkes herself.' His head turned to Effie and Anna, his scowl returning with added suspicion. 'Who are these?'

'I told you already, darling. Marie's daughters.'

He glared at them for a few seconds longer. 'I suppose you better come in then. Not this way, this is for the public; come around the back.' The curtains closed abruptly and he was gone.

They squelched their way to another opening at the tent's rear. Anna followed Effie through it and gasped – what lay within was so far from the tent into which they'd stepped that she couldn't help poking her head back out just to check they were still in the fairground. They were. Demdike's tent was not.

Inside, the room resembled a chamber within a grand manor from a different century entirely. It was lit with the light of gas lamps and candles throwing reflections onto the rich wood walls and the floor-to-ceiling shelves of books. A fire roared within a majestic stone hearth, in front of which Demdike lolled in a leather chair behind a desk messy with papers and books, its worn leather surface bearing the trails of cigarette ash and questionable dark stains. Opera music was crackling from a gramophone. Anna felt drawn in by the warmth and sumptuousness of the room but found herself on edge – perhaps it was the scent beneath the aromas of fire and leather; the scent of something feral.

Demdike breathed out as if the weight of the world were on his sloping shoulders. 'It's been a while,' he said to Selene in a voice deep and gravelly. He had the face of a broken poet – features that might once have been roguishly handsome but were now drawn and pale and beaten down, with broken veins along his nose and shadows curved beneath his seen-it-all eyes. He was wearing a loose dark shirt over tight leather trousers. He picked up a cigarette and lit it on a candle, running a hand through his long and unkempt hair. 'When was it last? Fernsby's banquet? Back when we were young and beautiful.'

'We're still young and beautiful, darling.' Selene reclined on a chaise longue to the side of the room. 'Now, whatever are you doing here? It's beyond the middle of nowhere.'

'Exactly,' he replied tersely, face darkening. 'Suits me. I'm not looking to be found these days. Funfair's a stinking shit-hole, I admit, but it's not so bad.'

'There's a man with a gun out there.'

'Oh, that's just Dennis. He's harmless, mostly, except the murder thing, but it's understandable when you hear the whole story. They're not such a bad bunch, though I wouldn't trust them as far as I could spit. Tricksters and fraudsters the lot of them.'

'Like yourself?' Effie took a seat in front of the desk and folded her arms.

He looked at her as if he had entirely forgotten the presence of the other people in the room. 'It talks,' he said to Selene. 'How did you wind up looking after children? Talking children.'

'We're not children,' Effie hissed. 'We're seventeen.'

He wheezed a laugh, a sound like air blowing through a blocked tunnel. He took another drag on his cigarette and leant forwards, eyes narrowed. 'I see a child before me.'

'I see a trickster before me.'

He laughed savagely. 'Go on then, a trick for a child. Give me your palm.'

Effie rolled her eyes but Anna could tell she was pleased to have won his attention. She stuck out her hand and he took it in his own. He ran his fingers over the lines of her palm, but then . . . the lines began to move. Anna stepped closer, not sure she'd seen properly in the candlelight, but it was true – the lines of Effie's palm were moving in response to his touch, like the pathways of her destiny were recalibrating or unravelling—

Effie's gaze went wide with unmasked delight. 'Cool. What does it say?'

Demdike dropped her hand, his scowl lines hardening. 'That your future holds greatness and great folly. You have much growing up to do, *child*.'

Effie pulled a face at him, though Anna could see the shine in her eyes at the word *greatness*, tunnelling its own new pathways. 'That's not a reading.'

He put his hands flat on his desk. 'I'm a cheap trickster, what can I say? Plus, I find it best not to read the future too closely, only gets into your head.' He tapped at his skull a little maniacally.

He and Effie stared at each other in silent battle until Anna spoke up. 'Can I have a go?'

Demdike twitched to her. 'Selene, the other one speaks too. It's alarming. How do you cope? Here – have a drink.' He moved his long fingers through the air like a lazy afterthought. A carafe of red wine rose from his desk into the air and poured two glasses, one floating over to Selene. He snatched up the other glass and tipped back half it, then turned to Anna with dark, sad eyes. 'Sit down.'

She took the seat beside Effie's, realizing she didn't want to know the specifics of her future, only to be reassured that there was one, that something was waiting for her beyond the curse. Demdike picked up a pile of shabby cards.

'Tarot . . .' Effie commented with intrigue.

He grunted, shuffling the cards and placing them back on the desk in a neat pile. 'Put your hand on top,' he instructed. Anna did so, feeling a thrumming cold rise up from the cards.

'Remove your hand,' he said.

A card began to draw itself up through the pack to the top of the pile. Demdike flicked a finger and the card moved onto the table in front of Anna, face up.

It was a blank.

She stared at it in panic, her worst fears confirmed, but Demdike was staring just as intently. It began to change. An image formed within it: two people. A tree with an apple. An angel overhead. It was not still. The lovers turned and twisted, smiling and weeping, switching places, reaching for one another, caressing, wrestling away; restless and distressed; together and euphoric. The apples began to fall from the tree, blackening and puckering on the floor . . .

Anna barely had time to take breath when the image began to morph again. A new card: a man mounted nobly upon a horse holding a colourful flag. *No. Not a man.* His flesh was dissolving to reveal a skeleton beneath. The flag flickered to black in the wind. In the background was a river – black waters – a boat and towers. It was snowing. Anna shivered with cold. On the floor, people were lying dead. They tossed and turned and groaned. *Am I hearing groaning?* The skeleton moved its head slowly and looked straight at her, eyes hollow as her endless nightmares. She felt terror clutch at the hidden places of her being but she could not tear her gaze away as the card morphed again.

The towers in the background moved forwards, blending to become one – a single tower in the centre, struck suddenly by lightning, windows on fire, two people falling. The scent of smoke. Black feathers flying like ash. The bodies falling and falling, spiralling to the ground – the bottom of the card never seeming to end, and then—

Anna felt a thud shudder through her whole body as if she herself had hit the ground.

All that was left staring back at her was a figure in a jester's hat with a stick on their back and a maddening grin on their face.

It took a moment to tear her eyes away. She looked up, surprised to find herself back in the room. Demdike's eyes were on her – no bleariness in them now, sharp as a fox on the hunt. 'The Lovers. Death. The Tower. And The Fool . . . Dark cards,' he said. 'But not without hope.'

'Demdike.' Selene sat up from the chaise longue, her voice taking on a hard tone. 'Stop frightening them.'

'What do they mean?' Anna asked.

'That you will face death and you must fall. But how do you land? Now that's the question.'

'Face death . . .' Anna's voice shrivelled like the flesh on the skeleton.

'Demdike,' Selene warned.

'It doesn't mean you're going to die, necessarily,' he replied flippantly. 'Just that a part of you must die. If I was going to be worried about any card in there, it would not be Death, but The Fool.'

'Why?'

He lit a new cigarette, looking as if he regretted what he'd started. 'Like I told the other of you, I don't do specifics. The future doesn't work that way. It's not set in stone, but like stone our lives are textured with a pattern. A pattern specific to us, a pattern we cannot escape, but a pattern that flows and shifts. The stupid fight it, the wise work with it, but most of us just plod along, entirely unaware of the forces dictating us. Awareness is power, awareness is how we live out our true destiny.'

'That why you're living in a deranged funfair in the back arse of nowhere?' said Effie.

Demdike returned to his glare. 'My destiny hasn't quite worked out, but, hey, you're the ones coming to speak to me.'

'Not for party tricks,' Selene chided. 'You know why they're here. You know they're Marie's daughters. We don't have all the time in the world.'

'Apparently there was once a witch who held all the time in the world in the palm of her hand. Shame she sprinkled it out so thinly.'

'Demdike—'

'OK. Marie,' he growled and jumped up. 'She was something. They haven't quite got her charm, have they?' He glanced at Effie, who glowered back. 'She came here and I showed her what she needed to know.' He lurched over his desk. 'Are you sure you want what she wanted? Are you sure you want to chase the shadows?'

'We're not afraid of shadows,' said Effie.

'You should be.'

'We're going to end the curse,' Anna stated. 'Once and for all.'

'Ha! End a curse.' Demdike spun away, putting a hand to his bookshelves. 'As if it were something we could blow out like a candle, shut like a book. I sensed it in Marie's blood before she even began speaking to me, moving through the dark tides of her veins. I could smell the futility of it.' He released a heavy breath. 'Why help you? I was no help to her.'

'It wasn't your fault, Demdike,' Selene insisted gently. 'What happened to her wasn't your fault.'

He ran a claw-shaped hand through his hair. 'I set her on a path. I might not have pushed her off the cliff but I damn well nailed the signpost up for her to follow.'

'My aunt killed my mother, not you,' said Anna with raw vitriol.

Demdike wasn't listening. 'I told her to run.'

'She wanted more than to run,' Anna said with unexpected force. 'She wanted to live. She wanted us to have a normal life. She'd have tried to solve the curse with or without you – and so will we. But it would make it a damn lot easier if you'd help.'

He looked at her at last, then crumpled into his seat, throwing Selene side-eyes. 'They're as implacable as she was, I'll give them that.' He turned back to Effie and Anna. 'I'll need your blood.'

Effie scowled. 'For what?'

'Because old secrets need fresh blood. I can trace your past – it's what I did for Marie.'

'I have this.' Anna presented the Everdell book to him. 'A book of our family history, only it's . . . empty.'

He reached for it and considered the blank pages with interest.

'You haven't seen it before, have you?' Anna asked.

Demdike glanced up. 'No. Marie never had this, but it's perfect. A blank canvas.' He laid it out on the desk, opening to the first page.

He looked up at Anna and went still. His features sharpened, a different energy rising up through his lackadaisical exterior, something intense and cunning. There was a clarity in his eyes that had not been there before – Anna could almost *feel* them, digging in, pulling at her heart, plucking at her veins and arteries as if they were strings, altering the rhythm of her pulse. 'Put out your hand,' he murmured.

She did so, unsure what was about to happen – whether he'd produce a knife or needle – but instead his penetrating gaze fell to her palm.

It began as a tingling – a tugging in its centre, gentle at first and then stronger. It didn't hurt but it was unlike any sensation she'd ever experienced. His eyes had closed and his lips moved lightly as if he were singing along to something no one else could hear. Anna's palm was hot now, the feeling intensifying – then, suddenly and painlessly, blood broke through her skin. A localized flood in the centre of her palm. Demdike wrapped his hand around hers and turned it sideways over the book. A drop fell from Anna's closed fist onto the clear page, like a rose petal onto snow. She realized what all the marks on his desk were made from.

He turned to Effie and Anna dried the blood on her palm, expecting to see a puncture mark beneath, but there was nothing. No signs of damage. The blood had simply risen through her skin.

Effie's offering landed on the page next to hers. Two drops, indistinguishable from one another. They began to run . . . a line extending between them – joining – threading them together and then branching. The blood flowed up the page, forming two new stamps of blood with names appearing alongside in sharp bloody script: *Marie Everdell and Dominic Cruikshank.*

Our parents.

The blood ran upwards from Marie's name to the top of the page. Demdike turned it over and the blood river split again, forming new branches, new names, grandparents, aunts, cousins . . . *a family tree . . . a blood tree* . . . The Everdell line. It was hard to keep up, it was moving so fast – Demdike turned the pages one after the other – quicker, quicker—

Anna watched the people and dates take form, drawn up against their will from the deep wells of time – all of the lives that had perfectly aligned for them to exist at all. Entire centuries in a drop of blood. Their roots. A map. A pattern. Suddenly, ideas of fate and destiny began to feel less foolish, more tangible . . .

It was then Anna noticed that some of the names were bleeding, the script overspilling – blood dripping down the page as if the words were open wounds, still. Demdike turned to the end of the book. No more names now. Instead the blood collected in the middle and began to spiral outwards into circles.

Seven circles filling up the final page of the book.

Even then, it did not stop. The blood ran beyond the page and onto the desk, dripping onto the floor and onto Anna's feet. She pulled them away but it had stained one of her trainers. Demdike's lips moved faster, silent but purposeful, and the outpouring slowed, then stopped, leaving seven circles in the centre of the page. The Eye.

'Guessing that's not meant to happen,' said Effie, her voice overspilling too – with fear or exhilaration Anna couldn't tell.

'In a word, no,' Demdike replied wearily, appearing displeased at the state of his desk. He spun the book around to them, then lit a cigarette and looked intently away.

They leant in closer. The blood of the Eye had begun to congeal and dry, its pattern setting. They turned back through the pages. There were bleeding names in almost every generation – the names were always two girls, born on the same day. *Twins.* But the dates of their deaths were not the same – one died young; one went on living.

'The bleeding names . . . they're the cursed,' Anna whispered, feeling sick, the scent of the blood in her nose.

One womb, one breath, sisters of blood, bound by love, so bound by death . . .

Had they always fallen in love with the same man? Had one always killed the other? Had the curse snipped their threads even as it tied them together? Anna looked away from the terrible, senseless loss, wishing she wasn't tied to it too. A loop that never ended. Was the curse mark on the final page the beginning or the end?

Demdike flicked a finger and the pages fluttered and stopped. 'There. That's where it starts. Before those names, there's no bleeding, no twins. They were the names Marie discovered too. Go back to the source and you might get your answers. I say *might* with great pessimism.'

'Is that it?' Effie spat. 'Just two names? No more information about them, no visions or glimpses into the past?'

Demdike scowled. 'I traced your blood back four hundred years. Isn't that impressive enough?'

Effie shrugged. Anna read the bleeding names:

Hannah Everdell (1628–1708)

Eleanor Everdell (1630–1651)

Effie blew air out from between her lips. 'So you were the bitches who started all this. The originals.'

'They weren't twins,' said Anna. 'They were born two years apart.'

Demdike nodded.

'But Eleanor gave birth to twin girls the year she died.' Effie pointed to the family tree. 'She was just twenty-one . . .'

Her twin girls' names were bleeding. *Cursed.*

There was no line extending from Hannah. She had not had children.

'Hannah lived on though, didn't she?' Effie remarked. 'Made it to eighty. Impressive for those times.'

Anna searched for something among the names, some sense of connection, some spark of understanding to leap from them and into her, as if she'd known them all along, as if their story was inside of her waiting to be discovered – but they meant nothing to her; they shared nothing but a name and a curse.

She narrowed her eyes at the name *Everdell, Everdell, Everdell*, appearing over and over. 'None of them take the names of their partners . . . husbands . . .'

'In our world, a wife does not take her husband's name. It's the name of the mother that's passed on to the children,' said Selene. 'I doubt it happened every time, though, but it seems magic has recorded them as Everdells and the name has survived through the generations.'

Anna turned back to the start of the book. To the names above theirs: *Marie Everdell—Vivienne Everdell.*

They bled, all too fresh.

'Why is my aunt's name bleeding?' Anna hissed angrily. 'She's not the one who was murdered.'

'A curse damages all who it touches,' Demdike replied soberly.

Anna pushed her chair back and moved away – away from the book, the webs of blood, the whisper of the Blood Singer's music in her ears. Away from the curse. And Aunt. *She shouldn't get to bleed! She did it! She was the murderer!* The one who had used the curse for her own ends. *Or had the curse used her? Where did one begin and the other end?* Anna could feel the curse pulsing in her own blood now, its threads spidering through her body, trapping her, holding her suspended. She couldn't escape it. 'There's no way out.' Her words fragmented with despair.

'I warned you,' said Demdike. 'Don't let it get into your head.'

'How can I not?' Anna cried. 'It's already inside of us.'

'Our blood doesn't define us,' Effie replied scathingly.

'Actually.' Demdike coughed. 'The truth lies between your statements. You don't have to let any one thing define you, but you can't discount the power of a witch's blood. Can't outrun it. It contains our magic. The secrets of our magic . . . our language and our seed. I can hear it as soon as a witch walks through my door, singing in their veins – thumping, swilling, murmuring, whispering . . .'

'What's . . . a seed?' Anna asked. She'd never heard the term before.

Effie jumped in. 'It's a witch's spell of power.'

'Power is too simple a concept for it,' Demdike interjected. 'It's about destiny. Each witch excels at a language, but within, there is a single spell that lives inside the beating heart of them. The spell their magic is destined to cast. For example, my language is blood divination, but my seed is what you've seen today – using blood to illuminate the past and future.'

'While my language is potion making,' said Selene. 'But my seed is my Passion Potion – my strongest creation.'

'I can hear it inside you.' Demdike raised a sensuous eyebrow to her. 'Swirling in your blood . . . the sound of summer rain, petals and spices at midnight, kisses along a neck—'

Effie made a disgusted noise. 'All right, put it away. Can you hear my language? My seed? What is it?'

Demdike's features flattened and his words faltered. 'It's not that specific; I can't detect exacts and your language hasn't come to fruition yet.'

'Well, what *can* you detect?'

His hands fell open. 'Like with Marie . . . I can't . . . hear anything.'

'The curse . . .' Anna said, *consuming it all.*

'I don't have the answers you need, I'm sorry,' he mumbled. 'I'm sorry about your mother too.' His voice seemed to catch and he coughed gruffly. 'You ought to throw that book away and move far away from one another. A curse can't catch you if it can't find you.'

'I thought you said you can't outrun your blood?' Effie challenged him.

'Yes, but I talk a lot of bollocks. It's how you end up a miserable old misanthrope like me. Right.' He sat back in his chair. 'I've delivered my services – you're free to go,' he said in a way that made it clear he wished for them to leave. Now.

'Wait,' said Anna. 'I had one more thing.'

Demdike frowned. 'Do I have the words "charitable organization" on my door?'

'It's only a small thing,' she continued quickly. 'I wondered if you knew anything about . . . the prophecy of the Hunters' return?'

Demdike laughed. 'A small thing, she says.'

Selene stood up. 'Anna, why are you concerning yourself with such things?'

Anna had known how she'd sound, asking about the prophecy – childish at best, paranoid at worst – but it had occurred to her that if anyone might know more about it, Demdike would. He was a divination witch, after all. 'Do you know it?' she prompted.

'Oh, I know of it.' He tapped his desk with twitchy fingers. 'But I can't say when I first heard of it . . . only that it's been rising up through the omniscient tides of time for the last few years and now, well, now it's drowning out everything else like a bloody earworm on the radio.'

'What do you mean?'

'It's on the lips of every divination witch. It's filling up the future like a dark wave no one can see past. It's a pain in the arse.' His face shut down in a scowl. 'I don't like prophecies, especially not insistent ones.'

'Aren't they part of your whole shtick?' said Effie.

'You really do just get more charming.' Demdike sneered. 'The art of divination is complex and intricate, uncertain and ambiguous. It's a whisper in the dark, whereas a prophecy is a big bragging bellow. It's poetry reduced to a headline.'

'But they have power.' Anna repeated Aunt's words.

'Of course they have power. That's the whole problem.'

'I know the gist of it,' said Anna. 'When the Hunters rise again, a cursed witch brings about the downfall of the world.'

'There's more to it than that.'

'Go on then,' Effie prompted.

'To be clear, I don't know the original wording. Prophecies are like Chinese whispers; they get chopped and changed and distorted until they reflect us more than the truth. But I can tell you that you are missing an important part: *When the Hunters rise again, a cursed witch will cast a love spell that will bring about the downfall of all.*'

'A love spell . . .' Anna frowned, turning to Selene. 'I thought there was no spell for love.'

'There isn't,' Selene replied firmly. 'Which is why this prophecy is poppycock.'

Demdike nodded, but his eyes were uneasy. He might hate prophecies but he obviously couldn't disregard it as easily as Selene.

Anna narrowed her eyes. 'You can feel it, can't you? Like the other divination witches . . .'

'I can feel something, but what exactly I don't know. Prophecies rarely lie, they just don't tell the whole truth.'

Effie snorted. 'Surely if the Hunters were real then the magical world would know.'

Demdike shrugged. 'People bury what is painful to them. Collective trauma. Even the magical world may create a blind spot.' He eyed Anna, who had drawn closer to him, drinking in his words. 'Why are you asking about the prophecy?' He shook his head at her. 'You don't think it's about you, do you? Curses might be rare, but there are plenty of other cursed witches out there.'

'No,' Anna replied defensively. 'But seeing as we *are* cursed, I figure we should be aware of it, considering the state of things right now.'

'Things are more turbulent than usual,' he admitted. 'But I wouldn't get lost in the world of prophecies and legend. Whether the Hunters are real or not, there have always been people who consider us an enemy, old prejudices polished up as new again. My life advice is: prepare for the worst because you're almost certainly fucked anyway.'

'How inspiring,' Effie snarked.

'Now, I hope there's nothing else I can help with because I have a busy evening of slow inebriation planned.'

'You both head back to the taxi. I'll be out in a minute,' said Selene.

Anna picked up the Everdell book, shutting it and its bloody pages delicately. 'Thank you, Demdike.'

'You're not quite as deplorable as you look,' said Effie.

Demdike snorted. 'Sugar and poison. A good sister team. Just . . . be careful,' he growled after them. 'Try not to kill each other.' With that, he turned away, glugging some more wine.

Anna took a last look at the room, knowing now what the feral scent was lurking beneath: *blood.* Then she followed Effie through the door, which confusingly became a curtain on the other side. It was bewildering to find themselves back in the fairground and not in the grounds of a manor. The sun had dipped low, darkening the scene and brightening the demented lights of the rides.

'Well, that wasn't what I was expecting,' Effie commented, as they started to walk back.

'At least we got something.' Anna gripped the Everdell book.

Effie shot her a cynical look. 'If by something you mean the names of two sisters alive several hundred years ago.'

'It's where Marie started. It's got to lead somewhere.'

'Maybe. I didn't see your question about the prophecy coming.' She raised an eyebrow to Anna.

'Well, Nana talked about it last year. It's about cursed witches. We ought to know as much as we can just in case—' Anna paused, still disturbed by Demdike's words. 'I wasn't even sure if it was well known in the magical community, but apparently it is. On the lips of every divination witch . . .'

'It certainly puts curses on the map, doesn't it?' Effie made eyes at her. 'Demdike's kind of hot, isn't he?' she said, already moving on. 'In that bedraggled, ex-rock-star kind of way.'

'I guess but I'm put off by the fact that he and Selene have clearly shared more than divinatory secrets . . .'

'Eugh. I know. The sound of summer rain, petals and spices at midnight, kisses along a neck—' Effie imitated Demdike. 'Oh Goddess, do you think they're at it now?'

Anna made a face at Effie. 'It's possible . . .'

Effie's pace had started to slow and then she stopped altogether outside the caravan belonging to MERYL THE MEDIUM. 'Whatever they're doing, I imagine Selene will be some time . . . what if we go on one last ride?'

Anna didn't like where this was going. 'What do you mean?'

Effie tapped the sign. 'I was thinking . . . we could take a shortcut. If we could speak directly to Marie, then we could find out where Attis's spell is or if there's any other way to break the curse without him dying.'

Anna shook her head, taking a few steps back, her feet sticking in the mud. 'No, no – I don't think that's a good idea—'

Would she give anything in the world to speak to the real Marie, to ask her all the questions she'd always wanted to? *Yes.* But not like that. Not speaking with the dead. The world felt darker around her – inside her – at the thought. Could it be done? Was it safe? What if it wasn't their mother who came to say hello . . .? 'I really don't think it's a good idea.' Her voice came out cracked. 'Is it even possible?'

'This is the magical world – anything's possible. I've heard of such things, but I don't know much about spirit magic.'

'This Meryl might not be a witch.'

'Have you seen this funfair? It's dripping with magic. She'll be a witch. Why don't we just go and see if she knows anything about it. What do we have to lose?'

My mother.

But Anna knew the mother in her head was an illusion while their reality was urgent and bloody. She'd just seen it dripping down the pages of the Everdell book. They had to break the curse. They *had* to save Attis. If the magical world could offer other avenues of knowledge – no matter how terrifying – shouldn't she at least explore them? Effie was looking at her with eyes entirely fearless, and Anna didn't know how to articulate her fears without sounding crazy. How to explain that she already felt haunted. That she already felt as if Aunt was still with her – wouldn't let her go.

Effie stuck out her hand. 'Together.'

Screams were going off in Anna's head, fear holding her in its grip, but she put her hand out towards Effie's. 'OK . . .'

Effie was already pulling her forwards. She knocked on the door.

'Come in,' a voice said from within.

SNOW

Do not fear the dead, but invite their presence into your life. Eat of the black fruit. Light the candles of the dead. Stare into the mirrors of eternity until you cannot separate yourself from the shadows who stare back.

Shadowing, Hel Witch Initiation Stage Two

Inside, it was low lit. The curtains were pulled to, like dozing eyes, and the light that struggled through the windows was caught in loops and coils of incense and dust. It looked exactly like a medium's den ought to look – rich, dusky fabrics covering the walls, heavy lampshades and winking candles, mirrors and unnerving pictures hung about the room; an expansive sofa upon which an equally expansive woman was sitting, who Anna presumed was Meryl. Amid the theatre of Meryl's surroundings, one object stood out – a crystal ball on the table in front of the sofa, lambent and swirling, vivid as a moon breaking through wreaths of cloud. Anna could not take her eyes off it until Meryl spoke—

'Welcome, welcome to my humble parlour, girls. Please, do take a seat.' She spread out her fingers towards them, indicating the armchairs opposite.

Effie remained standing. 'We know the guy in the tarot tent. We're like him . . . if you understand my meaning?'

Meryl dipped her head. 'I do indeed. I cater to cowans and witches alike. What is it you've come for?'

Effie took the armchair on offer. Anna sat on the edge of the other one, ready to spring up again.

'Can you actually speak with the dead?' Effie began bluntly.

'Can I glimpse through the Fabric to what lies beneath?' Meryl responded in a towering voice, fitting for the stage. 'Of course.' Her eyes were almost comically large but heavily lidded, set in a face that drooped like the fabrics of the room. Her hair provided a short and spiky counterpoint, dyed an abrasive orange.

'What about speaking with a specific person?'

Meryl interlaced her fingers. 'It can be done. But it's harder, a little more pricey . . .'

'How much?'

'Fifty.'

Effie sat back, arms crossed. 'Forty.'

'My dear.' Meryl's voice was light and yet implacable. 'I'm not open to bargaining.' She sat back too, testing just how desperate they were.

Effie's foot tapped up and down. 'Fine.'

'Effie—' Anna hissed. 'I thought we weren't sure we would do this . . .'

The woman's eyes rotated to Anna. 'Don't worry, my dear. We will only speak with a spirit of your choosing and they won't be able to reach you in any way. Their energy will be contained within my crystal ball. It's perfectly safe. I know what I'm doing. You must, when you are contacting Hel.'

Anna frowned. 'Did you say hell? Like . . . heaven and hell?'

Meryl hooted. 'Oh dearie, have you been living in the cowan world too long?'

'She wasn't brought up in the magical world,' Effie explained. She turned to Anna. 'She doesn't mean the Christian hell – that's just a perverted fantasy created by men with too much time on their hands. Getting spanked for your sins, come on. Like everything else, they stole the name from us and twisted it. She's talking about the real Hel. H-E-L.' She spelt the letters out. 'The true realm of the dead, the spirit world, where we go when we die.'

'You don't know much more than her, do you?' Meryl jeered, making Effie scowl. 'Hel!' Meryl declared loudly, fanning out her shawls. 'Also known as the Underworld, belongs to the dark side of the Goddess, Mother Holle herself, Snow Queen and Weaver of Bones. It's a place more ancient than time; merciless, terrible, sacred. And yet, it's not a different place at all. It is here. Among us.'

A shiver crawled up Anna's spine. 'What do you mean?'

Meryl held up the edge of one of her embroidered shawls. 'Imagine the world is made of fabric.' She ran her fingers over it. 'This side is the reality we experience every day – the physical world as we see it, woven with our own interpretation of it. While the Underworld . . .' Her fingers spidered to the underside of the cloth, feeling it, but not showing it. 'Is what lies beneath. Not another realm, but the underside of reality. Not so pretty. Full of knots and loose ends and stitches frayed and broken. The parts of ourselves we do not wish to see. But when we die, all souls must pass through it and many remain stuck there, tangled until they break their way free. If they ever do . . .'

The shiver seized all of Anna now.

'Perhapsss,' Meryl's voice susurrated, 'the person you wish to contact is still there . . . still with us.'

Her words sliced through the peaceful image of her mother that Anna had created, chopping it to pieces. Anna couldn't bear the thought of her mother being trapped, stuck, tangled for all time in this liminal place. She turned to Effie, whose expression was not as bold as it had been a moment ago, but the curiosity still burned in her eyes. The craving for magic. She looked at Anna. 'I think we have to give it a shot.'

Anna's whole body revolted at the thought. She gripped the chair, lifting herself as if about to run. But where could she run? The curse would be with her wherever she went. This didn't feel like the right path . . . but it was still a path. She forced a quick nod, her voice strained. 'Do it.'

Meryl raised a blunt, drawn-on eyebrow. 'Got cash?'

Effie rolled her eyes and reached into her bag, extracting a few notes. Meryl took them and tucked them into a drawer beneath the tablecloth. Then, she lifted her head and rubbed her hands together. 'Right, who is this spirit and what was their living name?'

'Our mother,' Effie replied, glancing at Anna. 'Marie Everdell.'

'Marie . . . Marie . . .' Meryl whispered as if drawing the name into her. She raised her hands dramatically into the air. The candles dimmed while the light of the crystal ball glowed brighter. She began to weave her hands around it as if she were manipulating the fabric of reality she had spoken of. It was hard to tell whether the ball contained liquid or air, but whatever its innards were formed of, they moved slowly and indecipherably, like mist in a graveyard. 'Mother Holle!' Meryl called out suddenly. 'We call on you today, to help us contact the mother of these here two sisters: Marie Everdell!'

Her mother's name did not sound right out of the lips of this woman, but twisted and broken. Anna tried to focus on the light of the ball, but it was the darkness around them that seeped into her eyes, that rose within her. None of this was right.

'Marie Everdell!' Meryl's voice soared. 'Are you here with us? Show yourself!'

The mists of the ball began to coalesce – darkening – forming a sense of something within. Shadows. Edgeless shapes. Hints of humanity but twisted and broken too. Black voids. They seemed to reach towards Anna, filling all of her vision, sapping the warmth from her—

I won't look down . . .

'Ah! I hear her!' Meryl announced. 'Marie is here with us!' She clamped her hands around the ball and her features slackened. Her eyes rolled back in her head. 'She wishes to speak through me!'

Effie shifted to the edge of her seat. 'What does she say?'

Anna could not move. The shadows were staring at her now; she felt no sense of her mother . . . only Aunt. Every formless face was Aunt. Her smile wide and mirthless and swallowing Anna whole—

'She says she can see you!' Meryl continued. 'She says that she loves you both very much. That she misses you. Wait. Wait. I'm getting something else. Something important—'

'What?' Effie urged.

'That you must go to the attic . . . there's a red box which contains something you must see. I don't know . . . I'm getting a vision of writing . . . perhaps a letter . . .'

Anna tried to hold onto Meryl's words, to the reality around her, but it was slipping away or she was slipping away, being dragged under, into the terrible world of the glass ball. Shadows and screams rising around her.

I won't look down.

I won't look down.

Oh Goddess—

All she could see was darkness . . .

In some other world, Meryl was screaming.

It jolted Anna back into the room. Meryl was staring at the crystal ball and it was no longer full of shadows, but snow. A terrible, eerie, drifting snow. Meryl appeared to be trying to remove her hands from the ball but they seemed stuck, as if frozen to it. She squealed like a turkey as the glass began to crack with a tearing, ripping sound. It shattered to pieces and the snow burst out, filling the small space of the caravan, spiralling around them fast as a blizzard – and then gone. The caravan just a caravan once more.

Anna still could not move – she was so cold, a cold like she had never known, so intense it felt inseparable from her, as if frost had risen up through her skin from inside her own bones.

Meryl's head dropped in slow, shocked motion to the destroyed crystal ball – a cut bleeding on her hand from the broken glass. She was trembling. Her head rose back up to them, horror and blame coalescing in her eyes. 'The snows of Hel . . .' she stuttered. 'What . . . did . . . you . . . do?' Her voice was no longer lofty but small and breathy. *Afraid.*

'Nothing!' Effie had jumped out of her seat. She looked curiously at Anna but then squared herself back to Meryl. 'Shouldn't *you* know what just happened? Aren't you the expert?'

'I'm no expert!' Meryl cried, shawls flapping. 'Why would an expert be working in this cesspool?!'

'What?' Effie growled.

Meryl breathed out raggedly and collapsed onto the sofa. She jabbed a hand at the broken glass. 'I was lucky enough to secure that crystal ball years ago and I've set up my business around it. It's not my magic, I don't contact the dead . . . but that ball *was* magic, a window to Hel, the Underworld. I just used it to put on a show and the rest was an act.'

Effie bore over the table threateningly. 'So that stuff you said about our mother . . .?'

'A load of old tosh. But what I just felt then—' Meryl's eyes moved between them. 'That was real.' She looked down bleakly at the glass-strewn floor and her face twisted. 'You two have ruined my livelihood!'

'I'm sure you'll find some new way of taking money off innocent people,' Effie spat.

Meryl glowered.

'We're sorry.' Anna stood up too. 'I'm so sorry. I – we didn't do anything intentionally. But, please, tell us, is there some meaning in it? The snow? Do you understand what happened?'

'The only thing I know is that I'd like you to get out of here!' Meryl inspected the cut on her hand, wincing.

'We'll go.' Anna put her hands up. 'But please, if you know anything, anything at all—'

'I don't know a damn thing!' Meryl snapped. 'There's only one grove out there who can help you.'

'Who?' Effie demanded.

Meryl's sunken eyes rose to them. 'The Hel witches. The Gatekeepers of Hel. The Raven Tongued, who speak with the dead.'

'How do we find them?'

'GET OUT!' Meryl squawked. 'Go on and don't come back – ever!'

Anna attempted to pick a few pieces of glass up from the floor, placing them back on the table, but stopped at the look on Meryl's face. She quickly followed Effie through the door.

The caravan spat them back out and all Anna wanted to do was to get as far away from the fairground as possible.

When Selene spotted them, she came running over. 'Where have you two been?'

'We got bored while you were otherwise engaged with Demdike.' Effie didn't stop walking.

Selene pulled a face. 'Come on, Travis is on the clock and it's getting late. I don't want to be here in the dark, *do you?*'

Anna could think of nothing worse.

'What do you know of the Hel witches?' Effie hit Selene with the question as soon as they walked through the door to the house.

Selene did not respond.

'Did you hear me?'

Selene eyed her with suspicion. 'Why do you want to know? What were you two up to at that fairground?'

Anna and Effie shared a glance but neither confessed anything. Selene gave Anna a look as if to say, *I'm used to Effie keeping secrets from me, but not you.*

'So?' Effie prompted.

Selene pouted. 'I don't know much about them; they're not the kind of witches who move in my circles. They practise necromancy – casting spells with the assistance of the spiritual world. Other witches dabble with such things, but the Hel witches . . . they are the purists, the originals. The only witches who can speak the Language of the Dead.'

Anna didn't want to know any more about these Hel witches, but Selene's words snagged. 'The language of the what?'

'The first ever written language, created to communicate with the dead.

Apparently, just hearing it is enough to drive a witch mad. Which is why any witch who knows what's good for them stays as far away from the Hel witches as possible.' Selene narrowed her eyes at them, then turned to her shelves of ingredients, which had been much depleted since Anna's outburst. 'Right. I have a client in half an hour, I need to prepare.'

She left Anna and Effie alone in the kitchen. Effie shot Anna a look, a smile glimmering along her lips. Anna wished she understood Effie's smiles but they ran away before they could be captured and left you chasing.

'What?' said Anna.

'Meryl was *scared*.'

Anna swallowed. 'I know, but it was just another hyper-magical episode. I think attempting to contact our dead mother might have, you know, been a bit of a trigger.'

Effie's eyes dropped. 'Sorry. You should have told me if it was too much.'

Anna didn't want to point out that she'd tried, but then she hadn't explained to Effie the whole truth either. She hadn't wanted to show Effie just how afraid she'd really been.

'I don't know why she was scared,' Anna mumbled.

Why was I so scared? The cold gripped her again as if it was still inside her. She thought of the snow of her dreams, always drifting, never settling.

'We could try to find out . . .' Effie suggested.

Anna shook her head emphatically, scattering the vision from her mind. 'No. If today proved anything, it's that we don't want to get mixed up with the Hel witches.'

'Even if they can talk to the dead . . .'

'No, Effie. I just think we ought to stick to our mother's path,' Anna insisted. 'We work out her next steps.'

'Why stick to one path?' Anna could see that glint in Effie's eye she knew well – a hunter on the chase, a hunter that would tear any path to pieces to get its prey.

Anna knew it was stupid but she'd been cradling a burgeoning thought. That if she could retrace Marie's footsteps back to the beginning . . . perhaps she'd find the real Marie at last. That somehow she'd be free of Aunt and free to love the mother she'd never known. Anna put the Everdell book on the counter with a pointed thud. 'Look, we've got the information Marie had now. We don't know what she did next, but we need to research these original sisters – Hannah and Eleanor Everdell. Find out as much about them as we can. Perhaps their stories contain the answers. We can go to the Library for research and look for Pesaycha there while we're at it. It's time we write Nana one of those letters with a Futhark Stamp, requesting a meeting.'

A Futhark Stamp – powered by the magic of the Runic Witches – ensured a letter would reach its recipient even if you didn't know where they were. It was how Anna had found Nana the year before.

Effie nodded. 'Sure. Fancy a movie?'

Anna was thrown by her invitation. *A movie.* It was the first time in a long time that Effie had suggested they actually hang out. An offering. Anna hesitated, looking down at the blood-soaked book. Shouldn't they be getting on with finding its answers?

'I won't bite, I promise.'

Anna raised an eyebrow now. 'You sure?'

'Not one hundred per cent. Come on. Let's go to my room.'

Effie grabbed a bag of Haribo from the cupboard and they made their way upstairs. Anna hadn't been in Effie's room since the year before. Apparently, Effie still didn't believe in tidying. Anna stepped across the debris on the floor to the unmade bed, behind which a painting hung. The dark, inky swirls of its purple and black colours were in a state of perpetual motion, like a sky that refused to settle. 'Where did you get this?' Anna asked, touching it gently. The paint reacted to her touch, spinning around her finger.

'I painted it.' Effie joined her on the bed, opening up her laptop.

'Really? You painted this? It's amazing. It moves!'

'Yeah.' Effie shrugged. 'I used to paint a bit. Got some friends in the magical art scene, they showed me some techniques. We should go to their gallery sometime, it's trippy.'

Anna could see Effie in the picture now, the colours were her – sultry and dangerous, bright shots running through like lightning strikes. The whole thing restless in a way that was hard to look away from – hunting, searching, feeding on itself; a suggestion of depths unseen.

'Aunt used to paint,' Anna said, not sure why it had come back to her. She'd been very young when Aunt had painted. She'd given it up eventually, replacing it with sewing and embroidery.

Effie raised her eyebrows.

'I mean, nothing like this,' Anna added quickly. 'In fact – the opposite. Still lifes. She captured things, locked them in place.' *Trapped forever.* Anna glanced back up to the painting. 'You should paint more though.'

'I should do a lot of things.' Effie lay back against the pillows. 'Nah. Outgrown it, too much fun to be had living life, not trying to capture it. What do you want to watch?'

Effie flicked on a movie. Anna quickly realized that Effie had little intention of watching it. She talked over it, messaged people on her phone, tortured the Haribo, stretching and squidging the sweets between her teeth. Eventually she turned the volume down and swivelled to Anna. 'I was thinking, do you reckon our language could be blood magic?' Her lashes were soft against the dark pulsing of her eyes.

'Er—'

'We saved Attis with our blood, remember? I think about it a lot.'

'Really?' Anna had done everything she could to block that moment from her thoughts. Images came back to her as sharp and sudden as they always did: Attis's blood pouring from his chest – *too much, too fast* – her and Effie slicing their palms, joining their hands, the beat of his heart beneath them – *too slow, too slow* . . .

'We brought him back to life.'

'Not quite back to life,' said Anna. 'He hadn't died—'

'His heart had stopped.'

'Paused.'

'Why do you do that? Deny our power?' Effie's eyes bore into hers. 'Do you remember how it felt?'

'No,' Anna lied.

'I remember it. The heat of our blood, magic surging between us, the power at our fingertips . . .' A savage smile formed on her lips. 'Feeling everything at once but joined by a single purpose: he can't die. Blood is a powerful language. I'm not saying blood divination like Demdike – there are other kinds of blood magic out there. It could be ours. *If* we have the same one.'

With the scent of blood still fresh in her mind, Anna recoiled at the thought.

Effie leant back against the pillow. 'I asked Selene about our mother's language.'

'You did?' Anna sat up. She'd been intending to do the same. 'What did she say?'

'You know Selene.' Effie rolled her eyes. 'Typically vague, said something about touch. That Marie used the power of touch – her hands – to cast spells. But she seemed keen to change the subject.'

Anna absorbed this new information. *Touch*. Selene had always said that Marie knew how to put people at ease. Perhaps touch made sense. It fitted into Anna's picture of her mother – she'd always imagined her warm and tactile, comforting.

'I'm not exactly the touchy-feely type,' said Effie. 'Do you know what your aunt's was? Selene said the Binders, but they're more of a cult than a true language.'

Anna shook her head. 'Aunt was one for keeping secrets. I don't think it would be touch though . . .' She thought of her aunt's tough, bony fingers. There had been no comfort in them. 'What if . . .' Anna tested her fears against Effie. 'What if we can't discover our language until we've stopped the curse? Perhaps Marie and Aunt never found theirs, the curse consumed it, and that's why Selene doesn't want to tell us, why Demdike couldn't sense anything in our blood . . .'

'No,' said Effie resolutely. 'Fuck the curse. It's already ruining everything, it's not going to take our language from us too. Our magic is more powerful than it.'

Anna nodded, wanting to believe Effie's words. 'How are you never afraid?'

'Oh, I am. It's just that—' Effie smiled, tongue moving over her sharp incisors. 'I like it. The breaking point of emotions is the point at which we're alive.'

Anna laughed. 'I'll try to remember that the next time you pull me into doing something crazy.' She leant her head against the wall, the words spilling out of her. 'I want to be brave.' She rolled her head to Effie. 'I want to be brave enough to finish what our mother started.'

Anna emphasized the words *our mother*. An offering of her own.

'Mother,' Effie repeated, as if she couldn't quite accept the word as belonging to her. 'Feels weird calling her that. It feels weird having a mother, full stop.'

'But you had Selene . . .'

Effie's mouth firmed. 'I never knew Selene wasn't my real mum but we never felt like mother and daughter either. I just didn't know why. I blamed Selene most of the time.' She laughed faintly. 'I guess, sometimes, I figured I was the problem . . . But hey, we know the truth of it now. It was all just a big lie.'

Anna frowned, feeling just how lost Effie had been too. 'I'm sorry, Effie.'

'Don't feel sorry for me. You were the one with the psycho aunt.'

'True.'

'And now . . . we have each other. Sisters. Still getting used to that word too.' Effie gave Anna a look that was half mocking, half tentative, waiting to see how Anna would react.

'Same,' Anna admitted. 'How do you become sisters?' She breathed out a laugh, not wanting Effie to see how much it might mean to her.

'We yell at each other for stealing each other's clothes and plait each other's hair?' Effie suggested.

'That could work.'

'We don't try to kill each other?'

'Also a good start.'

'Thanks for *not* killing me, by the way.'

'Sure,' Anna replied, and they laughed faintly at the absurdity of their conversation.

'You thought about it though?' Effie's voice remained teasing but her eyes sharpened.

Anna wanted to say no but she couldn't. 'I thought about it,' she said, slowly. 'Aunt painted a compelling picture, and I was angry and terrified and I'd always done what she told me to do my whole life. But no. It was never an option.'

'Can't entirely blame you. I'd lied, released the video and slept with Peter. And if you'd got rid of me, you'd be free now. You wouldn't have a curse or a bitch of a sister to deal with.' Effie smirked but it fell away. 'I'm sorry. I shouldn't have done those things. I was pissed at Darcey and then I was pissed at you. I was drunk and destructive.'

Anna hadn't ever expected to hear those words. 'I'm sorry too,' she said quickly, wanting to meet Effie halfway. 'I'm sorry if you felt I was coming between you and Attis . . .'

She wondered whether to tell Effie about their kiss, but it would ruin everything, and for what? Something that had meant nothing to him.

Effie searched her eyes and Anna began to grow uncomfortable, but then Effie smiled. 'I forgive you. I get it. He's hot.'

'It wasn't—'

Effie laughed. 'I'm just playing with you. Though he'd have died too if you'd sacrificed me. How do I know you weren't just saving him?' She arched an accusatory eyebrow.

'I wasn't going to let either of you die,' Anna replied seriously. 'I don't think one of you could exist without the other anyway. You're part of each other.' It hurt her to say the words, but they were true.

Effie nodded. 'We are. I couldn't live without him.'

Anna didn't know how to reply. Their conversation was the closest they'd ever come to honesty and yet it felt rife with cracks – one wrong step and you'd fall right through. 'Which is why we'll save him,' she said. 'Together.'

'Of course we will. The curse can go to hell and leave us to take over the world.'

'The world?' Anna laughed. 'I thought we were just getting used to the idea of being sisters.'

Effie's face gave way to a grin. 'OK. Well, you can borrow any clothes you want, my wardrobe is basically Narnia, and I can't plait hair, sorry.'

'Wait, you don't know how to plait hair?'

'Can you imagine Selene doing that? We just used magic.'

Anna thought over the evenings that had punctuated every day of her life – Aunt brushing her hair, plaiting it – sometimes severe, sometimes tender. It had been control, but it had been some of their closest moments too.

'I can teach you.' Anna nodded towards the floor-length mirror.

Effie rolled her head on the pillow. 'No, I'm too comfy.'

'Come on.' Anna cleared a pathway to the mirror. Effie dragged herself from the bed and slumped onto the floor. Anna sat down behind her and their eyes met in the mirror. They laughed, a little embarrassed. Anna ran her fingers through Effie's hair, teasing away the knots. It was as soft as her own.

'I like your real colour,' said Anna, looking at the black roots beneath the peroxide blonde.

Effie waved a hand. 'I get bored. Maybe I'll go red?' She pouted in the mirror. She pulled some of Anna's hair close to her face, considering the colour. 'We don't look much alike, do we?' She tilted her head. 'Maybe you have my nose.'

'I think you'll find you have *my* nose.' Anna grinned. She preferred to look at Effie's face in the mirror to her own. Her own red hair and green eyes reminded her too much of . . . *Aunt*. Whereas Effie, with her black hair and dimples, was all Marie. *Not just looks.* From Selene's stories, Marie had always sounded fearless and bold and entrancing. All the things Effie was.

'What if I'm like her . . .' Anna muttered, afraid to say it out loud. 'What if I'm like Aunt?'

Effie's eyes moved to hers. 'She's dead, Anna. Let her die. Anyway.' Effie looked back to the mirror, teasing. 'If anyone's going to be the bad sister, it's me. I'm the morally depraved one; you're the virginal wholesome one.'

Anna opened her mouth. 'Hey!' She refocused on the task at hand to distract from her burning cheeks. She picked up a few strands of Effie's hair. 'Plaits. Now, you select three even pieces of hair and you weave them together like this—' Anna demonstrated. 'You see?'

'I mean, magic is a lot easier, but it does feel nice. I'll give you that.'

Effie leant back, softening, closing her eyes and turning uncommonly quiet, her coiled energy unwinding as Anna plaited and unplaited her hair. A few minutes passed in silence.

'I guess,' said Effie, her voice as wistful as Anna had ever heard it, 'our mother might have done this to us . . .'

Anna nodded but they looked away from each other, the weight of their lost memories too much to bear.

Anna loosed the plaits with her fingers. 'We're all that's left of her now . . .'

Effie turned to her, cross-legged on the floor. She bit her lip. 'You wouldn't want to take up Demdike's suggestion . . . get as far away from one another as possible?'

Anna imagined it but she could feel the pull, the pull between them that had always been there. 'No. You?'

Effie shook her head.

'Maybe we need to learn how to trust one another again . . .' said Anna, her words trailing, not sure how they would be received.

'Trust.' Effie seemed to reel at the word. She traced her spider tattoo, which was running down her arm. 'I find it hard enough to trust myself half the time.'

'I find trust hard too, believe me. My aunt drilled into me my whole life that she was the only person I could trust, and look how that worked out.'

'Everyone lied to me too.' Effie's eyes went still. Hard.

'We could try . . .' This offering felt tremulous, close to breaking. How could Anna trust herself when she didn't know who she was any more?

Effie looked back up at her, eyes thawing. She nodded. 'Let's try. We don't let the curse come between us. We work together.'

She put a hand towards Anna. Anna went to take it but the spider of Effie's tattoo ran into Effie's palm. Without thinking, Anna put her hand to the side and it ran across into her own palm, the lightest footprints of magic.

Effie appeared surprised. 'Well, that's never happened before. Apparently, magic wants us to work together too.'

Anna smiled at the simple yet astonishing magic, letting the spider run back into Effie's hand. 'Together,' she said, not looking away, trying to believe in it. 'Besides, I need you.' She smiled. 'I'm always braver when I'm with you.'

'I'll have to try harder to terrify you.' Effie grinned. 'Speaking of, this hair plaiting has given me the perfect idea for our next coven session.'

'Should I be worried?'

'Indefinitely.'

When Anna returned to her room later, her head was full of Effie. She opened the Everdell book, seeing their names first.

Anna Everdell – Effie Everdell.

A line connecting them. A simple thread. But so far from simple. Even though Anna wanted it, perhaps more than anything, they would never be the kind of sisters who plaited hair and swapped clothes and shared secrets about boys. What they had was different – uncategorizable, complicated, turbulent. *Would the thread be strong enough?* They didn't have a past, they'd only known each other one fraught year and Anna felt like she was only ever seeing half of Effie; the other half hidden beneath restless waves. How could you know someone who turned knowing them into a game?

If you don't have trust, you don't have anything, my child . . .

Anna traced the line up to: *Vivienne Everdell.* That name she knew; that name was sewn on the inside of her heart. A bleeding name. *Dead, because of me.* Dead but not gone. Anna could still feel the threads between them, tangled, still beating and bleeding, so many she didn't know where she began and Aunt ended.

BLOOD, HAIR, BONE

To exert control over a spirit, its Death Name must be known, but not all can be uncovered. Some names are buried so deep even Hel fears to speak them.

Spirit Magicke, Books of the Dead: Tome 3865

Anna shut her locker door to find Peter approaching, a determined look upon his face. He was carrying a bunch of flowers, which he extended towards her. Roses. Without thinking, Anna flinched from them. They hovered in the air, as unsure as the look on his face.

'An apology,' he said in that voice of his, smooth as polished marble. 'Please take them.'

'Peter, I don't want flowers.'

He lowered them, his cheeks flushing in a way she'd never seen before. 'I know I don't deserve your forgiveness but I just hoped we could talk.'

Anna had dreamt for years of him uttering a single word to her and now, apparently, he was desperate to speak to her on a daily basis. She couldn't fathom why he was still interested in her. He could have anyone in the school, and she'd refused his advances once. He'd been quick to find a replacement then . . .

'I don't think a talk will change anything,' she said, her voice brittle as the memories of the ball flooded back through her.

He attempted a playful smile. 'You can't avoid me forever . . .'

I shouldn't have to avoid you! Anna felt like shouting, but his smile faltered and he looked so momentarily helpless that she bit her lip. *How am I the one feeling guilty now?!*

He stepped towards her, his cut-glass blue eyes sharpening with intensity. 'Please, Anna. I just want a chance to explain myself. Why don't we just go for a coffee? One coffee?'

'I'm in.' A hand appeared on Peter's shoulder. Smoke-stained fingers. Anna hadn't noticed Attis come up behind them. He put his arm around Peter in a friendly gesture that was also somehow incredibly threatening. 'You're very persuasive, Mr Nowell.'

Peter shrugged him off. 'Attis.' He nodded, releasing a controlled breath. 'Anna and I were just speaking.'

'Looked to me more like you speaking *at* her.'

Peter squared his shoulders to Attis. 'Really? You're talking to me about harassing girls? Isn't it all you do?'

'The difference is they *want* to talk to me.'

'I think we both know you're not interested in anything a girl has to say, Attis.'

'You're right, I'm just a rogue with one thing on my mind. Not a gentleman who hounds girls with flaccid flowers.'

Anna looked down at the roses in Peter's hand, which had suspiciously wilted, the stalks flopped over. She made a face at Attis. His smile quirked. Peter stared at the flowers in confusion.

'Don't worry, Peter. Happens to the best of us.' Attis patted him on the arm. 'Now, if you don't mind, Anna and I have plans to walk to class together.'

Peter's jaw stiffened. 'Anna and I were speaking—'

'Actually, Anna is leaving,' she said. 'I'll leave you two to work this out.' She brushed past them, feeling gratification at the looks on their faces. It gave way when she thought of what Peter had said about Attis. Anna had noticed him around school, back to his old tricks, a girl on his arm as he walked to class or sitting with another in the lunch hall, chatting, laughing, flirting with expert ease. Apparently, the rumours had only added to his allure. Did you really think it would be any different? That he would be any different?

'Anna.' She heard Attis's voice behind her as he caught up with her. 'Well, that was harsh.'

She rolled her eyes at him, knowing it was dangerous to look into his eyes for long, that she was far from immune to his allure. 'I was beginning to feel like a third wheel.'

'Peter and I just have a lot of catching up to do.'

'You need to *not* do magic in front of cowans.'

'I didn't do it on purpose. My presence tends to wither flowers, birds drop out of the sky, women run screaming. That sort of thing.'

Anna snorted. 'That adds up.'

They made their way outside towards the science building. She wasn't sure why he was still here; she didn't think he had a class there now. He stretched his arms to the sky briefly then turned to her as they walked. 'But seriously, you shouldn't let Peter harass you.'

'I'm not. He's just trying to apologize for—'

Anna didn't finish. They both remembered vividly what had happened that night. Effie and Peter together in bed. Attis driving Anna home, his hands unzipping her dress, their eyes too close for comfort, the feel of his lips—

Not helpful thoughts. She turned to the wind, breathing it in. 'I don't need your help with this.'

'He shouldn't keep bothering you, trying to woo you with tokens of his fuckwittery.'

Anna stopped. 'They were just roses, Attis.'

'It's what the roses represent.'

'And what is that?'

'That he'd like to . . . pluck you.'

'Attis!' Anna walked on quickly so he wouldn't see the bright hue of her cheeks.

'Anyway.' He caught up with her, chuckling. 'You know you're not a rose girl.'

Anna wondered if he was hinting at the conversation they'd had once, when he'd transformed Cressey Square garden into a secret wilderness for her. When he'd chosen a flower he thought represented her: *springwort*. A magical flower that summarized what that whole afternoon had been – nothing but an illusion.

'Maybe I'm not a flower girl at all,' she responded. 'Why is it girls are presented with something that was once beautiful but is now slowly dying?'

Attis considered her words. 'You have a point.'

She stopped at the science building door, then narrowed her eyes. 'Do you even have a class here now?'

He looked up at the building and shook his head. 'Nah, just fancied the walk. I can't remember where my next class is.'

'Attis!'

'Don't worry, they'll wait for me.' He grinned and made off in the other direction.

Anna watched him go, her smile wavering as she wondered if she was just another flirtation for him now. She turned and made her way into class, freezing as she opened the door—

Inspector Eames was sitting at the back of the room with his notepad at the ready. His gaze moved to her and for a moment the black depths of his eyes were all she could see. She stumbled towards a chair. *Keep it together.*

'Anna, you're late,' the teacher chided.

'Sorry, Dr Pinkett.' She tucked herself into a row.

'As I was saying,' Dr Pinkett continued, giving Anna a pointed look. 'Inspector Eames will be observing today's class. Nothing to worry about. We shall continue as normal—'

Anna took out her books, doing her best to ignore the man sitting behind, but he was all she could think about, all she could *feel* in the room. Why was he observing classes? It had been a few weeks since the start of term, and while Darcey's rumours were still on everyone's lips, they had begun to lose some of their initial fervour – but his presence, his *watching*, would only keep the questions alive. Anna moved her hands beneath her desk, her fingers tangling, gripping, as she tried to take her focus off the racing of her heart, but in her mind, bells were ringing in high warning and all she could feel was a cold nothingness creeping through her body, setting it on edge—

She'd been practising her magic. Forcing herself to open up to it. Last night, she'd formed ripples in the bath and then attempted to draw them back to their centre with magic. At first, nothing had happened. She'd gone through the motions of the spell easily enough, sensing the threads in the room – the shimmer of water, the unfolding ripples, the fertile steams of the bath – but when she'd attempted to reach for the magic inside herself – to raise her Hira – it just . . . wasn't there. She'd tried not to panic at the fact she couldn't feel anything, pulling the threads tighter, but they felt colourless . . . stretched too far. It had been easier in the sewing room with the others, but alone, with no one to face but herself, her magic was too distant. And yet, when she'd dashed her hand through the waters in frustration, the ripples had suddenly grown in force and number, rising up like a well overflowing, making a storm of the bath and spilling over the sides. It had been the same when she'd attempted to light a candle in her room and had set the curtains on fire. How could she control her magic if it kept acting so out of control? Giving her too much or nothing at all.

It might have comforted her if they'd made more progress with the curse but their new *plan* was getting nowhere. Anna had spent night after night ignoring her school work, researching the names of the original sisters instead – Hannah and Eleanor Everdell. Finding no trace of their existence. She'd written Nana a letter and attempted to make plans to go to the Library with Effie, but apparently Effie had been too busy partying and then sleeping off her partying. Things had been better between them since the trip to Demdike, and Anna was trying to keep relations amicable, but she found Effie's general lack of urgency infuriating. But then, Effie's dreams weren't tortured by ravens and a winding staircase to nowhere; Effie's magic wasn't exploding randomly; Effie believed they could beat the curse no matter what they did; Effie hadn't almost killed her own aunt—

'Ms Everdell!'

Anna cried out.

The whole class turned to her. Dr Pinkett was staring at her and frowning – she realized he was the one who'd said her name. He frowned. 'Anna, are you . . . OK? You weren't responding to my question.'

'Er – yes – sorry.' Anna pulled herself up, hearing sniggers, whispers, the scratch of the inspector's pen behind her. 'What was the question again?'

When she was finally released from the classroom, she felt as if she might explode. She put her head down and made straight for the music room, wanting to put as much distance between herself and the inspector as possible. She spotted Peter ahead. He was coming the other way but he slowed down.

'Anna—'

'Not now, Peter.' She carried on but he walked after her.

'Anna, what's wrong?'

She spun around. 'What's wrong? What's wrong? Oh, I don't know, maybe that I'm being accused of insane things, shunned and talked about by most of the school, and I just had to sit through a whole lesson with that – that inspector watching our every move. A man who's currently investigating me for bullying Darcey even though I've spent my entire life at this school being bullied *by* Darcey, your former girl-friend by the way!'

Peter looked taken aback at her outburst. She hoped it might scare him off but he moved closer, that straight line of concern appearing between his eyebrows. 'Of course, it's understandable you're stressed, you've been through so much.'

His sympathy caught her off guard.

'Come and sit down,' he said soothingly, moving her down the corridor to an empty bench.

Anna took a seat, crossing her arms around herself.

He shook his head. 'Ignore Darcey. She's always been an attention-seeker. I should have listened to you when you warned me about her last year. And what she did—' His voice thickened with disgust. 'Headmaster Connaughty, for God's sake.'

Anna lowered her eyes, guilt prickling at her skin, hot and cold. 'So you don't believe what she's saying? Any of it . . .'

'I don't believe what Darcey is saying, but do I think there's something going on at this school?'

Anna looked up.

His eyes flickered with thought. 'That video footage of the ritual on school grounds can't simply be ignored. I've seen *all* of it, Anna, and trust me – it's not . . . normal. At the very least it's a break-in, and at worst, evidence of some kind of cult. My dad's on the school board and he backed the inspection – thinks it's better to clean everything up properly rather than try to bury it. I'm just sorry you're caught up in it all.'

Anna turned away, not able to bear the way he was looking at her.

He sighed. 'I'm sorry for earlier, I just wanted to talk to you.'

'OK. Talk,' she relented.

'Now?'

'Yes.' Anna just wanted it to be over and done with so he would let it go. *Let me go.*

Peter shifted towards her, a look of focus settling on his face as if he had prepared for this. 'Firstly, I'm so sorry about your aunt.'

Anna stiffened.

'I wanted to talk to you over summer but, after how we ended things, I thought I'd be the last person you'd want contacting you. I can't imagine what you've been going through.'

It was all she could do to manage a nod.

He cleared his throat. 'And . . . that night at the ball . . .'

'When you slept with Effie,' she said. *My sister*. He didn't know *that* part.

He swallowed hard. 'I was a fool. An idiot. I thought you wanted me as much as I wanted you and then when you said no . . . I was reeling and stupid and I'd drunk too much. I just wanted to be alone and then Effie was there—' He could barely form her name; it grated against the polish of his voice. 'One thing led to another.' He shook his head, raised a fist as if he would strike himself. 'I wish I could undo it. I wish it had never happened. Except, that it's taught me some tough life lessons, made me realize what's important to me. I don't want to be that guy. The popular jerk. As of next year, we're going to be in the real world and all this school stuff is going to be meaningless. I want to make something of my life – myself. My dad didn't grow up rich. He built himself up from nothing. I want to stand on my own two feet too, to stand up for what's right.'

The blue in his eyes was set – clear and determined. Anna remembered the boy who'd once defended her when all the other *popular* boys were making fun of her.

'And I hope you do,' she said sincerely. 'But I don't see what it has to do with me.'

'Because you're not like the rest of this school either,' he replied, still impassioned. 'You're different. You aren't swayed by other people. You're strong and . . . you're good.'

For a moment Anna wanted to be the girl reflected in his eyes – not a witch, not cursed, not a murderer – but she was all of those things.

'You don't really know me, Peter.'

He tilted his head as if he wasn't so sure about that, his lips softening to a smile. 'Well, would you let me get to know you then? Properly this time? Just one date?'

Anna had watched him on the debate team in the past – she knew he had a way of pushing and pushing until he won. Perhaps, if she changed the terms of the negotiation, it might throw him off.

'This year is intense enough. I just don't want any complications right now.' She didn't know why she was making excuses. 'Why don't we just try being friends again? Like before the ball.'

Peter's smile tightened, but as he let her words sink in, it relaxed again. 'OK. Friends it is. I'll take it. It's a start.'

He put out a hand. Anna hesitated.

'Hey, don't leave me hanging here, Everdell.'

Anna put her hand out and they shook on it.

'Now.' He smiled, releasing her. 'Can I escort you to your next class?'

Rowan moved about Anna, arranging fresh greenery on their newly cleaned altar down in the depths of the sewing room. 'Eames was in my class yesterday too.' She shuddered. 'He gives me the creeping ivies. I just don't get the point. How is "observing classes" going to prove anything about bullying? What does he think I'm going to do – start a fist fight with someone?'

'Maybe it's giving him a sense of our social dynamics.' Manda glanced up from where she was working at a desk.

Or maybe it's simply meant to put us on edge, Anna thought.

'He was in one of my afternoon classes too,' said Attis, leaning against the wall. 'But I had the last laugh – his pen nib broke several times. He looked mildly irritated.'

'Attis.' Anna suppressed a smile. 'You need to stop doing cantrips on him.'

Knowing they couldn't draw any sort of magical attention, Attis was taking particular delight in casting the silliest, if most mundane, tortures upon the inspector.

'What?' He shrugged innocently. 'He had no idea. Just like the fact that his watch is either five minutes too fast or too slow at any one time.'

Rowan laughed. 'You're ridiculous.'

Attis bowed. 'I only deal in the ridiculous. Is that comfrey?'

'Yes, for mending friendships—'

While Attis and Rowan got lost in a discussion about the properties of comfrey, Anna was distracted by the snow globe on the altar. She reached for it and looked into it – a sensation that always felt more like falling, a miniature London waiting to catch her. She remembered picking it out with Effie in the memory shop the year before. The intricacy of its pocket-sized world still amazed her. Scraps of cloud moved through its sky, London peeking through beneath – roads and streets and skyscrapers, electric lights winking, cars moving like lines of ants and the Thames trailing dark glitter through it all. The snow inside it ever swirling – but trapped. She thought of the snow in Meryl's crystal ball with unease . . . but then a cloud blizzarded through the globe and Anna was distracted by something. A collection of tiny black dots. She peered closer and, for a moment, saw what they were . . . small birds . . . ravens . . . flying through the sky . . .

'PEOPLE!' Effie's voice rang out as she walked through the door. 'What are we doing?'

Anna almost dropped the snow globe and when she looked back down at it there were no dots in the sky, no ravens. *Am I going mad?*

'Adding some plants to the altar,' said Rowan.

'You've turned it into a bloody garden. Have you planted something in my goat skull?'

'Just livening it up.'

Effie stopped at Manda's desk. 'Manda, are you *working*?'

Manda covered the notes guiltily. 'I got here early, thought I'd use the time productively.'

Effie had heard enough. With a sharp click of her fingers, Manda's book snapped closed, the lights dimmed and the candles roared to life. 'We're not going to find our languages by wasting time. Let's do some Goddess-damn magic!'

Manda clicked her pen shut. 'What do you propose?'

'Well.' Effie sashayed over to the altar. 'I had an idea.'

'Always concerning,' said Attis.

Effie trailed her hands over the many objects, stopping at the Russian doll and looking back at them through her black hair – she'd removed the peroxide blonde. 'I propose an old language.' She cracked the doll open and plucked the next one out. She placed it down. 'An original language.' She took out the next one. 'A powerful language.' The next. 'A language of control.' She smiled the Russian doll of smiles.

Rowan folded her arms. 'Effie, what are you getting at here?'

'Imagic,' Effie responded, spinning her finger in the air and sending all the dolls toppling.

Rowan took in a breath. 'Thirteen black moons, I was worried you were going to say that . . . that's a highly questionable language . . .'

Manda looked as if she'd seen a ghost. 'You mean like voodoo dolls?'

'Voodoo dolls, effigies, mommets, poppets and pins, whatever you want to call it, Imagic offers us the power to take control of another human.'

'Hence it's not a particularly encouraged language,' said Rowan.

'We're not going to find our languages if we play safe, and Imagic is one of the oldest. One of the Goddess's original seven languages, and as such, we ought to familiarize ourselves with it.'

Rowan's eyes narrowed suspiciously. 'What exactly does that mean . . .?'

'Don't worry, my little poppets.' Effie smiled. 'We're not going to stick pins in Darcey, as happy as it would make me. I had something else in mind.'

She ushered them to the floor and they formed a tight, suspenseful circle in the centre of the room – the shadows at their backs, and before them: only each other, the candlelight throwing its illusions over them so that none of their faces were still, never quite settling on a single expression. Effie looked between them. 'I thought we could practise on each other.'

Rowan threw her hands up. 'Oh right. Now I feel totally reassured.'

Effie laughed. 'Come on, it'll be fun.'

'No.' Manda curled her legs up, clutching herself tightly. 'I don't want to explore this language. It doesn't feel right.'

Effie held her tongue, turning to Manda in an attempt at patience. 'Why not?'

Manda shook her head as if there was something she wanted to say but she didn't quite know how. 'It's playing God. You're not meant to play God.'

'Witches don't need to play God. Not when the Goddess can control him.' Effie winked.

'If it helps, Manda,' said Attis. 'Imagic isn't normally used for harm and control, it was traditionally employed for protection, healing, fertility and love.'

'Really?' Manda looked towards him, a hint of intrigue in her eyes.

'Love—' The word burst from Anna before she could stop it. 'There is no spell for love.' She didn't want to go near anything of the sort, considering what Demdike had said about the prophecy.

'Not *love, love*,' Rowan clarified. 'But lust, infatuation, fancy-the-pants-off-you sort of thing. I'm not proud but I desecrated several Ken dolls growing up trying to get various boys to fall for me. Didn't work because Imagic is hard, like, really hard. It takes great power to control a cowan, and to control another witch is next level. You have to get past their magical defences for starters.'

'Which is why I thought we could practise on each other,' said Effie.

'If we join our magic, the spell will have more power and we can lower our own defences. Rowan, you did tell me we needed to open up to one another.'

'I don't know if I meant it *this* literally . . .'

Effie shrugged. 'I take things rather literally, but it's just going to be a game.' She nudged Manda. 'No serious spell work. Come on, you know you want to . . .'

Manda was still holding herself tightly. She looked at Effie. 'OK . . .' Her voice squeezed itself out. 'Just a game.'

'Great.' Effie jumped up before Manda could change her mind, leaving them all to stew on her words, their circle far too close for comfort. All Anna could hear were the words *open up*, which was about the last thing she wanted her or her magic to do, but she thought of the inspector in her classroom, the feeling of almost losing it again, and knew she had to keep practising.

Effie returned and placed a bowl down in the centre of the circle. It looked to be made of smooth, grey stone, its centre deepening to black. 'An offering bowl,' she explained. 'For Imagic traditionally requires three offerings—'

> *Three ways, three keys,*
> *Can a man be owned:*
> *Red, black, white,*
> *Blood, hair and bone.*
> *Speak their name,*
> *Clear and true,*
> *Unite them all,*
> *And you have your fool.*

Effie finished her recitation, letting the silence settle. 'You create a representation of someone – an effigy – but for the spell to work you have to link it to them with their blood, hair and bone.'

'Bone!' Manda exclaimed. 'How do we give bone?'

Effie laughed. 'Nail clippings apparently suffice.'

'You can keep hold of your femurs today, Manda.' Attis nodded at her reassuringly. Then he took out his knife of many blades and held it up. 'If we're doing this, I can help with the blood and hair part. I promise, you won't feel a thing. It's what I say to all the ladies.'

He started around the circle. Anna waited nervously for him to arrive, trying not to think of all the potential dangers of her magic *opening up*.

Attis appeared before her. 'You look a bit peaky.'

'Magic and I don't have the best relationship right now.'

His eyes held hers; warm grey. 'Well, you should trust your magic, because I do.'

How could he do that? Flip between playful and disarming within moments? She put out her hand and he put his beneath hers, his touch distracting all her thoughts. She didn't even feel the blade move across her finger – soft as a feather's edge – but a drop of blood welled up. He let her hand go and she tipped it into the offering bowl. He moved the blade through the air and it changed to scissors. He took a lock of her hair between his fingers. *Why do they call it that? A lock of hair? Like it requires a key.* Their eyes met briefly, uneasily, like two passing butterflies tangling and flickering away again.

He handed her the hair as if it might fly away too. 'There you go.'

He was gone before she had time to answer. She leant forwards and dusted the hair into the bowl, swallowing through the tight, nervous rings of her throat. Then, she bit off an edge of nail and dropped that in too. *Blood, hair and bone.* The bowl had all of it. All of her.

'We ready?' Effie called.

They entwined hands and raised their circle with their usual chant, Effie adding:

> *By blood, by hair, by strength of bone,*
> *Blend our flesh and unite our souls,*
> *From me to you and you to me,*
> *Joined within ourselves, so mote it be.*

The magic between them began to circulate, a slow stir, the bowl responding. It had begun to stir too – their blood, hair and nails moving around inside of it, as if the bottom of the bowl had become a swirling, dark lake. Then, the offerings began to sink into its depths until . . . there was nothing left. *Consumed.*

Anna was still staring at it when Effie spoke. 'Call out each other's names and the spell will be complete!'

They began to incant each other's names.

'It's working!' Effie hollered. 'Can you all feel it?'

With the power of the group, Anna could feel echoes of the old magic she'd used to feel, faint but there – a pressure, a buzzing, a blurring of worlds. It felt as if the bowl were drawing them into its depths too. She didn't want to go but the currents of magic were unpeeling her fingers, loosening her grip, swallowing her up—

When she lifted her head, the room had faded away, the world shrunk to the tight bonds of their circle. All that existed now was each other . . . and it was no longer quite clear who was who. The magic was shifty, sly as the candlelight, blurring the lines between them too, as if their edges had unravelled – more of a question than a firm statement. Terribly open.

'I think we're in,' said Effie with the look of a puppet master. Her eyes settled on Rowan. Effie ran a hand through her hair, and, as she did so, her hair was no longer her own – its black silk shortened and turned dark brown and curly, a mirror of Rowan's wild spray.

Rowan's mouth fell open. 'That's – you've got my hair – wait, why can you pull off my own hair better than I can?'

Effie laughed, shaking the curls around her face. 'Go on. You try something.'

Rowan looked back at Effie with concentration and then she smiled and dimples popped up on either side of it. *Effie's dimples*. Rowan felt them with her fingers. 'I did it! Mother Holle, this is so *freaky*.'

Effie pounced on Manda. Manda's eyes were brimming with fear but an agreement seemed to pass between them and the magic did its work: Manda's skin lightened as Effie's grew darker.

'Lord in heaven.' Manda breathed, staring at her arms and hands. 'This is so . . . weird. It's not just the colour that's changed, it *feels* like your skin too. Can that be possible?'

'I think this spell runs more than skin deep,' Effie replied.

Rowan and Attis turned to one another with curiosity. The bright and dark clouds of Attis's eyes began to clear, replaced by Rowan's full eyebrows and the shape, and rich chestnut colour, of her eyes. Rowan smiled but her mouth was Attis's – her tongue running along the uneven line of his teeth, one a little off-kilter – Anna's favourite tooth. It was mind-bending.

'Anna, you haven't tried anything yet.' Effie searched her out with a knowing smile. Anna tried to dart from the tug of Effie's magic but it wrapped around her and Anna knew what it wanted. She relented, allowing her magic enough give to connect with Effie's. Their hair began to transform – Effie's turning red and Anna's black. Anna marvelled for a moment, reaching for a strand of it and realizing that it was no illusion . . . the hair she was holding was Effie's – its texture, its colour, each individual strand Effie's own.

'Weirdly, you two look more alike now.' Manda glanced between them. Attis was doing the same, his expression guarded.

'What about this?' Effie ran a finger up her own arm and Anna shivered. She'd felt Effie's touch on her arm as if their bodies were one. Intrigued, she eased uncomfortably into the magic and drew the threads of the spell towards her. She raised her hand up and wiggled her fingers – Effie's own arm mirrored hers, seemingly against her will.

Effie laughed, sounding genuinely taken aback. She sized Anna up and then twisted her head to the side – Anna's followed. Anna retaliated – turning Effie's head the other way, then up, then down. Effie was visibly delighted by their sudden battle of wills. She looked at Anna for a moment – then shut her eyes. Anna's world went black though her own eyes were entirely open. She put a hand out, suddenly afraid. 'I can't see.' Everything was darkness, not her own darkness, but Effie's.

Effie laughed and opened her eyes again and the world returned to Anna with sweet relief.

'This spell is even more interesting than I thought it would be. Think of the possibilities . . .'

'I don't want to think of any of the possibilities you're thinking of,' said Rowan, but Attis had started to tickle himself under the armpit and Rowan squealed in response. 'Gah! No – no! You know I'm ticklish, Lockerby! Right.' She turned to him. 'I'm getting you back . . .'

The spell descended into temporary chaos until Effie called out, 'How about we take things a bit deeper? Feel each other?'

'Er – that sounds highly inappropriate,' said Rowan.

Effie rolled her eyes and Rowan's rolled along with hers against her will. 'Hey!'

'I mean, feel each other's feelings,' Effie clarified.

Anna pulled back. Silly games were one thing but emotions were another. They were slippery, unclear, they did not abide by the rules – they hid, they lied, they masqueraded as one thing when they were something else entirely. They turned funerals to screams and set off bells. Panic surged through her.

'We should at least see if the spell runs *that* deep . . .' Effie reasoned. 'I'll start with Manda. Rowan and Anna, you can try.'

As Rowan turned to face her, Anna shrank into herself. Rowan nodded encouragingly in a way that made her feel worse – one look inside of her and Rowan might be left screaming. Anna clenched her fists and resisted the urge to pull away, allowing the spell to pull at her instead . . . down . . . down . . . inward and then suddenly – opening—

Anna could barely comprehend what was happening.

She was in a different world.

Inside Rowan? She couldn't interpret what she was experiencing – was she seeing it? Touching it? Hearing it? She didn't know, but she was immersed in a sense of Rowan-ness . . . like – like a pattern . . . a series of patterns she had no way to describe – like a poem in a foreign language or music made of instruments she'd never heard before. She gleaned a sense of lightness, the feeling of bubbles – fast and excited, childlike delight – things flitting this way and that, scattered like a rainstorm, all in a hurry and flurry, as unstoppable as Rowan when she couldn't stop talking about something. Yet, beneath lay other parts – like green grass and deep roots, and beneath, something smooth and grey and protective as stone. Heavy and sad.

Anna didn't have time to work out what it all meant; Effie was calling for them to move on.

Anna turned to face Manda and what met her felt like a wall. Prickly. No sense of lightness and heaviness like with Rowan . . . more like different textures flowing against one another with uneasy friction, a kind of desperation, a shifting fortress with tumultuous insides. What feelings were these? Anna sensed flecks of pain and bitterness and something so tenuous it looked as if it would tear apart to nothing . . .

Attis next. Their eyes met and for a fleeting moment the spell connected them without their bidding. Anna felt a wild energy filling her like a fever and then it was gone; withdrawn. They both retreated from the magic with silent, mutual agreement, turning their eyes away. Anna was desperately relieved. She couldn't bear the thought of him knowing what lay inside of her, as tempting as it was to unearth what his own inner worlds felt like . . .

Better left unknown.

Finally, Effie. Anna was still floundering in the strange, new magic but Effie did not give her a moment. Their magic entwined as if it had been waiting all along. This time it felt different.

Effie's emotions . . . they felt almost recognizable, as if formed from the same cloth as her own, but that was where the similarity ended. Her patterns were restless, electric, choppy and blade-edged, tearing through themselves. Blasts too quick to fathom, as if Effie were throwing everything at Anna at once to leave her dizzy and blindsided. Anna pushed deeper, sensing something . . . something . . . beyond all the chaos—

An edge. A black abyss like her own yet nothing like her own . . .

Effie called out suddenly, as if she'd felt Anna's probing. 'All right! Let's leave it there!' Their eyes met but Effie's were hard and darting. 'Time to bring this spell to an end.'

They chanted their closing circle and the magic spat them all back out again. Anna felt overwhelmed and strangely bereft. She tried to pin down the sensations she'd just experienced but they were already flying away from her, too strange to hold onto, the world solidifying everything back into place. What had that been?

She looked up at the others, the room behind coming into focus again. Normality returning, but nothing quite the same. At least no one was screaming. Only . . . they *were* looking at her strangely.

Rowan laughed a little uncomfortably. 'Well, I think an orgy would have been less intimate.'

'It was intense,' said Effie, who looked unusually dazed herself.

'Overwhelming.' Anna breathed out.

'Really?' Manda turned to her. 'Were you doing the spell? I couldn't tell – when it came to you . . . I wasn't sure if you'd pulled out.'

Anna frowned. 'I – I was doing it. I could feel you, I think. It wasn't like magic I've ever experienced but like – like—'

'I don't think I really got it, to be honest,' said Manda, sounding frustrated. 'I sort of felt something, like feelings that didn't seem like they belonged to me, but I couldn't make any sense of it.'

'Same,' Rowan agreed. 'I think I was tapping into something but I didn't really get it.'

Anna turned to her. 'Could you feel anything in me?'

Rowan's eyes shifted. 'Like I said, I don't think I was doing it right . . .' Her voice trailed and Anna knew she was trying to be kind.

'Effie?' Anna asked directly.

'I felt a lot. Powerful magic.' Effie's cheeks were flushed with magic, her eyes expanded. 'But, yeah, when it came to you, it was . . . harder to get anything . . . maybe your defences were up. The point is we pulled off Imagic. An original language.'

They began to discuss it in more depth but Anna had stopped listening. She'd opened herself up, fearing the worst, fearing the darkness inside her would spread to all of them . . . but instead they'd all felt . . . nothing. The emptiness she lived with now, confirmed.

'Oh shoot, I've got to go,' said Manda, standing up and wiping the dust from her knees. 'The librarian is waking in five minutes.'

Anna wanted to leave too, to go home and curl up in bed and forget the way they'd all been looking at her. 'I actually have to grab some things from my locker,' she mumbled to Effie and Attis. 'I'll meet you guys by the car.'

Manda had already shot out the door. Anna followed but she could hear footsteps behind her.

Rowan caught up with her. 'Hey.'

'Sorry, Rowan, I've got to hurry—'

'Anna, I know you're upset about what we said . . .'

'I'm not. I'm fine.'

Rowan ran in front of her. 'Look, you're making me run and you know how I hate that.'

Anna slowed her pace. 'I just want to get home.'

'Just stop.' Rowan put her hands out and Anna relented, leaning against the wall, fingers fidgeting.

'What do you want, Rowan?'

'It's just I brought something today that I thought might help you.' Rowan rummaged in her bag and pulled out what appeared to be a spinning top.

'A . . . toy?'

'No. Not a toy. A magical training tool. Well, also a toy, but the two aren't mutually exclusive.'

'I really appreciate you trying to help but nothing makes any difference.'

'Emotions are at the heart of magic, Anna, they *are* the heart of magic. Magical languages are only really a way of connecting with them, and you have to be connected in order to cast. When witches are young and aren't in tune with their feelings, parents help them along with little games and toys to hone them. Like this.' Rowan held up the spinning top. 'Simple but effective. It spins in response to a single emotion. It will help you tease each one out, learn to work with them again – not against them.'

'There's nothing to work with, Rowan!' Anna cried. 'Do you know why no one could find anything inside me? Because it's the truth. There's nothing inside me any more.'

Rowan's eyebrows fell apart. 'That's not what's going on, Anna. Your emotions are just – hiding.'

'Why would they be hiding?'

'Because . . . maybe . . . they're too big to face. Not because you feel too little but because you feel so much.' Rowan said it gently.

Too gently. Anna felt a surge of something which she choked back.

'You just need to find them again – draw them out. You unleashed a lot of power last year but you'd never learnt how to wield it. It's like you chopped down a tree, but now you have to put down the axe and learn how to carve the wood. Your magic will be stronger for it.' Rowan held out the spinning top to Anna.

Anna took it, not able to disappoint the hopeful look on Rowan's face. 'OK. I'll try to carve.'

'Thank you. Sorry I chased you down the corridor.'

'No problem.'

'I actually have to go back and get the rest of my stuff . . .'

Anna watched Rowan walk tentatively back to the sewing room, leaving Anna alone in the corridor, clasping a small wooden toy in her hand. Could it really help her? Could it bring her back to life? *Should my magic even be brought back to life?*

HIDE AND SEEK

In the coffin, may we discover freedom.
In the shadow, may we divine the night sky.
In the darkness, may we unveil infinity.
In death may we find what it means
To be alive.

Translation from Spiritual Communions,
Books of the Dead: Tome 5662

Anna twirled the spinning top and tried to focus on feeling happy.

It danced on its tip for a few brief seconds before falling onto its side. No matter what emotion she tried to draw forth, it was the same every time. The world of feelings she'd glimpsed inside Effie had been so bright and forceful and chaotic. *Why does Effie get to be so alive?* Maybe that was how the curse worked – it took from one sister and gave to the other. One of them expanded, while the other shrank to nothing. Turned hard and bitter like Aunt. *Like me.*

She heard Aunt's laughter, gloating and gleeful. Anna wanted to roar against it but she couldn't find the roar within herself. Then Aunt's voice too close: *my child . . .*

The spinning top sprang back to life suddenly, whirring mad circles on the floor – around and around. It flew off, hitting the walls, the ceiling – faster – faster – desperate as a silent scream – and then fell back down in front of her. Still, again.

Anna grabbed it and stuffed it in her drawer, breathing hard. Wasn't it meant to be helping her? Not reminding her how broken she was. She hurried from her room, running down the stairs to Effie's room. She knocked on the door but there was no answer.

'Effie?'

She opened it a crack – there was no one inside. It was early. There was no way Effie was up yet, which meant she hadn't come home. Anna fumed. They'd agreed to go to the Library today. She made her way down to the kitchen hoping to find Effie, but there was an unknown man instead, looking slightly lost. This was an ordinary occurrence. He was one of Selene's playthings.

'Oh – hello,' he said, surprised.

'Hi. I'm Selene's niece,' Anna replied, well versed.

'I'm a – er – friend of Selene's.'

'Sure.' Anna nodded. 'The coffee machine's over there. She likes it with a splash of milk, no sugar.'

'Thank you.' He gave Anna an appreciative look.

The kitchen looked remarkably normal, which meant he was a cowan. Whenever a cowan was around, Selene cast a series of well-worn chimeras to hide any magic. Her shelves of ingredients were now full of canisters containing dried lentils, beans and pastas.

Selene appeared in the doorway, a white dressing gown trailing behind her. 'Ah, darling, there you are,' she said to the man. 'I wondered where you'd got to.'

His face turned to mush at the sight of her. 'I didn't want to wake you.'

'I have to be up early today anyway. I've got a breakfast meeting with a friend.'

A breakfast meeting – Selene's go-to excuse for getting rid of unwanted lovers the morning after.

The man's face fell. 'But I just made us some coffee—'

At that moment, their quiet breakfast scene was invaded by the sound of the front door banging open and a voice laughing and singing loudly. Effie and Attis burst into the room – Attis swaying through the door, Effie on his back. Effie spread her arms wide and finished the song she'd been crooning. Her tights were ripped, she was wearing only one shoe and the end of her hair was on fire.

The man jumped up. 'Jesus! Is she on fire?!'

Effie looked down at her hair and tried to blow at it ineffectually. 'Don't worry, s'not really burning, just a little sizzlin' – sizzly hair accessory.'

Attis blew it out. Selene was mouthing words behind them while she reached for something on her shelves of ingredients, disturbing the chimera.

'WHAT?' Effie replied loudly.

'He's a cowan,' Selene seethed, pouring a few drops of something into his coffee.

'I'm a what—?' The man turned around.

'Darling, ignore them.' Selene leant distractingly along the counter towards him. 'Just kids playing a prank. Have some coffee and we can go back up to bed.' Her eyes filled with secret promises and she raised the cup to his lips. He took a sip and immediately turned blank-faced and stood stock-still.

'Thank you all.' Selene sighed dramatically. 'I've had to daze him now. He'll be out for a few minutes. Why *are* you on fire?'

Effie walked past her to the fridge. 'Equinox had some fire tricks last night, or this morning, what time is it? Mother Holle, I'm thirsty. I need a hangover elixir and a bacon sandwich.'

Selene looked them up and down. Half of Attis's T-shirt was burned away and still smouldering too. 'Well, you shouldn't have been out until this time, it's eight in the morning.'

Effie pulled a face. 'Since when did you care when we get home? You're never even here.'

It was true. Selene was never bothered where any of them were or what hour; the concept of time seemed barely to exist for her at all.

'You have . . . school and things. Homework. And—' Selene ran out of ideas, clearly unsure what kind of things a parent should chastise their child for. 'You should know better.' She looked at Attis accusingly. Anna realized Selene's displeasure was nothing to do with newfound rules but the fact he and Effie had clearly been out all night together, drunk and disorderly and up to who knew what.

Anna found herself just as irritated. She turned to Effie abruptly. 'Are we going to the Library today?'

Effie shut the fridge. 'The only place I'm going is to bed. We can go tomorrow.'

'Well, I'm going today, seeing as I'm the only one who seems to care about ending our curse . . .'

Selene huffed. 'I don't know why you two are putting yourselves through this.'

Attis picked up a can opener off the counter. 'I can do it right now. Sacrifice myself. Just say the word.' He inspected the mechanism.

They all scowled at each other, Selene's lover standing in the midst of it all, blissfully unaware.

Effie looked at Selene pointedly while speaking to Anna. 'Actually, I think I *will* go to the Library with you.'

'You haven't slept . . .' said Attis. 'And you're definitely still drunk.'

'Where am I?' Selene's lover started to come around.

'You were just about to head home,' Selene replied, giving him a pat on the hand. 'Let me show you to the door.'

'Are you coming with us, Attis?' said Effie.

'No. I'm going to sleep, like you should.'

'Convenient,' Anna retorted, not looking at him, though she wanted to scream at him – *why are you making jokes about sacrifice? Why do you not want to save yourself?* She turned to Effie. 'Meet you down here in twenty.'

Effie nodded, her hair sparking to flame again.

'Why is she on fire?' the man asked, aghast.

'Oh, for Goddess's sake!' Anna heard Selene cry as she left the kitchen.

Half an hour later, Anna and Effie had boarded a bus to King's Cross. Effie hadn't bothered to change out of last night's clothes but at least they were no longer aflame. She'd thrown on a leather jacket and put some sunglasses on. They sat in silence for a while until Anna's stewing got the better of her.

'So, did you and Attis have fun last night?'

Effie turned her head towards Anna slowly. 'Sounds like an accusation.'

Anna shrugged.

'I have invited you out, you know,' Effie pointed out. 'You choose not to come.'

'Yeah, well . . . there's a lot to do.'

'Just because we're cursed doesn't mean we have to remove every ounce of fun from our lives.'

'Like staying out all night?'

Effie smirked. 'This whole trust thing isn't going so well, is it?' She lifted her sunglasses away. 'Look. We're abiding by the rules. Attis and I aren't together any more, not in that way, and it's shit, OK?' The smirk dropped away at her unexpectedly honest admission, revealing something raw beneath. 'If you must know, we both got with other people last night.'

'Oh.' Anna didn't know what to make of Effie's statement. Irritation followed hot on the heels of relief. Apparently, Attis *was* back to his old ways.

'Next time, you should come. Have some fun of your own.'

Anna nodded, knowing she wouldn't. She forced painful thoughts of Attis hooking up with someone else from her mind and tried to focus on the task ahead of them. The Library. The secrets of the original Everdell sisters. As London whirred by beyond the window, she wondered where they'd lived . . . what life had been like for them back then – a witch in the 1600s. *If* they had been witches.

They disembarked at the hectic intersection of King's Cross. Anna went to cross the road but Effie put up a hand.

'Pit stop.'

Anna watched her disappear into McDonald's and return with a large bag under her arm. Effie stuffed a few chips into her mouth. 'What? You dragged me here early. I need sustenance. Want some?'

Anna took a chip and pulled Effie onwards. 'Come on.'

The British Library was bright and busy, fraught with students, its large foyer echoing with the rush of footsteps against polished tile floors, the chatter of discussion, the whirring of minds, the café's coffee machine working overtime. They cut through it, making directly for the silence of the highest floor.

Effie leant over the bannister of the top floor, looking down at it all. 'Busy, busy cowan bees.' She laughed. 'If only they knew.'

Anna approached the central bookcase that bolted through the Library's middle, where a small, dilapidated lift was waiting, barely distinguishable from the books around it. Anna pressed the button, her nerves taking over. The Library was vast and immeasurable and run by magic itself – there was never any knowing what could happen once you were down there. Beside her, Effie chomped through her burger.

Anna shook her head. 'You're really taking McDonald's into an ancient and unfathomably powerful library buried beneath the foundations of the city?'

'Appears so,' Effie replied, walking into the lift.

It wheezed under their weight and Anna tried not to wonder how old its mechanisms were. Effie pronounced 'Eneke Beneke' into the intercom and the lift began to freefall – too fast to be safe, too deep to be possible. Anna's stomach lurched with the descent and the knowing that there was no going back. They reached the bottom with a remarkably gentle bounce and the doors drew apart with the whisper-sound of a book opening.

They stepped into a different world. A world made entirely of books – mountains of them, quiet as stone, layered deep as sedimentary rock, ancient rivers of parchment and ink, tunnelling winds made of dust and letters unstitched, flying free as tearaway leaves. Anna breathed in the scents of old leather and secrets mossy and fertile as the innards of a cave. She tipped her head back to a ceiling so high she couldn't fathom it – glowing, nebulous light falling over them from unknown sources. Around them, the circular epicentre branched into different corridors – different pathways, like the points on a compass, and they, the dial in the centre, spinning, waiting for the magic to pull at them . . .

Effie was smiling knowingly at the look on Anna's face. Anna dropped it.

'You were marvelling.'

'I wasn't marvelling,' Anna retorted. 'We're here for business.'

'Actually,' said Effie, 'we don't get to decide what we're here for. The Library does, so buckle up.' She swept into the middle of the cavernous room and declared: 'We want to know more about our curse!' The Library absorbed her voice, like ink sinking into paper. 'Give us all you've got! Come on! We can take it!'

Anna wondered if Effie was still drunk.

'Also we'd like to speak with Pesaycha! Do you hear me? We want to talk to you, Pesaycha!' Effie reached into the bag and held something out. 'You hungry? I've got a McMuffin here with your name on it.'

Anna stepped beside her. 'Er – just to add to that, we're specifically after any information you might have on our ancestors Eleanor and Hannah Everdell. Thank you.'

They turned slowly, back to back, examining the many corridors – one was winking with candlelight though there were no candles to be seen, another glowed green, others were umbral, disappearing to darkness.

Effie elbowed her. 'Look.'

One of the corridors seemed to have reacted, though *how*, it was hard to put a finger on – had the light changed? Was it whispering? Had it grown larger or narrower? Anna didn't know, only that it was making itself *known*. It was stirring. Its shadows beckoning.

Anna inhaled. 'Let's go then.'

There were three open books on the floor before the corridor's entrance, like three stepping stones. They hopped across them and into the dark forest of words.

Hours later, Anna had the distinct feeling the Library was laughing at them. In fact, they *had* passed through a corridor of sniggering books several times.

'I think we give up,' Effie groaned. Her good mood had long since given way to a hangover. 'The Library is taking us around in circles. We've been this way already. Look.' She picked up a book and her face stared right through it. 'The corridor with the books with the holes in their middle.'

'Maybe it's this way then.' Anna pointed down another corridor. 'Oh no wait, we've seen those before too, haven't we?' The pages of the books appeared to be made of glass and were glowing faintly with opalescent light. 'Crystal magic.'

Anna was surprised she'd forgotten such beautiful books, but then, they'd seen so many other mind-boggling things in the last few hours it was hard to keep up: books small as fairies, books large as standing stones, books torn apart by unknown claws, books covered in scales, books that weren't even books – there'd been a corridor of tapestries, a corridor of cobwebs spun with letters, and a corridor completely empty except for the distant sound of scratching pens.

'If you think this is funny, it's not! Can't you just show us the way?' Effie yelled out to the Library as they turned another corner. 'I'm tired and getting hungry again.' Her head fell back to Anna. 'Shall we get out of here?'

Here, here, here . . .

Effie's voice echoed down the new corridor.

Anna narrowed her eyes. 'I'm pretty sure we haven't been down here yet . . .'

Yet, yet, yet . . .

The new corridor was an unsettled sort of dark, unknown lights flickering from above.

'Yo!' Effie shouted.

Yo, yo, yo . . . Her voice repeated.

'OK. That's weird.'

Weird, weird, weird . . .

Anna walked along the shelves – the books had no titles but were leather-bound. More like journals than books. She picked one off a shelf and unwrapped its leather strap, opening up to find – empty pages. *Again!* Why did the Library keep giving her blank books?

The darkness quivered with a sense of movement. Anna shot her head to one side but could see nothing.

Effie was looking through some of the books too. She ran her finger over a moon engraving on the front of one. 'I think I know what these are,' she muttered. 'Books of Shadows. I've seen them in shops.'

'What's a Book of Shadows?'

'A witch's journal. A personal spell book, where a witch can write down her spells, but the contents are concealed by shadow magic to keep their secrets safe. I'm not exactly sure how you uncover the words inside . . .' Effie gave the book a shake. 'Apparently, they last forever.'

Anna thought she saw, or felt something again, behind her. She swivelled to find nothing there, nothing but her own echo: her shadow.

'It's Nxy witch magic.' Effie's voice glimmered with awe. 'Witches of the night – their magical language is darkness and they do all kinds of mind-bending things with it.'

This time, Anna saw something move behind Effie. The journal dropped from her hand as she moved closer, realizing it was just Effie's shadow too . . . but . . . but—

Anna pointed, shaking her hand at it, managing to mutter the word, 'Shadow . . .'

Shadow, shadow, shadow . . .

Effie was still but her shadow was moving – jumping away and back again. It raised an arm, pointing back at Anna. Effie twisted around to look at it and the shadow darted from her, running undulant fingers along the shelf. Anna felt movement to her side again and spun around to find her own shadow tilting its head as if it were looking at her. Then it launched forwards, running after Effie's shadow.

Effie and Anna stared at each other until Effie smiled. 'Shadow magic. Shall we go get them back?'

They started to chase after their shadows, which flickered ahead, running wild, running free, scampering along and scaling the shelves – running too fast to catch. And then, reaching a crossroads—

Their shadows turned left.

Effie and Anna, hooting and laughing, sped around the corner after them, but they were gone.

The next corridor was not like the last. The light no longer flickered, the shadows no longer played. Everything was still, the books cloaked in dust. It had a forgotten feeling to it. A dark feeling.

'What is this place?' Effie muttered.

The books looked ordinary enough. Anna brushed a title clear: *Witch Trials, Essex County, 1560–1700*.

Effie roved along the shelf, murmuring other titles. '*Accounts from Germany Wiesensteig Trials, 1562*; *Hangings of Hartford, Connecticut, 1647 to 1663*; *Notes on the Flaying of Hypatia, 415 C.E. Alexandria*. Well, this is disorganized, even by my standards.'

Not all were books; some were booklets, pamphlets— 'I think,' said Anna with a strangled whisper, 'they're witch trial accounts . . .' Had they arrived here by accident or had the Library led them here? 'The dates . . .' Anna muttered. 'The Everdell sisters were alive during the last witch hunts! If I remember, it was gaining momentum in the 1600s, when Eleanor—'

'Died,' Effie finished Anna's thought.

'Maybe the hunts were involved somehow.' Anna's moment of revelation scattered into fear. *Beware smoke on the wind* . . . Aunt's laughter went off in her head.

Effie looked up and down the shelves. 'If they were caught up in a witch trial, then where is it?'

'I don't know,' Anna replied, overwhelmed by the number of books before them – the length of the corridor stretched interminably into darkness.

'Apparently, there've been a lot of witch hunts over the years . . .'

'Time and time again, you might even say,' Anna mumbled.

They walked up and down the shelves, hoping the Library would drop something into their laps, but nothing happened. The corridor had a strange scent that Anna tried to ignore, of smoke and burnt hair . . . it caught in her throat. She grabbed at any books that appeared to deal with English witch trials in the 1600s, searching contents and indexes, flicking through pages, hoping to stumble upon the name Everdell somewhere, but it evaded her. Instead, she found herself lost in a harrowing world she hadn't been prepared for – small towns and villages rife with accusations of witchcraft; desperate, deranged confessions; images of torture devices; lists of people tried and executed, mostly women but men too, all ages: imprisoned, starved, hung, drowned, burned and other more imaginative deaths that made Anna sick to her stomach.

One book, when she opened it, released a bloodcurdling scream that sent her staggering back against the shelf behind her.

Anna had heard Aunt talk of witches being hunted so many times but the reality of it splintered into the darkness of her mind. *Why? How could people have turned on one another like this?* But nothing answered her, except more books – more deaths. These books weren't dripping with blood like the Everdell book, but they should have been. There was blood in them. *Why hate us so much?* Though it was likely that many of the victims were not witches at all, but cowans wrongly accused. It didn't matter either way – they were all people and no one deserved such endings.

Anna had walked a long way down the corridor and found herself at the end of the books, although the sight ahead was more unsettling: empty shelves stretching as far as the eye could see . . . as if waiting to be filled. She took a step back and released a cry as she bumped into Effie.

'I guess we're done here,' said Effie, her voice uncharacteristically sombre as she took in the same unnerving view. 'If there was an Everdell in here the Library would have shown us by now—'

A slither of movement disturbed the darkness ahead. This time, not a shadow, but skin and bone.

Anna hurried after it. 'Pesaycha! Is that you? It's me, Anna Everdell. Please, wait.'

She stumbled into something. She screamed.

A scream met hers.

She looked down and there he was: Pesaycha. Crouching down on the floor. His arms over his head. Shrieking. Afraid of her fear.

'Oh my Goddess.' Anna dropped to him, trying to calm herself down at the same time. 'It's OK, I'm sorry Pesaycha, you just scared me, that's all. It's me, Anna, Anna Everdell, we've met before . . . do you remember?'

The figure unhunched itself and looked up at her. Anna held back her gasp. She'd forgotten how strange he was to look at – part man, part book, his grey parchment skin sheathed with words like he'd been sewn together with letter stitchings; his wide eyes deep pools in the hollow wasteland of his face. The eyes themselves were not hollow though, they dripped with words and feeling from his lettered lids – frightened but curious, darting back and forth between them like they were a book he'd just opened, wanting to understand, to be understood. His head cocked to one side. 'Anna Everdell, daughter of Marie Everdell. We met two hundred and fifty-two days ago, corridor of curses. My friend.'

Anna was too surprised by the accuracy of his response to reply as quickly as she should have. 'Er – yes, friend, friends. Thank you for helping me then, I—'

But his attention flitted to Effie. Anna had rarely seen Effie look shocked, but her eyes had ballooned, her lips were parted, her usual bellicosity temporarily disarmed by the man before her.

'My sister,' Anna explained. 'Effie Fawkes. Marie's other daughter.'

Pesaycha blinked as if something had just come back to him. 'Twins. Yes. Doublets. Couplets. Family ties can never be untethered. The pull of propinquity. Kin ships sailing back together like bobbing boats on an oligotrophic lake. Sinking.'

Effie threw Anna her best *what-the-fuck* face. Anna tensed, worried what Effie might say or do, but when Effie turned back to Pesaycha, she'd formed an encouraging smile. 'How about another friend, Pesaycha? Here. I brought you something.'

She offered the McMuffin and he took it greedily with an arm that was more bone than flesh. They watched as he ate it all with furious speed. 'Friends,' he concluded, spitting crumbs.

'Do you know what friends do?' Effie said. 'They play games and tell each other secrets.'

He released a dusty puff of a laugh. It had the excitement of a child in it. 'Hide and seek! Hide and seek! Never, never peep! Where shall we go? What penetralia shall we perambulate? I know as many secrets as there are books, secrets so secret they'll never be found.'

'How about I tell you a secret and then you tell us one?' Effie offered.

Pesaycha looked wary, skittish, but he nodded.

'When I was eleven, I was so angry at my mum that I went into her wardrobe and cut up all her silk dresses. One by one. Into teeny tiny shreds.'

Pesaycha laughed but then stopped and frowned. 'Why so furibund?'

'Furi–what?'

'Angry.'

Effie shrugged. 'She was meant to come to my school play. I was the lead role and she had tickets and . . . she missed it. It was for the best, I messed up my lines.'

Anna couldn't imagine Effie taking part in any kind of school play, but then again, it did sound like Selene.

'Sad little secret. All alone,' Pesaycha uttered glumly.

'Sure,' Effie dismissed. 'But now it's time for you to tell us a secret. Last year you told my sister here that our mother went to see Nana. Was there any more to the story?'

His face began to crumble and now it was tears that his eyes unloosed, his cheeks turning soggy as paper mulch. They stood there, not knowing how to comfort a man who was both frightening and utterly pitiable. Effie, to Anna's astonishment, moved a few steps forwards and put a hand on his shoulder. Pesaycha flinched but did not run.

'You can tell us.'

He scratched at his skin. 'There was something else . . . a book Marie found . . . back there . . .' Pesaycha's very apparent bones trembled as he nodded towards the shelves from which they'd just come. 'After she . . . died . . . it came back here to the Library—'

Anna knew that the Library magically took back books when it was ready.

'I found it.' Pesaycha's eyes darted. 'I hid it. Hide and seek. Never, never peep!'

'Marie would have wanted us to know,' said Effie. 'We're her daughters.'

'Best not to know. Best to be safe.'

'But we won't be safe. Our mother died because of the curse that's haunted our family for centuries and we're next. We don't want to die, Pesaycha. You don't want us to die, do you?'

Effie shook her head and Pesaycha shook his along with her, slowly but then faster. Nodding now, nodding with fear, laughing, but laughter like broken spokes. 'Only I have the keys to the chambers of this kingdom. Hide and seek! Ready or not! Here I GO!'

He ran off. A scarecrow made of sinew and words, disappearing into the shadows.

'Fuck's sake,' said Effie.

They launched after him, trying to keep up, to catch his wisps of movement in the darkness. It didn't help that the Library seemed to be moving too – corridors branching without warning, shelves shifting, sudden gaps opening up in them and revealing new doorways – as if the Library's gravity revolved around Pesaycha, as if they were connected like limbs on the same vast body.

Anna didn't know how, but it felt as if they were going deeper into the Library – their surroundings growing wilder. She craned her neck as they darted down a corridor with great archways of books formed overhead like the remains of an ancient castle. Another corridor had pages falling from above like a waterfall.

'Woah!' Effie cried out, stopping and catching Anna before they both fell down the chasm in the floor ahead of them – a crevasse edged with broken bindings and ripped pages. 'Is he trying to kill us?'

'It's possible. Jump?'

They nodded and leapt across the gulf in the floor. For a moment Anna thought they'd lost him but then she spotted his wraith-like form ahead.

She yanked Effie. 'This way!'

The corridor began to tilt now – a slow descent that quickly steepened, the books morphing into stairs. They stumbled down them, the steps uneven and treacherous, sheaths of paper flying out from beneath their feet. Anna had never expected there to be lower levels when they were already so deep below ground. At the bottom, she was desperately relieved to see Pesaycha's outline before them. He was standing next to a shelf of books no larger than the height of a small child. He glanced up and down the corridor as if someone might be there – watching – although they hadn't seen a soul for hours. Then he knelt down and began to prise apart two tomes on the lower shelf until there was a gap – a *tunnel* . . .

Pesaycha crawled into it, his thin ankle bones disappearing like rats' tails into its darkness.

'Really?' said Effie, but she didn't hesitate to follow him.

Anna paused. The darkness of the tunnel was so complete – so unknown. How many books lay above it? How much weight? How many words? Would it let them out again? But she could hardly let Effie go alone.

With a sharp breath, she dropped to her knees and crawled into the hole, finding her worst fears crystallizing around her – the tunnel was narrow and she could see no end to it. After several shuffles forwards, Anna could see no end behind her either. Her panic rose frantic, but the books pressed down and paper wedged itself under her fingernails as she dragged herself forwards, the air so thick she could hardly breathe. She could feel things falling onto her head – spiders? paper? letters? – as if the whole thing might collapse at any moment. *Buried by books.* It was one way to go.

Just as she thought she might lose it altogether, she saw a pinprick of light ahead. Her heart leapt towards it and she crawled faster, spilling out beside Effie onto the floor into . . . a cave made of books. A wild lair. The air was muggy, mulchy, damp with words, the walls and ceiling uneven as paragraphs, piles of books rising from the floor like loquacious stalagmites. Ancient-looking oil lamps burned here and there and Anna tried not to think of the dangers of flames in a paper cavern.

'Mind the books,' said Pesaycha.

Anna didn't see how you could mind the books in a room made of them, but she moved carefully around the piles stacked in very specific shapes, feeling bad for scuffing the pages beneath her feet, as if she were getting mud on his carpet. She spotted a thick nest of papers in the corner that looked well-worn and grooved – was it his bed? There was a stack of cans beside it, some Heinz baked beans and Spam that looked decades old. Was this his home? The thought was so sad and lonely that Anna didn't want to believe it.

'What do you do here?' she asked.

'My closest friends,' he replied, looking at the books with such tenderness it squeezed her heart. 'They help me seek. *Veritas vos liberabit*.' The words on his own heart were distracting as he spoke, flickering with the quick calibration of his pulse, spelling out: WORHEEN.

'What do you seek?'

He looked around like a sailor lost at sea. 'I don't know. I don't know. I knew once but I read too much to remember.'

Effie moved closer, impatient. 'Where's the book our mother found? Do you have it?'

Pesaycha looked startled, as if he might run and hide from her questions. 'Who are you?' he asked, suddenly afraid.

'Your friends, remember? Marie's daughters.'

'Yes. Yes. Marie. Where is she?' He sat down and began to pull up his trouser leg. 'She's here somewhere.' Anna watched with confusion as he searched the words on his right calf. He scratched at his skin, some of it coming away. 'Yes. There. Yes.' He appeared to have read something. He looked up and then darted towards the shelves and began to climb them, stopping halfway up to pull out a book. He scuttled down again and sat on the floor, placing it on his lap like a child. 'It's somewhere in here.'

Anna read the title of the book with confusion: *The Mechanics of Structural Geology*. It didn't sound like a book that held the secrets to their family curse. Pesaycha's knuckly fingers worked up and down its inner spine, and then they disappeared inside of it and he began to pull something out – paper edges . . . pages . . . a second book emerging from inside the centre of the other, a little rumpled but whole.

'The best place to hide a story is inside another story,' he said, turning to them, his face distraught. 'Your story. Don't read it. Dark words. Lethiferous words. Words are but pale nightmares, just bone, not the flesh of it, not the blood.' He extended his hands, offering it to them, but when they took it he ran away, hiding behind his largest stack of books.

Unperturbed by his display, Effie opened the book – it was only small, more of a notebook, the cover titled: *Court Reports, Surrey, 1651*.

Anna's heart leapt at the date. 'The year Eleanor died.'

'It's transcripts of interrogations and trials in the area . . .' said Effie, leafing through the pages.

Pesaycha yelped disconcertingly in the distance.

Anna jabbed at a page, barely able to contain herself. There it was, buried in the title, the name – *Eleanor Everdell*. The writing was barely legible – small and elaborate and written in Old English.

Effie raised the book to Pesaycha. 'It's gobbledygook. How are we meant to understand this?'

Pesaycha scurried out from behind the books and over to his make-shift bed. He pulled out a pair of spectacles and ran over to them, handing them over. 'They will translate. Any language. Don't read it.'

He ran away again.

'Genius.' Effie put them on and returned to the book. Anna waited in tense anticipation. Once she'd finished, Effie blew out a breath and handed over the transcript and glasses. Anna positioned them on her nose, and although the words of the book remained unchanged, she found they suddenly made sense in a way they hadn't before. She could read them – she just wasn't sure she wanted to.

Entries Regarding the Trial of Eleanor Everdell, 28 January, 1651

Eleanor hath confessed to the unholy acts of witchcrafte, whereby she hath been convicted by an Assize and consigned to death by burning in the county of Surrey on the 30 January 1651, in accordance with the laws of this realm.

Accused by denizens of her community amongst them her own sister,

Hannah Everdell, for transgressions including consorting with the Devil and his imps, diabolical sorceries and carnal seductions, interfering with the bonds of matrimony, enchantments upon the hearts of men and the dire murder of her own husband, Henry Merkel.

Confession, 20 January: The accused defends her innocence, laying blame upon her sister for her wicked crimes. She screams that she is cursed and does invoke the name Black Annis, attesting that the witch of the woods possesses knowledge of the truth she does speak of.

Confession, 23 January: The accused has confessed to the art of witchcrafte and malefice, recounting nocturnal visitations by shadowed imps which did crawl through her windows and into her bed whereupon they suckled from secret marks upon her body. She admits her heart has been ensnared by evil and that she is cursed and that her children are cursed also.

Confession 25 January: The accused confesses to the most heinous act – that at midnight on the 3rd of January the Devil appeared to her and she did renounce Christ and sign his book and was granted immeasurable power which she then used to overwhelm her husband, severing his throat. She saith she swore upon her Bible which does contain her most infernal secrets and spells, beseeching that it be bequeathed to her infants along with her necklace. She pleads with us to seek audience with Black Annis though Black Annis is no doubt a consort of the Devil himself.

Anna was breathing fast. She tried to slow her pacing thoughts. There was so much to take in. Eleanor Everdell had been tried for witchcraft, accused by her own sister, found guilty, and burned at the stake for her crimes.

'I know. They really didn't have a grip on punctuation in the 1600s, did they?' said Effie.

Anna turned to her, aghast. 'She was burned.'

Effie's face darkened. 'I guess the story of our curse wasn't going to be a light read, was it?'

'But it doesn't make sense.' Anna read it over again. 'Imps and secret marks and renouncing Christ . . .'

'I'm not sure you'd make sense either if you were being tortured for a confession.'

Effie's words plunged cold through her. 'You think she was tortured?'

'I mean, yeah. It's what they did back then, isn't it? Tortured suspects of witchcraft for fun. Forced them to say what they wanted to hear.'

Effie tried to sound nonchalant but Anna could feel her anger. 'It means we probably can't trust anything in this account.'

'There might be some truth in it though, even as she's forced to lie. At the start she clearly states she's cursed. Later she says her children were cursed too. It must be our family curse!' Anna's eyes trailed over the words. So much of the story felt uncomfortably familiar – two sisters, lies and betrayals, the death of the husband, like her own father. 'And at the end she mentions a necklace – asks for it to be given to her children. We know Selene obtained the stone for Attis's spell from a family necklace. Surely that's it. And who is this Black Annis?'

'Black Annis,' Effie replied, as if it were obvious. 'You don't know? She's like a legendary figure in the magical world. Every town has their own version of her, the frightful hag in the woods flying about by moonlight, eating children, spreading nightmares, casting curses, that sort of thing . . .'

Pesaycha squeaked suddenly.

They walked around the pile of books he was hiding behind. He wouldn't look at them. Anna narrowed her eyes. 'Pesaycha . . . do you know something about this Black Annis?'

'There is no Black Annis,' said Effie. 'She's a folk figure.'

'All shadows must be cast by something . . .' Pesaycha's voice was barely there.

'Pesaycha,' Effie said with a trace of threat. 'If there's a real Black Annis, you have to tell us who it is.'

His voice rose into the air, oscillating with distress. 'She has many names, she has lived many lives, the minacious night hag—'

He stuck out a bony arm, pointing with his other hand at a word among the myriad mutterings of his skin. They peered at the letters:

B – L – A – C – K – A – N – N – I – S.

They began to shift and shrink, becoming, slowly:

N – A – N – A.

'Nana!' Effie exploded and Pesaycha fled to the corner of the room. 'Black Annis is Nana? No way.'

Anna's thoughts flickered. 'She claims to be ancient . . . what if she is? What if she's caught up in the legend of Black Annis?'

Effie strode over to Pesaycha. 'Are you lying to us?' she yelled, her previous gentleness forgotten.

He shielded his head with his hands. 'I do not lie, I don't know how.'

'Well, if Black Annis is Nana then she was *there*!' Effie raged. 'She was obviously the one who cast our curse!'

Anna gave her a look, gesturing to Pesaycha, and Effie paced away, still fuming.

Anna knelt down to Pesaycha. 'That's why our mother went to see Nana, isn't it? You told her Black Annis was Nana too?'

Pesaycha's voice rose into a wail. 'I sent Marie to her and now she's dead. Don't go to her again! Leave it be. The truth is better buried. The truth is without mercy. Best forgotten, best forgotten.'

'We can't forget it,' Effie snapped. 'We're still trapped in it!'

'We have to, Pesaycha, you know that,' said Anna.

'That is all I know,' he whimpered. 'Now, let's forget all this. You can stay and look at my books. Books here with forgotten words so beautiful that time kept them to itself. Stories made of doors. Word-horizons. Paracosms beyond imagining.'

Anna sighed. 'We have to go, Pesaycha, I'm sorry—' He looked so desolate that she continued without thinking. 'Come with us! Leave! You don't have to stay down here. Out there, there's daylight and air and many more friends—'

Pesaycha shrank into his bones. 'No, no.' He touched one of the books with tender, wasted fingers. 'I can't go. I can't leave them. There is something here. There is—' He began to look at his skin, reading the words, picking at them. 'There's something I've forgotten . . . go I know not whither, bring back I know not what . . .' He looked up at them, suddenly stricken. 'And now – and now – too late, running out of time, the Dark Times returning—'

The Dark Times . . . Anna put out a hand towards him. 'What did you say? Pesaycha, are you talking about the Hunters? Are they returning?'

This time he didn't cry. He didn't run and hide or shriek or scream. It was worse than that. He simply disappeared. The life left his eyes, closing up inside of him like a book tucked away inside another book. His body crumpled to the floor and he fell on his side, not moving. A lifeless pile of bones.

'Pesaycha?' Anna's heart raced. *What have I done?* 'Pesaycha? Pesaycha!' She touched him gently, trying to rouse him, but his body didn't react. He had turned to a rock among the pebble-stacks of his books; crouched, desolate, broken.

TRICK OR TREAT

Drawn from the ancient tradition of our Helkappe, during Samhain children would wear a mask – half black, half white – and go door to door singing spirit chants and performing in return for food or money.

Traditions and Customs, Books of the Dead: Tome 8229

Anna and Effie resurfaced over an hour later.

'Hands down, *that* was the weirdest magical experience of my life,' said Effie.

The world was too bright around them, moving with busy ignorance of all that lay beneath it. Anna was still down there, in the dark tunnel of books, Pesaycha huddled on the floor, locked inside of himself. It was her fault. *I shouldn't have asked about the Hunters.* She hadn't known. She hadn't realized it would entirely immobilize him. *Why? Why had it done that to him?* The questions leaked their darkness into the outside world, turning the clamour and noise of the crowds into something menacing. People everywhere. Too many people. 'We shouldn't have left him there like that,' she repeated.

'We tried for, like, an hour, nothing worked. He was breathing, just in shock. He'll come around. He's survived down there for Goddess knows how many years. At least we got out . . .'

Anna was glad of that too. She'd feared they might be stuck down there with him, but the tunnel had been open when they'd returned through it, as if some part of him had let them go, even as he himself was trapped. *How long would he stay like that? A few more hours? Days?* Guilt burrowed its way into her stomach, like woodworm through the pages of a book.

Effie shrugged. 'Guess it was a touchy subject.'

'I think touchy might be an understate—' Anna's words cut off, choked by shock. The symbol of the Eye stared back at her. Effie leant back against the bus stop, blocking it out. It was so out of place that Anna wasn't sure if she'd seen it at all.

Effie frowned. 'What?'

Anna moved her aside and lifted her hand to her mouth. There it was. Entirely jarring on a busy street in the light of day. Seven circles – the symbol of the Eye on a poster stuck onto the glass of the bus stop. Beneath it, the words: STOP THE SPREAD.

'The Eye.' Effie grimaced.

'Why's the curse symbol *here*? For everyone to see?' Anna tried to keep her voice low through her surging panic. 'Stop the spread . . . the strapline of the WIPS.'

Effie ripped the poster down without a second thought. 'Reckon they're behind it?'

Anna looked about again. 'Probably!' If there was one . . . there would be more. Had the WIPS put them up? How many were across the city? How many had seen it? 'They're trying to get their message out there. The symbol of the Eye was found on the back of the necks of the Faceless Women, remember? It was all over the news last year. It's recognizable as a symbol of magic. They're turning it against us.'

'Come on, the bus is here.' Effie pulled Anna onto it, Anna's thoughts still sinking into the expanding circles of the curse symbol.

Fortunately, the bus was quiet. They sat down on the empty back row.

'People will just ignore it,' Effie continued. 'Who's got time to look at a poster? Relax.'

'Relax?' Anna repeated. 'I grew up with one message drummed into me: magic must be hidden. Its exposure will be our downfall – will bring the Dark Times back upon us. And I know – I know – Aunt was crazy, but you just saw what I saw – a corridor of the horrors witches have had to endure across the centuries. You saw what mention of the Hunters just did to Pesaycha. What was that? Why was he so afraid? You believe in the power of the Seven, right? Why not their opposite? A darkness that managed to overpower them, a darkness that might be rising now among us.'

Effie closed her mouth, no answer ready now, a flash of fear and intrigue lighting her eyes. Perhaps the Library *had* got to her too.

Anna still hadn't taken a breath. 'I can't believe they're using the symbol of the curse as a warning against magic. It feels . . . it feels . . .'

'A bit close for comfort.'

'Exactly. Not helped by the fact we just learnt our own ancestors were caught up in a witch trial.'

'But even if the Hunters are real,' Effie countered. 'It's a different world now. And that *was* just a poster.'

'Can I see the confession again?'

Effie took it out and they looked through once more – they no longer had Pesaycha's spectacles but, having read it once, it was easier to translate the archaic wording.

'It took place in Surrey. I wonder where . . .' Anna's thoughts overtook themselves. 'I still can't believe—'

'She was burned for being a witch, I know. This is what cowans thought we deserved back then. The devil's whores. Just like us.' Effie's bitter rage was back.

'It also mentions a Bible,' said Anna, still studying the transcript. 'Here, see. Eleanor claims it contains her "most infernal secrets and spells" and that it must be given with the necklace to her children.'

Effie knocked her knuckle against the window. 'We're looking for a written spell that went along with the necklace, right? What if it's in the Bible? If Eleanor was cursed then maybe she created the antidote – the spell for Attis. A woman living in some small town or village back then probably wouldn't have had access to, you know, paper, pens, stationery fucking sets . . . maybe she wrote the spell in the only paper she could get her hands on – her Bible. It was the most common book back then.'

Anna sat up. 'Yes! You might be right. That's why she wanted the Bible passed on with the necklace – the spell and the stone to end the curse together!'

'You forget I'm very clever,' said Effie. 'But then again, how did our mother locate a Bible from 1651? Seems unlikely.'

Anna's momentary excitement deflated.

'We could go and rip the truth out of Nana,' Effie growled.

'We don't know that she cast it—'

'She's a curse witch, Anna! And she was there! It's why she's been involved from the start because *she* bloody started it and she's still basking in it. It was probably nothing to her, just another curse, another family ruined for, oh, the rest of time.'

'Why would she help me then, last year?'

'Did she? She laughed in our faces and gave you a riddle. I don't see how that helped anyone.'

'The riddle helped me get into the third-floor room.' Anna had attempted to explain it before but it was difficult to capture . . . so many things she still didn't understand had aligned that night. Had Nana helped her? Or had she only sent her into the clutches of the curse? 'Anyway, she hasn't replied to my letter.'

'I'll write the next one.'

'I have a feeling it's not going to be very polite.'

'How do the words "*Fuck you*" work?'

Anna made a face at her. 'I'll write another.'

'Can you at least add: "*P.S. Fuck you*"?'

Anna laughed. 'I'll think about it.'

'She isn't going to reply. She doesn't want to help us.'

'Do you actually want to solve the curse or are you just doing this whole thing to piss off Selene?' Anna's earlier frustration returned.

'Bit of both.'

'Effie!'

'I want to solve the curse. Obviously. I'm just not as crazy about it as you.'

Anna's irritation was pricked further at the word *crazy*. 'If we don't find another way, Attis could kill himself again.'

'He won't.'

'How can you be so sure? He did it once already! Behind your back.'

Effie scowled, annoyed now too. 'Exactly,' she said coldly. 'Now I know the situation, I can make sure he doesn't do it again. You really think I'm going to let him die?'

'How do you know you can stop him? I can see it in his eyes, he's—'

'I think I know Attis better than you.'

Anna pulled back at the tone of her voice, full of contempt. 'I never said you didn't . . . I just—'

Effie laughed it off. 'I guess he's *our* touchy subject.'

They were back to uncomfortable silence as the bus arrived in Hackney.

'You enjoyed it though, didn't you?' Effie nudged her. 'The Library, the magic, the wonder and terror—'

Anna shook her head, but her lips twitched at the cajoling smile Effie was giving her. She hadn't felt that alive for a long time, running through the Library's dark corridors with Effie. 'We almost died several times.'

'Exactly. What did I say? Just because we're cursed doesn't mean we can't have fun.'

Anna laughed.

Effie lifted an eyebrow. 'Perhaps the magical world has other avenues we can explore, other ways to end our curse . . .'

Anna tucked the confession transcript into her bag as the bus reached their stop. 'I think we should stick to our mother's path, as planned.'

Effie followed her down the bus. 'But you know how I hate to follow plans . . .'

* * *

> *Witches, witches . . .*
> *What a bunch of bitches.*
> *They'll tittle, they'll tattle,*
> *They'll turn their skin green,*
> *And ride on their broomsticks,*
> *'Cause it's Halloween!*

Tom sang his latest rendition heartily as he passed Anna in the corridor, performing a full range of suggestive gestures involving riding on broomsticks.

Anna glowered at him and made for her locker. She opened the door and shut it immediately. There was an apple inside. No ordinary apple. *Effie!* Anna waited for the corridor to clear and then opened the door again – just a crack – and there it was: a black apple. Black as the darkest of moons, like it had just rolled out of the poisoned pages of a fairy tale. The words AN INVITE TO BITE gleamed along its skin.

'Anna!'

Anna slammed the door shut and spun around.

'Just me,' said Manda, looking stressed.

'You've got one too?'

Manda nodded, her eyes swollen with alarm.

'We should get rid of them.'

'What on earth is Effie up to?'

'What the hell am I up to would be a more accurate question.' Effie appeared, looking giddy with anticipation. 'Did you get your invitations?'

'What are they?' Manda snapped. 'Are you intending to poison us this morning?'

'They're deadly, but not *that* deadly. Where's Rowan?'

'She has a dentist appointment this morning.'

Effie looked mildly disappointed. 'Well, she can have hers later, but we can start the fun now. Come on.'

'It's assembly now,' Anna pointed out.

'So? I skip assembly all the time. Also, if you want to get rid of your apples, this is the quickest way . . .'

Anna hissed a breath and grabbed the apple from her locker, throwing it in her bag and following Effie down the corridor. They moved away from the main thoroughfare, stopping at a set of toilets by the school shop that were rarely used. Effie opened the door and they followed her in. The bathroom was long and narrow, a row of cubicles on one side and sinks and mirrors on the other. Anna walked down the cubicles, checking each of them – all empty. 'We agreed not to do any magic publicly. Only in the coven room.'

'This isn't casting, it's just a little magical gift . . . Anyway, the invites aren't from me.' Effie pulled a black apple out of her bag, holding it up to the light. It wasn't so much black as an absence of colour; a shadow that seemed to absorb the light. 'See? I have one too.'

Her excitement worried Anna. 'What are they?'

'Eughhh.' Effie's arm dropped. 'You know I hate ruining my surprises.' She gave Anna a coy look. 'The apples are a gift from the Hel witches.'

'What?' Anna pushed away from the sink. 'The Hel witches! I thought we agreed not to pursue the Hel witches!'

'No,' Effie responded. 'You didn't want to, but we never agreed not to.'

'*Who* are the Hel witches?' Manda attempted to interrupt them.

'Is this about speaking to our mother? It's madness!' Anna cried.

'Not necessarily our mother; we could talk to Eleanor or Hannah, or both. I don't know how death magic works, but the medium said we should go to them.'

'Death magic?' Manda exclaimed, looking at her apple with renewed fear. 'What do these apples *do*?'

Effie turned to her. 'They reveal what is on the other side of the Fabric. What is always there. Or who . . .'

Anna felt her hairs rise, thinking of the formless shapes they'd seen in the crystal ball. 'Effie, you saw me lose it before with the crystal ball, that could happen again!'

'Hence I'm warning you in advance. You don't have to bite your apple, but I'm going to, and Manda, you should too. Apparently, the effects only last a minute or so and are a taste of what's to come . . . They're given to all guests invited to their biggest event of the year, which includes – us. A party like you've never been invited to before.'

'Well, actually, I've never been invited to a party before so—' Manda stopped halfway through her retort, realizing how it sounded.

'Sure.' Effie shrugged. 'If you want to stay home with your parents and let them control you for the rest of your life . . .'

Manda stiffened, falling straight into Effie's trap. 'What's the party?'

'The Hel witches' All Hallows Dumb Feast.'

'What does that mean?'

Effie held her apple up. 'I don't know. Let's bite and see.'

'Gah!' Manda cried, breaking at the look in Effie's eye. 'Fine!'

They turned to Anna, who shook her head firmly. 'No way in Hell.'

Effie shrugged, then raised her apple up into the air towards Manda's. 'Trick or treat . . .' she cackled.

Manda let out a final – 'Oh Lord' – and then they bit into their apples. They cracked against their lips, the remaining apple disintegrating in their hands, falling away like ash.

Anna gripped the sink, looking between them. The difference in their reactions would have almost been funny if it hadn't been so disturbing. Effie spun around, her eyes getting wider and wider, swallowing the light of the room. Manda screamed, her eyes focusing just behind Anna. She raised a finger, her mouth forming indistinct shapes of horror. Anna looked to where she was pointing but there was nothing there.

When she turned back, Manda had dropped to the floor into a foetal position, on the edge of hyperventilating. 'Oh God, what are they? What are they?'

'Spirits!' Effie announced, trying to instil the word with her usual triumph, but her voice faltered. Her eyes darted about the room.

Manda began to recite the Lord's Prayer.

'Don't be afraid!' Effie rallied, though she'd backed up against the bathroom door. 'You are seeing through the Fabric into the next world!'

'I'M NEVER OPENING MY EYES AGAIN!'

Anna couldn't see what they were seeing but she could almost feel it: prickles on her arms, up her neck, a feeling of the air tearing open around her, something beneath . . .

She looked up into the mirror and Aunt's face was staring back at her.

She stumbled back into Manda, who screamed, 'Can they touch me? Can they get to me?'

'No!' Effie shouted shrilly. Her eyes were consumed entirely now by what she was seeing, as black as the apples had been, her fingers taut against the door.

'PLEASE LET THIS END.' Manda peeked out from behind her hands. 'Wait – are they going?'

'Think so . . .' said Effie, breathing fast.

It took another minute for the spell to wear off completely; for Manda to uncurl herself and Effie to unstick from the door.

Manda stood up and she and Effie stared at each other for a moment in shocked silence. Manda wobbled as if she might faint but Effie caught her, and then they burst into frantic laughter.

'What *was* that?' Manda gulped for air. 'Were they . . . were they really *ghosts*?'

'Only cowans speak of ghosts,' Effie replied. 'They were spirits. Spirits of the Underworld, of Hel.'

'HELL?' Manda looked like she might faint again.

'Not the hell you've been raised on, Manda. This is the true realm of the dead – the Underworld – and the Hel witches are its gatekeepers. They work with spirits, cast magic with them . . . and they don't open their doors often. It's taken a lot of work to secure this invite. I had to go through the Wild Hunt. They got me into a house party with two young Hel witches. Conveniently, I hit it off with one . . .' Effie raised a suggestive eyebrow. 'And Poppins did the rest.'

'Who's Poppins?' Manda asked.

'Basically the leader of the Wild Hunt. He knows how to pull strings and he's pulled this one hard for us. This is a once-in-a-lifetime opportunity, you might not get the chance again . . . until you die.' Effie winked.

Manda grimaced at her words but appeared to be considering them. 'I don't know how I'll sneak out with my parents the way they are . . .'

'I'm sure we can arrange something.' Effie turned to Anna. 'What do you think?'

'I think you've been planning this behind my back!' The fear of the last ten minutes burst out as anger.

'What can I say? I'm an opportunist who plans for everything.'

'Well, *I* say we don't mess with death magic!'

Effie shook her head. 'I don't get it. You're the one who's desperate every second of every day to break the curse. The one who says we need to do more. Then I present you with a perfectly good opportunity and you don't want to go.'

'You don't want to go to solve the curse,' Anna spat. 'You want to go because you've got the scent of new magic under your nose and you're on the hunt for it. You just can't leave any stone unturned.'

'Why should I?' Effie's voice rasped, her eyes still high on the magic. 'I'm a witch! It's our job to search beneath, to chase midnight into its darkest corners. Our souls are restless – they die if we stay still!'

'That doesn't mean we have to chase the dead!'

'Is that you talking or your fear?' Effie's eyes locked onto hers and twisted like a key so Anna had nowhere to run.

Anna tried to look defiant but she knew that Effie could see her fear, because she *was* scared, she'd been trapped in terror since the day Aunt died. Aunt was gone from the mirror, but she was still there. She was always there.

The bell went off.

'We'd better go,' said Manda. 'Assembly is ending.'

They left the toilets, Manda plying Effie with more questions. Anna was glad for the busy corridor – full of living, breathing bodies. *Unusually busy* . . . Students were running to and fro, jumpy whispers passing between them.

Effie stopped their classmate Lydia as she was going past. 'What's going on?'

'Locker searches,' she replied with conspiratorial thrill.

Effie scowled. 'Locker searches? Why?'

'Don't know. They did one a few years ago when they'd smelt cannabis smoke in one of the toilets. Apparently, this one is being directed by the inspector.' She shrugged and walked off to watch the action unfold.

Anna, Effie and Manda turned to one another.

'Rowan's locker!' Manda spluttered. 'It's got the apple in it!'

'Oh, fuck,' said Effie.

Anna's stomach dropped away, a different kind of fear surging through her. The very real and immediate fear of being caught. If they found an impossibly black, magical apple in Rowan's locker, it would expose them, it would confirm all of Darcey's wildest claims, it would turn the attention of the WIPS to them.

Anna could see then, through the crowds, the dark loping form of Inspector Eames working his way up the corridor, assisted by Andrew and Peter. Everyone watching on, whispering and muttering, riled up by the unexpected morning's interlude.

They were opening each locker in turn: systematic, meticulous – scouring the contents within. There was no way they'd miss an apple so black it could eclipse the night. *An apple to raise the dead.*

Anna struggled to breathe. 'We have to do something.'

She spotted Attis coming through the crowd. He made for them, brow furrowed. 'I heard there were locker searches, thought I'd come see what was going on.'

'There might be a Hel apple in Rowan's locker . . .' said Effie.

Attis's expression darkened. 'I told you to hand them out in the coven session!'

'I couldn't resist. What's done is done, we have to deal with it now.'

'It's too late!' Manda cried. 'Isn't that next locker Rowan's?'

Manda was right – they were only one locker away. Anna tried to rein in her own panic, to think straight.

'I'll do a cantrip,' Effie whispered. 'Break something. Set something on fire. Peter?'

Anna wondered if she could set the school bells off again, but she didn't know how she'd done it the first time, and could she really trust her magic enough to do it in front of everyone?

Andrew shut the locker they'd just checked and the inspector moved to stand in front of Rowan's.

'Open it,' he instructed Andrew.

'It's over!' Manda buried her head into Anna's shoulder. 'It's been good knowing you all!'

Effie moved as if to do magic – but Attis stopped her. 'I've got something.' He reached inside his pockets.

Andrew inserted the master key and turned the handle – but the door didn't budge. He twisted again, but still, it would not open. He jostled the key, yanked at the door, his features twitching with irritation. The door strained against its hinges but remained steadfastly closed.

Peter stepped forwards to help. Anna spied the magnet Attis was holding tightly in his hand.

'I think the lock's broken.' Peter inspected the mechanism. 'The door's stuck.'

Eames raised his head to the crowd. 'Whose locker is it?'

Andrew checked a sheet of paper. 'It's Rowan Greenfinch's.'

Eames's eyes registered the name with a tightening of his lips. 'Is she here?'

Heads turned, everyone bubbling with fresh excitement, a fury of whispers, but there was no sign of Rowan.

Andrew joined Peter in trying to pull open the locker. Attis held a look of interest on his face as if he were part of the crowd, but Anna could see he was beginning to strain with effort.

'*This* is your plan?' Effie hissed.

'I was hoping they'd give up,' Attis replied through gritted teeth.

Anna looked around desperately, wondering what she could do. Run out and confess now? Draw the attention onto her? Punished at last. Aunt's face laughing in the mirror forever.

Another boy joined Peter and Andrew and they heaved against the locker. Attis made a grating sound beneath his breath.

'I'm going to do something . . .' Effie threatened.

'No. I'll go in,' said Attis through clenched teeth. 'Make a scene, try to snatch it.'

'No.' Anna grabbed his arm. 'I'll do it. You make a scene. I'll get the apple. They won't notice me.'

'Anna. No.'

Their eyes locked in battle.

The locker door bulged – about to break.

'Trust me,' she urged.

Attis held out for a struggling moment more, then he nodded to her, releasing his magic and stepping out. 'There's a knack to it!' he declared in his most booming voice, drawing the attention of everyone. 'Happened to my locker last year all the time, just needs a little wrangling. I'll show you—' He strode with unquestionable confidence towards the locker, people stepping out of his way automatically. He blazed past Inspector Eames and began to bang his shoulder against the door, shouting at the top of his voice, 'YOU'VE JUST GOT TO HIT IT IN THE RIGHT PLACE! TAKES A FEW GOES!'

'That is not required.' But Eames's voice was drowned out by the growing excitement of the crowd.

'WAIT! HERE WE GO!' Attis took a run up. Peter tried to step in his way but Attis palmed him off and hit the locker. The door sprang open. He tumbled back into Eames, scattering the crowd.

Anna was ready. She'd moved herself close by and, with everyone momentarily distracted, she stuck her hand backwards into the locker and grabbed the apple . . . but there wasn't time to hide it. Eames was already getting back to his feet and Andrew was turning towards her.

There was only one thing left to do. The last thing she wanted to do in the world.

Anna bit into the apple in her hand. As before, it dissolved instantly to ash. She brushed it away as Eames called out.

'Everyone step back!'

Anna tried to draw back with the rest of them but Eames's eyes fell on her – two voids. But it was the voids opening up in the air around her that held her attention, burning away the reality before her with a searing cold. If she'd been able to scream, it would have frozen on her lips. She could see what the others had seen . . . *shadows* . . . but not shadows . . . more like shadows unstitched – torn and contorted and broken. There was the suggestion of humanity – tangled limbs, grasping fingers, gaping mouths – but warped, not human at all.

They lived at the edges of sight, at the edges of what the mind could fathom, on the fringes of nightmares.

Anna couldn't move.

Eames stepped closer towards her, his gaze tightening on her like a pincer.

Was he saying something? She didn't know. The spirits were everywhere, consuming everything, consuming her, her own edges leaking out—

She tried to hold his gaze but the shadows' mouths were twisting with laughter, twisting into the shape of Aunt's face—

Just as she was about to scream, a hand appeared on Eames's shoulder, pulling him around. 'Sorry about that.' She heard Attis's voice in some other world. 'Didn't knock you too hard, did I? But look – locker's open. I told you there's a knack to it.'

Attis presented the open locker and Anna managed to step back into the crowd, escaping the living, but not yet able to escape the dead . . .

* * *

'Hel's Bells,' said Rowan, pacing the sewing room later. 'I still can't believe that I'm there, getting my teeth cleaned, blissfully unaware that the entire school is about to discover a death apple in my locker.'

Manda shook her head. 'If Attis hadn't held the locker tight . . .'

'Hey, Anna's the one who swiped the apple and managed to keep it together in front of everyone. It was impressive.' Attis smiled at her.

Anna struggled to smile back. She'd spent the whole day trying to suppress the memory of what she'd seen – and felt – but the shadows kept prising their fingers through the gaps and drawing her back into their darkness, turning her slowly inside out. 'I didn't have a lot of choice,' she said, her eyes meeting Effie's.

'I didn't know *that* was going to happen.' Effie threw up her hands defensively. 'It wasn't like I was doing magic out in the open. I thought they were safe – there's never been a locker search before.'

'As much as part of me wants to scream at you right now, you have a point,' Rowan responded soberly. 'Why *are* they searching our lockers?'

'Trying to catch us out,' said Manda. 'Looking for anything that might link us to a cult?'

'The school's behaviour management policy stipulates that locker searches are permitted under special and time-sensitive circumstances,' Attis stated. 'But this seems like a stretch.'

Anna gave him a look. 'Since when have you read the school's behaviour policy?'

He smirked. 'Ramsden quoted some of it to me once during one of his tantrums. I thought it was best to read it so I could quote it back at him next time.'

Anna laughed. She could imagine how well *that* would go down.

'Do you think Ramsden instigated the whole thing or Eames himself?' said Rowan.

'I spoke to Peter about it briefly,' Anna replied, not wanting to admit they were back on speaking terms. 'He said their direction had come from the inspector. That they'd been called upon as senior prefects.'

'How very honourable of them,' Attis growled.

'We got away with it, is what matters.' Effie pushed herself from the wall, clearly wanting to move on.

'Maybe we lay off the magical items in lockers from now on?' Rowan suggested.

Effie clicked her fingers. 'Guess I'll cancel that vat of virgin's blood I had planned for next week.'

Anna had expected Rowan to laugh, but she didn't. Instead, she bobbed on her feet nervously. 'It's just there's been more . . . strange incidents in the news.'

Anna swivelled to Rowan. She'd been so wrapped up in the curse she hadn't been checking the news as closely as she had been before. 'What things?'

'I didn't want to say because I wasn't sure if they were anything, but—'

'Rowan, what?' Effie prompted.

'OK, since last year, there's been some magical suspicion surrounding Epping Forest, locals claiming some eco-warrior group had been doing rituals in the forest. Anyway, a couple weeks back, a handful of people were found collapsed across the woods. Witnesses have said they'd seen people out jogging that morning and behaving strangely, as if they . . . couldn't stop jogging. One witness had spotted someone running across the road without looking, others had seen someone running straight across the path and through brambles even though they were tearing at their legs. Another person said they'd seen their friend running and had tried to call after them but it was like they couldn't hear them, couldn't stop. It seems the people ran themselves to the point of collapse.'

Effie went to speak but Rowan stopped her.

'There's more. Last week, there were a few stories about a company in White City. Some financial services company or something boring that I can't remember. Anyway, at their offices, none of the staff went home one night. Cleaners found them later on . . . everyone still working as if it was the daytime, but erratically, strangely . . . someone walking around and around the room as if they were going somewhere but going nowhere; a row of people typing at their keyboards but too fast . . . nonsensically, slamming their hands against the keys; someone photo-copying over and over, paper flying everywhere. The cleaners said it was as if none of them could even see them, as if they were all in another world. Apparently, they had to call the emergency services to restrain them all because they just wouldn't . . . stop.' Rowan took a brief, fraught breath. 'I did some digging and there's been magical suspicion around these particular offices too. Apparently, a few months ago, an employee there accused a younger woman of using witchcraft to further her career. He'd filed a complaint that she'd used her "craft" to influence a promotion and inflict him with migraines to stop him being able to work. He wasn't being taken seriously by management. They'd forced him to take time off work with stress, but then last week this happens and now he's claiming it was her, the woman he'd accused, that she'd made her colleagues lose it too.'

'If I had to work in an office I'd probably lose it too,' Effie reflected.

Rowan made a face at her. 'I know it all sounds absurd, but when you put the incidents together . . . the construction workers knocking down the flats, the joggers running until they collapsed, these people working all night . . . there are threads of connection . . . everyone acting erratically, uncontrollably, and all these sites linked to magical suspicion already. Hopkins commented on the office story too, saying that due to its disturbing nature they're looking at opening a WIPS investigation there. I'm just concerned because their investigations have always been after big events that have been all over the news, but the offices . . . this wasn't a big story. If the WIPS start involving themselves in every wild suspicion of magic across the capital, it could get out of hand.' She picked up her phone. 'Hopkins also shared this on his accounts.' She turned it around, presenting the image.

It was the same as the poster Anna had seen with Effie out in London – the symbol of the Eye and the words: STOP THE SPREAD.

Anna felt the familiar sense of unease spread through her limbs, tighten around her throat. The incidents were all so strange, and Rowan was right, all too similar to discount.

'OK,' said Effie. 'I admit, it is weird, but it's only three events across a city as big as London, and we're looking for a link – other people aren't going to be. I bet most cowans aren't even aware of any of this.'

'There were the ravens in the Tower of London too,' Anna reminded her. 'The birds couldn't stop either.'

Attis exhaled a low, rough breath, still analysing the STOP THE SPREAD image on Rowan's phone.

'We should talk to the Wild Hunt about it all on the weekend, see if they've heard anything,' said Effie, her gaze piercing into Anna. 'A few of them are coming to the All Hallows feast.'

Rowan shut her phone off. 'Orrrr . . . you guys could come to mine instead? A Greenfinch Halloween is really fun. We grow magical pump-kins that carve their own faces, bob for toffee apples, do a ritual in the garden with the plants and trees we planted for relatives who've died—'

'Rowan.' Effie put a hand up. 'We have a chance to go into the depths of the magical world on the most magically potent night of the year – we can't stay home.'

Rowan nibbled at her cheek. 'I've just always been taught death magic is something to stay well away from. I'm a Wort Cunning. We like living things. Mum would freak out if she knew what we were doing—'

'I think we have to go,' Anna interrupted.

Rowan turned to her, surprised.

'You guys don't have to,' she clarified. 'But Effie and I. These Hel witches may be able to help with the curse . . .' Anna hated to admit it, but it was true. 'We at least have to explore it.'

She met Effie's eyes and Effie smiled like a cat that got the cream, like a greedy pumpkin on Halloween. Anna didn't want to go and she was still every shade of angry at Effie for going behind her back. She'd much rather be bobbing for apples at Rowan's – she'd much rather be doing anything else in the world – but she knew, deep down, despite her fears and the screams going off in her head, that if it could open up other doors to the curse then she had to. Besides, she'd been forced to face the spirits already today and survived.

I can do it again – can't I?

DUMB FEAST

Feasting with the dead, 'shaking of the feathers', ecstatic possessions and burial ceremonies are some of the performative rituals an Initiate will enact throughout their training in preparation for journeying into Hel.

Hel Witch Trainings, Books of the Dead: Tome 2714

Anna rang the doorbell of Manda's house. No one answered. From the outside, it was well kept, as twee as the other houses on the street, with mock-Tudor beams and leaded windows. The raked gravelled garden was decorated with plumes of shrubbery like iced gems on a cake. Aunt would have approved of its order but not of its ostentation – *too showy,* Anna could hear her mutter disdainfully, *those hanging baskets would take all day to water!*

Anna tried the doorbell again, wondering if Manda had locked herself away. She couldn't blame her, considering the evening that was awaiting them. But then, the door opened a crack and Manda peeked out. 'You're late.'

'Not a traditional greeting,' Anna replied with a smile.

'Come in.' Manda grabbed Anna's wrist and pulled her inside, shutting the door hastily.

'Are you . . . OK?'

'Yes, sorry, just hectic—' Manda replied, out of breath, glancing guiltily up and down the hallway. She was wearing a dressing gown and a lot of make-up – heavy, very un-Manda-like make-up: black eyeliner ringing her large eyes and dark purple lips. 'Could you take your shoes off? Mum likes it neat.'

'Sure.' Anna left them on the mat. The rest of the hallway was indeed impeccably tidy, if slightly cloying, with patterned wallpaper, fussy lampshades, a HOME SWEET HOME sign on the wall, staged family photographs and candles everywhere – the kind that had names like Sea Breeze, Cinnamon Dreams or Strawberries and Cream.

'Come on.' Manda ushered Anna towards the stairway, but stopped briefly to glance through an open door on the left.

Anna looked in too – Manda's parents were in there, stationed in front of the TV, staring at it with glazed eyes and slack mouths.

Manda yanked Anna onwards up the stairs, past photographs of Manda's picture-perfect family – her mum's dominating smile, her father's too-tight tie, pictures of Miranda trying to sustain a smile while squeezed between her older brother and sister.

'My impeccable older siblings,' Manda muttered bitterly. 'I was already the most disappointing child before the allegations of witchcraft and satanism, but they've really secured my position. Sorry about my room—'

'Ahhhh—' Anna cried as she stepped inside. Dolls – the creepy, antique, ringleted and rosy-cheeked kind of doll – were staring back at her from everywhere – *everywhere* – nestled among the flounce and frill of Manda's pink room. 'It's, er, lovely.'

'It's an embarrassment.' Manda shook her head witheringly. 'Mum decorated the whole thing when I was young and we collected the dolls together. I liked them back then but . . . well, Mum would be too hurt if I ever put them away. I've resigned myself to the fact they'll be here forever. You see why I can never bring a boy back here? That and the fact my parents would chase him out of the house with crucifixes.'

Manda turned to the mirror and took off her dressing gown. Beneath, her outfit was even more un-Manda-like: a mini black skirt, mesh top, snake choker around her neck. Anna must have looked startled because Manda shut her gown tightly again and spun around. 'It's too much, isn't it? Effie's brief was: gothic and slutty, two adjectives I've never tried to pull off before.'

Anna chuckled. 'You're definitely pulling them off.'

Manda looked pleased. 'Good. I had to do a lot of research to get it right. You look spot on too, I like the leather trousers.'

'Effie forced me into them.' Anna looked down at herself. She did not own either the high-waist black leather trousers or crop top she was wearing.

'Mum would keel over if she saw me—' Manda cut herself off, wincing and taking a few deep breaths.

'You know, you don't have to do this—'

'It's too late!' Manda barked. 'It's already done.'

It had been Effie's idea. She'd suggested administering Manda's parents some of Selene's daze concoction so they'd be out of it all night. Selene had advised on the dosage, apparently having no qualms about drugging the parents of her daughter's friend. Anna had offered to come around to pick Manda up beforehand for support and Manda had jumped at it. Anna knew how hard it could be to defy the ones who brought you up.

Manda chewed at her nails. 'Sorry, I didn't mean to snap, it's just I need you to encourage me or I won't go. I know it's safe, we've knocked out plenty of teachers before, but I've never done magic on my own parents. It feels so . . . wrong.'

'Then—'

'No! I need to do this, Anna.' Manda cut her off again, wringing her hands, pacing about her room. 'Effie was right. Am I going to let them control my life forever? I can't take it any more! They're driving me crazy, breathing down my neck every minute of the day as if I might start calling up Lucifer over dinner. I feel like I'm suffocating.' She raised coiled fists in the air. 'Sometimes I just – I just hate them – it's awful—'

'I get it,' said Anna. 'Believe me.'

Manda turned to her. 'I know you do, more than anyone. But your aunt was the worst. My parents, they're not like that – mean or cruel. They're just full-on. They want the best for me – a good job, stability, faith in a respectable religion. They might be right too. I may well be messing up my life and going against everything I've worked so hard for.' She stilled, drooping after her outburst. 'But I can't live this way any more, I've tried so hard for so long . . .'

Anna watched the battle play out across her expressive features. She took Manda's hands. 'Well then, we need to go out. The world needs to see these outfits.'

Manda blurted an excited laugh. 'OK, OK, let's do this before I have a nervous breakdown.'

Anna held her smile, trying to put on a brave face while Manda checked her outfit in the mirror, but Anna was just as scared about the night ahead. She and Effie had discussed it but they didn't have a firm plan – how could they when they had no idea what lay ahead? Anna intended to lie low, draw as little attention to herself as possible, while seeking out the right people to talk to or waiting for a window of opportunity that would allow her to find out more about how death magic worked, if there was a way they could unearth the secrets of their curse through those who'd already died for it.

'I honestly don't know how girls wear such short skirts,' said Manda, pulling hers down. 'It's a logistical nightmare.'

'Come on.' Anna laughed. 'Let's head. I'd rather face Hel than stay here with these dolls . . .'

They giggled their way down the stairs but Manda grew tense again. She didn't look in the living room as they passed. 'I've put their favourite TV show on,' she said, feebly. 'I guess it'll be over by the time they wake up. They'll think they fell asleep watching it. Oh Lord . . . no, no, no! No going back.' She moved in a fluster to the doorway, trying to untangle her coat from the others on the hook. It got caught and she cried out in exasperation, throwing several other coats on the floor. She turned to Anna. 'They'll be fine, won't they?'

'They'll be fine,' Anna replied, helping Manda pick the coats back up. Manda placed them back on the hanger in a specific order. 'They'll be sound asleep. While after tonight, we may never sleep again.'

'There you go.' Manda put on her coat. 'That's the encouragement I need. Let's do this. I'm ready. Bring on the dead! Freedom! Trauma for life!' She raised her voice and then silenced herself as she opened the front door, throwing her hood up and disappearing into it. 'The neighbours,' she explained as they made their way down the street.

'Every natural instinct in my body is telling me to run. Fast. In the opposite direction. Why are my legs not listening to my brain? WHY ARE YOU NOT LISTENING TO ME?' Rowan shouted at her legs, causing a man to skitter to one side as he passed the other way.

They made their way down the stairs of Tottenham Court Road tube station. Effie had insisted they meet in central London because apparently the journey was *part of the experience*. Effie ushered them onwards and they piled onto the train after her, Attis holding the doors apart for Rowan, who appeared to be hoping they might shut without her.

The carriage was full, the air hot and heavy with the breath and steam of too many bodies. All eyes turned towards them, which was not surprising considering what they were wearing. Effie had taken her dress code to the extreme with a dress that skimmed the top of her legs, slashed fishnet stockings and silver spiked boots. She'd formed her hair into two long plaits that fell to her knees, although it had only been shoulder-length the day before.

An older woman tutted in her direction.

Effie winked at her and pulled her dress up to reveal a hint of suspender.

The woman's scowl turned to open-mouthed shock and she looked away, flustered.

'Hey, Grandma, if you can't take the heat, get out of the cauldron,' Effie cackled and turned back to the others, biting her lips with excitement, plaits moving like cats' tails. The train jerked into action, plunging them into the darkness of the tunnel, electricity snapping like hell's fires beyond their window. Effie passed around a bottle.

'I don't eat or drink on the tube. Germs,' said Manda.

'It's vodka-based. It'll kill them all off. Drink up. You're going to need it.'

Manda considered Effie's words and then took the bottle.

'Why are we doing this again?' Rowan asked Effie.

'Because,' Effie replied, 'no one in their right mind turns down an invite from the Hel witches.'

'You've never been in your right mind.'

'True,' Effie laughed, 'but think of the magical potential – all that we can learn. Necromancy. Speaking with the dead. One of the Goddess's first spells of power.'

'I find I have quite enough to say to the living,' said Rowan.

'So what do they actually do?' Manda asked. 'Just talk to the dead?'

'Actually, they're more known for using the dead to cast spells,' said Attis. 'Or lending the power of the spirit world to spells to amplify the results, like spiritual batteries.'

Rowan nodded. 'Yeah, spirit magic's meant to be this powerful force that can take a spell to the next level. There are legends of it in the magical world. That a powerful coven of witches in the New Forest called on the spirits to help cast a spell to stop German invasion during the Second World War. It worked, apparently. Or that the infamous Mother Shipton used the spirit world to deepen and expand her prophecies.'

'Perhaps death magic could be my language,' Effie mused with a dangerous smile.

'Effie Fawkes of the Hel witches, Weaver of Bones, Queen of Death and all that is depraved.' Attis took a swig from the bottle with a grin. 'Sounds about right.'

Effie laughed devilishly at his words and clicked her fingers – the lights of the carriage stuttered out, blanketing everyone in darkness. There were gasps. Anna and Attis fell against each other. The lights flashed back on and they straightened up with awkward smiles, his gaze dipping briefly to her outfit and back to her face with a raised eyebrow that Anna didn't want to interpret. He was wearing all black, hair falling over his face, which was painted like a skeleton, highlighting the angles of his bones, the depth of his eyes. He flipped the bottle to her.

Anna took it, turning away to take a sip, feeling just as uncomfortable as the rest of the carriage looked – the people shifting warily at the disturbance, sensing the danger and magic among them but not understanding it.

'Effie!' Rowan hissed.

'Just testing out my deathly powers.'

'How about we don't test them out while we're travelling in a metal tube forty metres beneath London. Where are we getting out, by the way?'

'Oh, we don't *get out*,' Effie replied. 'We'll be getting off the tube but we won't be going above ground. Not tonight.'

'Hold the wand.' Rowan spun to Effie, almost toppling over again. 'What do you mean, we're not going above ground? I like above ground.'

'You'll see.'

'*What* does that mean?' Rowan looked at the others. 'Are the rest of you not as bleeding terrified as I am?'

'Yes,' said Anna, thinking of the crystal ball exploding with snow, of the shadows that had stripped back the veneer of her world, Aunt's face in all of them . . .

'Me too.' Manda nodded. 'But I think I might be more afraid of being alive than dead, so I've decided to embrace it. Death seems peaceful anyway. Neat. Like you've finally ticked off your to-do list.'

'Only you could put death on a to-do list.' Rowan shook her head. 'Be it on your own heads. The Hel witches are outliers for a reason.'

'Why are you here, then?' Effie asked.

'Well, I wouldn't want to miss out.' Rowan grinned. 'Obviously.'

The train pulled to a stop – the doors flew open and three additional witches stepped on. It was very obvious to Anna they were witches, not just because she recognized two of them, but because they stood out even more than they did, exuding a general air of chaos.

The first was tall, dressed in a tux paired with a long, tight black skirt. He wore a top hat on his head and was holding a black umbrella, which he wielded dangerously as he threw his arms into the air. 'If it isn't Effie Fawkes!' he declared, his red, glittering lips pulling into a wide, jester smile. His face was made of severe, hyperbolic lines that stretched in all directions and distracted from his clever, sharp green eyes that took in each of them in turn.

'Poppins,' Effie laughed. 'Meet my coven.'

He dipped his hat to them, revealing electric-blue hair. 'Charmed to meet you all, friends of Effie's. Attis, darling,' his eyes landed on Attis, 'have you missed me?'

'Always, Poppins.' Attis grinned.

The other two stepped through. Anna had met them last year – Ivor and Ollie from the Wild Hunt, a motley grove that claimed their magical language was hedonism but felt at times more like anarchy. Ollie moved straight to Anna. 'My sweet Dorothy.'

She smiled at the nickname he'd given her the year before, in ode to her hair colour. He took her hand and kissed it, looking up at her through his thick black locks with a whimsical smile and sweet, brown, twinkling-with-mischief eyes.

'Good to see you again, Ollie.'

Anna didn't think he'd dressed up, but his purple silk shirt and gold earring made him look a little like a pirate. 'Ah! You have not forgotten me! And nor I you. You are more ravishing than I remember.' He stepped back to take her in. 'Are those leather? Goddess, help me, I'm not sure I'll survive tonight.'

The train jolted, Ollie leaning towards her as he held the bar above. Anna caught Attis's eyes, which appeared to be noting the proximity between her and Ollie. Meanwhile the large and muscled Ivor was spinning Effie around and she was hooting loudly.

The old lady from earlier looked as if she was about to faint.

'I hope you're all ready for tonight,' said Poppins with a flourish.

'Er – not exactly,' Rowan piped up.

'Well, *be* ready, because it wasn't easy getting us in here and I had to pay a small fortune to bag us seats at the table, so to speak.'

'This cost you money?' Anna asked.

'The Hel witches don't come for free.' Poppins waved a hand. 'No matter. I throw money at anything I think will titillate and amuse me, especially if it's depraved—'

His laughter joined the sound of the screeching train as it came to a sudden halt.

The doors opened like an intake of breath, the darkness beyond seeping in. The other passengers didn't appear to have noticed the train had stopped at all, staring ahead or looking at their phones or reading.

'This is us!' Poppins stepped off cheerily.

'This isn't a station,' said Manda.

'It is.' Effie winked. 'Just not one you'll find on the cowan tube map . . .'

Effie followed Poppins out, dragging Manda behind her. Ollie offered Anna a hand, but she let go when she saw that Rowan had backed herself into the corner. 'You know what?' Rowan gulped. 'I think I'm going to stay on. I actually fancy a trip to Bethnal Green.'

Between Anna and Attis, they managed to prise Rowan off the train just in time. The doors snapped shut behind them, the train whooshing off and leaving them in absolute darkness.

'I regret my life decisions,' Rowan croaked.

A strip light overhead flickered like something struggling to life. Several other lights twitched weakly into being as the station woke itself up and revealed its innards – it looked like a tube station that had been gutted and left to dry out, the cylindrical walls rough, greenish brick, veined with old piping and stained with grime and the slow ooze of ancient damp. The railway line they had just arrived on was rusted and broken – the track twisted and missing in places. *How had the train even run on it?* Where on earth were they?

Anna walked over to a sign on the wall, the faded symbol of a skull and crossbones, and beneath the words:

Raven Row.
The London Necropolis Railway.

There was a tube map printed onto the wall to its side – faded black lines against a white background. It showed the major lines that Anna recognized but not the newer ones, and there, weaving among them, was a line she didn't recognize – vaster, blacker and more twisted than the others, displaying station names she'd never heard of: Tyburn. The Crypts. Bonehill. Ten Bells. Raven Row . . .

Attis came to stand beside her. 'The Necropolis Railway,' he said with fascination. 'I didn't know this was still in use . . .'

'Only by the Hel witches.' Poppins's voice echoed through the silence of the surrounding cavern, the only sounds the dripping walls and faint rumble of tube trains in the distance.

A voice rose up from the darkness.

'You've arrived.'

'HEL'S BLOODY FEATHERS!' Rowan shrieked as a figure stepped into view.

Anna's imagination had already built up its own idea of the Hel witches: old and fearsome, draped in black capes, hoods raised over sallow faces . . . but the girl before her was small, young – around their age or a couple of years older – and dressed in stylish, if severe clothing: wide black trousers, a white polo neck, her hair cut into a choppy bob; glassy, unearthly eyes peeping from beneath a heavy fringe. She smiled a neat smile like a ribbon on a gift.

'We've been waiting for you.' A second voice.

Rowan cried out again as another figure stepped into view. 'Why do they keep doing that?'

It was a boy this time. Again, he looked to be about their age – his features handsomely carved, beautiful in a haunting, hollow way with dark eyes and full, baroque lips. He wore trousers cropped at the ankles, heavy black boots and an oversized red jacket. His hair was dyed a shocking white and a silver crucifix hung on a thick chain around his neck.

'Welcome to Raven Row. I'm Yuki,' said the girl.

'And I'm Azrael,' the boy announced in a voice low and eloquent. 'We're so glad you could join us for All Hallows, the night when the Fabric is at its thinnest, when the dead are at their most alive.'

'How fabulous,' said Poppins. 'Ever thought about getting some heaters down here?'

'Yuki.' Effie nodded. 'Azrael.' She twisted the name around her tongue, smiling. Anna suspected he was the Hel witch Effie had become friendly with at the party.

Attis threw his arms around Yuki and Azrael from behind, pulling them together in a hug. They did not appear to be comfortable with hugging. 'Good to see you guys again.' His voice reverberated. He gestured to Anna, Manda and Rowan. 'This is our crew.' The rest of them made their introductions, Azrael and Yuki nodding at each of them. Ivor forced them into a second hug while Ollie saluted from behind.

Although they were not what Anna had expected, there was still something about the two young Hel witches that jarred and unsettled. Perhaps it was their placid, almost expressionless faces, or the other-worldly look in their eyes, or the stillness that surrounded them – their movements slow and considered, flowing but surreal, like oil swirling in water, as if they belonged to a different quality of reality altogether.

Yuki raised her head. 'A few rules before the evening commences. It will begin with the Dumb Feast – a silent feast for the dead. Make no sound until it is over. Do not unveil the mirrors. Do not ring the bells. Do not stray into the tunnels. Try not to scream. There is little point. Down here, no one can hear you scream. Let us go.'

Yuki turned and began to lead them onwards. Poppins strode ahead. Anna noticed that he walked with a slight limp, using his umbrella for balance. Rowan grabbed Anna and they made off after them, shuffling and afraid.

'Internally, I'm already screaming – very, very loudly,' Rowan whispered.

The pathway was treacherous – potholed and broken and falling away to the battered railway on one side. The light flickered on a few paces ahead of them and off again behind, forcing them to huddle together as they followed. Anna tried to focus on the warm smoke-trail of Attis's voice ahead as he asked Yuki and Azrael questions.

'So this is all part of the London Necropolis Railway?'

'Indeed,' Azrael replied.

'Built in the early 1800s, right?'

'Indeed.'

'For transportation of the dead out of London?'

Azrael took a breath. It seemed he wasn't used to being asked so many questions. 'Indeed.'

'I remember reading about it once. Extensive poverty and the spread of disease had left London's graveyards too congested. Cowans built the Necropolis Railway to transport their dead to cemeteries outside of the city.'

'They partly built it,' said Azrael. 'Hel witches were involved in its creation from the start. We used it to transport our own dead to sacred tombs across London and beyond, and to connect sacred spiritual sites across the capital. When cowans abandoned it in the mid-1900s, we took it over in its entirety, for transport and a private space to carry out our magic and to house our newly dead.'

Rowan gripped Anna's arm tighter. 'Did he just say a place to house their dead?'

They stopped at a door. There was a jangling of keys and then it opened with a brittle wail of rust. They moved from the railway line into a maze of dark and narrow tunnels. Anna could feel the air changing, no longer the dusty haze of the tube system but drier, thinner, colder. Much colder. Effie hung back to chat to them.

'What do you think?' she whispered excitedly.

'As horrifying as expected so far,' Rowan replied.

'You met these guys at a house party?' Anna asked, trying to imagine them in a normal setting.

'Yeah. They're cool. They work together at a death art gallery. It sells art created by spirits.'

'That's a thing?' Anna exclaimed, aghast.

'Apparently. Azrael's hot, right?'

'Technically,' Rowan conceded. 'But he seems kind of morbid.'

Effie raised her eyebrows. 'I heard death talk is the new dirty talk.'

'There's something wrong with you—'

Lights lit up ahead. The tunnel before them widened, marked by an entranceway that was decorated with an arch of white stones carved with—

Anna stopped moving, recoiling from the letters, but not able to look away. They latched onto her like barbs.

Could they even be called letters?

They were hard and strange, composed of stark, angular, irregular lines, finding no pattern. Letters formed of screeches and scratches, spreading shivers over Anna's skin, tiny incisions, curling her toes and twisting her stomach so that she couldn't breathe.

She tore her eyes away just as her legs gave way. Her knees hit the concrete floor.

'Anna.' Ollie helped her up. 'You OK?'

'I—' Anna looked around. The others appeared almost as distressed. Poppins and Ivor had turned away. Rowan had drained of colour. Manda looked as if she might faint. Even Effie seemed rattled. Attis was staring at Anna with concern.

'Best not to look at it for too long,' said Yuki.

'What is it?' Effie asked.

'The Language of the Dead,' Yuki replied, fondly.

'The first verbal language to ever exist . . .' Attis moved to study it, apparently without any aversion.

'Created by the Great Goddess in order to speak with the dead,' said Azrael. 'The language we still use to communicate and cast with them today.'

'What does it say?' Attis touched the letters.

Yuki translated: *'As you are now, we once were; as we are now, you shall be.'*

Rowan swallowed loudly. 'What an upbeat welcome message.'

Azrael looked at her intolerantly, clearly wondering how they had let such people into their sacred chambers, but Yuki smiled. 'Are you ready to meet our members?'

They passed beneath the words, Anna wondering if it was too late to turn back. She looked behind her – the lights going out one by one. She reminded herself why she was here: to solve the curse, to find a way out even if there was no way back . . . but then she noticed what the tunnel ahead of them was full of.

Boxes. *No, not boxes.*

Horror unfurled in her again as she realized they were coffins. They went on and on – coffin after coffin after coffin, measuring out the darkness in sombre increments.

Rowan whimpered. 'Please tell me they're empty.'

'Of course not,' Azrael replied with a touch too much gratification. He waved a theatrical arm. 'These are our members.'

Manda gasped. 'Ex-members . . . don't you mean?'

'We do not distinguish between our living and dead,' said Yuki. 'We are one.'

'That's great and all,' said Poppins. 'But I was expecting a more lively party, a more *alive* party . . .'

Yuki smiled. 'The party lies ahead. Let's keep going.'

Anna felt herself sinking as she looked at the coffins, imagining Aunt in each of them. *Herself.* Aunt's bones around her as she'd felt in her dreams so many times . . . pulling her down . . .

'Are you OK?' Yuki asked.

Anna realized she wasn't moving.

'Remember, they are only people. See.' Yuki pointed to a small table beside one of the coffins. There were a few objects upon it: a bottle of Chanel No. 5; a copy of *National Geographic*; a packet of digestive biscuits.

'Things she liked,' Yuki explained. 'Offerings.'

The display was touchingly human. Anna could see the other coffins had their own tables.

Yuki moved her gently onwards. 'The dead are nothing to fear. They are us. We do not forget our dead like cowans. We live beside them, feast with them, dance with them and love them still, for that is how we keep them alive. They will join us tonight.'

'I have a feeling you don't mean that figuratively . . .' said Attis, but then, a glow appeared ahead. Movements of light and shadow.

'Now, *that* looks more like a party.' Poppins clapped.

Azrael raised his voice. 'The time for silence is now!'

'WHAT?' Rowan called from the back.

'Shhhh,' he hissed.

'Oh, silence. Sorry. OK. Starting now.' Rowan zipped her mouth shut.

The tunnel opened up into a large, cavernous room – a crossroads with four tunnels leading off it, including the one at their backs. There was a vast dining table running down the centre around which people – *living people, thank the Goddess* – were gathered. All were silent.

It was easy to make out who was a Hel witch and who wasn't – some of the people turned to them with the same jittery, wide-eyed expressions Anna imagined she was wearing, looking as if they couldn't remember quite how they'd ended up here and were quickly deciding it might not have been a good idea. Whereas the Hel witches turned to them slowly, floatily, offering mild nods and smiles, their eyes strangely vivid and oddly detached. Their clothes marked them apart too, dressed in the same colours as Yuki and Azrael: white, black and red. They appeared to span a range of ages, from the elderly through to what looked like a child among them. The table was elegantly and tastefully laid with fine silver and cut glass catching the light from the tall black candlesticks down the centre. There was a magnificent spread of food – plates of meat stewing in juices, towering pies, roasted vegetables and bowls of freshly cut figs and grapes, punctuated by carafes of black liquid. *Wine?*

They, alongside the other guests in attendance, were escorted to their seats and unnervingly dispersed. Anna was led to a chair between Manda and a middle-aged man in round, bookish glasses, Rowan throwing Anna eyes of terror as she was placed on the other side of the table between two long-faced Hel witches. Once everyone had settled into place, the silence gathered around them, abrupt and heavy as a curtain falling.

The Hel witches turned with deference to the far end of the table, where the silence pleated tighter, denser. At the head, an old man was sitting in a wheelchair, though old was not the word. Ancient. Fossilized. For a sickening moment Anna thought he might actually *be* dead. His complexion was deathly pallid and his skin puckered around his bones as if he'd been left to soak too long in the vinegars of time. *He* was more like the Hel witches Anna had imagined. No one stirred. Everyone waited. And then, he moved – a nod, barely perceptible, but it appeared to be the signal. The Hel witches turned to their plates and began to serve out the food in a flurry of activity.

The man beside Anna poured her some of the near-black drink, then took her plate and began to heap food onto it. She scanned the table and saw that no one was serving themselves, but instead offering food to those beside them. She and Manda exchanged quizzical looks. Anna turned back to the man, indicating his plate. He nodded eagerly and she picked it up and began to serve food onto it. He took his plate back from her with an equable smile.

Anna stared down at her brimming plate, still feeling nauseated from the room of dead bodies they'd just wandered through. She hadn't realized the feast was going to be so formal, so silent, so impossible to get out of – everyone around her was tucking in, though her coven members looked as unconvinced as her. After the black apples, she wasn't sure she trusted anything the Hel witches served. She spotted Attis taking a few bites while Manda nibbled on some bread. Anna smelt the liquid in the glass. It smelt like wine, but stronger, perhaps. She took a tentative sip. It was pungent and sour but moreish – she took another sip and felt her head swim, her vision darkening, settling into the inky smoke and shadows of the room. She forced herself to pick at the food, not wanting to seem out of place, so that she could assess the people around her. Her eyes were drawn to the end of the table – sitting beside the ancient man was a tall woman with hair dark red and gleaming as a beetle's back, and, on the other side, the child Anna had seen earlier – perhaps only ten or eleven years of age but his small, serious face carrying the same gravitas and air of authority as those around him. Were they the people she needed to speak to?

Beyond the candlelight of the table, the room was dark, unknown objects around its outside covered disconcertingly with sheets. The four tunnels gaped like open mouths and, above them, the ceiling was adorned with bells. *So many.* Like the servant bells of old manor houses but in all shapes and sizes – glinting gold and silver, brass and iron. Motionless. Waiting. *For what?*

Anna looked down, surprised to see she'd eaten more than she'd realized. Manda turned to her with giddy eyes and raised her glass. Anna lifted her own and they drank – Manda gulping half of hers down in one go. As the feast went on, reality seemed to slip and slide, the candlelight bruising the air, the shadows spinning a carousel around them, drunk on their own darknesses. The food was half devoured now, its odours intensifying, something bitter wafting up between the succulent layers. Anna plucked at a handful of grapes, watching Effie feed Azrael a fig; Attis making a beautiful Hel witch in a backless dress beside him laugh silently – only he could manage to entertain people without the power of speech. Anna went to bite another grape but it blurred before her eyes, coming in and out of focus. She dropped it suddenly, managing to hold in her scream. She could have sworn it was mouldy. She rolled the grape on the table but its scarlet skin glistened fresh. She reached for her glass but dropped it too . . . the cup was no longer silver but white. *Bone.* She felt fingers beneath her fingers. The cup came back into focus and she could see it was formed of finger bones, curled around and melded together. This time it dropped from her hand, putrid wine fizzing all over the floor.

Manda turned to her, eyes dislocated now, fork loaded with food. Anna jerked back from it – the food was rotting . . . furred with mould and dripping. Manda smiled at her and took a bite, apparently not noticing. The Hel witches around the table were still eating and drinking quite happily. Anna wondered if she was going mad, but then she caught Rowan staring at her plate with unfettered horror.

Anna could see the table for what it was then, as if the veneer had been stripped away: the food was not luscious but dry and hard or slick and congealed, rife with mould and running with dark, putrid juices; the serving plates and cutlery were made of bones – the bowl in the centre a skull spilling over with soft, rotten fruit. The candles burned and bubbled like boiled fat. The smells were overwhelming. Anna saw that Attis had stopped laughing, a fork halfway to his lips. Effie's eyes were roving over the table. Ollie's face was caught in an expression of revulsion.

As the candlelight flickered, the table flickered too, between its two states: fresh then rotten, rotten then fresh. *Which was real?* Anna couldn't focus on one, her vision was pulsating, the room was pulsating, the shadows swirling now, faster and faster, the tunnels around them opening wider, sucking everything in—

'Dear Lord in heaven!' a high-pitched voice yowled, shattering the silence.

The whole table froze – the Hel witches turning their surreal eyes slowly towards them – to Manda, the owner of the voice in question, who was staring at her fork, apparently having finally realized the food was not as delectable as she'd thought. She dropped it with a clatter, shrinking under their gazes.

The silence had been shattered.

'Er, sorry—' Anna spoke up quietly, trying to distract attention from Manda but not sure what to say. The Hel witches shifted their eyes to her, unflinching, unforgiving.

And then – they erupted into laughter. A sound so at odds with the situation and setting that Anna didn't know whether to laugh along, or run.

The tall woman with the red hair stood up in the midst of the furore. Her dress was slick as wet tarmac, licking every curve of her statuesque body and clinging around the swell of her stomach. She must have been a few months pregnant. 'Honoured guests,' she said, her laughter sinuous as a black pearl necklace, her cheekbones high and carved as candelabras, 'how is our Dumb Feast suiting your delicate appetites?' She didn't wait for them to respond before raising her voice. 'We of the flesh know that all must rot, all must become death.'

'All must become death,' the others repeated.

Anna looked back at the table and was desperately relieved to see the food and tableware had returned to their former states and the dizzying smoke of the candles was clearing, although her head was still full of dark fumes and she wasn't sure her stomach would ever recover.

'Very few survive our Dumb Feast without breaking. We take bets on who will scream first.' The woman's scarlet lips twisted. 'All part of the fun.'

Effie chuckled as if she'd been in on the whole thing. 'It was certainly entertaining. A convincing chimera.'

The woman turned to Effie. 'Who said it was a chimera?'

Effie's smile faltered.

Attis banged his fork on the table. 'What I want to know is – what's for dessert?'

The woman smiled. 'You'll see.'

The Hel witches laughed, and Anna was sure the sound of a screaming crowd would not be as chilling. She didn't know what tricks were still to come, but the mood of the room at least began to ease. Now speaking was allowed, a flurry of chatter took over. Further food was brought out – cheeses, dark crimson jellies, lavish cakes – but Anna had no intention of taking another bite.

Manda turned to her, drunk and distraught. 'I ruined everything, didn't I? Why do I always ruin everything?'

'No, Manda, if you hadn't screamed, I would have. At least you ended it.'

Yuki, who was sitting on the other side of Manda, leant over. 'Yes, don't worry, no guests ever make it through the entire feast. As Mór said – it's all part of the fun.'

'Fun.' Manda seized onto the word. 'Yes. Fun. Fun. That's why I'm here. To have fun! To live my life! Drugged parents be damned!'

Yuki frowned. 'What?'

'Nothing,' Anna replied quickly at the same time as trying to stop Manda from drinking more of the wine. 'Is this even wine?' she asked.

'We call it the Waters of the Dead.' The man on the other side of her swirled the black liquid around inside his glass, blinking behind his glasses. 'For it looks as black as them.'

'What are the Waters of the Dead . . .?'

'Waters from the river of the Underworld. The Bone River. The River of Forgetting. It runs with the memories of all who have died. But, of course, this wine is not truly that.' The man laughed. 'It is our own homemade elderberry wine. A potent blend for opening up one's eyes to the underside of reality.'

The man was as unsettling as the rest of them but Anna engaged him in small talk, discovering his name was Paul and, when he wasn't a Hel witch, he worked at a creative branding agency, lived in Kent, owned chickens and had a passion for collecting vintage bow ties.

'So—' she said, trying to move the topic on from his collecting habits, but not knowing how to pose the question. 'Do you – er – speak to the dead then?'

'Oh no.' Paul shook his head. 'I'm not that advanced yet. I commune with the dead but only the Raven Tongued speak directly to them, for only they know the Language of the Dead.'

'Who are the Raven Tongued?' Anna probed.

Paul motioned to the far end of the table, where Anna's attention had been drawn earlier. 'Our most senior Hel witches. Those who have travelled to the Underworld and returned.'

Anna sucked in a sharp breath at the thought. 'So they speak that – that—' she wanted to say *abomination* but she managed to spit out the word, 'language?'

He nodded. 'It is in the journey to Hel that they learn it.'

Anna took in the figures at the end of the table again. It was them she needed to get to.

'Is he a child?' Anna asked, distracted by the young boy.

'Felix. He's twelve but has a natural aptitude for death magic.'

'He travelled to the Underworld at twelve?!'

'Eleven actually, but age has no meaning to death, although he will need to go home soon. It's past his bedtime.' Paul pointed to an old railway station clock above one of the tunnels. It appeared to have two minute hands – one ticking forwards and one backwards, as if two worlds were about to collide.

At that moment, the red-haired witch, Mór, stood up again. 'It is almost midnight,' she announced. 'The Crossroads Hour. One foot in the day, one in the night; one in the living, one in the dead.' Her voice moved like a black river in moonlight. 'Shall we play?'

'What's the game?' Effie heckled.

'Possession,' Mór purred. 'The question is – which of you wants to volunteer? A chance to truly connect with the dead . . .'

Anna's stomach plunged. She didn't know what this was but it could be her chance . . . Effie's eyes had lit too. They both went to speak – to volunteer – when another voice cut in—

'I'll do it!'

Anna's head snapped to her right. *Manda*. Manda had spoken. The girl who, last year, had threatened to throw herself out of the window when Effie had told her she was a witch, was volunteering to be possessed by a spirit.

'Manda, what are you doing?' Anna whispered.

Manda was drunk and on the edge, her chin was trembling, but her head was raised and her jaw set in her most obstinate expression. 'I need to do this.' She pushed her chair back and stood up. 'I volunteer!'

Mór clicked a long finger at her. 'You then. Come forwards.'

Anna watched in shock as Manda was led away by two Hel witches into one of the tunnels.

LIVE TO DIE

Bran the Blessed, ancient King of Britain and founder of the Hel witch grove, established the original gateway to the Underworld upon Londinium's White Hill, where the Tower of London now stands. After his death in battle, his bones were laid to rest under White Hill and seven ravens were born from them, clawing their way from the ground into the sky. From that day forth, it was declared that seven ravens must watch over the site, protecting London from spiritual attack forevermore.

Hel Witch Histories, Books of the Dead: Tome 2440

Yuki moved to sit beside Anna, offering her a silver tray laid with lines of a yellowy white powder.

'Oh – no thank you,' Anna said. 'I don't do drugs.'

Yuki tittered. 'This isn't a drug. It's spirit powder. A protective substance used when working with spirits.' She drew a finger along one of the lines, raising the powder into the air and then directing it into her mouth.

Anna's nose wrinkled at the aroma of sulphur.

'Don't worry.' Yuki passed the tray along. 'We'll also be encircled by it.' She gestured to the Hel witches pouring the same powder around the outside of their table.

Anna watched with concern. 'Is Manda going to be OK?'

'The Hel witches have been practising necromancy for thousands of years; we know what we're doing.'

'You didn't answer my question.'

Yuki smiled. 'There is nothing to fear. We work only with our own –

the spirits of our dead members. They will join the circle around us –
another barrier of protection.'

Anna gulped. 'So spirits are protecting us from the spirits?'

Before she had a chance to ask any more, the clock struck. The sets
of hands had met each other in the middle: midnight.

Midnights.

Manda was led back out.

Her face was set into the kind of focused expression she wore before
taking an exam. The table had been cleared and she was helped up onto
it, laid out like the final course of the feast. The room returned to silence.
No longer sombre but roused, pronged with anticipation. Anna wanted
to shout over it, *Stop! Stop!* But Manda had chosen this and it was all
just a game, *right? Could they trust the Hel witches? What if Manda couldn't
handle it? What if I can't?*

'Try not to be afraid. Spirits feed off fear,' said Yuki, her words the
very last thing Anna needed to hear.

Anna's terror intensified, every nerve end jangling and her heart
pounding so hard she could barely hear Mór as she spoke.

'Raven Tongues, Initiates and honoured guests – please join hands.'

Anna took Yuki's and Paul's hands. Everyone closed their eyes but
Anna kept one open, on Manda. Mór's voice was velvet and terrible:

> *We call on Goddess Hel!*
> *Raven Mother,*
> *Weaver of Bones,*
> *Crone of the Crossroads,*
> *Keeper of the Keys.*
> *We call on her gifts:*
> *The snows of Hel,*
> *The Shadow Moon and Bone Moon,*
> *The River of Forgetting.*
> *Join with us now, unveil your power,*
> *Upturn the Fabric at this midnight hour.*
> *Raise up our dead, let the feathers fly,*
> *Cross our hearts and live to die.*

'Live to die,' the others repeated.

Magic clawed its way into the circle. So different from the charged

and freeing magic they generated as a coven. It felt sharp and pressured
– a cold current shooting through Anna's hands, a noisy, needled buzzing
in her head. Almost painful. And then . . . it felt like cracking open,
like everything inside her was rushing out into the gaping darkness
behind them and a black cold was seeping in instead. Not the cold of
winter winds or ocean waves but a deeper kind – the hard, trapped cold
beneath frozen lakes; the cold of still forests buried beneath rotten leaves;
the cold that lives inside coffins. A cold Anna's bones already seemed
to know. It slowed everything down, drew everything out – her heartbeat,
her thoughts, her terror – holding them in place, her emotions trapped
like snowflakes in ice, frozen but dreadfully exposed.

Mór spoke again – a single word – and Anna couldn't breathe. It
could only be . . . the Language of the Dead. It sounded as it had looked.
Worse. As if the flesh of the words had been flayed. As if it had risen
from inside her and was tearing her apart too. It felt like the opposite
of music, like music mangled and shredded until it screamed—

The Hel witches at the top end of the table followed Mór, each
speaking a word, a terrible word, calling it out . . . like a name. Anna
needed them to stop. She wanted to howl, to run, but the words held
them all, like nails through their flesh—

'We have summoned our Guardian Spirits,' said Mór.

Anna shuddered with desperate relief that the Language of the Dead
was over, but it only lasted a moment. The room had turned so cold
they could see their breath, and inside their clouds of exhalation danced
small flecks of snow. A bell above rang out. Sudden and startling. Then
all of the bells began to clamour – a blizzard of sound, high and urgent
and deafening.

'They have arrived!' Mór called.

Anna could not move, but she did not need to look behind to feel
them – the empty, amorphous forms they'd seen when they'd eaten the
black apple. The darkness coming alive. The shadows. It wasn't so much
shivers up her spine as the feeling of her spine being unstitched, vertebra
by vertebra, of her marrow being sucked out. Anna knew then that they
were the final course of the feast – only they were no longer the ones
doing the devouring.

Mór spoke a last word in the Language of the Dead. A final call.
The bells rang louder, faster – faster, a frenzy of sound, pure as heaven,
damned as Hel. They stopped.

Sudden, paralysing silence.

Then, without warning, Manda laughed.

All heads turned to her, trembling snow-breaths rising.

Manda sat up. Her head tilted to one side and her smile curved like a hook. She laughed again. It sounded like Manda's laugh but richer, fuller – full of echoes, as if it were coming from somewhere deeper inside her. Her eyes opened. They looked like Manda's eyes, but far away as a story. They began to turn slowly in her skull – the pupils disappearing backwards, behind her eyelids, then rotating up again from the bottom, rolling around and around. Dizzying. Horrifying.

Anna was crying out in her head but the words would not come. *Stop! What are you doing to her?*

Manda moved forwards and then onto her feet. Her motions were not jerky like Anna had seen in the movies, not like a puppet on strings, but as if her fibres were stretching open, her body loosening, her movements unfurling into something flowing. Her head rolled around on her neck and her arms rose upwards as she began to dance – body swaying, hips undulating, limbs rippling, leaving shadowy imprints in their wake; black, liquid echoes. Laughter erupted from her again – free and gurgling, her smile a nightmare.

She dipped to her knees and crawled sinuously along the table, stopping before the beautiful Hel witch with the backless dress who was sitting beside Attis. Manda leant forwards and kissed her on the lips. Then she rolled onto her back and began to laugh again, the sound travelling up through her body like a wave on the edge of breaking. Her laughter deepened to a growl, then a retching cough, shuddering through her. She sat up and reached into her mouth, drawing something from deep within—

A black feather.

She held it up above her head – triumphant – and then fell back onto the table with a smile on her lips.

The Hel witches burst into applause.

The show was over.

'Did that just happen?' Rowan had already asked the question several times.

The coven had gathered together, waiting for Manda to return. Anna's voice still felt too far away to muster, to unfreeze from the magic they'd just experienced. What had it been? Why had it felt so strange and so familiar at the same time? *Because I'm already dead inside* . . . Anna forced the terrible thought from her mind, looking around the room, trying to spot one of the senior Hel witches to speak to . . . once she could speak again.

'Her eyes just rotated in her head. ROTATED!' Rowan cried.

'It was impressive,' said Attis, inspecting one of the bells hanging from the ceiling. 'As is the craftsmanship on these . . .'

Effie shook her head. 'The bitch stole my role.'

'You wanted that abomination to happen to you?! What if she's broken now? What if she's like *them* now?' Rowan made eyes towards the Hel witches. 'Creepy? Eerie? Lobotomizey? Is that an adjective?'

'She looks all right to me.' Attis nodded towards the tunnel.

Manda was walking back into the room surrounded by several Hel witches. She appeared chatty, relaxed, exhilarated. She exchanged a few more words with them and then made her way over. 'Hi guys.'

Rowan took her by the shoulders and started to shake her. 'Manda! Are you still in there?'

Manda frowned. 'What are you doing? Can you please stop shaking me? You know you can get an intracranial haemorrhage that way.'

Rowan narrowed her eyes. 'That does sound like Manda. Are you aware of what just happened?'

'Yes. I was just possessed by a spirit from the Underworld.'

'Why are you not freaking out?'

'Because . . .' Her eyes were still liquid, exultant. 'I've never felt like that in my life, like – like someone else, like for a while I was free of the burden of . . . me.'

'You do remember the bit where you regurgitated a feather?'

Effie laughed and threw an arm around Manda. 'My little Queen of Death. I always knew you had it in you.'

Anna was about to ask her own question when she spotted Mór pass by them. She hurried after her.

Mór turned as if she had already sensed Anna's presence. 'Did you enjoy the show?' Her voice was soft but authoritative, like silk that's strong enough to wrap around your neck and slowly leach the air from you. Anna was momentarily struck dumb. She'd never seen anyone as glamorous as Selene, but Mór could compare, only where Selene was golden, Mór was ruby and black lace, glamour balanced on the edge of a blade. The room moved around them, the table being cleared away, groups in discussion, the dark tunnel of coffins gaping behind Mór, but Mór's eyes held Anna captive.

'Er – yes,' she managed in reply. 'It was – unforgettable.'

Anna heard the others arrive behind her.

'I'm glad,' said Mór. 'We aim to please. Now please, do stay to dance. The night is young and the dead do not sleep . . .'

She began to turn away but Anna spoke up again. 'Er – Mór, I had a question . . .'

Mór swivelled slowly back to face her. 'Of course.'

'I wondered if there was – is any way to call upon a specific spirit?'

Mór smiled with thin patience, as if she'd been asked this question many times before. 'Who?'

'My mother—'

'Our mother.' Effie stepped beside Anna. 'We need to talk to her.'

'When did she pass?'

'About sixteen years ago.'

Mór shook her head firmly, though her eyes held consolation. 'I'm sorry, but no. Spirits don't work that way. They aren't . . . whole people.'

'What do you mean?' Effie asked.

'As souls move through the Underworld, spirits are what they leave behind – emotions too broken to be put back together. Fractured, unprocessed, unstitched, caught in the Fabric; stuck in a loop of their own undoing, the moments in their life that held great feeling . . . great trauma. Your mother's soul has moved on, even if parts of her remain behind.'

Parts. What parts of her mother were left? Anna thought of the room on the third floor. Was her mother there? Tangled in the Fabric, trapped in her moment of dying? Over and over? *Is Aunt there too?* Trapped in her moment of killing – endless stitches of terror and loss and betrayal weaving themselves back and forth through the Fabric of life and death, never to be unknotted?

'Can we not contact one of her parts?' Effie asked.

Mór breathed out. 'You do not understand. It has been too long . . . those parts are not your mother, not her soul, not her story. They would not know what you seek. They are but the shadow of an emotion left behind.'

'But you speak with spirits,' Anna said, grappling. 'You just called on spirits . . .'

'We may be able to speak with a soul who has just passed, who has not yet been fractured by the Underworld, but we rarely work with unknown spirits. It is too dangerous. For the most part, we commune with only our own members.' Mór raised her arm to the tunnel of coffins behind her. 'They are who we called upon tonight. The spirits of our dead remain whole in Hel for longer than most, for it is everything we spend our lives training for, what all of our Initiatory stages lead up to – for our souls to remain intact for as long as possible in the Underworld, so that we may be useful to those we've left behind. But eventually, even we fragment.'

'You live to die,' said Rowan from behind Anna, her voice strangled.

'We live to die,' Mór confirmed.

'We live to die,' Yuki and Azrael echoed from behind too.

'So there's nothing you can do to help us?' Anna tried not to sound as desperate as she felt.

'Secrets die with the dead. I'm sorry.'

'Technically, there are the Waters of the Dead.' Azrael spoke up again, trying to sound knowledgeable but earning him a look of censure from Mór.

'The Waters of the Dead.' Anna pounced on the words, remembering what the Hel witch had said earlier. 'Where the memories of the dead go? Are these waters . . . real?'

Mór raised a razor eyebrow. 'Yes. The Waters of the Dead carry the memories and secrets of those who have died. You need only take a sip and you can draw any memory you seek to you.'

'Perfect.' Effie clapped her hands together. 'Can we do that? There are memories we could really do with.'

Mór laughed without mercy. 'Hel witches are known for their patience, but you two do not give up easily, do you? There is no way on earth you can drink the waters, for they exist only in the Underworld.'

'You don't have any? Can't one of you Initiated go to the Underworld for us and collect some?'

'You still understand nothing. Hel is sacred. We don't use it for personal missions but to *learn*. Come.'

Mór strode through them, walking through the room and leading them into the tunnel opposite. They hurried after her.

This tunnel held no coffins but was filled with cabinets and display cases. They loomed out of the darkness at Anna, unveiling curious paraphernalia: skulls carved with strange markings, bone sculptures, bone instruments, a bell ringing silently, a display case swirling with a black, viscous liquid, quills made from black feathers, an egg timer filled with snow. Anna stopped in front of one cabinet, her heart lurching. A face looked back at her. It took her a terrified moment to realize it wasn't a face but a mask – long and smooth, one half of it black, one half of it white. The eyes were gaping holes to nowhere, slightly downturned, giving the mask a melancholic expression; a look of loss.

'A Helkappe.' Azrael stepped beside her, making her jump. 'Used in our more advanced rituals.'

'What is this place?' Rowan's voice travelled down the hollow tunnel. No echo returned.

Mór spun around, arms extended. 'Our Museum of the Dead. The heart of what we work for, what we seek.' As she moved further down, it opened out into rows and rows of shelves stacked with what appeared to be books. 'Our Books of the Dead. They are connected – containing all the knowledge the spiritual world has taught Hel witches about the afterlife since the Language of the Dead first came into being.'

The books looked as if they'd been buried and exhumed. They were white and dust-webbed and appeared melded into one another, as if time had grown over them like plaque.

Attis ran a hand down the paper of their pages. 'This isn't parchment. Is this—'

'Bone paper,' Mór interjected. 'Many of these books contain the Language of the Dead and bone is the only substance strong and pure enough to hold it. For bone remembers.'

'Bone remembers,' Yuki and Azrael echoed.

Effie huffed. 'What's the point in all this knowledge if there's no way of helping people who need it?'

'Because the world and its Underworld do not revolve around you,' Mór retorted.

'It's important,' Effie insisted stubbornly.

Mór looked between Effie and Anna with a candle-flicker of curiosity, but she extinguished it. 'Life is a brief wave, but death – death is the ocean. We seek to know what lives beneath the waters, not above.' She swivelled around and the shadows seemed to part for her as she walked back to the crossroads, her outline fading away.

'Goddess damn.' Effie stared after her. 'She knows how to make an exit.'

Yuki sighed. 'You should have been more respectful.'

'We're sorry,' Anna apologized. 'We're just desperate.'

'Can't you help us get the waters?' Effie turned her smile on Azrael.

'Even if it wasn't against our codes, we couldn't,' Yuki intervened. 'Azrael and I aren't anywhere near enough advanced to travel to the Underworld. We're Initiates with many stages and decades of training ahead of us before that.'

'Decades . . .' Rowan sounded almost desolate, looking around the dry and dusty room. 'Why would you want to spend your whole life focused on death?'

Yuki turned to her. 'It's not really a choice. Like any language, when it calls, you must answer. Although, in my humble opinion, death magic is by far the most fascinating.' Her face broke into a smile. 'We get to raise spirits, speak to the dead. We're taught how to keep our own souls conscious after death. One Hel witch managed to keep theirs intact in Hel for twenty years. That's the record. Can you imagine being alive for twenty years after you die? Looking back from the other side, casting spells as a spirit, seeing into the eye of eternity itself . . .'

Rowan appeared temporarily silenced. They all were. Anna's eyes travelled down the rows of books, which went on as far as the darkness would allow, before it swallowed them up.

Yuki put her hand to her ear. 'I can hear the band warming up. We had best go back.'

They returned to the main room, where the dining table had been cleared and a band had set up. Anna felt frustration at Mór's denials, but couldn't help feeling relieved too. The Hel witches could not help them. They could leave death magic safely behind.

'Where do the other tunnels lead to?' Attis asked.

Yuki gave him a shy smile. 'As you've seen, the one we just came from is the Museum of the Dead and the one ahead is where we keep our dead. That one' – she pointed to their left, where Manda had been taken – 'is our living and administrative quarters. And the other . . .' She paused, indicating slowly to the final tunnel on their right. 'That is the entrance to the Underworld.'

Anna turned her head to it, wondering how there could be an entrance to somewhere you went after death. What did it lead to? Its darkness seemed deeper than that of the others. For a moment, it felt as if it were moving towards her, as if gravity was no longer up and down but in its direction, and she was falling towards it.

'I was hoping it was just the toilets,' said Rowan, her voice tight.

Anna heard Attis ask something else, but they were jostled apart as everyone turned to watch several Hel witches move to the sides of the room. With a sombre flourish, they pulled away the sheets from the objects that had been covered over. They were mirrors. Their reflections exposed a sight Anna had seen before: spirits. The unformed shadows, the unfinished darknesses were everywhere around them, mingling among them. The shadows in the mirrors – in the room with them – began to move and sway and swirl. Dancing, Anna thought, but her horror did not muster itself as much as she'd expected. Perhaps it was not the strangest thing she'd seen that evening, or perhaps she was simply beginning to get used to the dead.

The music started with a bang.

The Hel witches, it turned out, knew how to party. They threw off their subdued demeanour and channelled their strange intensity into the dance floor. The music was rampant, the dancing wild, ecstatic, delirious – and inescapable. They were held captive by the crowd, twisted and turned and separated until Anna didn't know which way was up or down; the mirrors blurred the living and dead into a frenzy of movement until all was shiver and shadow. Even Rowan seemed to have forgotten her terror as the frantic rhythms jolted through them.

Ollie appeared through the crowd. He bowed low and stuck a hand out to Anna. 'I'm not sure they're ever going to let us leave this place, but in the meantime, would you care to join me in this madness?' He flashed her his most charmingly wicked smile.

'I could be persuaded.' Anna took his hand, laughing as he pulled her close and spun her away. Ollie was fun to dance with, matching the energy of the crowd, sending her flying in all directions but routinely pulling her close to whisper sweet flatteries in her ear. She flirted back, enjoying his easy attention.

She was dizzy and still giggling when another hand took hers, pulling her the other way. She came face to face with a spectre of death – a skeleton – Attis's make-up shifting through several devilish patterns as the lights flashed around them. His grey eyes looked hazy with drink. His hand was the warmest thing Anna had felt all evening. 'Sorry to drag you away,' he said, his gaze flicking behind her to Ollie, 'but we need to go.'

'What time is it?' Anna put a hand to her head, trying to keep the room still.

'No idea. The clock appears to have gone mad. Both fascinating and troubling.' Attis pointed up at the old railway clock – its hands were spinning around and around nonsensically.

'Manda's parents—'

'Exactly. We need to get her back.'

'You appear to have stolen my dance partner, Lockerby.' Ollie stepped between them, wearing a smile.

Attis put his hands up. 'I wouldn't dare, Moridi. Unfortunately, it's time for us to go.'

Anna looked around. 'But where is everyone?'

They managed to gather Rowan, Ivor and Poppins together at the edge of the dance floor. They discovered Effie and Azrael making out against one of the coffins.

'There's something wrong with her,' Rowan mumbled.

Anna was growing increasingly concerned at the lack of Manda.

Attis jogged back over. 'Yuki thinks there may have been a sighting of her going into the Museum of the Dead. I'll go and check.'

Anna nodded. 'I'll circle the room one more time in case.'

She walked the perimeter, searching for any sign of Manda, trying not to get pulled back into the fray. A group of Hel witches burst towards her from the crowd and Anna moved back against the wall. Only the wall wasn't there.

She turned to find herself staring into the abyss of the final tunnel. *The entrance to the Underworld.* Anna hadn't understood Yuki's words then and she still didn't now. Where did it go? Something caught her eye.

A snowflake.

A tiny snowflake rocking gently through the air.

The more Anna stared, the more of them she could see – snow crystals coming into focus through the darkness. Like the snow of her dreams, they did not move like normal snowfall, more like a lullaby . . . a broken lullaby . . . not peaceful but uneasy – the slowness of their motion, the softness, the way the flakes never settled, the way she could barely feel how cold she was . . .

It drew her in.

A piercing sound ripped through her. A raven. Anna's head snapped up to see ravens flying over her – out of the darkness of the tunnel and into the room, shrieking, tearing up the sound of the music, disturbing the bells and setting them jangling again.

The music stopped abruptly.

The ravens circled around and around – faster and faster – and then flew straight back at Anna – a racket and tangle of sharp wings. She dropped down, putting her arms over her head, as they careered over her, leaving a trail of feathers in their wake.

Slowly, Anna unfurled herself, and now everyone was looking at her. *So much for not drawing attention to myself . . .*

Mór's figure sliced through the crowd, her voice just as cutting. 'What were you doing?'

Anna looked behind her and back to Mór. 'I – nothing – I just – I saw snow and I must have stepped towards it—'

Mór's flint eyes contracted. 'You saw snow?'

Anna nodded. *Had it been real? Or her mind playing its tricks again?* She tried to gather herself together, though her whole body was shaking violently. She pulled a feather from her hair. 'The ravens . . .' she muttered. 'Why did they come out of there?'

'Because they are the messengers of the dead; they travel between our world and the Underworld.'

Anna knew she should let it go, should leave as quickly as possible, but, instead, she found a new question rising up in her. 'Do you know anything about the ravens at the Tower of London?'

'Of course,' Mór replied plainly. 'They were *our* ravens.'

'What do you mean, *your* ravens?'

Mór's lips tightened. She clearly wanted the interchange to be over, but she raised her head, indignant. 'Before we were forced out, driven underground centuries ago, the Tower of London was our original headquarters. We carried out our magic there before the Tower was even built, for the land there has always been a sacred site – a site of potent spiritual activity. We may have left, but we still keep watch over it to this day. Several key members of the Tower Guard are Hel witches, the nightly Ceremony of the Keys is an ancient ritual threaded with our magic, and the ravens belonged to us too. No ordinary ravens but messengers of the dead. They have kept watch over the Tower for hundreds of years. Until now.' Her face remained impassive and yet anger glinted at its edges.

'Do you know what happened? Why they died?'

'We do not,' Mór said abruptly. 'But as I said, those birds were formed from powerful magic, which means that whatever killed them was more powerful still.'

Effie moved towards them. 'Can you not find out?'

'We do not intend to get involved. There is too much attention focused on the Tower already right now.'

'The WIPS . . .' said Anna, aware that everyone was listening, murmurs spreading.

'They are a nuisance. They will not let the ravens be replaced. They are questioning members of our Guard. They have suspended our Ceremony of the Keys. All of our protections have been removed.'

'Then surely you have to do something?' Anna cried, frustrated by the expressionless faces all around her. 'The Tower is no longer protected.'

Mór laughed lightly. 'You miss my meaning. Those things weren't protecting the Tower. They didn't stop things from getting in – but from getting out. The Tower and its land are host to dark energies, ancient energies; spirits with names that even the Language of Dead fears to speak. And now – all is exposed.'

Anna felt the darkness of the tunnel behind her open up. *Exposed. Exposed. Exposed.* 'If the ravens leave the Tower, London will fall . . .' Anna uttered the superstition she had heard.

'Perhaps,' said Mór.

Anna struggled against her detached acceptance. 'What if everything going on is part of something bigger? What if London *is* being taken over? Some believe . . . the Hunters are returning . . .'

The room turned silent once more.

Felix, the child, spoke softly. 'When the Hunters return, the living shall die and the dead shall rise.'

Anna looked at him in confusion but Mór brought her attention back. 'Hel witches do not interfere with concerns of the living. People live and people die. Cities fall and are rebuilt. Shadows come and shadows go. But all is nothing in the face of death. We live to die.'

'We live to die,' the others repeated. A chamber of echoes.

Anna looked around them, searching for some flicker of fight. The old man in the wheelchair looked as if he may have fallen asleep.

Poppins stepped forwards. 'Perhaps we have outstayed our welcome. I think we'll just – go.' He laughed loudly, putting firm arms around

Effie and Anna, moving them along. Anna spotted Attis with Manda and Rowan.

'I think that's a good idea,' said Mór, turning from them with frosty abruptness.

The Hel witches began to talk and move once more but the shadows remained in the mirror. Still. Watching. Anna wondered if the spirits had always been the audience and not the other way around.

'Come.' Yuki ushered them quickly from the room into the tunnel of coffins.

Halfway down it, Anna heard the music start up. She turned back to see the dancing kicking off again, their presence already forgotten.

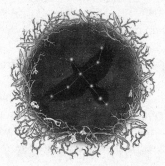

CONSTELLATIONS

Our Guardian Spirits are first and foremost information gatherers; storytellers – illuminating the other side of the Fabric so that with each passing year we uncover another layer of its limitless complexity.

Working with Guardians, Books of the Dead: Tome 7487

'Oh sweet Goddess, we're above ground!' Rowan exclaimed giddily as they burst out of a side door onto Folgate Street. 'Look! There are lights! There are people! The wind, I love the wind! I love you, sir!' she announced to a homeless man in a doorway.

'Love you too.' He blew a kiss.

'Can we never, ever, ever . . . ever go back there? No offence, Azrael.'

Azrael, who Effie had dragged along with them, managed a shrug in Rowan's direction, as if her opinion mattered little to him.

'Where did you go?' Anna asked Manda.

'We found her back in the Museum of the Dead,' Attis replied. 'Buried under a pile of books.'

Effie shook her head with disappointment. 'Only you would go to a library during a party.'

Manda's eyes shifted. 'I just popped in . . . there were so many books I couldn't resist . . . Death magic is so interesting . . .'

'You're not actually allowed to disturb the books—' Azrael began to say but Poppins cut in.

'I'm very glad you all found each other. My heart is warmed. But *what* just happened? I've never been to a party with so much drama. I lie. I've never been to a party where I haven't been the cause of the drama. I'm not sure I liked it.'

Effie shrugged. 'That's just how we roll.'

'But seriously.' Poppins's eyes flashed to Anna. 'What was all that about the Hunters? You don't really believe—'

'Look.' Anna interrupted him, pointing. There was a row of the Eye posters stuck along the side of the building they were passing.

STOP THE SPREAD

STOP THE SPREAD

STOP THE SPREAD

Poppins tapped the tip of his umbrella against them. 'What are these?'

'Anti-magic posters around London,' Anna said. 'You haven't noticed them?'

'Darling, we're rarely sober when out on the streets of London.'

'Well, they're out there. The work of the WIPS.'

'Ah, yes, the WIPS. I admit, it's a strong campaign message.' Poppins stopped outside Liverpool Street station. 'But are these really going to contain the magical world?'

'No,' Anna agreed. 'If it was *just* the posters. But the WIPS are opening investigations into suspicions of witchcraft. No one knows who they are or how much power they have or what this is all leading to—'

Poppins smiled – a jagged, menacing thing. 'So, what? You think witches are going to be hunted again? Hounded in the town square? Posters and pitchforks?'

Rowan joined Anna. 'We think that we ought to be investigating the WIPS just like they're investigating us.'

'Tit for tat.' Poppins pouted. 'Now *that* I can understand.'

'We can ask questions.' Ollie nodded to Anna. 'We know enough people and go enough places.'

'Every day's a party!' Ivor pumped a fist into the air. He looked very drunk.

'Fine!' Poppins opened his umbrella, surprising a woman walking by. 'I'll do some digging. See what these WIPS are all about. If there's real drama here, I'm not going to miss out on the fun. Now, come on, my Wild Hunters, we have somewhere else to be. Probably. Where are we going? Attis, you sure I can't steal you too?'

'You've already stolen my heart, Poppins.'

'Oh, how you tease me,' Poppins replied, throwing his arms around Attis, almost toppling the both of them over.

Ollie stepped closer to Anna. 'Till next time, sweet Dorothy. Unless you would like me to accompany you home . . .?' He raised his eyebrows. 'I know how dangerous the streets can be on Halloween.'

Anna laughed. 'I think I'll survive. I should probably get back with the others . . .'

Ollie pretended to be struck in the heart, smiling goofily. 'You wound me. It's OK. I need my beauty sleep too. Perhaps next time . . .' He kissed her hand again, fingers trailing beneath hers.

'Oliver Moridi, cease your seductions! I need you to carry me home.' Poppins put his arms around Ivor and Ollie and they swayed in a chaotic line towards the steps of Liverpool Street station, an umbrella bobbing in the air behind them.

The rest of them parted ways too – Manda and Rowan heading south together and Anna, Attis, Effie and Azrael north, to Hackney. *Home.*

Back at the house, Effie insisted they go to the roof, explaining to Azrael how it was their late-night tradition. He reluctantly agreed. Anna joined, not yet ready to go back to her room alone. Not after all she'd seen that night.

On the roof, they lazed on the tattered sun loungers. The stars above were distant, struggling through clouds, and the sound of traffic rose up from the streets below, but the air was cool, blowing away the feeling of claustrophobia that had pervaded the evening. Attis coaxed the fire into being and Anna felt her body begin to thaw out, the shivers finally dying away. The evening had given them little – no way to speak to their mother, no way to get hold of the Waters of the Dead and a cold shrug from the Hel witches when it came to the events of the magical world.

Anna glowered briefly at Azrael, though he wasn't personally responsible and his attention was directed elsewhere. Effie was sitting on his lap, the suspenders beneath her skirt exposed. She twirled the smoke of the fire around her fingers. 'Want to show us some more death magic? Call up another spirit?'

Azrael stiffened. 'You know that's not allowed.'

Effie made eyes at him. 'Well, it wouldn't be fun if it was allowed, would it?'

Azrael's stern expression relented but he did not budge. 'I can't.

I'm sorry. Only senior Hel witches are able to commune with spirits alone.'

'What do they do with them?' Effie asked, her fingers twirling his hair now.

Anna looked over at Attis but his face was unreadable across the fire. She guessed he was used to seeing Effie with other men and vice versa. It had always been their way. Part of their games.

'They speak to them, learn from them, cast spells with them, some have even had relationships with them.'

Effie opened her mouth wide. 'What? Like sexual relationships?'

Azrael nodded, his smile deepening through the cold structures of his face. 'An orgasm from a spirit is said to be the most intense experience you can have while alive. If you survive it . . .'

Apparently his exposition had seduced Effie. Anna didn't know what was more horrifying, Azrael's intimate knowledge of the dead or the sounds of them kissing. She wasn't sure where to look. She took a sip of her drink and was wondering whether she could creep off to bed when Effie jumped up.

'We're going to head.'

Azrael stood up. 'Goodnight,' he said, looking at Effie in a way that suggested he had no intention of sleeping. They made their way from the roof, Effie's laughter trailing behind them. Attis watched them go. He'd washed the skeleton make-up off but its shadows still clung about the deep gradients of his face.

Anna glanced at him and away again, trying to determine what he was thinking. Did he care? Was he jealous? Did he like it? Loathe it? She wanted to look at him again but she was suddenly aware that they had been left alone on the roof. They'd barely been alone together since the year before, especially not in the wake of two people furiously making out.

Attis broke the swelling silence. 'Do you think . . .' He turned to look at her meaningfully. 'They're about to have a threesome with a ghost?'

Anna snorted. 'I think there's a distinct chance.'

'Azrael probably needs the help,' he muttered. 'Dessert?'

'What?'

Attis reached inside his pocket and pulled out a bar of chocolate. 'I don't know about you but I didn't fancy any of the Hel witch dessert selection. Crème brû-decay, mildew-berry pie . . .'

'I thought the strawberries and rotted cream looked delightful.'

Attis laughed and handed her the bar. 'Dig in.'

Anna snapped off a row and gave it back. Their fingers touched in the interchange, only for a second, but enough to feel the deep warmth of his hands, the texture of his skin. She lay back in the chair, trying to distract herself with the chocolate, which was by far the best thing she'd tasted all evening. A giggle rose up inside of her through all of the fear.

Attis smirked over the flames. 'What?'

'I was just thinking about the look on that Hel witch's face when Manda started making out with her.'

Attis's head fell back with a laugh. 'It's in my list of the top five things I thought I'd never see.'

Anna ate another piece of chocolate. 'It was a weird night. For such a sombre grove they were certainly dramatic.'

'They're used to entertaining visitors.'

'What do you mean?'

'From what I can gather, they make a lot of money offering out their spiritual services.'

'So they put on a show, traumatize their visitors and win business? Is that ethical?'

'Most groves make money somehow. There's a whole magical economy out there and Hel witches have access to the primest of real estate: the Underworld.'

Anna thought of the dark tunnel entrance, crystallized with snow, and shuddered.

'Maybe I should join their ranks,' Attis considered. 'Start wearing black, get a trendy East London haircut, become extremely aroused by death.'

Anna chuckled. 'You couldn't pull off an East London haircut.'

He opened his mouth in mock offence.

'What about Effie?' Anna raised her eyebrows. 'She seems to think they might be her people.'

Attis shook his head, a knowing smile on his face. 'They're just another phase. Can you really see her as a Hel witch?'

Anna tried but it didn't fit. Their rules and initiations and unwavering dedication – it was all too rigid. Effie could barely focus on a movie for more than five minutes, let alone give her entire life over to one teaching.

And the darkness and stillness and death – Effie could not be contained by such things.

'She'd grow bored,' said Attis, matching her thoughts.

'Azrael might be able to change her mind . . .'

'She'll bore of him too. He's just a distraction.' Attis caught a burning spark from the air. 'The guy's dry as a gravestone in a desert.'

Anna laughed. 'He really is. I'm not sure he cracked a smile all evening.'

'We live to die.' Attis put a hand to his chest, imitating Azrael's grave pretension.

Anna's laughter flowed again. She cut it off. Talking to him, laughing with him, losing time with him was all too easy. *Far too hard.* The fire-light tangled with the copper of his hair as he looked back at her, the flames illuminating his face in distracting ways. She wished she knew what he was thinking but his eyes were as unknowable as the smoke that drew a hazy, uncrossable line between them.

She ought to leave but instead she whispered, 'What about me? Perhaps death magic is my language?' She thought of the darkness of the tunnel, the snow, the ravens above her, in her dreams . . .

Attis leant forwards. 'You're no death witch. You bring things around you to life.'

His words were painful to hear, the softness of them. Anna drew herself into the chair, tucking her knees up. It wasn't true. She'd brought nothing but death.

'Plus, you wouldn't suit all the black, pale redhead and all.'

'And I'd die of terror at every Hel witch ritual, not that anything appeared to scare *you* this evening.'

'It's just death. Not so scary.'

'So nothing scares Attis Lockerby?'

'Some things,' he said, his eyes still on her.

'What?'

'Flying ants. I mean, what are they? An ant or a fly? Why won't they choose? Why do they exist? What do they want from us?'

Anna shook her head, biting her smile. 'See, nothing scares you. You even looked upon the Language of the Dead without dying inside. How can you tolerate it?'

Attis shrugged. 'Perhaps because I'm not really alive.'

Anna hated the tone of his voice, so accepting, so apathetic. 'That's rubbish. You're the most alive person I know.' She hadn't meant to say it, but there it was and it was true. The world would be a colder, darker, deader place without him in it. A world that didn't bear thinking about.

He pulled back from the fire, into the shadows. 'I'm just stating the facts.'

Anna made a grating sound. 'Facts you've decided to be true.'

'Facts based on the evidence we have, which is better than the hope we can undo a hundreds-of-years-old curse.'

'You sound as fatalistic as a Hel witch.'

'There's a difference between fatalism and realism.'

The way he said it made her even more annoyed. There were a hundred things she wanted to scream at him in that moment but she chose cold silence instead, folding her arms stiffly and staring at the distant stars. They burned indifferently.

Attis sighed. He followed her gaze up to the sky. 'The old stories say that once there were no stars in the sky. It was entirely empty. Black, without meaning. They say it was only when the Goddess died that they appeared above – the stars a map of her body, her magic, her soul – a map back to her.'

Anna made a huffing sound beneath her breath. Did he think he could distract her with talk of the stars? What was more annoying was that it *was* distracting – his voice soft as ash, as musical as the motions of the fire. The sky seemed to come into focus with his words.

'My dad knew all the constellations,' he said. 'We'd use them when we went camping.'

'Use them?'

Attis lay back. 'Yeah. It's what I like about the stars. They're beautiful but all the more so for being useful. They help us to navigate. Their positions in the sky can signal the change of seasons, inform people what crops they should be planting. They guide us with stories too. My dad knew all of them. I can still remember falling asleep to the sound of his voice and the fire, as if the two were one.'

Anna smiled at the thought. 'Well, you seem to have inherited his knack for storytelling.'

He turned to her with a ripening grin. 'Want to hear one?'

'Do I have a choice?'

His smile grew wider. 'Of course not.'

She laughed. 'Go on then.'

He looked between the sky and the fire, and the next thing, tiny sparks rose up from the flames into the air above them. His eyes churned with concentration and the sparks began to move, to align themselves into shapes, patterns . . . constellations. *The* constellations. Attis had brought the stars to them. The night sky fallen to earth. Anna could hardly speak for the wonder of it. They were not quite still but moving gently above the flames, turning, hovering, sparkling—

'The seven major constellations of the Goddess,' he explained. 'The mirror, the bear, the cauldron, the raven, the poppet, the star and the apple.' Anna had never heard such names for the constellations before. 'Which do you want to hear?'

She looked at each of them, but she knew already – the word was already on her tongue. 'The raven.'

Attis raised an eyebrow. 'A dark story.' He drew the constellation closer to them. It was bird-shaped – wings outstretched. He rotated it slowly through the air as he began, his voice a low simmer. 'It starts in the time before stars, when the Goddess was spinning the first magic into the world. They say the world then shone silver as the moon and everything was full and ripe with life, but the Goddess knew the light already; it was the dark she wanted to uncover. The deepest secret of all: death. For how can you have power over life until you know the truth of what comes after? Plus, like all women, she was a meddler.' He smirked.

Anna narrowed her eyes. 'No ad-libbing.'

'And so the Goddess formed a bird strong enough to travel into the Underworld to speak with the spirits and bring their secrets back to her. The bird was pure of heart, with long feathers white as the moon and a song bright and dulcet as a bell. The bird flew from her hand to the world below.'

Attis moved the constellation above them as if the bird was flying. It swept down.

'It travelled deep into the Underworld until time lost all sense of meaning. It passed through the seven trials of Hel, losing seven feathers along the way. It travelled to the very centre of the darkness, where it sang to the spirits and the spirits spoke to it, telling it their secrets, until the bird knew all there was to know of death. It was ready to return. It began the long flight home. Only, as it was flying back, it spotted a river below. The waters were black as can be but the bird was so tired and thirsty from its travails that it stopped for a drink. But once it started drinking, it could not stop. It drank and drank so deeply that it fell right into the waters. It struggled back to the surface but it was too late. The bird was changed forever. Its feathers were now slick and black as the waters of Hel, and its voice – its beautiful voice, when it tried to sing – was all dried up, nothing now but a rattling, desperate caw.'

Anna shivered. Was the black river the Waters of the Dead? She recalled the fairy tale of the seven ravens she'd read – a raven had fallen into the waters then too, disappearing that time. Both tales felt like a warning.

'The bird returned to the land of the living and flew back to its Goddess. It tried to relay all it had learnt but all she could hear was its terrible, screeching song. It took time, but slowly she translated what the bird was saying, forming a new language just as terrible: the Language of the Dead. The first to ever be written down. At last, the Goddess understood what it meant to die and so she no longer feared it. From that day forth, the bird became the messenger of the dead, travelling to Hel on her behalf. But after the Goddess was gone, and the stars had risen, and time had moved on and on again, forgetting itself, the people turned against the bird. When they heard its song, they covered their ears; they shunned it and shot it and said that if you listened to it, you'd turn raving mad, and so the bird became known as the raven.'

The constellation flew above Anna's head in a sparking circle and then settled back among the others. Anna was silent.

'I can't help but feel you didn't enjoy my story,' said Attis. 'I normally receive a round of applause. A standing ovation is welcome too.'

'It was well told.'

His eyebrows met. 'You look afraid.'

'I am.' For a moment she wanted to tell him about all of it, but she knew how it would sound, like she was *raving*. Haunted by her aunt, ravens in her dreams, screams buried in the silences of her mind. 'I guess I'm still on edge after the night we just had. Is it true? The story?'

Attis made a questioning gesture with his hands. 'It's just one tale about that constellation. It has many others, depending on where you go or who you speak to. Who's to know which is more true? My dad used to say that the stars are a map of our imagination. Doesn't really matter what they mean, only that we make meaning of them.'

Anna considered his words. 'I think I'll choose another story for the raven then.'

He laughed. 'You hated my story that much?'

Her lips quirked. 'You just said we're here to make our own meaning.'

'What's your story then?'

'That the raven told the Goddess to sod off and, instead of going to Hel, flew away somewhere nice and warm. Mauritius, maybe.'

Attis's laugh billowed over the fire. 'Mauritius?'

'It's more realistic than agreeing to go to Hel.'

'So the Goddess never learns the secrets of the dead?'

Anna shrugged. 'But the raven's happy.'

'I'm not sure the true stories are ever the happy ones,' he said, his voice low, undoing her.

Anna leant back. The stars above were faint now, the morning light beginning to rise up from places deeper than the horizon. A thin tremble of moon remained, resisting the oncoming dawn, like the last note of a song. She didn't want the night to be over, but to remain in the limbo between night and day, not having to remember what had come before or to face what was coming.

She looked to him. 'What was your dad's name?'

Attis coughed and shifted in his chair. 'Like stories, what meaning do names really have?'

'I'd still like to know.'

Attis lowered his head and his stars fell back into the fire. 'My dad, the one who died, was called Sugata. Cancer got him in the end.'

'I'm sorry.'

'My other dad . . . the one I went camping with was called Herne. Herne Lockerby. Strong name, right?'

'You don't know where he is?'

Attis shook his head. 'We haven't been on speaking terms for a while.'

'Because you left with Selene? To break the curse?' Anna felt an old hunger rising up, a desire to know as much about him as she could.

'Yes. He'd agreed to it when he first took me in but I don't think I truly believed Selene would really go through with it. When Selene told him it was time . . . he lost it. He tried to reason with me, to argue with me, he begged me to stay but I wouldn't. I left and after that he left. I don't know where.'

'Is that why you went back to Wales over the summer? To see if he'd returned?'

'I went back to collect things from my old forge. But . . . I guess

I thought I might see signs of him, traces. I didn't think he would have returned but that he might have been back to the house. He hadn't.'

Anna knew he didn't want to talk about it any more, she could tell by the way his jaw was tensing, but she couldn't stop. She wanted him to see that there were people out there who loved him, who were worth fighting for. 'Don't you want to find him?'

'I don't think it would be useful. I haven't changed my mind.'

'You aren't actually serious about sacrificing yourself again?'

'Deadly,' he replied like a joke, but he wasn't laughing.

'But you've agreed to try! To find another way!'

'For now,' he stated, and Anna could feel her panic rise at his tone. 'And what if there isn't another way and I have to crush him all over again? Anna, this is one story you can't rewrite. My blood is how we end the curse. It's fine, it's cool. I made my peace with it a long time ago. I'm made of magic, remember?'

Anna scowled, remembering just how irritating he could be. With his hair gilded by the flames and his eyes dancing between light and dark, half smoke, half fire, his words felt all too true. He didn't look as if he belonged to the world. Was he the price that had to be paid? A star to be swallowed by the night? *No.*

'Don't flatter yourself,' she said. 'You're not *that* magical. Come on, Attis. You can't talk to me about the stars like that and then tell me you don't care about your life.'

'You know what the stars really are? Celestial bodies of gas, predominantly hydrogen and helium.'

'Thank you for the science lesson,' she snapped. She was sure if it had been the previous year, they would have been shouting and throwing their hands about, but a restraint held them in place, though Anna could feel the charge between them filling the air. 'Surely,' she said, trying to keep her voice steady, 'you want to at least try—'

'That's rich.'

'What's that meant to mean?'

'You don't play the piano any more. You don't want to practise magic. Are *you* living?'

'I – I haven't had time.' It was a lie and they both knew it.

'Busy summer?'

'Yeah! Trying to deal with the fallout of our bloody curse! Not running away on a holiday like you and Effie.' She couldn't keep the bitterness from her voice.

'You mean trying to stop Effie drinking herself into oblivion and holding her every night while she cried? Yeah, it was a real holiday.'

Anna's response stuck in her throat. She couldn't imagine it – Effie inconsolable; Effie crying. 'I didn't know,' she said, quietly.

'Effie isn't as strong as she pretends.' His voice had run out of fire. 'I hated leaving you, but I knew the only way I'd get through to her is if we got away, went somewhere she felt safe. You're not the only one in pain, Anna,' he said, more softly. 'But you can't just . . . stop.'

'You think I care about pain?' Her voice was rough. 'I was brought up on pain. Going and having a tinkle on the piano isn't going to change anything, isn't going to—'

Undo what I did.

Attis's face fell. Anna pulled at the loose thread on the cushion, not able to bear his expression like that – that she'd made it so – without a smile waiting around the corner. She stood up, needing to get away, needing to be anywhere but near him.

'You can't give up on who you are,' he said, looking up at her, his eyes glinting like his goddamn stars.

'Says the man giving up entirely.' She walked away, moving faster the closer to the door she got. As soon as she was through it, she ran down the stairs.

Her room was cold, the chill of the night coming back to her. She sat on her bed and tucked her knees up around herself, feeling a wrenching and twisting in her stomach, his words refusing to leave her head: *You can't give up on who you are.*

Who was he to talk? As if he was somehow staying true to himself by dying. It was ridiculous. And she wasn't giving up on herself, she was growing up. She couldn't go back to who she'd been. She knew now that stories couldn't save her, that magic wasn't only a place of wonder. Attis couldn't distract her with stories of the stars as if they held the answers when really it was all they could do to keep the darkness of the night at bay.

She picked up the spinning top Rowan had given her and let it go with a cry of frustration. It began to spin on its tip, fast and furious, as if the floor was on fire and it wished to escape. She held her anger steadily. It felt good, hot and pure, pricking her eyes with tears. It sped up. Faster. Faster. Balanced. *It's balanced! I'm doing it!* But then through the rush of her anger and triumph—

A vision of Aunt on the floor, the golem strangling her, fuelled by the same anger that held Anna now. Anna's body went slack, her cry dying on her lips.

The spinning top flew off its orbit, smashing against the window and falling to the ground. Anna fell back onto her bed, the walls shrinking with fear around her.

You'll never be free of me.

Aunt's voice again. Closer now. Laughing. In Anna's head. Her own private Hel. No way of escaping what she'd done, the ghosts that haunted her, the stars that had slipped her grasp and would never be hers again.

WRITING

To experience possession by a spirit is to transcend yourself and dance with the devouring energy of Mother Holle. Once possessed, your life will never be the same.

Possession, Hel Witch Initiation Stage Three

The end of term came too slowly and, just when Anna thought that things were settling down, they'd been informed that they had to attend a meeting with all parties involved in the bullying allegations: the coven, Darcey, and their respective parents. Anna could not imagine anything good coming from such a combination of people in a small space.

Her stomach turned over as she made her way to Mr Ramsden's office. They were so close to the end of term now, they couldn't afford for anything to happen. Rowan suspected that Darcey's parents had insisted on it, believing not enough was being done. Over the last few weeks, Eames had continued talking to people and observing classes, but nothing seemed to have come of it. Perhaps, it had been a box-ticking exercise after all. The rest of the school was losing interest in Darcey's rumours – Anna had actually been able to concentrate in class without everyone whispering about her, and a handful of people had even started talking to them again. Some of Rowan's band friends had joined them the day before for lunch. It had given Anna hope that things could go back to normal, a normal she'd never even known. Not that Effie had been impressed by *cowans* joining them. Anna had realized that Effie had never cared about being popular – the games they'd played the year before had simply been to piss off Darcey. To win.

At least Anna was beginning to feel more in control of her magic. In the coven room, Effie hadn't let up, making them try out language after language – stones and crystals, numerology and words of power. Effie had bought her own tarot set to practise divination and they'd attempted to scry with mirrors, but none of them had seemed particularly drawn to one language over the other. Anna's magic had stopped erupting at least, as if the pressure had been released, but something was still missing; a part of *her* missing. She hadn't mastered the spinning top and her Hira remained frail and distant . . . just out of reach.

Perhaps, that was just how it was now and she had to accept it, she told herself, trying to ignore the ache in her heart, the grasping feeling of wanting to hold onto something that was too lost to find. As long as she could keep it together until the end of term – that was all that mattered.

If they'd made more progress with the curse, she'd have felt better, but after the dead ends of the Hel witch night and the lack of response from Nana, Anna wasn't sure which way to turn next. She'd spent nights researching – even emailing history professors with witchcraft specialisms around the country – but she couldn't uncover any more about the Everdell sisters or their trial. It was infuriating that she could find no way to save them . . . *him*.

Did he even want to be saved?

She and Attis hadn't spoken for several days after their rooftop argument and then things had settled down to how they'd been – polite, friendly and with a strained distance Anna found exhausting. Night after night, she'd taken out his skeleton key from her drawer, studying the puzzle-pattern of its blade, running her finger over it as if it might somehow help her make sense of him – who he was. It wasn't even the lies he'd spun the year before, with Attis it was always more than that, a feeling that part of him was always unknowable; a flame that turns to smoke as you try to touch it; a key that can open every door except the one you want.

'Anna!' a voice behind her called.

She turned around to find Peter coming down the corridor towards her, a man she didn't recognize striding beside him.

They stopped before her and the man smiled knowingly. 'Ah, *this* is Anna.'

She saw it then – two pairs of blue eyes staring at her, the same piercing shade.

'You're not meant to say that, Dad.' Peter shook his head, his cheeks reddening.

'Oh, sorry.' The man winked at Anna and put out his hand.

Anna, still confused as to what was happening, took it.

'Good to meet you, I'm Reiss Nowell.' His grip was tight. 'I've heard lots about you, Ms Everdell.'

'Good to meet you too,' Anna replied, holding a polite smile through her discomfort. *Peter has been talking to his father about me?*

Peter jumped to her rescue. 'I'm sorry, Anna. As head of the board of governors, my dad is here for the meeting.'

Anna remembered Peter saying before that his dad had backed the inspection.

'I just came to see him for a minute and I'm now regretting it.' Peter laughed, touching his brow.

'Ah!' Reiss patted him on the back. 'It's good to wear your heart on your sleeve, son.' His voice was even more polished than Peter's. His looks were similar too, but more assured and at ease with their handsome features, cultivated with the kind of wrinkles that people say make a man more attractive as he ages. He boasted a light tan, as if he'd just come back from a skiing holiday, and his shirt was undone a few buttons, the sleeves rolled up. 'Just as it's good for a woman to keep a man on tenterhooks.' He winked at Anna again and, again, she was lost for words. 'But in all seriousness, Ms Everdell, Peter has never spoken so highly about a girl as he has about you.'

Peter coughed. 'I think it's time you go in, Dad.'

Reiss put his hands up. 'I know when I'm not wanted. I'll see you later, son.'

Reiss and Peter nodded in a strangely formal way at one another, then Reiss disappeared through the door towards Ramsden's office.

Peter gave Anna a bashful smile. 'I'm sorry about that. You know what parents are like—' He stopped, looking chagrined. 'Sorry, a stupid turn of phrase, I didn't mean—'

'It's OK, Peter. It was nice to meet your dad . . . and to see you embarrassed for once.' She did the smiling now. 'I'd better go though . . . .'

He nodded. 'Good luck in there. Darcey's parents can be vipers.'

Anna swallowed, remembering just what she was about to face. 'Thanks.'

By the time she went in, everyone was already there. A table had been set up with Ramsden at the head wearing his usual halo of gloom and everyone else sitting down the sides: Rowan and her mum, Bertie, Manda, Effie, Attis, Darcey and her parents, Reiss Nowell and Eames's secretary. Eames was at the other end of the table, his back to Anna. He turned when she entered, his eyes moving over her impassively but in a way that made her feel entirely exposed.

'Anna, come and sit over here.' Bertie, clad in a brightly coloured knitted jumper, patted the seat next to her. Anna had never moved so quickly. She sat down next to Bertie, who gave her a reassuring smile, filigree wrinkles creasing around eyes that didn't miss a trick. Anna wondered where Manda's parents were as Bertie took Anna's hand beneath the table and squeezed it. 'It's going to be OK, chicken.'

Anna squeezed it back, but the expression on Darcey and her parents' faces suggested otherwise. They were not the kind of people who took no for an answer.

Effie's laugh cut through the growing pressure of the room and Anna turned to see her whispering something to Attis. Anna did a double take at him. She hadn't noticed what he was wearing: a suit and tie – his suit the same grey and his tie the same lurid orange as Mr Ramsden's. What was he playing at now?

Ramsden began with a grating sigh. 'Inspector Eames thought it would be useful to gather you all together at this juncture in the inspection. A chance for you all to voice your thoughts.'

So Eames *had* been behind this. Anna cast a quick glance at him. He had his notepad in hand, long-nailed fingers stretched around it. Another chance to observe them.

'Well, I have some thoughts!' Bertie began punchily, shifting her woolly shoulders to Ramsden.

His lip curled with displeasure. 'As I'm aware, Mrs Greenfinch, from your many phone calls, emails and faxes. I didn't even know the school *had* a fax machine but you managed to find it—'

His sentence was broken by the door opening dramatically. Selene stepped through, arriving like a blizzard of gold. Her hair was blow-dried into billowing waves – how were they billowing? – and she wore a yellow blouse and high-waisted trousers; bright necklaces and rings twinkling. The institutional surroundings of the school seemed to crumple around her as if they were only made of paper that could never capture her colour. Anna hadn't noticed for some time just how magical Selene was. Mr Ramsden sat up straight, touching his tie. Mrs Dulacey looked her up and down with distaste that couldn't quite mask her jealousy. The inspector made a note.

Darcey's father summoned up a petty response to her arrival. 'The meeting has already started.'

Selene smiled at him as a lion might smile at a kitten. 'Darling, no party ever starts without me.' She sauntered into the room, taking the spare seat next to Ramsden. 'Please continue.' She leant back in her chair and crossed her legs in a way that Ramsden seemed to find highly distracting.

He coughed gruffly. 'I was just saying we have been called here to discuss the ongoing inspection—'

'This *inspection* is disrupting my daughter's life!' Bertie erupted. 'That man over there.' She could barely look at Eames. 'Has been questioning them, searching lockers, watching them in class, making their life at this school even more difficult than it already was. It must be brought to an end. The allegations were ludicrous to begin with, based on not a dandelion seed's worth of evidence. My daughter and her friends have never bullied Darcey or lured her into any kind of cult. My daughter poured orange juice on her cornflakes this morning instead of milk. Orange juice! This is not the first time it's happened—'

'Mum . . .' Rowan whispered, lowering her head behind her hand.

'And you think she's capable of cult coercion and brainwashing? Why can't this school have investigated this calmly and reasonably? Why bring in an outside inspection? It's only stirred up the ridiculous rumours surrounding this whole thing and made it impossible for these girls to focus during their final year in school—'

'Pah!' Mr Dulacey's fists which had been locked and loaded on the table the whole time could finally take no more. They banged up and down. 'It is our daughter who has suffered!' He was a leading criminal defence lawyer with a reputation for ruthlessness and Anna could see from the ferocious look on his reddening face why you wouldn't mess with him.

Darcey pretended to wipe a tear from her eye. 'They targeted me! They took everything from me!'

'Bullies! Bullies, all of them!' Mrs Dulacey turned to Bertie, contempt pulling at her too-smooth features, her broad jaw jutting forwards. With her blonde hair whipped into an updo, manicured nails and tailored outfit she couldn't have been more different from Bertie. 'They harassed my daughter and her friends all of last year. They started a hate campaign designed to smear her impeccable reputation, her good name—'

'Pffft,' Bertie dismissed. 'Everybody knows your daughter's name instils nothing but terror in this school. Do you know how many times I've had to comfort my girl over the years, coming home in tears because Darcey has conjured up some new way to taunt her?' Anna saw the hint of a smile tweak the edge of Darcey's lips and some of her old hatred for Darcey came surging back. 'Darcey's always been as cruel as knotweed wrapped in bramble!'

'I'm sorry, are you speaking in English or tongues?' Mrs Darcey turned to Ramsden. 'I can't understand her.'

'I can't help it if you can't keep up, Emily,' Bertie snapped. 'The point is, bullying happens, but it belongs in the domain of the school. I think we can put an end to all this now and return to sanity.'

Mrs Dulacey ignored her, screwing up her face at Ramsden. 'There will be no end to anything until this inspection achieves results. It's taking too long! Who knows what this bunch of . . . delinquents will do next! Their parents obviously have no idea what their daughters are up to.' She flashed a look of disgust at Selene. 'They can't control them. They need to be punished! Expelled! Before anything else happens!'

Mr Dulacey banged his fists some more. 'We give enough money to this goddamn school! We expect answers! We demand answers!'

The room descended into yelling and threats, Bertie outstretching her arms like a mother bear protecting her cubs from attack. Anna shifted her eyes to Eames, who was watching the unfolding chaos without a flicker of emotion.

'Everybody! Can we remain focused!' Mr Ramsden tried to restore order, ineffectually.

'PARENTS,' Attis shouted at the top of his lungs. The squabbling stopped at the surprising boom of his voice. 'Now. Mr Ramsden is trying to speak, can we all listen. He is the voice of reason here.' Attis turned to Ramsden, who glared at him. 'Perhaps a biscuit break then . . .' Attis suggested, taking out a packet of digestives and opening them noisily.

Mrs Dulacey looked at him as if he were some kind of imbecile.

'Mr Ramsden.' Selene's voice slipped through the momentary silence of the room. She put a hand on Ramsden's arm. 'Robert, is it?'

'Well – I—' Mr Ramsden's eyes bulged at her proximity.

'Good. Robert, darling. I understand exactly why you carried out the investigation – you're a man of action and action needed to be taken when your school was under threat by these claims. You were put under pressure by a clearly corrupt governing board but the inspection has been given its chance. No basis has been found to the claims. Letting this farce continue will only reflect badly on the school, and *you*, darling.' She smiled, her eyes entrapping him entirely. 'This is your school to take back. Your decision.'

Ramsden's head rose at her words, red flushing up through the strangled buttons of his collar, but it was Peter's father who spoke, his twinkling eyes landing on Selene lightly. 'Mrs Fawkes, is it?'

Selene released a low laugh. 'You insult me. It's Ms Fawkes but you can call me Selene if you promise not to offend me again.'

A smile twitched at his lips. 'Selene, then. A fine speech but the inspection was sanctioned by the governing board and must be discussed with the rest of the board before any termination can be agreed.'

'That's not actually true though,' said Attis, through a mouthful of biscuit.

'Excuse me?' Reiss's smile fell away as he turned to him.

'It's just—' Attis swallowed. 'External inspections are allowed to be commissioned by the board of governors but only up to the period of a single term to avoid any lengthened period of disruption. After such time, the decision defaults to the headmaster and the school's administrative team. The board of governors are permitted to carry out a review and submit their recommendations but it is Headmaster Ramsden, my personal hero, who has the final say.' Attis straightened his orange tie.

'I don't think you ought to be speaking on matters you don't understand.' Reiss smiled tightly.

'These aren't my matters but the matters of the school's behaviour policy, as delineated by section 89 of the government's Education and Inspections Act. A policy that is adhered to by both school management and the board of governors, and enforced by the law of the country. I've printed out a copy here.' Attis reached into his blazer and pulled out some papers. 'If you'd like to read it out to us, Mr Nowell? Or can I call you Reiss?'

Reiss's mouth had closed to a hard line.

Attis offered him the packet.

Mr Dulacey growled. 'Why are we listening to this *boy*?'

Effie snorted. 'Why is anyone listening to your liar of a daughter? Let's stop beating around the bush here, Darcey's not claiming we're bullies, she's claiming we're witches who drank her blood in a ritual to raise Satan. I mean, come on, we all know Darcey lost her mind last year and this inspection is paid for by her parents to try and cover up the fact she had an affair with the headteacher.'

'SCREW YOU, EFFIE!' Darcey looked as if she would jump across the table and strangle her.

Effie looked pointedly at Eames. 'Wait, am I the one out of control here?'

Before everyone else could erupt again – he put down his notepad and spoke.

'I'd like to reassure everyone that all allegations are being taken seriously. The inspection is not yet over. There is more evidence to gather and analyse before a final conclusion can be reached. I ask you to be patient; this is a delicate matter.'

'Thank you, Mr Eames.' Reiss Nowell nodded at him. 'We are so glad to have your expertise on board. Now, unless anyone has anything further to add, myself, Mr Ramsden and Inspector Eames will have a private discussion, taking everything said here today into account.'

The coven met in the toilets after the meeting, except Attis, who had to get back for a lesson at the Boys' School.

Rowan whistled. 'Well, that was intense. I thought my mum and Mrs Dulacey were going to end up wrestling on the table at one point.'

The meeting had ended with more shouting and further threats until the secretary had forced them all from the room.

'It was bullshit.' Effie's voice was scathing. 'Darcey and her parents throwing a tantrum because the inspection hasn't gone their way.'

'You shouldn't have brought up magic in front of the inspector,' said Anna.

'It worked,' Effie replied. 'It set Darcey off. Showed her up. Plus, it was fun to watch her squirm.'

'What do you think Eames meant by *all* the allegations are being taken seriously?' said Rowan. 'Like, he can't actually be taking any notice of Darcey's occult claims . . .'

Eames's words had been going around Anna's mind too, digging their nails in. She shook her head. 'I don't know. There's something not right about him, about any of this. It seems suspicious with the WIPS investigating witchcraft claims elsewhere . . .' She turned to Effie. 'Have you heard anything from Poppins yet? Have they managed to dig anything up about the WIPS since Halloween?'

Effie shook her head. 'He's got the Wild Hunt asking questions, but they haven't found much. Apparently, the WIPS *are* a black hole.'

Rowan chewed her cheek, her brow troubled. 'Still, maybe Attis and Selene got through to Ramsden. He might bring the inspection to a close at the end of term.'

'Oh Lord, let's hope so.' Manda clasped her hands together. 'We need to be focused on our applications over Christmas. They're due in when we get back.'

'How come your parents didn't come today, Manda?' Anna asked.

'Oh.' Manda looked startled. 'Dad couldn't get the time off work and Mum refused to come. Doesn't want to be associated with any of this. It's for the best; she'd have combusted on the spot if she'd heard Effie talking about Satan.'

Rowan managed a laugh. 'I was thinking, why don't you all come to mine for Christmas? After this term, I think we could all do with blowing off some steam. A Greenfinch Christmas gets a bit mad but, honestly, it's fun. We burn a Yule log, dance around the evergreens, pop divination crackers, eat until we can't function . . . There's nut roast and roast apples, mince pies and Yuletide cakes and candy canes big enough to fly on and so much wassail you could drown in it. Holly grows all through the house and Great-Uncle Aster refuses to wear anything on Christmas Day except ivy, just ivy. You have to see it. Not the Uncle Aster bit, but everything else.'

Effie smiled, considering Rowan's invitation. 'We always go away for Christmas . . . but perhaps we can make an exception this year.'

Anna beamed. 'Of course.' She could think of nothing better than a Greenfinch Christmas.

'I figured it would be tricky for you, Manda, with your parents.' Rowan gave her a sympathetic look. 'My mum would be happy to call yours but I don't know if that would help . . .'

'Doubt it,' Manda replied, bitterly. She tapped her fingers against the sink restlessly. 'But I'll see what I can do. They've talked about wanting to visit my sister so perhaps I can wangle something.'

'Let me know if I can help. I know Mum would love to have you all and she could do with the distraction. As you could probably tell from today, she's been stressed as of late. She's been downing cups of calming tisane and a glass of sherry every night—'

At that moment the door banged open. Darcey, Corinne and Olivia stepped through. They spread out, blocking the doorway.

'Well, look who it is.' Effie hooted. 'Couldn't stay away, Darcey?'

Darcey gestured to Olivia, who raised her phone and started filming.

'Wait.' Effie put a hand up, applied some lipstick in the mirror and swivelled back to the camera. 'There we go. I'm ready. Now, what do you want me to do? Whip out my wand? Mutter a spell? Call up the devil?' She raised her arms. 'Ave Satana!' She snorted.

Darcey didn't reply. Her old sarcasm had soured into something bitter and hard and there was nothing but hatred in her eyes. 'You think you're so funny, Effie, but you're playing with fire. I can't wait to laugh in your face while you burn.'

The best thing they could do was leave, but Effie turned to Olivia and Corinne. 'You two aren't buying this whole magic thing, right?'

Olivia said nothing. Corinne tried to look righteous. 'We believe Darcey.'

'Do you?' Effie narrowed her eyes. 'Or do you just struggle to have minds of your own? I'd seriously consider your allegiance. Darcey's kind of an embarrassment these days. Maybe it's time to forge your own paths. Olivia, you've got your fashion drones. Corinne, you've got your whole hippie, kale-juice, pretending-to-help-the-planet shtick. There's still time for you both before she drags you down into obscurity. She was always just using you, anyway.'

'That's rich,' Darcey spat, looking like she might slam Effie's head against the mirror. 'You don't know any other way but to use people.' Her eyes moved with disgust over Manda, Rowan, Anna. 'She doesn't care about any of you but you're all too pathetic to realise, aren't you?'

Anna stepped between them. 'Look, why don't we just all stay out of each other's way and get through the year? Then you'll never have to see us again.'

Darcey's hollow laugh was lined with blades. 'You have to be joking. You're not getting away from me! You took everything from me! Now, I'm going to take everything from you. I'm going to make sure you leave this school destroyed—'

Effie cut in. 'The thing is, nobody's listening to you any more, Darcey. The girl who cried witch too many times. Putting on a show is all about the anticipation, the timing . . . and you've blown your load. I mean, devil worship, bloodletting, orgies? Too big, too soon.'

'There's truth in it,' Darcey spat, her stony face crumpling with revulsion. 'I know you're not normal. I know what's inside you all. Evil.'

Anna stepped back, cringing at her words.

'Then surely you ought to be careful . . .' Effie smiled coldly but Darcey didn't look away from Anna, sniffing out her fear as she always had.

'Sometimes I think I have it all wrong.' She stepped closer. 'Sometimes I think you might be the real mastermind. After all, you went from *nobody* to somebody in less than a year. You stole Peter off me. You stole Attis off Effie. And Effie still hangs out with you even though Attis is clearly into you.' She laughed with something of her old amusement. 'That's before we get on to the dead parents and dead aunt.' Darcey's smile fell, her lips white around her teeth. 'Are you killing them all or is it simply your presence that has that effect? Perhaps you're the one who ought to be careful, Effie . . .'

Darcey's words sliced into Anna just as they'd been designed to do, too close to the truth. As Anna bled out, Aunt's laughter rose up and all Anna could see were her own hands wrapping around Aunt's neck—

Effie bore down on Darcey, inches from her face. Darcey was breathing fast, a fervent look in her eye. The room felt on the edge of breaking, magic crackling in the air—

Effie moved suddenly. Olivia stumbled back. Corinne screamed. But Effie had only raised her hand. She blew a red-lipped kiss at the phone and turned back to Darcey, smiling. 'Did you really think I was going to break that easily? You've got to build the tension before the big finale, you know.'

With that, she pushed past them and out of the door. Anna, coming back to her senses, bolted after her.

Anna ran to catch up with her. 'Effie, Effie – don't let Darcey get to you. She's just—'

Effie turned to her sharply and Anna tried to read the lines between her smile but she couldn't. 'Did I look out of control to you?'

'No,' said Anna, but she'd felt it. She had felt the magic in the room ready to snap. *Was that mine or Effie's?* She didn't know. 'She's just getting desperate, she's trying to bait us, to catch us in the act.'

'I know that,' Effie barked. 'When magic hits Darcey, she won't see it coming . . .'

She won't see it coming . . .
   She won't see it coming . . .
   She won't see it coming . . .

Effie's words would not settle in Anna's head as the day wore on, the threats of the morning hanging over her. She'd thought that tensions had been dying down but now she could see that they'd only been building . . .

Something was building inside her too, something that needed release. With a free period ahead, she took herself to the music room.

She missed escaping here.

Her fingers twitched as she looked at the piano. She missed that too, the ache in her heart radiating through her whole body, Attis's words coming back to her – *Are you living?*

She wandered to the piano and sat down. She breathed in the scent of its old wood, its hollow tunnels of sound. She put her fingers on its keys – a light touch that made her realize how much weight she was carrying. She wanted to play but she didn't know how, how to let go . . . as if releasing a single note might break her entirely. That Aunt might flood in through the cracks. Waiting to laugh. Waiting to cry. Waiting to take it all from her just when she thought she was free—

Darcey's words tripping her up: *Are you killing them all or is it simply your presence that has that effect?*

I won't look down . . .

I won't look down . . .

I won't—

A scream fractured the silence of the room.

Anna jerked her hand away. *What have I done?*

There was no sound and for a moment relief rushed through her – it had just been in her head—

But then – another cry. Beyond the door. Anna jumped up. She could hear a raised voice, commotion. She ran from the room into the empty corridor, trying to locate where it was coming from.

A few doors away.

Anna ran towards it but was not ready for the sight that met her.

The teacher was panicking, her back against the whiteboard, head shaking, eyes peeled wide. 'They won't stop – I – I – they won't stop. They won't stop.' She wheeled to Anna. 'Call someone! Get someone!'

Anna stared into the room. The class was only small, a handful of girls, and they were writing. Or perhaps they had been writing but Anna didn't know how to put into words what they were doing now. They clutched their pens tightly, hands moving furiously – one girl scribbling over the same sheet of paper – tearing it to bits – another had run out of paper and was scoring her pen into the desk itself. Heads down. Writing. Writing. Writing.

'GET SOMEONE!' the teacher shrieked.

But Anna couldn't move either. Couldn't think straight. The floor had given way and she was falling. It wasn't just what she was seeing . . . but the feeling . . . the feeling in the air. As if everything was being torn apart. A blind cold. A numb terror. *Magic*. Rotten magic. She tried to wade against it but she was drowning too. A hundred Aunts waiting below to catch her – laughing and shrieking.

No. No. I won't look down—

She managed to stumble from the door, head rocking up and down the corridor. Mr Archer was passing in the distance. 'HELP!' She cried the only word she could articulate. 'HELP!!'

He sprinted down the corridor. 'What's going on?'

Anna fell back into the room. The girls had grown more furious – arms rigid, pens scribbling, scrawling. One had moved, writing along the wall now in big, unhinged loops. The words: *Ave Satana*. Mr Archer rushed over, trying to stop her, but the girl struggled against him, flailing wildly, still trying to write, turning the pen on him – on anything.

Another had started to dig the pen into her own arm—

Anna tried to move towards her but the girl looked up and her eyes held Anna frozen. *Her eyes. Her eyes.* They were not there. Not in the room. They were lost – lost somewhere incomprehensible, as if the girl were looking up at her from the bottom of a well – so far away – and yet something around their edges, or in their very centre, fought against it. Pulsed. Clawed. Raged. But couldn't break free.

Anna could hear more people pouring into the room behind them. Voices. Cries. Commotion. But Anna was held as trapped as *the eyes*.

A teacher pulled her away. 'Get back!'

Anna did not resist, watching as the girls were restrained one by one.

She bumped into someone in the doorway. She turned around and Inspector Eames was there, looking down at her, shifting his attention back up to the room. Watching with keen interest. His Adam's apple fluttering, his empty eyes stirring, rippling; measurements being taken.

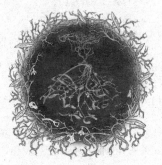

FALLING

Through pre-sleep rituals and extended trances, Initiates invite Mother Holle's ravens into their dreams as a way of bridging their shadow psyche with the realm of the Underworld. A practice that must be carried out with great caution else the shadows spill over into the waking mind.

'Raven Dreams', Hel Witch Trainings,
Books of the Dead: Tome 5933

Attis was looking up to the light. Anna traced the puzzle-pattern of his features. He turned and took her by the wrist, pulling her close. His lips were sweet as ever but his eyes . . . his eyes were not his own. His lips opened and the sound that flew from them was a raven's call, brittle as bones picked over. Effie appeared from behind him, encircling him, entwining with him. They sank into the earth together – buried, writhing roots. Anna tried to pass over them but they reached for her, grabbing at her ankles, clawing at her legs.

She kicked herself free, running blindly – scrabbling up the stairs before her – up and up – the Language of the Dead screaming on the walls around her – ravens calling her onwards – up and up in a spiral of dread. She wanted to run but her legs would not move faster, she wanted to scream but her voice would not come. Around and around. And then—

A door.

She'd never arrived at a door before and she knew this one well.

The door to the third-floor room.

Why is it still locked? It shouldn't be locked!

Ravens flew through the keyhole like shadows contorting to nothing, their sounds shredding to pieces. A feather fell free. Anna picked it up and put it in the lock but the lock began to scream. Blood gushed from the keyhole, splashing up the sides of her dreams – too much to contain – too much to hold back. She fell backwards . . . only there was nothing behind her and she was falling – falling—

Anna jolted up in bed, a scream she could not translate on her lips. Something was making a whirring noise – the spinning top on her floor, spinning erratically. As she stared at it, it twisted faster and then spasmed around the room and slammed against the wall, falling back to the floor.

Her own magic was taunting her.

Anna squeezed her eyes shut but all she could see was *the eyes*. The eyes of the girls at school.

They'd been lost. *Where had they been?*

They'd been trapped. *By what?*

They'd felt too familiar, like a mirror, as if Anna already knew the place they were lost and trapped. *My magic? My darkness? Had it unleashed itself again? Did I finally lose all control?*

The school had closed early for Christmas, describing the incident as an episode of 'stress-induced hysteria'. Anna feared how it would play out with the inspection, which had been so close to wrapping up. But she had bigger worries. She took out her phone, bringing up Hopkins's channel. The event at their school hadn't made the main news, but local news sites and more unorthodox sources had given it coverage:

Fresh disturbance at St Olave's School for Girls

St Olave's pupils mysteriously hospitalized

Students suffer from hysteria at Dulwich school

Witchcraft inside our schools?

Hopkins had shared the last story, along with the words:

Our children are at risk. Stop the spread.

Anna stared at the line, still not quite believing it – that the eyes of the WIPS were on them.

She tucked herself back under the duvet, not sure she ever wanted to come back out, Aunt's laughter vicious around her. *I warned you this would happen . . .*

Anna tried to think it all through again, to make sense of it. There'd been magic in that classroom, she was sure of it. But had it been hers?

Another eruption? She didn't know. *Was it yours, Aunt?* Anna had begun to wonder if she was truly haunted, if Aunt was working through her somehow. She thought of how Mór had spoken of spirits – not as something whole but something fractured. Well, the curse had no doubt created many spirits as it had torn through her family. Souls shattered to pieces as they passed through its darkness, rippling above and below the Fabric . . . into the depths of Hel . . .

Or had it been something else?

Anna tried to recall exactly what had happened but it all felt so fragmented. The girls – the writing – convulsive movements – *their eyes* – everyone else flapping around them. The only composed person among them had been the inspector, his blank-paper eyes, reading the room while the girls wrote and wrote and wrote—

After they'd finally stopped struggling, the girls had been taken to hospital, while Anna and others who'd been caught up in it had been taken to the Ebury wing to calm down. After a few hours, Anna had been questioned by Eames's secretary – where had she been, what had she been doing, what had alerted her to it, what had she seen, what had she done.

Not enough. Why hadn't I done more? Why hadn't I found a way to stop it? Why had I been so frozen? So useless.

The secretary had given her a cup of tea and smiled sympathetically and for a few crazy moments Anna had wanted to tell her everything – to confess, to scream that it was magic, terrible magic – that they all needed to get away, from the school, from her. That somehow it was her fault. But she hadn't. She'd answered the questions quietly and carefully until they'd let her go.

A knock at Anna's door set her nerves firing again. 'Who is it?' It was too early to be Effie, who'd been trying to get her out of her room all week.

'Darling.' Selene's voice.

'Come in—'

Selene frowned, soft lines dimpling her forehead. 'You're still in bed.'

'It's early.'

'Yes, but I know you, you don't just stay in bed.'

'I think it might be better for everyone this way.'

Selene sighed. 'You're not to blame for what happened.'

'We don't know that.' Anna twisted the duvet beneath her hands.

'Five students lose their minds and I'm just around the corner. My magic has been erratic, dangerous—'

'It wasn't you, darling. You'd said it was getting better, that you were practising magic again.'

Anna lowered her head. She'd already had this discussion. 'Either way, it's not good, Selene. It's going to draw the exact attention we didn't want.'

Selene came over, sitting on the bed and pulling the duvet away. 'The school is saying it was just stress. They're not going to want to cause alarm among parents. They're going to do everything they can to let this pass quickly.'

'What if the WIPS don't let it pass?'

Selene's neck tightened. 'The school isn't going to want them getting involved either.'

Anna nodded a few times, trying to let Selene's words make her feel better, safer. Perhaps it would blow over. Perhaps the school would push the whole thing down. *But what if it happens again?* Anna could feel her panic rising all over again – the spinning top did a little whirr on the floor.

Both their pairs of eyes moved to it.

'You see,' Anna remonstrated. 'I'm not in control of my magic. Rowan gave me that damn spinning top, said it would help me work with my emotions, but I can't keep it balanced, it either does nothing or flies off!'

Selene stared at the spinning top. 'I think control might be the whole problem. My mum used to say, the more you learn, the less you know; the more you force, the less you flow. Now, she was a complete sixties hippie, but she had her moments.' She looked back at Anna. 'You're gripping too tightly, darling. Your magic can't breathe and when it does . . . it's gasping. Magic doesn't respond to force but to *feeling*.'

'But I can't feel it!' The outburst shuddered through Anna. 'That's the whole problem. When I try . . . I – I – don't feel what I used to feel and it just makes me feel worse.' She choked back tears. 'I can't feel anything any more. That day – that moment at the Binders' ceremony when I undid the knots of my Knotted Cord . . . I gave everything away, I lost my magic and I'm never going to get it back.' She took in a sharp breath, the ache in her heart seizing at the admission, not knowing how deeply it had burrowed into her, how much pain it was carrying.

Selene took her hand. 'No. The Goddess does not punish. Magic does not take, it does not run out, the more you give to it, the more it gives to you. You didn't lose your magic that day – you freed it.'

'Then why do I feel this way?'

'Because you undid the knots in your hands, but they're still in your mind. Vivienne never taught you to face your feelings.' Selene tried to catch her eyes. 'Goddess knows it isn't easy, for anyone. You need to find a way to let go, let your magic flow . . .'

Let go. Everything inside Anna seemed to contract at the thought. 'How can I let go of something I can't even get a hold of?'

Selene smiled at the riddle of her words. 'Do you know what Hira truly is?'

Your will. Your inner force. That's what Anna had been told.

'It's belief,' said Selene. 'Belief in your magic; in yourself, for the two are the same thing. Trust is how you let go – magic won't let you fall.'

But Anna was falling, all the time falling . . . How could she trust herself after what she'd done that day? How could she trust her magic when it had turned from her in silence? How could she step forwards when the path was lost in darkness?

'What does your Hira feel like?' she asked Selene.

Selene's smile turned hazy. 'Like colour. It feels like the place where the colours run together, where they clash and create and make chaos beautiful.'

Anna found herself distracted by the vividness of Selene's magic, it was so perfectly *her*.

'Do you remember how yours felt . . . before?' Selene asked.

'Like threads.' Anna's heart tugged. *My Hira is needle and thread.* 'Like I was sewing the worlds of things together. You told me that, Selene, that everything has a world inside of it.'

'Then you already know that you can't thread a needle with force.'

'How then?'

'You think I can sew? I have no idea. How do *you* thread a needle?'

Anna thought of the many times she'd sat beside Aunt sewing in the silence of their living room.

'Trust in what *you* know, Anna.'

Anna heard her name repeat in her head. *Anna. Anna. Anna.* Calling her from somewhere deeper too. 'What was my mother's language?'

Selene pulled back. 'Why do you ask?'

'I just want to hear it from you.'

'She cast spells through the power of touch.'

'How? What kind of spells?'

'She could heal, comfort, soothe people . . . oh, I don't remember it all, darling. We were apart so much after school.' She was being evasive again. 'All I can tell you is that your mother's magic was beautiful and good, like yours.'

'No,' Anna combated, like a reflex. She dropped Selene's hand. 'It's not, it's—' *Unstable. Broken. Haunted.* 'Cursed.'

'I've told you before, you bear a curse, you are not your curse. It does not come from inside you—'

'But it finds a way in.'

Selene rubbed her forehead, trying to ease out the creases. 'I know the curse has power, Anna. I have seen and lived through its consequences, but I've also seen what can happen if you let it consume you . . .'

Anna knew what Selene was inferring. *Aunt.* Anna remembered Aunt sewing the symbol of the curse into her skin, like a brand, a shield. Letting it become her. How many times had she done it? How deep had the stitches gone? Anna could still feel the stitches in her own chest that Aunt had once given her as punishment. She never, ever wanted to become her. 'I'm trying,' Anna replied desperately. 'I'm trying.'

'Well, promise me over Christmas you'll stop *trying* for a bit. Take some time off worrying about *everything*. Have some fun. It's what you need.'

'But that would involve me leaving the bed . . .'

'And what good are you doing to anyone from your bed?'

Anna released a tightly held breath, knowing Selene was right. That she couldn't escape what had happened. That the more she tried to hide, the worse she felt.

'Why don't you come with me to Mexico? We can drink palomas at sunset, eat freshly grilled shrimp on the beach, you can have a fling with a surfer. They're always fun – for a very short period.'

Anna laughed. 'I can't. I've already promised to go to Rowan's with the others.'

Selene's face fell. 'Yes, Effie has made it very clear she doesn't want to spend Christmas with me this year. Do you think she's going to be mad at me forever?'

'She'll come around eventually.'

'Oh, I don't know.' Selene tried to smile but it wavered. 'I fear she's capable of holding a grudge forever. I suppose I deserve it.'

'You're her mum. She needs you. So does Attis . . .'

Selene ignored her words. She stood up, her dress smoothing perfectly into place. 'Right, I must get back downstairs, I have a cauldron on the boil. I'm batch cooking – trying to get all my client orders done before I go away.' She moved towards the door. 'Demand is high during the holidays. 'Tis the season of heartbreak and hedonism.'

'I'm pretty sure that's not what the Bible said.'

'Well, you have to read between the lines a little.'

'Ho! Ho! Let's go!' Attis whooped, sporting a large Santa's hat. Effie was sitting in the front beside him while Anna was among the bags in the back of the small Peugeot 206. They sped off towards Rowan's house in Forest Hill, but before long were stuck in the traffic of Londoners escaping London. Drizzle fragmented the reflections of street lights and headlights in the windows, the wipers beating back and forth. Attis sang along cheerfully to Christmas songs blaring from the radio. Anna still didn't feel like celebrating but she'd decided to try and follow Selene's advice – to attempt to enjoy the holidays despite everything.

Effie, whose feet were on the dashboard, kicked at Attis. 'You're not remotely in tune.'

'Subjective,' he replied. 'To my ears, I sound marvellous.'

Anna thought of Selene singing loudly and off-key in the shower – apparently he'd inherited her singing voice too.

Effie turned back to Anna. 'He gets like this every year.'

Attis smiled his most boyish smile, catching Anna's eyes in the mirror.

'Remember that Christmas in Hong Kong when you grew an actual Father Christmas beard?' Effie snorted.

'I wanted to immerse myself in the Santa experience.'

'And remember when we had to stay with that posh twat Selene was seeing? The old guy who hated Christmas?'

'In California,' Attis recalled.

'Yes! And he refused to get a Christmas tree and I wanted one and then when he and Selene were out one night you came back with this huge tree.' Laughter burst between her words. 'And we put it in his bedroom and decorated it with expensive things from around his house.'

'Oh, yeah.'

'But then we got tipsy on leftover eggnog and—'

'I tipped it over into his bed . . .' Attis chuckled.

'When they came home he lost it. "THE PINE NEEDLES ARE EVERYWHERE! IS THAT MY CHANDELIER?" Selene couldn't keep a straight face either.'

They fell into laughter. Anna laughed along but was keenly aware she wasn't part of the memory.

Effie nudged Attis with her foot and gave him a more significant look. 'Remember New York?'

He glanced at her. 'I remember,' he said, then cleared his throat and turned to the wheel, concentrating on the road.

Anna pretended to look at her phone, trying not to think about what might have happened at Christmas in New York. Their lives had been entangled long before she'd arrived.

'I don't think I've ever actually spent Christmas in London,' Effie mused.

'Really?' Anna asked. She'd never spent Christmas anywhere else.

'Selene doesn't like being here for Christmas. We go away, she gets drunk, distracts herself with men. We've never done the whole Christmas thing either, you know – stockings, turkey, carols around the fucking piano. Is that what normal families do?'

Anna didn't reply. She didn't know what normal families did. Christmas Day had always been dictated by Aunt's mood – their measured and repetitive festivities sometimes enjoyable and other years . . . other years were better not remembered.

'Well, this is underwhelming,' said Effie.

They'd just pulled into Bertie's driveway and Anna could see what Effie meant. Rowan's house emerged out of the rain-swept night. There was a string of colourful lights bordering the wrap-around porch, a wreath on the front door and . . . nothing else. Anna hadn't expected it to look so *normal*.

They clambered out. The garden, at least, was wild as ever – the meandering stone pathway surrounded by bushy greenery, trailing trees and weeds growing up through the cracks. Attis rang the doorbell, bottles of wine under his arm, breath swirling in the air. It flew open with such exuberance that the wreath fell off. Bertie stood before them in a pair of antlers decorated with flashing lights and swinging baubles, which tangled with her mane of runaway black and grey hair. She had a large, steaming mug in her hand which spilt over as she threw her arms wide. 'CHICKENS! YOU'RE HERE AT LAST! CHRISTMAS CAN BEGIN! Merry Yule! Happy Solstice! Abundant tidings to the Green Goddess! May the Green Wheel Turn! Come in, come in,' she fussed. 'You look half frozen. I've got cake enough to feed an army of elves and mulled wassail by the barrel. I'm on my third – mug, that is, not barrel. Not yet, but the day is young!'

Attis laughed and met her open arms, lifting her up off the floor, Bertie releasing a raucous squawk. 'Is it just me or is Father Christmas more handsome this year?'

'You know you're on my naughty list, Bertie.'

Bertie hooted. 'Mother Holle! You've got to watch out with this one, haven't you?' She laughed at Effie and Anna, ushering them inside.

Anna was bundled into her own tight squeeze, which proved a precarious manoeuvre considering the antlers. When it was done Bertie took her hands. 'Anna, dear, I'm so glad you're here. You deserve a proper, magical Christmas with all trimmings and I have every trimming known to man, woman and the Green Goddess!'

'She's not lying.' Rowan smiled as she came down the hallway in a Christmas jumper bearing the words: MERRY WITCHMAS. 'She loses all control at Christmas.'

'And I have very little to begin with!' Bertie cackled. 'Come on!'

As they moved further into the house, Anna's mouth fell open. Inside, it was a festive jungle. Holly and ivy, laurel and evergreen firs covered everything – hanging from the ceiling, twirling down the bannister, weaving over the walls, along the surfaces, wrapping around picture frames and encircling the many red and green candles that burned with plump flames. Anna looked closer and could see that the plants weren't cuttings, but living, growing, breathing decorations, bursting with berries.

'I thought, this year, I might keep things a little more reserved on the outside.' Bertie's smile tightened momentarily. 'It gives me all the more reason to go bigger on the inside. We don't want another incident like a few years back when holly grew all over next door's house over-night.' They followed the beckoning scents of the kitchen down the corridor. 'Self-decorating decorations are much easier and Christmas isn't about holding back. The darkest days need the brightest lights! And the biggest of baubles!'

'Mum! Don't say big baubles!' Rowan shook her head.

'There is nothing wrong with the word baubles, Sorbus! Now, Attis, you better watch yourself. We've a horde of young cousins arriving and they'll be all over you like ivy up a trunk.'

'MUM. Don't say trunk either!'

'CAN I SAY ANYTHING IN MY OWN HOUSE?'

Anna walked through the kitchen doorway alongside Rowan and, inexplicably, they turned to each other and kissed on the lips. Rowan chuckled at the startled look on Anna's face and pointed upwards. A plume of mistletoe hung above them.

'Mum's kiss-me-quick mistletoe,' Rowan explained. 'Does it have to hang in such a busy doorway, Mum? I've kissed half the family this morning.'

'There's nothing wrong with sharing Christmas, love. Now who wants some wassail?'

The greenery ran through the kitchen too, lights sparkling over the purring Aga which was buried under sizzling pots and overflowing pans. The rest of the kitchen was already brimming with plates and bowls of delicious temptations, Anna's stomach rumbling at the scents of cloves and citrus, butter and marzipan, roasting nuts and bubbling apples. Bertie waved a hand and a row of mugs lined up above the wassail. 'It's got over thirty herbs and spices from the garden and more apples than an orchard.' She ladled it into the mugs. 'It won't run out either – self-refilling – although one year Uncle Archie did manage to beat magic itself and empty the pot, but I've made the spell more robust since then.'

'That sounds like a challenge,' Attis quipped.

'NOT a challenge.' Bertie eyed him. 'One cup each! I can't cope with drunk teenagers *and* mad family members. Help yourself to food too but watch the mince pies – packed so full they're known to explode.'

Attis cut off a small branch of what appeared to be an upright chocolate Yule tree cake. 'Can I marry you?'

Bertie laughed. 'An offer I expect most women can't refuse, but alas, here comes the love of my life—'

The back door clattered open.

'The light of my existence—'

Two barking, bounding dogs ran through, followed by two men.

'BILL! YOU'RE GETTING MUD EVERYWHERE – BACK OUT! OUT! CLEAN THE DOGS!'

The men grabbed at the dogs and retreated. Bertie clapped and the mud from the floor swirled up into the air and into one of the witch balls hanging from the window. The men and dogs bundled back through. The large black dog dropped in front of the Aga and the small one barked viciously at their feet. 'Don't mind Yapper, lost her teeth years ago.' Bertie pulled the youngest of the men into a hug. Anna recognized him from family photos as Rowan's brother. He was tall and gangly with sleepy eyes weighted down by the same bristle-brush eyebrows as Rowan. His dark hair sprouted thick and curly from his head. 'This is my biggest baby,' said Bertie. 'Rumex.'

'I'm legitimately and legally too old to be called a baby, Mum,' Rumex replied, suffering a kiss on the cheek.

'Say hi to Rowan's friends.'

'Hi Rowan's friends.' He waved, looking at them with the studied disinterest of an older brother.

'Rumex thinks he's too good for my friends these days.' Rowan poked at him. 'He's at *university* now and only socializes with *university* people.'

'I'm just surprised you *have* so many friends.' He swatted back at her. There was an undertone of teasing that suggested they were well practised at such exchanges.

'Rumex is studying horticulture at Greenwich College,' Bertie announced proudly. 'He came top in his chemical analysis and plant physiology modules. So clever. How did you get to be so clever? Not that I can understand half of what these cowans are teaching you about gardening, they seem to make it all very complicated. You can learn a lot more by having a good chat with the plants.'

'Knowledge can enrich magic, Mum.'

'So long as you remember magic goes places knowledge can't reach.' Bertie spun towards the door. 'Mr Greenfinch, don't sneak off!'

Rowan's dad was halfway out the room, cookie in hand.

'Come and say hello. He doesn't like crowds.'

Mr Greenfinch sidled back into the room with a sheepish look on his face. He didn't look like the rest of his family. He was a slight man with grey hair and a gentle expression set with lucent, blue eyes and wrinkles that seemed to have been formed in all weathers. His clothes were crumpled and his hands were muddy from the garden.

'It's your favourite time of year, isn't it, Dad?' Rowan smiled.

'It is my duty to survive it,' he replied with a congenial sigh. 'Hi there, everyone.' He nodded bashfully. 'I'm Bill.'

'A man of few words,' said Bertie.

'You learn to be in a household like this one, never get a word in edgeways . . .' He pinched another cookie, Bertie batting at his hand.

Rowan's younger sisters ran in, brandishing wooden wands with glowing stars on top.

'MUM! GERANIUM IS WEARING SPARKLES BUT I WAS WEARING THEM FIRST!'

'I WORE SPARKLES YESTERDAY!'

'Geranium! Gardenia! You can both wear sparkles!' said Bertie.

'BUT IF SHE WEARS SPARKLES NO ONE WILL BE LOOKING AT MY SPARKLES!'

'Bibbity,' Effie snarled, grabbing Geranium's star wand. 'Bobbity.' She aimed it at the twins. 'BOO!' They screamed and ran out of the kitchen. Effie turned to the rest of them with a smile. 'I'm good with kids.'

Bertie narrowed her eyes at the mug in Effie's hand. 'Effie, is that your second cup of wassail?' But before she could finish her inquisition, she put a hand up, nose sniffing. 'Ah! The gingerbread poppets are ready!' She grabbed a tea towel with one hand and opened the Aga door with the other. 'And Bill, don't try and sneak off again! Entertain the guests!' Geranium and Gardenia ran back through, knocking a plate of muffins onto the floor, which Yapper started snaffling. 'NO! Yapper! No!'

The kitchen descended into chaos that didn't lift for the next hour – a whirlwind of noise and chatter and wassail and eating far too much food. Anna was glad she'd come.

Afterwards, they retreated to Rowan's bedroom. Manda, who'd arrived late, joined them, while Attis remained downstairs chatting with Bill and Rumex. Rowan's four-poster bed was draped in the same festive greenery growing all over the house. Rowan swatted at some holly that had begun to creep onto her pillow. 'It keeps doing that. Makes for a very prickly night's sleep. I'm so glad you're all here. It's going to be the best Christmas ever.'

'It already is,' said Anna, drinking in the cosiness of Rowan's room – the furniture decked with family photos and plants, fairy lights in the fireplace, a desk cluttered with books and papers, pictures and posters of bands and boys on the walls. A lava lamp on Rowan's bedside table rotated red and green colours over the whole scene.

'I'm so glad you could come, Manda.' Rowan grinned. 'You sure you didn't drug your parents for the entire holiday season?'

'No,' Manda replied sharply. 'Like I said, they decided to go and visit my sister and I begged them to let me come here, told them I couldn't spare the time going away with applications. Anyway, my mum rang your mum and it was all sorted.'

Effie opened up a small music box on Rowan's mantlepiece. Instead of a ballerina, a miniature plant began to grow up from its centre along to the music. 'I thought your mum wasn't letting you out of your sight right now.'

'I thought so too but apparently they can't stand the sight of me any more,' Manda replied bitterly.

'I'm sure they'll miss you,' said Anna, but Manda turned from her words, looking as if she'd rather not have heard them. She sat down on the bed and pulled at the blanket tassels.

Effie picked up a family picture. 'Your brother's kind of hot, in that university, weed-smoking, just-rolled-out-of-bed kind of way.'

'No.' Rowan shook her head emphatically. 'No, Effie, brothers are off limits. Especially to you.'

'I'll take that as a compliment.'

'Haven't you got enough to occupy yourself with Azrael?'

Effie put the picture down. 'We've been keeping busy.'

Anna was well aware. Azrael had been coming and going to their house and spending a lot of time in Effie's bedroom. He was a fourth awkward party in their already awkward living arrangement.

'Do you not find him unsettling?' Rowan asked.

'Yes. That's why I'm into him. He's intense.'

'Intense,' Anna repeated. 'I offered him toast for breakfast the other day but he said it wasn't part of his purification diet. That he was only drinking water mixed with ash for the next three days.'

Effie sniggered. 'He's very dedicated to the Hel witch path. He's carrying out a week of silence too. It's for his next stage of Initiation. Possession, I think—'

Manda sat up. 'Possession. Their second stage of initiation. It's way more advanced than the possession you saw me do. He'll be able to channel spirits, help cast spells while possessed, with the help of Senior Hel witches of course, for they are the only ones who can command spirits and speak the Language of the Dead.'

They all stopped to stare at her.

'What?' Manda shrugged, her hands pulling at the tassels. 'I've been doing some research.'

'Should we be worried, Manda?' Rowan poked a toe at her. 'Are you leaving us for the dark side? You'd have thought that after undergoing possession by a spirit, you might have been put off.'

'That was one of the most freeing moments of my life.' Manda's mouth hardened, her chin dimple resolute. 'I have seen behind the Fabric. I know the truth now, of life, and death.'

'Goddess, you're starting to sound like Azrael.' Effie rolled her eyes. 'Maybe you two should hook up instead.'

'Well, actually.' Manda spoke quietly. 'I think Karim and I might have something going again . . .'

'What?' Rowan dove to the front of her bed. 'WHAT? How?'

'Thanks,' Manda retorted.

'I think what Rowan means to say is,' said Effie, 'how did you get past the restraining order?'

Anna couldn't contain her laugh. Manda tried to keep a straight face, raising her nose. 'He and his girlfriend broke up and we've started messaging again.'

'For how long?' Rowan grilled.

'Not long, the last week . . .'

'You kept this gossip from me *for a week*!'

'I don't want to make it into a big deal until I see where it's going. I think we might meet up after Christmas.'

Effie stretched herself out on the floor. 'A bit of Christmas nookie, hey? I'd recommend it.'

Rowan sighed loudly. 'Please let me live through you vicariously. What's Azrael like in bed?'

Effie lifted her head onto her hand, a smile trailing across her lips. 'He's very into pleasuring me. Takes it *very* seriously, and it's great, except when he stares into my eyes and talks about how we're going to be together in life – and death.'

Rowan managed to laugh and shudder at the same time. 'So, I've not managed to get a boy to take me on a date and you've got one willing to bind his soul to you for eternity. How is life fair?'

Manda giggled, putting a hand over her mouth. 'Is he the best you've ever had?'

'No,' Effie replied without pause.

'Who then—' Manda stopped when she realized what the answer might be.

'Attis,' Effie replied anyway.

Manda stuttered. 'Oh, yeah I—'

'What?' Effie shrugged. 'It's no big deal. We're not a thing any more. For obvious reasons.'

Anna pretended to study the flower press prints on the wall, trying to force unwanted images of Attis and Effie from her mind.

The door opened and Attis stepped inside with a plate of biscuits. 'Cookie, anyone?'

Anna groaned internally.

Rowan spoke quickly over the awkwardness. 'Come in, Attis, before my mum can pile you up with any more treats. We were just discussing Manda and Karim potentially getting back together.'

'What?' Attis's mouth dropped. 'And here was me hoping I'd be the next recipient of your love letter series.'

They gathered together on Rowan's floor, nibbling at the biscuits in the centre. After a few quiet moments of munching, Rowan spoke up. 'So . . . are we going to talk about school?'

Everyone's eyes shifted to Anna and away again.

'Mum's scared about it all, I can tell,' Rowan continued. 'The episode of stress-induced hysteria . . .'

Anna breathed out with friction. 'It wasn't stress-induced hysteria.'

'I'm not saying it was, but that's the official line. It's not what Darcey's posting all over her channels or what most of the rumours are saying either.'

'What's the latest?' Anna muttered. She hadn't been able to bring herself to check the full fallout of everything.

'As hysterical as you'd expect from St Olave's students, not helped by the fact Darcey's acting all vindicated, claiming it as proof of witchcraft. It's all circulating – that the pupils were attacked by a dark spell. Mind control. Demonic possession. That we cast it, obviously. Everyone's saying the school's trying to cover it all up, that it could strike again, that no one is safe, that—'

'I'm still not convinced it isn't just attention-seeking,' said Effie bluntly. 'Darcey's been filling everyone's heads all term and now these unknown Year Sevens are going to return to school just as famous as her. They probably just put it on for show.'

'No,' Anna responded sharply. 'They weren't in their right minds. I felt magic . . .'

'You were in shock though,' said Manda. 'Maybe you're not remembering it clearly.'

'I am remembering!' Anna's words burst from her, but Manda's insinuation made her doubt herself. She'd heard the screams first, what if they'd set her on edge? What if her own fear had coloured everything? Made her feel something that wasn't there? She turned away. 'What if I was the one who snapped?' The lava lamp had turned black, bubbling fiercely.

'It wasn't you,' Rowan insisted. 'You said it wasn't like the other times you experienced a hyper-magical episode, and you weren't even there, you were several rooms away. And, we do have the other events to consider. This isn't the only case we have of people losing control at a site of magical suspicion . . . the construction site, the joggers in Epping, the people working in that office . . . and now our school . . . they can't all be putting it on.'

Manda leant in. 'Maybe it *is* genuine hysteria then. These are all places where people are already spooked. People do weird things when they're scared. Like, when I was younger I had to open and close all the drawers in my room and my wardrobe five times before I could go to sleep.'

'Sounds exhausting,' said Effie.

'Try living in my head for a day.'

'Mass hysteria,' Attis murmured. 'Collective delusion – group psychosis brought about under conditions of anxiety.'

Rowan nodded. 'I learnt about that in psychology last year. There' ve been episodes of mass hysteria throughout history. There was once a convent of nuns who couldn't stop screaming and a whole medieval town that couldn't stop dancing – they called it the dancing plague. Darcey's claims have put everyone on edge all term and even if most people don't believe any of it, there's still a part of their minds that might have been taking it all in. Perhaps they just – snapped.'

'Cowans *are* like sheep.' Effie spoke with authority. 'Set one off and the rest will follow.'

It had been a kind of hysteria, and yet, Anna was sure she'd felt magic, had seen it in *their eyes*. 'Whatever it is, it's drawn the attention of the WIPS on us.'

'It was just one comment from Hopkins,' said Effie.

'One comment with thousands of comments in response,' Rowan countered.

'Yeah, from crackpots.'

'But crackpots bang the loudest pots.'

Effie made a face. 'What?'

'Attract the most attention. Hopkins's online followers are calling themselves the anti-mals – it stands for anti-malefice. They're starting to piece together these different hysteria incidents too, questioning what's going on, sharing videos, "evidence". The WIPS have launched an official investigation into those offices in White City, which is drawing more scrutiny there, and apparently other people who work there have now come out against the woman originally accused of witchcraft. *And* there've been charged stories about a patient who has accused a doctor at a central London family planning clinic of using questionable herbs and "magical substances" to help terminate pregnancies.' Rowan put her biscuit down as if she could no longer face it. 'I don't know if there's truth in any of these stories but I've just never seen so much open discussion of magic . . . malefice before.'

'Male-fuck them,' Effie growled.

'I'm not sure that's going to stop the problem.'

Effie shrugged but Anna could see she was agitated, that denial and anger were her ways of dealing with it, that she hated the idea of the magical world being contained more than anyone. Attis's brow was heavy too, his eyes moving back and forth, as if he were trying to pin down the solutions that evaded him.

'We can't let this – all of this that's going on – ruin our lives, OK?' Manda spoke up, her voice strained, as if it were trying to keep itself together too. 'I haven't worked this hard for seven years for it to all be destroyed by hysteria!'

'Ironic, seeing as you seem to spend your life hysterical over school work.' Effie snorted.

Manda pulled a withering face at her. 'Are you really not going to do any applications?'

Effie shrugged. 'Once I don't *have* to be in an educational institution, I don't intend to choose to be in one. Attis and I had always planned on going travelling after school, discovering the magical world – New Orleans for All Hallows, party with the brujas in Mexico, stumble on some shamanic rituals in Siberia. Who knows.'

Anna looked down, wondering if it was still their plan. If they broke the curse, would Effie and Attis up and leave her behind again?

'Well, I want to go to university,' Rowan declared. 'It's going to be my time to shine. Redefine myself. No longer Rowan the oddball – but Rowan the party animal, Rowan the player, Rowan the . . . OK, I'm still working on the branding. I just have no idea what to do with my subjects. Rumex is studying horticulture, so I was thinking something like that, maybe botany or agricultural studies? Surround myself with farmers. I bet it's, like, four men to every woman, and those are odds I could work with . . .'

Manda shook her head at Rowan. 'Anna, have *you* at least filled out an application?'

Anna nodded. She hadn't. She intended to.

'Still going for medicine?'

'Yep.' Anna nodded again, Effie catching her eye as if she sensed Anna's reticence.

'You people,' Effie tutted. 'Working so hard just so you can work even harder. It's like you've forgotten we're magic.' She snatched the last biscuit. 'I have a solution to our problems.'

'What?' said Manda.

'Drink more wassail.'

Rowan laughed. 'Works for a lot of my family members. I'll go swipe some. They're all playing chimera charades downstairs – they'll be distracted.'

They spent the rest of the evening drinking wassail and camping out in Rowan's room, until they dragged the mattress and pillows onto the floor and fell asleep together. Anna shared a pillow with Effie, Effie's head falling against her shoulder.

'How are you finding our first Christmas together?' Effie whispered.

'All good so far. Maybe we should try it again next year.'

They smiled at each other in the dark.

ROOTS

If daisies grow above the grave,
The soul be merrily on its way.
If nettles thrive and shake and rattle,
The soul has found itself in battle.
If snowdrops rise, with them we weep,
For the soul has sunk too deep.

'Ravenstone' Nursery Rhyme, Source Unknown

At Rowan's, it was easy to forget the rest of the world existed. By Christmas Eve, or what everyone kept referring to as Mother's Eve, the house had reached new levels of mayhem. People had been pouring through the door all day and showed no signs of stopping. Anna wondered how the place could fit everyone in, but, like one of Bertie's all-encompassing hugs, it seemed to expand to accommodate.

Anna bumped Rowan's shoulder. 'How many people are in your family again?'

'Who knows.' Rowan shrugged. 'I lose track. We call family friends aunts and uncles too so it's all a bit of a blur. Doesn't help that all the Wort Cunnings look as unhinged as one another . . .'

The people surrounding them were certainly unique. Between them they seemed to be wearing about as much foliage as the house – there were holly and mistletoe crowns, pine-cone necklaces, capes trailing ivy or trimmed with pine fur; one man had berries dripping from his beard and Anna spotted a woman with lit candles perched atop her green headdress. Anna noticed they all had green brooches pinned to their chests too – each sprouting a little flower or plant.

'They go all out for Mother's Eve.' Rowan nodded as if this were her life and she'd long ago accepted it. 'May as well put a poinsettia on my head and be done with it.'

Anna laughed. 'Why do you call it Mother's Eve?'

'In honour to the Great Mother Goddess and also the fact that mothers do all the bloody work at Christmas.'

At her words, Bertie sailed back into the room like a many-armed Goddess balancing trays of food while welcoming new arrivals, wiping Gardenia's face and checking the latest cake. The dogs ran underfoot. As per Bertie's predictions, a flock of cousins chased Attis about, strategically planning their entrances and exits so he'd be forced to kiss them beneath the mistletoe. While, much to Effie's displeasure, Geranium and Gardenia trailed her everywhere, having decided that as much as she scared them, they wanted to be her.

The day flowed onwards, buoyed up by a river of wassail, Anna weaving from room to room, meeting more people than she'd ever met in her life. Everyone was cheerfully busy – preparing food, wrapping gifts, weaving wreaths, stringing bay leaf garlands, while singing a medley of carols she'd never heard before. She soon knew all the words to 'The Twelve Worts of Christmas' . . .

Twelve fir trees dancing!
Eleven birch trees swaying!
Ten oaks a-creaking!
Nine pine cones dropping!
Eight cloves a-popping!
Seven nutmegs roasting!
Six rosemary sprigs!
Five ivy leaves!
Four cinnamon sticks!
Three mistletoes!
Two holly boughs!
And a Yule log from an ash tree!

In the living room, the fire roared and a colossal Christmas tree grew out of the ground itself. *We move it inside from the garden*, Rowan explained – Anna accepting that the explanation made little sense. It was decorated with witch balls filled with twinkling starlight and snowfall. Fairy lights flew around it and a shining pentacle sat atop it. Great-Grandfather Basil dozed by the tree in a rocking chair – *that chair will rock you to sleep whether you like it or not* – while a gaggle of kids sat on the floor practising their magic with paper-chain making and chasing flying candy broomsticks around the place.

After lunch, Rowan gathered the members of the coven together and chivvied them into the garden.

'Why are we going outside?' Effie flicked a wind chime hanging from the porch. 'It's cold out here – it's warm in there, with food and drink and sofas we can nap on . . .'

'Because,' said Bertie, standing stoutly before them in wellies wrapped in tinsel. 'It's a Christmas tradition. On Mother's Eve we all work in the garden and sow seeds for the coming year.'

'Why?' Effie remained unimpressed. 'It's winter, everything's dead.'

'Dead!' Bertie wielded a towel animatedly. 'It's never been more alive! Life has simply gone beneath the soils. Just because we can't see it, doesn't mean it isn't there. You ought to have a word with my husband. His entire magical specialism is soil – how to nourish and care for it, for there is nothing more alive on this earth than soil. The roots are feeding on it as we speak – burrowing, searching, preparing.'

'To be fair,' said Anna. 'Your garden doesn't look particularly dead.'

Winter did not appear to have dampened Bertie's garden. If anything, it was more beautiful than ever, still thick with foliage, the colours soft and deep as a winter's sunset – long grasses, burnt-colour stalks, vivid flowers and bright volts of berry. Above, the evergreens murmured dark green songs while bare branches wore gauzy veils of winter light.

'A good gardener knows how to work with the seasons, not against them. A touch of magic never hurts either.' Bertie winked.

'Frost and snow, probably even a hurricane, couldn't stop Mum's garden from thriving,' Rowan added with pride.

'But, my chickens, it all begins with this.' Bertie held a tiny seed up between her fingers. 'My garden, my plants, everything we create from it, starts here: a seed. An intention. The first word of a spell. In winter, we must sow seeds not only with our hands but with our hearts, because everything that we plant now will grow forth from the darkness into the light. Am I boring you, Effie?'

Effie had begun to kick a stone over. 'Nope. I'm with you, seeds are great.'

Bertie narrowed her eyes. 'Did you know that witches used to hide spells inside of seeds?'

Effie looked up. 'Really? What kind?'

'Powerful ones.' Bertie's voice rose to the wind around them. 'Spells to send a whole city to sleep, or to cast storms as big as a continent, or deadly, torturous hexes too terrible to utter. You might want to think about that when you plant this.' She handed Effie the seed in her fingers.

Effie looked down at it. 'What is it?'

'A hydrangea, my dear.'

Effie made a withering face. 'Very funny.'

Bertie chortled. 'Actually.' She rocked on her wellies. 'There is a little magical game we can play, if you wish. A Mother's Eve special.'

Effie perked up again at the sound of game and magic in the same sentence. 'What?'

Bertie went over to the windowsill. The wind chimes above her had started to play what sounded distinctly like 'The Twelve Worts of Christmas'. Bertie chuckled indulgently. 'Bill's little hobby – making wind chimes.' As she came back over, she now held a basket in her hands. It appeared to be full of seeds of all shapes and sizes, from bulbs through to seeds hardly bigger than a grain of sand. 'It's even deeper than it looks. Now, it's said if you ask the Green Goddess a question on Mother's Eve, she will answer in the way she does best. Ask your question, pick your seed and whatever plant grows will be her way of replying.'

Effie's excitement deflated. 'So we have to wait for a plant to grow?'

'Goddess forbid Effie should have to wait for anything. But no, you won't have to wait.' Bertie tapped her nose. ''Tis the magic of Mother's Eve.'

'It's basically seed lucky dip,' Rowan beamed. 'We normally ask it what's going to happen in the year ahead. Remember that year it gave me poison ivy and we wondered why the spell would give me a plant that causes a painful, itchy rash?'

'Then in January you caught the chicken pox and couldn't stop scratching for weeks,' Bertie chortled. 'Oh, I remember.' She looked to the others. 'Sometimes the Green Goddess takes the request *rather* literally and other times she can be infuriatingly cryptic. Anyway.' She held the basket out. 'Fancy a go? Or a sow, I should say.' She chuckled at her own joke, the way Rowan often did.

'I have an idea.' Effie looked at the others. 'Why don't we ask what our languages are? It might give us something to go off. I'd take even a hint at this stage.' Her voice roughened with pent-up frustration.

'Ooo, yes!' Rowan clapped. 'I'd never thought of doing that.'

'I'm in,' said Manda.

'Me too,' Anna agreed, figuring it couldn't hurt.

Attis took a step back. 'Seeing as I know mine already, I'll leave you guys to it.'

The others, Anna included, peered over the basket and spoke in attempted unison: 'What are our magical languages?'

Then they dipped their hands in. Anna's disappeared deep into the basket – she got the feeling that it might not have a bottom. There were thousands of seeds and she had no idea why she picked the one she did, but when she pulled it out, her hand was cradling a small white bulb.

'Chop, chop,' said Bertie, putting down the basket and leading them deeper into the garden. 'Let's get digging.'

The soil was soft beneath their wellies and their breath softer in the cold air. The garden felt different to when Anna had last seen it, as if it had rearranged itself – the wild, flowery patches moved around, new paths and archways had sprouted up, the stream twisted a different, glittering path through it all. Everything moving and stirring and growing – Wort Cunnings dotted among it all, working fervently as Christmas elves.

'Are they sowing seeds too?' Anna asked.

'Some,' Bertie replied. 'Some have simply come to sit with my plants, for their greatest power is in this form, when they're alive and growing.'

'Living spells are Mum's forte,' Rowan explained. 'She's the best of all of the Wort Cunnings.'

Bertie waved a modest hand.

'People just . . . sit with them?' Effie looked unconvinced.

'Well, I'd advise it over sitting on them.'

Effie rolled her eyes while Attis stepped alongside Bertie. 'Surely the plants need to be ingested or absorbed in some way for their healing properties to be transferred?'

'Oh, there's much to absorb in being with a plant. Take Uncle Alfalfa here.' Bertie pointed to a man lolling in a chair.

'He's asleep,' Manda stated.

'Exactly!' Bertie responded. 'Alfalfa suffers from insomnia, but a nap with my lavender will sort him out for months. There's nothing more peaceful than my Lavandula Somnum, my sweet dreamer, elf's pillow. It likes to be sown in soft, chalky ground and I feed it on my own dreams in summer. It loves being sung a lullaby at sunset too.'

Attis raised a quizzical eyebrow. 'Plants like to be sung to?'

'Well, not all of them. Some prefer music played to them. My lemon balm devours Bach, while my bergenias love Bowie, but my Eyevain here likes its peace.'

Bertie nodded to a sprouting of tall, nimble stalks with clustered purple-black flowers on their ends. 'Don't be deceived by its delicacy though, it's one of the toughest plants in my arsenal.'

Another Wort Cunning was sitting beside the Eyevain. Bertie nodded at her supportively.

'Auntie Juniper here is going through a tough time at work. A nasty colleague who's repeatedly undermined her. I suggested she spend some time with my eyevain, Faen, eye of the Goddess—' Bertie spoke the plant's names like a litany of devotion. 'It's an ancient variety of vervain, one of the sacred herbs of the Goddess. Highly protective.' She brushed her hand through the flowers and they closed up into tight buds. 'It'll charge up her inner defences, give her the strength to take action. Best planted in silence beneath a waning moon, ideally with your eyes closed if you can manage it.'

Bertie moved them on. 'You see? Plants are generous with their wisdom and feeling. My grandpapa used to say they wear their hearts on their leaves, but it goes deeper than that, right down into the roots.'

Attis shook his head.

'Am I confusing you?'

'Always, but mainly impressing me. How do you learn all of this, Bertie? All the plant names, the different varieties, growing method-ologies, what all their favourite pop hits are . . .'

Bertie chuckled. 'I don't. It would be impossible to learn it all. The real magic is in paying attention, listening to the plant's story and letting it hear yours. The tale told is different every time. It's why plants must have so many names, so there's room for them to move and grow and play.'

'But how can you communicate your knowledge, if everyone's version is different?'

'Your questions are trying to cut paths through smoke. When you're in your forge, how do you speak with your fire?'

Attis closed his mouth, considering her words.

'You see. That you cannot explain. You speak its language and it speaks yours and therein lies the magic. At some point you have to let go and simply feel.'

Attis's smile widened. 'How do you make sense while making no sense at all?'

'It's a woman's skill.'

'I need to work on my woman skills.'

Rowan snorted. 'A line Attis Lockerby has never said.'

Bertie stopped at a clear patch of soil towards the back of the garden near the whisper of the river. 'This'll do nicely.'

After some instruction, Anna was soon on her knees, digging a trowel into the earth. It was cold and hard and didn't look particularly inviting for the little bulb in her hand. She dropped it into the darkness of the soil and covered it over. *Buried.* Her mind wandered to her conversation with Selene about her mother's language. It hadn't been the truth, not all of it. *But why?* Why not tell them what their mother's language had been? What was so wrong with it? Had Aunt's been the same? Had it been part of the reason she'd joined the Binders? To repress it? Or had the curse consumed their language from the start?

Suddenly, Anna wasn't sure she wanted to see what would grow up from the ground.

Manda gasped. 'Mine is coming!'

A little green leaf had sprouted from the section of ground where Manda had planted her seed. Several further leaves erupted, unfolding like tongues, then a spray of shoots followed by a final flourish of purple flowers that Anna didn't recognize.

Manda looked to Bertie eagerly. 'What is it? What is it?'

Bertie's head tipped to the side, her brow lifting with faint surprise. 'Why, it's mandragora . . . mandrake, devil's apple, alraune . . .'

'Mandrake! Devil's apple!' Manda exclaimed. 'Isn't that the plant with the root that looks like a human?'

Bertie nodded thoughtfully.

'What does that mean?'

'Hard to say. The mandrake is an extremely magical plant with a hundred different uses.'

Rowan cupped one of the flowers. 'Wasn't it one of the first anaesthetics? Maybe you'll be a healer? But then ingesting too much is fatal . . . it was also used as a poison . . .'

Manda did not look comforted by her words.

'Its roots were often carried around or kept as a charm for love magic, fertility and wish fulfilment,' Bertie muttered.

'Aren't they meant to scream hysterically when you pull them from the ground?' Effie commented. 'Just like you every time I try to push you out of your comfort zone, Manda.'

'Thanks, Effie.' Manda glared.

Bertie gave her a kind smile. 'I wouldn't overthink it, love. I suggest you all spend time sitting with your plant and seeing what it has to say to *you*, and you alone.'

'Hey.' Effie's voice spun them all around.

Two green shoots had sprouted from the earth: Anna and Effie's patches. They grew quickly up into long, thin and delicate stems and then . . . they flowered. Anna knew it instantly.

A snowdrop.

Two snowdrops.

'They're the same.' Effie stated the obvious. 'We've chosen the same seed.'

If Bertie had looked taken aback by Manda's plant, she appeared even more surprised now. 'Well, leaping lilies, that's never happened before.'

Anna and Effie turned to each other. The invisible threads of their magic tug-tugging again, tying them together even as it tore them apart.

'Guess it's confirmation we share the same language,' Effie surmised.

'I would make few presumptions when it comes to the Goddess,' Bertie responded frankly.

'What does it mean?' Anna asked, finding herself not able to look away from the snowdrop. So small and defenceless and sad.

'Well.' Bertie looked uncomfortable. 'It's the flower of loss, of heartbreak and death. But so, too, comfort and hope – new beginnings.'

Death . . . the word shouted louder than all the others from such a quiet flower. Anna shivered and not from the cold air encircling her.

'What's that meant to mean for us?' Effie's exasperation was back. 'Our language? *Our* seed of power?'

'I know I may look it, but I am not a Goddess,' said Bertie, attempting to lighten the situation. 'I don't have the answers.'

Effie threw her hands up. 'Ugh! What is the point in this?'

She spun around, almost toppling into Rowan, who'd crouched down and was staring at her patch of earth.

'What's yours, Rowan?' Manda asked from the other side, not yet able to see what Anna could see – that no plant had grown from the ground.

It took Rowan a moment to realize they were all looking down at her. She raised her head, a forlorn dip between her eyebrows. Her eyes moved to her mum's. 'Nothing's coming, is it? It's never taken this long before.'

'Oh, Sorbus, baby, it's just a game. I wouldn't take this to heart.'

Rowan looked back down as if she were willing something, *anything* to grow. They waited uncomfortably until she stood up. She turned to them all with a smile. 'You're right, Mum! I managed to pick the one dud seed in the whole damn basket. Classic me.' She laughed. 'I think I'm going to go in and have another mince pie rather than stand out here staring at the ground like a crazy person.' She laughed again and walked backwards a few paces before turning around and heading quickly towards the back door.

Bertie gave them all a concerned look before going after her.

It wasn't long before Effie had given up and gone back inside too, Manda following. Anna and Attis ended up helping a group of nearby Wort Cunnings, who were pruning and mulching a section of the garden. Anna was glad for the fresh air and the hard work, letting it clear her mind of the questions going around it . . . *death . . . why the flower of death? Is death magic our language after all? Or is it simply the curse reminding us what's in store?*

Attis spun around holding his spade up behind his neck. 'Well, I'm officially an expert mulcher.'

Anna laughed.

He narrowed his eyes. 'What?'

'You've got soil on your nose.'

He grinned. 'It's meant to be there. It's part of my new Wort Cunning look.'

'You're not pulling it off.'

'Well—' He reached out and wiped a line of soil down Anna's cheek.

'Really? That is not the act of an honourable Wort Cunning.'

'Good job I am a man of no honour.'

Anna flicked her hand, sending his spade flying from his. His eyes widened with mock incredulity. 'And you are a woman of low cunning!'

'Still a better Wort Cunning than you.'

He laughed. 'Harsh but fair.' He wiped the soil off his nose with the back of his hand. 'Better?'

Anna assessed his face, distracted by how his eyes were as grey as the sky above, but brighter – brighter. 'Better.'

'Good,' he said, brushing his hair back and smearing fresh lines of soil across his forehead on purpose.

Anna shook her head, trying to control the smile on her face as she turned back to her work. It felt easier being around him out here in the open air, focused on their respective tasks, where she could joke and talk with him without having to look at each other, with room to escape if need be, their breath occasionally meeting but nothing more.

When Bertie returned later, she hooted. 'By the Green Goddess and her fruitful loins, what have you two been doing? You've bloomed my winter roses.'

Anna looked at the bush of white roses beside them and felt her cheeks flush. It did look suddenly abundant. 'Just . . . mulching,' she said hurriedly.

'Well, you've both obviously got the Wort Cunning knack.'

Attis saluted her. 'The knack but not the honour.'

'That I'm aware of. Now, if you want to ask Bill some questions about soil management – he's free.'

'Really?'

'Go on, I know you're desperate to talk chemical compositions.'

Attis moved away, shouting back at them. 'I'll be sure to rap to the bergenias on the way!'

Bertie snorted. 'He's trouble, that one. You should come in, chicken, you look freezing.'

'Is Rowan OK?' Anna asked.

'Oh, she's fine. She knows how fickle the plants can be sometimes.'

Anna nodded. Bertie took her elbow and they wandered back through the garden, Bertie pointing out some of her other magical plants until they passed the patch where they'd planted their seeds. Anna stopped next to her snowdrop, its white bell-shaped head still hanging down to the ground from which it had come, as if it knew no other way to look, as if it hadn't realized yet the sky existed. It rang with a silence that seemed deafening.

'It's so . . . still,' Anna whispered. 'Everything else in your garden is in motion but it's so still. Why is it so still?'

'The snowdrop, Hel's Bells, Holle's tears,' Bertie replied solemnly. 'There are many suspicions surrounding the snowdrop. That if you bring it inside there will be a death in the family. If you hear its bell ringing in the wind, the dead are nearby. That it has the deepest roots of all the winter flowers – so deep they reach Hel itself and take its colour from its snows.'

The snows of Hel. The snows of my dreams . . .

'But I believe the snowdrop is a flower of courage,' said Bertie softly. 'After all, it blooms in winter. Even with frozen roots it fights its way back to life. How does it feel to you?'

Anna stared at it. 'Like it's stuck. It can't go backwards, can't go forwards. It's had to grow still.'

'Perhaps it needs to be still, to grow its roots deep enough.'

'Deep enough for what?'

'To feel its grief.' The kind crispness in Bertie's voice had a way of bringing tears to Anna's eyes. 'Grief doesn't live on the surface – it can't or we wouldn't be able to function.'

'I don't feel grief, Bertie, I don't feel anything except afraid. Is there a plant for that? That will take away the fear? Can't you make me a tisane? Something to cure me. Something in this garden has to help. Please, Bertie. Please—' Anna's voice rose and she found herself clutching onto Bertie, everything coming up at once.

Bertie pulled her into a hug, rocking her side to side. 'Oh, my dear, you don't need curing. There is nothing wrong with you.'

'Then why – why – do I feel this way? How do I make it go away?'

Bertie sighed – a long, slow, heavy thing. 'That's the thing about feelings. You can't make them go away. Sometimes you have to just . . . be with them. Do you know, for many years I couldn't even look at a marigold flower?'

'Why not?'

'They were my brother's favourite. He died when I was a teenager, tore my whole family apart for a while, tore my heart up too.'

'I'm so sorry, Bertie.'

'I'd like to tell you the pain goes away over time, but it doesn't. Emotions don't work that way. They never lose strength, we just learn how to grow stronger around them. It's why I was able to face the marigolds again, and now—' She pointed to the bright yellow flower on her brooch.

'A marigold?'

Bertie nodded. 'This is my living brooch. As you might have spotted, when Wort Cunnings get together we all wear one – a way of sharing with each other the plant that speaks to each of us the most. Our seed.'

'Your marigolds are your spell of power?'

'Yes. My sunshine flower. Nobody can resist smiling in my marigold patch. I feed them with sun-charged water and share my happiness with them. If I'm ever down, I come out here and they share theirs with me.'

'I can't imagine you ever being down,' said Anna, without thinking.

Bertie lowered her head, chins tucking together. 'Believe me, chicken, I'm not happy all the time. That's not possible for anybody. I've given this garden all of my feelings over the years – blood, sweat and tears.'

Anna looked back down at the snowdrop. 'What about . . . fear? How do you grow stronger against it? Escape it?'

'Fear is one of the trickier emotions, I'll give you that.' Bertie's mouth closed briefly into a firm line of thought. 'It's like a frost that covers everything – freezing, burying.'

'So you have to dig your way out?'

'Or dig deeper. Fear has lessons to give. It's a map of our limitations, it shows us the places we must run towards, not from. After all, a seed must be buried to grow.'

Anna looked back at the snowdrop. 'All the way to Hel . . .'

'Perhaps not quite *that* deep,' said Bertie, the wrinkles around her eyes softening. 'Now come on, you're shaking. It's time for some herby hot chocolate by the fire. If you're lucky, I'll add some wassail to it.'

Anna managed a laugh and Bertie wrapped an arm around her, guiding her back down the garden path through the fading light.

CRACKERS

As part of their training, Initiates will enact a ritualistic descent into the Underworld, drinking of the 'Waters of the Dead', being separated and left in the bowels of the Necropolis Railway where they must find their way through the labyrinth of darkness and back to the light by moonset the next morning.

'Night of the Descent', Hel Witch Trainings,
Books of the Dead: Tome 8740

On Christmas Day, somehow, though Anna still hadn't worked out *how*, everyone gathered in the lounge. The fire roared a merry hymn, Christmas cocktails were passed around, stockings taken down from the grate. The tree had tucked itself into the bay window to make more space and giddy jubilation permeated every corner of the room. Except Great-Grandpa Basil, who was still snoring in the rocking chair.

'THE GIFT GIVING IS INTENSE!' yelled Rowan over the noise, as a plant and its dangling roots were passed over her head.

'Why are all the gifts plants?' Effie grimaced as the Wort Cunnings exchanged pots and bulbs and wicker baskets filled with cuttings.

'It's how the Wort Cunnings do Yule. Only the young get gifts, everyone else swaps plants and cuttings. It's their way of sharing their magic with each other.'

'A nice idea,' said Anna.

'Most of the time.' Rowan nodded. 'Though it occasionally gets political, like when Aunt Aloe bought Aunt Columbine a plant for success with love just after her divorce, or when three people gave Uncle Salix a variety of eucalyptus specifically for bad breath.'

'A shadow puppet!' cried Geranium, pulling a gift from her stocking.
'Storm marbles!' Gardenia squealed.

'It's easier with the kids,' said Rowan. 'The stockings decide which gifts they get.'

'What do you mean?' Manda looked entirely baffled by everything unfolding.

'All the gifts go into the stockings and then the stockings decide who gets what between them. Avoids arguments.'

The coven collected in a corner to exchange their own gifts. Rowan gave them all a PMS tisane made by a Moon Sower witch she knew. Manda gave them diaries for the coming year in which she'd helpfully highlighted all important school dates – which grew larger as the date approached. 'So you won't miss it,' Manda explained.

'Wow. It's as annoying as you,' said Effie.

'Hey, it's fun too! I put winking smiley faces next to birthdays. See—'

Effie had bought them jewellery from a recent trip to Camden Market. Anna opened hers, it was a small solid gold ring. 'How does it . . . work?'

Effie took it off her and moved the gold ring to her own nose. It slipped around the skin and sealed tight as if she had a piercing there. She pulled it off with no apparent pain and then did the same to various places on her ear. 'You can wear it anywhere. Get creative.'

Anna laughed. 'Well, now I can look as cool as you.'

'That was my general thinking.'

Anna's gifts weren't magical. She'd found a red beret for Rowan that she'd thought would suit her. A book of poetry from a vintage bookshop for Manda. For Effie, she'd sewn a small, circular embroidery with a black moon in its centre and *Bitches of the Dark Moon* written around the outside.

Effie eyed her. 'I thought you were over the whole sewing thing.'

'I am, but I sewed this in spite of my aunt. She'd have thought it crude.'

Effie smirked. 'I guess I'll have to put it up on my wall then.'

For Attis, Anna had found some dark chocolate truffles, which he looked delighted to receive.

'Your favourites, right?' she asked as he opened them up.

'Absolutely,' he replied, popping one in his mouth and offering her one. Anna shook her head and waited, but he didn't move to give her a gift in return. 'You sure?'

She shook her head again, curtly, and turned away, her stomach hollowing. Had he really not bought her anything? She hadn't spotted if he'd given any of the others gifts, but she couldn't imagine him not buying Effie anything. Anna thought of the year before, when he'd bought her the piano book that captured the musical notes of the song you were playing. It had been so magical, so wonderful . . . but that was when he'd been trying to seduce her. He obviously had no need of such gifts now.

After the gift giving, the focus moved to the preparation of the Christmas feast, Bertie overseeing all with the skill of a commander bringing a fleet of ships into shore.

'I don't know how she does it,' said Rowan as they scored brussels sprouts. 'You know like how cows have three stomachs? I think Mum might have three brains all whirring at once.'

'Three?' said Anna. 'I think you're limiting her.'

'I'd vote for the Wort Cunnings to run the country.' Attis threw a sprout over his shoulder and caught it with the other hand.

'Can you imagine?' Rowan snorted. 'They'd flatten all schools and replace them with gardens, force everyone to wear flower headdresses.'

'At all times!' Bertie declared.

Soon Anna was squeezed around the dining-room table, festive greenery winding through the dishes and plates and up the candlesticks, flames bouncing merrily from one candle to the next. Anna could hardly take in the feast before them – bowls of crackly potatoes, buttery vege-tables, sauces of every colour and herb, and a humongous nut roast candied with dates and berries nestled in the centre.

Bertie stood up. 'Before we begin our Yuletide feast, Bill will cut the roast!'

'But he didn't do any cooking!' a red-cheeked Wort Cunning heckled with a wink.

Bill nodded. 'Exactly. This is the only thing she trusts me to do.' He stood up looking a little cowed but his voice had a calm composure that drew everybody's attention. 'And it gives me the opportunity to say a few words—'

'Have you ever said more than a few words, Bill?' Uncle Aster, who was indeed clad only in ivy, jested.

'Quiet, Aster, or I'll confiscate your wassail.'

Aster put his hands up in surrender, shoulders jumping with laughter.

Bill continued. 'Firstly, I want to apologize for the jumper I'm wearing.

It was just bought for me and I have been forced to wear it on pain of death.'

The jumper in question bore the words: *You're my soil mate.*

'Suits you, Bill!'

'Secondly,' said Bill, quelling the rising noise. 'A huge thank you to my wife, Gilberta Greenfinch, not only for this appalling article of clothing, but for making everything more magical than magic itself. She outdoes herself every Yule, and beating Bertie is no easy task.'

'TO BERTIE!' everyone cheered.

'BERTIE FOR PRIME MINISTER!' Attis banged his hands on the table.

'And, finally, to the Green Goddess.' Bill raised a glass. 'On these shortest of days and these darkest of nights, we thank you for your abundance and light!'

Everyone raised their glasses. 'To the Green Goddess!'

Bill cut into the nut roast and a fresh round of 'The Twelve Worts of Christmas' kicked off. Bowls were passed around, food piled high on plates, glasses filled and filled again. Crackers were pulled, unleashing little spells of mischief around the room – setting people off into sneezing fits, or giggling fits, or forcing people to spout riddles and tongue twisters.

Anna picked up her cracker and turned to the red-cheeked Wort Cunning man beside her.

He cackled, 'Ah! What mischief does this one hold?'

They pulled it – it went off with a snap. Anna had won. She pulled out a paper flower crown which immediately began to grow real flowers . . . but she could hear something else inside . . . something rattling around. She tipped the cracker up and an object rolled out onto her hand.

A cotton reel wound with black thread. She glanced about the table – the other crackers hadn't given gifts.

She was about to ask the Wort Cunning man, who'd turned to talk to the person next to him, what it was, but then a piece of paper fell out of the cracker too. Wondering if it was a joke, she opened it up:

Q: What will follow you no matter how fast you run?
A gift for you and your coven, should you dare to use it . . .

It took Anna a moment and then she worked it out: *your shadow . . .*
She had no idea what the thread was, nor who had sent it. *Selene?*

Nana? The Wild Hunt? Someone else? She rolled the spool on her palm, thinking of Jerry Tinker's moonthread, but where one had shone, this one was black as midnight . . .

'What's that?' The Wort Cunning sitting on her other side peered over.

Anna slipped the thread into her pocket, sensing it wasn't something to be shared. 'Oh, nothing. So, what do you do?'

Anna soon regretted her question. The woman, an Aunt Winifred of Rowan's, proceeded to describe the intricate complexities of hedge keeping to her for the next half hour. *A hedge isn't just for Christmas, it's for life!*

Anna was glad when a flaming Christmas pudding was brought out, distracting everyone, Winifred included. Anna was served a slice – still burning.

'Do you eat it like this?' she asked Winifred.

'Well, it's polite to use a fork,' she replied tersely.

Anna smirked and, following everyone else at the table, took a bite. The flames didn't burn, only tickled, enriching the deep flavours of the spices. The warmth of the room radiated; scents of treacle and roasted nuts and coffee filled the air. Just as the post-meal lethargy was beginning to set in, someone pointed upwards.

'It's snowing!'

Anna looked up. It was true. Small flecks danced this way and that above them, the whole room falling silent. The snow fell over the table coating everything in sparkle. Bertie stood up with a sly smile. 'Go on! Out with you all so I can clear up!'

The bay doors blew open and the snow flew out into the garden in an animated swirl.

Rowan shook her head. 'She likes to plan a surprise every year. Or several.'

They spent the rest of the afternoon having snowball fights, not with each other – but with the snow, which turned out to have a life and mischievous will of its own.

Anna wanted the day never to end, but slowly evening soaked into the snow and collected against the windows. Everyone piled back into the lounge for the ritual burning of the Yule log, which seemed to involve lots of cheering, drinking wassail and chanting: 'May the Yule log keep burning! May the Green Wheel keep turning!'

'I have no idea what is going on,' said Manda. 'My family would usually be playing a fraught game of Scrabble now.'

Rowan laughed. 'The log is ash wood. It'll burn in the fireplace for twelve days and then we'll sprinkle its ashes around the house to bring us prosperity and protection for another year.'

A Wort Cunning band struck up, all fiddles and pipes, and dancing took over. Great-Grandfather Basil had finally risen from his chair and started doing a jig in the middle of the room to surrounding cheers. Rowan dragged them all into the fray.

Several hours later Anna's head was spinning in different directions as she made her way back to the kitchen in search of something quenching. Her hair had fallen loose and her cheeks were hot, laughter still in her throat. She rounded the corner as someone was coming the other way. She looked up to see Attis but it was already too late.

The mistletoe had them in its intractable grip.

Their eyes met in mutual panic as Anna's head tilted upwards and Attis's lowered and their lips collided.

It happened so fast and yet the kiss felt excruciatingly slow. *Too slow, too sweet.*

It released them but it did not leave Anna's lips, nor her body. With his face still close enough to kiss again, a hundred unbearable sensations rushed through her – her stomach falling away, heart galloping in her chest, her throat tightening, her nerve endings like sparks on a drum. The kiss sank deeper, thrumming through her like a wild call. Attis stared down at her, deep grey eyes full of complications.

The silence went on too long to put back.

He laughed. A short, stilted sound. 'It seems I keep getting caught in this doorway . . .'

As quickly as they had exploded, the feelings in Anna's body collapsed to a pinprick of acute embarrassment. He probably thought she'd planned the whole manoeuvre like one of Rowan's kid cousins. 'I was just getting a drink – I—' She ducked past him but they collided again.

Attis put his hands up and took a step to the side. 'You go first and I'll cut down the mistletoe.'

She tried to laugh but no sound came out. She hurried past him, hearing him go the other way. She turned the tap until the water ran cold, filled up a glass, drank it all, filled up another one and drank that too. She ran from the room through the other door and struggled her way through the crowd until she spotted Rowan. She grabbed her hand. 'I need to talk to you. Now. Please.'

Rowan froze mid-dance move. 'Of course. I'm coming.'

She followed Anna up the stairs to her room. Once inside, Anna shut the door behind her and banged her head on it several times.

'Anna!' Rowan cried. 'What's wrong? What's going on?'

Anna spun around. 'Attis and I kissed.'

Rowan's mouth fell open. 'What? When? How? Oh Goddess, I thought something like this might happen, this—'

'It was the mistletoe.'

The frazzled, fearful look disappeared from Rowan's face. 'Oh! The mistletoe! Well, that's OK, then. I mean, Attis has kissed about four hundred people under it over the last couple of days. Including me once. OK, twice. OK, THREE TIMES. But I didn't plan the last one.'

Rowan smiled but Anna remained distraught. She paced the room, the drumbeat still inside her. 'I'm aware the mistletoe is just a spell and doesn't mean anything. It obviously meant nothing to him—' She had to keep moving. 'But that's not the point. The point is . . . it's . . . your mum should really take the mistletoe down, you know! It's not fair, catching people out like that—'

'You're worrying me now,' said Rowan. 'You're talking more than me. Sit down.'

Rowan patted the bed and Anna joined her on it, still not able to stay still. The lava lamp spat red, frantic bubbles.

'What is it?'

Anna took a breath. 'It's just . . . it meant something to me. More than I realized, I think.' She stilled at the words, holding them away from her.

'Yeah,' said Rowan, as if it were obvious.

Anna looked at her. 'What do you mean – yeah?'

'Well, Anna, you're in love with him.'

Anna shook her head, steeled herself against it. 'I can't be.'

'Can't doesn't mean you aren't.'

'I'm seventeen!' She threw her hands up. 'I still don't know anything about life. I don't even know who I am. How can I be in—' She refused to say the word. 'It's a teenage crush, an infatuation.' She fell back on the bed and put her face into the pillow, releasing a scream.

'Was it a good kiss?'

'Not helpful,' Anna replied, her voice muffled.

'Sorry.'

Anna sat back up, breathing out and looking at Rowan. 'It was brief, but, it was . . . like that moment you cast a spell and the world comes alive.'

Rowan blew air out between her lips. 'I want a kiss like that.'

'I'm being a dramatic, ridiculous teenager—'

'You *are* a teenager and it's not ridiculous.' Rowan looked at her. 'Trying to avoid your feelings for him any longer would be ridiculous.'

Love who laughs at locksmiths. Well, it was laughing at her now and threatening to break down the door. Anna lay back on the bed, knowing she'd been trying to push how she felt about Attis away for so long. But the off-guard kiss had broken through her defences and brought it all back. An echo of another kiss. That fateful evening in Effie's bedroom – Attis's fingers unzipping her dress, their eyes meeting with slow inevitability, an urgency in their hands. In that moment, Anna had let go of everything she'd held onto. Years of pain and restraint and fear of love instilled by Aunt. She'd undone it all for him and afterwards had come everything Aunt had promised: betrayal, pain, punishment. Not a kiss but a curse.

'Love killed my parents,' Anna whispered. 'It sent my aunt mad. Love and magic. Magic and love. They're at the centre of the storm and I'm not going to drown like they all did. I'm certainly not dragging Effie and Attis down with me. It's just the curse. This is what it does.'

'It's just—' Rowan bit her cheek.

'What?'

'It's just that seems kind of convenient.'

Anna looked at Rowan, stunned. 'What about this is *convenient*?'

'That you can blame all your feelings on a curse.'

'So it's just a coincidence that Effie and I love the same guy? That my mother and Aunt were in love with the same man? Generations and generations before that—'

'I'm not saying you're not cursed, just that whatever the circumstances are – love is still love.'

'But what if it's not real—'

'Looks pretty real to me. I've never seen you scream into a pillow before . . .'

Anna sank her head into her hands and Rowan put an arm around her. 'I'm sorry this is so complicated, Anna. I just think you need to cut yourself some slack. Firstly, Attis Lockerby is Attis Lockerby. It's hard *not* to fall in love with him. Secondly, we don't get to choose who we love, only what we do with it. Your aunt spent her whole life fighting it and it destroyed her.'

'But my mother opened herself to it and it destroyed her too.'

'Love didn't destroy her, your aunt did.'

Anna sighed. 'I can't be with him. It's not an option. Effie is my sister.'

'Of course,' Rowan agreed. 'You *could* tell him how you feel though.'

'Tell him!' Anna's face prickled with heat at the thought.

'Mum always says better out than in.'

'I think when it comes to a curse it's better locked in a box with a hundred keys and buried in Hel where no one can find it.'

'Unless burying it just makes it stronger . . . buries you instead . . .'

Anna groaned, wishing she could drive his face from her mind. *His lips.* She wished she didn't want to kiss them again more than anything.

'I'd love to have all the answers for you,' said Rowan. 'But I'm not exactly experienced with the whole love thing.'

'You seem pretty good at it to me.'

'I've watched *a lot* of romcoms. And if I'm destined to have no life of my own, I may as well help others in need—'

'Now *you're* being ridiculous. You have a great life. These last few days, here with your family, have been some of the best in my life.'

'That's my family though, not me.' Rowan slumped. 'Did you see my mum out there tonight? She can transform a garden, cook up a feast and command a room, all while tipsy. She practically runs the Wort Cunnings these days, they all look to her and—' Rowan shook her head. 'I know she plays it down, pretends it's all simple as spring rain, but she can do things with plants that the chemists of this world can only dream of. What can I do?'

Anna frowned, bewildered by Rowan's speech. 'You're a great Wort Cunning too.'

'Ha!' Rowan laughed but the sound of it was like hard grit in soil. 'You just think that because you don't see my magic compared to the rest of them. I'm OK at everything, exceptional at nothing. A jack of all trades . . . gardener of all spades. Mum doesn't admit it but these days I'm the worst at Botanical magic in my family. My plants always end up stunted or wonky or weird and—' She stopped, her voice lowering. 'You saw what happened yesterday with the seeds . . .'

'Like your mum said, it was just a silly game.'

'It's never not worked before. What if – what if it wasn't just because my magic's weak, what if it's because . . . I don't have a magical language *at all*? I'm not going to find one?'

Anna didn't know what to say. She didn't know where it was all coming from; she'd never heard Rowan question her magic before and Anna had never thought to question it either. She couldn't imagine Rowan being anything other than a Wort Cunning. 'But you're so magical, Rowan, you love plants so much—'

'I do. My Hira lives in the soil and the roots . . . but I'm not sure plants love me back. Why have I never connected with any particular type of Wort Cunning magic? Why do I find it so hard to focus on any one thing?'

'Hey, you love plants, that's what matters. As you just explained to me, love is love, no conditions attached. Don't put too much pressure on yourself; your language will come in time.'

Rowan attempted her best smile, and it really was convincing. Her face was so naturally cheerful that it was hard to tell the difference. Anna wondered how often she might have been fooled, missed the truth, too wrapped up in her own worries. 'You're probably right. I'm just behind is all, but hey, story of my life. Still, things could be worse. I could be in love with Attis Lockerby.'

Anna laughed this time. There was little else left to do. 'I'm doomed, aren't I?'

'There's always chocolate.'

'I'm going to need a lot of chocolate.'

'Shall we go back down then?' Rowan suggested lightly.

'I might just stay here, scream into the pillow some more.'

Rowan stood up and put her hand out. 'You aren't hiding away. The sooner you face him and his dreamy eyes and taut biceps the better.'

'*Still* not helping.'

'Sorry.'

They walked down the stairs laughing, but as they approached the living room, Anna's insides tightened and twisted. The party had died down, everyone had collapsed on the chairs and sofas, singing a final incoherent rendition of 'The Twelve Worts of Christmas'. Attis was laid out on the floor in front of the fire, Effie beside him, snowflakes still glinting in her hair. Anna's eyes met Attis's and they both looked away, quick as the sparks of the fire. Anna tried not to think of the kiss but it burned on her lips and her stomach burned too, jealousy searing into the yearning as she watched the light and shadow move over Effie and Attis, entangling them. Even if they weren't together any more, deep down, Attis still belonged to Effie. *He always would.*

Anna and Rowan dropped down next to Bertie on the sofa.

'Where have you two been?' Bertie threw a warm blanket over them. The blankets were always toasty warm in the Greenfinch household.

'Escaping the relations,' said Rowan.

'Well, don't escape too far.' Bertie snuggled her close. 'Another year over. I can't believe it. I remember when you were no bigger than Geranium and Gardenia, wearing your best red velvet dress, lighting the Yule log.'

'Was that the year I had accidentally tucked the dress into my pants and the cousins taunted me for days?'

Bertie hooted. 'No, I think it was the year your dress caught on fire after you stood too close.'

Rowan shook her head. 'I can't do anything right.'

'Nonsense.' Bertie dismissed her. 'You bring the flair! And speaking of – Geranium! Gardenia! No more marshmallows. It's time for bed.'

'Noooooo,' they whined, quickly grabbing toasting, floating marsh-mallows from the air and stuffing them in their mouths. 'Christmas can't be over!'

'I don't want to go to bed! Can you tell a story before we go?'

Bertie grinned, her cheeks redder than ever. 'Just one. After all, Christmas wouldn't be complete without a story. But which story is the question?'

'The story of the Goddess!' Geranium replied eagerly.

'Yes! The Goddess! Please tell that one, pleeeease!'

'Ah.' Bertie's smile dipped like a quill into the ink of her thoughts. 'The story that began it all.'

Mince pies were passed around. The fire stretched itself out into a low purr. The last stragglers gave up their song and the room stilled as people cosied up and turned to Bertie, who took a sip of sherry and began.

'Once upon a time, before time existed, the world was made of magic. The moon ruled the sky, the stars had not yet settled and stories moved like leaves in the wind, not yet given form.' Bertie's voice had a way of making the words twinkle. 'In these times of formlessness – there lived a woman with a wild heart and a curious mind. She craved to know the secrets of the world. She set off for the Impenetrable Forest where the deepest secrets grow. Eventually, she came across a little grove among the trees and in its centre – lit by moonlight – was a spinning wheel. She sat down at the wheel and, with nothing but threads of moonlight itself, she began to spin magic.

'First, she needed time, for nothing could truly take shape until time had put things in place. And so, she spun the language of the planets and with it learnt the power of the seven planets and the spell of time – to weave past, present and future betwixt her fingers. The sun joined the moon in the sky, night and day separated and everything began to align to the new rhythm of things.

'As evening drew in, the woman lay in the grove, the wind blew, the ground was hard. She wished she could make a fire to keep her warm and find water to drink. And so, the next day she sat down at the spinning wheel and spun the language of the elements and with it learnt of the seven elements and the spell to wield them and command the natural world.

'The next night, she lay beside the spinning wheel, tired and hungry, and as her body ached she wished she would never grow old, so she would never have to stop learning. And so, the next day she sat down at the spinning wheel and spun the language of botanics and with it learnt of the seven sacred herbs and the spell of eternal life and healing. Us green-fingered witches say that as she wove this spell her fingers turned quite green and never went back . . . but I digress.'

Bertie took another sip of sherry.

'Now that she could live forever, she pondered on death, for don't we all at some point wonder what lies in the darkness beyond? And so, the next day, she sat down at the spinning wheel and spun the language of words and with it learnt the seven words to speak with the dead and the spell to travel to the Underworld and unearth its secrets.'

Anna thought of Attis's story of the raven sent by the Goddess to Hel to unravel its secrets, returning black-winged and cawing the Language of the Dead.

'The woman was all-powerful now and people came to her with their griefs and woes, asking for her help. And so, the next day she sat down at the spinning wheel and spun the language of imagic and with it learnt of the seven centres of the body and the spell to enter another's soul, so she could soothe their hearts and give them strength.

'But the world was changing. She had spun magic from it and things had divided and grown and taken shape. With the sun in the sky, the shadows had taken form too. The woman became known as the Great Spinner and watched over her creation, keeping the Balance, but the darkness grew and grew. And so, she sat at the spinning wheel and spun the language of symbols and with it learnt of the seven sides of the sacred star and the spell to protect others from harm.'

Gardenia sat up on her elbows. 'The next bit's my favourite.'

'No way, the best bit is when she talks with dead people,' Geranium bickered.

'No interrupting! The Goddess had many demands on her now, but her heart was lonely. She wished to have another with whom she could share her knowledge and magic. And so, with one of her ribs, a drop of her blood and a cutting of her hair, she formed the Horned God, cooked into creation by the light of the sun. They fell deeply in love – a love like the world had never seen. Filled up with it, the Goddess sat down at her spinning wheel and spun the most powerful language of them all – the language of emotions – and with it learnt of the seven emotions that govern us and how to cast the spell for a love as true as hers.

'For a time, the Goddess and the Horned God ruled over the world and all was balanced. But even their love could not hold back the darkness forever. The Goddess knew her magic was too powerful to contain, that the darkness would find a way to it eventually. And so, by night, with the shadows on her heels, she returned to the Impenetrable Forest and sat down at the spinning wheel one last time. Only this time, she pricked her finger upon the spindle and fell into a deep, eternal sleep. They say, that night, as her body dissolved into the land, she dreamt the Moonsongs and the stars finally settled in the sky.

'The Horned God came after her but it was too late. He found her blood upon the spindle and knew what she had done. He turned the spindle upside down and a drop of her blood fell onto the forest floor. Where it landed an apple tree grew – expansive and beautiful with leaves as green as her eyes had been and roots as deep as her love. Seven apples grew ripe upon it.

'The Horned God called upon six wise women, the wisest in all the world. He plucked six apples from the tree and gave each of them one. As the women bit into the fruit they each came to speak one of the languages of the Great Goddess, the Great Spinner: Planetary, Elemental, Botanical, Verbal, Imagic, Symbolic . . .

'The Horned God took the final apple for himself, the language of Emotion, but before he could bite into it, a seventh wise woman appeared. Angry at being left out, she snatched it from him but, before she bit into it, she placed a curse upon it: that every emotion would have its opposite, every light, its dark. And then – she took her bite.

'And so, the women became the Seven. The first witches. They took magic into the world, released it and spread it far and wide, scattering magic like seeds on the wind, so that all who lived came to taste it and from the original languages many more were born, sprouting forth like new shoots. The Seven lived on, watching over us, guarding the secrets of the Great Spinner and maintaining the Balance to this very day.'

'What about the darkness?' said Effie, bringing the story to an abrupt end. The fire snapped behind her, a snarl of flame.

'The darkness remains,' Bertie replied. 'For therein lies the Balance.'

'If the Seven are gone, what happens then? Does the darkness tip the scales?'

Bertie's lips firmed. 'It's just a story, Effie.'

'But how can the Seven be beaten if they have the power of the Goddess's original spells?' Manda frowned.

'They don't. Not any more. Over time, their power has lessened. It was said that there were some bloodlines, some witches, who were gifted with the power of one of the original spells, but such claims are lost to myth these days. Gardenia and Geranium, time for bed.'

'Noooo!'

'Tell another!'

'I couldn't. Yule is spent and so am I.'

Bertie ushered the girls from the room. Great-Grandpa Basil woke up with a start. 'Is it Christmas?' he garbled and then fell promptly back to sleep.

Everybody laughed and began to talk among themselves, Bertie's story dissolving into the happy blur of the day. Anna's eyes passed over the figures of Effie and Attis by the fire – and into the flames, the smoke unfurling and forming shapes. She saw black feathers and ravens – wings spreading, flying up the chimney into the darkness that lay beyond the light and warmth of the room.

She blinked and they were gone.

A GIFT

It's said in the building of the Tower of London, its walls were interred with the bones of dead Hel witches, which were first shattered and then mixed directly into mortar; the bone-walls providing a further layer of protection against the intensity of the invocations and evocations carried out within.

'Buildings of Power', *A Macabre History of London*
(Published 1940)

Anna had expected the festivities to calm down on Boxing Day but the Greenfinches were far from done.

'Twelve days.' Rowan laughed as new visitors arrived. 'Did you not get that from the song yet?'

Anna spent the morning doing her best to avoid Attis, vigilant not to use the kitchen door with the mistletoe. She knew she'd have to face him sooner or later, to pretend everything was fine – she just needed time. To prepare herself. To get the kiss out of her body. It was fluttering still in the pit of her stomach like an escaped thing that wouldn't settle now it had been set free. He seemed to be avoiding her too, she'd only caught glimpses of him and apparently he'd gone out on some errand.

In the afternoon, she busied herself in the kitchen, helping Bertie cut out biscuits from swathes of dough, the cookie cutter changing shape each time she used it: a sun, star, crescent moon, full moon, heart . . .

She was on the fourth batch when a Wort Cunning she recognized as Aunt Iris came in looking flustered. 'You should probably come and see the news,' she said to Bertie, grim-faced.

Anna stopped, the cookie cutter still shifting beneath her fingers.

Bertie wiped floury hands against her apron. 'I'm coming.'

Anna followed. A group of Wort Cunnings were gathered in front of the television. The coverage was live, in front of the ice rink at London's famous Somerset House.

The reporter was interviewing a young woman who looked to be in shock. 'I came with friends this morning – I – I – went to get some hot drinks but when I came back . . . something wasn't right. Everyone on the ice rink – they – they were skating around and around, faster and faster. Everyone on the sidelines started screaming, screaming at them to stop, but they wouldn't. They just got faster, they started slamming into the sides, colliding with each other, falling, skating over each other, getting back up, going again like – like they couldn't stop. People were getting hurt but no one was stopping. It was horrible, so horrible—'

'Are you aware of anything that might have caused the strange behaviour?' the reporter asked.

The woman shook her head. 'No, everything was fine one minute and the next there was just a feeling in the air, like – like – dread.'

The interview cut off, returning to the studio.

Dread. That was how it had felt at school, the room full of dread; the eyes of the girls lost in it, as if they would never claw their way free again. They watched until the report began to go around in circles with no new information. People had been injured – nasty cuts and gashes, broken bones, a severed finger. They briefly showed the ice rink, empty now, its white glass surface streaked with blood.

Bertie switched off the TV. 'Rowan, Rumex, why don't you go next door and keep the cousins company? We need to have a quick chat in here.'

'Mum!' Rowan and Rumex began to protest but stopped at the look on Bertie's face.

They were ushered from the lounge, the door shut behind them. They joined the young cousins in the other room, the coven immediately gathering together.

Rowan's eyes jumped between them. 'Another hysteria outbreak.'

'Right in the centre of London.' Manda's eyes were wide. 'It's the same as the other incidents, isn't it?'

Rumex looked completely lost. 'What are you all talking about?'

Rowan turned to him. 'Have you not realized something is going on out there?'

'I know there's been stuff,' he retorted. 'But what are *you* lot going on about?'

Rowan leant in. 'There have been incidents like this, hysteria around the capital, like what happened at our school – people not able to stop, it's like they're—'

'Out of their minds,' said Anna.

'Possessed.' Manda bit her lip.

Rumex's eyebrows met in a thick thatch. 'Why haven't I heard about all of these incidents?'

'Not all made the main news,' Rowan replied. 'People are only just beginning to connect the dots. We think it might have begun with the ravens at the Tower of London that couldn't stop circling until—'

Until they died. Anna felt dread thicken in her stomach.

'And what happened at our school – it might have been part of all this.'

Through her fear and anguish, Anna felt a small breath-release of relief. Perhaps it wasn't her magic, perhaps she wasn't connected to everything going on.

Rumex rubbed his neck. 'I don't know. It all seems kind of far-fetched.'

'Well how do you explain today then? What just happened on that ice rink?'

'It was crowded, people started panicking and the panic spread. That kind of thing does happen.'

'We've considered it might be cowans losing their shit,' said Effie. 'Genuine hysteria . . . but it's getting suspiciously persistent . . .'

Beyond the window, the garden lay beneath a mask of white, snow angels still flapping in the snow. They heard the living-room door open, the adults filtering back into the house.

'MUM!' Rowan called as Bertie passed by in the corridor.

'I need to get back to the kitchen—'

Rowan shook her head. 'Come on.' They followed her into the kitchen, where Bertie was taking a batch of the cookies out of the Aga. They were completely burned.

'Oh, Mother Holle! These are ruined.' Bertie promptly took her apron off and started putting it on inside out. 'If you have a calamity in the kitchen, put your apron on the other way to turn your luck around!'

'Mum!' Rowan pulled the tray of cookies away. 'What's going on? You have to talk to us, we're not children.'

Bertie rubbed at a dusting of flour with a towel, hands still fussing, then she stilled. 'I know that, Sorbus.'

'Do you know what that was today? Is it the same as what happened at our school? That's been happening across London?'

Bertie stared at them all. 'Nothing misses you lot, does it?'

'Well?'

Bertie dropped the towel. 'We don't know.' Her voice was uncharacteristically quiet. 'It could be genuine hysteria or it could be magic. If it is, it's a dark spell we're dealing with.'

Effie picked up a cookie from the tray, a black moon. 'What do you mean dark?'

'I don't know.'

'Who would be casting it? Why?'

'I still don't know. We're reaching out to other groves to see if anyone knows anything.'

'What about the Seven?' Manda asked. 'Are they responding yet? Can they help?'

Bertie's fingers fiddled again. 'We haven't heard anything further from them.'

'So they've abandoned us!'

'Of course not. So long as there is magic in this world, the Seven will never abandon us.'

'So where the hell are they?' Effie spat.

'We don't know!' Bertie's hands erupted, spraying flour into the air. Breath rushed out of her as if she'd been holding a taut balloon inside of her. 'Sorry.' She rubbed her forehead. 'It's just, we've never been in a position like this before, without the Seven to turn to. After what happened last year and the message of warning they sent and the – the WIPS building against us, we need to be vigilant.'

Effie crumbled the cookie beneath her fingers. 'So you reckon the WIPS are the Hunters too? The Wolves in WIPS clothing.'

Bertie took too long to reply. 'We need to be open to all possibilities right now. We must step slowly, carefully, wisely.'

'Let them walk all over us, you mean.' Effie shook her head, disgusted. 'Shouldn't the magical world retaliate?'

'How do you know it isn't?' Bertie snapped. 'This hysteria could be exactly that! Some grove taking matters into their own hands, getting revenge against the WIPS. It will only draw more attention. We need to know more about the WIPS, understand who they are and how they work before we can overcome them. If you want to be treated like adults then you must accept, like adults, there are not always easy answers!'

Rumex put his hands over his mum's shoulders. They dropped. 'Mum, it's OK.'

She reached up to pat his hand, sighing. 'Of course it is. This isn't for all of you to worry about.'

'You at least need to talk to us, Mum,' said Rowan.

Bertie nodded. 'I will. I would tell you more if I knew more.'

'What about the Binders?' Anna asked. The mention of a grove taking measures into their own hands had made her think of them. They were the sort of messed-up lengths they'd go to.

Bertie's shoulders winched back up and she looked to the window. 'We've tracked the majority of your aunt's coven down. Protections have been put in place with the help of the Warders, but there's still one we haven't found yet . . .'

'Who?'

'Lyanna Withering.'

Anna gripped the kitchen counter to keep herself steady. She'd known it would be the name Bertie would say. Withering had always been sly, slippery, clever. Anna could see her now – her scornful gaze seeking out all the broken parts of her. She knew all of Anna's sins. They'd been partners in Aunt's death. Anna couldn't bear the thought of her out there. What if she'd run off to unite with other Binders around the country? There could be a network beyond her aunt's coven.

'We'll find her.' Bertie gave Anna a reassuring look but her eyes betrayed her, spilling over with concern.

'Why are we guarding the Binders?' asked Effie, still riled up. 'Shouldn't they be thrown in some sort of magical jail?'

Bertie appeared almost amused. 'The magical world doesn't quite work in the ways you want it to, Effie. There are no jails. If there were, we'd need rules and regulations, laws other than natural ones. There is the GoldiLocks grove who deal with small, personal disputes, but anything more than that would be too complex. Who would be in charge? Who would decide the rules? The punishments? Who would dole them out? It is the will of man to carve up the world into what is wrong and right, to decide who gains and who suffers – but magic cannot, should not, be controlled by such things, and to give certain witches that kind of power would be far too dangerous.'

'Don't the Seven have that power?' Effie contradicted.

'The Seven do not own the power of magic, they were chosen by magic itself and cannot be separated from it. They are its balance in living form and through them magic redirects the pathways from those who cause harm to those who maintain peace. Of course, other groves often take it upon themselves to sort things out . . . revenge, retaliation . . . but that is not the right way. Not *our* way. If we did that, we would be no better than the Binders themselves.'

Effie huffed as if she wasn't satisfied by Bertie's explanation but she said no more.

'Now.' Bertie tied her loose apron strings. 'How about a cup of living tea? I think we could all do with something soothing. I can probably bring those biscuits back from the brink too . . .' She waved a hand over them and the burnt covering crumbled away, transforming them back to golden.

That evening, the coven gathered in Rowan's room. Attis had returned from his mystery outing, his brow dark and his body wound as they watched the fallout from the day's events. The news was soaking up the panic and churning it back out again, asking the questions that kept people clicking, wanting to know more. Videos of the incident were spreading, everyone sharing, commenting, adding to the hysteria, whispers of magic fizzing up through the fractures . . .

Hopkins had reposted several alarmist stories about the ice rink but had also shared a link to a podcast episode in which he was being interviewed. An episode titled: *The truth about malefice: Should we be afraid?*

They'd decided to listen. Rowan pressed play. The host made his own introductions before enthusiastically welcoming Hopkins.

'We are so pleased to finally get you on the show, Mr Hopkins! Now, tell us, you're the lead researcher at an organization known as the Witchcraft Inquisitorial and Prevention Services? Quite the name.'

Hopkins laughed lightly, and yet the sound had a depth that prickled the back of Anna's neck. He said nothing, waiting for the interviewer to continue.

'What is it you do in your role exactly?'

'Exactly?' Hopkins repeated, that hint of laughter still there, laughter and threat. 'I lead investigations into allegations that go beyond the remit of our pre-existing services and institutions. My teams compile, analyse and present the research. And propose potential solutions.'

'Intriguing. What kind of *allegations*?'

'Allegations of occult practices – cults, rituals, witchcraft, malefice.' He spoke directly, but there was a magnetic gleam to his voice.

'And you believe such dangers are on the increase?'

'I don't like the word *belief*. I'm more interested in the facts, the evidence, and it's all there, people simply haven't been looking. But I think eyes are beginning to open to the rising threats we are facing.'

'You've stated elsewhere that the increase in these threats began with the deaths of the Faceless Women at Big Ben?'

'Look. I think these dangers have always been with us, but that event certainly marked a turning point. An uptick. Our investigation into the women revealed that their self-inflicted deaths were highly ritualized, with the aim of unleashing dark forces of malefice across the city, forces that are now gaining in strength and power and spinning out of control with devastating consequences. We've been tracking this for a long time and we have a substantial amount of data. The statistics are deeply troubling. Do you know we've received over three hundred reports of witchcraft in the last year? Even if half of those are true – the growing numbers are alarming.'

'People might question what you mean by dark forces and malefice.' The host stated it in a way that suggested he wasn't one of those people. That he was already bought in.

'Supercalifragilisticexpialidocious!' Hopkins's laugh came this time as a forceful boom. 'Is that what you're getting at?'

'Well, I – er – no—' the host stuttered.

'This isn't a new force.' His words sharpened. 'This is a force that's been with us always. It's been called many things in the past, given many names: the work of the devil, the dark arts, sorcery, alchemy, voodoo, hoodoo, hocus-pocus. It's recorded in myth, in religion; belief in and fear of such forces playing out in every culture and community that we have on record. And yet, these days we wheel such ideas out for entertainment or pretend they don't exist. In our material world, if we can't see it, it's not real, right? But I think we all still *feel* it, in our gut, our animal instincts, in our nightmares . . .' His words hammered and yet his voice was as much mead as muscle – it could be soft, sinuous, it knew when to draw you in and when to contract and strike, leaving you gripped, holding onto everything he said as if he had all the answers. 'People are reawakening to the truth – that there are things we can't understand, that there are people among us who don't belong. Those who are able to use and wield these forces against us.'

'Do you believe enough is being done about this threat?'

'Not even close. We've got malefice attacks around the city, growing in force and number, and putting lives in danger. We've got fresh reports coming in all the time – suspicions in local neighbourhoods, places of work, key institutions. We've got a doctor at an abortion clinic using magical substances against patients' wills. We've got a London school with a witchcraft cult. Teenagers, especially females, are particularly vulnerable to the lure of malefice. We're doing everything in our power but we need more power. The populace is beginning to wake up but the government must act with us. Together we must stop the spread.'

'Powerful words there, Mr Hopkins. We've been saying for a long time on this podcast that we're being repeatedly let down by those running this country. People feeling simply not listened to, and it's just so refreshing to hear you speak openly and plainly about what's really going on.'

'We're listening,' Hopkins replied in a way that felt like he was talking personally to each individual listener, as if he were reaching out a hand to them. 'We're here to cut through the lies and tell the truth that no one wants to hear.'

The episode went on for a while longer, but nothing was said that hadn't already been said, it was only repeated and emphasized further, Hopkins smiling and growling in turns.

'Well.' Effie leant back against the headboard. 'He's certainly a good frontman.'

'I've never heard anyone talk so publicly, so seriously about . . . the magical world.' Rowan looked dazed. 'Not that it *was* the magical world; the things he was saying were . . . wrong, so wrong. He mentioned a school, *our* school.'

Manda took in a shaky breath. 'It's just a podcast though, right?'

'A popular podcast. It always covers controversial topics and people lap it up. This has already got thousands of listens and it's only just gone up.'

'Can't blame them.' Effie shrugged. 'It's more interesting than all the other depressing shit in the news. Ancient evil forces, witchcraft on your doorstep.'

Attis exhaled gruffly. 'He said a lot without saying anything of any substance.'

'But he said it well.'

Attis moved away to the window, releasing untamed energy, his jaw working. Anna could still hear Hopkins's charismatic voice curling around them like a vice: *Teenagers, especially females, are particularly vulnerable to the lure of malefice.*

'I've got more news,' said Effie, drawing their attention back to her. 'Poppins messaged today and he *finally* has some information on the WIPS. Says they still don't know who they are but they've found that they've been receiving vast amounts of funding from all over – heads of corporations, politicians, people in positions of power and so on. They've also recently taken up residence on a floor of the Shard to run their operations out of.' Effie gave them all a look. 'Friends in high places and an office in the highest building in London.'

The Shard. A symbol of power in itself.

'And a lot of people online supporting them too,' Rowan mumbled. 'The anti-mals are all over the ice rink thing.'

'Do you think the hysteria *is* some kind of dark spell?' Manda looked between them, biting her nails. 'Who would be casting it?'

Effie considered the question with curiosity. 'There are the Hexen witches. From what I've heard, they're a pretty vengeful bunch.'

'The Binders,' Anna stated. 'No one fears the rise of the Dark Times more.'

Effie met her eyes. 'They're pretty good at vengeance too, but they don't seem like the type to do something so public. They prefer torture in their own homes. If there *is* some other grove behind it, we can't entirely blame them; no one else is doing anything.'

'You can't just attack cowans!' said Anna. 'That's not a solution to this.'

'I'm not saying it's right.' Effie put her hands up. 'Just that magic isn't meant to be contained. Maybe it's the Seven themselves . . . after all, no one knows where the hell they are or what they're up to, and if the WIPS killed them then they've got good reason to be pissed.'

Rowan's head was shaking. 'The Seven wouldn't unleash that kind of magic.'

'You don't know that. No one seems to know anything about them. Maybe they've become corrupted.'

'They can't be—' Rowan began to protest but Effie bit back.

'*Everything* can be corrupted.'

'We still don't know that it isn't just hysteria,' said Attis firmly. 'With the WIPS drumming up the kind of fear we just heard in that podcast, it's no wonder cowans are getting afraid.'

'On an ice rink on Boxing Day?' Rowan said doubtfully. 'This time it wasn't even a site of magical suspicion like the others.'

'What if it happens at our school again?' Manda wrapped her arms around herself.

Anna thought of the eyes, fear appearing before her like a sheer slope she couldn't get a grip on, falling down – down—

She needed something to hold onto.

That was when she remembered. The cracker. The spool of thread. Distracted by all the magic and the kiss of yesterday, she'd forgotten about the strange gift. She went over to her trousers and pulled it out.

'What's that?' Effie walked over.

'I don't know. I got it yesterday in my cracker along with this.' She pulled out the note. They passed it around, working out the answer was shadow as she had done.

A Christmas gift for you and your coven, should you dare to use it . . .

'For us?' Effie took the thread off her. As she pulled it loose from the spool the blackness of the thread became less . . . concrete, became something fluid and intangible, like smoke, *like shadow . . .*

Rowan's eyes cinched. 'I think I know what that could be . . . but it can't be . . .'

'What?' Effie asked, the thread disappearing and reforming around her fingers.

'Shadowthread . . .' Rowan sounded awed. 'I've heard about it in stories. A thread of shadow like that can make—'

'Shadowrobes.' Attis's eyes contracted onto the thread.

'A shadowrobe!' Effie looked at the spool with fresh excitement. 'Nxy witch magic, right?'

Rowan nodded. 'Shadowthread is woven from shadow itself. Not just any shadows. Shadows from the Impenetrable Forest, the wild moors, caves so deep no one has ever found their endings. Untameable shadows. According to the stories anyway. Apparently, shadowrobes were widely used during the last . . .' She looked up at them all with alarm. 'Witch hunts. So that witches could move about unseen, shrouded in shadow.

Supposedly, the Nxy grove helped witches in many ways during that time. It's said they created the spell for Books of Shadows to help a witch conceal her spells too. I always wanted one when I was younger.'

'Books of Shadows,' Anna repeated. 'We saw a whole shelf of them at the Library . . . but why was *this* in my Christmas cracker?'

None of them could answer that.

'Could someone here have planted it?'

Rowan shook her head. 'Unlikely. This doesn't have the work of a Wort Cunning about it. We can't ask Mum, she'd definitely confiscate this. This is seriously powerful magic.'

Effie clutched it tightly in her hands, releasing an ecstatic laugh that flew around the room. 'Whoever sent it wants us to *act*. If we can conceal ourselves, we can start finding out some answers of our own. Anyone know how to sew a shadowrobe?'

The next day, they gathered at the front door, everyone more tense than when they'd arrived. Anna didn't want to leave – she hadn't stepped out of the Greenfinch enclave all Christmas and didn't feel ready to face the real world beyond. Or Attis, for that matter.

Rowan hugged Anna tightly. 'It's been so great having you stay. Best Yule ever. Next year, we'll go even bigger.'

'I can't imagine how *that* is possible.'

'Bigger baubles.' Bertie smiled, her eyes creasing with the lines that Anna had come to know. She bundled Anna into a tight hug too. 'Take care.' She looked as if she didn't want them to leave either. 'And don't forget, I'm always here.'

'Can we take you with us?' Attis asked. 'I'm not sure I can live without your cakes. Life will hold no meaning any more.'

Bertie chortled and shook her head. 'Love to, but I think I'd best stay here. Bill needs me.'

'I'd get by, for about two hours,' Bill confirmed, smiling kindly but folding his hands beneath his armpits and stepping back as if to indicate he wouldn't be joining in with all the hugging.

Effie embraced Bertie in a rare burst of gratitude – and then, they left, the outside air a shock of cold.

Effie had Attis drop her off at Azrael's on the way home. She didn't say when she'd be back – apparently they had a lot of catching up to do.

Not wanting to place herself any closer to Attis than was necessary,

Anna didn't move to the front seat after Effie had gone but leant her head against the window and pretended to fall asleep. When they arrived back, Attis seemed to have returned to his usual high spirits. He bounded out of the car and opened the front door for them. The house was dark and cold – he flicked the lights on and turned on the heating, banging a radiator as he passed. 'I'll get the forge fires going. It'll be balmy in no time.'

Anna assessed the fridge. 'We'll need to get some food.' Selene wasn't due back until later, and even then, she rarely remembered to buy groceries.

'Order pizza?'

'Sure.'

Attis hovered, smiling strangely, hints of mischief about his lips.

'I'm going to unpack . . .' said Anna, taking herself from the room, but he followed her out of the kitchen and into the lounge.

She stopped.

The room was different. Selene's large, velvet purple chair had been pushed aside to make way for a new presence – a piano stood against the far wall, opposite the cocktail bar.

Anna was silent for several moments and then, in a strangled voice, she managed to say, 'What's that?'

'People traditionally call them pianos,' Attis answered. 'But you can call it whatever you like – it belongs to you.'

'Why? How?'

'It's your Christmas present.'

'Christmas . . .' Her voice trailed. She could feel him looking at her, his smile waiting for her response. The piano dominated the room, sturdy and beautiful, its rich caramel wood shining brightly. She turned to him. 'You bought me a piano?!'

'I procured one. Getting it here was most of the battle.'

Anna realized that must have been what he was doing when he'd disappeared on Boxing Day. He went over to it and brushed his hand along its top tenderly. 'It's an old Bösendorfer. Incredible pianos. They're handcrafted with spruce from the mountains of Austria.' He opened the lid and dust swirled. Its keys were the light and dark of his eyes. 'The bass strings are hand-wound too, which gives the sound greater depth and warmth. Needs a bit of tuning but—'

'It's too big,' Anna interrupted.

'It's difficult to make pianos smaller, they come piano-sized.' He grinned.

'I meant the gift is too big,' Anna stammered. 'I bought you chocolate truffles . . .'

'Hey, I'm passionate about chocolate truffles.'

'Why – why—' Anna's heart was beating too fast, her words coming out too slowly. 'Why would you buy me this?'

Attis looked up from the piano, confused. 'So you can play again.'

'But I don't play any more.' Her words turned hard now.

'That's like saying you don't breathe any more.'

Anna's hands clenched together. 'I'm sorry, but I don't want it.'

Attis's face fell and that only made it worse. His voice turned stubborn. 'You need to play again.'

'No. I need you to stop assuming you know what's best for me.'

'Anna—'

'I don't want it, Attis!'

The light went from his eyes. His jaw clicked shut. 'Well, it's not going anywhere. It's staying. It's heavy.'

'Fine!'

'Fine!' he retorted, trying and failing to keep the anger from his voice. He stalked past her down the stairs to his forge.

By the time she made it to her room she could already hear the *thwack, thwack, thwack* of his hammer from below. She imagined it was the piano he was hammering, tearing it apart with his hands. Wooden shards; broken music.

She curled up on the floor, clutching at her stomach, wanting to cry.

A LETTER

*From the fertile soils of death grew the first letters of the first language; the
dead could speak before the living for the end has always been the beginning.*

Language of the Dead, Books of the Dead: Tome 579

The next morning Anna stayed in her room for as long as possible. There
were more ice rink videos online, more witnesses spouting their versions
of what they'd seen, rumours of malefice rumbling beneath the official
verdict of *mass panic*. Meanwhile, Hopkins's podcast had racked up
hundreds of thousands of listens.

When she'd grown too hungry, she crept downstairs. Effie wasn't back
yet and she didn't want to face Attis alone. She didn't know what to
say. She knew he would never understand. The piano was still in the
lounge – still whole, still lovely, still too much to bear. She thought of
his face falling as she'd thrown his gift back at him and felt wretched.

In the kitchen there was no sign that Selene had returned either.
Anna cut herself some bread and went to the toaster—

It pinged suddenly, something flying out from it and landing on the
counter.

A letter.

It looked singed at the edges. The name *Anna Everdell* was written
on it. No address. Then again, it had arrived through a toaster. *Could it
be from Nana?* Anna turned it over – the back of the envelope was sealed
with a black mark scorched into the paper. Seven circles. Fear twisted
her insides.

The Eye.

She went to rip it open but stopped. She brushed a finger over the circles – the mark was no stamp but a kind of burn into the fibres of the paper, and yet, it seemed not to have come from the outside but as if it had risen up from within. From the letter itself. *Was it safe?*

Anna paced around the kitchen, wrestling with herself, and finally deciding she had no choice but to face him. She went downstairs to the forge. Attis wasn't there. The door to his bedroom was shut. She walked up and down the hallway several more times then knocked on it. Quiet at first, then louder, louder—

It opened. Attis stood before her in low-slung jogging bottoms. His chest was bare and his horseshoe tattoo glinted, silver threads over taut, tanned muscle. He rubbed his eyes. They were dark-ringed, lashes heavy and soft with sleep.

'S-sorry, you're sleeping—' Anna stuttered, not sure which way to look.

'I *was* sleeping,' he replied, running a hand through his hair, making a mess of it. She could feel the warmth of his body straight out of bed.

'I thought you never sleep.'

'It's rare.' Attis frowned, seeing she was holding something in her hand. 'What's that?'

Anna held it up. 'I – I had a letter. I was going to open it, but then I thought I better check with those more magically informed than me that it's OK to open.'

His eyes narrowed onto it. The sleepiness flew from them in an instant. He snatched it from Anna's hand. 'You can't open it!'

'Attis!' Anna tried to grab it back. 'That's mine! Give it back!'

He held it above his head. He was annoyingly tall. 'We need to burn it.' He moved past her down the hallway towards the forge.

'ATTIS!' She ran after him. 'YOU CAN'T! I need to know the contents of that letter! It's probably from Nana!'

'It's a Devil's Letter, Anna! A Curse Letter. It intends to do you harm.'

She tried to reach for it but he held it back. 'What's a Curse Letter?' she fumed.

Anna could see the fire of his forge lighting up behind him as he explained, 'It's not actually a curse, that's just what people call it. It's a hex really – a letter that contains a hex that will be unleashed on opening. There's no way of knowing what the hex will be. It could be something small, an inconvenience, or it could be something terrible – cover you in boils, steal your memories, stop your heart beating in your chest, kind of terrible.' His eyes were on her with a furious intensity. 'There's no way you're opening that letter.'

'I have to! It might help us stop the curse. The curse that's going to kill us anyway. It's worth the risk. Nana's just playing games. She won't hurt me.'

'We have no idea *what* Nana would do!'

Anna gave up on holding back. She ran after him and he darted away, weaving between the forge equipment. He placed the anvil between them. She circled it, jumping and swatting at the letter. He moved towards the fire.

'NO!' Anna screeched and leapt onto his back, arms around his neck.

'ANNA!' he shouted – shocked – trying to swing her off. She reached for the letter. He tried to hold it higher but lost his balance and they both fell, sprawling onto the floor. Anna scrabbled for it but Attis snatched it, jumped to his feet and ran to the fire.

'Attis, no! Please. Please.'

He stopped at the desperation in her voice, staring at her, warring with himself. He turned and ripped the envelope open himself.

'NO!' Anna ran for him but it was too late. He'd opened it.

His eyes darted over the words inside and then he dropped the letter to the floor. She ran to him and hammered her fists against his chest. 'No!' He caught her hands and they froze in their entanglement. 'Attis. No! What have you done? Why? Why did you read it?' Her eyes moved over him in panicked terror, waiting to see what horror would strike, not wanting to let him go. She could not lose him again.

He went to say something but his mouth struggled with the words. His lips would not open. He tried again, but it looked as if he were chewing the words, his shut mouth straining.

Anna stepped back.

He grappled at his lips with his fingers, trying to prise them open but, though his knuckles strained white and his cheeks puffed, he could not.

'You can't speak.'

Attis nodded, eyes wide.

Anna breathed out, steadying herself. 'Is that it? Is that the entire hex? Oh thank the Goddess.'

He looked at her as if he wasn't quite so thankful. Anna was so relieved he wasn't hurt she hadn't yet considered the repercussions – was his mouth sealed temporarily? Or . . . forever? He needed his mouth, to speak, to eat, to drink . . .

Attis looked back at her grimly. He reached for his knife of many blades, curled it through the air. The blade that appeared from it was thick and jagged and sharp.

'The hex-cutter . . .' Anna remembered it.

Attis nodded. He turned the blade towards his mouth and she screamed. But as he drew it towards his lips the blade bent backwards, the metal folding like paper.

'Nana . . .' Anna breathed out. Only her magic could be that powerful.

Attis was still staring at his blade, incredulous, furious.

'We have to work with it, not against it.'

Attis threw the blade at the wall and made a face at her as if to say *HOW THE HELL DO WE DO THAT?*

'The letter.' Anna reached for it on the floor and read it aloud:

> *What can spin but never gets dizzy?*
> *Meet me tomorrow at the devil in disguise,*
> *to wash your socks and sins of grime.*
> *HA! HA!*
>
> *P.S. Don't be late.*
> *P.P.S. Bring jelly babies.*

'Definitely Nana,' said Anna.

Attis fumed through his nose. He nodded his head towards the door and Anna followed him through to his bedroom. The bed was still unmade where he'd jumped out of it. He grabbed a white T-shirt and threw it on, then went over to his wooden desk, moved aside a stack of books and took out a piece of paper. He wrote something down and held the paper up to Anna:

I HATE HER.

Anna nodded. 'Considering the current circumstances, I'd say that's fair, but we still need to find her.'

TO STRANGLE HER?

Anna bit back a laugh. 'So she can undo this hex – so you can speak again. And to talk to her about the curse – so you can live. It's a win–win.'

Attis made a withering face and sank onto the bed. He wrote something else.

FOOD.

'But you can't eat . . .'

YOU CAN AND I NEED A DISTRACTION.

'OK, but let's hurry. The letter says we have to meet tomorrow.'

YAY!

They left the house, walking as far as the local supermarket, where they stocked up on food. On their return, Attis clattered around the kitchen. Toast. Poached eggs. Sliced tomatoes. He whipped up a hollandaise sauce and put it all together on a plate, pouring the sauce over and sprinkling parsley on top.

Anna eyed him. 'Was this necessary?'

HELPS ME THINK.

She sat down at the table, not wanting to eat around a man who couldn't open his mouth, but her stomach was rumbling. Attis nodded encouragement and she shrugged and tucked in. Her mind sharpened as the food entered her system. She talked through the riddle, trying to make sense of it.

'What spins but never gets dizzy . . . never gets dizzy . . . wheels? The earth? A fan? A yo-yo?'

A spinning top . . .

Anna could feel Nana as if she were inside of her, as if the dizzying force of her magic had seeped through the letter; as if Nana were watching and already knew her secrets. Attis raised his head suddenly, picked up the pen and wrote:

A WASHING MACHINE

'Wash your socks and sins . . .' said Anna, growing excited. 'Yes! That works! But how can we meet her at a washing machine?' She sat back, brain whirring. 'A laundrette!'

Attis nodded along with her.

'At the devil in disguise . . .?'

Attis shook his head. They cleared away the food. He went to feed Mr Ramsden. Anna ran upstairs to get dressed, the riddle ticking in the back of her mind. She brought her spinning top back down, twisting it idly at the kitchen counter, hoping it might somehow spin sense from the riddle.

A laundrette . . . presumably in London . . .

The devil in disguise . . .

A place . . . a place name . . .

Attis came back in and marched about the room. Anna watched the bright colours of the spinning top pour into one another.

London was mapped around the tube . . .

A tube station?

The devil in disguise . . .

What would the devil disguise itself as?

Blackfriars . . . Victoria . . . Shepherd's Bush . . . Angel . . .

The spinning top took off, hitting the cupboards. 'Angel!' Anna exclaimed. 'It could be Angel.'

'I was thinking along those lines,' Attis replied.

They both stopped speaking, their eyes mirrored in mutual shock.

'You can talk!' Anna exclaimed.

Attis stretched his mouth open, touched his lips. 'Seems so.'

Anna laughed, suddenly euphoric, relief pouring through her like spring rain, not realizing how terrified she'd been. 'It must mean we solved the riddle!'

He cracked a smile back and Anna was glad to see the uneven line of his teeth again. 'Don't pretend you didn't prefer me mute.'

She ran over to him but stopped a few paces short, remembering that throwing her arms around him was the last thing she should be doing. She pointed a finger instead, recalling her anger. 'I can't believe you read my letter! It was very clearly addressed to me! You had no right—'

'I think *I* preferred it when I was mute,' said Attis, putting his hands up in defence or surrender, she wasn't sure. 'You're right, I had no right, but I still wish I'd burned the damn thing. Nana's insane. We shouldn't go.'

'Of course we have to go!'

'Do we? The woman just hexed me.'

'It was a practical joke. You love them, remember?'

'And what if she has some more practical jokes in store for us? Ones that involve the loss of limbs or lives?'

'Nana helped me solve the curse.'

'If you hadn't, then I'd be dead now and you'd be free!'

Anna breathed in sharply at his words, taking a few steps back. The fear and confusion that had propelled their morning were slowly losing momentum, the wedge between them hammering back into place. She went to pick up the spinning top.

Attis sighed roughly. 'Anna, I don't want to fight again.'

'Neither do I,' she muttered. 'I need to go and research laundrettes in Angel.'

She went through the lounge but he followed her. 'I'm sorry if you felt the piano wasn't an appropriate gift and I know I have no place to give it . . .' She turned to find him looking almost embarrassed. 'But I still think you should play.'

'Attis—'

'I know it's hard, after everything . . . but you can't give up on your music.'

Anna could feel it all rising up again but this time she wasn't sure she could hold it down. Nana's letter had left her frazzled, had unspun her defences. She didn't want his kindness, his pity. 'There's no music left in me.'

'That's not—'

'Attis!' she erupted. 'It's broken, I'm broken, OK? There's no way back.'

'Broken?' His own voice broke on the word. Anna wanted to crumble before his eyes. To make him see that she wasn't worth his time, his energy, his fight. That it was too late. Why wouldn't he see? But he kept speaking. 'Your soul is made of music, Anna.' Every word an incision straight into her heart. 'You're running from yourself! Your magic—'

'Good!' she cried. 'I should! My magic is cursed. I just want it gone!'

'So you solve the curse, you give up magic. What then? Will you play music then? Will you allow yourself to live then? Or do you intend to punish yourself forever?'

Pain and punishment. Punishment and pain. 'I'm not punishing myself . . .'

'You are!' He moved towards her. 'Your aunt spent her whole life punishing you, and now she's dead, you're doing it to yourself.' Looking down into her eyes. 'Don't you see? So long as you're not living, she's still winning.'

Aunt's laughter rose up with its own merciless music. Anna couldn't take it. 'That's rich coming from someone who intends to die!'

'At least I enjoy life! I have hobbies. Cooking. Heating up metal. Trampolining.'

'That's right, make a joke of it all!'

'What else am I meant to do? Spend the entire year in despair? In denial? It's my fate. I didn't choose it. But there it is.'

'Bullthistle!'

'Blood, Anna.' His eyes were implacable as a cliff face. 'Your mother said *my blood* is required. When they say bleed a pig out they don't generally mean give it a bubble bath.'

'So you're throwing your life away on a word?'

'I'm not going to wait around for you or Effie to die.'

'No that's right, be the big hero, give up, kill yourself!'

'I have no choice! The curse exists because I exist! And it's ruining your life!' He paced away.

Anna stilled. 'You're not the reason I'm this way and it's not your responsibility to fix me.'

'Fine.' He looked back at her. 'Screw what I want. Screw your aunt. Screw magic. You owe it to yourself to live. You deserve it more than anyone.'

'I deserve nothing.' Anna's words wrenched through her with a sob. 'I killed her! I killed her!'

Attis looked confused for a moment and then his brow crumpled above his eyes. *One light. One dark.* Tearing her apart. He looked as if he might reach for her. 'You didn't kill her, Anna.'

She fell onto the sofa, fell into her hands. 'I wanted her to die,' she said, the fight in her dying too as she spoke the words that had been haunting her for so long. 'I wanted it.'

Attis's eyebrows rose, his lips parting. Shocked. *Good.* Anna wanted him to see her darkness, to see who she really was and to hate her for it.

'Still think my soul is made of music?' She laughed as coldly as Aunt.

He sat down beside her, his eyes steady. 'Yes.'

She shook her head, not wanting his kindness, but he did not look away. 'You might have wanted her to die but you didn't kill her. It wasn't your fault.'

'No—'

'None of it was your fault.'

'No—'

'The punishments she put you through your whole life weren't your fault.'

'No – no—' She'd been trying to hold it together for so long but she didn't want to any more. She wanted to break apart. The tears came at last. They fell as if they would never stop, as the pain sliced through her – clean, sharp lines – everything pouring out. She crumpled against him and Attis caught her. She sobbed into his warmth – wracking sobs, tears wetting through his T-shirt. She didn't know how to stop – with every shuddering breath the pain seemed to refill and spill over again as if she would drown in it. His arms tightened around her, keeping her afloat. She wanted to dissolve into their heat. To give in to everything she'd been holding back for so long. To let the curse consume her.

She pulled back sharply, startling him. 'Attis. I need to tell you something. I *have* to tell you something.'

'OK.' He nodded. His hands were still on her. His eyes moving over hers.

Anna grappled with the words, how to translate it all. In the end, there was only one way. 'I love you.'

His mouth shut, as if he'd been hexed all over again. Silence. The music of her soul bleeding out for him to see and he – nothing but silent. He lowered his eyes and she was left in the limbo of wondering what she wanted – for some part of the year before to have been real, for some part of him to love her too. But when he looked back up all she could see in his eyes were guilt and pain, *pity*. 'Anna—'

Her words ran on in a senseless stream as quick as the beats of her heart. 'Don't. Please. Don't. I just wanted you to know because I – I want it to be out there, in the open, so it doesn't have power over me. I don't expect anything from you. I know you don't love me. I know that it's impossible. I'm not telling you because I have any kind of agenda. I don't. I just, I can't live with things the way they are between us. I don't want to be held hostage to this curse.'

His eyes moved through shades she couldn't understand. His hands were on her, still.

He looked down at them and they dropped, his body slumping. 'You shouldn't be held hostage to anything,' he muttered then looked up. 'You know I care for you very much—'

'Attis, really, you don't have to say anything. I think I'm humiliated enough. I just bared my heart. I've sobbed into your T-shirt. I'm red and puffy.'

'Hey,' he said, though he couldn't muster any humour into his voice. 'Some women pay a lot of money to look as puffy as you right now.'

She laughed and he smiled briefly at the sound. Silence fell between them, but Anna was no longer suffocated by it. She could breathe.

He looked towards the door as if he should go but he didn't move. 'If we're airing everything . . . I wanted to say that I'm sorry about last year. I've been wanting to say it since the start of the summer—'

'You mean tricking me into loving you so you could ignite a centuries-old curse and then sacrifice yourself in a deadly ritual?'

'Is that all?' He breathed out a ragged laugh but it wasn't convincing. 'If it helps . . . you didn't make it easy.'

Anna swallowed, not sure what to make of his comment. 'What I don't understand is why help me with the bindweed, help me uncover my magic? Surely it would have been easier for you if it had remained suppressed?'

Attis's face twisted in pain, his eyes moving over her, something sad beating behind them. 'I could see that you needed your magic . . . to feel. To love.'

'So it was just part of the plan?'

'I would – I would never try to contain you, Anna.' As she tried to work out what he meant, he looked away. 'You should find someone else to be with. Someone who'll make you happy.'

Anna pulled back. Of everything he'd said, that hurt the most. He wanted her to move on. To get over him. To be with someone else, like it was that easy.

He stood up. 'I better—'

'Yeah – I need to—' She wished she could think of something faster.

'Got a new hex-cutter blade to make.' He grinned. 'Now, just checking, you're not going to attack me in my forge again? I still can't believe you jumped on my back.'

'You left me no choice.'

'I was naked and vulnerable.'

'You were NOT naked . . .'

'Half naked. Emotionally exposed. Tackled to the floor in my own man cave.'

'Nowhere is safe.'

'I vow never to cross you again, Dr Everdell.' Attis quirked a smile and headed towards the door.

'Attis—' Anna stopped him. 'Wait.'

She ran upstairs and returned with his skeleton key. She offered it to him. 'I found it in Aunt's house. Sorry . . . I don't know why it's taken me so long to give it back to you.'

He reached for it, their fingers briefly meeting. It was hard to ignore the feeling of his touch, her skin coming alive beneath it.

'Thank you.' His eyes flitted to the piano behind her. 'It's your choice. I just wanted you to know that I built my first forge after my dad died. It was basically a scrap bucket with some fire in it and a stone for an anvil, but it was everything. For a while that fire was the only thing I could find to speak to, that spoke back to me. I just think that your music could help you with your magic, help you find your way back.'

'I'll try,' she said, her voice catching.

His smile lifted—

'If you will.'

And fell again. He understood what she meant – that she would try to live, if he would try not to die. He stared back at her and then nodded faintly. 'OK.' He lowered his head and disappeared down the stairs.

Her body ached after him. She sat down and tucked her legs up, remaining that way for a while as the silence condensed back around her. She was glad she'd told him the truth, it made her feel stronger in the face of the curse, but it didn't make loving him any easier.

She turned back to the piano – feeling it tug at her too.

She shook her head and stood up, bracing herself, walking around the room in slow circles, moving closer to it the way one might approach a wild animal so as not to startle them.

She sat down at the stool. The piano smelt like old books and copper and dust. Up close she could see that its wood was scuffed and scratched in places, one of the keys a little chipped. Even so, it was beautiful. She rested her fingers on the keys and then moved them up and down feeling their peaks and troughs and little flaws and ridges, finding the colours in their monochrome landscape. No piano ever felt quite the same. No piano ever sounded quite the same.

Her hands tensed.

Tears threatened again.

So much longing in her fingertips, but how could she play? Easier to punish herself than to face it—

Aunt's laugh. Aunt's scream. Aunt's silence . . .

Anna felt for a moment as if she might explode, as if were she to let it all out, it would tear her to pieces, leaving nothing. She put a trembling finger back on the centre key: C.

She had to try.

It was the hardest note she'd ever played.

It rang out and Anna felt herself shattering, over and over, but the sound of the note held her together too. Her heart breaking but not diminishing, rising to meet it – the note a little out of tune, but pure. She played a few more before she could stop herself. They were stilted and broken but as they joined together there was music in them. They settled into a phrase she used to play, comforting as an old blanket. Over and over. Keeping her together. Her other hand joined – bolder, braver – and the song lifted, throwing off the blanket and taking flight, running up and down the keys – hands expanding, fingers stretching, flexing, flying—

The notes seemed to tune themselves as she went as if . . . by magic. Anna could feel it then – so many threads, so many melodies, so many songs all held back too long, all wanting out at once—

She lifted her hands abruptly. Shocked. Dazed. Scared. Tears falling onto the keys.

Silence stumbled back into the room but she could hear something else. On the floor, the spinning top was spinning in perfect balance. It slowed and came to rest on its side with something like relief.

That evening, Anna left the spinning top out on her chest of drawers, its colours reminding her of earlier, when, for a brief moment, she'd *felt* her magic, its threads finding their colours again. Like breathing after so long beneath ground. She wanted it again . . . she wanted it like she wanted the touch of Attis's hand again, his lips again . . . but could she trust her magic? Could she trust herself?

Should she unleash what she didn't understand?

She pushed the thoughts away, double checking the location of the laundrette in Angel. She'd found one not far from the station called Socks & Spins, which fitted with Nana's letter: *wash your socks and sins of grime* . . .

She and Attis had told Effie the plan to go early the next morning, omitting some of the events of the day before. Anna didn't know what they would be met with but was sure it would not be pleasant. She could still feel traces of Nana's energy moving about inside of her – little, chaotic whirlpools in her blood. Her hand reached for the book of fairy tales by her bed, hoping Nana's madness might tip the stories upside down and spill out something new.

The black feather was not in the page she had left it, but had moved to the start of the third fairy tale . . .

The Ice Coffin

Long ago, before plants had roots and still roamed free, there lived a king made of shadow and a queen made of ice. The queen was proud and beautiful and every day she liked to roam about her palace gardens, admiring herself in her water fountain and asking her reflection who was the fairest in the land.

Her reflection would smile and reply: 'You, my queen, with skin of ice and heart as cold as stone, you are the most beautiful the world has ever known.'

One of the young maidens who looked after the gardens had a special way with plants and flowers. They would bloom and grow at her touch and sometimes even speak with her.

One fateful day, the queen asked her reflection who was the most beautiful. The water rippled and her reflection replied: 'Your young servant with a heart like a flower opening and eyes green as the trees, she is the most beautiful we have ever seen.'

Enraged, the queen touched the water, freezing it over and creating a blade of ice. She gave it to one of her huntsmen, instructing him to take the young maiden to the forest and to cut out her heart. The huntsman followed his orders, but when the moment came, he could not do it and bade the girl to run. He cut out the heart of a deer instead and presented it to the queen.

The young maiden ran deep into the woods. At first, she was scared of its wildness and ferocity, so different from the gentle palace gardens, but then she began to listen – to the trees and the plants along the path; and they quietly whispered to her, leading her to a little house. It was surrounded by a tangled garden of its own, abundant with plants and flowers she had never seen.

Inside, the house was neat and orderly but cosy, with a burning fire and bubbling cauldron and seven little beds all in a row. Exhausted from all she'd been through, the maiden sank into one of the beds and fell asleep. When she woke, six small men were before her. She sat up and said hello.

They said hello too – they had bright eyes, kind smiles and green fingers. They each stepped forwards and introduced themselves.

'I am Una.'

'I am Wergulu.'

'I am Maythen.'

'I am Faen.'

'I am Belene.'

'I am Rugge.'

Una added: 'Our brother Springwort is not here right now. You may stay here with us and sleep in his bed, in return for helping around the house and garden.'

The girl agreed and the wise men taught her many things until she knew the names and could speak to the hearts of all the strange plants in their garden and could tend them just as well as the flowers of the palace gardens.

Meanwhile, the queen consulted her fountain and was overcome with rage when it answered as it had before: 'The young maiden with a heart like a flower opening and eyes green as the trees, she is the most beautiful we have ever seen.'

The queen decided to take matters in her own hands, snipping a rose from her garden and touching her finger to it, turning its heart to ice. She dressed up as a flower seller and went to find the maiden. She searched far and wide and eventually came to the little house in the wild woods. She saw the girl working in the garden and knew it was she.

The queen approached her and offered her a flower from her bunch, pretending to be poor. 'Its scent is sweet as summer, go on, see for yourself.'

Taking pity on the old flower seller, the maiden took it from her, putting the rose to her nose and smelling deeply. Immediately, she fell down dead. The queen laughed with wretched triumph and left her there on the floor.

Slowly, the ice heart of the rose, still in the maiden's hands, spread over the girl and formed an ice coffin around her.

When the men returned from the woods they found her that way, her loveliness preserved. They knew what they must do. They set off to find their brother, Springwort, the wisest of them. It took many years and a day, but they found him hidden among the shadows of the woods.

When all seven brothers arrived back at the house, they heated up their cauldron over a fire. Once it was hot, they jumped into the boiling mixture one by one. The liquid fizzed and bubbled and turned the green of spring shoots and out of the cauldron stepped a man who was just as green, with a heart of fire. He walked out to the maiden and touched her coffin. Its ice melted. He took her in his arms and the maiden's heart began to beat again, fire returning to her cheeks and lips.

From that day forth the green man and the maiden lived in the house in the woods tending to their plants until those who came past could not distinguish them from the garden at all.

Anna had read the tale before and knew that springwort was in it – the flower Attis had chosen for her the year before. She remembered his words vividly: *It produces but a single flower, which blooms only once, but when it does the whole world falls on its knees for the beauty of it.* He had plucked it from the storybooks and offered it to her with his silver tongue. But now . . . he'd bought her a piano. He'd fought for her magic. He'd held her while she cried. Had the year before really all been a lie?

The questions drifted into her dreams – but all that was waiting for her was a staircase and a locked door, cold as ice.

WASHING MACHINE

Mother Holle, Mother Holle,
Oh the stories we can tell!
Mother Holle, Mother Holle,
lives at the bottom of a well!
Mother Holle, Mother Holle,
knows your terrors and your fears!
Mother Holle, Mother Holle,
makes a river of your tears!
And when she shakes her bed out,
oh, how the feathers fly!
It snows above, it snows below
and the ravens cry, cry, cry—

Old English clapping rhyme, repeats

When Anna woke the next day, there was a string of increasingly hysterical messages on her phone from Rowan:

> Go to the WIPS website!
> It's changed!!
> It says they're due to INVESTIGATE our school!!!
> OUR SCHOOL!!!!

Anna took out her phone and went directly to the website. The WIPS logo met her, but now you could click through to a landing page. Her eyes moved rapidly over the new information, her mind chasing to catch up with it all, what it all meant—

They'd uploaded a mass of 'reports' – detailing their research, findings, evidence of malefice and statistics on the growing threat it posed to the UK. There was a section where you could submit your own suspicions of witchcraft or malefice through an easy form with a promise they would be in touch within twenty-four hours. A section called *Join Us*, inviting people to sign up to join their team of *Watchers* . . . whatever they were. And an area listing their current and new investigations – four so far: the Tower of London, the White City offices, the Whitechapel construction site and—

St Olave's School for Girls, Dulwich.

Allegations of a witchcraft cult and ritualistic practices. Originally thought to be targeting one pupil but levels of malefice are increasing with a recent attack against an entire classroom. Our contacts on the ground have been monitoring the situation, but considering the substantial risks to children, we are now opening a full investigation.

Downstairs, Anna showed Effie and Attis. Effie grabbed Anna's phone, reading it again, her eyes expanding, taking it all in. Attis stilled, hands on the kitchen counter, fingers raised as if ready to pounce. Anna was lost in her own thoughts of school – a classroom full of girls writing, faces twisted, eyes lost. Malefice in the air.

Effie walked away. 'Do you think it's true? That they'll open an investigation? They might just be making claims.'

'It says: *contacts on the ground,*' Anna pointed out, trying to hold back the waves of terror. 'They're talking about Eames. The inspection was just a ruse. They've already been investigating us . . . watching us all along.'

Anna was sure of it. She'd known something wasn't right about Eames but she hadn't wanted to see it. Surely the school hadn't known, or perhaps some of them had . . . either way, it was all out in the open now. Eames had been recording them for months. A thought knocked the remaining air from her. 'Do you think the WIPS know about our curse?'

Attis's head shot up.

'No . . .' said Effie. 'How could they? They're just focused on the cult rumours.'

Anna nodded but she felt like she was in one of her dreams, like if she took a step back the world might no longer be there and she'd fall and fall and fall. No safe ground anywhere. The eyes of the WIPS on them all along. *The Ones Who Know Our Secrets.* 'Rowan and Manda are coming over . . .' she managed to say.

'I thought we had to go and see Nana now,' said Effie.

'We do, but I couldn't stop them.'

Attis dropped onto a stool and began scanning the website. Effie paced back and forth.

'Do you know where Selene is?' Anna asked.

Effie shook her head. There came loud knocks at the door. Anna went to answer it and Rowan and Manda bolted through, expressions of panic on their faces that Anna was sure her own matched.

'We're being hunted!' Manda declared.

'Manda, not helping my anxiety here!' Rowan ran a hand through her frazzled hair as they made their way into the kitchen. 'We don't know what's happening yet. Mum's going to the school today, demanding to speak with Ramsden. Apparently Selene's going to join her.'

'Selene's back?' Anna asked.

'Flew in yesterday apparently.'

'Good of her to stop by,' Effie huffed.

'They'll stop it, right?' Manda looked between them for assurance. 'They can't *actually* open a WIPS investigation at a school? It wouldn't be allowed.'

'Friends in high places and financial connections,' Rowan repeated what Poppins had told them about the WIPS. 'Perhaps they've convinced the school board it's necessary or maybe the board wants this. You saw Darcey's parents, they wanted retribution.'

'And the WIPS might already be there,' said Anna. 'We think—'

'The inspector?' Rowan had obviously come to the same conclusion. Anna nodded.

They all stared at each other, thinking of the magic they'd been carrying out in the sewing room, the recklessness of it, bells going off, black apples in lockers, Anna being caught near the site of the school hysteria.

'He hasn't found anything solid,' said Effie, defiantly. 'No evidence of a damn thing. Anyway, fuck St Olave's. If they're escalating things then we just don't go back. I've moved schools plenty of times before.'

'It might not be that simple,' said Rowan. 'If they're investigating *us*, what's to stop them following us to another school? And if we move now it's only going to make us look guilty. The WIPS are bigger than our school – they're across London.'

Effie folded her arms, rocking back and forth, rage growing on her face, hardening her features.

Anna breathed out. 'And if they *are* the Hunters then their power could be greater than we know.' She looked to the door. 'We need to go. Nana's waiting and I don't think she'll appreciate us being late.'

'We'll come too,' said Manda.

'No. You guys shouldn't. It's our curse, no reason to put more of us at risk seeing her.'

'You might need back-up.' Rowan pulled a karate move. 'We're pretty threatening.'

Anna smiled. 'It's better if you guys wait here for Selene and Bertie. Find out everything you can. We won't be long, hopefully . . .'

She tried to maintain her hope as the bus trundled them towards Angel but Effie shot her a look. 'She's not going to help us, Anna. The bitch just hexed Attis and she probably started our curse. She's laughing at us.'

'You could be right but we still need her and we need to be careful – respectful—'

'We need to show her we're not afraid of her.'

'We can't threaten an ancient curse witch of unimaginable power.'

'Everyone has a weakness . . .'

'Effie—'

'Don't worry.' Effie rolled her eyes. 'I'm not stupid. I'll be my most charming self, as always.' She smiled in a way that was entirely unreassuring.

Anna tried to imagine Nana having any weakness. Last time they'd met, she'd bombarded them with dark visions, breaking everything apart, and yet, Anna didn't think Nana could be broken – her force pushed outwards and held no cracks.

'If all fails, I'll pelt her with dirty socks,' said Attis as they disembarked.

Anna led the way down the street from the station to the laundrette on the map. They faced it from the other side of the road – a shabby corner building that looked lost in time compared to the many coffee houses and lifestyle shops along the street. Some of the retro letters above the muggy windows were missing, spelling out: So ks & S ins.

They crossed the road and Anna spotted a trolley crammed full of detritus parked outside the laundrette. Nana's trolley. There was a man leaning against the front with a dog curled in his lap. His clothes looked like they hadn't seen the inside of a washing machine for some time. Anna looked through the windows but it was hard to see through the murky, soap-sudded glass. As she moved towards the door, Attis swerved in front of her.

'I'll go first,' he said, but he'd barely touched the handle when the man jumped up and slammed his hand against the door. The dog began barking ferociously, teeth snapping at Attis.

'Who do you seek?' said the man. He had a deeply lined face, prominent ears and several teeth missing.

Attis tried to stop the dog from chewing at his trouser leg.

'Nana,' Anna answered quickly, 'Nana Yaganov.'

'Are you here by your own free will or by compulsion?'

'Both.'

The man turned to her, hard-eyed, then his face split with a smile that reached from bulbous ear to bulbous ear. 'Go on then, but it's on your own head.' The dog came to rest next to him.

'This is a bad idea,' Attis muttered as he pushed the door open.

They went in one after the other, rattling the bell. The door swung shut behind them and so did the morning. With lurching disbelief, Anna realized that the street outside the windows was now dark as if it were night. Inside the laundrette, the lights were garish and ghoulish – bright, but stripped of warmth, flickering intermittently. The stacked washing machines on all sides were whirring, their hollow mouths chewing up the clothes inside. It smelt of laundry detergent, damp and grease. The place was empty save for a hunched bundle at the far end. The bundle shifted, revealing a figure within the layers of clothing and rags. A face more wrinkle than feature – folded in on itself like a riddle that answered only with a sickening laugh as a toothless slash of a smile opened up like a sinkhole and swallowed them all. It contracted back into a tight, disgruntled scowl. 'You're late.'

'Good to see you too, Nana.' Attis tilted his head. 'It's been too long.'

The caverns of her face turned on him. 'Are you still alive? Shame.'

'Ditto.'

'Sorry we're late.' Anna stepped forwards, glaring at Attis. 'We weren't sure exactly what time you meant—'

'Oh don't make excuses, girl.' Nana pointed at Anna's feet. 'WHY ARE YOU STILL WEARING YOUR SHOES? SHOES OFF. Off. Off. All of you – off!'

Anna put her hands up, appeasing. 'OK.' She knelt down and unlaced her trainers. She stepped out of them. Attis followed suit.

'Really?' Effie mumbled but complied, kicking her shoes off. 'Let's make ourselves at home.'

'You're not going to join us, Nana?' Attis gestured towards Nana's feet, which were hidden beneath layered rags of clothing.

'As if you could handle my toenails, boy.' She cackled and the sound tore up the air like a storm made of knives. 'RIGHT. LET'S ON WITH IT.' Nana heaved herself up. Her small, hunched figure moved surprisingly quickly, picking up baskets along the bench and emptying clothes onto the floor. 'Get sorting! Whites. Blacks. Reds. Delicates. Indelicates. You know the drill. No time to waste! No time to waste!' She turned to the washing machine beside her and started pressing buttons, seemingly at random. The machines began to spin faster, louder—

Anna looked down at the pile of clothes and knelt down, starting to sort them. Attis joined her, picking up a giant pair of grey knickers with a questioning eyebrow. Effie sat down grudgingly.

'Nana,' Anna began. It was hard to talk over the racket of washing machines. 'I hoped I might be able to speak to you again—'

'Hope. Pfft,' Nana spat. 'Hope is flimsy cartilage. It rots away. Where you're going . . . you're going to need bone.'

'I'll keep that in mind—'

'What do you want?' Nana snapped.

Anna bit her lip to stop it from trembling. 'I want to know the truth.'

'Can't tell the truth, I'm afraid. I might be an ancient curse witch of immeasurable power, but I'm human too and humans are incapable of such a thing.'

'Well – then – I'd like to know what you know.'

'A better request. About what?'

'About our curse.'

'What curse?'

'Nana.' Anna gritted her teeth, trying to remain controlled as she folded and sorted item after item. 'My family curse, the Everdell curse, we spoke about it last time we met—'

'Did we? When was this?'

'Around March.'

'Which century?'

Anna squeezed the cloth beneath her fingers. 'Last year.'

Nana slapped her knees. 'Well, I don't remember last year – too recent!'

'You were there when our curse began,' Effie growled.

'Was I? When was that?'

'1651,' said Anna.

'Don't remember that either. Not my favourite century.'

Effie stood up and moved towards Nana, losing patience. 'My sister here might believe you intend to help us, but I want to know what you – *Black Annis* – were doing there when our curse exploded all over our family for the rest of time? I don't even care if you did it, just tell us how to end it!' She forced out a final, 'Please.'

Nana poked her tongue out. 'Why should I?'

'Because!'

Nana stepped towards Effie. 'Because, because, because . . . because of the wonderful things he does—'

Effie raised her head. 'I'm not afraid of you.'

'Oh no, no, no, no, Effie fears nothing but herself and there's nothing worse than that.' Nana's eyes were black with threat; a bottomless, merciless pit.

'Shut up!' Effie spat. She stepped closer to Nana but Nana didn't budge. 'Don't you—' Effie's voice cut off, giving way to fear.

Nana laughed, her eyes devouring Effie. The lights above flashed with the motion of the room.

'No!' Effie roared. Her hands flailed out as if she would hit Nana but Nana moved nimbly back. 'No!' Effie's voice was crumbling now.

Attis and Anna ran to her. Anna wondered what visions Nana was showing her.

'Don't. No!' Effie screamed suddenly.

'What are you doing to her?' Attis yelled.

'No . . . please . . .' Effie's voice lost hope as she sank to the ground.

Attis lunged at Nana but she clapped her hands and the world went dark.

Anna had faced many kinds of darkness in her life, but nothing like this. It was not the kind of darkness you could shut your eyes against, you could close your fear off to. It was *made* of fear. Total and complete, consuming, fracturing – she had an item of clothing still in her hand but it made no sense to her fingers any more, not whole but threads—

'Three blind mice, see how they run.' Nana's voice made terrible music of the darkness. 'Lost in their curse, not knowing who is who is who, who to hold onto, no way out . . .'

She clapped her hands again and the world came back into focus. A dingy laundrette. Angel. London. Reality careering back into place but nothing quite making sense yet. *What had that darkness been?*

'No . . .' Effie's voice, from somewhere, so small and afraid.

Attis spun around. 'Effie, where are you? Anna, are you OK?'

They spotted Effie crouched in the corner of the room. She stared up at Nana through the black curtain of her hair, seething, silent. Attis ran to her.

'Whites! Blacks! Reds!' Nana cackled. 'Come on. I haven't got all day!'

Anna looked down at the item of clothing she was still holding in her hands and screamed. It was Aunt's blouse. The one they'd buried her in. Blood dripped from it. She threw it to the floor but when it landed, it was only a pair of jeans . . .

She picked them up again with shaking hands and folded them into the pile. She wouldn't let Nana derail her. She had to go on for the sake of them all. 'Do you remember our curse now, Nana?'

Nana plopped down on the bench, scratching her balding head. 'Do you know how many curses I've witnessed over the ages? Enough to shrivel all the spleens in London. Tell me. What was it again?'

'A curse to love the same man and one of us to kill the other over it,' Anna stated. Little point in hiding from it now.

'Ah yes,' Nana replied cheerily. 'I recall it now. I prefer something with a little more pus and boils, but still, nicely twisted as curses go. Could be worse, hey, ladies? At least he's a pretty one. I knew a woman once who was cursed to fall in love with a rat.'

'You haven't seen my boils,' Attis replied darkly.

Nana laughed like a cracked kettle on a bonfire. 'FUNNY TOO! WHAT A CATCH YOU ARE, JACK! HA! HA! HA! Why don't you choose your Jill and we'll send the other tumbling down the laundry chute. Go on, pick, pretty boy, or shall I do it for you?'

Attis leapt back onto his feet, looking between Effie and Anna, a wild animal not sure which way to run. The lights around them shuddered. The washing machines pounded.

He moved towards Nana. 'Don't you dare hurt them.'

'Or what?'

Though Attis towered over her small, stooped frame, somehow Nana seemed the larger figure as she shambled towards him, eyes latched on him now, screwing tighter. Attis held her stare. His jaw locked – but he held it. His fists clenched – but he held it. She laughed an empty, soulless sound, the lights flared wildly, and finally he roared, turning to punch the wall beside him, his knuckles bloodying against it. He crumpled to the floor.

Nana shrieked and the lights blinked out again, the darkness returning, but thicker, heavier, crunching them to nothing but despair. Anna couldn't breathe, couldn't hold onto herself – she heard Attis cry out from somewhere but his voice had unravelled—

Nana's sliced through it. 'They all ran after the farmer's wife! Who cut off their tails with a carving knife! Three blind mice!'

She clapped her hands and they were back in the laundrette.

Attis was the one on the floor now. Anna wanted to run to him but she turned to Nana. 'Eleanor and Hannah Everdell,' she called out over the washing machines which were pummelling faster. 'They were sisters. Hannah accused Eleanor of witchcraft and Eleanor was burned for it.'

Nana looked at Anna and for a moment Anna thought she saw something almost human in her eyes, but it quickly churned itself up. 'Did she now?'

'Before her death, Eleanor claimed she'd been cursed but we think she created a spell to end it. We need to know that spell – if there's a way to break the curse without Attis dying.'

'No pus, no fun.'

'Nana, please. There has to be another way.'

'Please! Pretty please!' Nana moved towards her. The lights flickered and Nana was Aunt, bearing over her. Anna couldn't move. 'Do you intend to be pathetic forever, my child?' The cold stillness of her voice. 'You know I haven't gone, don't you? You know I'll never, ever leave you—'

Aunt's face lit up in the lights – light then dark; flesh then bone.

I won't look down . . .

I won't . . .

Anna stumbled back but the floor wasn't there – she was falling and falling, landing at the bottom of a grave. Bones wrapping around her, Aunt's laughter in her ear.

'I'll never let you go.'

The lights flashed again and Anna found herself flailing on the floor among a pile of clothes.

'Don't listen to her, Anna!' Attis thundered from somewhere. 'Don't believe it!'

Anna scrabbled to her feet.

'Tell me!' she cried to Nana, trying to hold herself steady as the washing machines spun faster, warping everything.

'Why should I?' It was Effie before her now, tilting her head. 'How can I trust you, sister? How can I trust anything you say? Do you think I don't know? Do you love him? You do, don't you?'

Effie slammed Anna back against the wall, her face changing to Marie's and back to Effie's. 'He'll never be yours, never, and you'll never be enough for him—'

'NO!' Anna raged.

Blood poured suddenly out of Effie's mouth. Anna looked down and saw the knife in her own hands, stuck into Effie's chest. 'Anna—' Effie spluttered.

Anna screamed for her sister, tried to reach for her but the lights went out.

Darkness.

Anna's name echoed – Anna. *Anna. Anna* – tearing apart – *A – n – n – a* – until she couldn't remember who she was, why she mattered, why anything mattered. In this darkness it was so easy to let go . . .

'Let go . . .' Nana whispered.

Anna hung on, clung on, reaching for Nana. Not letting her go. 'Tell – me—' her voice squeezed through the darkness.

The lights flickered and Nana was so close, their faces almost touching. 'Tell me.'

Nana grabbed her and Anna was somewhere else. A corridor. *In a house?* Candles burning on the walls. Doors shut. Three figures walked past – men, grave-faced, darkly dressed in old-fashioned clothing. They stopped at a door. Necklaces hung about their necks with a symbol Anna knew.

One of the men produced a bunch of keys and opened the door. They went in. The door shut behind them and Anna was left in the hallway. She could hear the voices of the men inside – and a woman's voice – the rhythm of their conversation like questions, like threat. Anna didn't know what was going on beyond the door, only a sense of time passing and fear building against it. She could taste it, could hear the woman's voice rising. Then – screaming. Screaming. A raw sound – nothing left but pain and fear. Anna could feel all of it as if it was hers.

'I remember the smell of her flesh burning!' Nana cawed. 'Snap! Crackle! Pop!'

Anna could smell smoke now, could see the crowds – a woman at the stake, flames licking at her skirts.

'The whole town of Afeldale came to see it! Lighting her up like a beacon!'

Anna could hear the chants, her screams, but then it was Anna screaming and she was the one in the flames and the crowd was larger, filling up the streets of London. Pain like she'd never known consuming her entire being. The fire roaring in her ears—

The washing machines were roaring, shrieking, blood whirring and pulsing inside of them, pouring down the sides, like the blood of their curse through the centuries.

'What goes around comes around,' Nana hissed. 'They're coming for you again . . .'

'Eleanor . . .' Anna's voice rasped as if smoke was caught in it.

'You can't suffer a witch to live, can you? The town's sins washed away by her screams. They buried her quickly so they wouldn't have to face themselves.'

'How – how do we stop the curse?' It was hard to speak through the pain still in her body.

'How do you thread a needle through itself?'

'I thought you were going to help me!' Anna raged.

'How do you know I'm not?' Nana snapped, her face still close. 'If you're going to face the darkness, you've got to be ready and you're not ready yet, none of you are!' She shook her head. 'Did you get my little Christmas gift?'

Anna's mouth dropped open. 'That was you.'

'HO! HO! HO! The only way out is through. How about a clue? A riddle to drive you mad?'

'Fuck your riddles!' Effie snarled from behind them.

Nana spun to her. 'How else do you get out when you're lost in the maze?'

Effie blazed. 'I burn it to the ground.'

'Effie, Effie, always burning, never learning. Wrong answer. You go beneath. Come on.' Nana clicked her fingers. 'Take off your socks. I'll need three socks for a riddle.'

'Go to Hel,' Effie spat.

'I've been, it's lovely at this time of year—'

'Look.' Anna interrupted their quarrelling. She'd taken off her socks and held them out to Nana. 'You can have two of mine instead.' She shot Attis a pleading look. He shook his head but pulled a sock off and handed it to Anna. She offered the three socks to Nana. 'Three socks for a riddle.'

'I wanted a sock each!' Nana stomped her foot like a sulking child.

'You didn't stipulate that.'

Nana eyed Anna beadily then laughed wryly. 'Now you're learning.' She threw the socks into a washing machine and slammed the door shut but, as she spoke, the machines turned slow and the world around them spun cold—

> Mary, Mary, so contrary,
> How does your garden grow?
> With silver bells and yew tree dells,
> And ravenstones all out of row . . .
>
> One grows up beyond the boundary,
> How deep – how deep did she go?
> Unearthed God's word, truth dark nor light,
> The shadows, the shadows they know . . .
>
> You must go down to come back up,
> Learn the truth where all forget.
> The mirrored book knows the way to the dead,
> But heed his offer, hold tight your thread!

The machines were silent now. Their contents had disappeared and all Anna could see inside their deep hollows was snow – snow drifting gently as despair. The doors opened and white feathers flew out, filling up the whole room and coming slowly to rest.

Effie spat one from her mouth. 'Can we leave now? She's never going to tell us if she ever cast our curse or not.'

Nana's face screwed tight. 'A curse cannot be cast by just anyone, only one bound to the victim by love. For there is love in a curse, twisted into a hate so deep the centuries fall into it.'

Anna could still smell smoke. Could still hear Eleanor screaming in the flames – but it had been her own skin burning. 'The Hunters . . .' she whispered.

Nana cackled. 'You're seeing it now, aren't you? Your fates are tied to theirs, my three blind mice.'

'What do they want with us?'

'Your howls. Your hearts. Your light. Your dark. Your curse, of course.' Nana's eyes moved with delighted destruction between Anna and Effie. 'The beginning of the end. A tale! A tale! They cut off their tails with the carving knife!'

'How do we stop them?' Anna demanded.

But the washing machines convulsed back into life once more, around and around. Nana started to spin, a mad shuffling dance beneath her thick layers, shrieking. 'Did you ever see such a thing in your life as three blind mice?'

Everything thrashing and churning. Lights frenzied. The room filling with shadows, darkening again—

'THREE BLIND MICE!'

'Let's GO!' Attis hollered.

Effie swung the door open and they ran out, Nana's voice deafening behind them.

'THREE BLIND MICE!'

And then gone – the slam of the door chopping off the rabid tail of her words. It was daytime. The street was full of people, Nana's shopping trolley still outside and the man from earlier asleep against the wall, his dog curled up on his lap. Anna spun back to the laundrette, half expecting to see blood and darkness and Nana's cackle swishing around inside, but instead its lights were on and it appeared to be empty.

'You might need some shoes,' the man croaked, raising his head and laughing at them.

They looked down. They were all shoeless. Attis was only wearing one sock and Anna's feet were entirely bare. They glanced between each other, mutually acknowledging that – socks or no socks – they would not be going back into the laundrette ever again.

They took the bus back in a ruptured kind of silence, not yet ready to discuss what they had been through, what they had *seen*. Effie was bleached of colour, Attis's body hunched and taut. There had been no way to fight Nana's weapons – they weren't tangible, but formed of your own nightmares. Anna couldn't get the images from her head: Aunt bearing on her, blood running from Effie's mouth, the knife in her own hands, Eleanor in the flames, the feeling of her own flesh burning . . .

She'd wanted a moment of connection with the original sisters, but it had been too much, far too much to bear.

When they got back to the house, the air was too still after Nana's energy. The mood sombre. Bertie and Selene were sitting at the table, Bertie cradling a cup of tea, Selene a glass of wine. Rowan and Manda ran towards them.

Rowan made eyes at them. 'How did it go?' she mouthed.

'Some fresh leads,' Anna whispered. 'What's going on?'

'It's true,' said Manda. 'The WIPS are launching an official investigation into St Olave's. The school will be sending out letters tomorrow.'

Rowan nodded gravely.

'WHAT?' Effie erupted, striding towards Bertie and Selene. 'How can you let this happen?'

Selene stood up. 'Darling, we've tried but the school say their hands are tied.' Her usual smooth and easy expression was marred by lines of concern.

'Not hard enough!'

'The board of governors is backing it,' said Bertie. 'If we push too hard, we risk making you look guilty. *That* very fact was made abundantly clear to us by your headmaster, who seems to be very supportive of this investigation too.'

'Ramsden,' Attis spat. 'He's just enjoying the power.'

'How can you not stop this?' Effie was no calmer. 'We have the world of magic behind us!'

'We still don't know the full extent of the WIPS' power,' Bertie replied gravely. 'The fact they've managed to open an investigation in a school suggests their reach and influence is growing. We are looking into . . . magical options against the WIPS, but we need to ensure nothing becomes exposed.'

'So we're just going to play by their rules?'

'Ultimately, they've already had a presence in your school – Inspector Eames. We've been reassured he will continue to head this all up. No one new is coming and we don't believe they have any new information. I imagine things will feel different . . . but you need to continue to stay out of his way, do no magic, while we buy ourselves time.'

'Or wait until it's too late!' Effie spat.

'There's no reason for panic,' Selene said in an attempt to console her. 'Nothing has come out of these WIPS investigations except reports.'

'And what about the hysteria?' Effie stared back at her, unrelenting. 'What if there's another attack?'

Selene seemed to crumble then, turning to Bertie, each struggling to hide their fear, neither one knowing what to say to make it OK.

'We're looking into that too,' said Bertie.

Effie huffed and shook her head. 'Come on.' She jerked her head to the others. 'Let's go to the roof.'

They sat outside as the light dwindled, Effie restless and railing against everything happening like a cat clawing at the bars of a cage. Anna found herself surprisingly still, as if the day had pummelled her so much that there was nothing left to do but accept everything, like on some level, she'd known it was all coming and now she could finally face it.

'What if the WIPS find us guilty?' Manda panicked. 'What do they actually want?'

Rowan spoke in a low voice, shaved of its usual character:

> Five wolves are out in the woods tonight,
> You better beware, the fire burns bright,
> Eyevain in the garden, iron in your bed,
> Or they'll gobble you up
> from your toes to your head . . .

She shook her head. 'My grandma used to threaten me with that one whenever I was misbehaving. Never *actually* believed it.'

'So, what?' said Manda. 'If they're the Hunters they want to gobble us up?'

Rowan sighed. 'I don't know, it's just a rhyme, but we can't ignore the fact there's more going on than we know and now we're in the middle of it. Like Mum and Selene said, we have to keep our—'

'We can't just keep our heads down like blind fucking mice!' Effie exploded. 'There's clearly more going on than they're telling us. This is exactly like Selene, lying all over again, treating me like we're the same bloody age half the time and a child who can't handle anything the rest. Meanwhile we've got enemies like Darcey and everyone already suspects us – including the inspector. He's not going to give up until he finds us guilty. If we let them contain us, they've already won.' Her eyes moved rapidly, already plotting, planning, rebelling.

'Except, this isn't a game,' said Anna sharply.

'It's always a game! The rules are simply changing and we need to be ready. We need to be smart. We need to be powerful. If the wolves are out in the woods, I'm not going to be the little girl looking through the window, I'm going to be the one with the fucking axe.' Effie's restlessness had turned to fuel for her burning words. 'We're witches. We don't cry – we howl! We don't cower from the dark – we wield it! And if they push us into the shadows – we become the shadows!' Her words took flight around them, refusing to be pinned down.

'The shadowthread . . .' said Anna.

Effie nodded hungrily. '*If* it works, that is.' She looked to the others. 'Turns out Anna's secret Santa was Nana.'

Rowan's mouth dropped. 'Really?'

Anna nodded. 'She certainly implied it.'

'If she's not messing with us and it *is* real shadowthread, then we make ourselves some shadowrobes so we can move unseen if we need to,' said Effie. 'Perhaps, we ought to consider using our magic against Eames too—'

'No.' Rowan jumped in. 'Way too risky.'

Effie looked as if she wanted to argue, but she bit her lip. The moment was broken by Bertie calling Rowan from downstairs.

'I better go too,' said Manda, still looking jumpy.

They said their goodbyes and headed off. Anna realised she hadn't asked Manda about her parents, if they knew anything yet. She imagined they wouldn't take news of the investigation well. She collapsed into one of the seats, thoroughly exhausted. The sky was dark now but nothing compared to the darkness Nana had shown them. That had not been darkness, it had been an emptiness that could have swallowed the sky whole.

Anna could still hear Eleanor's screams.

'Nana showed me something,' she said, scared to voice it but knowing she had to.

Attis released a low, charred sound. 'Don't believe anything she showed you. We should never have gone to see her.'

'A waste of time,' Effie spat.

'It wasn't a waste of time,' Anna snapped back. 'Nana admitted she was the one who gave us the shadowthread and you seem more than happy to use that.'

Effie folded her arms. 'Go on then . . .'

'Nana may have told us where the original sisters lived. She said the whole town of *Afeldale* came out to see Eleanor burn. And what she showed me . . . it wasn't . . . it wasn't like her other tricks. I think it was *real*. It felt real. I think she showed me Eleanor being interrogated, which tallies with the confession we read. And I saw her—' Anna tried to stop her voice from shaking. 'I saw Eleanor burning. Then I—'

Attis knelt down to her, his brow contracted. 'What?'

'I felt myself burning. And it wasn't the same – 'And it wasn't the same – all of London was watching—'

Attis's head was shaking. 'It wasn't real. This is what she does, she gets into your head, to drive you crazy.'

The look in his eye told Anna that Nana had done just that to him. She knew he was right, that Nana's visions were designed to feel real, to find your weak spots and blast them open, but she could still feel the echoes of the flames on her skin.

'There was something else,' she said. 'In the vision of Eleanor, the men who went to interrogate her, they had necklaces around their necks . . . necklaces that showed the symbol of WIPS.'

A cross inside a circle. She'd known it instantly.

Effie's eyes narrowed now. 'So the Hunters were after Eleanor and Hannah and now they're after us too?'

'Symbols are often repurposed. The WIPS may have taken an old symbol and made it their own,' said Attis, but his voice had weakened, fear making it rough. 'That's *if* Nana's vision was true, which it probably wasn't.'

'Nana also said the Hunters will want our curse,' Anna reminded him. 'What if it's all connected?'

Anna didn't like the way Effie's eyes lit up at the thought of them being linked to everything going on. 'Perhaps the prophecy really *is* about our curse . . .'

'No.' Anna tried to quell Effie's rising exhilaration. 'That's not what I'm saying, but that considering the prophecy, *all* curses are of interest to them.'

'Do you see what she's doing?' Attis's voice was fire now. 'Sending you down her many rabbit holes – they're all traps!'

'Or she's trying to warn us.'

'You're too trusting, too naive to see that she's just messing with you—'

Anna spun to Attis, feeling some of Nana's wildness inside her. 'Naive?! I grew up on lies and threats, OK? I know how to handle them.'

He looked a little cowed, the steel of his eyes relenting. 'I just – I don't want you getting hurt . . . not when I can solve all this—'

'Attis! You promised!' Anna's words erupted. 'I try – you try.'

Effie's eyes narrowed. 'What *promise*?'

Anna looked back at Effie, momentarily flustered. 'Nothing. I just told him to stop offering to die . . . that it's annoying. Anyway, come bane or boon, we have to at least consider Nana's madness or we'd be the fools.' She spoke the start of the riddle again.

> *Mary, Mary, so contrary!*
> *How does your garden grow?*
> *With silver bells and yew tree dells,*
> *And ravenstones all out of row . . .*

'I know the word ravenstone,' said Effie. 'I've heard Azrael use it – it's what the Hel witches call graves.'

'Really? *Graves all out of row* . . . some kind of cemetery?' Anna wondered.

'You do get yew trees in graveyards,' Attis admitted begrudgingly. 'Ogham witch tree magic – yews protect the dead, help their souls move on.'

'To Hel.' Effie's mouth twisted.

'Why this is Hel nor am I out of it . . .' Attis muttered grimly. Anna recognized the quote from somewhere. 'Look, I'll leave Nana's riddle to you two – I've had enough of her riddles for a lifetime.' He sighed, his eyes moving to Anna's. 'But I can look into Afeldale if it helps. There's a magical map shop in London. I'll contact the owner, see if she has anything.'

Anna nodded. 'Thank you.'

He dipped his head in return and left.

Effie rolled her eyes. 'Any excuse for him to get his hands on a map. He loves them. Always has.'

Anna turned back to the empty fire, worried at the look in Attis's eyes as he'd spoken of himself as a solution, wishing she hadn't told him about Nana's vision now. 'He's stressed.'

Effie nodded as if this was normal. 'He gets like that when he feels like things are getting out of his control, like he can't protect everyone.'

'Well, we can't let him believe he is the only answer to all this.'

Effie eyed her sharply. 'Of course not. I told you I won't let Attis hurt himself again.'

Anna held back her response. She didn't want to get into an argument over him. 'We have to keep going. Our mother went to see Nana and she found the spell for Attis. We can do the same. If we can stop our curse, there's a chance we can get through this year, get on with our lives.'

Effie stared at her, as if she knew Anna didn't believe her own grasping words. 'Go back to being *normal*? Off to *university*?'

'Why not?'

Effie's dark eyes lit up again. 'Because we're meant for more.'

'Is that just a way of getting out of revising for exams?'

Effie snorted. 'Maybe.' She edged forwards in her chair. 'Or maybe I can feel what you can feel . . . something's building.'

Anna didn't answer, Effie's words creeping under her skin. Anna could feel darkness on all sides, everything spinning out of control, herself somehow tangled in it all.

'A witch is only limited by her imagination . . .' Effie put her hand towards Anna, her spider tattoo in her palm again. 'Together . . .'

Anna met Effie's eyes. When they were together she felt like she could be *more*, she just didn't know if it was a good thing or not.

'Together,' she replied, putting out her hand.

The spider tiptoed onto her palm trailing threads of magic. As she tried to grasp it, it crawled back to Effie.

Effie smirked. 'We should get matching tattoos, you know.'
'How about the words: *Beware of my sister?*'
'I wholly approve.'

SHADOWTHREAD

Can you see through the snows of Hel? Can you pierce through the blizzard? Can you capture the fractured pieces of your own being? Can you see how intricate this bone-lace be? How the maze was spun by you yourself; how that which ensnares you – sets you free.

Translation of the Words of Ra-webenes, Hel Witch and Guardian Spirit,
Fourteenth century BCE

Anna managed to carve out some time at the end of the holidays to send off her university applications and do *some* school work. In between catching up and doomscrolling on the internet, she'd found herself drawn to the piano – again and again – trying to free herself from the darkness of her dreams.

They were getting worse. The night before, she'd arrived at the door once more but it had still been locked – covered in locks, in fact, so many and yet none she could open, like a riddle she could not solve. When she'd tried to reach for it she'd found her arm would not move. She'd looked down to see threads tied to it . . . not around, but through her flesh. She'd pulled against them but they'd pulled back. As she began to flail she'd realized her body was tied – every limb – threads coming through the keyholes, holding her suspended, motionless like a fly in the web of a monster she could not see. *Captured.*

Her hands moved freely now, flexing up and down the keys as if they'd never left. The spinning top spun steadily on the top of the piano. She'd been trying to focus on the feeling of happiness – joy, working on a melody that contained all the warmth and safety of Christmas at

Bertie's – the hum of the fire, the taste of hot chocolate, carols and laughter echoing through every room, the snow and the quiet grace of the garden beneath the stars. She filled the sketch lines of the song with all its richness, letting them deepen, sink into her, feeling colours she hadn't felt for so long; feeling her magic. Everything connected, reaching outwards—

But then darkness.

The spinning top flew away. The magic severed. The song shrank beneath her fingers. Every time she started to flow it was the same – her magic would hit a wall, darkness and silence would surround her. *What is it? Why won't it let me through? Is it out there?* The threats they faced. *Or inside me?*

Anna was left torn in two – longing for her magic now she had started to feel it, but fearing it. Fearing that as it expanded the curse would slip through again. Nana's vision flashed before her – Effie bleeding, the knife in her own hands . . .

She wished Nana had not made a game of their curse again. She had no idea where to start with the riddle. Who was Mary? Where was her garden? Why did it have graves in it? She'd researched Afeldale. It no longer existed as a town. A couple of search results had stated that it had once been located in the county of Surrey but there were no maps showing where. She'd pestered Attis about his map shop and he'd said it was in progress. She hoped he wasn't stalling.

There was just one line of the riddle that she thought she might have cracked. *The mirrored book knows the way to the dead . . .*

She believed it was referring to the book of fairy tales with its golden mirrored tree on the front. It had helped her before and she knew its tales contained many secrets, but was this a secret she wanted to unearth? There was little choice, not with their own WIPS inspection waiting for them back at school and Attis starting to believe he was the only way out.

When they returned to St Olave's, the Eye was the first thing that met Anna. Staring at them from the poster nailed to the entrance noticeboard.

STOP THE SPREAD.

Effie released a growl beneath her breath. 'Isn't it nice they decorated for us?'

Anna had the urge to run. There were too many things that could go wrong. What if the hysteria struck again? What if it *had* been her magic? What if Eames already knew about their curse? What if the Hunters were after them just like Eleanor and Hannah? She tore her eyes away from the poster and forced herself to move forwards.

Attis followed, wearing a deep scowl. The Boys' School sixth form had been called to join assembly, which didn't bode well. Ramsden wanted everyone there. The whispers rose as they walked through the corridor, surrounding them like a net, but different now – no longer excited and hungry but rattled, laced with real tremors of fear. Even Attis wasn't receiving his usual warm welcome, people turning away from them as they made their way to the Athenaeum. Anna lowered her head, not wanting to scare anyone more than they already were.

Her heart contracted at the sight of Inspector Eames on the stage, holding the lectern as if he'd been there all holidays. Waiting. He was dressed as always – black suit, red tie, lacquered hair carefully combed to one side like a schoolboy's – and yet there was a fresh confidence in his stance, a new polish in his black shoes, a shine in the dark shadows of his eyes. He could declare who he really was at last.

Behind him, in Darcey's usual spot, sat a row of senior prefects from the Boys' School, including Tom, Andrew and Peter. Darcey had been moved to the other side of the stage. She looked different, softer – her make-up pared back, her hair tied into a low ponytail, her uniform abiding by all the rules for the first time: skirt below the knee, unheeled black shoes slippering her feet. Her hands were clasped in her lap demurely, vindication in her eyes.

Eames's stillness stilled the crowd. He cleared his throat – a tight, dry sound. 'As you have all been informed, I will be continuing my work here at St Olave's but now under the direct guidance and direction of the Witchcraft Inquisitorial and Prevention Services.' His words rolled out tersely, shaved to the bare bones. 'It is necessary. The levels of threat in this school have increased and we must respond. We have last year's evidence of a potential Black Sabbath on school grounds, allegations from a student who believes she was targeted by the same cult, and now, what might be a wider malefice attack at the end of last term.'

His statement was bold, unafraid, countering the school's verdict of *stress-induced hysteria*, proclaiming things that had only before been allowed as rumour. The darkness reared around Anna again and she lowered her eyes, playing the melody she'd been working on in her head, trying to keep herself calm.

'I don't wish to unsettle you,' he continued. 'But we need to be aware of the threats we face. I am here for *you*. To protect you from those among us who are not like us, who threaten our safety as a community and school.'

Among us.

'If you have any knowledge that might enlighten my investigations then you must share it, either with Headmaster Ramsden, myself, or, if you'd feel more comfortable, Ms Dulacey has set up a group for those impacted by the effects of malefice where you can speak freely about your fears and suspicions. And to those responsible – there is still time to end this now.' He looked out over the crowd, eyes scanning steadily. 'To confess.'

Confess. Confess. Confess.

The Athenaeum had never been so silent. Held in the shock of his words. But Anna could feel the fear vibrating beneath, shaking the walls around them, the foundations of life at school as they all knew it.

Ramsden proceeded to take Eames's place, thanking him for his *expertise* and listing off a new set of school rules with spiteful pleasure.

Nobody is allowed on school grounds before or after school hours . . .

Nobody is to remain in classrooms after class . . .

No personal items are allowed at school except what is required for your studies . . .

'Inspector Eames has also requested the help of a select number of senior prefects.' Ramsden gestured to the row of boys behind him. 'Please do adhere to their requests at all times.'

Peter was sitting almost as still as Eames himself, hands on his knees. He raised his head at the words, his broad shoulders an inflexible line.

'I have a question, Mr Ramsden.'

Anna's head snapped the other way – to where Attis had just stood up, her heart leaping into her throat. *Attis! What was he doing?*

Ramsden's face twitched. 'No questions, Mr Lockerby.'

'Is it only senior prefects who are able to assist Mr Eames with his investigation? Because I'd like to volunteer my services.'

'Sit down, Lockerby,' Ramsden ordered.

'What's the screening process? Do you have to be as stuck-up as that lot? On course for Cambridge? Have money? A certain haircut?'

'LOCKERBY! YOU ARE PLAYING WITH FIRE!'

'Big dick energy?'

'TAKE HIM OUT!'

A couple of prefects moved towards Attis. *Don't fight them, please, don't fight them.* Attis put his hands up in surrender, but his voice turned low and his performance mask fell away. 'No, Ramsden,' he growled. 'You are the one playing with fire, you're just too stupid to realize it.'

There was no sign of Attis as they left the hall. The crowd remained quiet but jittery, as if everyone had too much to say but were too afraid to speak it.

'What was he thinking?' Anna whispered hoarsely.

'He doesn't always think when he's angry,' said Effie.

'Well, he should!' she fumed, worried what he'd be facing now. *Why did he choose to put himself in harm's way?*

Anna looked around for Rowan and Manda but her eyes landed on a group of Year Sevens who were passing by – among them were some of the girls she'd seen that day in the classroom. Anna froze and they froze too. She wanted to say something – *sorry, sorry I couldn't help you, I don't know what it was either—*

But one of them began to scream. It set the others off, the girls erupting like jack-in-a-boxes wound too tightly – shrieks splintering the silence as they shook and quaked with terror. Anna's own terror held her still – she didn't know what to do, what was happening—

Not again . . . not again . . .

She turned to Effie but Effie appeared just as lost.

Peter's voice broke through the clamour. 'What's going on?'

He strode towards them, his eyes moving between Anna and the hysterical Year Sevens. She shook her head as if to say *I don't know.* Several other prefects arrived from assembly, attempting to quell the chaos. The girls began to calm down, their screams fading, looking dazed by their own outburst. They huddled together. Anna couldn't feel the magic she'd felt before and the look in their eyes was shaken but lucid.

'Take them to the nurse's office,' Peter instructed several of the prefects. 'And then to the Ebury wing.'

He turned to Anna and Effie.

'Oh, come on,' Effie spat. 'They were putting it on.'

Tom stepped beside Peter. 'Except how do we know that you didn't mutter some of your dark spells at them?' Tom rocked on his heels, fully enjoying his raised prefect status. 'Where there are witches, there's always trouble . . .'

'Kellman.' Peter's voice was firm. 'This is not a laughing matter. None of this is.'

Anna found her voice. 'Peter, we didn't do anything.' She desperately hoped it was true. 'They just started screaming . . . they're young and they just had a terrifying assembly—'

'I still have to report any incidents of hysteria directly to Eames and take anyone involved to him. I'm sorry, I'll do my best to explain to him what likely happened here.'

'There was no likely about it,' Effie retorted. 'They started acting crazy for attention and we're getting the blame. What do you think you're doing working for him?'

Peter scowled in her direction. 'We were asked,' he replied archly, 'and extra school responsibilities always play out well on university applications.'

'Oh yeah, I'm sure you're doing this for your *applications* and not the power trip. How's your hard-on right now?'

Tom leered at Effie. 'Mine is always ready to go when you're around.' She shoved him away.

'She does look like a witch, doesn't she?' Tom elbowed Peter. 'Black hair. Evil stare. Big mouth.'

'Wow.' Effie glowered. 'We have the finest of witch hunters on our hands here . . .'

Seeing the growing look of anger on Peter's face, Anna jumped in. 'Come on then. If we have to go to the Ebury wing, let's get it done with.'

She moved ahead with Peter, leaving Effie to bicker with Tom behind them. Anna tried to take deep breaths, to hide the shake of her hands. This was the worst possible start to term – already off to see Eames, more evidence stacked against them.

She shot Peter a look. 'You don't have to help Eames. Your applications hardly need bolstering.'

Peter turned to her. 'Do you remember what happened at the end of last term?'

Her skin shrivelled at his words. She tried not to show her fear, forcing a smile. 'You don't really believe in magic, do you?'

Peter did not smile back. 'I don't know what's going on. But there's more happening out there than most of us are privy to.' He lowered his voice. 'My dad runs the biggest surveillance company in the UK. He always has his finger on the pulse. He's told me that things are changing, that there are threats right now we can't understand, that the WIPS are the ones we should be looking to.' His voice had risen. 'I told you I wanted to do more, *be* more. If I can help with this then I want to.'

Anna bit her tongue, not knowing what to say that wouldn't give anything away. His words disturbed her. He'd always had an intensity to him but it had been anchored by rationality. Now something else was breaking through. Peter's expression softened, as if he was worried he'd scared her. 'I know it's a lot to take in but I'm here to help you, I promise. If the real culprits are found, you'll be free.' Anna didn't like the way his eyes flashed back to Effie.

'What's going on?' Eames's secretary asked when they arrived on the second floor of the Ebury wing.

'There's been a small outbreak of panic after assembly,' said Peter.

The secretary's lips firmed as if she didn't want to have to deal with this on top of everything else. 'Eames is busy at the moment. You can wait here.'

After a few minutes of uncomfortable silence, Darcey exited Eames's room. *What was she doing in there?* When she spotted Effie and Anna she unleashed a look of malicious glee, a smile that said: *I'm going to win this war.*

Peter strode to the door. 'I'll go and speak to Eames first.'

'I'll stay here and watch the witches,' Tom snorted, still entertaining himself.

'You can go, Mr Kellman,' the secretary barked. Anna smirked at the dismissive tone in her voice.

By lunchtime, Anna just wanted the day to be over. She'd had to face a fresh round of questioning from Eames. She'd sat alone in all her classes and been stared at wherever she went. She met the others on a bench outside, glad to be away from a hundred prying and fearful eyes. Attis wasn't there – he'd been given a full day of detention by Ramsden.

Manda glanced between Anna and Effie, looking stricken. 'What was Eames like? Was he different now? Did he think we're guilty?'

'He was the same creep as always,' Effie replied scathingly. 'And yes, he does think we're guilty, but no, he still can't prove it.'

Anna had paid close attention to the inspector, trying to work out what he knew and didn't. His questions hadn't tiptoed around malefice any more. They'd been direct, cutting. But as she'd looked into his eyes, she'd seen something she hadn't noticed before. That their strange blankness wasn't emptiness . . . it was that they were entirely full, but full of just one thing – one motivation, one purpose: the search for the truth. Not the kind of truth that allowed for shades of interpretation, for humanity, but a hard, cold, nailed-down truth. He wanted it, he craved it. Like Effie said, he certainly suspected them, but Anna didn't think he knew for sure that they were witches. Which meant the WIPS probably didn't know they were cursed. She hoped. 'I think it helped that Peter downplayed this morning's incident to him,' she said.

'Because it was bullshit.' Effie kicked at a stone. 'I told you those Year Sevens were attention-seekers.'

Anna shook her head. 'This morning was different from . . . before. I think today they were just scared.'

'Maybe, maybe not. We still don't know if any of this hysteria isn't just cowans being crazy.'

'To be fair, *I'm* feeling hysterical after Eames's assembly,' said Rowan.

'He said Black Sabbath!' Manda cried, a bundle of nervous energy. 'Do you know what that is? A satanic meeting of witches! He can't say things like that.'

'He said *potential* Black Sabbath.' Effie walked up and down in front of the bench. 'He didn't directly go against the school's whole stress-induced hysteria thing, just added layers, offered an alternative, enough to—'

'Scare everyone shitless?' Rowan suggested despairingly.

'Surely parents will be up in arms?' said Manda, clearly trying to hold onto the school she thought she knew.

'I don't know,' Rowan replied. 'I mean, some will be, but I bet plenty are afraid to speak out. The board of governors has got a lot of sway with parents and most of them probably just want something to be done, to feel like their kids are being kept safe. Plus, like with us, it's presumably being implied that if you take your child out of the school, it'll make them look guilty. I overheard that some of the teachers have been complaining too, but Ramsden's no doubt threatening them to toe the line as well,' she sighed. 'Mum's started to keep tabs on where I'm going now, which she's never done before. How are your parents coping, Manda? I'm surprised they haven't tried harder to take you out.'

Manda appeared startled at the mention of her parents. 'They have, but I think they're terrified to draw more attention to it all.'

'How are things at home?' Anna asked.

Manda shrugged. 'They're not really talking to me. I've been distracting myself with Karim . . . we've been speaking every day.'

'Ah.' Rowan managed a smile. 'Love in the midst of war.'

'Or boinking in the midst of battle,' Effie snorted.

Manda pulled a face at her.

'Sorry, I'm sure you'll end up happily married, et cetera, et cetera.'

'Like you and Azrael?' Rowan teased.

Effie wrinkled her nose. 'To be honest, his intensity is starting to get a bit much. Don't get me wrong, in bed it's all good, but out of bed, he really does talk about death a lot.'

Rowan laughed then looked to Anna. 'Peter still seems pretty enamoured with you. You should be careful there.'

'We're just friends,' Anna insisted. 'I don't even know why he's into me.'

'I do,' said Effie. 'Because you didn't let him have you and Peter is the sort who doesn't like being denied what he wants.'

Her deduction made Anna uncomfortable. She diverted the conversation. 'Peter said his father thinks we should be listening to the WIPS.'

Rowan's eyebrows knitted together. 'That's worrying. His dad's a big shot. The exact kind of person we don't want supporting them. I can't believe Peter and his stupid jumped-up friends are running duties for Eames . . .'

'Makes sense.' Effie shrugged rancorously. 'They're young, conceited . . . easy to control.'

Manda dropped her head into her hands, her bitten nails pulling at her temples. 'We should be focusing on our exams right now. If our universities find out we're suspects of witchcraft, we might all lose our places before we even get them.'

Rowan put a hand on Manda's shoulder. 'We can get through this.'

'Not with people randomly losing their shit around us, we won't,' Effie bit back. 'We need to get to the bottom of what's going on. I've found out how we can make the shadowrobes. Emilia from the Wild Hunt is obsessed by the Nxy witches – wants to be one but no one knows if they exist any more. Anyway, she's confirmed it. Apparently they sew themselves. Amazing, right? You just need to sew a single stitch and the shadowthread takes it from there. But—' She put a finger up. 'It needs potent, powerful shadows to work with. It's recommended the thread is left in a room charged with magic and that hasn't seen daylight for at least a hundred years.'

'OK . . .' Rowan narrowed her eyes. 'Where do we find that?'

'We already have it!' Effie presented a smile. 'Our coven room. This school is centuries old and the sewing room is underground. Plus, it's amped up with our magic.'

'I'm not sure. We'd have to get in and out of there unseen—'

'Only until our robes are made,' Effie said quickly, 'and then – we're free. Nobody will see us going in or out and the door is hidden by Attis's chimera. Besides, we need to keep practising our magic somewhere private, and we all live on different sides of London. It's easiest here – we can meet straight after school without either of your parents getting too suspicious.'

Effie's rationale sounded convincing but Anna knew the real reason Effie wanted to keep practising in their coven room: pure stubbornness. They'd been here first and there was no way she would let Eames drive them away, not if it killed her.

'Let's meet Friday. Get sewing . . .' Effie started but her words were interrupted by a voice.

'Hey . . .' Karim was coming down the path towards them.

Manda stood up. 'Hi,' she said coyly.

He nodded to the others, but his eyes were on Manda. 'I've been trying to find you.'

'Ah! Young love.' Effie clapped her hands together. 'We'll leave you to it. You can have this bench but remember – no canoodling on school grounds.' She wagged a finger at them.

'Effie . . .' Manda glowered at her, but Karim just laughed, sweeping back his black hair and smiling at Manda goofily.

'Shall we?' He presented the bench to her.

Anna, Effie and Rowan walked away, managing to giggle despite everything going on.

On Friday, Anna left school as usual and walked several streets away, where she met the others. Manda hadn't known if she'd be able to make it but she was there.

'I don't have long,' she said, chewing at her nails.

Anna would have asked how she'd managed it, but she was too distracted thinking about what they were about to do. With the unknown darkness inside her own magic, Anna wasn't sure she should be working with any kind of shadows right now . . . but she'd spent her whole life running and hiding – she didn't want to any more.

No way out but through.

Attis came down the street, his body tense and alert. 'The entrance looks all clear.' He'd sussed out an old, little-used side door that could be accessed from a quiet street. It was right next to a stairwell so they could run straight down to the abandoned lower ground floor of the school. They nodded at each other like comrades then followed after him.

The shadow of the school fell over them. It had felt like a prison all week – everyone on edge. Ramsden walking around like he owned the place. Even the teachers in some of Anna's classes had been wary of her, while Darcey had been delighting in it all. She'd started her group for victims of malefice, *to help process their trauma*, Anna had overheard Corinne saying in her cloying voice. Apparently, Darcey was encouraging everyone to share their *fears* and *suspicions* online, feeding the rumours about them, while she passed them on to Eames directly.

They stopped at the door. Attis took out his skeleton key and with a single click they were in.

They ran, shadows chasing at their heels. Anna had sneaked down to the sewing room so many times before, but it felt different now . . . the school heavier above them, the darkness more knowing. There was something else too – something that ran deeper than the jittery energy of the day, something that shouldn't be here at all—

Rowan's bag swung against the metal bannister, making a clanging noise. They all stilled, hearts pounding in unison.

'Sorry,' Rowan whispered.

Attis waved a hand. 'Come on. Almost there.'

They sprinted down the final corridor, Attis temporarily removing the chimera from the door, long enough for them to rush inside.

He put it back in place and Anna breathed out, feeling safer in the deepest bowels of the building, in the gloom of the sewing room, than she had all week.

'See?' said Effie. 'Easy-peasy.'

Rowan slumped onto a chair. 'I think I might die.'

Effie made for the headless mannequins that had stood quietly in the room for so long. 'As if it was meant to be . . .' she said, beginning to strip them of their old rags of cloth. 'Everyone find a needle.'

They joined her in the ring of mannequins. Anna pulled an old needle out from one of them. It trembled in her fingers. Such a small thing – about to weave great power.

Effie took out the spool of shadowthread and pulled the thread away. It was hard to even see it in the gloom of the room, indistinct from the shadows around it. She snipped five lengths from it – emptying the spool as if Nana had given them just enough for their purposes – and passed the threads around.

'Now.' Effie faced her mannequin. 'You just need to thread the needle, then prick your finger and sew a single stitch.'

Anna turned to her own mannequin, its blankness staring back at her like a reflection. Was this how they were seen now? Not people any more, objects to analyse and gossip about, to fear.

'OK, not to sound stupid here, but how do you thread a shadow?' Rowan asked, holding up a needle in one hand and the undulating, vaporous thread in the other. She tried. It failed.

Manda groaned a noise of frustration. 'Yeah, I can't do it.'

Effie frowned, trying to force thread and needle together.

Anna unravelled her own thread and watched it move about her fingers – there and not there, shadow and silver, air and shiver. *My Hira is needle and thread* . . . Selene's question before Christmas came back to her: *How do you thread a needle?*

Anna thought of the many times she'd sat beside Aunt, sewing in the silence of their living room. *Stillness.* Even when Aunt had been angry, had been testing her or cursing her, Anna had been able to find a small kind of steadiness, a stillness. A place where Aunt couldn't get to her. *Freedom in the eye of the needle.* She'd done it a thousand times over. She could do it with her eyes closed.

She closed them now and emptied her mind, letting the furore of the week fade away. When she opened them again, nothing was left in the world except the thread and the eye of the needle. She breathed out and moved them together. The thread slipped through, like a shadow through the bars of a cage. It felt strong, like mist made of steel, the needle hanging from it, locked and loaded.

'How did you do that?' said Manda, looking over.

Anna smirked. 'I've threaded a lot of needles.'

She helped the others, one by one, except Attis, whose finely tuned fingers had managed it, and then they turned back to their mannequins. Anna pressed the needle to her finger and released a drop of blood with a sharp prick, then threaded the shadowthread through the fabric of the mannequin. One stitch.

Effie stepped back rubbing her hands together. 'Apparently we just leave them now – let the shadows complete their side of the bargain.'

They looked between one another and Anna sensed no one else wanted to leave the sewing room either. Here they could become anything they wanted. Out there they were *the witches among us*.

'I could probably stay a little longer . . .' said Manda.

'Really?' Attis stepped forwards. 'I actually had something I wanted us all to work on.'

They turned to him and he moved beyond the circle of mannequins, eager to begin. 'With everything going on, we need to learn how to protect ourselves. I know we covered the basics of circles last year but there's a lot more to them. Whether you're facing an oncoming attacker or a dark spell, your circle is your first line of defence. Think of it as your magical armour – it needs to be quick, strong and flexible. Let me show you.' The tension across his shoulders seemed to loosen as he moved with purpose, clearing the desks to the side and taking a glass bottle out of his bag. 'Effie, could you help demonstrate?'

She moved to the centre.

'There are three basic types of circle. Last year we worked with the first – the circle as a barrier.'

He threw the bottle towards Effie, as he had demonstrated to them last year. It broke with a blinding shatter before it reached her, tiny pieces of glass falling around her.

'Nicely done.' Attis nodded. 'Now, the second kind is not only a barrier, but it returns the attack too. Effie's favourite.'

He raised his hand again and the scattered glass shards lifted up into the air. He moved his fingers around, drawing the pieces back towards him, then propelled them with force towards Effie again. They flew fast – dagger-edged – but as the shards reached the boundary of her circle, they rebounded, turning back towards Attis, with more speed, more force, growing sharper as they cut through the air—

Attis threw a hand up and held them still just before they could reach him.

'Mildly terrifying,' Rowan murmured.

Attis put a finger up. 'Ah. But there's another option and the most complex by far. A circle that doesn't just return the attack but morphs the spell into something else. Ready?'

Effie nodded.

He flared his fingers and the shards flew again towards her. As they touched the edges of her circle, they rebounded, but this time forming new shapes, soft shapes, fluttering wings – little glass butterflies dancing around Effie. Attis caught one from the air and then pulled his finger away sharply. It had cut him.

'Thank you, Effie, for showing us the attack can be returned as boon *or* bane.'

She smiled sweetly. 'You're welcome.'

He swivelled back to Anna, Rowan and Manda. 'You see? Circles can be much more than simply deflective, they can be an opportunity to—'

'Change the rules.' Effie completed his sentence with a flourish.

'Now it's time for you all to have a go.'

'If it's all the same,' said Manda, 'I'd rather not have glass thrown at my face.'

Attis laughed. 'I thought we could start with something less permanently disfiguring. Pair up.'

Anna and Manda turned to each other.

'Now, the game is called Pinch, Punch,' he explained.

'Ooo, I know this one. We used to play it as kids! Wait—' Rowan frowned. 'I hate this game.'

Attis smiled. 'It's based on an old hex spell, but to be clear – we're not trying to hurt each other. In the game, one of you is the attacker and one of you the victim. You don't touch, but the attacker uses their magic to try and land a pinch on the other person. I want the victim to experiment with the three types of circle. First, see if you can stop the pinch getting through. Then, try to send the pinch back to your attacker. Finally, try to turn it into a punch. A gentle punch. Got that, Effie?'

She waved a hand. 'Too many rules.'

They began. Anna took up the attacking position first. It took her a few minutes to work out how to even land a pinch. She was reticent to call on magic with the intention to harm – drumming up a prickle of spite and focusing it at Manda – but slowly she got used to it and it felt good to release after the week they'd had. Manda managed to block most of her pinches but struggled when it came to rebounding them or turning them into a punch.

Anna could hear Rowan receiving a battering from Effie. 'Ow! Ow! I remember why I hate this game!'

'How am I meant to make my circle rebound the spell?' Manda complained when Attis came to watch them. 'I've only ever used my circle for protection, I don't know how to make it turn inside out.'

'We're not trying to turn it inside out,' he said. 'We're just trying to make it more flexible. You want to maintain the protection of your circle, keep it strong from the outside, but let it become permeable from within, so that your magic can find a way through and push outwards.'

'Pull inwards and push outwards?' Manda looked as if she were trying to solve an impossible maths equation.

'I know it's hard to wrap your head around at first and even harder to teach because circles are highly personal. Shaped by your Hira. Think about how you imagine yours and use your visualization to help – mine is a ring of fire, so I know it's strong and can repel, but it's not still, it allows my magic through like smoke through flame.'

They continued, and slowly Manda began to send Anna's pinches back to her. Attis walked away to help Rowan and Anna swapped with Manda to let her have a go at attacking.

It had been a long time since Anna had cast her circle. She drew on the strands of magic in the room – the candlelight, the shadows, the focused silence between her and Manda – letting it weave around her. Manda started throwing magical pinches at her. A few slipped through and Anna tightened the circle to stop them.

'Try and send some back,' said Manda.

But Anna couldn't. She couldn't see how to either.

Attis stopped beside them again, assessing, which only made her more flustered. 'My magic's not strong enough!' She grated out a noise of frustration between her teeth.

He shook his head. 'This isn't about strength. How do *you* imagine your circle?'

'Like threads woven and pulled tight, forming a barrier around me.'

'I think they might be too tight. You need to trust your magic – that

it will protect you – but let some light in so it can breathe. Let me try.'
He moved Manda aside and faced Anna.

That was hardly going to help her focus.

Anna did her best to defend herself against his oncoming pinches,
though she sensed he was going easy on her. She tried to send some
back, but again, nothing.

He frowned, circling her. 'I think part of the problem is you're drawing
your magic from everywhere except . . . yourself. Here.'

His arm moved over her and touched the space between her heart
and her stomach, both of which leapt at his touch, making it even harder
to concentrate.

'That's where your power is. It'll be easier once you know what your
languages are, then you can draw on them. Like a word witch might
chant words to raise her circle, a wind witch might call on the wind.
Other witches might carry a little of their language with them – a vial
of blood, a bone charm, a wand – so they have the power on hand when
they need it.'

'It's part of the reason why the Wort Cunnings wear their brooches,'
said Rowan, 'so they have their plant of power with them at all times.
Chlorophyll mojo.' Her smile faded and Anna sensed she was worrying
about her own language again.

'And even if you don't have something of your language to use,' Attis
added, 'just knowing your language strengthens your circle, because your
language is also inside you, in your blood. It connects the magic out
there with what's within.'

'But we don't know our languages,' Manda complained.

'We will soon!' Effie threw a pinch at her.

'Ow!'

'Put the foundations in place now and your circles will be unstoppable
later, when you do know them,' said Attis. 'Which is why we'll be
practising over, and over, and over.'

Rowan groaned.

'I'd rather you struggle now and be able to protect yourself later.'

'I'd rather procrastinate now and struggle later.' Rowan flashed him
a smile. 'My life philosophy.'

They carried on for a while longer taking turns with each other, but
Anna's magic had no chance against Effie. She had them all surrendering
by the end. 'We'll be a shadow army in no time!' she declared in her victory.

'An army with a maniac commander,' Rowan wisecracked.

'Sometimes a little madness is necessary.'

When it was time to go, Anna was the last to leave. As she closed the door, she stared into the narrowing darkness of the room. She swore she could already see – or feel – the shadows of the room swirling towards the mannequins. She shivered, more with wonder than fear.

She turned to find Attis standing behind her. He nodded at the door, smile askew. 'Just going to check my nails.'

Anna smiled back at him, feeling a different kind of shiver entirely. 'Sorry.' She stepped out of the way.

'No worries.'

She waited for him as the others moved ahead towards the stairwell. 'I've been meaning to ask, what's happening with the—'

'Map shop?' he replied with a grin. 'It's on. I've heard back from the owner and it's open this weekend. We can go.'

'Yes!' Anna whooped.

'We still have to find the shop, of course.'

Anna gave him a look, not knowing if he was joking or being serious. His smile quirked. 'Don't worry, my navigation skills are excellent.'

'Come on!' Rowan called to them, and they focused their attentions back on getting out of the school unscathed.

They all spilt out onto the street again, everyone breathing giddily with exhilaration at their act of rebellion. Effie threw an arm around Anna and they laughed, thick as thieves of the night as they walked back down the street, until Attis halted suddenly.

'There's someone in the school.'

Anna followed his gaze up to the main building, which was in view again. A light was on.

'The Ebury wing,' Anna murmured.

They all stared at it in mutual alarm, imagining Eames creeping around while they had been carrying out magic just below.

Rowan breathed out into the cold air. 'Why would he be there *now*?'

MAPS

Many believe the officially charted map of the Necropolis Railway is only half the story. That the railway has continued to spread beneath the City of its own accord and design. That those who use the line without permission may never be seen again – caught on one of its infinite loops . . . or a direct line to Hel itself . . .

Excerpt from London Above, London Below (Published 1978)

By the weekend, another hysteria incident had struck. A meeting about the contentious and supposedly cursed construction site in Whitechapel had quickly broken down into shouting . . . but then no one had been able to stop, everyone yelling, louder and louder, higher and higher, until they were screaming and shaking and quaking, voices tearing apart with the strain of it—

Anna had watched some of the videos spreading online. The sound had been too terrible to take – screams formed of the very dread she'd felt in that classroom. It was the same spell, she was sure of it. The eyes of the hysterical crowd were just as tortured; trapped from within. The incident had been covered everywhere this time, newspapers grappling over the most attention-grabbing headline.

LONDON LOCKED IN GRIP OF TERROR!
A CITY ON THE EDGE!
MADNESS OR MAGIC – WHAT ARE WE FACING?

The frenzy was gaining momentum, people interested . . . scared, wanting to know what was going on. Debates and theories raging and clashing online. For as many disbelievers as there were, there were plenty of others claiming all sorts: that the events were linked to mobile phone rays targeting the city, that London's water was being poisoned, that it was the work of witchcraft and malefice and that people ought to turn to the WIPS who *know the truth!*

Hopkins welcomed them with open arms on his feed, confirming it as *another act of malefice. We must stop the spread!*

After the week she'd had at school, Anna didn't want to sit in bed and watch the comments multiply – she wanted to move, to *do* something. She went downstairs and tried Effie's door but, of course – no Effie. She spotted Attis feeding Mr Ramsden in the garden and marched out to him.

'Attis!'

He turned around, the early morning sun bronzing the wayward strands of his hair.

'I need to go to that map shop. I can't get anywhere with this riddle and it's driving me mad and I just need *something*. Unless you have better things to do with your Saturday morning than break a Goddess-damn curse, because I don't. I don't want to wait any more. Everything is going to shit and I just need to get out of this house!'

He patted Mr Ramsden on the head. 'OK. Let's go then.'

'What, now?'

'Yeah.'

'Where's Effie?'

'I think she stayed at Azrael's last night.'

Anna exhaled loudly. She didn't want to go without Effie, but who knew when she'd be back. She couldn't spend the whole weekend waiting. 'OK, let's go.'

'I'm all for that, but—' He looked down at her. 'You might want to change. I think it's a good look, personally, but the general public may be disconcerted.'

Anna followed his gaze down and realized she was still in her dressing gown. 'Let's go in ten minutes,' she said, backing hastily out of the garden.

They took the bus into central London. Anna tried Effie's phone again to no avail. She checked the news instead and then wished she hadn't. 'Did you see—'

Attis nodded before she finished. 'More hysteria.' He pressed his lips into a hard line and looked out of the window, lost in dark thoughts, his fingers tapping against his leg.

They disembarked at Shaftesbury Avenue and walked down St Martin's Lane to a busy six-way crossroads with signs for Leicester Square and Covent Garden. London was lively, sunlight spilling through the streets as everyone rushed in their different directions, getting in the way of the traffic. Tourists gawked at a street entertainer dressed in head-to-toe gold. A few of them turned from the entertainer to Attis, who had covered his eyes with one hand and started to spin around with his other arm extended outwards.

'What are you doing?' Anna said through a forced smile, as if to reassure everyone this was entirely normal.

'I'm trying to get lost,' he replied, a concentrated frown on his face. He stopped and opened his eyes. He was facing Long Acre Street. 'This way, I guess.' He strode off down it.

Anna hurried after him, doing her best to ignore a row of STOP THE SPREAD posters along one building. 'You're not filling me with confidence that you know where you're going.'

'I hope not. If I know where we're going, we won't find it.' He turned at a corner pub down a smaller street. 'You have to get lost to find the map shop, it's part of its whole thing.'

Anna tried to keep up with him as he turned down another alleyway. 'That makes no sense.'

He stopped and spun around again, disorientating himself. 'I agree, but it's how we get there.'

They cut through a few more back streets, Anna hurrying to keep up with Attis's veering. Here, away from the high street shops, an older London opened up, tucked away between the forgotten backs of places – lost-in-time cobbled streets, Victorian hanging lamps, antiquated signs. Anna was busy taking it in when Attis stopped suddenly and she knocked into him.

'Here we are,' he said with relief. 'It gets harder to get lost every time.'

In front of them, in an alleyway that showed no other signs of life, was a red-fronted shop called THE LOST MAP SHOP.

Attis opened the door and Anna, still in shock at the shop's sudden appearance, went inside. The room seemed to unfold like a map around her – much bigger than she'd expected and yet with the feeling of the whole world crammed within it. There were maps of great scale and vivid colour hung on the walls, wooden units stacked with small drawers, shelves crammed with books and rolled-up maps and globes of all shapes and sizes among it all – some, disconcertingly, were not round. There was even a map underfoot and another papering the ceiling above. The shop smelt of rich woods and brass polish and – freedom: of desert sands and the air above the ocean and the wildflowers of mountain tops. Smells Anna had never even smelt.

'Well, well, well, what brings Attis Lockerby through my door?' A low voice spun them around. It belonged to a very attractive woman. She looked to be in her early twenties, with sleek black hair tied into a plait and crystalline eyes that caught the light and made a joke of it. She was smiling with one hand hitched on her hip, wearing a loose shirt tucked into cargo trousers.

'Terra!' Attis replied, opening his arms. She threw the hand off her hip with a laugh and they hugged. 'Anna, Terra, Terra, Anna.'

Terra took Anna's hand and shook it firmly. 'Welcome to my store.'

'You own this place?' asked Anna, awed.

'Well, it was my father's but he's retired, again, and is travelling the world, again, so I've stepped in.'

'It's never looked better,' said Attis, taking a deep breath and becoming distracted by a map that was open on one of the tables.

Terra gave Anna a look of warning. 'I hope you're patient. I've known him to spend hours here.'

'Really . . .' Anna could imagine a shop full of maps and a beautiful woman held a great deal of fascination for him.

'So,' Terra continued, friendly but businesslike, 'what can I do for you?'

Attis turned back to them. 'Anna would like a tour first. I mean, you can't go to this map shop and not have a tour.'

Terra smirked. 'Come on, then.' She moved them further into the shop and pointed upwards. 'First thing to know, you can't get lost here.'

Anna followed her finger upwards and saw that where they had walked, footprints had appeared on the map above them. *Their footprints.* The map above was a mirror of the map below.

Terra smiled at Anna. 'Now, the maps. Things are generally organized. We've got London over here, Britain here.' She pointed to the different areas of the shop. 'World maps, seas, stars, other dimensions and uncategorizables.'

She stopped at a map lying on top of one of the cabinets. It showed the whole of Britain, drawn with skill, tracing roads and train lines, rivers and mountain ranges. 'The thing to know about all the maps in this shop is that they have a hidden map beneath them. You just need to look deeper—'

They continued to stare at the map. Then Anna began to see it – a new set of pathways rising up, threads of silver, not altering the map but adding a new dimension to it, extending all over Britain and gathering together at certain points. 'What are they?' Anna asked, reaching out to touch the new lines, which seemed to have a different quality to them, as if they were made of light.

'Magical pathways of Britain,' Terra replied. 'Moonsongs, or ley lines, as cowans call them. Unseen but felt each day by all of us, created by the land itself.'

She beckoned them onwards and opened up one of the drawers, removing a map and unfolding it carefully on the surface. This one was of Somerset. 'Look deeper,' she said. Feathery lines and patterns began to appear over the map, almost as if flying above it. 'A map capturing the flight paths of birds as they're happening.'

Anna barely had time to marvel before Terra walked them on and presented one of the maps hanging on the wall. It was of London. Anna gasped as this map revealed itself too – expanding to accommodate new roads and streets and pathways and place names she'd never heard of. 'That,' said Terra, proudly, 'is the magical world – all the magical locations of London . . . or most anyway. Not all are known and not all want to be found.' Some of the pathways moved as she spoke, snaking and rerouting, a few place names hopped about, rivers glittered. 'Doesn't like to stay still.'

She moved on but Anna remained staring at it. *The magical world.* She'd spent so much time hiding away in her bedroom when all this was out there.

'Not for sale,' Terra called back to her. 'Sorry. There aren't many like it. Anyway, it's best to uncover it all in good time, on foot, with sturdy shoes and a mind open to surprises. I walk the city every day and never get tired of it.' Anna looked down at Terra's boots. They were light but strong, made of leather sculpted to her feet.

They moved on, their footprints tracking them as Terra illuminated different maps: weather maps and starlight maps; tree root maps and hedgerow maps; maps of lost places and places that didn't exist yet but would; historic maps tracing battles and bloodshed; a map that showed how the world would have looked if certain events had not taken place; maps that didn't map things along the normal planes but up and down or under and over. Maps of other even less tangible topographies – happiness or grief; maps made of stories or imagined places; maps that let you feel the textures of the land or smell its scents. A map Anna couldn't look away from that traced the music of a city . . . her fingers moving over it as if she were playing a song.

'I just sold a dream map I would love to have shown you,' said Terra. 'From the Astral witches, very rare, never had one before. Dreams are not easy things to pin down, as you can imagine. Anyway, I think you've probably heard enough from me. Shall I leave you to browse?'

'Actually,' said Anna, recalling her purpose, 'I'm looking for something specific.'

'Hit me.'

'A town by the name of Afeldale that existed in the 1600s. Most likely in the county of Surrey.'

Terra nodded again, her eyes moving over the store. Anna began to worry she didn't have what they needed when she jerked her head and made off. They followed. Attis helped Terra take down a sizeable book from one of the shelves. She put it down and pulled up her sleeves. Anna could see the beginnings of a moving tattoo on her arm – the lines of a map forming. She wondered briefly if Attis had ever traced its pathways but drove the thought from her mind.

The book was titled *The Complete Atlas of Great Britain*.

'Extremely complete,' said Terra. 'It's got the whole of Britain mapped out since the first manmade pathways were carved out on our little rocky isle. Now, Surrey, 1600s . . .'

She searched the index and then flipped through the book – through the different areas of Britain, eventually landing on a page that covered the county of Surrey, its landscape riddled with roads and motorways and densely populated towns.

'I know,' Terra spoke before they could, 'not the 1600s . . . but this is just the start.' She kept the page open but turned the book upside down and flipped it around. Now, when she began to flick back through the pages the map remained on the same area, and yet, it began to change – the latticework of roads and streets and buildings slowly disappearing, filling up with green areas, Surrey expanding and the towns shrinking smaller and smaller – woodland and rivers spreading—

Attis's eyes were completely absorbed, mouth falling open. 'It's Surrey going back in time. Remarkable.'

'It gets bigger . . .' said Anna.

'Yes,' Terra replied. 'Surrey used to cover a much wider area. It contained counties like Merton, Sutton, Kingston, Wandsworth—'

Anna's head snapped up. 'Wandsworth. That's where I grew up.'

Where my mother bought our house.

'OK,' said Terra, unsure of the significance. 'Do you have an exact date?'

'1651.' The date of Eleanor's trial.

Terra landed on a page that claimed to be Surrey in 1651 exactly. The map was entirely different from the one they had first seen. It looked like it had nothing to do with London at all, but was rural, scattered with small towns and hamlets.

Anna and Attis leant in closer, their cheeks almost touching as they searched and then Attis's finger landed on the map. 'Afeldale.'

Afeldale. The name hovered above a town near the top of the county – barely a town, it looked more the size of a village, with a small river running through it and fields all around. There appeared to be little of note within the town itself – a town hall, a market square, a bridge running over the river, a church called St Mary's—

'Mary . . .' Anna whispered. 'Mary, Mary, quite contrary, how does your garden grow.'

She locked eyes with Attis. Terra frowned at them both with mild concern.

Anna's thoughts had whirred ahead and she couldn't believe where they were going. 'St Mary's . . . that's the name of the church right by the house where I grew up.'

Attis began to turn back through the pages of Surrey – forwards in time – the map shifting once more. As the centuries passed by, one thing remained.

'The church . . .' he muttered.

'It's there the whole time.'

'Actually, it briefly disappears.' Attis flipped between the pages. 'See. Around the start of the 1800s, but it comes back bigger. Maybe it was rebuilt; most churches are rebuilt on older sites. Can I borrow your phone?'

'Sure.' Anna handed it over. Attis typed in something, his eyes scanning quickly.

He nodded. 'St Mary's church . . . demolished some time in the late eighteenth century and rebuilt in 1818, but it still stands on the same site as the original church.'

'Could that mean that the town of Afeldale, where it all began, was right where I grew up? My mother could have chosen the house there knowing it was the source . . . perhaps she thought it would help her solve it. Or maybe the cu—' Anna stopped herself saying curse in front of Terra. 'The spell drew her back there . . .' The dark gravity of the curse pulling them all back to the centre. The threads of the old family ties tugging at their strings.

'Maybe a bit of both,' Attis suggested gently.

Anna returned to Nana's riddle, saying it aloud.

> *Mary, Mary, so contrary,*
> *How does your garden grow?*
> *With silver bells and yew tree dells,*
> *And ravenstones all out of row.*
>
> *One grows up beyond the boundary,*
> *How deep – how deep did she go?*
> *Unearthed God's word, truth dark nor light,*
> *The shadows, the shadows they know.*

'If ravenstone means gravestone then it could be referring to the grave-yard of St Mary's church. Perhaps Eleanor was buried there back in 1651? *One grows up beyond the boundary . . . How deep – how deep did she go?*' Anna paused. She thought of her dreams – clawing through the earth, soil beneath her nails. 'Unearthed God's word . . .'

She didn't want to trace these footprints.

'My mother—' she said haltingly. 'Do you think she could have unearthed the Bible from Eleanor's grave? Dug it up? Eleanor wanted it passed on to her children but maybe they buried her with it?'

The Bible in which she might have written Attis's spell.

'Is she OK?' Terra asked Attis.

Attis sighed, looking at Anna. 'Anna, I'm not sure. A grave from 1651 would be long lost by now.'

Anna's excitement tripped up. Attis might be right. But it all added up . . . or was she only trying to make sense of something senseless?

'Let's go there then. If there's no such grave, I'm wrong and Nana is just having her fun.'

Attis rubbed the back of his neck, looking unsure. 'We can . . .'

'This seems serious,' said Terra. 'I don't think I've ever seen Lockerby look so concerned.'

Attis smiled at her. 'Better?'

'Much.' Terra smiled too, her eyes lingering on his face.

'Thanks Terra.' Anna stepped between them. 'You've been really helpful.'

'It's my job.' She clapped her hands against her thighs. 'Need anything else?'

A thought struck Anna. She tried to push it from her mind but it stuck tight, like gristle on a piece of bone. If Nana's riddle led them nowhere, they might still need other options. 'That map of magical London . . . does it show the magical rivers of London?'

Terra nodded. 'Yes, its rivers and springwells. There are many hidden beneath and within the city.'

'Beneath . . .' Anna repeated. 'Are any of the rivers connected to the River of the Dead?'

Terra blinked, as if she couldn't believe what Anna had just said. 'There are many magical rivers on that map but I can tell you now, the river of Hel is not one of them. It doesn't exist in this world at all and that's the only one I deal in, I'm afraid.'

'You just spoke about a map of dreams. Dreams don't exist in this world.'

'Dreams are drawn from the living, from tangible thoughts and feelings; the Underworld is drawn from the dead.' Terra's face darkened. 'There is no map for Hel. It is not a real place. You should speak to the Hel witches if such things interest you. They are Gatekeepers of the Underworld.'

Anna and Attis shared a look. Anna thought of the entrance to the Underworld she had seen in the Hel witch lair. *If Hel wasn't a place, then where did that lead to?*

'I'll show you out,' said Terra.

Anna followed Attis and Terra back through the shop, his finger trailing through a globe as he passed, producing a wave through its waters. Anna could see why he loved it here. He bought a few maps he couldn't resist and, as he handed Terra some money, he commented, 'You must get that map in for me too.'

'Which one?' she asked.

'The one for your eyes. I got lost in them again.'

She laughed, shaking away her former seriousness. 'Are you going to say that line every time you come here?'

'Probably.'

She turned to Anna. 'I hope you know what you're in for with him. There's no map for Attis Lockerby either.'

Anna felt herself go distinctly red. 'We're not – it's – er—'

'My point exactly.'

As they bussed and trained their way to the other side of London, Anna's eyes felt expanded, knowing now just how many secret places were hidden within the city, folded into the fabric of the everyday, a sense of possibility around each corner . . .

And yet, it was a graveyard they arrived at. The deadest of ends. Bare plane trees lined the street, chopped back to knuckles of bark against a sullen white sky. Anna knew St Mary's well – she'd walked past it almost every day on the way to school. She'd even asked Selene to enquire about burying Aunt there but apparently it was full, no longer open to the freshly dead. The church dwarfed its boundaries – constricted by the spread of houses on either side – as if it had once commanded a much bigger area. It was made of three parallel sections with a high spire and belfry rising from the central nave. The graveyard encircled it, giving way to a quiet church garden at the back.

As they stepped through the gate, Anna was struck by the silence, that strange and unnerving twilight silence that all graveyards seem to embody no matter what time of the day. Silence like a stopped watch. Like a final breath. Like the dead were still listening. The graves were old and worn by the slow storms of time, many of them askew or half-buried as if they were sinking back into the ground. They were scattered about in no order at all—

Ravenstones all out of row . . .

Above them, hung the webbed branches of yew trees, and below, nestled against the graves, sprouted solemn plumes of snowdrops—

With silver bells and yew tree dells . . .

'It's here, I know it,' said Anna, feeling the shadow of her mother move between the yew trees. The rustle of her footprints.

She began to search, navigating the uneven ground, the cries of ravens puncturing the air as they flitted between branches. She tried not to let their calls drag her back into her dreams – or remind her of the spirits she had seen amid the Hel witches. *Were they here now?* Was the Fabric thinner in places like this – places of stillness and silence and death? Were the shadows staring back at her as she stared into their graves? Saying her name as she uttered theirs. *Anna* . . .

Attis put a hand on her shoulder and she spun to him with a cry.

He put his hands up. 'Sorry. Probably shouldn't creep up on people in a graveyard.'

She smiled. 'Maybe don't creep up on people full stop.'

'Noted.' He looked out over the graves, his smile sinking. 'None of them are old enough.'

'There's one here from 1798.' Anna tried to make out the name. 'That's only a century off.'

'More like a century and a half. I've not seen anything before that. I don't think we're going to find any graves from the 1600s. It's just too long ago.'

'Let's keep looking.'

Eventually, they ran out of graves.

Attis gave her a kind but resolute look. 'I don't think—'

'We might have missed one,' Anna interjected, holding onto Nana's riddle, to her hope, to the shadows of her mother. She sat down on the wet grass, trying to think but the ravens kept distracting her with their squawking. 'The riddle says: *One grows up beyond the boundary*, so maybe it's not here at all . . .'

'Wait,' said Attis from above her, 'this woman was killed for being a witch, right?'

'Yeah . . .'

'Of course. It's likely they wouldn't have buried her on consecrated ground. Often witches, criminals, prostitutes, women of "sin" or ones who just, you know, just talked too loud, were banished, buried outside the church's boundary . . . which means, we won't find it here at all. It's probably under one of these houses.'

Anna looked around distraught. A raven called again, wings black as a curse as it flew beyond the graveyard, over the archway that marked the entrance to the church garden, landing on the branch of a distant yew.

'Yew . . .' she said.

'Me?' Attis replied quizzically.

'No, yew. Another one. Look.' She pointed to the back of the garden. 'You said that yews were planted where the dead lay. Well, there's another down there.' She stood up, moving towards it. 'Maybe that's where the other graves were, the unholy, the lost and hopeless. Beyond the boundary . . .' She passed beneath the archway, Attis following behind.

The back of the church garden turned slowly into a wild tangle – brambles and nettles and the gnarled yew tree trunk bound up in an old wire fence. The raven cawed above. Anna couldn't see any gravestone but she was drawn deeper in, kicking at the weeds and rubble. Her foot hit something hard. A rock.

She fell to her knees and tore back the nettles, stinging her hands.

'There's something here,' she called.

A rock . . . small and withered, barely emerging from the ground. Its face was covered with an old map of moss. Anna rubbed at it, peeling the moss away with desperate hands . . . sensing something – something looking back at her—

An eye.

She fell back and Attis caught her, stopping her from falling over entirely. Anna pulled herself upright again, breath shallow.

'It's . . . it's . . . the Eye.'

Carved deep into the battered stone were seven circles.

'It's a grave, Attis! A grave marked with the curse symbol.'

He looked entirely shocked. Anna reached out for it and as her hands touched the symbol, she felt it all. The graveyard by night. Her mother. Raw desperation, raw hands digging into the earth, throwing the shovel away, clawing—

I won't look down . . .

Anna pulled her hand away with a cry, the ravens shrieking into the sky.

Attis dropped down beside her. 'What's wrong?'

She looked at him but she was still lost in what she'd just felt. 'I – I – think she was here. My mother.'

'You look pale.'

'I feel it,' she said, scrabbling back towards the grave.

'How would the grave still be here? It's impossible . . .'

'You just took me to a shop that had a map made of music; anything is *possible*.'

'It must be enchanted,' said Attis. 'Protected.'

'So that it could be found,' Anna whispered. 'But who enchanted it? Who marked it?'

They had no answers.

Anna dug her fingertips into the soggy ground, thinking of the riddle. *How deep – how deep did she go.* 'I think Marie dug the Bible up.'

'That's crazy. Surely she wouldn't have done that.'

'Desperate people do crazy things for the ones they love.' Anna didn't want to point out that Attis had attempted to kill himself for the girl he loved.

'If she did dig the Bible up, where would it even be now?'

'The house,' said Anna heavily. 'Marie lived there before she died. All her possessions would have been there.'

What if Aunt had thrown it out? She'd never tolerated clutter but she would have kept things too, coveting her sister's possessions, *like my father in the third-floor room* . . .

She forced the words out. 'I need to go back.'

She was being called home.

It wasn't far. They walked the few streets to Cressey Square. It was as if she'd never left – the neighbouring houses looking down on them with distant disdain, Anna feeling eyes in the windows although there weren't any, Aunt's warnings still trailing her. Anna was pleased to see the front garden was entirely overgrown with weeds, standing in unkempt contrast to the rest of the square. Still, its old silence remained – withered, but just as poisonous. She turned to Attis. 'Could you wait here?'

He frowned. 'I can help—'

'I know – I'd just, I'd rather go alone.' Anna didn't really know why, only that this house, the life she'd led here . . . she didn't want to share it with anyone. She wanted to keep him away from its shadows.

He chewed his jaw but relented. 'I'll wait in the garden.' He nodded behind to the garden in the centre of the square, then grinned. 'I haven't broken in there for a while.'

Anna watched him as he jogged across the road and jumped the fence with ease. She turned back to the door, her smile dropping away. She swallowed the coarse knot in her throat and took the keys out from where they were buried in her bag. She turned the door key in the lock and the door shuddered open. The air was stale and stifling, as if the house's containment had only made the rot at the heart of it stronger. She could still smell a whiff of Aunt's perfume, the scent of decaying roses. Dust covered everything like a fine veil. She kicked back the pile of post from the door and ignored the unbearable silence, looking up the stairway, through the layers of darkness, feeling the press of the third-floor room. She moved into the living room.

The room was cold, the blinds half closed, shredding the light into strips across the floor. She began searching through the books on the shelves, looking for any signs of a Bible. Perhaps it was in Aunt's room or the attic . . .

Then her eyes fell on it.

A book still laid out on the table by Aunt's armchair. *Aunt's Bible*. Anna hadn't even thought of *that* book. It had been one of Aunt's instruments of torture, Aunt selecting damning passages from it for their embroideries. Anna had never opened it herself.

She walked over to it. It was smaller than she remembered, bound in dark, soft leather. She trailed her finger over it, imagining Aunt's fingerprints on it still, little maps of spite. Anna lifted it and opened it up – the paper was thick, old and brittle. She turned to the front, her finger scouring for a print date: 1601.

It was impossible.

Aunt's Bible.

Perfectly preserved. *Had Aunt known the significance of it?* She couldn't have. It had been her mother's secret and Aunt had never known of Attis's existence.

Anna rifled through the pages, searching for a spell – writing, words scrawled in the margins or the back pages. Clues. Traces of life. But there was nothing.

She hung her head, breathing out with frustration. She'd found it and she was still lost; the riddle unravelling but not yet solved. In her moment of defeat, she suddenly felt the darkness of the room keenly, her aloneness in it. Aunt's shadows all about her – sitting in the armchair, watering the roses, standing by the dark encumbrance of the piano, disapproving, merciless—

Tick. Tick. Tick.

Anna screamed. The metronome on the top of the piano had begun ticking.

Tick. Tick. Tick.

She picked up the Bible and ran. Down the corridor. Out of the house.

Tick. Tick. Tick . . .

The ticking chased her across the road. She kicked open the garden gate and sprinted down the path. Attis was leaning against her old oak tree, head cast to the ground. He looked up at the sound of her steps and she dived into his arms. He jolted with surprise but then his arms responded, wrapping around her, holding her tightly. She could feel herself trembling against him.

'Anna,' he breathed.

He held her the way the oak tree used to hold her, without question or judgement.

She pulled away. 'I'm sorry – I – I—'

He took her hand and traced a symbol on her palm. She felt it spread through her, pulling her with gentle, solid warmth back into her body, down her feet and into the earth; a feeling like everything inside her was settling, falling back into place. Rooted.

'What was that?' she asked, her voice returning.

'A grounding symbol. It helps with panic.'

Anna took a deep breath, the world coming back into focus piece by piece: the muggy smell of the garden, the breeze through the leaves of the oak and her hair; their fingers – still joined. She dropped his hand.

His eyes did not leave hers. *One light, one dark.* Questioning. 'What happened?'

Anna didn't know how to explain it, if she even could. She'd admitted her madness to no one. 'I felt her in there . . . Aunt. It's not the first time . . . she haunts me. Every day, in some way, big or small, she haunts me. It's like – like – she's even more alive now she's dead.' Anna shut her eyes, running trembling fingers across her brow, trying to swallow back the tears. Her voice dropped to a whisper. 'I'm so scared all the time, Attis. I'm going crazy, aren't I? Just like her, I'm going crazy.'

'No.'

'I'll never escape her.'

'You will.'

'I won't. She's inside me now and I can't get her out.'

Attis looked into her eyes, suddenly fierce. 'I don't see anyone in there, but you, Anna. Now take my hand.'

She took it without question and the chimera spun open around them, swallowing the garden, the fence, the street, Aunt's house, the whole damn city. Only the oak tree remained beside them, but bigger now, with room to stretch its branches, its roots thickening beneath their feet, churning up the ground. The tired light, the hard lines of London were gone – replaced by a vast and soft undefined wilderness: a meadow surrounding them, giving way to fields and the curves of hills, distant mountains dusted with trees, dreaming themselves into a sky of golden, unending light.

Anna shut her eyes again, hardly daring to believe she was back here. With him. His creation was too perfect to be true, a dream, and yet, when she opened her eyes, it was no dream. It felt entirely real, and she didn't feel floaty or swept away, but present and grounded, as if it was her own body coming into focus now. As if she hadn't felt it for a long time. 'Thank you,' she murmured.

Attis shrugged, looking a little abashed. 'Figured you needed to get away from it all, just for a moment.'

'Do I ever have to go back?' she said without thinking.

He grinned. 'I'm not sure my magic can stretch quite to *forever*. But I can probably sustain it for a little while.'

They moved away from the oak tree and sat down in the long grass which was tangled with wildflowers. There was the feeling of spring in the air, not just in the buds and the blue of the sky, but something else – beneath them – a feeling of things burgeoning, ripening, deepening, coming undone. Attis stretched his arms back to the sun, lying down in the grass as if he'd arrived home. Anna breathed in the air – stem and blossom, earth and smoke – and followed the path of a ladybird along a strand of grass. Since the end of last year, whenever she'd thought of the garden, it had felt like an illusion, a trick she'd fallen into, but now she remembered how real it felt. *How could he create something like this?*

They didn't say anything for a while, Anna listening to the music around her – the wind carrying the stray tunes of birds, a stream wandering somewhere, the rise and fall of his steady breath. She could have fallen asleep to it, but Attis spoke.

'So, you have the Bible?'

He looked down and Anna realized she was still clutching it tightly. 'I do.'

'And?'

'I don't know yet – I couldn't see a spell, but I'll find it.'

'You're sure it's it?'

'The dates match. It's the key we need to break the curse, to set us all free.'

He didn't say anything.

'I know you don't believe it's possible . . .'

He sighed, turning towards her. 'I don't know what's possible, Anna. I just don't want you setting yourself up for a fall.'

Too late, she thought – seeing then how his eyes were not grey but the colour of the sky behind him: slate and teal and mauve and green and so many other hues that she couldn't separate them all, smoky and wind-blown and undulating between light and shadow. Normally the world seemed to pale against him, but here it matched his aliveness, his richness. It was as expansive as him – the trees moving with his power; leaves messy as his hair; his voice musical as the wind; the wildflowers sweet as the freckles on his nose. Everything that had felt so complicated suddenly seemed so simple. How easy it would be to pull him towards her and kiss him again.

If only a kiss would be enough.

She looked away, fighting her longings, knowing it was too dangerous to stay here. 'Is it real here? Or only a spell?' She regretted the words as soon as she'd said them. He believed he was only a spell.

Attis turned his head to the sky and the clouds began to change above them, from rough drifts into a form – a ship with large, billowing sails, clouds dashed beneath it like waves. 'I could make ice cream grow on the trees or swap the rivers and the sky or have unicorn deer wearing French berets frolic through the fields.'

Anna laughed.

'But I like how it feels real here. Somewhere between a memory and a daydream.'

'What's the memory?'

He continued looking at the sky. 'No specific time or place, but just a gathering of . . . memories, I guess. Maybe a little of where I grew up in Aberystwyth, or places where my dad and I used to go camping. We went almost every weekend after my other dad died. We'd just up and leave, head to the hills. Pitch a tent, light a fire. He made these amazing stews. He's the one who taught me to cook and sometimes when I'm cooking, to this day, it feels like he's right there next to me. I'm not sure the dead ever quite leave us . . .' He gave her a meaningful look. 'Anyway, I wish I could tell you this was real, but it's only a chimera.'

'But are we still in the garden in Cressey Square? Can we walk around? Why is it warm here when it's cold there?'

'Chimeras are strange magic. Hard to pin down. The strength of them depends on the force behind it. Some are no more than an imprint over the real world, like a mirage, but others – more tightly woven with magic – can become something more . . . like another layer of fabric on top of the fabric of reality, their threads connected but the patterns distinct. Its own world. Some witches live entirely inside their chimeras.'

'I can see why. The real world isn't so great.'

'I don't know.' Attis released his crooked smile. 'It can be.'

Anna turned back to the sky. 'I'd like to be able to do magic like this.'

'This is nothing compared to what you'll be able to do.' She heard him say it but she didn't look back at him. How could she meet his eyes when he said things like that? He did not make loving him easy.

She pulled some grass between her fingers. 'We should go.'

'You sure you're ready?'

She turned back to him. 'No.'

He laughed and the dream he'd created drained slowly away around him, the world returning with all of its hard lines and complications. Anna didn't know why he'd taken her to the garden, why he sometimes looked at her the way he was looking at her now. They turned to walk down the path. She closed the gate behind them, breathing in the mug and mud of Cressey Square garden, knowing she would never return again.

Effie was in the kitchen when they got back. She looked up as they bundled through the door, her voice prickly. 'Where have you been?'

'We tried to find you but you weren't here,' said Anna quickly, wrestling with her coat. 'We went to the map shop.'

Effie's eyes hardened. 'Oh. Curse-solving behind my back, are we?'

Anna felt several stabs of guilt pierce through her. 'You weren't here and I just needed to get out. The news was driving me crazy and Attis offered to help. It's a long story but we found the Bible back in Aunt's house. Eleanor was buried at the church I grew up next to, our mother dug it up from Eleanor's grave – her ravenstone – just like Nana's riddle said.'

Anna put the Bible down on the kitchen counter, like an offering.

Effie looked down at it. 'So? Where's the spell?'

'Well, I haven't found it yet—'

Effie laughed and walked away. 'OK.'

'What do you mean – OK?' Anna replied with irritation.

'It just sounds like a lot of leaps. How do we even know this is *the* hallowed Bible?'

'It is from the 1600s,' Attis stated.

'Then why doesn't it contain the spell?'

'Nana's riddle led me to it, it's not going to fail now,' said Anna.

'That sounds exactly like something Nana would do – lead you halfway then laugh in your face. We can't trust Nana. Don't you agree, Attis?'

Effie looked at him sharply.

His eyes darted between them, caught in her trap. 'Er – the riddle does seem to be leading somewhere . . . but, no, I don't think we can trust Nana.'

Anna snatched the Bible back. 'Well, I believe this Bible has the answers. I can feel it. Our mother—'

'Do you think you have some kind of divine connection to *our* mother? You're obsessed.' Effie laughed unkindly. 'All you're doing is Nana's bidding.'

'I don't!' Anna snapped back, Effie's words striking uncomfortably close to the truth. 'Our mother found Attis's spell, I just want to do the same before Attis does something stupid or the curse catches up with us.'

Effie paused. 'The curse feels under control to me, does it not to you?' Her eyes flashed to Attis and Anna knew what she was implying – that Anna's own feelings for him might be getting the better of her.

'It does.' Anna swallowed tightly. 'But we still can't trust it.'

'I agree with that,' said Attis, his expression dark. 'Which is why me doing something stupid might be entirely necessary.'

'Don't get your knickers in a twist, Lockerby,' Effie dismissed him. 'Anna and I are going to sort the curse out, we're just having a bicker. It's what sisters do. Right, Anna?'

Anna forced a smile. The last thing she wanted was Attis seeing the curse getting to her and Effie. 'Right. You should see us playing a board game.'

Attis grinned. 'I've seen Effie playing a board game. It isn't pretty.'

'Hey.' Effie threw her arms around him. 'Just because you can never win against me.'

The mood began to relax, their bickering giving way to chatter.

The front door shut and, a few moments later, Selene swanned into the room, an array of shopping bags in her hand. She smiled at Anna and Effie brightly, her eyes passing over Attis with her usual indifference.

'Ah, you're both here!' She dropped the bags down on a stool. 'Where were you this morning? I came to see if you wanted to go shopping.'

'Out,' said Effie.

They hadn't told Selene about their trip to Nana yet. Part of Anna wanted to open up to her about it all, but with the investigation at their school and the hysteria, Anna didn't think Selene would appreciate knowing they had been putting themselves in further danger going to see a curse witch behind her back. She would probably only be dismissive, reminding them all that Attis was the only way to break the curse, which was the last thing Anna wanted right now.

Selene went to pour herself a wine and Effie pulled out a black silk dress from her shopping bag. 'I see you're very busy tackling the problem of the WIPS.'

Selene made a face at her.

Anna resisted pointing out that Effie had been at Azrael's half of the weekend.

'I have a date this evening,' said Selene with a smile. She pulled out another dress from the bag – this one a wine-coloured velvet. 'Which do you think?' She held them both up.

'Who's the victim?' asked Effie flatly.

'Reiss Nowell, actually,' Selene replied, considering the two dresses.

Anna almost choked. 'Nowell! As in – Peter's dad?!'

'Yes.' Selene shrugged smoothly. 'We got talking after that meeting at your school. He's quite charming.'

'No. No.' Anna shook her head. 'Not Peter's dad. You can't date Peter's dad.'

'Why ever not?'

'Because!' said Anna. 'Peter is—'

'Obsessed with Anna,' said Effie.

'A twat,' Attis suggested.

'Well, I'm not dating Peter.' Selene smiled. 'I'm dating his father.'

'Please, Selene,' Anna pleaded. 'Not Peter's dad. It's weird. And, anyway, Peter says that he's supportive of the WIPS.'

'Darling!' Selene turned to face her. 'It's just a date. He's just a man. I'm not talking about matrimony here. The only commitment I'm making tonight is whether I'm going to be a damsel in Dior.' She held up the wine-coloured dress. 'Or femme fatale.' She held up the black dress. 'I think I'll go damsel. He seemed the type to like that. You see? It's all just fun and games.'

'I tried to warn you about her,' said Effie with an *I-told-you-so* look, while she poured herself a glass of wine too.

Anna huffed with growing irritation. 'Well, I've had enough fun and games for one afternoon.'

She took the Bible back to her room, channelling her frustration into it instead. She couldn't believe Selene – going on a date when there'd been a hysteria attack this morning. Surely there were more important things to do? Aunt's contempt for Selene came back to her. *You could never leave her alone with a member of the opposite sex and expect her not to go chasing. The worst kind of woman . . .*

Anna shook her head. *No. I won't listen to you!* She knew if the date hadn't been with Peter's father it wouldn't have got to her so much.

She reached the end of the Bible, having found nothing again. She screeched with frustration. The spell had to be in there somewhere – encoded? Hidden? She had what she needed and yet the truth still evaded her. She thought of Effie's words – *You're obsessed* – and she knew she was, that she was consumed by their curse, as if, by thinking about it all the time, she could somehow keep it at bay. But was it getting to her anyway?

She was annoyed at Effie for accusing them of curse-solving behind her back when she was the one who'd gone behind Anna's back in contacting the Hel witches. And if she waited for Effie she'd never solve the damn thing. Anna had to keep things moving. If Attis had come with her, so what? Effie and Attis spent plenty of time together, why couldn't she and Attis? Nothing had happened or ever would. But the light of the garden fluttered through her and Anna knew a part of her longed for it . . . craved it like she craved her magic. *If he'd reached for me – would I have resisted?*

She pulled the mirror out from under the bed and unwound the sheet from it. Aunt stared back at her and then began to laugh.

Anna wrapped it back up quickly and stuffed it away.

I won't become you!

I won't!

I won't look down . . .

But Anna knew she couldn't keep running. That perhaps it had never been the curse she'd been running from, but herself.

CONCERT

Who are we without our shadows?
What is the painting without its shading?
How burns the fire without its coals?
What is a song without its sorrow?
Music that spins without no soul.

'What Is a Shadow?', Traditional Folk Song

'What's going on?' Effie grabbed the girl in front of them. They were stuck in the rain in a queue outside the school entrance.

The girl's eyes bulged as she realized who was talking to her. 'Bag searches,' she stammered.

'Fuck this.' Effie pushed her way to the front.

It wasn't hard – nobody wanted to be near her. Anna followed.

Andrew and another prefect were standing behind a table set up in the foyer. He held up a hand towards her, fingers spread wide. 'Stop there, Fawkes. Everybody on entry is subject to a bag search. New school policy.' He looked down his long, ratty nose at her, not able to mask the relish of his newfound power from his face.

Effie stared at him and Anna could feel her rage, could see it in the way her fingers were curling.

'You've got something in your bag you don't want us to see?' Andrew prodded. 'Used condoms? Herpes cream?' he sniggered, his eyes too small and his teeth too big for his face. 'Or, perhaps . . . items of malefice?'

'I think there is something actually—' Effie began searching through her bag. 'Ah, no. I thought I had your balls in here, but I guess they belong to Inspector Eames now.'

Andrew's sneer flickered with viciousness. 'A comment like that might require reporting. Eames told us that any unruly, lewd behaviour could be a sign of—'

'Of what?'

'A witch,' he said, his voice clear and travelling down the queue like a shiver down a spine.

'Effie,' Anna hissed beneath her breath, 'let's just get this done.'

Effie threw her bag at Andrew suddenly, unsteadying him. 'Go on then. Have a good rummage. You know you want to.'

Andrew's face tightened. He handed the bag to the other prefect to check. Once it was done, Andrew creased his nose, leering over Effie. 'I expect you to be more compliant tomorrow morning.'

Anna stepped between them before Effie could retaliate and Andrew's eyes fell on her – ran all over her, slippery as a rat's tail. He'd known her for years and had never taken the least bit of notice. Anna suspected his newfound curiosity was motivated by Peter's interest in her – he'd always been jealous of Peter.

'Are you going to put up a fight too, Anna? Or do you have more sense than that?'

She handed her bag over.

'Good girl,' he said in a way that made her want to punch him square in his snide face.

She held her breath until it was done then pushed Effie onwards through the door, releasing her breath bit by fuming bit. There were more STOP THE SPREAD posters lining the corridors.

'Bag searches now,' Effie spat.

A couple of girls whispered furiously as they walked past them and Effie stamped a foot towards them. 'BOO!' The girls screamed and ran away.

Anna dropped her head to Effie. 'Don't.'

Effie's anger gave way to laughter. 'Did you see the look on their faces? If we can't have some fun with this I'll go crazy. I just had my bag searched by fucking Andrew.'

'We're being watched all the time.' Anna nodded to some other prefects stationed down the corridor.

It was the same the rest of the week, Eames's prefects taking it in turns to patrol the corridors between classes or watch over the canteen at lunchtime. His eyes had multiplied. As if he was waiting for someone to break. Encouraged by Darcey, the rumours had multiplied too, everyone commenting or sharing personal, emotional videos detailing their own experiences . . .

I've had nightmares every night since the hysteria . . . they chase me in my dreams . . .

It felt like I couldn't breathe in class – I turn around and who's sitting behind me? Rowan Greenfinch . . .

I heard them whispering Ave Satana in the toilets . . .

I heard screams coming from the old gym hall . . .

I can't concentrate, I keep forgetting everything, like my head is filled with this dark fuzz . . . like this school is cursed . . .

Anna's school work was certainly suffering and she couldn't even think about starting revision for exams. At home, she was caught up with trying to solve the riddle – searching the Bible – or drifting towards the piano, returning to the song she'd been working on. The melody had expanded, wandering accidentally from Christmas . . . to the garden with Attis . . . entering new territory, weaving in smoke and cloud, roots and shoots, the bright sparks of bird flight, the song swelling and breaking open into the colours of the sky that Anna had tried to memorize but could not. The music knew them though, so like the colours of his eyes. She'd tried not to imagine her fingers exploring his skin as they'd moved up and down the keys, breaking her apart and drawing her back together, the spinning top dancing free upon the piano, no longer simply spinning – but moving, as if forming something . . . patterns . . . But before she could understand them, the darkness contracted around her, turning the skies of her music to dust. Burying her back under the ground. The spinning top flying away, over and over, like she'd never break through . . .

Towards the end of the week, they were finally able to sneak back into the sewing room after-hours, Attis double – triple checking that no one was in the Ebury wing this time.

'Yessss.' Effie ran towards the mannequins, arms outstretched and grasping. 'They're ready!'

'Mother, maiden and unholy crone . . .' Rowan murmured, as she approached them.

The mannequins were each wearing a garment, as shadowy and intangible as the thread had been. Effie ran her hand over the billowing material and her fingers went right through it. She made a noise of pure exhilaration, ripping the garment off her mannequin.

It wasn't a robe, but a short jacket, with silver buttons.

'I thought they were meant to be shadowrobes,' said Manda, looking over hers, her face gaunt in the sallow light.

'Seems not,' Rowan replied, taking hers off too and holding it up. It was a trench coat. 'Cool.'

Anna approached hers. It was not quite a robe either – but a hooded cape, falling in thick, undulating folds to halfway down the mannequin, the material swirling like the surface of a lake at midnight. A faint embroidery covered it – spirals and roses and vines. Its neck was held together with a little clasp – a small silver apple. The tailoring, the stitching, the details, all were exquisite, like in fairy tales where the clothes have been made by silver-fingered elves overnight. Only these had been spun from the shadows by the hands of darkness.

'How do I look?' Rowan threw her trench coat over her shoulders but as she did the shadows flared around her and swallowed her, not all at once, but slowly, as if she were dissolving, becoming part of them.

'We can't see you,' Manda stated.

'Therein lies the whole point.' Effie shook her head, shrugging her own jacket on. She disappeared too.

Rowan appeared again, trench coat in hand. 'Could you guys not hear me either?'

'No,' said Anna.

'I was talking the whole time. Trying to tell you all that I looked like a fabulous, but extremely deadly spy.'

Attis undid his from the mannequin – a long, heavy coat with a high, turned-up collar. The shadows of it seemed almost grey with metallic hints. He put an arm through it and was gone.

Manda's was a neat shoulder cape with little pockets and a red-hued ribbon tie. Manda tucked an arm into it, fading into the darkness too.

Anna was left in the silence of the room. She narrowed her eyes trying to pick anything out – a hint of movement or a feeling of someone there – but the room felt entirely empty. She reached for her own cape, her fingers passing through it. She could barely feel it at all, except a faint sense of something – like the way you might feel drizzle in mist; the texture of darkness in a shadow. She threw its shiver of magic over her shoulders with relish, the clip fastening itself around her neck. It fell just below her knee but felt weightless and supple as a second skin. She could hear their voices now.

'Hey,' Anna called. 'Can you guys hear me?'

Rowan laughed. 'Anna's joined the party!'

'So we can hear each other when we're wearing the robes?'

'Woven from the same thread,' said Attis with fascination. 'The shadows must somehow be bound together, linking us while we wear them . . .'

Effie's voice was dark with delight as she declared, 'We're free at last!' Anna couldn't see her, but her voice felt everywhere, ricocheting off the walls with euphoria and vengeance. Effie threw off her jacket. She was standing on one of the tables. 'We're free, bitches!'

The rest of them took off their garments, appearing back in the room.

Rowan gave Effie a wary look. 'These robes aren't an excuse for us to be reckless. The WIPS have opened a new investigation this week into that abortion clinic Hopkins has been highlighting – specifically the female doctor who's been accused of "killing unborn babies" as he put it. They're growing, recruiting. Apparently, they've expanded their offices in the Shard already. I've tried to talk to Mum about it all but she says they haven't learnt any more. I don't know if it was the truth.'

'On that note, I think the Wild Hunt have come through with some info on the WIPS,' said Effie. 'Poppins says he'll only tell us if we all go partying with them this weekend.'

Rowan gave her a wry glance. 'Did he really say that?'

'It's important for us to build bridges with these guys,' said Effie. 'They have a lot of standing and access in the magical world. We all game? You're not too busy with Kariiiiim, Manda?'

Manda rolled her eyes. 'We're officially back together if you must know, but I'm playing it cool this time.'

Effie snorted as if she didn't believe a word of that. 'Well, at least you have your shadowrobe now, so sneaking out should be easy.'

'Why not party?' Rowan threw her hands up. 'My grades are already spiralling, I can't focus on revision, I've had to quit the band—'

'You quit?' Anna turned to her.

'Well, sitting in a room for an hour while no one talks or looks at me wasn't so fun any more. Plus, they're performing in assembly tomorrow. How am I meant to stand up in front of everybody with everything going on? It's bad enough just walking around the school.'

'I quit all my extracurricular activities too,' said Manda.

'Hold the wand.' Rowan's mouth dropped. 'You quit your extracurriculars? *All of them?* You were the only member of some of those clubs and I thought they were *vital* for your university place.'

Manda shrugged defensively. 'I've already done my applications and my grades are perfect. All that's left to focus on is exams. I don't care about the rest any more. I've given everything to this school and what has it got me? We've been shunned and labelled witches. Screw them.'

'Finally.' Effie climbed down from the table. 'Someone seeing my point of view.'

'I've had to quit all my extracurriculars too,' said Attis solemnly.

Rowan snorted. 'What were they? Annoying the shit out of teachers club?'

'Cheerleading with Ramsden?' Anna suggested.

'The Sex God Society actually.' He nodded. 'Very exclusive. Only for people who like blood rituals and goats.'

They laughed, but Anna could feel the tension in it, as if they were all thinking the same thing. How would the year come to an end? Would they be free to move on with their lives? Or was it all going to get worse?

Freedom felt a long way off. When Anna entered assembly the next morning, Eames's prefects were standing outside the entrance to the hall, while others were studded between the rows of seats. Anna knew most of them by sight – there was Hutton, Digby, Andrew – but they all looked different, were carrying themselves differently – a new air of self-importance, their eyes distant and hard, as if a line had been drawn between them and everyone else. She spotted Peter. He nodded at her.

The band were on stage preparing their instruments, and Anna realized it must be the performance assembly Rowan had spoken about. She was relieved – at least they wouldn't have to face Eames. Rowan waved at them from a back row and they joined her.

'You all right?' Anna whispered to Rowan, who looked forlorn watching her old band mates with their instruments.

'Yeah, just feels weird not to be a part of it.' She shrugged, giving Anna an unconvincing smile. 'Nothing's the same though, is it?'

It was true. Normally, the crowd would be chatting away but the hall was subdued, everyone holding in a breath they all seemed too afraid to let out. Mr Ramsden blustered onto the stage and grunted through his daily updates, eventually introducing the band in a way that made it clear he had little patience for music.

The band began – a merry song that clashed with the feeling in the room, the conductor's hands jumping up and down. The drumbeats followed his rhythm, trumpets and trombones flared, flutes and clarinets braided a tune through it all, a few of them dragging out of time.

'Wow, we're not very good, are we,' Rowan whispered.

'They were better with you,' Anna muttered back, then shut her mouth. One of the prefects had snapped his head to them.

She closed her eyes and let the concert wash over her, moving her fingers in time to the music, thinking of her own piano, her own melody, stirring her magic as she played.

The band started on their final song – a marching tune, the drum pounding beneath. A few minutes passed but the song didn't come to a close. *Pounding, pounding, pounding—*

Anna felt suddenly cold. It crawled up from her toes, forming little crystals of unease over her skin. There was a feeling . . . a feeling of discomfort growing, like a nail slowly drawing down a chalkboard. She opened her eyes – the band were still playing. *Pounding, pounding, pounding.* Some of the instruments dropping out of time. They were a minute over the end of assembly. Her thoughts began to slow, her body frozen in place as the dread pressed down against the horror rising up inside her.

It's here.

She managed to turn to Rowan and Rowan's eyes flickered over hers, back and forth. Effie shifted forwards. They could feel it too.

The band ploughed on, crashing through the song now – faster – faster – the conductor's hands a blur. The music unravelling – drum erratic – *pounding, pounding, pounding* – trumpets flatlining, flutes and clarinets squealing. *The eyes.* The eyes of the band members staring ahead as their hands and fingers moved too fast, as their faces slackened or grimaced too tight. Their eyes disappearing to somewhere terrible, as if the life in them was falling away as the song drove them on. The music screaming and in it Anna could hear Aunt's laughter, deranged and delighted.

Panic began to spread across the crowd. Cries and shrieks. People covering their faces and ears or trying to run. The band wrestling with the instruments now, beating against them, wrenching at strings, tearing and thrashing. The notes of the song twisted and torn apart like a pile of bones.

Teachers began to run onto the stage, but the band members were wielding heavy instruments and the spell that drove them on would not let them stop. Mr Ramsden gibbered, turning this way and that, doing nothing effective. Some pupils had taken out their phones to record the chaos. Anna saw Eames among it all, watching with keen, detached interest. Only his eyes moved, inching slowly around the room and landing on them.

Anna, Effie and Rowan were still sitting, held by the furious, frenzied force of the magic. Anna wanted to reach for her own magic but she could feel nothing – not her magic, not her body, not even herself – everything locked, numb, torn open and shredded to pieces like the music.

Rowan stood up. 'We have to help.'

'No,' Effie hissed. 'We shouldn't get involved.' Her eyes were on the spectacle, consumed by it.

Anna forced herself up. 'We have to!' But she could not move against it. The spell had her trapped. Burying her.

A group of prefects ran up the row towards them. They had Manda already.

'Come with us!' they yelled, surrounding them. 'Now!'

'Don't resist, Anna.' Peter's voice in her ear. 'Eames's orders.' He held her arm as she was pulled from the room.

Anna, Effie, Manda and Rowan sat in silence, heads bowed. They'd been taken to one of the rooms of the Ebury wing, the door shut, prefects stationed outside. They'd been frantic for the first hour, not knowing what to do, arguing, banging on the door, but eventually, they'd given in to the shock inside their bodies and had slid to the floor, powerless.

'I hope they're OK.' Rowan's voice was frail. 'We should have done more . . .'

'What could we do?' Manda snapped. Her eyes were wide, her cheeks hollow. She was clutching herself as if she might start to rock or shake at any moment. 'If we'd resisted being brought here it wouldn't have looked good. If we'd tried to use magic to help . . . it could have exposed us. *Everyone* was there.'

Rowan didn't reply. Manda was right, but it felt wrong. Lives were at risk, they couldn't just watch on and do nothing. But what could they do? How could they fight something they couldn't see? Couldn't understand?

Effie kicked the door again from where she was sitting. 'They can't just keep us in here.'

'Who cares about us right now?' Manda glowered.

That was true too. Everyone would be distracted with the chaos of what had just happened. No one would be fighting their corner. If anything, most of the school would be happy to see them locked up. The prefects had all but thrown them in here – except Peter. He'd taken Anna to one side, away from the others. He'd held her hands. 'I'm sorry I have to leave you here.'

'I could be helping!' Anna had cried. 'In there!'

'There are enough people to help. Eames wanted you removed. You have to understand, you're under suspicion.'

'We didn't do anything, Peter! You have to believe me.'

'I know.' He'd held her eyes. 'I believe you, but it would have been worse to resist. You're safer here anyway. I have to go now.' He looked to the door, terror and exhilaration battling on his face, blue eyes sharper than she'd ever seen them. 'I – I hadn't quite been sure until now. But that was *malefice*, Anna. That was it.'

Anna hadn't bothered to deny it. What was the point in trying to claim it was only hysteria? Peter was convinced now, she could see that.

She turned to the others. 'You've all felt it now. The magic I felt before. It was like it was then . . . but worse. Bigger. Deeper.'

The others nodded, no one able to deny it. Anna could still hear the music, torn and turned inside out so that the melody was twisted into something monstrous . . . Aunt's laughter erupting through it . . .

'It definitely isn't your magic,' said Rowan, startling Anna from her thoughts. 'That was . . . I don't know what it was. Like no magic I'd ever felt. Extremely powerful.'

Anna shut her eyes against the force of it, its cold still running in her veins. She hated how it had held her captive in her own fear, how helpless she'd been again.

'So powerful,' Effie reiterated, 'if they hadn't started to restrain the people on stage, I don't think they would have stopped. I think they would have played until it killed them.'

Rowan buried her head in her hands. 'What if they're not OK?'

'There were plenty more people in that room than those lost in the spell; I'm sure they managed to stop them,' said Anna, trying to comfort herself as much as Rowan.

'They were my friends . . . the way they looked . . . the terror . . .' Rowan's words gave way to sobs.

Anna put an arm around her, letting her cry against her shoulder, not knowing what she could say to make it better.

The door opened and Eames's secretary bustled in with Attis. 'You're to wait here,' she instructed.

Effie leapt to her feet. 'You can't keep us locked in here like animals!'

The secretary turned to her, looking somewhat in shock herself, but she clasped her hands together, attempting composure. 'You're not locked in here, Ms Fawkes.'

'So we can leave?'

'Of course you can leave . . . only, after what just happened, it wouldn't reflect well. It might look like you were running away.' She moved her goggly eyes between each of them, making her point – or warning – clear. If they ran Eames would only have more reason to catch them. 'I suggest you stay put,' she added as if she were trying to help them.

'We just want to go home,' said Rowan.

'I understand, but Eames is waiting to speak to each of you.'

'We're being singled out!' Effie yelled.

'You were singled out before this investigation even began. We've just had a severe malefice attack; questions have to be asked. I'm sorry,' she added, biting her lip and looking to the door as if she feared Eames's imminent arrival. 'I'll bring you all some water. Now, I gather you're happy to wait here a little while longer?'

'Perfectly content,' Attis replied gruffly, moving a fuming Effie away from the secretary.

Once she'd left, Effie released a roar. 'They've got us trapped and, unless we do something, they're going to find a way to pin this all on us!'

'Is everyone OK?' Rowan asked Attis.

He nodded. 'It's still bedlam, but from what I can gather, no one's been seriously hurt. By the time the police arrived most of those . . . affected . . . had been brought under control. They've been taken to hospital.'

Rowan leant back against the wall. 'Thank the Goddess.'

Relief coursed through Anna too. *No one hurt.*

Attis moved away from the door, his voice hushed. 'I did find something though.' They gathered around him. He reached deep into his pocket and took out a glass vial with a small layer of pale yellow powder at the bottom. 'Spirit powder.'

They all stared at it, until Manda broke the silence, her voice breathless. 'What? Where?'

'As soon as news of what had happened reached the Boys' School I took advantage of the chaos, grabbed my shadowrobe from the car and made for your hall to check it over. Couldn't see anything, but then, around the edges of the stage, I spotted traces of what looked like powder. I gathered as much of it together as I could.' He opened the vial and put his nose to it. 'From the sulphurous smell alone, I'm fairly certain it's spirit powder. Would have gone to the chem lab to check but figured they were probably looking for me and thought it best to show myself before anyone discovered I was missing.'

'You can't have that vial on you,' said Anna, panicking for him. 'If they find it—'

'Don't worry. I have very deep pockets.' He tapped his nose and dropped it back inside his blazer.

Effie took a few steps back. 'Death magic.'

Attis nodded. 'Looks likely. Spirit powder generally precludes working with spirits. Does what it says on the tin. Whatever this spell is, someone is using the spiritual realm to give it power.'

Anna felt dizzy, realization sinking through her. *Of course.* The feeling of the spell . . . the dread, the panic, the paralysis . . . it was like the magic that night with the Hel witches, when the shadows had risen through the Fabric. Only this had been so much more intense, as if the Fabric had been clawed open entirely. Is that why the magic had felt so impossible to counteract? To comprehend? Because it didn't belong to this world at all . . .

'So someone is raising spirits in our school?' Rowan's eyes flickered with confusion. 'But it's not just our school – the hysteria is striking across London . . .'

Anna spun to Effie. 'The Hel witches! You've spent more time with them, with Azrael. Have they said any more, *anything*, about what's going on? If this is all linked to death magic they must know something!'

Effie frowned, speaking sharply. 'What's that meant to mean? If I'd known anything I'd have told you, wouldn't I? Azrael and I don't exactly do a lot of talking.'

'Well, we need to talk to him,' Anna insisted. 'To all of them.'

'If they're behind it, they might not want to talk,' Rowan pointed out.

'We have to try.'

'Fine,' Effie snapped. 'I'll call him as soon as we get out of this damn room and I get my phone back. Though I doubt he'll be pleased to hear from me . . .'

'Why?'

'I've been kind of ghosting him.'

'Bad choice of words,' said Rowan grimly.

'I'll bring him around.'

It was after lunch by the time Inspector Eames opened their door, his delayed arrival making it clear to them they were at his mercy. He was wearing his usual expressionless mask, his eyes moving over them impassively, as if they were all the same to him. Suspects not individuals. Creatures of malefice to capture.

Effie stirred from where she was brooding but she did not unleash her rage.

Rowan stood up. 'When do we get to go home? Our parents will be worried.'

'They've been informed of the situation,' said Eames, without a hint of sympathy. 'You will be free to go home once you have been questioned. Miss Richardson first, please.'

Effie tilted her head to him. 'Are we the only ones being questioned?'

'At present,' he replied tersely. 'Now. Miss Richardson.'

Manda got to her feet shakily.

Effie spoke again. 'What if you're wrong?'

Eames's hollow eyes twitched back to her, irritated by the insinuation.

'The suspicion against us is based on the word of one girl,' Effie continued.

'I assure you, it is more than just one,' said Eames, his Adam's apple tightening.

'But it began with one. What if you're focusing on the wrong people? What if the real witches are just playing with you? I'd hate to see you mess up your job here.'

Eames's look darted again, discomforted, as if he couldn't handle the ambiguity of her words. 'All possibilities are being explored.' He snapped long fingers at Manda. 'Now! Miss Richardson.'

They were each taken through until only Effie and Anna were left.

Effie's restlessness had turned hard and as Anna looked over at her she tried to work out what Effie was thinking, what was stirring behind those shadowy eyes. It was strange how she could feel so close to her sometimes and so like a stranger at others. They needed to stay together in all this.

'You OK?' Anna asked.

'I'm not used to being caged, I'm not sure I like it.'

'I can imagine that.' Anna, on the other hand, had spent her life caged. She knew how to be still, how to wait, how to hold onto loose threads of hope. That didn't mean she liked it either.

'So,' Effie's eyes shifted, 'what did Peter want with you?'

'You know, the usual, checking I was OK.'

'It might not be a bad idea to keep him on side, you know . . .'

Anna frowned. 'What does *that* mean?'

'Just . . . it might be sensible to keep him pliable. He could prove useful. He's clearly one of Eames's favourites and if Peter has one weakness – it's you. You've got him hooked, all you need to do is reel him in a bit. Men are easy to manipulate, they're simple creatures really, just play the game – flatter, flutter those lashes, pretend you need him to be your hero. It won't be that hard, it wasn't so long ago you liked him.'

'That was different,' Anna replied abruptly. Peter was not a game she wanted to play. 'I don't want to complicate things with him. Anyway, you hate him.'

'I do, but we need all the help we can get right now. You're expecting me to call Azrael when we get out of here, aren't you? Get him to help us. What do you think that's going to involve?' She gave Anna a pointed look, then shrugged. 'Just think about it. This is about the bigger picture, the safety of all of us, the coven.'

Anna turned to look out of the window, angry, feeling betrayed by Effie but caught in the tangle of her words. Did she not see what position she was putting her in? Did she not care? She knew how intense Peter could be. But then, like Selene, Effie didn't see things like flirting and sex as a big deal, just fun to be had, opportunities to be gained.

The worst part was, Anna knew she was right – they did need Peter on their side.

OUIJA

Employing the Language of the Dead in written form, Initiates begin to commune with the spirit world directly, building relationships with Guardian Spirits and performing spells alongside them. Our Guardian Spirits will then continue to teach Initiates the foundations of the written language.

Communing, Hel Witch Initiation Stage Four

The moon was soft and sly as it rose above the school ahead of them, hiding from the darkness behind a gauze of cloud.

'I don't have enough fingers to count the reasons why we shouldn't be doing this.' Rowan looked down at her fingers as if she didn't know what to do with her hands, with herself. 'Mum's been in panic mode all evening and if she finds out I've sneaked out – sneaked out to go back to SCHOOL – she'll kill me. If I don't die by the end of this evening anyway . . .'

'We have no choice,' said Effie, looking down the road.

Anna couldn't believe they were back here either. Her eyes rose up to the Ebury wing, all its lights were off now. Only hours ago, she'd been sitting in the centre of Eames's office, his chair positioned between her and the door. Notepad in hand, he'd questioned her relentlessly, mercilessly, going around in circles, trying to trap her in her own answers. Then, without blinking, he'd described the state of the pupils who'd been taken to hospital – how some hadn't stopped screaming, how some had tried to claw at their own faces – prodding, watching her for a reaction, his nails tapping on his notebook.

Are you responsible for the malefice?

Do you wish to confess?

On the outside, Anna had kept it together. Inside, she'd been crumbling. She knew it made no sense that she was responsible – the strikes were across London, the magic they'd all felt had been far beyond anything she was capable of – and yet, why had it felt so personal? Why did it feel as if that cold already lived inside her? Why had it held her so still? Why had she heard Aunt's laughter so clearly?

'I can see them,' said Effie, pointing to two figures in the distance, walking up the street: Azrael and Yuki were coming to meet them, coming to help them go back into the school they'd only just escaped from.

'This is madness,' Rowan muttered. 'We should have told my mum about the spirit powder.'

Bertie and Selene had met them outside the school gates after they'd been released – Bertie frantic, Selene livid. Apparently they'd been trying to get to them for hours but hadn't been allowed and, short of resorting to magic, they hadn't had any choice but to wait.

'Your mum would never let us do this,' Effie retorted.

'For good reason!'

'Then we'd never have any way of knowing what's really going on. You don't have to join. You can wait here.'

Rowan looked up at the school too. 'I'm not leaving the rest of you to go alone. All in. We stick together, come bane or boon or me running away flailing and screaming like a wild banshee.'

'That's the spirit,' said Attis.

Rowan groaned. 'Please don't mention spirits.'

Anna looked to Manda who was leaning against the wall, uncommonly quiet, arms folded around herself. Karim had been there earlier, waiting for them to be released, but her parents had not come. She'd said that they'd been too ashamed to show up, to deal with her. Anna had wanted to ask more but they'd been swept up by all the chaos. She felt guilty they were lying to Selene, but Effie was right – all Bertie and Selene cared about was that they were safe, but Anna couldn't wait around and watch while some sort of death magic took over the school, threatening the lives of everyone in it.

'Greetings,' said Yuki solemnly as they arrived. She wore a long black coat and white gloves, hair severe around her delicate-as-glass face. A backpack was secured to her back, almost half the size of her small frame. Azrael was wearing a frown and a slouchy wool black jumper, frayed sleeves pulled over his hands and his crucifix necklace resting over it. Neither one smiled.

'Thanks for coming.' Effie walked over to Azrael and gave him a kiss on the cheek. 'We really appreciate it.'

He appeared slightly mollified.

Yuki turned to Attis. 'You are sure you found spirit powder within the school?'

Attis nodded with certainty. 'I've carried out a test on it, fairly rudimentary – added iron powder, heated it up. It formed iron sulphide which indicates the existence of sulphur, the predominant ingredient of spirit powder, right?'

Yuki nodded. 'Do you have some?'

Attis reached into his pocket and pulled out the vial. Yuki opened it and placed a dab on her tongue. She nodded to Azrael. Their eyes locked in silent debate.

'We should not be here,' said Yuki. 'It goes against all of our codes.'

'Do you know what's going on?' Anna asked.

Yuki's wide eyes turned on her. 'No.'

Anna didn't know how to tell if a Hel witch was lying, they already belonged to a different version of reality.

'We've been following the hysteria outbreaks,' Yuki continued, 'but none of the senior Hel witches will speak of them. If this is death magic, we want to know the truth too.'

'We don't do everything they tell us,' said Azrael, with a toss of his hair. Anna sensed his rebellious comment was for Effie's benefit.

Manda moved towards them, livelier now the Hel witches had arrived. 'What are you going to do?'

'To contact the spirit world,' said Yuki. 'To speak with them and learn what might be going on here.'

'Sounds swell.' Rowan smiled tightly.

They took out their shadowrobes. Effie lent Yuki her jacket and then joined Attis beneath his wool coat, while Rowan gave Azrael her trench coat and sidled over to Anna, who wrapped her cloak around the both of them, Manda slipped on her cape and they disappeared into the ripe midnight darkness.

They moved up the street towards the back entrance to the school. Anna could hear Rowan's teeth chattering beside her. They held hands tightly.

'This way,' Attis instructed, leading them up into the main corridor, the suspects returning to the scene of the crime.

The skin of Anna's body tightened and prickled as they drew closer to the Athenaeum as if the coldness of the spell still lingered, still beckoned . . .

The hall was still caught in its state of panic – the rows of chairs scattered about, some on the floor as people had jumped up and run; some on the stage, the instruments strewn about looking like pale, twisted limbs in the moonlight. The night pressed up against the surrounding windows as if it were watching their every move. They took off their cloaks, appearing one by one.

Effie gestured to the carnage of the stage. 'They were up there when it struck. They went loco, wouldn't stop playing.'

Yuki nodded. 'We must communicate with the dead.'

'Er – I don't think we want to communicate with the force we witnessed earlier today . . .' Rowan stammered.

'Don't fear. We will only be contacting our Guardian Spirits. They may be able to illuminate what took place here.'

'I thought you couldn't speak to the dead?'

'Only senior Hel witches, our Raven Tongued, who have travelled to Hel, can speak the Language of the Dead and communicate with spirits directly. However, there are indirect methods—'

Yuki took off her backpack and extracted a plain white board from within. The board was so thin it was almost transparent. *Bone.* Anna recognized it from the Museum of the Dead.

'No.' Rowan moved away from it. 'Hel, no. A ouija board? Have you guys watched any horror movie *ever*? Ouija boards never end well.'

'Do not equate what we have here with Hollywood trash,' Yuki responded, her voice disapproving. 'This is a Hel board and it's a reliable way for Initiates to contact spirits. I am trained in this.'

She pulled up her sleeve and extended her arm towards them. Travelling up her wrist were four black markings. The Language of the Dead.

'I have passed the first four stages of Initiation, the last of which – communing – allows me to commune with the dead through symbols.'

'You're so close to the fifth stage,' said Manda with awe.

'What's the fifth stage?' Anna asked with foreboding.

'Journeying to Hel.' Yuki's eyes gleamed. 'But I still have many years to go until I am ready.'

Anna glimpsed again at the marks on her arm, recoiling instantly. They weren't tattoos but sunk into the skin, black and puckered.

'Formed by death itself,' Yuki explained. 'The flesh rotted away.'

'At this point, I'm not even surprised any more,' said Rowan.

'How many have *you* got?' Effie asked Azrael.

He looked affronted. Unwillingly – poutily – he pulled up his sleeve to reveal two marks. 'Yuki is unusually advanced,' he added hastily.

'Six is as many as you can have while you're alive,' Yuki added with a wry smile. 'The seventh and final mark is given when you die. It denotes your Death Name.' At the looks on all their faces she continued. 'In death, you take on a new name, decided by the Language of the Dead. When we call on our Guardian Spirits, it's their Death Names we use.'

Anna thought of the ritual at Halloween, the words the senior Hel witches had called out. They'd been Death Names.

'I will lead the spell,' Yuki continued. 'It would be useful for some of you to join, for additional power, but you don't have to partake. We need people keeping guard too.'

Rowan stared at the board again and nodded. 'I'll keep guard.'

'I will too,' said Attis, his head already moving reflexively between the entrances and exits.

Manda was eyeing the board covetously. 'I'll join.'

Anna nodded before she could stop herself, trying not to think of the magic they'd experienced earlier that day. Music strangled until it screamed. Screams still echoing inside her.

Azrael and Effie were having a hushed conversation in the corner of the room.

'Azrael!' Yuki called. 'Are you two joining?'

They came back over. 'Course,' said Effie.

'Oh Mother Holle.' Rowan wrung her hands. 'Please be careful. No possessions. No eyes rolling back in anyone's head. No ectoplasm erupting from anyone's mouth, OK?'

'Ectoplasm doesn't work that way,' Azrael scoffed. 'It's a cowan misunderstanding. It's not something that occurs when you're possessed by a spirit, but a symptom of Death Sickness.'

'What's Death Sickness?' Anna asked, not sure she wanted to know.

'It's what can happen if you do not work with spirits safely. They can feed on your energy, drain you, rot you from the inside out, resulting in the emission of ectoplasm – a black, viscous substance – from the mouth, nostrils, even the ears sometimes.'

They all stared at him, terrified.

'Surely that's a bit extreme . . .' Manda gulped.

'Do I look like I'm joking?' Azrael replied. Anna suspected he'd never made a joke in his life. 'There's a reason we take so many precautions.'

They moved the chairs away, creating a space in the centre of the room, beneath the moonlight which streamed through the stained-glass window above, a pale echo of its daylight colours. Yuki poured a neat circle of spirit powder around them. Azrael took off his crucifix necklace and unscrewed it. He tapped some yellow-tinted powder from inside onto his finger and placed it on his tongue, letting it dissolve. He tipped some more out, offering his finger to Effie. She licked it off with a dark laugh. He passed the crucifix around. 'I highly advise you all to take some spirit powder. For protection.'

Anna tried it this time, wanting all the protection she could get. It tasted sour and eggy, a tang of festering earth. Hard to swallow.

Yuki's smartwatch lit up. 'It is midnight. It is time.' She picked up the planchette that came with the board. Anna caught Effie's eye and could see that she too was terrified, invigorated but terrified. They joined hands as she began to speak, Yuki's voice hollow in the empty acoustics of the room.

> *Goddess Hel,*
> *Raven Mother,*
> *Weaver of Bones,*
> *Crone of the Crossroads,*
> *Keeper of the Keys,*
> *Join with us now, unveil your power,*
> *Turn o'er the fabric at this midnight hour.*
> *Raise up our dead, let the feathers fly,*
> *Cross our hearts and live to die.*

'Cross our hearts and live to die,' they repeated.

Yuki looked down at the board. Waiting. The magic passed between their fingertips, slowing down, scraping against the flow of reality, turning cold as their breaths began to quiver with little snowflakes. That feeling of death magic rose into the air again, too similar to earlier that day, flaying fresh shivers over Anna's skin. The magic tightened like a twist of barbed wire. The Hel board stirred.

A row of letters appeared along it, as if they were rising up from somewhere beneath it. *Not letters. The Language of the Dead.* Anna felt its horror rush through her – its symbols the etchings of screams, whispers made of blades, slicing her open.

Yuki placed her fingers on the planchette. It began to move over the letters which were flickering and changing, running through an alphabet that seemed to have no end.

'What's she doing?' Effie's whisper was as frail as the snowflakes rising from her lips.

'Spelling out the names of our Guardians – calling them forth,' Azrael replied.

Anna felt them arrive.

That sensation behind her of the world disappearing. The Athenaeum falling away like crumpled fabric, the living emptinesses growing up through its tatters. *Terrible shadows.* Dead and numbing; alive and writhing; the feeling of fingers smudging up and down her spine.

Friends not foe, Anna reminded herself through the pain of the magic. *Here to help us.*

'They are ready to speak with us,' Yuki announced. 'Join me.'

It took all of Anna's strength to move her finger onto the planchette alongside the others. It felt weightless beneath their touch and yet the magic that ran through her was powerful, dizzying, black and endless, stitching them together with threads of bone, plucking at their goose-pimpled flesh and holding them in painful paralysis. The letters still flickered – infinite combinations. The planchette began to move – as if invisible fingers had joined theirs – slowly at first and then faster, building words that had no meaning to Anna besides horror. She wanted to clasp herself, but she couldn't let go of the planchette. It trembled now. Faster. Scraping across the board with a toe-curling screech.

Yuki sucked in a sharp breath. 'Something is wrong. They want us to stop.'

'We can't stop,' Effie urged. 'Tell them we need to know.'

Yuki's head shook, her eyes lost as the planchette moved faster and faster beneath their fingers. Anna could feel all the wrongness inside herself. She wasn't sure they could stop the spell now even if they wanted to – it had them gripped, its darkness sucking them in . . . down . . .

The planchette clawed over the bone of the board as if it were being dragged down too, the letters whirring so fast Anna could no longer distinguish between their broken shapes, could no longer separate them from the broken parts of herself.

And then, the letters stopped flickering. Only four remained. The planchette moving between them, over and over, carving deeper and deeper into the board.

Over and over.

Faster and faster.

Anna could feel herself fragmenting, letter by letter—

She wanted to move but couldn't.

Needed to scream but couldn't.

The same letters.

Over and over.

Faster and faster.

The shadows engulfing them.

Then a shattering sound as if the world had broken.

They fell backwards from the board. Anna looked up. Above, the glass of the vast stained-glass window was shattering – and reforming – shattering – and reforming—

Caught in a loop of undoing. And noise. Everywhere noise. Anna realized she was screaming but they were not her screams, nor those of the others. *Bells.* Bells were going off. All of the school bells.

'Run,' Attis shouted over the clamour. 'We've got to go! Now!'

Attis lifted Anna to her feet and she registered she could move, that the deadly magic had released its grasp. She ran with the others for her belongings, Yuki stuffing the board back in her bag. The bells had woken the whole school and they would be coming. *Eames* would be coming. The window was still shattering – reforming – shattering – reforming—

Anna grabbed Rowan's hand and threw the cloak over them. She couldn't see the others now but could hear panting and gasping between the clang of bells as they ran out of the Athenaeum, down the corridors. They would have to go past the front entrance – there was no other way. Anna could see flashing lights arriving outside. Rowan tripped up beside her and the cloak tugged off her—

'Rowan!' Anna screamed, reaching for her.

Rowan scrabbled for her hand and Anna pulled her back up, managing to throw the cloak around her as the front doors burst open. They didn't stop to see who was arriving, fleeing down the corridor – following the frantic footsteps of the others until they reached the back door. Outside, the sound of sirens wailed, uniting with the mayhem of the bells.

'To the letterbox!' Attis's voice boomed in the darkness.

They ran down the road into Dulwich, away from the lights and the cars until the night was silent again, arriving at the old Futhark Letterbox they had sent the letter to Nana from the year before. It was tucked away in a cobbled back street. They removed their cloaks but no one could speak for several minutes through their ragged breathing. Anna tried to put back together the pieces of what had happened, but her mind was still shattering and reforming too, the letters still embedded beneath her skin like pieces of shrapnel.

'What – what was that?' she managed to say.

Rowan lifted herself from where she had been bent over, trying to catch her breath. 'Was it the hysteria spell?'

Yuki shook her head, her eyes wider than they'd ever been. 'I don't think it was the full force of the spell. Just an echo of its earlier magic.'

'*That* was only an echo . . .' Rowan repeated with disbelief.

'The letters,' said Effie, trying to hide the tremor in her own voice. 'What did they say?'

Yuki looked at them, her face moon-white and broken in the black night. 'Fear. The letters spelt: fear.'

Anna's heart jolted like a struck bell, as if she'd expected Yuki to say those words. 'What does that mean?'

'I don't know exactly.' Yuki's mouth searched for answers. 'I suspect we're dealing with a spirit formed of fear. We must speak with the senior Hel witches . . .'

'Can they be trusted?' Attis looked between Yuki and Azrael.

'I don't think they are behind this if that's what you mean,' Yuki replied sternly, and then more delicately. 'But . . . perhaps we can talk with Mór first. She's our living mentor.'

'I'm undergoing training tomorrow alongside other Initiates,' said Azrael. 'Mór will be there.'

Effie grabbed his arm. 'You have to get us in.'

Azrael released a breath. 'She won't be pleased.'

'If we don't stop the spell, people are going to die,' said Anna forcefully. 'We have to tell her what we know.'

'Fine,' Azrael replied flatly. 'But you might want to bring a coat. It gets cold down there.'

They arrived in front of the grandly pillared church of St Martin-in-the-Fields right in the middle of London, Trafalgar Square buzzing at their backs. The church's steps were busy too – workers eating lunch, people taking in the view of the square, pigeons pecking at the dust. To the side of the church, indicating down a set of stairs, there was a sign for: CAFÉ IN THE CRYPT.

'See, it's just a nice café.' Effie nudged Rowan.

'IN A CRYPT,' Rowan cried. 'A CRYPT.'

The five of them began down the stairs, leaving the light of day behind them. Anna hadn't slept well, the school bells clanging all night in her mind, just as they'd done when she'd set off the bells before . . . *Why? Why these threads of connection?*

The café was situated beneath the church – a low-lit, underground room, thick pillars descending from its brick vaulted ceiling, as if the church had grown roots beneath its foundations. There were dark alcoves and corners, giving the room a sense of unendedness, as if anything could be lying in wait. Utilitarian tables, plastic chairs and a food counter clashed with the unsettling atmosphere, the people in the café taking little notice of the tombstones forming the ground beneath their feet.

Rowan grimaced. 'How can people eat with dead people beneath them?'

'The scones look good,' Effie commented. 'Actually, Attis, could you grab me a coffee? Black as Hel, please.'

Anna laughed at the expression on Rowan's face. She looked down at the tombstones, the words on them almost too worn to make out, names and half-formed dates. The dead among the living. There was no sign of Azrael.

Manda sat down at a table. She looked as exhausted as Anna felt. They waited for Attis to return with some drinks. Effie had taken a sip of coffee when Yuki stepped behind them.

'Mother Holle alive.' Rowan spilt her juice down herself. 'Where did you come from . . .?'

'We know subterranean London like no one else,' Yuki replied. 'There are other entrances and exits to the Crypts of St Martin's. Shall we go?'

'Never big on small talk, are they?' Rowan muttered as they followed her.

They walked in a line down through the café, into one of the alcoves which contained a small door at the back. It led into a narrow corridor, then through another door, down several flights of stairs, the air chilling with every breath.

'The Crypts is one of the stations of the Necropolis Railway,' Yuki explained. 'The dead that were taken to the church above could be shipped out on the train below. But we're not going as far as the platform today – only to here.'

She opened another door with a shriek of rust and they stepped into a stone corridor with a vaulted ceiling like the café, electric bulbs dripping wan pools of light down the walls which held doorways on both sides. A figure was standing in the centre, cutting a tall and severe shadow against the light. *Mór.* She turned and glided towards them, her long crimson hair pouring over her shoulders, her skin cold pearl, her eyes flint as they moved over each of them with displeasure, somehow impatient and yet containing all the time in the world. 'How is it I am facing you five again?' Her voice was frosted velvet, her hand coming to rest on her bump – larger now.

Yuki stepped forwards. 'I am sorry, I—'

Mór put up a hand. 'Azrael has told me. I am aware of the circumstances. You carried out an unsanctioned Hel board in a cowan school.'

Yuki lowered her head but Effie spoke up, her voice almost as cold as Mór's. 'Yeah and there's a big, fat, unsanctioned death spell spreading across London right now, turning cowans into quivering wrecks. I think that might be the bigger issue, don't you?'

Mór pursed her lips.

Yuki found the courage to speak again. 'We believe it is death magic, Mór. The ouija board—'

Mór cut her off. 'I know what the spell is.'

Yuki's mouth formed a little halo of surprise. 'You do?'

Mór walked away, heels clicking like icicle points on the ancient stone beneath. 'The senior Hel witches are aware of what's been happening across the city. We have carried out investigations of our own and believe we have established the spell involved.'

She checked the locked doors as she walked. Anna could see now that the doors were far from ordinary – large and ornate, lined with ivory tiles scored with the Language of the Dead. She flinched away, perceiving what the doors were . . . tombs, the entrances to tombs.

'What spell?' Yuki asked.

Mór stopped and turned back to them. 'An unleashing spell.'

Yuki inhaled, her breath catching.

'Want to tell us what an unleashing spell is?' Effie prodded.

Mór looked up to the light. It fell upon the taut lines of her face like snow on bare branches. 'When we engage with spirits we are always in control, we know their Death Names and we work with them, alongside them. An unleashing spell is entirely different – a spirit is released from Hel into our world, rupturing through the Fabric, uncontrolled and untameable. This particular spirit is formed of fear and feeds voraciously upon it.'

'Formed of fear . . .' Manda repeated in a whisper.

Mór moved down the tunnel again and they followed. 'Hel is not where our souls go to rest, but where the restless parts of us are left behind. As I explained before, that is what spirits are – shards, shadows of broken emotions, repeating their moment of shatter over and over.

'In this case, a spirit made of fear – ancient, pure and potent beyond measure, beyond recognizable – dredged up from the darkness of Hel into the cold light of day. Its well runs deeper than you can imagine and when it spills over into our world, all who feel it are undone by its despair, spiralled into madness.'

Effie blew out a breath. 'That sounds about right. What we want to know is, who did the unleashing? It's the magic of *your* grove after all.'

Mór's eyes snapped to her. 'This was not cast by a Hel witch. It goes against everything we stand for. This spell is reckless to the extreme. It has no control over the spirit it has unleashed and it can't be undone. The spirit will continue to terrorize this world, feeding on the fear that it creates, until eventually its energy wears out.'

'When will that be, do you suppose?' Rowan asked delicately.

'I couldn't say. Months, years, perhaps.'

'Years!' Anna exclaimed. 'We can't let this go on for years! There must be some way to stop it.'

'There isn't. In order to command a spirit, you must know its Death Name. This spirit was released without such control – we doubt those who unleashed it know its name.' Her head shook. 'Sometimes we are able to draw out the names of spirits we don't know but not one like this. This spirit is buried too deep. Its name can only be learnt in the Underworld itself. The spell can only be stopped in Hel.'

'OK.' Anna nodded. 'Then there *is* a way.'

Mór looked taken aback. '*That* is not an option. Such a journey would be madness.'

'So you're just going to watch while the world descends into madness? Can't you go? Or one of the other senior Hel witches? Many of you have travelled to the Underworld before, haven't you?'

Mór lifted her sleeve to unveil six Death Marks travelling from her wrist up her arm. 'I have been to the Underworld. We train for decades. We go just once. It is a personal journey. We do not go for magical missions. We do not seek out dangerous spirits. To interfere with such things is not the Hel witch path and never has been. We will not break our codes now.' Mór pulled her sleeve back down.

Effie laughed. 'Oh, so you claim it wasn't a Hel witch who released this spirit at the same time as saying you won't do a damn thing about it. We can't trust a word you say.' She paced away but at that moment one of the tomb doors was flung open, the darkness within spitting out a terrified and disorientated-looking man.

'Are you OK, Angus?' Mór asked, quite calmly.

'I – I – I – I—' he stammered.

'Go and sit beneath the light and practise your trance breathing.'

Angus managed a nod, stumbling away and sliding to the floor, huddling in a pool of electric light as if it were the only warmth in the world.

Rowan looked between Angus and Mór, aghast. 'What are you doing to them?'

'Our Initiates undergo various forms of training over many years to help them prepare for their eventual journey into the Underworld. This is one of the harder exercises.'

Anna was drawn to the open door of the tomb, to the darkness within – a darkness that seemed to shift and stir and softly suffocate like a quilt of feathers, like the darkness of her dreams . . .

Mór stepped beside her, breathing it in. 'The Initiate must go into the tomb and stay in its darkness for as long as they can take.'

'Sit in a dark room. Doesn't sound very hard,' Effie scoffed.

'It isn't ordinary darkness . . . is it?' said Anna, her voice feather-thin.

'No,' Mór replied, looking at her curiously. 'It is created with magic, designed to emulate True Darkness.'

'True Darkness?'

'You have heard cowans speak of the seven circles of hell?'

'It is written into many mythologies around the world,' said Attis.

'It is drawn from truth. In journeying to Hel, a person must face seven trials – seven layers of fear, each one stripping away your sense of self. If you can't hold onto yourself, you may be left to face the True Darkness of Hel – a darkness unlike any other, indescribable for those who have not experienced it. It exists only in the Underworld.' She looked through the open door to the tomb. 'The darkness in there is only a weak emulation, but it can help an Initiate to mentally prepare.'

Another door was flung open and a girl came running out screaming.

'Yuki, go and calm Chastity,' Mór instructed.

Anna turned from the tomb, trying to suppress the chills of Mór's words. 'Mór, if a Hel witch isn't behind this spell, then who is? Who else is trained in death magic?'

Mór's eyes moved evasively. She seemed to be considering how much to tell them. 'The Hel witch path is tough. Not all make it through. And not all who travel to the Underworld survive the journey. They may return . . . broken. Not everyone can put themselves back together. Many leave us afterwards.'

Effie laughed coldly. 'So what you're saying is that there are a load of demented ex-Hel witches out there with a bone to pick and spirits at their fingertips?'

Mór scowled at her. 'You have a way of twisting things, Effie. They do not leave because we throw them out, but of their own choosing and most never practise death magic again, but it is possible that some *could*.'

Attis breathed out angrily. 'So an ex-Hel witch could be behind all this?'

'The unleashing spell is powerful, ancient magic. We do not think it could have been done alone, more likely a group of witches – a ritual. We think the spell was carried out at London's most spiritually potent site – the Tower of London – the death of its ravens marking the beginning.'

Around and around – falling – dying.

'We also think whoever cast the original spell may be helping it spread across the city. Witches acting like lightning rods – drawing the spirit's energy to them and causing the hysteria in each case. The fact you found spirit powder within your school suggests that such a person may be at St Olave's.'

'An ex-Hel witch at our school . . .' Rowan reeled.

Anna struggled to imagine it. To imagine *who*.

'Perhaps. Or someone working with one,' Mór clarified. 'We don't know exactly.'

'But why?' Rowan cried. 'Why are they doing this?'

'We don't know that either.'

'Can't you track them down?' said Attis.

'We do not keep track of the whereabouts of ex-Hel witches and do you know how easy it is to hide in the magical world? Anyone can change their name, but magic makes it easy to change your appearance too. If they don't want to be found – we won't be able to find them. Besides, as I've told you before, we do not interfere with the affairs of the living.'

Attis slammed his hand against one of the tomb doors. 'You can't just do nothing! The spell is in our school, it could kill anyone, it could kill one of us!'

Mór closed her eyes and opened them again, unruffled. 'As I said, the spell cannot be stopped except in the Underworld itself.'

Effie went to speak.

'And before you ask.' Mór put a finger up. 'No. None of you can go. There is only one entrance and we are the Gatekeepers. It would be a death wish. You would not make it out again.'

A third door burst open and Azrael crawled out, pale and panting, his handsome face a broken grimace of pain.

Mór frowned. 'I must attend to my Initiates. I have told you what I know and can do no more.'

There was another cry. This time – among them.

They spun to Manda who'd fallen to the floor.

Attis dropped beside her. He checked her over then raised her legs. 'I think she's fainted—'

Manda began to come around, eyelids fluttering, putting a hand to her head and groaning.

'We should take her to fresh air,' he said.

They helped Attis lift Manda to her feet, while Yuki opened up the door for them.

In all the commotion, Anna held back, calling after them, 'I'll be out in a second.' She was not yet done with Mór.

Mór looked at Anna curiously, like a raven cocking its head.

Anna tried to find the words as she held Mór's gaze. 'Is it – is it possible to be haunted by a spirit?'

'Why do you ask?'

'Because – because sometimes I feel, as if a presence is near me, within me, I don't know – and my magic seems connected . . . to death – to bells and snow and I dream of a darkness like that—' She nodded to the tombs. 'But worse, deeper.' She didn't know whether to admit the last part. 'When the hysteria spell strikes, I feel the spirit with me, inside the spell, but I'm not doing anything, I swear—'

Mór's eyes moved between Anna's, slow as a pendulum. 'Sometimes those who have experienced death in life – a near-death experience, the death of someone close to them, or a part of themselves – can become . . . attuned to the other side of the Fabric. They may be able to feel Hel's echoes more keenly, their magic may carry the shadow of death within it.'

'The shadow of death . . .' Anna's voice trembled, as if snowflakes would start to rise from it.

'Your connection to death may mean you feel the fear spirit more intensely. Perhaps it wears the face of that which, or whom, you fear most.'

Aunt.

'It may not last forever,' said Mór, 'but until you learn how to pass through the shadows.'

Anna wanted to know what that meant, *how* to pass through them, but the tunnel door banged open behind them.

'Anna?' Attis called. 'Are you OK?'

'Yeah . . . I'm coming . . .' She turned back to Mór. 'Please, if you won't help with the hysteria, then can you at least tell the magical world what you know of the spell? They won't believe us but if it comes from you, it'll make them pay attention.'

Mór nodded. 'I'll see what I can do. In the meantime, I advise you to leave your school.'

'We can't,' Anna replied fiercely. 'We're being investigated by the WIPS, another enemy that threatens all of us.'

Mór lowered her head. 'We are archivists, not anarchists. I'm sorry.' She turned away, moving to help Azrael. Anna stared after her, feeling the shadows of death creep out from the open tomb doors, uncurling their fingers towards her.

She found the others in a nearby café, trying to ply Manda with food to help her recover from her fainting episode.

'The Hel witches are a useless pile of goat shite and *that* is an insult to Mr Ramsden,' Attis declared, releasing a forceful breath.

Effie slurped on a cola. 'They were never going to help.'

'At least we know some of what we're dealing with now,' said Anna.

Rowan shook her head, dazed. 'A group of crazed ex-Hel witches have unleashed a spirit and are now drawing its energy to different locations around London setting off mass hysteria wherever it strikes.'

'A spirit of fear . . . feeding on fear,' Anna muttered.

'Like the Pied Piper,' Manda whispered, leaning against the wall, her eyes still too wide and her voice strange and distant. 'He played his pipe and the children couldn't stop – they danced and danced and followed him to the river where they all drowned.'

'Great,' Rowan groaned. 'A phantom Pied Piper. What are we meant to do?'

'We find the person in our school drawing the spirit's energy,' said Anna. 'We might be able to get them to stop the spell.'

'Why would they want to stop the spell?' said Effie. 'If it's some group pissed at the WIPS, perhaps they won't stop until the WIPS back off?'

'We still need to try and find them. We can at least hand them over to the magical world.'

'But who would be doing this inside *our* school?' Rowan still looked flabbergasted at the thought.

'Mór said it might be one of the ex-Hel witches or someone working with them . . .' Anna tried to think through all the possibilities, but the school was vast, with pupils, teachers, administration staff, governors, even parents all having access.

Effie's eyes narrowed. 'Darcey,' she said. 'She vowed to bring us down. If we fall – she triumphs.'

'Darcey's many things but she's not a witch,' said Rowan.

'I'm not saying she's doing the casting herself, but she sure does believe in magic these days and she's got money and connections, maybe she's got caught up in all this, started working with this ex-Hel group . . .' Effie stopped, her eyes widening. 'Wait. Or perhaps we're not seeing the bigger picture here? Who's benefiting the most from these hysteria attacks?

The WIPS themselves. Drumming up hatred and fear against the magical world so they can consolidate their power. Maybe it's them.'

'But everything they stand for is against magic,' said Rowan.

'No one's above dirty tricks.'

'It did start when Eames joined . . . Do you think he and other WIPS investigators around the city could be sowing the hysteria themselves? He really doesn't seem like a witch though.'

Anna thought of Eames's dead eyes, the way he'd described the state of the band members' suffering to her as if it were nothing . . . but then . . . the disgust that disturbed his features when he spoke of malefice. She could not imagine him casting. 'I don't know . . . he *loathes* magic.'

'Or he's very good at pretending,' said Manda bitterly.

Attis knocked his knuckles against the table. 'It could be any number of possibilities. I can search the school, and Eames's room, for traces of spirit powder.'

'We all go,' said Effie. 'We've got our shadowrobes now. We can do some hunting of our own.'

'Yay. More break-ins,' Rowan groaned. 'I'll agree only on the condition that we tell Mum and Selene about everything we learnt today too so they can take it to their connections. Maybe we omit the whole carrying out a ouija board on school grounds though.'

'Sure,' Effie replied. 'But from what I've seen Bertie and Selene are going to just keep pussyfooting around it all. Anyway, we've got our night out to prepare for now. Let's not forget Poppins has fresh WIPS information for us.'

Still lost in subterranean darkness, Anna had forgotten they were due to meet with the Wild Hunt that evening.

Rowan nibbled her cheek. 'Feels weird to party right now . . .'

'A night out is more than just a good time,' Effie countered. 'It's about information gathering, teasing out secrets, networking, forming alliances and remembering what we're fighting for.' She banged her can of cola down. 'Magic.'

'I thought you were going to say my dance moves,' said Attis.

Effie nudged him. 'Those too, of course.'

Anna turned to Manda. She looked better for the food, but still worn out, her skin stretched too far over her bones. 'Maybe you should stay home and rest . . .' Anna suggested gently.

'No,' Manda replied abruptly. 'I'm not missing tonight. I'll be fine, I just didn't eat breakfast this morning.'

Anna was sure it was more than that. The stress of everything going on was eating at all of them in different ways. 'How are things with your parents?'

Manda stiffened. 'Fine.'

'It must be hard though—'

'I'm over it, OK?' Manda snapped. 'I'm over them. If they think I'm a witch then so be it.'

'OK.' Anna pulled back. 'I'm here if you want to talk is all . . .'

'You know the only thing I want to do?' Manda replied, banging the table herself now, an echo of Effie. 'Get drunk.'

GLITTER

During periods of purification, an Initiate should abstain from rich foods, alcohol and narcotics, consuming only water or diluted vinegar mixed with ash and small portions of fermented fruit and vegetables.

'States of Purification', Hel Witch Trainings,
Books of the Dead: Tome 8311

They stood looking up at the vertiginous white walls of London's prestigious Dorchester Hotel.

'The den of the Wild Hunt,' Effie declared.

'Doesn't look much like a den to me . . .' Rowan's neck tipped back further to take the building in. Its capacious entranceway was sleek with lights, two green-coated and black-gloved doormen standing on either side, eyeing them suspiciously: a gang of teenagers, Effie barely dressed, Attis attempting a winning smile as he curled a bottle of beer into the crook of his arm.

Effie marched up the stairs.

One of the doormen blocked the entrance, gloved hands folding neatly together. 'Can I help you?' His eyes travelled up and down Effie unfavourably.

'You most certainly can, Derek.' Effie pointed a finger at his name badge. 'We'd love to go inside.'

'Do you have a reservation?'

'We do not.'

'I'm afraid you need a reservation.'

'We're here to see a friend – a resident.'

Derek looked as if his patience were wearing thin. 'And what would your friend's name be?'

'William Calthorpe,' Effie replied, and Derek's eyes jolted.

He stiffened upright. 'Mr Calthorpe?'

'Yes. He's expecting us if you want to ring and check. I don't think he'll be happy about how long you've kept us waiting.' She tutted and tapped her wrist.

'Your name?'

'Effie Fawkes.'

The doorman hurried off and returned promptly with a flustered, apologetic smile. 'Do come in, Ms Fawkes. Mr Calthorpe is expecting you. I will show you up to his suite.'

'Thank you most kindly, Derek.' Effie flashed him a smile that put him entirely in his place.

'Could I take that for you?' the other doorman said to Attis, nodding at his bottle.

'Cheers, Tim,' said Attis, handing it over.

They were directed through the revolving doors into a vast and sparkling foyer, all Art Deco magnificence, everything black, white and gold; cut-glass chandeliers reflected upon the floor below.

Derek led them through to a lift and pressed a polished brass button. 'He's residing in our Terrace Penthouse. The views are quite spectacular.'

'Naturally,' Effie replied, looking at herself in the lift mirror as they stepped inside, completely at home among the surrounding grandeur. She could go anywhere and make it hers, thought Anna, play any part while somehow remaining unbudgingly Effie.

On the top floor, they were presented with a long corridor with rooms on both sides, reminding Anna briefly of the Crypts earlier and yet this couldn't have been more different. She could see from a window that they were perched above the city, its lights all aglitter below.

Derek stopped at the door at the very end, with a sign dangling from its handle that read: DO NOT DISTURB. Derek knocked gently.

After a few moments, the door burst open, the doorframe struggling to contain the force of the presence behind it – Poppins dressed in a black tux lined with red sequins, a shock of long electric-blue hair and cocktail glasses in both hands. He smiled his jester smile, eyeing them all greedily. 'Oh good. Fresh meat.'

The room behind was an explosion. Music and noise, people yelling and shrieking, confetti flying about in the air, people dancing on a table that was stuck to the ceiling . . .

Derek tried to speak.

Poppins leant into him. 'Darling, what you didn't see won't hurt you.' He formed a threatening smile. 'Run along now and keep this between us.'

Derek, alarmed, nodded and swivelled back down the corridor, footsteps quickening into a run.

'I have them all in my pocket,' Poppins cackled and dispensed one of his cocktail glasses into Manda's hand. He grabbed Attis by the T-shirt, pulling him into the room. 'Welcome, friends of Effie! Welcome to the party!' He raised a razor eyebrow at Effie's outfit. 'Effie, doll. You appear to have forgotten half your clothes. No matter. We prefer them off than on here. Speaking of, Attis, my light, my love, when will we be together?' He draped himself over Attis's neck.

Attis grinned. 'Soon, Poppins. Soon.'

'How you tease me. How I love it.' He laughed a laugh thick as treacle, quick as a pocket knife.

'Who's William Calthorpe?' Manda asked quizzically. 'This is his room.'

Poppins's snakeskin-green eyes snapped to her. 'Never heard of him.'

'It's Poppins's real name,' said Effie.

'Never!' Poppins declared. He lowered himself to Manda. 'Tell me your name again?'

'Miranda.'

'I deny it! I shall call you Cupcake!'

'But that's not my name.'

'And these aren't my eyebrows. Do you see? This is the Wild Hunt – here you can be anyone, you can become your wildest dreams . . . and everyone else's worst nightmares . . .'

Ivor ran full pelt towards them, picked Effie up and threw her over his shoulder. She squealed with laughter, legs kicking as he carried her off.

'Well, that's the rest of her clothes taken care of,' Poppins hooted. 'Now, have some champagne.'

He moved them towards a bath – which was sitting incongruously in the middle of the floor – Poppins's uneven gait more pronounced now he didn't have his umbrella to balance on. He dipped a glass into the bath. It was full of liquid that appeared, from its colour and bubbles, to be champagne. A blow-up flamingo floated through it and another one several feet above it.

Anna took a glass, distracted by the rest of the room, which looked like a hotel room that had been taken apart and put back together so that nothing quite fitted or made sense any more: everything out of place, brightly dressed people lazing on lavish sofas watching people dancing on a table hanging from the ceiling, one of the room's pillars bent over into a U-shape, ornaments exploded to pieces, the noble figure in the portrait above the fireplace wearing a pink feather boa which Anna was sure did not belong there. On the other side of the room, a group of people in various states of undress were gathered around a dining table, cheering and laughing as they played cards, a girl swinging from the chandelier above. The balcony doors behind were thrown open, the London night blowing in, circulating explosions of confetti around the room. There was the feeling in the air of barely contained chaos.

Someone took Anna's hand and twirled her around. She landed face to face with Ollie, who was bare-chested with a shimmering cape draped over one of his shoulders. He bowed, his mop of ebony hair falling forwards, his whimsical smile lighting up his sweet brown eyes.

'Dorothy!' He stepped back and threw his cape over the other shoulder. 'You have returned to me!' He revealed a gold coin in his hand. 'Now, heads you kiss me, tails you marry me.'

Anna laughed. 'Marriage might be a bit of a leap.'

'The heart wants what it wants, Dorothy, we cannot deny its whims! But OK, I shall change the terms – heads you kiss me, tails I buy you drinks all night. How about that?'

'Deal.'

He threw the coin high into the air. As it spun upwards it appeared to pass through many colours, sizes and types of coin – and landed as a small bronze coin with foreign script. It showed heads.

Anna narrowed her eyes suspiciously. 'I sense the odds are always in your favour . . .' She gave him a kiss on the cheek.

He put a hand to it and pretended to stumble backwards, cartoonish. 'A kiss as sweet as the face from which it came. I would cheat a thousand times over for another.'

'I knew you were a cheater!'

'A cheater? Or a fool in love?'

'Maybe just a fool,' said Attis, coming over and slapping a hand on Ollie's shoulder.

'Takes one to know one,' Ollie replied, patting him back just as firmly.

Attis conceded a smile. 'You're right there.'

'Come on.' Ollie gestured to them all. 'Come and meet the pack.'

As they approached the uproarious dining table, a girl threw her arms around herself, her dress disappearing into thin air. 'I've only got two items left!'

'You think you've got it bad . . .' Ivor stood up to reveal he was no longer wearing any trousers. Effie, who'd sat down beside him, laughed along with them all.

'What are they playing?' Rowan asked.

'Strip poker,' said Ollie. 'Once you're in, there's no way out. Magic does the stripping and it's ruthless. Ivor always ends up starkers. He's terrible at bluffing.'

'At least I'm allowed to play!' Ivor boomed, his wedge of jaw set in a grin.

'They don't let me play any more,' Ollie explained. 'Because I always win.'

'Because he always cheats!' the girl attached to the chandelier chirped as she swung brazenly. She began to shuffle the pack upside down, her body small and lithe and Lycra-clad. Anna watched, mesmerized, as the cards moved between her hands like mini acrobats, jumping and flipping, hovering in the air and forming elaborate patterns that were impossible to track and fantastical to behold.

'That's Picatrix – or Trix.' Ollie caught a card and threw it back at her.

She caught it and flicked them a grin, made even more impish by her pixie haircut.

'You won't ever find her in a normal position. Her body and its impossible contortions are her magic.'

She finished the shuffle with a final flourish, the cards fanning out and landing face down in front of each of the players.

Ollie moved around the table, stopping at a girl with thick golden locks of blonde hair braided into plaits on either side of her head, clad only in her bra. 'This is our lovely Bridy.'

Bridy picked up her cards and smiled warmly at them. Her face was soft as flour and her eyes blue as flax.

'Her language is bread,' said Ollie.

'Bread?' Manda repeated.

'Bread making is one of the oldest magical arts in the book,' Bridy replied.

'She owns a bakery in Bethnal Green,' Ollie added. 'You should go. Her muffins are delightful . . .'

Bridy looked down at her buxom chest and smiled. 'Best muffins in all of London.'

The boy next to her picked his cards up and assessed them.

'That's Jeudon,' said Ollie. Jeudon gave them a cool nod. He appeared to still be wearing most of his clothes and Anna could see why – the contained features of his face were entirely unreadable, as sharp and defensive as an ace of spades amid the havoc around him. Only the cornrows of his hair moved, weaving different patterns as he assessed his cards.

'He's not a talker,' said Ollie. 'He works with thought forms.'

'What are thought forms?' Anna asked.

'Thoughts so powerful they take on visual forms you can work with to create magic.'

'I fold.' Ivor threw his cards down. 'And yes, now I am entirely naked.'

They all shrieked with laughter.

'And who's she?' Manda nodded towards the girl at the far end of the table. She was leaning back, considering her cards with casual confidence, a cigarette between her lips.

'She's none of your business,' the girl in question murmured, not looking up. Her eyes were ringed with black that swirled around her eyelids like a dark mist.

'Emilia,' said Effie.

Emilia took a slow drag on her cigarette and breathed out – but the smoke did not come out of her own lips, but Manda's, and it was darker than smoke, more like shadow.

Manda coughed and grimaced, making Emilia laugh darkly.

'She's all bark and very vicious bite.' Ollie grinned. 'I wouldn't cross her.'

'He'd be right,' Emilia responded, assessing her cards.

'Fold!' Bridy threw her cards down, losing her bra in the process. She looked down at her bare breasts then undid the long plaits of her hair and covered them with it.

'Now *that's* cheating!' Ollie declared.

Jeudon pushed a stack of chips into the centre. Everyone chorused an *Ooooo* of suspense.

'Jeudon's going big!' Ivor bellowed.

'Jeudon always goes big.'

'He's bluffing.'

'I wouldn't go up against him—'

The others folded but Emilia leant forwards. She flicked a hand and her own chips moved into the centre. 'Raise.'

From above, Trix revealed the final card of the round. Jeudon and Emilia eyed each other across the table. The rest began to drum roll as the tension rose.

Bridy gasped as Jeudon laid down a perfect royal flush.

Emilia roared and threw something in rage – a knife which spun through the air and lodged itself through one of Trix's upside down cards. Its hearts began to bleed, red dripping down over them and onto the table.

'Em doesn't like to lose,' said Ollie.

Emilia growled and stood up, lifting her glass above her head as her jacket disappeared revealing arms swirling with shadowy tattoos. She downed her drink. 'I've still got plenty of layers left. Let's go again.'

'And I've got nothing to lose . . .' Ivor laughed.

The others cheered as Trix drew all the cards back together.

'So everyone's a different language?' Anna asked Ollie. 'But still a grove.'

Poppins reappeared, answering her question. 'A grove doesn't *necessarily* have to be bound by one language. It can be bound by values, beliefs, moral principles. In our case – Anarchy! Debauchery! Mayhem! Madness! A unique ability to Fuck Shit Up!' He raised his umbrella and confetti shot out of the end of it. The rest of them laughed and banged the table. Ivor streaked around it to further hoots.

Anna laughed as she jumped out of the way. 'And what's your language, Poppins?'

'*Moi?*' Poppins spidered a hand across his chest. 'Why, my language is chaosssss.' He hissed the word seductively. 'Wherever I go – it surely follows, like a bad habit.'

'And he gets around,' Emilia quipped.

'I can't deny it.'

'Speaking of . . .' Effie eyed him from the table. 'You told me you had some information to share with us.'

'I might do.' Poppins smirked. 'But for what price?'

'We have information to share with you too.'

'Intrigue.'

They faced each other, hard-eyed, the table silencing. And then, they snorted with laughter.

Poppins raised an eyebrow. 'You go first. Spill the magic beans, darling.'

Effie leant back in her chair. 'The hysteria outbreaks occurring across London are death magic. A spirit unleashed.'

Trix's cards, hovering in the air, fell to the table; everyone turned to Effie.

'It's true,' said Effie, basking in the attention. 'Confirmed by the Hel witches themselves, who claim not to be behind it but believe it was cast by a ritual of several witches. They have ex-members who are capable of such things.'

'If it's their magic,' said Poppins, 'they should fix it.'

'Apparently there's no way except by going to the Underworld.'

A few of them laughed.

'She's not joking,' said Attis.

Poppins put a hand to his chest, taking in a dramatic breath. 'To Hel itself! The land of Mother Holle. Queen of the Dead! Surely not?' He smiled and popped his umbrella open. It flared behind him turning black on the inside, contrasting with the sharp, white teeth of his smile. 'They say a single cry from one of her ravens can flay the skin from your back!'

'That she eats the souls of children for a snack!' Ivor boomed.

Ollie threw his cloak out. 'No, she eats the memories of the dead – crunching our lives between her teeth and flossing them with our bones!'

'No.' Bridy joined in. 'She makes a crown of our bones and weaves herself a cloak from snowflakes to pass the centuries!'

Emilia's voice came low and threatening. 'They say her snowflakes are a maze you get lost in until you turn as mad as her and forget your own name.'

Trix extended herself from the chandelier. 'And when Mother Holle shakes her feathers – it snows on earth! The snows of Hel!'

The glitter in the air stopped its swirling motion and began to fall slowly over them, everyone's faces raised towards it—

They all began to laugh at the theatrics, except the coven who'd felt death magic too recently to find the humour in it.

Anna spoke up. 'This is no joke. It could kill people.'

'The spell is in our own school,' Rowan added bluntly.

Poppins snapped his umbrella shut. 'And we're sorry, but I'm not sure what the likes of us can do. This seems a matter for the Hel witches, or the Seven.'

Attis released a rough breath. 'If only they were options.'

'We can offer you our information at the very least. Cillian!' Poppins called loudly across the room. 'Where are you, my little Cillian?'

A girl with pigtails, in a leopard-print dress, came over with a boy. 'He was looking through the bathroom cabinets,' she explained.

Poppins tutted. 'Cillian, I told you to sit still.'

'I find bathroom cabinets interesting,' Cillian replied.

Effie looked him up and down with a judgemental frown. '*Who* is this?'

Poppins smiled dryly. 'Our newest member of the Wild Hunt.'

He did not look like a Wild Hunt member. He was not brightly dressed – his slight frame was enclosed in a long, black leather coat. His hair was scruffy blond and his eyes hidden behind round-rimmed, shaded glasses.

Poppins put his hands on Cillian's shoulders. 'He's the best ShadowNet hacker in London.'

'In the UK,' Cillian corrected.

'Sorry. In the *UK*.' Poppins made eyes at the rest of them. 'We've been trying to track information down about the WIPS as per your request, Effie, but, despite my legendary ability to draw gossip out of a stone, it's been hard to find much. Cillian, however, came to my attention. He has ways of finding out things that even the best gossipers among us cannot. He's been feeding us information and in exchange we've allowed him to join the Wild Hunt, as per *his* request.'

Cillian scratched his spray of hair and shifted his glasses further up his nose. Anna was surprised he wanted to be a member of the Wild Hunt. He didn't look like the partying, hedonistic sort. 'What's the ShadowNet?' she asked.

'A magical area of the internet used by witches,' said Rowan.

'A layman's explanation,' Cillian commented, earning him a glare from Rowan.

'Go on then, Cillian,' Poppins prompted. 'Tell them what you know.'

Cillian turned his head towards them, though Anna couldn't tell where he was looking behind his glasses. 'I've been researching the Witchcraft Inquisitorial and Prevention Services for some time,' he said, as plainly as if talking about bathroom cabinets. 'A near impossible task – they are shrouded in darkness. I've recently uncovered further aspects of their organizational setup. They're made up of five departments: Communications. Investigations. Security. Some kind of legal arm. And another branch – secretive – I don't know what it does. They have five members in charge. Halden Kramer, Head of Communications. Marcus Hopkins, Lead Researcher and Head of Investigations. Packton Lancre, who seems to head up the legal side of things. Norman Remy, Head of Operations and Security. And a final member – a shadow member – identity unknown. They've buried their pasts but they were all established, successful figures in the cowan world before joining the WIPS. Kramer worked at a senior level within GlobeMedia and as a political advisor. Hopkins is a businessman, who seems to have worked across a variety of different sectors – technology, energy, construction, even aerospace. Packton Lancre was a High Court Judge. And Norman Remy worked in commodities trading focused on developing countries. They have their fingers in a lot of heavy-weight pies.'

'Five heads,' Rowan muttered. 'Legend has it there are Five Hunters.' She recalled one of the old rhymes. '*Five wolves are out in the woods tonight, you better beware, the fire burns bright—*'

'I don't deal in rhymes, I deal in data,' said Cillian, earning him a second glare from Rowan. 'But five appears to be the number and, from my research, I believe that the magical world is certainly under attack.'

'You're not seriously suggesting the WIPS are "the Hunters" of legend . . .?' said Emilia.

'Yes, we are,' Anna replied, the words coming out of her mouth before she could stop them. She was tired of holding back, of worrying that she sounded like Aunt. 'Witches have been hunted before and they could be hunted again. Whether the hunts are all connected doesn't really matter right now – we just need to look at the threats we're facing – the WIPS are opening investigations into witchcraft across London and they're turning cowans against magic, against us.'

The Wild Hunt stared back at her as if she were either mad or a bit simple.

Effie leant forwards at the head of the table. 'Anna could be right.' The attention shifted to her. 'There may be truth in the old stories and warnings. You all believe in the power of the Seven? Why not their opposite? A darkness that overpowered them, a darkness trying to build cages around us.'

Anna recognized the words – she'd once said similar to Effie.

'I work near Whitechapel and there *is* a lot of uproar around there about magic at that construction site . . .' Bridy admitted.

Effie nodded. 'The WIPS may be no passing inconvenience. The magical world might be facing something it's not had to face for hundreds of years and we're on the frontline. We're under investigation in our school and we're being targeted, singled out, scapegoated for the malefice there. What will happen to us? Where's it going to lead? Will the WIPS stop or will they continue to grow their power?' She stood up, getting carried away now, all eyes latched onto her. 'What are we going to do about it? Accept these attacks on us? Or fight back? Show them what we're made of! Show them that we truly *are* their worst fears . . .'

The table burst into uproarious cheers and hoots.

Poppins assessed Effie with a sharp smile. 'Aren't you blowing things a little out of proportion, Fawkes?'

'You love blowing things out of proportion, Poppins,' Effie replied with a flick of her own smile.

'I do, but only when it's fun.'

'Who says it can't be fun?'

Poppins chuckled darkly. 'Point made.'

Anna wasn't sure the conversation was going in the direction she wanted it to. She shared a glance with Attis, who looked as concerned as her. She turned to Cillian. 'Please, if you can keep gathering information – or any of you – then we start to know our enemy and how to fight them . . . when the time is right.'

The Wild Hunt nodded and murmured between themselves.

'After all.' Effie smiled. 'Nobody hunts the Wild Hunt. Am I right?'

Ivor banged his barrel fists on the table. 'I'd like to see them try!'

The others roared in response. 'We hunt! We ride! We hunt! We hunt! We ride!' They raised drinks and tipped them back, chanting, whooping, chasing away the discomfort of the conversation.

'Fuck the WIPS!'

'Flash our tits!'

'We hunt!'

'We ride!'

'Go big until we die!'

'And look at the time!' Poppins thrust his umbrella towards a clock on the wall. Its glass face exploded – Anna suspected who had shattered half the ornaments of the room. 'It's time to go a'hunting!' He stopped and looked at the coven with mock fright. 'But first – you lot need . . . work.'

Half an hour later, Anna, Effie, Rowan and Manda stared at themselves in the mirror of one of the suite bedrooms.

'As above, so below – fabulous hair, fabulous shoes,' Rowan squealed, turning around on some high heels Poppins had lent her, her hair bigger than ever.

Anna looked at herself, in a purple dress that brushed the tops of her thighs and silver glittery heels with straps that had wound their way up her legs. Her hair had never been so voluminous either, her nails never so long – they'd grown and sharpened as Trix had applied the nail brush to them. Poppins had turned Effie's hair blue to match his while Manda was now wearing a pink halterneck top and flare skirt. Anna could see just how thin she'd grown from the stress of the year.

'Tonight is all about colour at Equinox, which means you need a little finishing touch. Fairy dust . . .' Poppins laughed gleefully.

He opened a pot of glitter and blew a cloud of it towards Anna's face. She squeezed her eyes shut, expecting a mouth and nose full, but instead the glitter took on a life of its own, whirling through her hair and landing on her lips, turning both of their reds to sparkling and then swirling a silvery-green pattern along her cheekbones and around her eyes.

'Woah,' she said, leaning forwards and looking at her glistening form in the mirror. She touched her lips but the glitter did not come away – it had become part of her features, had dissolved deep into the strands of her hair.

Poppins dusted the rest of them, the glitter turning different colours and forming unique shapes as it landed on their skin. It spidered a black-glitter pattern down Effie's neck and along her clavicles, then tunnelled into her eyes, turning her irises from black to glittering granite.

Effie blinked in the mirror. 'Cool.'

'You all look spectacular,' Attis announced.

Poppins raised a hand. 'A-moon.'

'Shall we head?' Attis opened the door.

'Don't think you're getting away so easily, lover boy . . .'

Anna chuckled as Poppins hooked Attis's neck with his umbrella and dragged him towards a seat. A few minutes later his eyes were lined with dark eyeliner and his fingernails were glowing different colours.

'Perfection,' Poppins cackled and blew a kiss from his lips, which landed on Attis's cheek, leaving a red mark. Then Poppins and Effie hooked elbows and bustled from the room in a cloud of glitter.

Anna went to pick up her bag and caught Attis looking at her in the mirror, his eyebrows rising higher as they travelled down the straps wound around her legs.

'I'm not sure I'll ever get free of them,' said Anna, turning to face him and feeling a flush of warmth at his gaze; a rush of excitement. Why did he have to look at her like that? It was so confusing.

'They suit you.' He smirked, but his smile wavered, the look in his eyes changing to something less tangible. 'We better go before Poppins and Effie start some kind of a riot.'

Before long, they'd all stampeded out the door and through the quiet foyer of the hotel amid chants of – *We hunt! We ride! Go big until we die!*

They took a bus back up Oxford Street, Poppins filling its interior with confetti and managing to get most of the passengers dancing, cowans and witches alike. Compared with school, it felt like freedom. *This is how it's supposed to be*, Anna thought – the magical world not exposed but not contained, glimmering at the edges of reality, sometimes flaring like a firework, there and gone again before anyone could quite work out what had happened. It was what she'd been missing her whole life and she didn't want it taken away. She didn't want to fight Aunt's fight against the magical world, she wanted to fight *for* it.

They poured off the bus and down Carnaby Street which matched them with its bright, glittering signs and colourful buildings. Anna noticed a few STOP THE SPREAD posters stuck up here and there but she did her best to ignore them. They turned down a side street and halted outside a wooden door to a café that appeared to be closed for the night. When Ivor pulled it open, Anna realized what it must be – an elder door. They were hidden around the city – doors that led somewhere else entirely. It wasn't the same door they'd used to get to

Equinox the year before, but when they emerged that's exactly where they were.

Equinox, and yet, different. It was still bell-shaped with the dance floor in the centre and dark, secretive alcoves around the outside, but now the walls were made of glass, the floor of mirror. The room was an eruption of colour – the colours of the flashing lights, the vibrantly dressed crowd, the rainbow – what looked like a real rainbow – which arched across the ceiling, its light rebounding in the mirrors and reflective tiles beneath, creating a thousand tiny prisms as if they were all caught inside a giant mirror ball.

A man with a tray of glasses came up to them with impeccable timing. 'Drink?'

Anna took one, dazed. 'Thank you.' The liquid in the glass was bright pink. She took a sip, tasting berries and marshmallows. When she brought the cocktail away from her lips it had transformed to a blue colour, the next sip tasting distinctly of plums and the sky on a clear day.

'It tastes different every time!' Rowan exclaimed, swirling her drink through different shades.

Anna's had turned green now – with a flavour of apples and four-leaf clovers – as she followed the Wild Hunt to a seating area, who promptly sprawled across it as if they owned Equinox.

'Darlings.' Poppins moved towards them, leaning on his umbrella. He was wearing a pink feather boa which Anna was sure he'd taken from *inside* the portrait hung up in the hotel room. 'I have a little offering for you.' His smile sliced through his cheeks as he put out his fist and revealed a pile of colourful tablets. 'My magical beans.'

'What are those?' said Rowan, warily.

'Drugs!' Manda gasped. 'They look like drugs! We can't take drugs, can we? I get weird when I drink coffee.'

'Just when you drink coffee?' Effie muttered.

'They're not *drugs*,' Poppins replied. 'They're little spells with a whole lot of fun inside.'

Attis lifted his brow. 'What kind of fun?'

'Well, finding out is *part* of the fun. You have to jump to fly, darling.'

'What classification do they fall into?' Manda asked. 'Are they A class magical drugs or more like C class?'

Effie rolled her eyes. 'Let's take the drugs, people.'

'I don't know . . .' said Rowan. 'We were down in a crypt earlier today; drugs might tip me over the edge.'

Effie waved a hand. 'Sorry, Poppins, my coven doesn't know how to live. Maybe later.'

He shrugged. 'Sure, there are plenty more . . . I have a very long beanstalk.' He winked, dragging his feather boa over Attis's shoulder and moving on to the next group of the Wild Hunt.

Attis laughed and gestured to the dance floor. 'You guys don't need drugs anyway, only my insatiable dance moves. Shall we?'

'We shall.' Effie grabbed his hand and pulled him through the crowd.

They were soon lost among the charged and pulsing mass of luminescent bodies, the rainbow dripping its colour over everything so that everyone's skin glowed with kaleidoscopic patterns. The music seemed to be coming from beneath their feet, sending bright shockwaves of sound up through Anna's body. It had been so long since she'd allowed herself to dance, to let go, but here it was impossible not to. Her body responded to the music – the thump of the bass, the motion of the crowd swaying with them as they laughed and danced and spun until the room was a hurricane of colour. At one point, Anna came face to face with Attis. She faltered. He halted. The last time they'd danced together flashed through her mind – his hands on her silk dress, moving over the curves of her hips . . .

He put out a gentlemanly hand and she took it, twirling beneath him, maintaining the ever-careful distance between them.

Soon, the Wild Hunt stormed into the crowd and Anna lost sight of Attis. She danced and danced until her feet were on fire and her head was blissfully empty. Rowan grabbed her hand and pulled her through the crowd – they emerged breathless and laughing.

'I just needed—' Rowan panted, 'a moment. Those guys can dance.'

'They can,' said Anna, still dizzy from Ollie's whirling.

Rowan leant against the wall, giggling. 'Did you see me on Ivor's shoulders?'

Anna nodded.

'That man is strong. Strong enough to handle me and I like it—'

Rowan bumped into a figure behind. He turned around and it was Cillian, his coat turned up at the collar giving him the look of a dark-winged vulture, his head scanning the room as if he were always on the lookout for danger. 'Cillian,' said Rowan, 'you having fun?'

'Not particularly, but I've been assessing the speaker configurations of the sound system here.'

Rowan frowned. 'You're strange.'

Anna shook her head. 'Why do *you* want to be in the Wild Hunt?'

'They're a powerful grove,' he replied. 'Plus, their combination of interdisciplinary magic and absence of any rules or group regulation makes for fascinating social dynamics.'

'Not for the glitter and free drugs then?' Rowan smirked.

Cillian considered her words. 'No. Although I would be interested in running an analysis on their recreational substances. You know, they're all rich. That's why they can do whatever they want all of the time, the freedom of money, no repercussions. Poppins's father owns the hotel group that includes the Dorchester. Oliver Moridi receives a two thousand pounds monthly allowance from his parents.'

'How do you know that?' Anna balked.

'I can't disclose that information.'

Rowan looked at him, exasperated. 'Who ARE you?'

'Cillian. I told you.'

'What kind of witch are you, then?'

'My language is information – data.'

Rowan made a face. 'How do you do magic with *data*?'

'I don't *do* magic with information. I find the magic within vast quantities of data.'

Anna and Rowan stared at him. 'Huh,' Rowan said, eventually.

He turned to her. 'Would you like to dance?'

Rowan's mouth dropped open. 'I, er – I'm OK, thanks.'

He shrugged. 'There's a speaker in the basement I wanted to assess anyway.' He raised his shades, to reveal startlingly blue, piercing eyes. 'From my estimations, your coven is in danger. You need to be careful to expose no magic at your school. Even then, I would recommend running away if you can. I don't think there will be a way out.'

Anna struggled to reply to the unexpected terror of his words.

He pulled his leather coat tighter, backing away. 'I'll be in touch.'

'You don't have our numbers!' Rowan called out to him.

But he was gone, into the shadows.

Rowan turned to Anna. 'It's hard to find a witch weirder than a Wort Cunning, but there you have it.' Her brow creased with little lines of worry. 'Do you think he was just trying to scare us?'

Anna shook her head. 'No.'

Rowan breathed out. 'Explains why I'm living with this sick terrified feeling in the pit of my stomach all the time.'

'Same,' Anna agreed.

'We need a drink.'

Anna turned and stopped dead, knowing the last thing she ought to be worrying about right now was Attis Lockerby, but he was leaning against the wall with a girl she didn't recognize. He was laughing, running a hand through her long blonde hair. Anna could see that look on his face, the one she knew so well – charming, flirtatious, irresistible; a fey smile and eyes drinking the girl in, full of dark designs. Anna turned away, a different kind of sick feeling taking over. She knew this was what he did, what he'd always done, but she hadn't been ready to see it.

Rowan had spotted it too. 'Are you OK?'

'Yeah.' Anna managed a reply. She felt stupid, thinking of the way he'd looked at her earlier, believing it might mean something.

'We can go outside for a bit,' Rowan suggested.

'No.' Anna turned back to her. 'We need that drink. Now.' She grabbed two drinks from a nearby tray, drinking hers in one go and taking another. She needed something else. A distraction to take away the pain. 'You know what? I think we should do those drugs.'

'I'm not sure that's a good idea . . .' Rowan began to say.

'It's our one night off before . . . who knows what. We have to live.' She took Rowan's hand and pulled her into the crowd.

They found Effie and Manda, who was currently tangled up with Jeudon.

'Heyyy,' Manda slurred, thoroughly drunk. 'I was enjoying that. He's a good kisser, you know.'

'I do actually,' Effie replied. 'What's going on?'

'I think we should do the beans!' Anna yelled.

Effie raised an eyebrow. 'Well, this is unexpected.'

'The DRUGS!' Manda squealed.

Anna nodded.

'OK.' Manda shrugged. 'Let's do the drugs!' She laughed giddily.

Rowan looked between them. 'How have *I* become the voice of reason?'

Effie snorted. 'Come on—'

She led them through the crowd to Poppins. Manda tapped him on the shoulder. 'WE WANT YOUR BEANS!'

He turned around with an arched eyebrow, sharp as a boomerang. 'Cupcake, what's happened to you? You look crazed.'

'She's always crazed,' said Effie. 'She just represses it by day.'

Poppins reached into his pocket and pulled out another handful of the pills. Bright capsules of colour in his palm. 'Fee fi fo fum, screw your worries and have some fun . . .'

They gathered around him.

'Oh, go on then.' Rowan released a breath and reached for one.

The rest of them followed and Anna selected a green one. They looked at each other, giggling nervously.

'To the Coven of the Dark Moon!' Effie proclaimed.

'Coven of the Dark Moon!'

Before she could have second thoughts, Anna threw it into her mouth and swallowed it with her drink.

'When does it kick in?' Manda looked down at her body. 'I feel normal. Should I feel normal? I still feel normal. Nothing's happened yet. Should something have happened—'

'Woah,' Rowan interrupted.

Anna turned to her. 'What?'

'I don't know, something just feels very different.' Rowan put her hand against the wall. 'Like . . . like maybe—' She put out a foot and stepped onto the wall.

Anna blinked, not sure if her head was still spinning or if Rowan was walking up the wall. No. Rowan *was* walking up the wall. 'How – how are you doing that?'

'I don't know.' Rowan shrieked with laughter. 'It feels like . . . gravity is just something to play with.'

Anna looked on disbelievingly as Rowan carried on towards the ceiling, Rowan's heart leaping with every step. *Her heart . . . how can I see her heart?*

Anna stepped back, her eyes widening as she took in the room. The whole crowd was beating . . . their hearts . . . inside their chests. She looked at Effie and Manda, and Anna could *see* their hearts too, though she wasn't quite sure *how* she could see them – it was more of a sense of them, something glowing, pulsing. She could *feel* them.

'What are you looking at?' Anna heard Effie's voice in her ear, though Effie was standing several feet away and her mouth hadn't moved. Effie smiled. Her voice came again – a whisper in Anna's ear – or in her head – it was hard to tell: 'This is going to be fun.'

'How are you doing that?' Anna shouted.

'Not entirely sure,' Effie spoke out loud.

Manda looked between them. 'What are your powers? What's going on?'

'I can speak inside people's minds,' said Effie. 'Like this.'

Manda pulled a shocked face at whatever Effie had whispered to her.

'I can see people's hearts,' said Anna, watching Manda's with concern – hers was racing, but almost as if it was struggling, a weaker, erratic pulse than Effie's which beat strong and sure.

'Well, what's my power? Why isn't it working?' Manda tapped Poppins on the shoulder and the next moment she *was* Poppins. Poppins staring at Poppins.

'Well, aren't I dazzling?' Poppins smiled.

Manda stumbled back looking down at herself. 'What – in – the – name – of – Our – Holy – Lord – I'm – I'm you, I'm you!' She grabbed Effie's arm and her form shifted into Effie's. She started to laugh hysterically. 'I can be anyone I want! Anyone! How long does this last?'

'A couple hours.' Poppins blew them a kiss. 'You're welcome.'

Manda squealed with glee and skipped into the crowd. Rowan was already walking on the ceiling above. Anna and Effie turned to each other giggling, Effie's heartbeat radiating brighter as she looked at Anna. Anna wrapped her arms around her – she wasn't sure why – perhaps the feeling of all the hearts in the room or the magical drugs seeping into her mind, making everything seem impossibly possible – throwing open all the doors. Effie squeezed her back, laughing in her ear, in her mind.

They let go and looked out at the dance floor. Anna spotted Attis dancing with the blonde girl now, their bodies far too close for comfort. Effie's voice came again in Anna's head, beckoning. 'Shall we show her who he really belongs to?'

Anna narrowed her eyes at Effie.

'What?' Effie shrugged. 'You know you want to. *I* know you want to . . .'

Anna shook her head but she felt that slipping-sliding feeling of possibility again. They couldn't. Couldn't they? There were rules. They had rules. *Rules.* The word seemed to rise above her, liquefying, coalescing with the colours, conveniently fragmenting.

Anna took Effie's hand. 'Let's.'

They pushed through the shimmering wall of heat towards Attis. Anna couldn't hold back the feelings as they approached them – they were pouring straight out of her heart as the girl writhed over him . . . jealousy and anger, vivid and dense as the colours around her . . . he wasn't hers . . . desire and fire and something far more complicated. Hatred as the girl put her arms around Attis's neck, pulling him close. They didn't fit.

Effie circled them, sussing out her prey. She trailed a finger along Attis's shoulder, his head seemed to move with the motion as if he sensed her presence. She shifted to dance beside them. The girl's eyes flashed to Effie uncomfortably. She tried to guide Attis away, but he'd spotted Effie too. Anna saw how his mouth curved, his eyes welcoming the game. How many times had they played it? How many victims had they discarded? Effie moved behind him like the darkest of beats, sliding along his back; sinuous and sultry. Attis laughed. The girl seethed, trying to pull Attis away but he spun her beneath his arm and Effie, ever the opportunist, slunk into the gap. Attis shook his head, trying to make room for both of them – the girl on one side, Effie on the other. The girl tried to bring his attention back to her, dancing more animatedly, but the game was already lost. Effie barely had to move – only to inch closer and Attis's body responded, syncing to hers: motion, rhythm, shape, instinctive as lock and key.

Effie threw out a hand towards Anna.

Anna stared at it, startled, remembering she was to be part of the game. She took it and Effie pulled her into the tangle of bodies.

Attis seemed suddenly surprised – captured on all sides. He raised his eyebrows seeing it was Anna. She gave him a look of challenge back and laughed as Effie pulled her closer, encircling him entirely. The other girl huffed and walked off.

And then there were three. Attis's arms were still thrown wide at the siege. Effie grabbed Anna and they danced in front of him, moving together, all hands and curves and Effie's hair flying, her laughter reverberating in Anna's head. Attis's eyes moved between them the designs behind them dangerous now. Anna could feel the force of him, drawing them in. Effie moved closer and Anna followed, pressing herself up against his body, her heart racing faster than the music at the sudden heat of him curling around her like one of his symbols, melting her from the inside out. The music pounded. The colour dripped over them, their skin glowing with the friction – branding rainbows into their skin. Attis's hand slid down her side, resting on her hips. Anna ran her own hand down her neck, imagining the trail of his lips. Her body felt more alive than she could remember, her heart moving with the music, Effie's heart burning through a hundred colours—

Anna spun around and Attis's heart was a hot white sun – blinding. She reached out to him, putting a hand to his chest and their eyes met – a brief moment – too dark, the lights too bright to see clearly. Then Effie threw her arms over his neck, laughing, and Attis shook his head, droplets flying from the mess of his hair. He pulled away from them and put his hands up.

'I surrender!' he yelled over the music, then turned away, swallowed up by the crowd.

Effie cackled in Anna's mind. 'We won,' she whispered but Anna didn't feel victorious, she felt suddenly hollow. Cold at the lack of him.

'Come on,' Effie urged. 'We've got spells in our veins.'

Anna followed the restless whirr of Effie's heart back into the centre of the dance floor. They found the Wild Hunt – Rowan walking along the ceiling above and throwing down handfuls of rainbow to the cheering crowd – and Manda, as Jeudon, making out with Jeudon. Effie began dancing suggestively with Emilia. Anna watched the throb of hearts around her, how they released waves and spirals of colour with the music, patterns she couldn't understand but, right here, right now, somehow made complete sense.

At some point, she spotted Attis with the blonde girl again and it was her neck his lips were moving down. She danced harder through the gut-punch pain of it, trying not to wonder where they were going . . .

When Ollie appeared before her again and put his hand out she took it. 'Dorothy, I knew I'd find you here.' He threw back his cloak and gave her a dazzling smile.

'And how's that?'

'Because I know everything five seconds before it's about to happen.'

'Magical beans?'

Ollie nodded. 'The power of foresight is proving extremely fun. Care to dance? Wait. Don't answer. You've already said yes.'

Anna pulled him towards her. 'I did,' she replied into his ear.

It was easy dancing with him, not just because he knew what she was going to do ahead of time, but because there was no ache in it. He moved around her, quick-footed and ostentatious, spinning her and throwing her and catching her at just the right moment, every single time. As the song came to an end, he lifted her with a flourish and brought her down close to him, his hands around her back.

'You're going to kiss me,' he whispered.

'Am I now?' Anna laughed and realized she wanted to.

He was charming and fun and maybe he could take away the pain entirely. She leant in and they kissed. His hands moved gently around her back, pulling her closer. He smelt of aftershave and purple flowers. It didn't burn and ache and tear and when she pulled away, Anna found she could still stand, still breathe.

He pulled her back in and Anna gave in to the sweetness of his kisses.

Several hours later, the Wild Hunt and their guests erupted from Equinox – delirious, dishevelled and drunk – colours spilling out of the door and pouring down Carnaby Street like an explosion from a party popper, mingling with the pink-peach glow of dawn above.

That was when the real chaos began.

CRUSH

Religion teaches us to fear hell, while those who have been to the real Hel know there is nothing to fear but themselves.

Ursula Aldhelm, Hel Witch and Guardian Spirit,
1811–1893–1906

The stairs seemed to go on forever but when Anna reached the door she did not feel relief. She felt too much, as if the door were pushing outwards, threatening to break open. The Language of the Dead was scored deeply into its wood, ravens crying from inside. She held a key made of shadow in her hand. It fitted the lock like a foot into the softest of slippers.

Click.

The door had never opened for her before. She stepped inside and wished she hadn't, but when she turned back, the door was gone and she was trapped in the third-floor room – only different . . . like the turret of a castle. Shadows danced upon the walls, twisted half-raven, half-human shapes. Effie and Attis were standing before her with sly-as-feather smiles. They reached out their hands and Anna took them. The shadows began to dance around them and they began to dance too. Together. *Close. Too close.* A tangle of limbs. *No.* Anna realized it was only her who was tangled. Caught. The threads on her again, sewn through every limb and flaring off into the darkness of the room, vast and complex, as if her nightmares had been spinning them the whole time and she'd only been walking towards a trap of her own making . . .

'Help! Help me!' Anna's arms flailed against sheets. 'No – no – no—'

'Hey, Anna—'

Anna's eyes shot open, vaulting her from the dream into a room she didn't recognize. She sat up, looking down at herself as if half expecting to still be covered in threads.

'You OK, Dorothy?'

She turned to see Ollie looking back at her, troubled.

Ollie.

Anna realized where she was – a hotel room. The Dorchester. She was in a bed. *In a bed with Ollie!* She pulled the sheets up around her.

'Either a bad dream . . . or you're really regretting last night.' Ollie's smile returned. He was still wearing his cloak and not much else. As he brushed his hair back she noticed a signet ring on his little finger with the symbol of a flower on it.

'Last night . . .' Anna tried to piece it together through the multi-coloured muddle of her memory: kissing Ollie in Equinox, beating hearts, had Poppins turned all the pigeons pink on the way home? Taking Ollie's hand, pulling him into the bedroom, kissing him on the bed . . .

'Don't worry, sweet Dorothy, my honour remains intact. Nothing happened. I'm pretty sure we passed out making out.'

Anna glimpsed beneath the sheets and saw she was fully dressed. She remembered much the same.

'I also spent the night on the floor,' he added. 'Apparently, I fell out of the bed and was too drunk to realize.'

Anna managed a smile at last. She ran a hand through her hair, which glittered in the sunlight streaming through the window, not half as bright as last night but still full of magic.

Ollie caught her eye. 'Bad dream?'

She nodded. 'I get them. It was nothing.'

'It looked like something.'

'My dreams just have a vendetta against me.'

'Maybe they're trying to tell you something. I never remember my dreams.' He shrugged. 'So I don't know.'

'You don't?'

He shook his head. 'Not for a long time. Too busy living them out in real life.' He laughed and pulled his gold coin from thin air. 'Now. Tails – we sleep off our hangovers. Heads – we carry on where we left off . . .' He rolled towards her.

Anna pulled back. 'I should probably find the others.'

'That sounds far too sensible. I think you should throw that sense out the window and come back to bed with me. I'll let you wear my cloak . . .'

She laughed, wondering what it would be like to kiss him by daylight, to play and explore and *forget* . . .

But she couldn't. Nothing felt the same in the light of day as it had done the night before. Her feelings weren't so . . . fluid. She knew she didn't truly feel about Ollie the way she felt about *him*. More images flashed through her head making her heart thump all over again: Attis's body against hers, the colour of his heart, his lips trailing down a blonde girl's neck. 'I'm sorry, Ollie. I have to go.'

'You have nothing to apologize for. If you must go – you must go. I shall remain here.' Ollie threw himself back on the bed. 'And pine away at the loss of you, bleeding my heart out, until I eventually fall asleep and wake several hours later just as hungover and probably craving some sort of bacon-based product.'

She chuckled and leant forwards, kissing him lightly on the cheek. 'Goodbye.'

He took her hand suddenly, looking up at her. 'As foolish as I might be, I do like you, Anna.'

She bit her lip, feeling guilty for leading him on. She'd thought it was just fun. 'I . . . I like you too, Ollie, it's just—'

'Go,' he said, releasing her. 'Leave me in the sweet, crushing hope that one day you'll come to love a fool like me.'

By the time Anna had freshened herself up in the toilet and gathered herself together, Ollie was snoring from the bed, clutching his cloak like a child dreaming they're a superhero.

She crept back into the central room hoping for a quiet reception – but everyone was in there. The room was as destroyed as her memory recalled, people passed out everywhere, someone asleep in the now empty bath. Effie, Rowan and several members of the Wild Hunt were gathered on the sofa feasting on a room service breakfast. Effie was draped over Emilia. She sat up and pointed accusingly.

'See! I told you all Anna was with Ollie. I saw you two disappearing in there last night.'

Bridy whistled. Poppins chuckled saucily. 'Naughty, naughty. I love it . . .'

'So,' said Effie, loudly. 'Tell us everything. Is he a tender lover? I always imagined him a tender lover . . .'

Anna knew her cheeks were burning at their brightest. She spotted Attis watching from the table behind. Their eyes met and he looked away.

'Nothing happened,' she mumbled.

'Oh, don't be coy.' Effie wiggled a finger at her. 'Manda and Jeudon are still at it somewhere.' She snorted.

Anna remembered Manda with Jeudon or Jeudon with Jeudon. Her head hurt. She took a croissant from the buffet and sat down on the edge of the sofa, trying to disguise the heat in her cheeks, a pink pigeon waddling past her feet.

'They're in bedroom number three,' said a voice. Cillian appeared from behind one of the side sofas.

'Goddess and all that is unholy.' Poppins jumped in mock shock. 'He always pops up from nowhere. What are you doing here?'

'I was sleeping on the floor,' Cillian replied as if this was sufficient information. His blond hair was messy as a haystack. Without his shaded glasses on, he looked young, his eyes a startling blue.

'Shouldn't you get back to your parents' basement or wherever it is you live?' Poppins sniggered.

'You're the one living in your parents' penthouse,' Cillian replied.

Poppins's face puckered.

'We should go,' said Anna, looking to Effie and Rowan.

Rowan lifted herself up. 'You're right. Mum's already texted me, oh, four thousand times.'

Anna turned to Cillian. 'Thanks for your help. Please do let us know anything else you find out about the WIPS, no matter how small.'

He blinked with the faintest hint of concern. 'There is something else. I didn't mention it yesterday because it's tangential, but if you wish to know everything—'

Anna stepped towards him. 'We do.'

Cillian sat down on an armchair. 'There have been some threads on the ShadowNet discussing the possible disappearance of two witches. The witches aren't connected in any way, except, they both happen to be cursed.'

Anna and Effie's heads jerked up, their eyes meeting.

'As in . . . cursed witches?' Attis came forwards, putting his hands on the back of sofa.

'Yes.'

'One is a witch based in Gloucester – female, late sixties, not seen since last month, but her family are said to be cursed with madness so no one knows if she is missing or if she's just gone wandering in the wilderness. The other is a witch based in London – male, early forties, not seen since last Tuesday. His family haven't reported it to the police yet but people have been asking questions online to see if anyone in the magical world has seen him. Apparently he's cursed by his ex-wife to be wracked with pains every full moon.'

'What does this have to do with anything?' said Poppins.

Cillian's eyes narrowed. 'There's a prophecy surrounding the return of the Hunters of legend that states a cursed witch will also ascend and cause the downfall of the world. Therefore, it is interesting that two witches marked by a curse should disappear as the WIPS rise to power. Then again, it may be an entirely spurious correlation. The ShadowNet is full of them. I am simply presenting the data.'

Anna's tiredness had been replaced by thumping adrenaline coursing through every limb. 'Has there been anything to connect them to the WIPS at all?' she asked.

Cillian shook his head. 'There is nothing to suggest the WIPS are involved. If I discover any more I will report. They may well turn up unharmed.'

'Sounds far-fetched to me.' Poppins waved a dismissive hand. 'Prophecies and curses. I know this is the magical world but *really*, has anyone ever met a cursed witch?'

The coven did not meet each other's eyes.

As they walked back to the station, the high of the night before had tumbled back down to earth with a hungover bump, no one knowing what to make of Cillian's parting words. Anna glanced at Attis. He hadn't spoken to her yet. He dragged a tired Effie along, who'd thrown her arms around his shoulders. Manda was subdued but surprisingly calm considering she was arriving home looking as if she'd been partying all night long. She hadn't even bothered to remove the glitter from her hair or the lipstick from her lips.

Anna checked the time. 'Isn't it a bit late for you to be sneaking back in, Manda?'

'No. They'll have gone to church early and won't be back before I am.'

Rowan nudged her. 'What are you going to do about Karim?'

Manda stared at her. 'What do you mean?'

'Well, you and Jeudon . . . last night . . .'

Manda shrugged. 'What happens in Equinox, stays in Equinox.'

Effie snorted. 'She's learning so well.'

'But it wasn't *in* Equinox,' Rowan pointed out. 'It was back at the hotel – in several rooms, I believe.'

Manda made withering eyes at her. 'It was just fun. Karim and I are in love, it's different. You wouldn't understand.'

Rowan looked affronted. 'Oh right, I wouldn't understand the difference between sex and love because I've not experienced either . . .'

'Exactly,' said Manda pointedly.

Before the bickering could continue they were distracted by a crowd gathering outside Oxford Circus. The entrance appeared to be shut, a metal gate pulled across it.

'What's going on?' Attis asked a man beside them.

'Looks like the tubes are shut down – all of them. Bloody hell! How am I going to get home?' The man walked away, stabbing numbers into his mobile.

They shared a troubled look. Rowan took out her phone. 'Something's happened.'

They moved away from the agitation of the crowd into a shop doorway.

Rowan's hand rose slowly to cover her mouth. 'A crush . . . at London Bridge tube station . . .'

'What do you mean a crush?' Manda cried.

'Like a crowd surge, people pushing, panicking . . . Oh Goddess—' Rowan kept reading. 'People were pushed onto the tracks . . . there've been fatalities.'

'Fatalities,' Effie repeated. 'How many?'

'They don't know yet. Witnesses are saying that people just began to walk towards the platform . . . and wouldn't stop. It's the hysteria, isn't it?' Rowan looked up, eyes spilling over with terror. 'Isn't it?'

'Only this time,' said Manda, 'the Pied Piper has taken lives.'

'Come on.' Attis assessed the swelling and increasingly irate crowd. 'It's best we're away from here.'

They walked away from the centre towards quieter streets where Rowan and Manda boarded a bus going south. They gave them anxious looks as they waved goodbye. Anna, Effie and Attis took an overground train back to Hackney. They didn't speak much, each of them looking at their phones, trying to work out what had happened.

Videos of the supposed crush were already appearing – a swell of people pushing down the stairs towards the platform, cries and screams. Witnesses posting accounts online.

I don't understand this . . . it was busy but not anything out of the ordinary. People just started to push and push—

My hands are shaking as I type. I can't believe this. I was at the back, I saw it all happen #LondonBridgeHysteria

All I could feel down there was fear, overwhelming fear. It was malefice! I KNOW IT!

Anna was sure it was magic too. There'd been no reason for the people to start pushing. It had the fingerprints of the hysteria spell all over it.

When they arrived home, she paced the kitchen. 'What are we going to do?'

'Plenty,' said Effie. 'But we can't do anything right now. I need sleep.'

'But there's just been another hysteria attack! People have died! How do we stop it? How do we stop the WIPS? Did you not just hear Cillian talking about cursed witches going missing too?'

Effie's eyes contracted, her mouth hardening as if she'd been thinking of little else. 'Of course I heard him. But even if two cursed witches have gone missing and this isn't just some basement-dwellers online trying to make something out of nothing . . . we have no reason to link it to the WIPS. Not yet. And our curse remains a secret.' She moved towards the door. 'You should get some sleep, sis, I doubt you got much last night . . .'

Anna was left with Attis, stewing in the awkwardness of Effie's words. She talked quickly. 'Rowan is telling Bertie everything now. We need to make sure Selene knows the truth of the hysteria – that it's a death spell. We need to make a plan to find the person casting the hysteria in our school—'

'We need to not go back to that damn school,' Attis growled, finally looking at her. His face was wracked with tension. 'It's too dangerous now.'

'We can't not go back!' Anna replied, sharper than intended. 'We have to find who's responsible, and anyway, the WIPS aren't just going to let us go. They'll follow us. You heard what Cillian said last night, what we might be up against.'

'I heard *everything* Cillian said. It puts you and Effie in more danger than ever before. The curse needs to end.' Anna didn't like the hard and distant look in his eye.

'It will. I'm trying. But we can't do nothing before that happens.'

'So I just have to watch while you both repeatedly put yourselves in danger?'

Their eyes locked, the grey in his fracturing.

'You shouldn't have disappeared last night with everything going on!' he blurted, walking away, running his hands through his hair and making a mess of it. 'We didn't know where you were.'

'I was with Ollie!' Anna shouted after him. 'I was perfectly safe!'

Attis turned. 'Oh yeah, what's Ollie going to do if something happened? Throw trick coins at an oncoming attacker? Dazzle them with his cloak? Ollie couldn't keep you safe if he tried, which he wouldn't, because he's a layabout.'

'A layabout!' Anna laughed. She couldn't believe it. He sounded almost . . . jealous. He wasn't allowed to be jealous. 'I don't need Ollie, or *you*, Attis Lockerby, to keep me safe. It was my choice to go to his room and I'm glad I did. I'm allowed to have fun too, you know? If I recall you were off gallivanting with some blonde girl, whoever she was.'

'Her name is Camilla – no, wait – Camille.'

'Oh well, I'm sure you showed *Camilla* or *Camille* a good time.'

'As always.' He smiled, but it had none of its usual lightness. 'Look, it's what I do, OK? I haven't ever tried to pretend I'm someone else. I like women. They like me. We all have fun.'

'Sounds lovely.' Anna grated an exhale and went over to the sink, pouring herself a large glass of water with as much clatter as she could make. She turned back to him. 'Be with whoever you like, do whatever you like, just don't stop me from doing the same. Those are the rules, right? So long as none of us are with each other, anything goes.'

'I'm not sure you and Effie were playing by the rules last night when you ambushed me on the dance floor.'

Anna felt the heat flood into her face again, his words catching her off guard. '*That* . . . was just fun.'

'It was unfair.' He breathed out, looking tired. 'Entirely unfair.'

'Come on, you and Effie play these games all the time! And what? I'm not allowed to join in? Because I'm Anna – too *sweet*, too *innocent* for all that. Well, I'm not so sweet and I'm not so innocent.'

He was still staring at her, the smallest, most frustrating of smiles twisting at his lips. 'I never said you were sweet *or* innocent. After all . . . I felt how you moved.'

Anna's mouth opened but no words came out.

He left the room, leaving her reeling. She tried to think through the hysteria . . . the attacks . . . but he clouded her mind, the way his body had felt against hers, the way her heart had beat out of control . . . exactly like it was right now.

Eventually, Anna retreated to her room and gave in to sleep. When she woke, her head wasn't pounding quite so much and the swirling colours of her mind had begun to settle.

She took out her laptop and saw that the WIPS had already responded to the tube crush hysteria. Hopkins had been interviewed on a major news channel, live on air, brought in as an 'expert'. She clicked on the clip – his powerful form filled the screen, his black hair carved, his pale skin flushed and mottled. Those same dark eyes embedded beneath a shelf of brow, strong jaw, broad mouth – no lip, all teeth.

'Here we have Marcus Hopkins, Lead Researcher of the Witchcraft—'

Hopkins interrupted. 'Actually, I'm now Lead Inquisitor of the Witchcraft Inquisitorial and Prevention Services—'

Anna paused the video. His title had changed. *Inquisitor* had an entirely different, alarming ring to it. He wore a black suit and as he sat back in his chair, Anna could see his shoes were polished black – they rode up his legs beneath his trousers . . . like boots. His red tie was sharp as an arrow and something lay upon it – a necklace – dark metal chain and a pendant. She peered more closely, her heart racing again. It was carved with a circle with a cross in the centre, the symbol of the WIPS. The same necklace the men had been wearing in the vision of Eleanor that Nana had given her. Anna could feel worlds colliding – the past and the present, reality and legend – the foreboding sense of being tied to all of it. *Tangled.* She pressed play again.

'In your opinion, what has taken place here today?'

'Another malefice attack. A direct provocation that has achieved what we have long feared would happen: the loss of human life. Deaths that could have been prevented.'

'How can you be sure this was malefice?'

'It has all the markers of attacks we have been recording and analysing across London. People don't throw themselves en masse off a tube platform with no reason now, do they? These people were being controlled by darker, cursed forces. The loss of life is devastating.'

'And you believe this can be prevented from happening again?'

'We warned it would happen and we fear it will happen again. The situation is getting worse – we're under attack from the enemy within; witches among us. We're facing an ancient sort of evil in a modern world, a new kind of terrorism borne from the fabric of terror itself. I do not wish to spread further panic, only to raise the alarm. We must wake up to this threat. The government must act now to give us the powers we need to put counter measures and protections in place, to take the necessary steps to stop malefice before it takes more lives. We need your voices – to call for action so that we can fight back. Together, we can stop the spread.'

Anna played the clip again and again until Hopkins's dark eyes were all she could see, as if they were staring right into her. Through her. She tucked her knees up, appealing to her hammering heart to stay calm. She couldn't see through him. Did he really hate the magic he spoke of? Or were the WIPS behind the attacks? Using them to further their power? Either way, if they could find a way to stop the hysteria it could disrupt their rise or at least slow down their message and give the magical world more time to retaliate.

Anna turned from the screen. She couldn't panic now. They had to keep moving forwards. Effie was right – their curse remained a secret, but the sooner they were free of it, the better . . . before Attis concluded he *was* the only solution. She took out the Bible and had begun wrestling with Nana's riddle again when someone knocked on her door.

'It's me,' said Attis from outside. 'Can I come in? Are you decent? You're not wearing those tartan pyjamas again?'

'One minute!' Anna called, not feeling at all prepared to face him. She'd stripped out of her purple dress but wasn't wearing much at all. She threw a long T-shirt over herself. 'OK.'

He stepped inside, eyes taking her in. She scowled. 'Attis, what do you want?'

He put his hands up, they were sooty with ash. 'I came to say sorry for earlier. You have every right to call me a fuckwit if you wish.'

Anna tried to remain composed though she was taken aback at his apology. 'I do already,' she replied. 'Regularly.'

He laughed. 'That's fair—'

'Look, Attis, nothing even happened with Ollie—' she began to say, but he stopped her, putting his hands up.

'You don't have to justify anything to me. I'm just overprotective at the moment, losing my cool.' He looked away, uncharacteristically flustered. 'And, not that you need my permission, but I just wanted to say that if you want to be with Ollie you . . . should.' He blew out a breath as if he'd got out what he needed to say. 'He's still a layabout,' he mumbled. 'But he's a good guy. If he makes you happy . . .'

Each word was an incision straight into her heart. She didn't want to be with anyone else. She didn't want him to want her to be with anyone else. She wanted him to look at her the way he had last night.

'OK,' she replied, her voice faint, flat. She breathed out. 'And I'm sorry for ambushing you on the dance floor. I don't know what I was thinking – I wasn't thinking . . .'

His lips twitched. 'It wasn't entirely unwelcome.'

She turned away, annoyed that he could apologize so perfectly and then say things like that. Things she had no defences against. How could she reply when all she wanted was for him to pull her towards him and feel the heat again? It was still alive inside of her. It couldn't be. Effie was downstairs.

He's my curse.

My curse.

Only my curse.

But when she turned back, he was looking at her with an expression so open-hearted that her own heart felt as if it might burst, spill out all its colours and patterns on the floor before them.

'Hopkins,' she said, throwing a bomb between them. 'Have you seen?'

He frowned and shook his head.

Anna grabbed her laptop and showed him the video statement.

'They're seeking more power,' he said, looking at Anna though his eyes were darting, searching for solutions he couldn't find, his smile replaced by a deep frown. 'And *Inquisitor?* What kind of name is that?'

They were sitting on her bed, poring over the laptop, reading everything they could, when the door burst open and Effie walked in.

'Anna—' She stopped, looking momentarily shocked to see Attis. Her eyes tightened at their proximity. 'What's going on?'

Anna held the laptop out like a shield. 'Hopkins has—'

'Released a video, I know,' Effie snapped. 'I was coming to talk to you about it.'

Attis jumped up. 'I'll make some coffees. Let's discuss downstairs.'

Effie gave Anna a cold look then followed Attis down. Anna threw some leggings on and came after, veering between guilt and anger. They'd only been researching the WIPS . . . *while you, sister, dragged me on the dance floor and made me dance with him last night!* Effie only liked playing when the rules were hers.

In the kitchen, Anna tried to suppress her irritation, focusing on the fallout from Hopkins. 'It's not just his video. The story is being covered across all major news channels and – this is everywhere.'

She scrolled down her screen, showing Effie how cowans were sharing the black and white STOP THE SPREAD image en masse, its stark words filling up social feeds. A call to action from the people.

'Fucking sheep,' Effie spat.

'They're scared,' said Anna. 'It's hard to convince people it was just a crowd surge when the station wasn't overcrowded, there was no terrorist attack, no reason for people to just start walking over the edge of the platform . . .' Her stomach twisted at the thought.

'Hopkins is calling for government action again,' Attis said. 'I haven't seen the government shutting any of this down and if it's playing out well with the people . . . I fear they could align with the WIPS. It might strengthen their position before the election. And you heard Cillian last night – the WIPS have major connections. Kramer's worked for GlobeMedia, who own half the news sites out there *and* he's been a political advisor. They could have influence from the inside.'

Anna nodded weakly, seeing how the WIPS could have been pulling the strings all along. 'There was something else too,' she added, pointing at the screen. 'You see Hopkins's necklace? It's the same as the necklaces the men were wearing in the vision of Eleanor Nana showed me.'

Effie lowered the coffee from her lips and peered closer. 'If they're the Hunters, who are they? Some kind of cult? Brotherhood?'

They looked between each other darkly, not sure what it all meant, what it would mean for them, but knowing, feeling the age-old danger drawing closer.

Anna was relieved when Selene arrived home.

'Have you seen the news or have you been off with Peter's dad again?' Effie took a swipe.

Selene did not look in the mood. 'Reiss and I are still dating, thank you, and, yes, I have seen the news—' Selene looked smaller somehow, as if she wasn't used to worrying and her body didn't quite know what to do with it. She dropped her bag on a stool, rubbing her forehead over and over. 'I've seen it all.'

Anna, ignoring the mention of Peter's dad, spoke up. 'Did you see my messages? We need to tell you something. The hysteria, it's a spell, a death spell—'

'I know,' said Selene. 'The Hel witch grove has worked it out and informed the magical world. We hope they'll be able to help.'

Anna, Effie and Attis shared a glance. Mór had followed through on her promise.

'So what is the magical world going to do? Does anyone have any idea how to stop it?' Anna tried not to sound desperate.

'It's in discussion, darling. In discussion.'

'What does that mean?'

'Very little in Selene terms,' said Effie scathingly.

Selene breathed in, trying to maintain her calm. 'I don't know how you lot found out about the death spell – Rowan has been telling her mum too. I hope you're not conversing with Hel witches. You just need to—'

'Keep our heads down. Yes, we know,' Effie snapped. 'Only we're the ones who have to actually attend St Olave's!'

The bickering went on for a while, going around in circles, getting nowhere until they all eventually dispersed. Perhaps it was how families worked, Anna thought. She and Aunt had never argued – there had been little point.

Anna went to the piano, needing to relieve the tension that had been building all day. She could hear the ring of Attis's hammer below, striking the anvil as if with enough force he could drive away the dangers that surrounded them.

She started to play. She didn't get very far before the spinning top – still upon the piano – seized up and flew off. She was too rattled, too full of fear, her song giving way to the darkness. She put the spinning top back in place and rested her hands back on the keys. She wanted to feel her magic stretch and strive and strengthen, but if they weren't solving the curse, what was she doing? Merely charging it up? Feeding the darkness? Opening up to the feelings that would soon consume her? But it didn't feel that way when she was playing . . . it made the feelings bearable, it felt as if she were slowly expanding into the darkness—

She stretched her neck, flexed her fingers and let herself wander, the song weaving through the shadows. She could still hear Attis's hammer, like a dark beat beneath the melody, and it took her back to the night before. The charge she'd felt between them, flashing like falling glitter. Was it real? Or a trick coin? The melody turned liquid, into the colours of desire, twisting with jealousy and guilt, tangling her while the song set her free, the spinning top rotating off the piano and onto the floor – forming shapes . . . patterns . . . patterns that seemed to make sense as she was playing . . . as she was feeling . . . growing deeper, stronger . . .

Then suddenly, too tight.

Suffocating.

The darkness all around her, spilling out from inside of her—

Aunt's laughter. Aunt's screams. Ever waiting. Anna moved her hands away, thinking again of Mór's words . . . *Sometimes those who have experienced death in life . . . the death of someone close to them . . . can become attuned to the other side of the Fabric . . .*

'Do you have to play that thing all the time?' Effie's voice spun Anna around. Effie was in the doorway.

'It's called a piano.' Anna tried to regain her composure but the melody was still running through her, sumptuous with desire. She and Effie hadn't discussed the piano since it had arrived in their home. 'It's helping my magic.'

'Good. We need to be powerful.'

Anna lifted her fingers from the keys. 'No. *We* need to break the curse, remember?'

'In my defence, there's quite a lot going on right now.'

Anna breathed out. 'I know.'

'So . . .' Effie smirked, 'did you hear from Ollie?'

'No. I'm not – we're just friends, despite all your insinuations.'

Effie laughed. 'Just because we're cursed doesn't mean you can't have fun, remember? But maybe it's best to save your feminine charms for Peter. Don't forget – we need him on side.'

Effie threw the spinning top back at Anna. She fumbled to catch it just in time. Effie was gone before she could respond. Anna fumed, playing a loud, dark chord, the spinning top twitching and stuttering in her hand.

TOUCH

In the fifteenth to eighteenth centuries, cowans were known to string the cemeteries and graveyards of London with bells, believing they would ring out and aid in the catching of witches supposedly communing with or digging up the dead. The practice, although ineffectual, gave rise to the name of London's Bellgravia which was once home to an ancient cemetery.

Hel Witch Histories, Books of the Dead: Tome 9728

'STOP THE SPREAD!'

'STOP THE SPREAD!'

'STOP THE SPREAD!'

The protestors were gathered around the school gates. Not a big group, but angry – venomous. Several were waving placards, all of them shouting. Anna stared, not quite able to believe the sight. Were there really anti-magic protests outside St Olave's?

Attis put his hands out, halting their approach. 'Let's use the side entrance.'

Anna was still too shocked, too confused to speak, but Effie pushed past. 'Screw that.' She strode towards the gate. Attis and Anna chased after her, the placards blaring their warnings:

THROW THE WITCHES OUT

SOS – SAVE OUR SCHOOLS!

WITCHCRAFT IS A SIN

Anna flinched at the word *sin*. It was Aunt's worst nightmare come true . . . or would she have loved this? Loved to have seen magic turned against, the punishment she'd always been craving.

The protestors shouted louder as they got closer, rattling their placards. They knew who they were – they'd been waiting for them. Their eyes were almost as lost as those caught in the hysteria spell, blinded with hatred, not seeing *them*, only what they wanted to see: *witches!*

Effie stuck a finger up at them. 'Is this the best you can do with your time? Intimidating schoolgirls? Get a day job, losers.'

Anna could hear their enraged shouts as they started up the hill. Her legs were shaking.

Attis was growling. 'Why the hell is Ramsden not having them cleared? We aren't using that entrance again, it's too dangerous.'

'I'd like to see them try something,' said Effie.

'Part of my concern.'

Within the school, they were met with just as much hostility. Bag checks. Locker searches. STOP THE SPREAD posters everywhere. Everyone moving in slow silence, as if they were all afraid to disturb the cold ripples of fear about them.

The fear intensified as they were syphoned down the corridors towards assembly – towards the room where the last hysteria had taken place. You could still feel it – ice beneath the creaking floorboards, shadows lurking in the stage wings. Anna could hear the twisted music, the scratch of the ouija board, the window shattering over and over.

It was boarded up now, its colours stripped away, darkening the whole room. Eames took to the stage and Anna's insides contracted. He had something new around his neck – a necklace, like Hopkins's. She could just make out the symbol of the WIPS. He touched it briefly before he began.

'This room, and everyone within it, has been witness to a malefice attack. If anyone doubted the presence of witchcraft in this school, you have now seen it for yourself, felt its darkness. Your doubts must be put aside. We must come together to face what threatens not only this school, but all of London.'

There were no whispers, only a feeling of the room sucking in its breath and holding it. Eames knew what he was doing, pulling at the strings of all their fears. Had he cast the hysteria spell? Anna tried to imagine it but there was such a fervour in his eyes, like a priest at the pulpit; a man who believed himself a saviour from the darkness he spoke of.

'I know you are all afraid, but it is vital that we control our emotions at this time, for they will use them against us. Witches are emotional creatures. They crave our fear and division, and we must not give it to them. I will now be conducting this investigation according to the latest structural changes within the WIPS, operating under my new title of Inquisitor Eames.' The flat line of his mouth twitched with hidden pride. He gripped the lectern. 'If you have any information that will be useful, you must come forwards. Share your suspicions, share your fears. I am here to listen. And to those responsible – there is still time to confess.'

Ramsden put everyone even more on edge by announcing that the school had been broken into over the weekend and that school-wide internal surveillance was due to be installed over the course of the week. His latest set of rules seemed intent on crushing any remaining life left.

No one allowed to leave the school grounds at any time.

No one to leave classrooms during lessons for any reason until break time.

During breaks and lunch hour, everyone to gather in appointed social areas.

All extracurricular activities and clubs cancelled with immediate effect.

The walls of the Athenaeum pulled tighter around them. Their every move would be watched. The rules were pinning them all in, trapping them inside with the spirit with nowhere for the fear to go. Sitting ducks with a whirlpool to Hel spinning furiously below them. *Is it what Eames wants? Or could someone else be behind it all?* Anna scanned the prefects. Peter. The teachers, looking just as lost as the pupils. Darcey, demurely composed on stage, her hair tied low. A school of so many people, but who was capable of such a thing? Beside Anna, Effie's eyes were latched onto Eames, wearing a hostile smile as if she would not let him break her.

They were dismissed abruptly. There wasn't even the pretence of discussion any more. These were the orders and they were all to follow. *Or else.*

The day continued as normal but everything felt surreal. Lessons were subdued and silent, most of the teachers no longer interacting with Anna at all. There was no milling in the corridors, no chatter and laughter. Instead, everyone filed through them, chivvied between classrooms and social areas by the watching prefects. Pupils had begun dressing like Darcey – prim and proper, lowering the length of their skirts, swapping heels for flats, as if they feared drawing any attention to themselves, or perhaps Darcey still set the fashion trends even during a witch hunt.

Before lunch, Anna was called to meet her head of year teacher who informed her that her examinations and applications had temporarily been put on hold until the investigation came to an end.

'I'm sorry, Anna.' Mrs Davies shook her head. 'There's nothing I can do. It's been decided from above.'

'THEY CAN'T DO THIS!' Manda was apoplectic at lunchtime. The edges of her nails were raw and red, her face gaunt, an untethered look in her eye. 'They can't cancel our futures!'

'Manda, keep it down.' Rowan glanced behind them. 'Everyone's looking.'

'Everyone's always looking! I don't care any more!'

The canteen was crammed now that every sixth former had to spend lunchtime here, but nobody was sitting near them, a wide and vigilant berth left around their table. Darcey's table meanwhile was surrounded and Anna had heard that her trauma group was packed out too, everyone scrabbling to speak, to relay their own suspicions and experiences of *malefice*, to have Darcey comfort and assure them; give them their moment in the spotlight.

'I've done everything, everything right!' Manda raged. 'And now they're taking it all away! Destroying it all! We should – should destroy them all back!' She laughed to herself, a little madly.

Anna tried to take her hand but Manda snatched it away. 'They said it was just temporary, Manda.' Anna attempted to console her, but she couldn't give her words conviction. Would it be temporary? Would any of this go away? Anna's own work had already fallen apart and she hadn't so much as picked up a book for her exams. She found it hard to care. What was going on eclipsed everything.

'At least we don't need to bother with revision any more,' said Effie. Manda scowled at her.

'Mum's going to go ballistic when she finds out.' Rowan shook her head. 'It's not like I can concentrate on work anyway. Whenever I go on my laptop, I end up reading everything being said about us. Apparently, we're haunting their dreams, whispering in their ears from afar, muttering curses, giving them headaches, stabbing pains, delirium in our presence. They've seen our shadows flying about the school—' She took a breath. 'Darcey's been really stirring the bloody pot. But it's not just in school, is it? There's *real* press about our school now and those anti-mal protestors outside. They've been organizing protests across the city, at various investigation sites since Hopkins's speech on the weekend. There are plenty of journalists out there questioning everything and challenging the WIPS, but it doesn't seem to be stopping it all.'

'Fear sells,' said Effie flatly. 'The WIPS are setting the traps to catch us in. I'm sure Eames is setting off the hysteria in this school.' She banged a fist on the table. 'He's getting a kick out of all of this.'

Anna leant in. 'Then we move on with our plan – search the school.'

'We should wait until surveillance is installed, apparently it'll be going on after-hours,' said Rowan. 'I'll need my shadowrobe to sneak out of my own house too. Mum's getting suspicious.'

Effie made a dismissive noise. 'Well, we're not going to sit still while they have more *discussions*.'

At the end of lunch, they made their way out of the canteen, but they timed it badly, managing to walk past Darcey.

Effie leant into her, muttering, 'Thanks for all the coverage.'

Darcey looked back at Effie, her eyes entirely lucid, and then – she screamed.

The room spun to them. Darcey didn't stop. She screamed again, stumbling back, cowering, hands rising up her body into her hair, tearing at it, screaming louder. Olivia and Corinne copied her and then it spread in shockwaves of fear through the canteen. More people screaming. Panicking. Plates smashing. Everyone rushing to the door, trying to get out, pushing and shoving, clambering—

Anna and the others ran in the opposite direction, to the far corner of the room. Anna closed her eyes, trying to detect the death spell, but she could breathe, she could think. It wasn't the spell but the leftover fear of it running in everyone's veins; hysteria conducted by Darcey. Olivia was filming the whole thing.

'Fucking typical,' Effie hissed.

The prefects arrived in force, restraining people, shouting orders, barking at everyone to stay still. Darcey needed holding up, apparently too weak to stand. Anna could see her pointing at them.

Andrew strode towards them with several others including Tom. They grabbed them, dragging them from the room, through the furore and past Darcey's barely concealed smile.

As they reached the hallway outside, Effie's arms erupted, throwing Tom away from her. 'Get off me!'

'Just trying to get you out of there alive.' Tom forced one of his buffoonish laughs, but it sounded strained. 'It was crazy in there. Girls are crazy.'

'Crazy?' Effie spat. 'This school is being driven crazy by that man!'

'Eames is a nutjob too.' Tom sniggered but the others didn't join in. Apparently insulting Eames was a line they didn't cross.

'Just keep her controlled, Kellman, you don't know what they're capable of,' Andrew ordered. His fingers tightened around Anna's arm as he led them down the corridor.

A prefect at the back began to sing:

> *Witches witches*
> *Just a bunch of bitches*
> *They'll tittle, they'll tattle*
> *They'll give you the fits*
> *So tie up their hands*
> *And feel up their tits . . .*

Andrew stopped, looking around, and opened the door of an empty classroom. He pushed Anna inside and the rest followed.

Tom remained in the doorway, dithering. 'I thought we were taking them to the Ebury wing . . .'

Andrew's lip curled. 'I think a search is in order first, don't you? You coming?'

Tom looked torn but shook his head and entered the classroom with the other prefects, who spread out, blocking the door. The coven shrank back from them, magic at their fingertips but not able to use it.

Andrew appeared momentarily unsure, as if he didn't know what to do now he'd got them here. He pointed at Manda. 'Remove your blazer.'

Manda stared back at him, aghast.

'Can you not hear me? Take your blazer off.'

A few of the others snickered under their breath.

'No.' Manda raised her head, her old, indignant self.

'You're not going to find anything in there, Andrew.' One of the prefects laughed. 'She's too skinny.'

'She's got the body of a child,' another snorted.

Manda tried to keep her head up, but her chin trembled. There was hatred in her eyes.

Anna stepped forwards. 'Andrew, for God's sake, leave her be!'

'Andrew, come on—' Tom tried to laugh.

Andrew whipped his head around to him. 'Kellman! Whose side are you on?' He turned back to Anna. 'Fine. You then. Get it off. I don't want to have to ask again!'

Fuming, Anna took her blazer off. 'There. Are you happy?'

'Now the shirt.'

Anna froze, looking at the other prefects, wondering when one of them would stop this madness. How far they would go. Tom looked between them too, but he said nothing.

'For fuck's sake.' Effie strode forwards. 'Here you go!' She ripped her blazer off and threw it on the floor. 'Is this what you want?' She moved towards Andrew, unbuttoning her shirt. 'If you're so desperate to see some tits . . . let's see if you know what to do with them.'

Andrew stumbled back, caught off guard by her outburst.

'Effie.' Tom put his hands up between them. 'Don't.'

But Effie shoved him away. 'No!' she shrieked, half laughing, flinging her shirt on the floor, kicking a shoe off and throwing it at Andrew.

Tom put his arms around her, dragging her back. 'Effie! Stop!'

'*What* is going on in here?' a voice rang out. They turned to find Peter in the doorway, eyes scanning the scene.

Anna pulled free from the prefect holding her. 'They're harassing us! Searching us with no cause!'

Andrew pointed at Effie. 'She started taking her clothes off and attacked me. You know what she's like . . .'

Peter looked at Effie in her bra. He turned to Andrew, pursing his lips. 'I thought you were taking them to the Ebury wing. What was your reason for searching them?'

'I thought I saw something suspicious—'

'He's lying!' Anna cried.

'Anna, please!' Peter raised a hand. 'I'm trying—'

But then Attis charged through the open door behind Peter. 'Get your hands off her.' He ran at Tom, ripping him away from Effie and shoving him to the floor. Two of the prefects rushed at him but Attis threw them off.

Peter stepped forwards. 'Lockerby, if you don't—'

Attis turned on him, face thunderous. He grabbed Peter by his blazer and pushed him against the wall. 'What the hell is going on?' He must have heard about the canteen outbreak and come looking for them.

'They were searching us!' Effie cried. 'Stripping us! Forcing us against our wills!'

'No—' Anna tried to shout over her, but Effie's words had riled Attis up further.

He banged Peter against the wall again. 'WHAT DID YOU DO TO THEM?'

Anna grabbed his arm and tore it from Peter, placing herself between them. 'ATTIS! No! Peter didn't do anything. He just got here!' She tried to get him to look at her through the blazing haze of his eyes. They flickered, seeing her at last. 'You're just going to make it all worse!'

Attis's nostrils flared and his jaw worked but, unwillingly, he let Peter go, his eyes still burning as they moved between Peter and Anna.

Effie ran to him and Attis put his arms around her protectively.

Peter pushed himself from the wall, shrugging his blazer straight, his face stiff with rage.

'Peter—' Anna began but he moved past her.

'Get him out of here,' he barked at the others.

The prefects took hold of Attis. Too many for him to fight off without magic. His eyes darted around the room between the members of the coven as if to make sure they were all unharmed.

'You can all go with him!' Peter snarled at the prefects.

Attis growled in Peter's direction but he gave in. He was removed from the room. Peter watched him go, like they'd managed to chain up a wild animal and the world was the better for it.

Anna spun to Peter. 'What will happen to him?'

He scowled. 'I imagine attacking prefects isn't going to go down well. Another strike against you all. Then again, so is a canteen full of pupils losing it.'

'You mean Darcey riling up a room of terrified people,' Effie spat back at him. 'She knew what she was doing.'

Peter's eyes turned on her coldly. 'That is for Eames to decide.'

'Peter, please.' Anna put a hand on his arm, catching Effie's eye. She pulled him to one side, speaking quietly. 'Darcey started all that in the canteen, I swear. Olivia was even filming it. Everyone's so on edge . . .'

Peter breathed out slowly, looking down at her hand on his arm. It took him a moment to calm down. 'I know Darcey is making the most of all this. I just – I don't think it's a good idea for you to spend time with people like Effie and Attis. They are making it all worse for you, don't you see?'

It was perfectly clear to Anna that Attis attacking prefects and Effie egging him on was helping no one, but she said nothing.

Peter shook his head. 'I'll explain as much as I can to Inquisitor Eames. He understands that emotions are running high.'

'Of course they are when he's making speeches like that in assembly!' Anna bit her lip, reining in her own emotions. She squeezed Peter's arm. 'Sorry, I know you're just trying to do your best. I know you aren't like the other prefects.'

Peter's eyes shone at her words, drawing them into himself. He nodded. 'I will be speaking to them too. They shouldn't be acting this way. I'll do what I can for you,' he added, with a secret smile between them. 'But now, I'm sorry, I'll have to take you all to the Ebury wing.'

Anna had known it would be coming.

She left with Peter, the others following. Effie raised her eyebrows at her but Anna looked away, furious – furious at Effie for making her use Peter, for riling up Attis when the stakes were so high. He could have injured one of the prefects! Carried out magic! What was Effie playing at? Why was she always *playing*?

They'd been made to wait in one of the old rooms of the Ebury wing until they were escorted up to the next floor. Eames's secretary looked concerned as she typed on her laptop and flustered with papers. There were voices coming from inside Eames's office.

'What's going on?' Effie asked her.

'I'm not privy to all of Eames's plans,' she replied tersely, but Anna sensed she had some inkling of what was about to take place. Something that was making her uncomfortable.

Anna looked back to the door with increasing dread. She'd grown used to Eames's questioning, but was this something else?

When they were called through, the room contained Eames, Darcey, several prefects, and a row of pupils. Anna recognized them instantly – some of the Year Sevens and band members who'd been caught up in the hysteria attacks. They looked terrified.

Eames spoke from behind his desk, his voice a dry scratch. 'Taking into account the increased stakes we are dealing with, it is prudent to introduce some new strategies to aid the investigation. Ms Dulacey has brought together some of the key victims of malefice from her trauma group and we will be using them for a brief Touch Test.'

Darcey looked so smug she was practically glowing, her hands clasped in front of her as she stood next to Eames's desk, a smile struggling against her lips.

Effie cocked her head. 'Do you want to tell us what a Touch Test is? Because it sounds messed up.'

Eames showed no response to her impertinence. 'According to the WIPS guidelines on the detection of malefice, victims of witchcraft will often elicit a strong reaction when coming into physical contact with a witch. I wish to examine the reactions of our own victims here at St Olave's.'

Anna looked around the room, at the fear on the faces within it. Surely this wasn't approved . . . did anyone know it was happening? Did Ramsden? Was Eames losing it? Or simply growing confident in his new role? At least none of the prefects in the room were the ones they had encountered earlier. She hoped Peter had warned Eames about them, but would Eames even care? How was *this* any better?

'Could Lilith Knight step forwards,' Eames instructed robotically.

The girl who responded was one of the Year Sevens. Small and timid, she was already shaking all over. Anna could barely look at her without remembering her scrawling on and scratching at the walls. *Her eyes.*

'Make contact with one of the suspects,' Eames prompted.

The girl, as if in a trance, moved forwards, stretching out a tentative, trembling hand. Her fingers made brief contact with Manda – she jerked her hand away as if she'd been stung.

'What did you feel?' Eames asked, notebook ready.

'Pain,' the girl whispered, scurrying back to the line. 'Like an electric shock through my body.'

'She's lying!' Manda stammered. 'I didn't do anything!'

'Could Suyin Huang step forwards and make contact with one of the suspects.'

It was a girl from Rowan's band. She took several deep breaths before moving forwards towards her old friend. She placed a hand on Rowan's arm. She yanked it away and cried out. 'I felt it too . . . something terrible. A darkness . . .' She began to shake her head, but it seemed to spread through her whole body. 'No. No. I don't want to do this—'

'You have to stop this!' Anna shouted. 'You're terrifying them!'

'I think you'll find you're the ones terrifying them!' Darcey bit back.

Eames ignored them both, continuing to write down his observations, calling out further names.

The victims stepped forwards one by one. The next, touching Anna and then stumbling away and squealing: 'Malefice! I felt it! Is it in me now?'

Another daring to touch Effie. She shrieked and began to hyperventilate. The terror of the room began to tilt into something like agitated excitement, nervous exhilaration, the reactions growing – the next girl tipping her head back, eyes rolling around her skull, another collapsing onto the floor as if her legs had given way, another shaking as if she were having a fit, as if they were all trying to outdo one another.

'They're faking!' Effie roared. 'This test is bullshit!'

But Eames was caught up in it, livelier now, writing fervently, Adam's apple quivering, a gleam in his eye that remained in place as he called the test to a close. Darcey gathered the victims together, drawing them back into her fold.

The coven huddled together too, clasping hands. Anna didn't know who was more frightened – the girls, or them.

'You can't actually be taking that as serious evidence?' Effie snapped at Eames.

Eames's eyes moved briefly to hers. 'This is one of the latest guidelines sent through directly from the WIPS, so yes, I am taking it seriously. They have asked for an immediate report on my results.'

'What happens then?' Anna asked, her voice faint. 'When does it end?'

He shifted in his seat. 'When the WIPS decides it ends.'

'What?' She narrowed her eyes. *Did he even know?* 'And what happens if we're found guilty? What then?'

Eames blinked. His throat tensed. He raised his head and ran a hand across the straight, combed line of his hair. 'That information is classified.'

Anna felt a stab of shock. 'You don't know, do you . . .' she whispered. 'You don't even know . . .'

His eyes blanked her as he looked over them. 'Now. Do any of you wish to confess before I send off my results?'

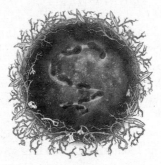

FOOTPRINTS

Spirits haunt not where they died, but where they lived. Where they felt so much that even in death the footprints of feeling still walk over and over, growing stronger in their entrapment, while seeking release—

Spiritual Energies, Books of the Dead: Tome 6658

Anna faced Effie, but if there were any cracks in her armour, Anna couldn't find them. Instead, Effie's circle seemed to push back, firing in all directions at once like a series of explosions – disorientating, distracting, burning with so many colours that Anna's magic was blinded and rebounded at the same time.

They'd finally met in the sewing room, practising circles while they waited for the coast to clear before they could search the school for themselves.

'Come on,' Effie goaded. 'You know you want to . . .'

Anna did want to. She wanted to push against everything entrapping her. To release it all.

The school week had been unbearable, Anna trying to make it through each day without losing it, not knowing what Darcey would do next, or Eames, or if the real hysteria would strike again. She still couldn't believe Eames had carried out that test. It had been madness. Had he truly believed he was gathering evidence? Or had he just wanted to watch them struggle and squirm? But then . . . the look on Eames's face when she'd asked him what would happen if they were found guilty. He'd tried to hide it, but he hadn't known. *That* was more terrifying than him knowing. The WIPS were a black hole even to those working for them. Was he simply following instructions he didn't understand? Was one of those instructions to cast the hysteria spell, no questions asked? Another madness.

Meanwhile, the protestors had not let up outside the gates and the prefects had smirked and muttered comments at them whenever they'd passed by, knowing there had been no real repercussions for their actions. No one else came near them, except Karim. He was so intently focused on Manda these days that he didn't seem to care he was being shunned by association.

'What are you waiting for?' Effie taunted. 'Why are you always holding back?'

Anna released her magic, but Effie blocked Anna's pinch instantly, sending it back as a punch. It landed on Anna's arm. There'd been several in the same spot and she was starting to bruise. She didn't show Effie that it hurt, but breathed out a hiss of frustration.

Effie raised an eyebrow. 'You'd better try harder.'

It was infuriating. Anna knew her magic was growing stronger, but it wasn't enough to break through Effie's. She gritted her teeth, dragging her magic back together.

'Aren't you angry?' Effie baited her. 'You should be. Your whole life has been controlled and now it's being controlled all over again.'

'Quiet, Effie!'

'First, your psycho aunt and the Binders . . . the curse . . . now the Inquisitor . . .'

Anna tried not to think of them all, bearing down on her. Aunt. Mrs Withering. The crush of the curse. The Year Sevens pawing and clawing at her. Eames's dead eyes. *You!* Anna thought. *You! Effie! With your tricks and traps.*

'Let it out!'

Anna roared and the magic coursed from her, hot and red.

'Ow!'

Anna was just as surprised as Effie to find that Effie was the one who had cried out. 'You pinched me, you bitch.' Effie rubbed her arm.

Anna released a breath and, despite their squabbling, they shared a charged smile at the feeling of their magic clashing and connecting.

'Is it safe to approach?' Attis moved towards them slowly, with his hands raised.

Anna had begged the others – mainly Effie – to play down the Touch

Test to Attis, knowing he'd be apoplectic, that it might push him over the edge he was already teetering on. He'd seethed for days about it all anyway – the prefects, the tests – hammering in the forge for hours every night. His eyes were shadowy, looking as if he hadn't slept for days, as if he were the one being hammered until he cracked.

I can't let him crack.

Anna had spent her evenings with the Bible, aware she'd been distracted by everything going on, redoubling her efforts, determined to find the answers to the curse before Attis decided he was the only one. She'd searched every page, scoured every word. She'd gone to the Library one evening, requesting any books on how to uncover hidden messages, break magical protections or codes, half wondering if she might find Pesaycha again, if he could help. But he hadn't appeared and the Library had only led her in useless circles, as if it were laughing at her, just like Nana. She'd gone to Rowan's to try out a series of spells Rowan had thought might work but none of them had. She'd asked Effie to start calling on her own connections to see if there was anyone who might have the know-how. Effie had laughed too, as if she saw the Bible for what it was – a trick. At least, in the end, she'd agreed to help.

'Finally, someone breaks through Effie's defences,' said Attis, bringing Anna's attention back to the room. He looked at Anna. 'Good work.'

'It won't happen again.' Effie pouted.

Attis's eyes were still on Anna. 'Try to take in the magic you just cast, how it felt.'

Anna shut her eyes, but all she could feel was her anger, still crisp, like the surface of magma, and yet, it had not been an eruption, it had run deeper than that, from many places, many rivers all leading to the surge she'd felt. With it, there'd been a sense of something . . . she tried to grasp at the threads . . . but the threads had not been threads . . . they'd formed a shape, a pattern . . .

'You're connecting with yourself now.' Attis nodded. 'But you're still unbalanced; there's something still blocking your way. You need to find your centre.'

Anna nodded back, wondering how to find her centre when the world was always spinning around her.

'And Effie.' Attis turned to her. 'It's not all about power— ow.' Attis squeezed his arm. 'No pinching the instructor.'

'You're lucky I only pinched you *there*.' Effie's mouth twisted wryly but they were distracted by Rowan's cries.

She was still battling with Manda. Manda was winning but her attacks seemed erratic, sometimes breaking through Rowan's circle, sometimes not, and from the look on Rowan's face, Manda was not being gentle.

Rowan put her hands up, defeated. 'I surrender. Everyone can beat me, it seems.'

'It'll come,' said Attis. 'It's important we keep practising, seeing as we have spirits, inquisitors and . . . prefects on the loose.' His jaw clenched. He kept moving, as if his whole body would seize up were he to stop and think about it all. 'I actually wanted to run through something else – a few defensive Warder moves.'

Manda cocked her head. 'I thought the Warders worked with symbols.'

'They do, but not only written ones, they work with physical symbols too – creating symbolic gestures and movements with their body to generate specific effects.' He curled a finger at Rowan. 'You can help me.'

'Sure.' She shrugged, still downbeat.

Once Rowan was in place, Attis raised his arm, keeping it bent, and moved his other wrist up to it, and then fired them both down, splaying his fingers.

Rowan stood still and Anna wondered if it had worked, but then she realized Rowan wasn't just still . . . she was motionless – completely frozen, except her eyes which were blinking rapidly with concern.

'The freeze symbol,' Attis explained. 'It immobilizes your opponent. I didn't put much magic into it, so it won't last long.'

After a few moments, Rowan began to stretch her neck, then her lips loosened. 'Gah. I can speak again. I didn't like that. Who am I without the power of speech?'

Attis grinned. 'You have to be careful with the freeze symbol. It's very similar to the tickle symbol but has entirely different effects. However, the jolt symbol is a useful one—'

This time he crossed his arms above his head and brought them down. Rowan was shoved back. 'Woah. Didn't like that much either.'

'You can move an opponent a little or a lot, depending on how much force you put into it.' Attis clapped his hands. 'Now, let's give them a go.'

He'd made the symbols look easy but Anna soon realized the motions had to be carried out with precision and required a certain kind of magic too, one that slotted into the feeling of the symbol like a lock into a key. It was challenging but Attis had them practise over and over, freezing and jolting, and sometimes accidentally tickling, until they all managed a faint replication of what he'd done.

'Let's go one more time,' he said, and Anna realized how he could work in his forge for such long hours. When focused, he was relentless.

Effie waggled a finger. 'No more. It's time to search the school. Attis, check the coast is clear.'

He looked to the door, his body tightening, his expansion collapsing. He slipped, heavy-browed, through it. Anna felt her magic wither at the thought of what they were about to do. Surveillance had now been installed in every main corridor. But they had to. Eames was out of control. Anna had found out the day before that her favourite teacher, Mr Archer, was due to leave along with several other teachers. Apparently, they'd spoken up against everything going on and had been dismissed by Ramsden and Eames.

Effie looked to the door darkly. 'I was thinking . . . maybe Darcey and Eames are working together. She looked very comfortable in his office while we were forced into that little show of his. When she's supposedly reporting back all the suspicions against us, maybe they're planning the next hysteria attack . . .'

'She sure is loving every moment of our downfall,' Manda seethed, tightening her arms around herself.

Anna tried to pick through Effie's theory but too much didn't add up. There was *something* they were missing.

After a few minutes, Attis came back. 'All clear.'

They nodded and slipped on their robes, blending into the darkness, becoming the shadows that everyone so feared.

Back in the main school, the cameras were watching with silent judgement, each lens as blank as Eames's eyes. They moved slowly and carefully, spreading out to check different classrooms. Attis split off to search the lockers while the rest of them met at the staffroom door. It was open and they were able to creep through easily enough. Anna was disturbed to see a STOP THE SPREAD poster on the noticeboard. It wasn't only the pupils who were being targeted. They searched quickly through belongings, filing cabinets, pigeon-holes, looking for spirit powder or any signs of magic.

There was nothing.

They left and moved on towards the destination Anna had been dreading. The Ebury wing. Attis met them outside. Anna was overcome with a feeling of powerlessness as they sneaked up the stairway. At least there were no cameras. They searched each of the old classrooms and then went up to the next floor. The secretary's desk held the only signs of life, messy with piles of papers, packets of biscuits, tea mugs stained deep ochre, and, among it, a framed picture displaying two smiling children. Anna began going through her drawers.

'Attis, can I get some help with these cabinets?' Rowan's voice rose up in the darkness.

Anna heard the sound of metal clinking against metal.

'Woah,' Rowan exclaimed. 'There are files on each of us. Very thick files. It's got records of every suspicion raised against us. There are *a lot*.'

'That's it. I'm going into his room,' declared Effie's disembodied voice. The door to Eames's office swung open.

Anna was still searching the secretary's desk, rifling through papers on its top. Her hand paused over one – an invoice from R.N. Security Services with a note.

Thank you for choosing R.N. Security. We are honoured to be partnering with the Witchcraft Inquisitorial and Prevention Services and look forward to growing stronger together in future.
   Warm regards,
   Reiss Nowell

Nowell. Peter's father. So his company was behind the surveillance. The invoice was clipped to another piece of paper beneath, showing that it had been paid – the secretary's name, Laura Wilmore, printed and signed at the bottom. Peter's father had supported the inspection all along but now he was actively helping it. The piece of paper lifted into the air and Anna could feel someone else standing beside her, a warmth she knew. *Attis.*

Then, the sound of footsteps coming up the stairs.

Anna froze, fear charging through her but with nowhere to go. *Where could they go?*

'Oh Lord,' Manda wailed.

'Quick, get back!' Attis commanded.

The paper dropped to the desk and Anna felt an arm wrap around her and pull her into a corner of the room.

The door opened and the secretary came in, her hair frizzy from the rain and her nose dripping. She wiped it and went over to her desk. Attis pulled Anna closer against him, his body taut behind her, as if he were ready to attack. She could feel his heart beating against hers, her own leaping about in an unsteady rhythm. His fingers lay across her ribs. The secretary picked up the invoice they'd just been looking at and went over to the shredder. She dropped it in. The whirring sound of it filled the room for a few seconds – then silence. Anna could feel Attis's breath on the back of her neck, the heat of him clashing with her cold fear.

The secretary started to leave but stopped suddenly in the centre of the room. She turned to Eames's office – to the gaping door. She frowned and walked towards it, stepping inside and flicking on the light.

Anna held her breath. *Don't move, Effie . . . please don't move . . .*

After a few moments, the secretary turned the light back off and shut the door behind her, scanning her own room with narrowed eyes as if she could sense something. Witches in hiding.

She shook her head and left, her footsteps disappearing back down the stairs.

No one spoke for several long moments. Attis did not let Anna go.

'Mother, maiden and – I think I may have momentarily lost consciousness,' Rowan wheezed through the fabric of their shadows. 'Are we all OK?'

Attis's grip finally loosened and they moved apart . . . back into the centre, everyone colliding with everyone else. Eames's door opened and shut quickly as Effie joined them.

'I thought you said coast clear, Attis!' said Manda accusingly. 'That could have been the end of us.'

'I'm sorry.' He breathed out heavily. 'It was. She must have come back.'

'What did she shred?' Rowan asked.

'It was an invoice from Peter's dad for the school surveillance . . .' Anna replied. 'There was a personal note from him saying he was glad to be partnering with the WIPS and looked forward to doing further work together in the future.'

'Ominous,' Rowan replied. 'Do you think she was asked to shred it? By Eames or by Peter's dad? Why?'

'I've no idea,' said Anna, trying to see the bigger game at play. 'They don't want a paper trail?'

'The Nowells can't be trusted,' Attis growled.

'Maybe we could try to talk to the secretary about Reiss's connection?' Anna wondered out loud. 'It always seems like she hates working for Eames, perhaps she could be a way in . . .'

'Too risky,' said Attis.

Anna knew he was right, it was just the temptation – or desperation – of getting information from someone close to Eames.

'We should go,' he added.

'We haven't finished searching,' said Anna.

'OK, let's search fast, then get the hell out of here.'

Anna finished checking the desk then went into Eames's room. It was entirely bare inside but for his desk, a storage unit and the chairs used for questioning. No personal items. No picture frames. No signs of life. She opened up the storage unit to find a blazer, red tie and a pair of black boots. She recognized them as the shoes he wore every day but she hadn't realized they were boots. Did he change before going home? Or were they a spare set? They rose high, their bases sturdy, thick-soled; a hard footprint to stamp things out. Not part of your typical suit and shoe combo. She put them back with unease and continued the search.

They found nothing.

'Gah!' Effie roared. 'I'm sick of this, scurrying about in the shadows like rats. Let's use what we've got in our arsenal! Do some magic! Banish Eames.'

'Effie—' Rowan began.

Effie spoke over her. 'Look, if we send him away and the hysteria stops, we've confirmation it's him. We can report him to the magical world. If not, we still have good reason to send him packing. You just saw all the evidence he has against us and he's getting desperate. What's he going to do to us next after his little Touch Test? Meanwhile, his prefects are running rampant. If we send him away it might buy us time while the WIPS find a replacement.'

'A replacement who could be worse,' Rowan pointed out.

'A risk we have to take. I know a banishment spell, I've done it before. We can go to the roof and cast it.'

The thought of going to the roof and unleashing all their pent-up magic was tempting, to send Eames far away, to never have to look at his face again. But would it really make any difference? Was Eames behind the hysteria? *Did Effie really think it was him? Or did she just want to get rid of him?* Revenge was her favourite dish after all. Anna wished she knew who Effie was, wished she could trust her. 'What do you mean by banished? Is it dangerous?'

'No, I promise,' Effie replied. 'It won't be anything dramatic. He'll just get called away, transferred to another department, or decide he has to quit suddenly, or get ill and have to take leave.'

'Those could still look suspicious.'

'The school band went insane on stage. I think people are already suspicious enough, don't you? There's nothing to lose now.'

'I'm in,' said Manda with vicious relish. 'Let's banish the bastard! No one tells us what to do!'

'Says the girl who used to have the school rules laminated on the inside of her locker . . .' Rowan muttered.

'They weren't laminated!'

'ARE WE GOING?' Effie yelled.

Anna and Rowan agreed, although neither one of them sounded convinced.

'Not until I've gone ahead to check there's no surveillance up there,' said Attis.

Once they got the message from him, Effie cackled with glee. 'TO THE ROOF! Freedom awaits! Come on!' Her voice moved away and the door flew open.

Manda laughed from somewhere and Anna could hear their footsteps already slip-slapping away, speeding up. There was nothing for it. She followed them out the door, Effie whooping ahead.

'TO THE ROOF! THE DARK MOON IS CALLING!'

Anna began to run after them. Tentative at first and then faster. Faster. It felt freeing after weeks of shuffling, head down, through the corridors. Now, no one could touch them, the school was theirs. Her cloak spread out behind her as she chased the laughter and lure of magic upwards, propelled by rage and fear and hatred for all that had been done to them, STOP THE SPREAD posters flickering in her wake.

The door to the roof was open. Anna burst through it, embraced by the night which met her with a wildness of its own – buffeting winds and clouds rolling above and the moonlight tearing through it all with vengeful silver claws.

'They may take our lives, but they can't take our magic!' Effie bellowed. 'Over here. Gather around.'

Anna followed the sound of communal breathlessness to the centre of the roof.

'I don't think I've run through the school halls like that since I got my period in the middle of physics class in Year Nine,' Rowan panted.

They all laughed, looking at each other in the darkness, but seeing nothing. Concealed as a dark moon above.

'There are no cameras up here,' Attis confirmed. 'But let's play safe.'

'Sure,' said Effie. 'We need to not trip into one another though. This is a footprint banishing spell and it involves a lot of energy. Follow my lead.'

She cast their opening circle.

> Energies joined, joined we stand,
> May none enter our ring of hands.
> Between the worlds we now roam,
> Take us there and safely home.
> As above so below, as within so without,
> Weave our circle without doubt!

Then, Effie began to stamp. Anna could hear it – *stamp, stamp, stamp.* She could see Effie's footprints scuffing the dust on the roof, sending it up in little shivers. The rest of them joined in – *stamp, stamp, stamp* – stamping shadows, the night rushing around them like a black wind as Effie spoke the words.

> We call on the Goddess of the Dark Moon.
> Goddess of all that cannot be known.
> Feel us stamp. Hear us roar.
> Shut the windows. Close the doors.
> Get him gone with all his bane.
> Take his footsteps far away.
> Return to the hell from whence he came!

Stamp, stamp, stamp!

'Join hands!' Effie called out.

They reached out, feeling for each other's fingers in the darkness.

They began to move in a circle, stamping their feet harder, faster, as Effie repeated the words over and over, channelling everything they'd been holding back into their magic.

Anna didn't know how, but she began to sense the others at the edges of her vision, glimmers of magic, shadows alive and twisting, as if they were spirits themselves. And yet, this was nothing like death magic. There was no sense of emptiness, but as if the whole world was filling them up – expansive, moonlit and star-fuelled, theirs to twist to their will.

Stamp, stamp, stamp!

Faster, harder – charging up the magic, their footprints disturbing the dust and then . . . breaking away—

Anna blinked. But it was true – their footprints were rising as shadows around them; footprint-shadows spiralling into the air. She marvelled as they swirled in the wind like black flags cut from the night, as dark as their despair and their hate and their rage.

Effie continued:

> By North, South, East and West,
> Banish him as you know best!
> May fire turn him to smoke!

'May earth swallow him up!' Manda answered.

Anna knew what to say next, as if the words were waiting for her. 'May water wash him away!'

Rowan last. 'And wind disperse him!'

Attis released a howl.

Their footprint-shadows whirled higher and higher, silver-lined with moonlight, twisting and turning and flying off – escaping from the school and everything in it.

And then – gone.

Banished.

The spell was over, but they didn't stop. It felt too good. Their feet hammered as they laughed and howled. Howls of hatred. Howls of rage. Howls of hysteria. Howls of power. Unleashed shadows on a rooftop – so loud and yet silent to the rest of the world. Anna could feel the sound rising from somewhere deep inside of her, hollow places she'd thought were empty but she now realized were only tunnels – channels – deep wells of power.

They howled until there was nothing left, until they collapsed onto the floor, delirious and feverish with laughter.

Effie removed her cloak.

'Effie,' Attis warned.

'Chill, darling. No one can see us from up here.'

They all removed their cloaks, dousing their skin in moonlight, glancing between each other and laughing. Anna caught Attis's eye and found herself smiling at the look of him out here – his hair all wind-blown, a wild mischief back in his eye.

'Noises just came out of me that I didn't even recognize,' said Rowan.

'Don't think I've ever howled before,' Manda mused. 'I should do it more.'

'I have,' said Effie.

Rowan snorted. 'OK, *when* have you howled?'

Effie threw a pointed glance at Attis and laughed unashamedly.

He lowered his head and coughed, then laughed too. 'Hey, I don't make women howl. Now barks, brays or quacks, I can do.'

Anna forced a smile through a gritted jaw, not knowing why Effie always had to do that, remind them all that Attis had been hers long before he'd been theirs. *Mine.*

He was never mine . . .

'I know that spell is going to have worked,' said Effie with unshake-able confidence. 'It was powerful. *We* were powerful.'

Anna had felt the power of it too. The power of witches freed from their chains for one night, but . . . would it work? Would the hysteria stop? Would it buy them time? Or would the WIPS quickly replace Eames with another . . . an identical copy – black suit and boots . . .?

Anna realized something had been playing on her mind. 'What was that old rhyme one of you said last year, Rowan? *Beware, beware . . .*'

'*The wolves are here,*' Rowan jumped in. '*There's smoke, there's smoke, in the town square . . . Red thread and boots, prepare the noose . . . The big bad wolves are roasting goose!*'

'*Red thread and boots,*' Anna repeated. 'Like the uniform of the WIPS – red tie and black boots. Hopkins wears them and I just saw a pair in Eames's room.'

Attis frowned. 'In the past, red thread was thought to protect against magic. People would tie it around their neck or wrists or put it some-where outside their home.'

Effie tilted her head back to the sky. 'Inspired by the old legends? Or they *are* the old legends?'

Roasting goose . . . Nana's vision gripped Anna again – Eleanor burning in the flames . . . herself burning . . . flame and smoke all around her—

'I actually had some news,' Rowan interrupted the dark spiral of her thoughts, 'Not good news.'

They turned to her.

'I got a message from Cillian this afternoon.'

'Cillian?' Effie repeated. 'Poppins's puppet? Why is he contacting you?'

Rowan shrugged. 'I don't know. I don't even know how he got my number.'

Effie snorted. 'Rowan's got a boyfriend.'

'NOT my boyfriend.'

'Whatever you say . . .'

'He wears a full-length leather jacket, non-ironically. Anyway, he has new intel. Apparently, the WIPS are trying to follow through on Hopkins's call to action – they're lobbying to become a government organization. If it happens . . .'

Attis dragged a hand over his face. 'They could have new levels of power. They'll be able to influence law making.' He howled to the sky. 'Screw our government for letting it get this far!'

The night seemed suddenly colder, darker, the hints of spring in the wind extinguished by Rowan's words.

'Did he have any updates on the missing witches?' Attis asked before Anna could.

'Didn't mention it but I'll go back to him and ask.'

They carried on discussing the situation, getting nowhere, but none of them wanting to go back inside, to face another day.

Rowan wandered over to the edge of the roof, staring out at the sky. Anna went over to her. It wasn't like Rowan to choose to be alone.

'You all right?'

Rowan exhaled. 'I don't know. The spell was fun, but it feels like we're only moving chess pieces ineffectually around a board.'

'I know what you mean. Getting nowhere with anything . . .' Anna thought of the curse.

'I just – I just feel so lost. Maybe we could fly away?' Rowan threw her arms out, the wind bringing the wildness of her hair alive. 'I used to dream I could fly when I was little . . . made me feel so . . . invincible, like nothing in the world could get to me.'

Anna smiled. 'Sounds like a nice dream.'

'Yeah, and then I grew up and I became . . . just me.'

'Just you! Rowan, you don't see how amazing you are, do you?'

Rowan looked at her but her smile couldn't sustain itself. 'If I'm so amazing, why can't I beat any of you at circles? It's the same at home in the garden. I'm falling behind. I'm still not feeling drawn to any particular area of Botanical magic. My magic always felt so stable, but now it's like . . . I'm losing my way, getting stuck somehow . . . I don't know . . . sorry, I'm rambling. It's the night air and all the howling, I'm not making sense.'

'It makes sense to me. I couldn't even feel my magic at the start of the year, but thanks to your spinning top and relentless encouragement, it's coming back. None of us know what our languages are yet, what kind of witches we're going to be. We're all just as lost.'

'I just want to be of some use in all this.'

'You already are. You're our resident spy.' Anna nudged her shoulder, but Rowan shook her head.

'I want to be more than good at gossiping and eavesdropping. Although, speaking of, what are they talking about?' Rowan threw a glance to Manda and Effie who'd migrated to the other side of the roof, talking quietly. 'Plotting to take over the world?'

Anna chuckled but the intense look on Manda's face made her pause. What *were* they talking about?

'You're not planning more banishing spells, are you?' Rowan yelled over to them. 'We're thinking of going flying over here. If only we had broomsticks . . .'

'Flying?' Effie walked over. 'Technically, witches *can* fly, you know. Well, some . . .'

'So it's said,' Rowan acknowledged. 'Though I've never met one.'

Effie stood up onto the edge of the roof and began to walk along it. 'Perhaps I'll give it a go tonight. A taste of true freedom.' She leant over the edge. 'Sure is a long way down . . .'

'Effie!' Anna yelled hoarsely, not only terrified Effie would be seen, but that she'd slip.

'Effie, get down!' Attis ran over but Effie just laughed and put a teasing foot out over the edge, wobbling. 'Effie!' His voice thundered.

She cackled and stepped off . . . into his arms. He caught her and she threw her head back, laughing. He growled and spun her around, his growl turning to frustrated laughter as he held her tightly in his arms. He put her down.

'You see,' she said to him with a teasing smile. 'I need you to stop me doing stupid things.'

'How about you stop doing stupid things?'

'Not possible, sorry.'

He shook his head, but the smile he gave her was familiar and forgiving. A smile that said he would always be there for her no matter what she did.

HAMMER

The fifth stage of the Hel witch path is often referred to as the point of no return, for once embarked upon an Initiate cannot look back, cannot go back. Hel will hammer, Hel will fracture, Hel will dissolve. May only the broken survive.

'Journeying to Hel', Hel Witch Initiation Stage Five

Anna lay in her bed, the spinning top forming patterns on the ceiling above her. She wasn't playing the piano, but the song was running through her mind, sustaining the magic, feeding it with the anger she'd felt earlier. The anger of stamping feet and moon-howling. Anger at protestors and prefects and *inquisitors*. The anger of being held in Attis's arms and not being able to give in to them. The anger at the way Effie had fallen into his arms as if she expected them to always be there. Demanded it. Deeper anger Anna hadn't even known was there, that had become so much a part of her she couldn't separate herself from it – at her aunt. Everything Aunt had done to her, *inflicted* on her. At herself, for staying small, staying quiet for too long.

She fed it all into the song and the anger moved through her body, breaking down its own defences – flaming in her stomach, licking its way up her throat like a scream made of fire, rising defiant through the melody. The spinning top responded, a reflection of her rage, moving around and around but not still . . . forming a pattern, like a clue, like the way out of the maze she was stuck in . . .

I want to get out! LET ME OUT!

But Aunt's voice answered hers, ever ready: 'This is what anger does. It hurts others more than it hurts you.'

No. No. No.

Where did anger get me, child? Dead! Dead! Dead!

No! No! No!

The spinning top fell to earth. It could not fly. A deep silence swallowed the anger, a deep cold extinguished it. Anna lay still, wondering why she could not break through this darkness . . . whether she even should . . .

It felt as if things between her and Effie were becoming strained all over again and she didn't know how to stop it. Anger and mistrust coming between them, but was it only the curse? Twisting everything? Trying to drive them apart? She couldn't let it.

She reached for the book of fairy tales and took out the black feather from within, turning it in her fingers as she read 'The Seven Ravens' again, trying to draw meaning out of it, anything that might illuminate Nana's riddle. Nothing new leapt out at her. She flicked to the next fairy tale – 'Trit-A-Trot':

Once there was and thrice there was not, a land over which a tyrant king ruled. One day, he called all the men of his kingdom to his castle to ask if any had a daughter who could spin straw into gold. A miller, who wanted to appear important, boasted to the king that his daughter could perform such a feat. He was commanded to bring her to the palace.

Immediately regretting his claim, the miller fetched his daughter and left her at the king's mercy. The king took the maiden to a room stacked high with piles of straw. He pointed at the spinning wheel and commanded, 'Now spin this straw to gold, else you'll be put to death.'

Left alone, the girl had no idea where to start and began to despair when a strange man with large ears and straggly hair appeared before her. He asked her why she was so upset and she told him of her task.

He smiled a devil's smile. 'I shall help you, child, but in return you must tell me your name and give me the black comb from your hair.'

In her desperation, the girl told him her name and then took the black comb from her hair and handed it over. He snatched it from her and got to work, the spinning wheel whirring around and around until all the straw had turned to gold and the room glistened from end to end.

In the morning, the king was delighted to see his fortune, but he wanted more. The maiden was taken to a bigger room, stacked higher with straw. The king warned: 'Now spin this straw to gold, else you'll be put to death!'

She began to fret but the strange man popped into the room once more. 'I shall help you again, child,' he chirped, 'but in return, you must give me one of your white teeth.'

The girl knew she had no choice. She opened her mouth and let the man wrench one of her teeth free. He got to work, the wheel whirring around and around even faster than before until all the straw had turned to gold and the room sparkled like a lake at sunrise.

In the morning, the king came and was delighted to feast his eyes upon his treasure, but he wanted more – more! The girl was taken to the biggest room she'd ever been in, stacked so high with straw she could not see the top of it all. The king ordered again: 'Spin this straw to gold, else you'll be put to death!'

The young maiden had not been left alone long when the strange man burst into the room. 'I shall help you this last time, maiden,' he snickered, 'but in return you must give me the red heart of your firstborn child.'

The girl agreed, deciding she would bear no child to give him. The man got to work, the wheel whirring around and around so fast she thought it would fly away until all the straw had turned to gold and the room seemed to burn with its colour.

The next morning, the king was so overjoyed he demanded the maiden sew a golden dress out of the thread she had spun, and then – marry him.

The maiden did so and before long the new queen fell pregnant. Yet, more than her new husband, she feared the return of the strange man and return he did.

After the baby was born, he appeared one night beside the cot and demanded its heart.

'No!' the young queen cried. 'Please, is there no other way?'

The man smiled and began to dance and sing upon the spot. 'By black, by white, by red, you see, you already belong to me! But three days I'll give thee, to guess my name or forever mine you'll ever be!'

He left and the girl wondered how she could ever learn his name when it could be anything.

The next night the man appeared again and the young queen tried *as many names as she could think of but he just danced about laughing. 'No, no, no you miss the mark, two days left or I'll have his heart!'*

He disappeared and the girl fetched one of her maids. She asked the maid to travel far and wide to see if she could learn the man's name. When the man appeared the next night the maiden tried out all the names her maid had given her but he just hooted. 'No, no, no you miss the mark, one day left or I'll have his heart!'

He disappeared and the girl wandered about the castle in despair trying to think of a way to learn his name. When the man appeared on the final night the maiden noticed the man's shadow upon the wall. While she recited possible names and he danced and jigged, distracted, she whispered to the shadow – asking what his true name was. His shadow replied: 'I know not much but know a lot, his true name be Trit-a-Trot!'

'Trit-a-Trot!' the girl called out and the man froze.

He turned to her with a look of rage upon his face. 'How do you come to know my name?'

The maiden smiled. 'My black, by white, by red, you see, your shadow told your name to me and now forever mine you'll ever be!'

She made the little man dance around and around, whirring faster and faster until the ground tore in two and swallowed him up.

Anna lay back in bed, something about the tale tugging at her. *Black, white and red . . .* where had she heard that before? But it was the shadow that beckoned her attention. The man's shadow as alive as their own footprint-shadows had been earlier that night . . . as if shadows could hold secrets the light of day, the light of reason, was not privy to . . . the words of Nana's riddle coming back to her . . .

Unearthed God's word, truth dark nor light, the shadows, the shadows they know . . .

She sat up, struck by a sudden idea.

Could the Bible be . . . a Book of Shadows?

She thought of the corridor of the Books of Shadows in the Library. Effie's words . . . *A witch's journal. A personal spell book, where a witch can write down her spells, but the contents are concealed by shadow to keep their secrets safe . . .*

Perhaps Eleanor had turned the Bible into a Book of Shadows to conceal it from prying eyes, so only witches could find the spell within – only her children who she'd wanted the book passed on to. Effie had said Books of Shadows last forever which could be why the Bible was still intact, protected by the spell.

Anna took out her phone and texted Rowan:

Hey. Hope you're still up! Random Q. How do Books of Shadows work?

Rowan didn't take long to respond:

Of course I am. Who can sleep any more? I've just binge watched three episodes of Dress the Bride and I'm ready for a fourth. They can only be read by shadowlight – it's like moonlight but in shadow. Moonlight + Shadow if that makes any sense. I'm aware it doesn't. Why you asking? WAIT. The Bible?!

Anna typed back:

Maybe. I don't know yet. Enjoy Dress the Bride.

Rowan messaged again. Anna could sense the reticence in her words, as if she didn't want to tell Anna.

KEEP ME UPDATED. Also . . . Cillian came back. Still no word on those two cursed witches who went missing and he thinks there may have been a third . . . he's trying to confirm the details. Sorry. I hate this.

Anna stared at the words, not quite able to believe them. Three missing cursed witches couldn't be nothing.

There was no time to lose.

She picked up the Bible and went over to the window. The moon was tucked behind clouds. She turned to the back page, which she knew was empty – the most likely place for a spell to be written down. She waited. The moon began to creep out like a secret from its shell, Anna's hand forming a shadow over the page below. *Moonlight + Shadow.* Something gleamed on the page – a slice of silver. Her heart thudded, her breath quickened. There was something there – something written – everything she'd been waiting for. The moon came out in full and it appeared in silvery, webbed script. A spell.

The spell.

The words shone with innocence but they were dark words. Terrible words. The only words Anna had ever read that were worse than the Language of the Dead:

> *By the curse and by my blood,*
> *Here be a spell to draw their love,*
> *Born of iron, born of fire,*
> *He shall be all they desire.*
> *Release this curse with his blood,*
> *His death restore this hate to love,*
> *Into this stone let this spell go,*
> *And so shall it be swallowed whole:*
> *A mother new, a womb fresh sown,*
> *So give him life and let him grow.*

His death.
  His death.
  His death.

Anna had barely slept but when she woke the next morning, the words hit her all over again like a hammer to the head, throwing her back into despair, back into the paralysing threads of her dreams. *No way out.* She felt sick. Betrayed. So full of rage her howl could have swallowed the moon.

After everything, *everything* she'd done – following her mother's footsteps dutifully, patiently solving Nana's riddle, clutching onto her hope, and then the spell had declared it loud and clear. It didn't just want his blood. It wanted all of him. His sacrifice. *His death.* Just as Selene had predicted. The terrible truth her mother had known all along.

The curse had encircled her and trapped her in the very darkness she'd been trying to escape. Attis had to die to end it – to save them.

There'd never been a way out, had there?

She shut out Aunt's laughter, reminding herself of what she'd decided last night – that she had to keep the spell to herself. She'd already messaged Rowan to say it had come to nothing and she had no intention of telling anyone. If Attis found out, he would take it as confirmation that his sacrifice was the only option and would do it all over again. She knew he would.

He could not know.

She stayed in her room, her despair only deepening as she discovered there'd been a fresh hysteria attack. More deaths.

Fatalities after buses lose control in tourist hotspot
London buses plough into onlookers in Piccadilly Circus
Malefice kills again in London's centre!

Six bus drivers had acted erratically in London's busy Piccadilly Circus causing damage, injuries, fatalities. *And what are we doing?!* Casting spells on rooftops and hoping that Eames might be banished. It wasn't enough. None of it was enough.

The internet was overflowing with hysteria. Fear of magic was rising, propelling itself, churning its own bile and spilling over like a well full of poison. Too much now. No way of pushing it all back down. And amid all the chaos . . . cursed witches going missing. Why couldn't Anna stop all the things that were happening? Why couldn't she stop the curse? Why couldn't she save Attis?

His death.
His death.
His death.

Anna threw her phone across the room. She couldn't read another word. She went downstairs. Effie's door was open which wasn't surprising. She'd gone to meet Azrael after their rooftop spell last night. Anna reached the ground floor and went straight to the piano, trying to release it all but not knowing if the song was helping her or merely charging up the curse; not knowing where she ended and the darkness began. Not caring any more, just wanting to dig deeper, to break through it, even as the spinning top careered away, again and again, her fingers moving so fast and furiously that she began to fear she would never stop playing, that she would turn hysterical and be lost in it forever—

A sound broke her trance.

A creak of the floorboards behind her.

She turned around fearing it was him and it was – Attis leaning against the doorway, wearing a faint smile. The last person she wanted to see, that smile breaking her heart.

His death.
His death.
His death.

Anna looked back down to the keys.

'Sorry, didn't mean to disturb you. I'll just be a second . . .' He walked into the room, knelt down beside her piano and began hammering a nail into it.

She jumped up. 'What in thirteen moons are you doing?'

'Just ignore me.' He took out another nail. 'I'm not here.' He started to hammer that one in too.

Anna thought about running away but her curiosity got the better of her. 'Why are you hammering nails into my piano?'

He looked up with a nail in his mouth and a madness of his own in his eye. 'Don't worry, I can remove them without leaving a mark.' He hammered it in.

'That didn't answer my question . . .'

'For protection.' He showed her another nail. The iron was dark and roughly wrought but the head was carved with an intricate symbol. 'The metal is formed from old coffin nails mixed with a small amount of iron sulphide, stamped with a Warder symbol designed to protect against spiritual energy.'

'The hysteria won't strike here . . .' Anna said, though she heard the waver in her own voice.

Attis stood up – he looked as if he hadn't slept either – his bright eyes splintered and weary, his hair flying in all directions. 'We don't know that. We don't know how it works. I'll put them around the house too and here—' He reached into the pocket of his jeans and pulled out a handful of the nails, handing them to her.

She frowned. 'Er – thanks.'

'Stick them into the soles of your shoes. Now, I should hammer a few more in—' He went to lower himself to the piano again but she took his arm.

He stopped and turned to look at her.

She didn't know what to say. She looked down at her hand on his arm, feeling the solidity of him. He was real. *Real*. No spell. She wouldn't listen to it. It didn't need to be true.

'When did you last sleep?' she asked, removing her hand.

He forced a smile. 'I don't remember.'

'I think you need to take a break from the hammering, for safety reasons if nothing else.'

His laugh deflated into a sigh, scratching a hand through his hair again. 'What else am I meant to do? I need to do something.' He breathed out, his body slumping. 'I just want to keep you all safe.'

'I know,' Anna replied, wishing she could wipe the fraught lines from his brow. 'But that's impossible right now . . . for anyone,' she admitted to herself too.

'OK, distract me then.' He hitched a smile. His eyes travelled to the piano and back to her. She knew that look – inquisitive, as if he were trying to work her out, but in a way that made no demands of her, a way that made her feel more than she was. 'What was the song you were playing? It was different . . . it was coming straight from you, wasn't it?'

Anna looked away, not knowing how he'd pinpointed it so accurately. 'It's just something I'm working on . . .' she made light of it. She didn't know how to explain it – how the song flowed from her and yet refused to flow; how it had been helping her magic, bringing the broken parts of her back together; how she couldn't complete it because there was a darkness at her centre which her music refused to touch. Something she feared more than anything.

'Could you play it to me?'

'It's not ready for public listening.'

'You sure? I did buy you that piano after all . . .'

She flicked a glance at him. 'You're saying you only bought me a piano so you could force me to play for you at your whim?'

'Of course. I am a piano pervert, after all, remember?' He grinned.

Anna did remember their joke from long ago. She narrowed her eyes and the tune of Chopsticks started up on the piano. The song he'd played her when they'd first spent time together in the music room.

He laughed with something of his old lightness. 'You'll be in the Royal Albert Hall before we know it.'

She took a bow.

'But seriously.' He raised his eyebrows. 'You can play the piano with your magic now? Impressive.'

'It was only chopsticks.'

'I think there's a lot more than Chopsticks in you. When you finish that song, I'd like to hear it.'

She nodded, trying not to think of all the parts of him she'd woven into it. 'I will, if my piano still works with all these holes in it.'

He laughed, then rubbed the back of his neck. 'Right, I better get on.' He nodded down the stairs towards the forge.

'I thought you were going to take a break?'

'I just did.'

Anna shook her head, trying to think of something else to say. She didn't want him to go. She felt better with him here, like the spell couldn't possibly be real if he was with her, like it had all just been a terrible dream. A dream of shadows.

'Want to help me?' he asked, the look on his face tentative.

Anna felt her eyebrows rise in surprise at his offer. She hadn't been alone with him in his forge since the year before. He had a tendency of not wearing many clothes down there. Not a good idea.

'I'll let you make something,' he said. 'I find hammering the shit out of metal very therapeutic.'

'OK . . . just for half an hour,' Anna agreed before sense could catch up with her. 'It's not like I've got exams to revise for.'

She followed him hesitantly down the stairs into his forge. The fire was blazing. The room was busy – the surfaces and workbenches covered with various projects, tools and nails strewn about, everything glinting and rippling with the dancing light, moving as quickly as Attis's mind. Anna walked around it, exploring. She stopped at a vast chart hung on one of the walls, full of symbols – curving, complex and yet incredibly precise. 'Are these Warder symbols? There are so many.'

'That's not even the half of them. There are around four thousand in total.'

'Four thousand! Do you know what all of them mean?'

Attis came over, looking at the chart beside her. 'Give or take. Some can be quite general like the power symbol or the protection symbol, others can be very specific, like this one—' He pointed at the chart. 'Which will increase the strength of the metal it's carved into three times over, or this one which will give metal the ability to bend, or this one which repels thievery, making whatever you've forged impossible to steal. You don't have to stick with one symbol either, you can play around with different combinations – create even more specific meanings through their interactions.'

'Sounds complicated.'

'That's before you take into account the alloys you use, the design and techniques you employ, and the magic of the fire, of course, which has its own language.'

Anna shook her head. 'How long have you been doing all this, Attis?'

'Herne and I built my first forge when I was eight.'

'Eight!'

He smiled to himself. 'I wouldn't stop asking. Of course, it wasn't much at first . . . just a lump of metal for an anvil and a fire in a barrel outdoors, but it expanded. Before long, I'd started up a trade selling locally. Herne was so supportive, always buying me new tools . . . I went to pick some up over the summer but I think – I think I just wanted to be back there. To feel his presence—' Attis swallowed, drumming his fingers against the workbench. 'Anyway, I work with the Warders now, sell most of my wares through them. They entrust me with their symbols and I make protective items in return. We split the profits.'

'I didn't realize you were making money.'

'Of course. I make to sell, except what I need for myself. How did you think I could afford all my designer outfits?' Attis waved his hand with a flourish over his ripped jeans and smoke-stained T-shirt.

Anna laughed. 'I always wondered.'

'I need the money.' He shrugged. 'My dad left some to Selene for my schooling and she obviously puts a roof over my head, but after that I make my own way.'

'Selene doesn't give you money?'

'I think money barely occurs to her as a concept. I'm sure she would if I asked, but I'm not going to. I'd rather not be beholden to her any more than I am.' His face darkened.

The rift between them cut through Anna, that they couldn't see just how brilliant each of them was, how alike they were.

'So.' He came towards her. 'What do you want to make?'

'What do you suggest?'

'Why don't you try a horseshoe?' He waved an arm at the many covering the walls. Anna reviewed them – they were stamped with multiple Warder symbols. 'They've been used as protective charms for thousands of years.'

'I'll give it a go. Now, where's the hammer?' She raised an eyebrow.

He pretended to look affronted. 'You can't just start hammering. You need to be kitted up first. Safety first.'

'You didn't make me kit up last time.'

'That was under my instruction – and protection from the sparks – now, you're on your own. Stand here.' He moved her to the side of the anvil and looked her up and down. She was aware of his proximity but his gaze didn't make her uncomfortable – it was focused on its task, assessing her as a master might his apprentice. 'Long sleeves, cotton . . . good. You'll need this.' He picked a leather apron off a hook and put it over her neck. Anna tied it at the back. 'And these—' He presented her with large boots and gloves which she slipped on. 'The hair – it's a fire hazard.' She lifted her loose hair up and tied it back. He stepped forwards and pulled a pair of goggles over her head, tucking a strand of hair that had slipped loose behind her ear. They looked at each other for a moment, the heat of the room condensing around them, then he stepped back. 'As always, you look ravishing, Dr Everdell.'

She made withering eyes at him.

He smirked. 'I think you're glaring at me but it's hard to tell through the goggles.'

She looked down at herself. 'This feels excessive.'

Attis put a finger up. 'Number one rule in my forge. Respect the power of the fire.'

'What's the number two rule?'

'That's all I've got.'

He put a long strip of metal into the heat and took her through some of the basic techniques – the different parts of the flame, how to heat metal but keep it malleable, how to know when the fire was ready to work with and how to cool it before hammering. He demonstrated how to shape a horseshoe and then took her over to the workbench and showed her how to carve a Warder symbol into it, working with quick, light taps.

She should have been paying more attention, but she was watching his fingers, how expressively they moved in the rippling light of the room, forming patterns of their own, patterns she wanted to decipher. He looked up. 'You see?'

'Er – yes. Totally.'

He handed her a fresh piece of metal to work on. 'Your turn.'

She didn't get off to a good start, dropping the hammer after the first hit.

He picked it up. 'Remember, hold it between your thumb and forefinger.' He adjusted the grip of it in her hand, moving close so that all she could smell was the clean pine of him, the ferrous tang of him. She wiped away a trickle of sweat from her brow – it *was* hot in here and his body was emitting just as much warmth as the open flame. 'Use your shoulder and let the hammer rebound. Hard strikes will make the metal brittle or crack. Gentle but consistent hammering creates the strongest metal.'

She tried a few times, getting a feel for it. He retreated to a work-bench, leaving her to it. Anna still didn't really know what she was doing but she enjoyed the satisfying thrum of the hammer through her body. She hummed her song and felt the tightness in her chest release, the fire burning a little more of the cold inside her away. Occasionally, he looked over and she could feel him watching. She liked the way that felt too. Thankfully, he was still fully dressed.

Once she'd formed something that looked vaguely like a horseshoe, she called him over. 'What do you think?'

'Very good.' He nodded, holding it up. 'I'll make a blacksmith of you yet.'

Anna tilted her head. 'It's wonky.'

'It's characterful.'

'You're being kind.'

'Never. I'm a hard taskmaster in my forge. Now, get carving.' Attis pointed to the Warders' chart. 'You've got plenty of symbols to choose from.'

Again, Anna didn't really know what she was doing but as she concentrated on the small and demanding task she relaxed into it, welcoming the emptying of her mind, nothing to concentrate on but four little symbols – four little worlds.

When Attis came over again, he looked at her clumsily formed symbols, nodding encouragingly but then frowning at the last one. 'Which symbol is this?'

Anna looked at it, surprised by the symbol herself. She hadn't really noticed what she was creating. It wasn't like one of the Warders' distinct symbols but something less defined, more like a pattern, as if it were only the beginning of something more complex. 'I don't know.' She shrugged. 'I guess I made my own.'

Attis turned to her, bemused. 'You had hundreds of symbols to choose from and you made your own?'

'Yeah . . .'

He shook his head, half exasperated, half impressed. 'What does it do?'

'I – I don't know that either.'

He laughed. 'Of course. That would be too simple.' He ran a finger over it and looked back at her, that penetrating look of his.

'Is it going to make the wall?' she asked, diverting his gaze.

'Of course . . . I've got an area over there for all the wonky horse-shoes.'

'Hey.' She nudged him. 'So, what are you working on?' She wandered over to his workbench which was covered in nails and various blades.

'Just sharpening some of my blades,' he said, a low rumble of unde-fined threat entering his voice.

'For your knife of many blades?'

'Exactly. I've been polishing up my hits-any-target blade and trying to make a new one that can cut through spiritual attack.' He frowned.

'How's it going?'

'Not well.'

'Do you ever make anything for yourself, Attis?'

He looked up at her as if caught off guard. 'Sometimes. Not for a while . . .'

'What would you make for yourself, if you had all the time in the world?'

He leant against the bench, brow furrowing then relaxing as his eyes travelled somewhere else. 'I'd make a weather vane.'

'Really?' She hadn't expected that.

He nodded eagerly. 'Yeah, I've done a few designs in the past . . . but never got around to it.'

'Like, to indicate the weather?'

'Well, it would be more than that. I imagined it having several different pointers. One for the direction of weather, another for the type.' He grew animated. 'One to function as a magnetic compass and another for the direction of magical energies. There could be one to track the migrations of birds, another to point to any animal life nearby; another to track the positions of the moon, one to work with the stars – I haven't quite worked that out yet, but I imagined watching it move to the stars when I'm out in my garden at night—'

'Your garden?'

'Yeah, somewhere in the countryside, by mountains and the sea. I'd like to build my own house and I'd have a big forge, open to the outdoors. I'd work there. Sell my wares all over—' He stopped, realizing he was getting ahead of himself, wary suddenly of the way she was looking at him. Full of pain, perhaps, trying desperately not to think of the words: *his death.*

'You should make the weather vane, Attis,' Anna said, her voice faint, as if she could flatten the emotion in it. 'You deserve it . . . all of it.'

He stared back at her, fierce and sad, but then the fire went out of him. 'Maybe one day.'

'You get to choose, you know,' she found herself saying, 'what you believe in. You can believe in yourself, your right to live.'

'Anna—'

She moved back from him, all of it suddenly too much. The proximity of him. The warmth. The pain. He did not deserve to die. 'I should get back. I've got a song to finish.'

'I want a full performance soon!' he called after her.

She ran up the stairs, tears spilling from her eyes.

Selene was in the kitchen, the cauldron stirring itself, bottles everywhere, the smoothie maker whirring a misty substance. Anna wiped her eyes as Selene turned.

'Darling . . .' But then Selene spotted her hands blackened by the forge and her smile faltered. 'What have you been doing?'

Anna went over to the sink to wash them. 'Just helping Attis.'

The cauldron stopped stirring. 'I'm not sure that's a good idea.'

Anna spun around to face Selene, the emotion she'd been holding back getting the better of her. 'Why not? I'm not going to throw myself at him if that's what you're worried about. I can control myself.'

Selene frowned. 'What's that meant to mean?'

'Are you still seeing Reiss?'

'You know I am.'

'Why? I've asked you to stop.'

'We're simply enjoying each other, darling, I don't see the harm.'

'You never do! You just carry on doing what you want no matter the consequences! He's working with the WIPS, you know? He provided the surveillance system at our school.'

'He's on the school board and owns the biggest surveillance company in the country. It was inevitable.'

Anna shook her head, biting her lip. She couldn't tell Selene about their break-in, about the invoice. 'It's more than that. Peter says he believes in what they do.'

'I've dated plenty of cowans who would be terrified to find out I'm a witch.'

'It's different now, you know that. Our school is under attack! You know what Attis is doing down there? Forging nails to protect against spiritual attack, trying to protect all of us, while you're making love potions or off with Peter's dad.'

Selene's eyes flashed with anger. 'I am doing what I can, but I still have a life! I can't just stop!' She bit her lip. The cauldron trembled with bubbles.

Anna moved away, trying to collect herself, to steady her breathing. She had a question she needed to ask Selene, something she needed to know. 'Selene. The spell to create Attis . . . the only thing you knew of it was that his blood was required? My mother never said anything else?'

Selene's eyes narrowed, spilling violet. 'Why do you ask? Have you found something?'

'No,' Anna lied instantly. Part of her wanted to tell Selene what she'd read, to cry in her arms and have Selene tell her everything would be OK. But that wouldn't happen. Selene would see it as further proof that his death was necessary. 'We're still searching – I just – I want to know everything.'

'She didn't say anything else, just that his blood was required. Well . . .'

'What?' Anna stepped closer, the cauldron's spiced scents overwhelming.

'She said that she intended to find out more out about the spell if she could. I don't think she wanted us to ever have to sacrifice him, but she thought she had time, all the years of you and Effie growing up . . .'

Anna clung onto Selene's words. Marie had known the spell but she hadn't wanted to accept it as it was.

'But you are grown up now,' Selene's voice grew urgent. 'And the curse has already begun. We are running out of time. He's . . .' she turned away, 'the only way.'

Anna's emotions finally took over. 'He is not a solution! He's a boy – a man – a person with hopes and dreams and you're his mother. For the first time in your life, maybe it's time you started acting like one!'

Selene's mouth dropped but Anna was gone, storming out the door and back up the stairs. It was their first real argument but Anna didn't regret her words. She hadn't realized just how angry she was at Selene too, that she'd never really forgiven her either. She couldn't just stand

and watch her treat Attis like that any more. Like he was nothing when he was *everything*.

I will not let him die.

I will not let him die.

I will not let him die.

Her mother had wanted to find another way and she would too. There was more of Nana's riddle, wasn't there? Perhaps there were other paths she could still take . . .

You must go down to come back up,

Learn the truth where all forget,

The mirrored book knows the way to the dead.

But heed his offer, hold tight your thread . . .

It was the part of the riddle she'd been trying to ignore, the part that beckoned all her fears to the surface and prickled her skin with frost.

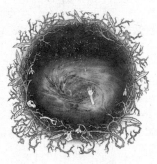

SINKING

How deep do the Rivers of the Dead run? As deep as the memories we try to forget. A single sip – a baptism of oblivion, to dissolve, to absolve, to cleanse the soul so it may be free. But who are we without the memories that unmade us?

Rivers of Forgetting, Books of the Dead: Tome 4993

Andrew banged Anna's locker, startling her. 'Move along to class or do you want me to perform another search?'

Anna tried to ignore him and the way his stare followed her down the corridor. Everyone was moving in single file, the whispers replaced by a deep but delicate silence on the edge of shattering. Anna didn't see the point in going to class. All the teachers she'd liked had been replaced by temps who seemed fully on board with what Eames was doing in the school. Her exams were still cancelled and she spent most lessons scared to speak or move lest she set off some kind of hysteria. Mini outbreaks were occurring all the time – pupils screaming if one of them came too near, Darcey setting off a crowd in assembly, a group of girls falling into fits when Anna had been working in the library on the table next to them. Not the hysteria spell but genuine hysteria – the lines blurring between the two now.

It was the same across the city. The outbreaks were increasing but it was hard to say how many attacks were the spell. Anna was sure at least two were the real deal – a protest march against the family planning clinic under WIPS investigation had unravelled. The protestors had descended on the clinic, unable to stop – shouting, screaming, louder and louder, smashing the glass windows of the building with their own hands, attacking the people inside. Lost in the mists of their hatred, gripped by the fear of the spirit – a toxic, volatile combination. Fortunately there'd been no fatalities, but then, two days ago, revellers in an underground club in Soho had drunk and danced themselves to death. They'd been found the next morning.

Anna thought of how they'd danced on the rooftops, shadows unloosed, *stamping, stamping, stamping* . . .

So much power unleashed, but nothing had come of it yet. It had been over a week and Eames was still running the school. Anna had seen him only yesterday in the corridor speaking to Peter's dad. The sight had made her shudder, to see them allied. Reiss had spotted her looking and winked.

Peter was waiting for her when she got out of her first class. They'd been spending more time together. Just little moments – letting him 'escort' her to class, eating outside at lunchtime away from the cameras, working on the same table in the library when he was stationed there to watch over them all. The lines were beginning to blur between them too. Anna didn't know why she was doing it, whether it was all just for Effie's plan, to keep him sweet as the dangers tightened around them – he seemed to be Eames's prefect of choice – or whether it was to distract herself. So she didn't have to think about Attis.

'Hey, Everdell.' He smiled. 'Free period next?'

'Yep.' Anna smiled back. 'I've got two hours to revise for exams I'm not allowed to take.'

Peter's face fell. 'You will. Once the real culprits are discovered your exams will be reinstated. You'll be free again.' His eyes were earnest.

Anna nodded, wishing he didn't see the world in such black and white terms, thinking he was on the side of the righteous, that he was somehow protecting her, when the truth was so much more complicated. That Eames himself might be casting the very spell they were fighting.

'I'm not on duty in the library but I can take you there if we're quick,' he said, scanning the corridor.

They started to walk together. 'I feel like I'm getting special prefect treatment,' said Anna.

'I'm just keeping a close eye on potential suspects.' He winked in a way that reminded her briefly of his father. 'Especially the hot ones.'

Anna shook her head at him. 'Oh, I saw your dad with Eames yesterday. Do you know why he was here?'

'Just checking over the surveillance system.'

She nodded, not sure how to dig any further. 'So . . .' she said, changing the subject. 'How are you feeling about him and . . . Selene?' She hadn't yet brought it up with him directly, but she'd overheard Effie taunting him about it.

Peter's jaw stiffened. 'Can't say I'm thrilled but my father's love life is his own. I don't think he's likely to settle down with anyone, he's too busy with his work and since—' His voice grew tight. 'Since my mother left us I don't think he's been interested in all that . . . Finding someone, marrying again.'

Anna stopped outside the library. Peter had never opened up to her before about his mother. The tautness of his features hinted at hidden pain. 'I'm sorry that she left.'

He shrugged, his eyes a cold blue. 'She cheated on him. A two-year affair. Then, she walked out. I wouldn't have chosen to live with her anyway. I'm happy with my dad.'

'Well, I'm glad you have him. And you'll be glad to hear that Selene isn't the settling-down type either.'

'I can believe that.' Peter looked down the corridor, at an approaching set of pupils. 'Anyway, I better go. Keep your head down and your chin up, Everdell.'

'I'll try not to lose it entirely.' She made eyes at him as he moved away before heading into the library.

When the coven met that evening, Effie appeared to have already lost it. 'Why hasn't Eames gone? Why is his ugly face still parading the corridors?' she shouted, the lights of the sewing room flickering with her rage.

'It might still happen,' said Rowan, ever the optimist.

Effie kicked at a mannequin. 'No. He's resisting our spell somehow. It's proof that he's got magic up his sleeve, he's using it to protect himself while he casts the hysteria.'

Attis was sitting on one of the desks with a deep frown, as if some-thing were playing on his mind, but he couldn't work out what. Anna still hadn't spoken to Selene since their argument over him and she'd been avoiding Attis too. Whatever she'd claimed to Selene about being in control, she knew it wasn't true. That her feelings for him were spiralling, tangling, holding her hostage to the curse. A curse that demanded his death. Effie, meanwhile, seemed to have forgotten their curse even existed, channelling her restlessness into distraction – partying and drinking with Manda, seeing Azrael. But then Anna hadn't told Effie about finding Attis's spell in the Bible. She wanted to, she desperately wanted to open up to her sister about it all, but she didn't know what Effie would do. If she'd tell Attis.

'What I don't understand,' said Rowan, falling into a seat, 'is why not just find us guilty now? Eames has enough to pin on us. Why wait?'

'Because he's enjoying it,' Effie spat. 'Ramsden under his thumb, the prefects at his bidding, the protestors outside. He's enjoying squeezing the life out of everything and everyone. And when he sets the hysteria off again – he'll enjoy that too.' She banged the desk, making Manda jump, which wasn't hard. Manda was permanently jumpy these days, a jittery echo of her former self – thin and colourless, her eyes sunken with exhaustion, the kind you can't shake off. The look in them was far away, dislocated.

Effie looked pointedly at Anna. 'Has Peter given away anything about Eames's plans? You two are spending a lot of time together.'

Anna stiffened, staring hard back at Effie. 'Peter hasn't said anything,' she replied bluntly, glancing at Attis but he'd looked away.

Anna moved away too, picking up the snow globe from the altar and turning it upside down – London on its head, the snow lifting from it and sinking downwards, finding no way out.

You must go down to come back up,
Learn the truth where all forget . . .

The final part of Nana's riddle felt like her burden to bear now, she was the only one who believed in it any more. *The mirrored book knows the way to the dead . . .* If the mirrored book was the book of fairy tales then how could it show her the way to the dead? Some sort of death magic spell to help stop the hysteria? Or something . . . worse? *Heed his offer, hold tight your thread!* Whose offer? What thread? Why did Nana's riddles make no sense until they did?

She flicked the snow globe back over, the city carrying on as if nothing had happened, the tiny lights of cars driving on the roads, the River Thames chasing its own black, serpentine waters through the centre. When would the next hysteria strike? And how many people would die?

'Cillian's messaged,' said Rowan.

Effie pulled a shocked face. 'Sexting again . . .'

'Haha. He wants to meet this weekend. He says there's something we need to know.'

Effie put her hands together, steepling her fingers. 'The plot thickens. Tell him we'll be there. Saturday afternoon?'

The others nodded in agreement. Anna's hand was gripping the snow globe tightly. 'Any more from him on the missing witches?'

Rowan bit her lip. 'No. Perhaps he wants to talk to us about it.'

Attis rubbed his face, his jaw clenching. 'Let's carry on with training. If the hysteria strikes here again your circles won't be strong enough to withstand the death magic entirely but they might buy you enough time to run.'

Anna wasn't so convinced. Attis hadn't felt the spirit's magic for himself – he didn't know how powerful, how paralysing it could be. Circles, nails, blades of protection . . . none of them would be enough. Still, if it made him feel better, she would do it.

Anna faced Effie. She could feel the rapid pulse of Effie's emotions, but Anna was beginning to understand Effie's bursts of power, to sense the patterns in them, finding their weak spots . . . giving her time to break through here and there and send her own pinches back. Today, almost as many as Effie had landed. Effie grew frustrated, though she laughed as she growled, as if she still welcomed the challenge, the game, even as she intended to land the final punch, which she did. A hard thump on Anna's arm.

'You still haven't managed to turn any of my pinches to punches,' Effie gloated.

'I'm aware,' Anna retorted. She didn't know how. She was finding it easier to hold her circle against Effie's attacks and to rebound Effie's magic, but to use her own magic to transform the attack seemed to require something . . . deeper . . . but when she sought it out, she found nothing but darkness and silence.

'Forget what's holding you back,' Attis urged, sensing her frustration. 'Focus on your magic instead. Trust it.'

They swapped over and Anna started against Rowan but they hadn't been playing long when Manda started to cough dramatically. They turned to her – she was bent over, a hacking sound coming from her.

Attis rushed over. 'Manda, are you OK?' She put a hand to her head, looking as if she might faint again. 'Why don't you rest for a bit?'

She yanked her arm away from him. 'I'm just hungover. I'm fine.'

He seemed taken aback by her sharpness. Anna hadn't seen Manda touch school work for weeks as if, now that their futures had been put on hold, she'd finally snapped. Was she simply losing it like the rest of them? Or was it something more?

'It happens,' said Effie, throwing an arm around her. 'Especially when you go out with me.'

Manda rolled her eyes. 'I can handle it.'

'Maybe we can *all* go out after meeting Cillian?' Effie suggested.

'I don't really feel like partying right now, Effie,' Anna snapped, exasperated.

Effie turned to her scowling but, before she could retort, Manda spoke up.

'I can't do Saturday night anyway. Karim and I have a special dinner date planned.'

Rowan swivelled to her. 'Wait, you have a special date planned . . . in the middle of everything going on?'

Manda lifted her chin stubbornly. 'It's important. I wasn't going to say anything but—' She smiled suddenly, her cheeks too hollow to carry it. 'We're engaged.'

'WHAT?' Rowan's mouth fell open and stayed there. 'Engaged to what?'

Manda flickered her eyes disdainfully. 'Each other, obviously.'

'Are you . . . sure?' The words fell out before Anna could stop them.

Manda glared. 'What? Because no one could possibly love me enough to want to marry me? Yes, I'm sure. I thought you'd all be happy for me. Is that too much to ask?'

'We are . . .' Rowan tried to recover. 'Just in an extremely concerned way. Isn't this a weird time to get engaged?'

'Karim asked, OK?' Manda snapped. 'It's not like we're getting married next week. He's going to buy me a promise ring. It's a symbol of our commitment that we'll be married one day.'

Effie snorted. 'Come on, Manda, you don't even like Karim. You were making out with someone else last night—'

'Shut up, Effie! We love each other!'

Anna tried to reason with her. 'You're seventeen – are you sure you want to commit to something like this *now*?'

'Are you sure you haven't fallen on your head recently?' Rowan added.

'Are you sure Karim isn't tied up in your basement?' Attis tried to keep a straight face.

Manda stood up, her own face contorting. 'You're all just jealous!' She jerked her head towards Rowan. 'Because you can't get a boyfriend if you tried.' Then to Anna and Effie, 'And you're both in love with Attis and none of you will ever, EVER be happy!' Her words turned into another coughing fit as she grabbed her bag and ran out of the sewing-room door.

Rowan called after her.

'I'll go.' Effie jumped up. 'Try and knock some sense into her.' She ran out of the door after her.

Anna could see Rowan trying to cover up the hurt on her face as she shook her head. '*What* is going on?'

'I have no idea any more.' Attis exchanged a brief, uncomfortable glance with Anna, Manda's words still reverberating around the room.

'They haven't got their shadowrobes,' Anna realized with fresh alarm. Manda running about unconcealed in the state she was in wasn't safe. At least surveillance hadn't made it to the lowest floor.

'Mother, maiden and crone!' Rowan exclaimed. 'Let's go!'

They all leapt up, Anna grabbing Manda and Effie's robes as they each covered themselves and headed out of the door.

'I'll go right, you guys go left,' said Attis. 'See if we can find them.'

Rowan and Anna edged down the corridor. There was the sound of voices coming from the stairwell.

Rowan went to open the door but Anna whispered, 'Don't.' She wasn't sure why – it was something about the fraught tone of their voices. Anna could see through the window Manda against the wall, Effie bearing over her.

'Leave me alone,' Manda hissed. 'You can't make me.'

'I can!' Effie snarled back. 'You have to listen to me, get yourself back under control. It's gone too far, the others are going to realize—'

Rowan moved too close, rattling the door handle, and Effie's voice cut off. They both looked towards the door and Rowan opened it, feigning ignorance. She took off her shadowrobe. 'Just me! We brought you your shadowrobes.'

Anna took off her robe too.

Effie backed away from Manda. 'I was just telling Manda how I fundamentally disagree with the institution of marriage, how she'll be chaining herself to a life of mediocrity . . . but apparently, this is what she wants.'

Manda ducked free of Effie and snatched her robe off Anna. 'I don't care what any of you think!' She lurched for the door, disappearing into the shadows.

Effie turned back to Anna and Rowan with a shrug. 'I tried, but I don't think she's coping well with everything going on.'

'Seems not,' said Rowan, looking after Manda with worry.

But Anna held Effie's gaze, trying to read it, trying to see through the facade, but Effie's defences were too tight. 'I'm sure you did your best.'

Effie smiled at her and it landed like a punch. The kind of smile you use to lie to your sister.

On Friday, Anna sat in the library, pretending to work but it was impossible. It wasn't only the whispers around her but the whispers in her mind, muttering with her own suspicions. *What had they been talking about? Why were they keeping it from the rest of us?* She wanted to trust Effie, but the truth was – she didn't. There was still too much between them and so much of Effie she couldn't fathom. Effie had used magic for her own games last year; who was to say she wouldn't again? But how was Manda involved? And was it something to do with the way Manda had been acting?

The whispers around Anna grew more frantic, people shooting her nervous looks, the tension rising in the room, as if they could sense her unease. The last thing she wanted was another outbreak of hysterics. She looked down at her paper, startled as she realized that the words she'd been distractedly scribbling had begun to resemble something like the Language of the Dead . . .

Anna scrunched the paper up and stuffed it in her bag, making for the door. She needed to get out. *Now.* According to the latest rules, you weren't meant to be outside of one of the allotted areas if you weren't in class, but she couldn't breathe in there. She would go to the sixth-form canteen, that was allowed, it might be quieter . . . only, she found herself slowing as she passed the music room. She stopped. *Just two minutes* . . . she told herself . . . *two minutes won't hurt.*

The piano started playing before she'd even sat down, the music rushing out of her. Anna joined it, her fingers uniting with the keys, feeling the release she'd been craving, the tightness in her throat easing, her heart free to beat again—

The door opened behind her.

'Well, well, well, caught in the act.'

Everything closed back up. Anna turned slowly on her stool to find Andrew in the doorway. He must have seen her enter. *Stupid, stupid, stupid.* She jumped up, reaching for her bag. 'I was only practising the piano . . . I'll be on my way.'

But he stepped into the room and let the door shut behind him. 'I think you know as well as I that you're not allowed in here, don't you?' He let the question sit between them, tilting in the direction of his power. 'You're smart, I remember that from class. Not smart enough, it seems.'

'Andrew, come on.' Anna kept her voice light. 'It was two minutes, let me go. What's the point in reporting this to Eames? He has enough against me already.'

'True,' he said, his eyes travelling over her in a way that made her skin shrink. 'Reporting you being in the music room is something and nothing, but then again, I could tell him I saw you doing magic in here. There are no cameras. Your word against mine.' He raised his eyebrows, his lip curling over his teeth.

Anna backed up against the piano, heart hammering – the room around her had always felt like an escape, but now it felt as small as a trap. 'That's not true.'

Andrew shrugged. 'Truth feels a little more malleable these days, doesn't it? Of course, you might be able to change my mind . . .' He snorted as if embarrassed by his own suggestion, but his eyes ran over her again – quickly, excitedly. Anna's body prickled at the rising threat. She looked past him. He wasn't big . . . she could try to get around him . . .

'Andrew, *please*—'

He stepped closer to her. 'I just want to see what all the fuss is about . . .'

Anna would rather anything than *this*. She threw her bag at him and tried to dart past him towards the door, but he grabbed her and pushed her against it. His hands roved roughly over her as he tried to kiss her, his breath hot against her cheek. She kneed him between his legs. He keeled forwards, giving her enough time to grab the door handle and shove her way out.

She fled down the corridor and around the corner. She could hear

Andrew chasing after her. Another corner and then – *Peter*. Peter was standing guard outside a doorway. She ran to him, hands shaking.

He took them. 'Anna, what's wrong?'

'Andrew—' she breathed as Andrew appeared behind them. 'He tried to force me—'

'She was in the music room alone.' Andrew tried to catch his breath, to sound confident. 'I was just questioning her when she ran.'

'No!' Anna spluttered. 'He pinned me against the wall, he tried to – to—' Her whole body was shaking.

Peter's head snapped to Andrew. 'Did you touch her?'

'Not really.' Andrew shrugged. 'Come on, Nowell, I was just having a bit of fun. You know how it is . . .'

Peter's eyes narrowed, looking between them, weighing and measuring the situation. 'Go to Eames's office now,' he said to Andrew, slowly, coldly. 'He'll be hearing about this.'

Andrew forced a laugh, hard and hateful. 'You're blind, she's as much of a whore as Effie—'

'Go!' Peter roared.

Andrew bit back his response, his teeth chewing at his lip in anger as he hunched his shoulders and left. Peter turned back to her. 'Anna. That should never have happened. I'll make it clear to Eames what really went on, insist that Andrew is removed as a prefect. He won't get away with it.'

Anna breathed out, but everything in her body still felt tight, on guard, strangely separate from herself. She looked back down the corridor. 'I need to get my bag, I left it back there—'

Peter nodded. 'OK. Let's go and get it.'

They walked to the music room in silence. Her bag was on the floor, the contents spilt. Peter helped her pick it all up. They stood up straight, facing each other. Peter looked beyond her to the door.

'You shouldn't have been in here alone. Anything could have happened.'

Anna pulled back from him, feeling a flush of anger at his words. 'I was only playing the piano.'

'I know.' He reached for her but she wrapped her arms around herself. 'I just can't protect you if you make yourself vulnerable.'

'Protect me?' Anna cried. 'It's you lot we need protecting from! Eames is letting this all happen!'

'I've told you,' Peter replied, more sternly. 'I'll deal with Andrew on your behalf. He doesn't represent us, or Eames. The school is under attack and we are needed – we are his eyes.'

'Why not use teachers? Don't you see?' Anna tried to reason with him. 'He wants you young and pliable, drunk on the power.'

Peter stiffened. 'You really think so little of me? That I'm doing this as some sort of power trip when all I've done is my best to look out for you?' He looked at her, wounded.

She held back her response, gripping her arms. 'Peter . . . I know you believe in what you're doing, I just don't trust the people you're working for, or with.'

'I understand,' he said, as if she didn't. 'But the WIPS are the experts in these matters. They are putting systems in place to keep us all safe.'

Anna wanted to scream at him that the system was the very thing they should be scared of but she knew there was no point, that getting into an argument would only distance him. 'You're right. I know they're trying to keep us safe, it's just – it's a confusing time.'

He nodded, his eyes softening. 'I'm sorry, I'm stressed too. Just the thought of something happening to you—' He moved towards her. She let him put his hands on her.

'Thank you for helping.'

He drew her into his arms and held her for a moment. Anna sobbed against his shirt, realizing that she was still shaking.

He pulled back. 'I've wanted to tell you something.'

'What is it?'

'I don't want to drag this all up again, but I'm tired of people taking advantage of you. That night, at the ball, when Effie and I—' He stopped and Anna nodded for him to go on. 'I just want you to know that Effie came to me. She kissed me. It's no excuse for what I did, but I just want you to be careful. Like I said, your association with her isn't helping you—'

'Peter.' Anna pulled away, trying not to let his words get under her skin. 'She's my friend. I'm not going to turn my back—'

That was when they heard the screams.

The sounds of terror Anna hadn't realized just how intently, how fearfully, she'd been waiting for, knowing they would come.

'It's here,' she whispered, feeling the rising cold, her legs turning rigid, her body beginning to tremble with fresh violence.

Peter looked up, alert. The screams were coming from beyond the window. 'Wait here,' he instructed, but Anna had no intention of waiting. She'd been waiting too long.

She cast her circle, trying to defend herself against the feeling of death magic as they ran towards it, seeking it out. They rushed through a door to the outside, where students were running from the sports building, screaming. Peter seized a girl. 'What's happening?'

'Swimming – swimming pool . . .' Her voice quaked.

Peter let her go and ran in that direction. Anna could see the glass conservatory of the swimming pool ahead . . . commotion inside. The screams were coming from inside. She followed Peter's pathway through the doors and into the pool. So much was familiar – the wet floors, the smell of chlorine, echoes rebounding off the walls – but everything was wrong. The echoes were formed of cries and the pool was full of bodies. Bodies swimming, splashing, flailing, floundering, around and around and around, as if some great well was sucking them down into the centre. There were too many people in there . . . too many . . . some in swimwear, some in uniform as if they'd jumped in . . . clambering over one another, dragging each other under, swimming downwards . . . as if trying to drown themselves . . .

People ran from the room as others joined – some teachers and prefects. Anna was pushed aside – the noise growing as people started trying to drag those in the pool out. She saw Peter, without hesitation, throwing off his blazer and start reaching for people. Anna wanted to do the same but she could feel her body slowing down, coming apart as the paralysis of the magic took over, so potent, so dense with darkness that her circle could not keep it out.

A hand landed on her shoulder. She turned to find Effie, her eyes as wide as a scream, her face battling with the magic too. Side by side, they joined hands.

In the midst of the chaos, Anna closed her eyes, feeling Effie's power blast through her, their fear unite, their magic unite, her own circle growing stronger – expanding – deflecting the darkness and pushing outwards.

Anna opened her eyes and gasped. The vicious swirl of the water appeared to have slowed down and . . . the pool was snowing. *Snowing upwards.* The top layer of water rising up as snowflakes into the air above, filling the conservatory. For a moment, the sight held Anna mesmerized – but the bodies below still thrashed desperately.

Anna and Effie let go of each other and moved forwards. Anna dropped to her knees and grabbed the arm of a girl swimming by. The girl raged against her, not wanting to be saved, but Effie joined the struggle and together they pulled the girl from the water. The girl's limbs were flailing madly. She tried to claw herself back into the pool but they held her down through her sodden uniform. Her eyes held the dread of the spell, trapped in a tunnel with no end. A teacher dragged the girl further from the epicentre of the hysteria and Anna went back to help more people. But it was too late to save them all . . .

Bodies were already floating. It had been too long. The spell had beckoned them too deep.

In the reflection of the water, Anna saw Aunt's face, not her own.

WELL-MEET

The Tower of London's Ceremony of the Keys is reputed to trace its origins to an ancient and protective spiritual rite carried out by Bran the Blessed and his followers upon White Hill. The annals of lore maintain that the shadow-keys used in the rite were bestowed upon Bran by Mother Holle herself – the same keys employed today to secure the fortress gates of the Tower.

'Locks, Keys and Riddles', Mysteries of the Metropolis (Published 1893)

'We may have no choice but to enact a plan we have been considering for a while.' Bertie looked at them frankly across the table in Selene's kitchen, her apple cheeks sunk low. 'Escape.'

Rowan stared at her mum. 'What do you mean . . . escape?'

Bertie's fingers hovered about her tea cup, too unsettled to hold it still. 'Take you all into hiding in the magical world. There are places we can go.'

'So, run away?' said Effie in a scathing tone.

'Give up our lives?' Rowan stuttered.

'There have been deaths now, Sorbus,' Bertie replied, holding firm, though her voice threatened to break. 'You are not safe, from any of it – the spell, the investigation. People are angry, parents are up in arms, the press is ravenous, people want answers, retribution—' Bertie looked lost for a moment, her mouth still moving but no words coming forth. 'This may be growing too big for us to contain.'

Anna looked down into the steam of her coffee cup, waves of despair rolling through her, a feeling of needing to cry. When she shut her eyes, all she could see were the bodies floating in the pool, the snow drifting upwards, Aunt's face in the water. Her own fears reflected back at her, her own shadows of death chasing her.

She'd been waiting for the shock of it all to settle but it wouldn't. It rocked and roiled as if she were a body in that water too and in her dreams the waters were black and filling up the third-floor room but she couldn't swim, her limbs were threaded. She was drowning – drowning—

They'd known the hysteria spell could take lives, but part of her hadn't really believed it would ever happen at St Olave's. But now, two pupils were dead. Two lives snatched by the spirit. A swim training session turned into a nightmare.

After it all happened, they'd escaped being dragged to the Ebury wing. Police and the emergency services had arrived and everyone had been sent home. St Olave's had called it a swimming accident and announced that it was to remain closed until after the Easter break, if it reopened at all.

Pupils swim themselves to death in latest hysteria outbreak!

Dreaded malefice leaves two pupils drowned at St Olave's

Are our schools safe? Schoolchildren sucked into madness of malefice

There was almost too much information, too many videos, too many questions for anyone to know what was happening. And they were at the very centre. Hopkins had released a statement that left no shadow of doubt as to what was going on:

'It has finally happened, the lives of our young lost to malefice. We will not let this go. We will find the witches responsible and we will bring them to justice. Support us, join us, help us to stop the spread.'

Bertie took a sip of tea. 'If a plant is threatened, sometimes you have to move it to the garden, into a pot for a while . . .'

'No one is potting me,' Effie hissed.

'What about Manda?' Rowan asked. 'She has cowan parents, she can't just . . . leave.'

'Manda may have to explain the situation to her parents,' said Selene, looking over her cup as if she were hiding behind it. 'I'm sure they'd—'

'Pah!' Manda laughed. She looked the worst of them, her skin thin as lace, dark shadows carved beneath her eyes. 'They would never understand. If I tell them I'm a witch on the run, they'll tell me to never come back.'

'Why can't the magical world find a way to stop the WIPS before they gain more power?' Effie banged the table. 'Now is the time!'

Bertie and Selene shared an uncomfortable glance. 'Attempts have been made, but it's proving difficult—' Bertie bit her lip, as if to stop herself saying any more.

'What you're saying is they're the Hunters returned!' Effie exploded. 'The very thing we've been trying to tell you all year, not that anyone's been listening. The magical world needs to do more! Aren't there groves out there who can deal with this sort of thing? Blow the WIPS to smithereens?'

'I don't think I need to explain why we aren't blowing things to smithereens, Effie.' Bertie tucked in her chin, giving Effie a steely look, but then she sighed. 'It's not that simple. There isn't some magical MI5 out there. The magical world doesn't operate by systems. If anything, quite the opposite. Witches are fierce individuals, each one leading her or his own life. Yes, there are groves, but you'd be lucky as a seven-leafed clover to get any sense of organization there. They operate in different ways – some are strict, some are secret, some are undefined, some are plain barmy – and straightforward lines of communication do not exist between them. The magical world operates in an entirely different way, more like the roots beneath our feet – connected, synergistic and a big old, wonderful mess. The Seven were our only form of management, but in their stead we are trying to bring the magical world together to fight this and we *will* fight this.'

'You have to trust us,' said Selene.

Effie shot Selene a look that said she was the last person in the world Effie was about to trust.

'We're not saying you're definitely being taken into hiding. Not yet,' said Bertie, 'but that we need to start considering it seriously and you need to be ready if that's the decision that's made. In the meantime, I've got something for you.' She reached for her handbag. She dug into it, pulling a variety of items out and onto the table – a packet of seeds, a Tupperware of cookies, keys, tissues, receipts, lip balm, a toy tiara and what appeared to be a gardening trowel on the table – before she found what she was looking for: five dark glass bottles. 'There's one for you each.'

Anna took a bottle and opened it up to find clear pills inside, a green powder within.

'Eyevain,' Bertie stated. Then listed its other names like an old habit. 'Faen, eye of the Goddess, witch's ally—'

'One of the sacred herbs of the Goddess,' said Anna.

Bertie nodded with a smile. 'You remember my teachings. Yes. As I told you, it's highly protective, but not just out there – within too. Take just one pill a week and it will keep your magic hidden from any kind of detection. It's just a precaution. And don't worry if one or two of the tablets starts to germinate; that happens occasionally. Just throw them away – or into the garden.'

Rowan was still staring at her bottle of Eyevain when they retreated upstairs to Effie's room, leaving Bertie and Selene muttering to one another downstairs. 'I can't believe that we're having to conceal our magic. Witches haven't had to use Eyevain in that way since . . .'

'Let me guess, the last witch hunts?' Effie barked.

Rowan nodded, her head dropping to the floor. 'Do you think we should run?'

'We have to,' said Attis, his brow so furrowed that Anna had begun to wonder if it was permanently dented. 'We don't know for sure who's behind the hysteria, we can't stop it and we're going to be blamed for it, especially now there have been deaths. The WIPS are growing more powerful and, as far as we're aware, cursed witches may be going missing.'

'We should have told Mum and Selene about that . . .' said Rowan.

'No,' Effie replied vehemently. 'Then they'll definitely force us to run. Let's not give them any more reasons to freak out. We don't even know if it's true.'

Rowan picked up a rogue shoe from Effie's floor, tapping its heel against the floor as she thought out loud. 'What would it even mean to run? Is it just me going into hiding or do my whole family have to join? Where do we go? For how long? I know my life is non-existent but I'm not ready to give it up . . .'

'Are you really so against disappearing into the magical world, Effie?' Manda asked. 'Would have thought you'd like it.'

'The magical world is a place of freedom. It shouldn't be a cage,' Effie replied from the bed. Her painting on the wall boiled with colour behind. 'If it's the Hunters we're facing, then face them we must.' There was a look in her eye that Aunt used to have when she spoke about the Hunters. An electric thrill. The lure of threat. Crisp aliveness. 'I said at the start of the year, I won't cower, I won't give up. I'm not going to let Eames win now.'

'No one is winning now!' Anna replied, harder than intended. 'The only thing we should be focusing on is stopping the hysteria spell before it kills again.'

'How?' Manda's voice rasped. 'Even *they* don't know how.' She gestured downstairs.

Anna breathed out. She didn't know but she could feel the spell drawing her in, as if its darkness had become an opening . . . *You must go down to come back up . . .*

'We find out what it is they're not telling us.' Effie cocked an eyebrow as if she had a trick card behind her back. 'Poppins has been in touch. Apparently, there's a Well-Meet happening tomorrow evening, the first in over two decades in London. I suspect Bertie and Selene are planning on going and we need to be there. In secret, of course.'

Anna frowned. 'What's a Well-Meet?'

'A traditional meet of witches,' Rowan explained. 'Not within groves but across groves, a kind of assembly. They meet at a well of truth – a well that runs with magical waters. They don't happen very often, only in times of crisis. I think, normally, the Seven would be there . . .' She looked down. 'I can tell Cillian to meet us there instead.'

'Yes,' said Effie with renewed exhilaration. 'We're not missing the action – and we're not running.'

Anna sat back, the bodies bobbing up through her thoughts again. She didn't care about leaving the cowan world behind – she hardly had much to lose – but she didn't want to hide away, not while people were dying.

'Clerkenwell,' Attis stated. 'The key is in the name. The area is named after the ancient well here.'

'Really?' Anna leant forwards from the back seat of the car. 'Clerkenwell is named after a magical well?'

He nodded. 'We call them Mother-Wells – sacred springs of ancient and magical rivers. There are several across London, but from what I've read, this one was once an ancient meeting site beyond the city, originally in a wooded grove, where Well-Meets were traditionally held, but that was centuries ago. As the city was built up around it, cowans adopted the well for their own uses, predominantly Christian clerics who believed its sacred waters were holy, and so it became known as Clerk's Well.'

'And now it lies in a pub?'

'Almost entirely forgotten,' Attis replied, 'but apparently still in use by our kind.'

'Ideal really,' said Effie. 'Find out the magical world is under attack and then get pissed.'

Attis pulled the car up on a quiet side street. They stepped out and walked to the corner they'd all agreed to meet at, the sign for Farringdon station visible further down the street, edged with the on-coming darkness of evening. Rowan arrived first, the words spilling out of her.

'Mum left half an hour before me and was very vague about where she was going . . . so I'm sure she's going to be here. I can't believe she didn't tell me.' Rowan looked around the street guiltily. 'I'm sneaking on her sneaking.'

'She's just trying to protect you,' said Anna. 'Selene went out too, so we suspect she's headed here.'

'That or a date,' Effie said. 'Hard to know.'

Manda arrived, bundled up in a coat though it wasn't particularly cold – spring had begun to warm the air, to drive away winter's stubborn cold. Anna hadn't been sure she'd come.

'So . . . did you and Karim decide to call off the engagement dinner celebration?' Rowan asked tentatively.

'No. It's happening tomorrow instead,' Manda snapped.

'Madness . . .' Effie muttered.

Anna was thankful for the sight of Poppins coming down the street, leaning on his umbrella. He was flanked this time by the flaxen-haired Bridy and Jeudon. No Ollie.

Poppins stopped and propped his umbrella out in front of him, an eyebrow raised to them, arched and conspiratorial as a cat's tail. 'We meet again.' He cast a smile. 'And what an occasion – a Well-Meet. I haven't heard of such a thing before, not in our lifetimes. The magical world must be quite discombobulated.'

'That's one word for it,' Effie replied dryly.

Poppins cleared his throat. 'I'm sorry to hear what happened at your school.'

'So awful,' said Bridy, her features dimpling.

Jeudon nodded, silent as ever.

Attis put a hand on Poppins's shoulder. 'Thanks, and thank you for informing us about today.'

Poppins's smile snapped back into place. 'Well, we can't miss out on all the gossip, can we?'

'Is Cillian with you?' Rowan asked, looking behind them.

'No.' Poppins eye-rolled. 'He's very hard to keep track of, tends to turn up unannounced, usually at some inconveniently timed moment. Apparently, he has fresh information for us. How exciting. Now, shall we sneak into this thing?' He looked at a watch on his wrist – its glass face was missing. 'It's about to kick off.'

'We're going to wear our shadowrobes,' Effie explained. 'It's probably better we're not seen tonight for various reasons . . .'

'You sneaky little devils, you.'

The Coven of the Dark Moon disappeared into the evening and followed the Wild Hunt to a compact, green-fronted pub with an anti- quated sign declaring it: *THE JERUSALEM TAVERN*. A few after-work drinkers were gathered outside, gripping pints, too engrossed in their own conversations to notice Poppins, Bridy and Jeudon slip through the door.

Inside, the pub was small and dimly lit with dark green walls, scrubbed wooden floors and rickety tables dotted with a few customers. A tiled mosaic above the fireplace showed an image of a woods with a slice of moon above it. There was the head of a Green Man carved in wood above the bar. The smell of beer suds and old peat pervaded. The land- lady nodded at Poppins and the others and placed three empty glasses on the bar. They picked them up and ducked through a small doorway to the side which led down a corridor and out into a pub garden. Surrounded by stone walls, it looked more like a courtyard and it was already full of people, around fifty, some robed and some in ordinary dress. *Witches.*

Anna weaved through the throng, careful not to touch anyone, tucking herself with the others to one side, against the wall. In the centre of the courtyard was a low, round stone protrusion – a well – surrounded by a small fence with a plaque. A row of witches were gathered behind it; looking out. Anna counted seven, but not *the* Seven, for Bertie was among them in robes of green lined with fresh vegetation; and another witch Anna recognized too – Mór – standing poised and self-contained in black robes, embroidered with snowflakes.

Anna scanned the crowd slowly. She spotted Selene's golden hair, her head bobbing up and down as she chatted to the witch beside her. She saw a few Wort Cunnings she recognized from Christmas and a small cluster of Hel witches – still and solemn among the animation of everyone else – Yuki and Azrael among them.

It wasn't long before one of the witches in front of the well stepped forwards. He was small in stature with a mane of white-grey hair, a greyer beard and a purple robe patterned with silver letters. Yet his presence drew the attention of the onlookers who quickly quietened their gabbling as he began to speak.

'Welcome and moon-blessings friends,' he began in a voice so gentle it seemed to ruffle the leaves on the trees, so commanding it seemed to shake the very foundations of the courtyard. Silence fell to its knees before it. 'Thank you all for leaving the hustle and bustle and restless rustle of the city streets to meet us here, in this small alcove of peace, this secret slip of evening. Though it may not be the ancient wooded grove of old, the sacred waters still run beneath our feet, the old friends of the stars still stir above us and this pub now stands behind us, with the best selection of ales man can offer.' As he spoke, the deep lines of his face became mere instruments for the expression of his words, adding to their depth and humour. The crowd cheered and laughed. But then, the old lines of his face drew inward. 'There has not been a meeting of such a kind in many years, for as long as most of us can remember, and yet circumstance, and happenstance perhaps, demand it must be so. The magical world is always in a state of motion, ever riding the storms of time and change, but we find ourselves in deeper and more turbulent waves than we have known for some time. As you see for yourselves, the Seven are not yet beside us, are not yet here to guide us through this tempest, but in their lieu, seven representatives from seven ancient groves will stand and speak tonight. Be still and listen, let their voices be heard and you will all be given the opportunity to speak too. Remember, we are all one and in our oneness we are all, bound by the threads of the Great Spinner. I am Taliesin of the word witches and by the maiden, mother and crone, I declare this Well-Meet begun.'

In response to the reverberation of his voice, the power of his words, the fence and plaque around the well disappeared and greenery grew up over its old stones – moss and ivy and weeds, as if they had always been there, the cowan world giving way to the magical world beneath. The row of witches stepped forwards to join him.

By the Goddess of all and one,
We call forth your waters deep,
Rise up and fill our cups,
May only truth we speak.

There was the sound of gurgling as water rose up through the well. The witches each dipped their cups into it and held them aloft, the well water sparkling silver in the moonlight above. They each took a sip.

'Truth water,' Rowan whispered through their shadowrobes. 'It means when they speak they will only be able to tell the truth, which doesn't necessarily mean the whole truth. People can still be careful with their words.'

The rest of the crowd held up their own empty glasses and though they had not dipped them into the well their cups filled up too with the same silver water. Everyone drank.

Taliesin continued, his words more matter-of-fact but his voice still rich. 'The magical world has remained a peaceful place for centuries, quietly under wraps from the majority of cowans. This appears to be changing. As you may be aware, since the Seven were killed that fateful night, an organization known as the Witchcraft Inquisitorial and Prevention Services has come to light, gaining power in the cowan world and becoming vocal against our kind.'

Disgruntled murmurs ran through the crowd.

'In addition, we have uncontrolled magic spreading across the capital which we have reason to believe is—' he paused briefly, his voice descending an octave as he spoke again, 'death magic. A spirit unleashed.'

Murmurs turned to gasps.

'Cowans are dying. Magic has blood on its hands but who, what, why – the questions remain unknown.'

The witch beside him stepped forwards. He seemed near twice the height and bulk of Taliesin, bald, heavily pierced and with a tattoo crawling up his neck, against which an incongruous white robe flowed. 'I am Jacques of the Warders, Protectors of the City.' He cleared his throat, clearly not as confident at speaking as the word witch. 'My grove has been looking into the WIPS but it has not been easy. They are shrouded in secrecy. More recently we have made magical attempts to infiltrate both their internal intelligence, and their physical location at the Shard, which have been unsuccessful. It is as if—' he coughed again, 'as if they have magical protections of their own. A boundary we cannot cross.'

His statement set off further gasps.

Bertie stepped forwards to quell the crowd, putting her hands up. 'I am Bertie of the Wort Cunnings and I know it is a lot to take in, but the only conclusion we can draw is that the WIPS have access to magic. Coupled with their power and standing in the cowan world this makes them a tricky foe indeed. Who are they? What do they want? Should we be at least considering the possibility that what – or who – we are facing may be . . . the Hunters.'

This time the crowd exploded.

'Your voices will be heard!' Taliesin called, his voice soothing the rising racket.

A witch in a red robe stepped forwards. 'We should not be adding to the hysteria out there!' she declared, giving Bertie a blazing look.

'Declare yourself,' Taliesin reminded.

The red-robed witch turned to the crowd. 'I am Brigid of the Elemental witches and in these unsettled times we call for balance, not panic. Just because the Warders cannot penetrate the inner workings of this organization does not make them a definitive threat. We can't leap to such a conclusion and we shouldn't call on legends to explain what we don't understand . . .'

'With all due respect,' said Jacques, 'our magic is robust and no cowan organization would be able to withstand it.'

'Perhaps they *are* utilizing magic in some way but that does not make them the Hunters!'

'The Seven themselves said that they were hunted—' Bertie began but Brigid interrupted, the lining of her robe flaring with flame.

'According to whom? The Ogham? A grove that hardly anyone has seen or heard from in decades.'

Another of the line spoke up. 'We are here.' A woman clad in a brown robe stepped softly forwards. She had a plain, round face and a voice that creaked like the branches of a tree. 'We have always been here. We are never gone.'

'Did the Seven speak with you?' someone yelled from the crowd. 'Have you seen them?'

'We have not,' she replied. 'They sent us messages through the roots.

They are with the roots – resting, healing, regaining their former power. Such things take time.'

'Whether or not the Seven are speaking through roots,' said Brigid, looking flatly unconvinced, 'we should not be making rash decisions that impact the entirety of the magical world without them. We *should* be taking our time—'

'We may not have it!' Bertie cut her off, hands rising now to her hips. 'The WIPS are calling for power within Parliament, a move that could give them concrete influence within the cowan world. They're already running investigations against *witchcraft*. My own daughter is involved in one and—' She stopped, swallowing back her emotion. 'She has been questioned, held, subject to cruelties no teenager should have to face. Is this just the beginning?'

'We see no end.' Another stepped forwards in robes of dark navy, a mirror of the sky above. 'I am Non of the House of Fortune and the future is unclear. For some time, our Diviners have been struggling to see beyond the individual. When we look to the collective . . . we are met with darkness. Black waves and shadows. A prophecy that consumes all else – the prophecy of the Hunters' rise.'

'With all due respect,' said Taliesin, trying to quell the bristling crowd, 'prophecies tend to match the fears of the moment, do they not?'

'It is true, collective fear may have brought this particular prophecy to the forefront, but its persistence, its stubbornness, its *vastness* cannot be ignored.'

Anna's heart was beating loudly beneath her robe.

'The hysteria attacks across London are playing directly into the hands of the WIPS,' Bertie moved on. 'We must find a way to stop them.'

Jacques nodded. 'We are employing the use of protective symbols against spiritual attack, but the spell is immensely strong and as the fear swells, so too does its force—'

'She should stop it!' Someone in the crowd pointed at Mór. 'This is the Hel witches' mess to fix!'

Several others piped up alongside them.

'My friends, let us hear from Mór herself.' Taliesin gestured to her, forcing Mór to step forwards and, finally, speak.

'I am Mór of the Hel witches,' she said, straightening herself up, her voice so chilled Anna could imagine it freezing the well water that ran beneath their feet. 'It is with deep apprehension that we have learnt the origins of the hysteria spell are death magic, and yet it has not been cast by any in our grove, and the spell itself cannot be stopped.'

'It's your magic, you must end it!' someone shouted.

Mór looked at them and Anna could see the heckler shrink into their own robes beneath her gaze. 'The spell cannot be stopped this side of the Fabric. We are happy to assist in investigating its origins, in tracking down any ex-Hel witches or other practitioners of death magic who may be involved, but we are not willing to interfere with unknown spirits of the Underworld. It goes against all of our codes.'

'Your codes be damned!' The cry from the crowd set everyone else off – voices rising, clamouring to be heard.

'We will open up to all of you in just a moment.' But even Taliesin's voice could not quite calm the noise this time.

'OI!' Bertie bellowed. It appeared to do the trick – the crowd turning back to her. 'We will get nowhere arguing amongst ourselves. We do not have time. We're right in the middle of the nettle patch right now and we must forge a path out. We must spread word and gather representatives from each major grove in the country, forming a temporary council until the Seven have returned. We must establish quick lines of communication and unite the magical world against the threats we are facing—'

'We need to find the Seven, not attempt to replace them!' Brigid's temper flared.

'The Hel witches must work beside us to stop this—' Jacques began.

'We must look to the prophecy to guide us—' Non added to the fray.

The crowd kicked off again. Panic. Anger. Denial. Accusation. The magical world driven into its own form of hysteria. They began to turn on the Hel witches among them, and in the chaos Anna saw Mór slip from the edge of the row, walking swiftly along the wall towards the door.

'I'm going after Mór,' she said to the others.

Back out on the street, Anna yanked her robe off and ran. 'Mór!'

The dark figure of Mór stopped and swivelled, surprise managing to break through the cold composure of her features. 'Anna. What are you doing here?'

'We're always here.' Effie appeared too – followed by Rowan, Manda and Attis.

Mór's eyes turned over them. 'I should have known.'

Effie folded her arms. 'At least we're not running away like you.'

'I have done all I can,' Mór sighed, looking back towards the pub.

'Not enough!' Anna railed. 'People are dying.'

'Death is not the end—'

'That doesn't mean people shouldn't get to live!' said Anna, the emotion in her voice surprising herself and Mór, again. 'Everyone deserves to live! Goddess knows I've seen enough darkness in my life already, but I've seen so much light, so much wonder. Death may be eternal but life, life is precious. Every single life—' Anna stopped herself, her eyes catching Attis's. He looked away. Mór did too.

'You had your baby,' Anna said quietly, catching Mór off guard.

'Yes.' Mór's hands fluttered to her missing bump. 'A girl.'

'Congratulations.' Anna waited for Mór to look at her. 'The fight we're in might be bigger than just one spell. It might be the fight for our future, the future of all witches. It might be time to change the rules that have gone before . . . before it's too late.'

Mór stared at Anna, unflinching but something in her eyes giving way, just a little, before she left them all standing on the street in Clerkenwell.

Cillian appeared from around a corner, swirling his signature leather jacket around him.

'Mother Holle!' Rowan put a hand on her heart. 'Where did you come from?'

'I've been watching,' he replied.

'How reassuring.'

'You all attended the Well-Meet.' He stated it more than asked. He was wearing his shaded glasses again. 'So you already know that the WIPS are using magic.'

Before they could answer the pub door swung open and Poppins, Bridy and Azrael exited, coming down the street towards them. Effie must have told them they'd left. On arrival, Poppins fanned his hand in front of his face. 'It's getting heated in there, dolls. Achieving very little though. I told Jeudon to stay in case there's anything we miss. Cillian, my poppet, I see you have appeared. You have new information, no?'

Cillian's head turned up and down the street with vigilant suspicion. He beckoned them into a side alley. 'I do. I finally know what the fifth organizational arm of the WIPS is.'

They drew closer to him.

'It appears to be referred to as the Penitent. It's a magical department. They've been gathering witches to work for them, to fight on their side against the world of magic.'

'So the very people decrying malefice, calling us evil, depraved, are using it for themselves?' Effie snarled a laugh.

'Fight fire with fire,' Cillian replied matter-of-factly.

'They must have witches providing strong protections if the Warders can't break through,' said Attis. He asked the next question just as Anna was about to. 'And the missing witches?'

Cillian nodded. 'No new information. Still three witches missing as far as I'm aware, which is not a huge number across the entirety of the UK, but somewhat concerning when you consider the rumours they may all be inflicted with curse magic.'

Anna's mind sped ahead. If the WIPS had witches working for them, perhaps they had sources that could inform them about cursed witches. Could they have tracked them down? Taken them? To what purpose?

Bridy looked between everyone. 'What does this all mean?'

'I believe it means we're all in the deepest of shit,' Poppins replied. 'As I think they've all just worked out in there too.'

'It means I was right.' Effie spun around. 'The WIPS are behind the hysteria and Eames is one of the Penitent.'

They descended into the same fraught chatter as the witches inside the Well-Meet, no one truly knowing what to do. Anna walked to the mouth of the alleyway checking the pub – but no one else had left yet.

Rowan followed her. 'Should we go back in, do you think?'

'I reckon we heard everything we need to hear. While they're arguing among themselves, more people are going to die.'

'I can't believe this is happening . . .' Rowan whispered.

'I know.'

Rowan looked about suddenly. 'Has Cillian gone?'

There was no sign of him.

Rowan shook her head. 'How does he do that?'

As Anna scanned for him her eyes fell on Effie and Manda who were now talking quietly with Azrael. Anna thought she saw something being passed between them – something made of glass. *A bottle?* It glinted and was gone.

'Did you see that?' she hissed to Rowan.

'What?'

'Do you remember the other day . . . when we heard Effie and Manda talking in the stairwell?'

Rowan nodded earnestly.

'What do you think they were talking about?'

'I don't know, it sounded—'

'Tense, right? And Manda isn't herself.'

'I know. She's acting so weird. At first I thought it was just Manda pushed to the edge but . . . I don't know any more.'

'They're keeping something from us.'

Perhaps it was the bitterness in Anna's voice but Rowan gave her a serious look. 'I agree, but we can't fall apart right now.'

'They're the ones keeping us out of the loop,' Anna replied defensively.

'Why don't you just talk to Effie? If she knows something, she might open up to you.'

'It sounds so simple, doesn't it?'

Rowan gave Anna a wary face. 'You two have to stick together right now. I really don't like what Cillian is saying about cursed witches going missing, Anna.' She grabbed her hand. 'Whatever is going on with Effie and Manda, I'm sure it's nothing earth-shattering. Everyone is just having a really hard time.'

Anna nodded, but she glanced back at Effie and Manda with a suspicion she couldn't shake off. Effie could drink a well full of glittering truth water and still find a way to hide her lies in the shadows.

A KISS

Light the candles of the dead and pierce ten fresh pigs' eyes with bone needles.
Call up the Guardian Spirits and speak the following words ten times over:
'May they only have eyes for me. By flame and bone, so mote it be.' Seal the
spell with a kiss upon the shadow-lips of each Guardian Spirit. Bury the candle
ashes and eyes together beneath a waxing moon in the grounds of a graveyard.

'Spell of Infatuation', *Spirit Magicke, Books of the Dead: Tome 3777*

The next morning, Anna knocked on Effie's door, but no one answered.
Anna had tossed and turned all night. Inside her dreams – inside the
room on the third floor – Aunt had been waiting for her. Waiting and
laughing while the ravens cawed and clawed around her, sinking their
talons into Aunt's skin, tearing her back to bone. Anna had tried to
scream, but she'd had no voice, and when she looked down she was
bone too. Nothing but bone and threads left of her.

She could feel herself breaking. She needed to speak to Effie – to
confront the suspicions, to lay everything out before the curse pulled
them apart. *But where was she?* They'd all gone home last night after
the Well-Meet . . .

Downstairs, Anna was met with silence from Attis's floor below. She
thought of Peter's words of warning about Effie . . . *She came to me, she
kissed me* . . . Anna's suspicions sharpened, warped in a new direction.
Was Effie down there? With him? Was everything a lie?

She crept down the stairs. The door to Attis's room was shut. Anna
made towards it, but then she heard something clang in the forge. She
spun around and walked towards its door. Attis was in there, carving at

one of the workbenches with concentrated focus. He looked up, his eyes turning their focus to her. 'Are you OK?'

'No.' Anna shook her head, wondering how her thoughts had spiralled. She needed to get a grip on herself. 'You?'

'Nah.' He looked as if he hadn't done a lot of sleeping either, his hair stuck up like a mad scientist's. 'Last night was . . . a lot to take in.'

'Have you seen Effie?'

He rubbed his eyes. 'I think she's gone to see Manda.'

'Really?'

'Why do you look like that?'

Anna shrugged. 'It's just . . . they've been spending a lot of time together lately—' It was on the tip of her tongue – she wanted to tell Attis about the conversation she'd overheard between Manda and Effie, about what she'd seen the night before, but she held it in. 'Manda isn't herself, don't you think?'

Attis put his tools down with a weighty sigh. 'She's not. She's unwell – not eating, not sleeping properly, behaving erratically. It could be anxiety from the stress of everything. Manda needs order and routine to cope and, well, that's been blown apart.' He looked back down at what he'd been working on as if none of it made sense to him any more.

Anna followed his gaze, but her eyes landed on some papers to the side. She tilted her head. 'What are they?'

'Nothing.' He sounded guilty, trying to move the papers away, but she picked one up.

It was a design of something. 'It's your weather vane . . .'

'Just some old ideas I dug out the other day.' Attis took the paper off her, shuffling it away with the others. 'Stupid.'

'It's not stupid.'

'It is,' he said, sharply. 'A waste of time, just like everything else I'm doing. None of it's enough. You were there last night. The magical world talking openly about witches being hunted, the WIPS using magic for their own purposes, cursed witches—' He stopped as if he couldn't bear to say it out loud, shaking his head and pacing away.

She went after him. 'Attis—'

He spun around. 'If the WIPS . . . the Hunters find out about you and Effie . . .'

'They won't.' Anna tried to sound convincing.

Attis looked at her, desperation, fear fracturing his eyes. 'If I'd just done my job last year, ended the curse, then you and Effie would at least be free of that. Instead, it's got a hold of you, and with everything going on, you're both in more danger than ever—'

Anna took his arms. 'Don't talk like that.'

'How can I not?' he cried, his voice breaking.

'Because you promised me! You promised me you were going to try to live! You deserve to live, you deserve a house, a garden, a future, a Goddess-damn weather vane! You deserve it all and more.'

'Not at the cost of your lives!'

She dropped her hands, shaking her head. 'You never believed it, did you? You never really believed there could be another way.'

His jaw clenched, but the resigned look in his eyes betrayed him. 'I tried. I'm trying.'

'Not hard enough! Effie was right, Selene convinced you into all this when you were just fourteen. You were too young to know what you were doing, but now—'

'It wasn't like that. Selene never forced me. She told me the facts and I made the decision, because I knew. I knew even then that this is what I was meant to do. *My* design.'

'How could you have known? You were fourteen!'

'I just did! It just . . . it slotted into place, the gaps that had been there my whole life finally making sense. Effie and I had grown up together, she was my best friend and . . . already more than that, and when Selene told me what this curse would do to her, how it would destroy her, I knew what I had to do. A part of Effie had always been missing too and you were the answer.' He looked up at her, eyes hard and soft. 'If I died, Effie wouldn't only live, she could become whole. She'd have you.'

'Effie doesn't want *me*!'

'That's because the curse is keeping you apart!'

Anna wanted to tell him it wasn't true, but how could she deny it? She could feel the curse, its darkness beckoning, twisting her thoughts, asking her to give in to all her feelings, all at once. She wanted it now, wanted him now, to break apart and let him put all her pieces back together.

Attis breathed out, his voice a low murmur that reverberated through her. 'It was my choice to leave my life behind, my father, even though it broke his heart. I felt it, the way I know a piece of metal is ready to be shaped. I knew it was my purpose.'

'Do not compare this decision to your fire, Attis!' Anna shook her head, tears filling her eyes. 'There is nothing of your fire in this. Giving in to death when there's so much to fight for?!'

'You think I want to die?' He thumped his chest, moving towards her. 'You think I don't know that I love the world more than most people in it! There's so much I want to live for! So much I want to see and do and make and the thought of leaving Effie, leaving you—' His voice caught, ripped a little.

Anna had been driven against the anvil by his speech and he was bearing down on her, not angry, but overcome, his eyes so full she could see nothing but his world. She raised a hand to his face, touching his cheek, and he gave in to it, closing his eyes, breathing out between his lips. A moment of respite, but when he opened them again – there was fire in them. Fire for her. Anna could feel it, no trick, no illusion. *Real. Undeniable.* She knew if she moved an inch it would be too much to fight against. She didn't want to fight it, it hurt too much to fight it—

There was a knocking sound.

Sharp and insistent.

Upstairs.

The front door.

They lifted their heads as if confused that the world out there still existed.

Attis moved away and Anna pushed herself from the anvil. They looked back at each other and away again.

'Er—' She spun around, unsteady. 'I'll get it.'

'I'll come.' He cleared his throat and followed her up the stairs.

Sometimes Effie forgot her keys ... *Effie. Effie! My sister Effie ...* But when Anna opened the door, it wasn't Effie.

'Peter,' she gasped, not able to hide her shock. Her defences had been blown apart. *Peter.* Peter was here. He couldn't be here.

'Anna.' Peter smiled.

'What are you doing here?' Attis's voice came low and threatening from behind.

Peter's eyes moved to him, his face curdling with hatred. 'Don't worry, Lockerby, I'm not here to see you.' He looked back to Anna. 'Could I come in?' He stepped inside.

'Er – sure,' she said, making eyes at Attis to go and hide any magic around the house.

Attis's jaw clenched but he moved into the kitchen while Anna distracted Peter, showing him where to leave his shoes and coat.

'You didn't tell me you were coming . . .' Anna didn't even know how he knew her address.

'I had to see you.' He took her hands. 'After what happened at school. I wanted to make sure you're OK.'

Anna's words fled from her, seeing the floating bodies in her mind all over again. 'I guess, like everyone else . . . I'm in shock. Scared.'

'Can we go somewhere to talk?'

She nodded and took him through into the kitchen, but Attis was there, leaning against the counter, arms folded. All signs of magic had been covered over. 'This way,' she said, trying not to look at Attis as she took Peter upstairs. She stopped outside her door. 'Wait there. It's a mess.'

'I don't mind.'

'Two minutes.'

Peter nodded and she darted into her room. She didn't own many magical items, but she quickly shoved the fairy tale book and the Bible beneath her bed. Peter knocked on the door.

'OK – come in.'

He stepped into her room, his eyes moving over it. 'So this is where Anna Everdell lives.'

'It's not really *my* room,' she said, hastily. 'I'm just . . . borrowing it.'

'I understand. It must be hard to make a home here.'

The way he said it made her feel suddenly defensive, protective. This *was* her home. At least, it had begun to feel like it, most of the time. 'It's not so bad. What's going on, Peter?' she said directly. 'Will they reopen the school?'

He nodded.

Anna knew they would. Reopening would ensure more attention. 'Even after what happened?!'

'It's happening across the whole city. It's better that we're all there under the care of the WIPS than left to fend for ourselves.'

She bit her tongue. She couldn't tell Peter the truth about the WIPS. 'But gathering us all together puts everyone at risk. More people could die—'

He walked forwards and put his hands on her arms. 'Anna, I knew you'd be this way. Concern for everyone but yourself. You *need* to be concerned about yourself.' His brow furrowed. 'I told Eames you were with me when the swim outbreak happened, but it's not convinced him that you and the others aren't responsible. He says evidence has come to light – evidence against you all.'

Anna's heart stopped. 'Really? What evidence?'

'I don't know, there wasn't time for me to find out, but I think it's going to make things much harder for you.'

Evidence. Her knees felt weak. She dropped onto the bed and he sat beside her.

'I'm trying to do everything I can for you. I've had Andrew removed from his position. I told Eames he was abusing his power.'

Anna breathed out, a shred of relief among everything. 'Thank you.'

'But you have to look out for yourself now.' Peter raised his eyes to hers. 'Perhaps you could tell Inquisitor Eames that the others have been coercing you, forcing you this whole time . . . with your confession I could secure you—'

Anna pulled back from him abruptly. 'I am not turning my friends in! We're all innocent!'

'Do you know that? How do you know they won't betray you? You can't trust Effie.'

'I can,' Anna replied defiantly. 'I won't lie. We're not responsible for the hysteria, none of us. If they go down, I go with them. You can't help me without helping them.' He did not look pleased, but she held her eyes steady – wanting him to see she meant it but not wanting to drive him away when they might need him.

He lowered his head. 'OK. I hope I don't get to say I told you so. I just care about you. A lot. A lot more than a friend . . .' His eyes moved back up to hers. Those blue, earnest eyes she'd liked for so many years. Not full of the complications and impossibilities of Attis's grey eyes. Peter wanted her and her own heart was so full of longing and pain she didn't know what to do with it all.

He shifted closer. She could smell his lemon-pepper scent. Could see the fan of his light eyelashes as his eyes lowered to her lips, the flush of his cheeks.

He moved towards her.

They kissed. Nothing like their kiss before, but tender as the hand Peter put to her cheek, his lips tentative, as if he was afraid to scare her away. He closed the gap between them, pulling her closer, the kiss deepening—

She broke it off, pretending to be breathless.

'Anna,' Peter whispered against her ear, his lips gliding over it.

They kissed again and Anna tried to relax, but all she could think of was Attis, and thinking of him made her want to cry. Peter shifted his weight, pushing her down onto the bed, but she stopped him, a hand to his chest. 'Could we take things slowly?'

He made a low noise in the thick of his throat. 'Of course.' He straightened himself up. 'There is nothing more exquisite than being teased by you, Anna Everdell.'

He smiled and she assembled one back, moving away and crossing her arms around herself. A hollow place had opened in her chest.

Peter looked at her with unfinished intensity. 'I should go anyway. I'm meant to be helping my dad. Things are very busy for him at the moment, as you can imagine.' He took her hand, his fingers moving over hers. 'I'll do everything I can for you, Anna. I just—' He looked down, shaking his head as if lost. 'I need to know you're not just using me. You know I've earnt Eames's trust and you seem to care more about the others than you care about me . . . I want to protect you and your *friends*, but it's not easy for me . . .'

Anna stilled at his words, trying to work them out. They were justified; she knew her whole heart wasn't in whatever this was with Peter. Effie's trap was always there, reminding her that they needed him. But had she detected a fraction of threat? He raised his eyes and she tried to see through their clear, unequivocal blue. Did he know what he was doing? Did he know what she was doing? Or was he simply looking for reassurance?

She laced her fingers through his. 'I do care about you. A lot.'

He smirked at her. 'A lot more than friends?'

Pushing him away now would be a danger to them all.

She nodded and kissed him again. The hollow place in her chest opened further. She felt far away from her body.

She took Peter back downstairs, taking him through the lounge to the front door to avoid the kitchen. She watched him leave, realizing she was trembling.

When she went back into the kitchen, Attis was still there. She lowered her eyes, not knowing how to face him, still feeling Peter's kisses on her skin.

'Why's he coming around here?' Attis seethed. 'It's not safe. He's against us.'

Anna tried to move through the kitchen towards the door but Attis stood in the way. She couldn't take this right now.

'He's my friend, Attis,' she said, still not looking at him.

'He can't be trusted, Anna.'

A hostile noise burst from Anna's lips. 'That's rich! Can Effie be *trusted*?'

Attis scowled. 'I've known Effie my whole life. You barely know Peter!'

'Neither do you!' Anna bit back. 'And what's it to you? You can insist on your title of coven protector, but you don't get to say who I can and can't date.'

'So you are dating then?'

'That – that – wasn't what I meant.' How could she tell him that Effie had encouraged her to use Peter? Attis would never let her go through with it. He'd be sickened. How could she tell him that loving him hurt too much, was too dangerous, that it would be better for them all if she tried to move on? 'I thought you wanted me to be with other people!' she cried, turning her shame to anger. 'You made that abundantly clear!'

'Not him!'

'Oh, OK!' Anna threw her hands up. 'Do you want to draw up a list of who I can and can't be with so I'm super clear?'

'It's a very simple list: anyone but Peter.' A strained wire of pleading entered his voice. His mouth moved as if searching for the right words, his expression pained. 'He doesn't understand you, Anna. He will never let you be who you are.'

His words struck her deep and she pushed him away. 'No, Attis! *You* will never understand me!'

She ran up the stairs. Into her room. It still smelt of Peter and she couldn't stop moving, haunted by the look of pain in Attis's eyes, Peter's kisses spreading all over her. Effie's games driving her mad. She tried to calm herself, picking up the pieces of her song, holding onto it, playing its melody in her mind. The spinning top began to move around her – over the floor, the ceiling, the walls, forming patterns she could feel within her, but could not understand. But then, spinning too fast—

The darkness swallowed her and it careered off its path and slammed against the wall opposite with a smashing sound, Aunt's laughter echoing about the room.

She fell to her knees before it but the damage was done – the spinning top was broken.

When Effie arrived home Anna was ready for her. She waited in her sister's bedroom. The Christmas embroidery she'd made Effie looked down at her from the wall mockingly – an attempt at being sisters. When Effie finally arrived back, Anna clambered to her feet.

Effie raised an eyebrow. 'Anna.'

'Where have you been?'

'Hi, sis, nice to see you too, sis . . .'

'Where have you been?'

'Who are you? My mum?'

'With Manda?'

Effie's eyes sharpened. 'We were just hanging out.'

'Is that all?'

'What's that meant to mean?'

'Do you know who came to hang out with me?' Anna snarled.

'I guess you're going to tell me.'

'Peter.'

'Oh. Hope you said hi from me. Is he thoroughly enamoured by you now?' Effie smiled.

Anna wanted to wipe it from her face. 'We kissed. We kissed and you're the one making me – making me—'

Effie grimaced. 'I'm not making you do anything, Anna. It's your choice, you know the stakes as well as I do.'

'Well, the stakes just got a whole lot higher.'

'What do you mean?'

'Peter says Eames has evidence against us.'

Effie rolled her eyes. 'Peter is trying to scare you, and anyway Eames already has plenty of evidence he can use against us. We just need to work out how to beat him.'

'No! We need to work out how to end the hysteria spell!'

'That too.'

Anna stopped pacing and looked at Effie, wanting to shock her, wanting to wake her up to the threats they faced; wanting to hurt her. 'I know Attis's spell. I found it in Eleanor's Bible.'

Effie's eyes went still, finding their dark, hungry centre. 'What is it?'

Anna recited it word for word.

His death.

His death.

His death.

Anna had thought she might feel something like relief, finally telling someone, but she didn't – she felt worse. 'He has to die, Effie. He has to die to save us.'

Effie bit her lip, then shrugged. 'Well, that's that then.'

'What do you mean, that's that?'

'Nana's led you to a pointless spell for the fun of it. A big fat full stop. Death. It's the joke, get it? Actually . . .' She smiled faintly. 'I think I *am* beginning to get Nana's sense of humour.'

'Effie!' Anna raged. 'This means there could be no way out of the curse!'

'The curse has no control over me,' Effie spat back. 'I know I'm more powerful than it.'

'But the curse is *real*. Do you not remember what happened at the end of last year? Do you not think Attis wouldn't do it again to save you? The way you treat him doesn't help!'

Effie's face darkened. 'What's that meant to mean?'

'You use him! Treat him like a pet who has to do everything you say!' The words rushed from Anna with the fury she'd been holding in. 'You play with his good nature and make him feel like his only use is to stop you doing reckless things, but you do them all the time anyway!'

Effie squeezed out a humourless laugh. 'Me, using Attis? The kettle calling the cauldron black, *sis*. You use him just the same as me. Your whole helpless, please come save me act,' she mocked. 'Trying to get his attention, trying to take him from me!' She growled suddenly then reined it in. 'Why can't you just accept he'll never want you the way he wants me?'

They were face to face now and Anna wanted to hit her, to slam her against the wall. The rage was pulsing through her so hard. Anna turned away, her fingers curling, the curse blackening all her thoughts like a match to paper. She closed her eyes, the world spinning.

'At least I don't lie to myself,' said Effie, behind her. 'At least I face the darkness in myself, but you're too scared for that.'

Anna walked out, not looking back. Afraid if she did, she would do something she regretted. Afraid if she looked back, Effie would see it on her face – that she *was* scared . . . terrified of the darkness she spoke of.

I won't look down.

She rampaged up the stairs to her bedroom, throwing her arm out – the mirror flew out from beneath the bed and into her hand.

Anna looked into it: Aunt's face looked back at her.

She screamed at it and the glass cracked to pieces, but then – it reformed.

Aunt's face.

Anna howled at it.

It cracked – and reformed.

Aunt's face.

Cracked – and reformed.

Aunt's face.

Aunt's face.

Aunt's face.

POPPET

The Initiate will be taught the art of holding various 'death postures', pushing the psychical body to its outermost limits in order to experience the limitlessness of the soul.

'Death Postures', Hel Witch Trainings,
Books of the Dead: Tome 9364

The people fell one after another, dark as ravens, flying towards the ground.

Flying – falling – dying.
Flying – falling – dying.
Flying – falling – dying.

Anna hadn't been able to watch. It had happened just before they returned to school – residents in one of the Barbican Centre's towers had woken one morning, opened their windows and proceeded to step out into thin air. En masse.

Another attack. The official figures weren't in yet but at least twenty people had thrown themselves out before security teams had managed to stop everyone else and shut the skyscraper down. The Pied Piper was at the height of its power, feeding to kill now and picking over the remains. Mór had said its energy would run out eventually but it was only growing stronger. How many more would have to die before it consumed itself? Was the magical world going to wait to find out? Was anyone going to do anything?

As Anna walked to the Ebury wing, in a state of despair, too tired to be as afraid as she ought to be, she knew the hysteria would strike at St Olave's again. She could feel it. There was too much fear here, drawing it in. The school that had been her hell for so many years was giving way to Hel itself.

They might not be here when it happened. They may have already been forced to escape into the magical world. Anna knew the plans were in motion, she'd heard Selene talking to Bertie about it on the phone and Rowan had reported that her mum was in a state of frenzied busyness – calls, meeting with different groves, sorting through the house as if she were preparing to . . . leave. It was only a matter of time, and then what? They'd leave the rest of the pupils in the school to face the spirit alone? Anna knew she owed none of them anything but she couldn't just leave them to die either. But the longer they remained in danger, the more she feared Attis would decide there was nothing left to do but to sacrifice himself again. She'd seen it on his face as he'd pushed her back against the anvil – waves of panic crashing against a hard rock of resignation. Her own desire crashing back, being sucked down into the abyss of the curse. Time was running out on all sides.

Effie, Manda and Rowan had been summoned too. They were gathered in silence in the secretary's room as she typed away at her computer, sipping on a cup of tea, until a set of prefects came out to take them through to Eames's office.

'It's time,' said the secretary, giving them a brief, anxious look.

Anna's mouth had gone dry, her body beginning to tremble. *What was coming this time?*

The first thing that Anna noticed was that the blinds at the windows had been pulled down and, as the door shut behind them, the prefects fanned out, positioning themselves around the room. Her heart began a rebellion in her chest. Whatever was about to happen wasn't for anyone else to see. She thought of what Peter had said about the evidence against them and felt gutted out, as if those eyes of Eames had finally sucked the life from her.

Meanwhile, he looked livelier than ever, as if the pupils' deaths had rejuvenated him with fresh and fierce conviction. He sat them in a circle – chairs facing each other, a small table in the middle, their eyes darting uneasily between one another, Rowan gripping her chair, Manda picking her nails to nothing. Anna shared a quick, loaded glance with Effie and looked away. They hadn't spoken since their argument. Anna had wanted to get all her feelings out but instead their words had compacted them inside her, left them to fester.

'I think you're all aware of how serious this investigation is now.' Eames looked eager. His tie was not knotted properly as if his fingers had been trembling that morning. The necklace dangled around his neck – the circle with a cross in its centre. 'Two deaths on school grounds and malefice out of control across London. No one is on your side, not any more.'

Effie looked up at him, chin jutting. 'Which presumes we're the witches you're looking for, when we're not.'

Eames said nothing but went over to his desk. Anna scanned the room again. The prefects were staring straight ahead, not at them. Andrew wasn't among them, at least, but neither was Peter. She wished he was there so she could get some sense from the look in his eye what was going to happen. Tom was present but there was no hint of humour on his face. In the waiting silence, Anna thought she could hear the shouts outside – there'd been more protestors than ever that morning, spitting and snarling at the gates.

GET THE WITCHES OUT!
SAVE OUR CHILDREN!
STOP THE SPREAD!

Eames came back over with something in his hand. He dropped it on the table in front of them. A doll. It was made of fabric, roughly stitched together, pins stuck into its hands and mouth. Anna's own mouth dropped before she could stop it.

A poppet.

'Evidence,' Eames declared. 'Miranda Richardson and Effie Fawkes were seen by Ms Dulacey with this item of malefice in an empty class-room just before the swim attack.'

Anna tried to keep her face expressionless but her eyes moved to Manda who was squirming in her seat.

'They were seen leaving the classroom without the doll but we searched the room thoroughly and it was found buried at the bottom of the bin.'

Eames picked the poppet up and turned it over in his hands, his long nails fingering it as he revealed what was stitched onto its back – a symbol, a letter that belonged to an unspeakable language. The Language of the Dead.

Anna couldn't hide her shock now. She pulled away from the poppet, her chair creaking. Manda's face had darkened, sweat sheening her forehead, her legs shaking. Anna's eyes moved to Effie but Effie did not look back at her. The poppet had been one thing but . . . *death magic*. Was it true? Were they using death magic? *Why?*

'You see, you are caught now,' said Eames, to all of them, to none of them in particular. They had never been people to him. 'All that is left to do is confess. Confess and this can all be over.'

He walked around their circle, his words tightening around them.

'You will be treated more leniently if you come forwards.'

Anna looked back to the others searching for answers she couldn't fathom. Rowan, white as a snowdrop, her mouth hanging open. Manda's head trained to the floor. Effie's eyes as full of unknowable shadows as ever. The threads between them all stretched too far, breaking, *already broken*.

'I only need one of you to confess,' said Eames. 'Whoever does so will be treated more leniently. Perhaps you were coerced by the others . . .'

Anna realized she wasn't breathing. Terrified that someone would speak. *Confess.*

Effie opened her mouth and Anna's heart leapt into her throat.

'Darcey?' Effie spat. 'Really? What a coincidence. The girl who accused us from the start, who has been controlling this investigation all along, has now very conveniently found evidence to damn us. She's playing with you, Eames, and you can't even see it.' She laughed.

Eames winced at the sound, his hand squeezing the poppet. He placed it down on the table and went back over to his desk.

'I had anticipated that none of you would comply, that additional measures might be necessary.'

Additional measures. Anna's eyes moved back to the closed blinds. Eames took a candle out from his desk and a lighter from his pocket.

'What kind of measures?' said Effie, not sounding quite as confident as she had a moment ago.

Eames lit the candle and pulled a glove over one of his hands. He took off the necklace from his neck. 'Iron,' he replied, concentrating on the task – taking the necklace in his gloved hand and then moving it over the flame. 'Heated iron will not burn a witch.'

Rowan released a cry. Anna had made a noise herself though she wasn't sure what, something unintelligibly afraid.

'The WIPS are updating their guidance regularly on how to detect and deal with potential suspects of witchcraft.' Eames dipped the necklace with clinical detachment into the flame. 'But this particular method hasn't yet been officially released. It will be, of course, once they secure their rightful power. But considering the circumstances we find ourselves in, I believe it is prudent to . . . take the initiative.'

Effie's hands gripped the chair, knuckles white, face draining whiter. 'You're going to burn us?'

'Wait . . . you can't – you can't do this—' Rowan's voice shook.

Eames held the pendant in the hottest part of the flame. 'If you claim it was me no one will believe you, or care, I imagine.' His eyes were mirrors of the fire before him, it danced in his black pupils. 'Not with deaths making the front pages.'

Anna had known he was losing it but she had never imagined he'd go this far.

'So if we burn, it's proof we're not the witches?' said Effie.

'Not necessarily,' he replied plainly. 'You could be using charms to interfere with the test.'

They looked between one another desperately, knowing there was no point in replying – his logic was too warped to argue with. It didn't matter to him if they burned or not. He only wanted a confession. Anna could see it in his eyes – he needed to know. To know he was right about them. To extinguish the doubt. She didn't even think the test was true. In theory, iron would sizzle if it touched their blood but they were all taking Eyevain now which would conceal their magic from detection. But even if they weren't . . . would heated iron not burn them? Anna had never heard such a thing with regard to witches. Attis had always made sure she was careful in the forge because she *would* burn. Any of them would.

Her breath came fast and shallow, her limbs tensed as she surveyed the situation, trying to work out if there was a way out. Too many prefects . . . and Eames was right, the test could be covered up. If they tried to tell people about it he could claim it was simply a cry for attention or an attempt to twist the investigation. And nobody would care. They could use magic to get away, but what if he had his own magic to stop them? Attis wasn't with them . . . even if they escaped . . . they could seize him as leverage . . .

'You're really going to let him do this?' Effie called out to the prefects.

'You're just going to watch while he burns us? Tortures girls in the name of protection? Tom? Really? I know you're an idiot but I didn't think you were a completely spineless sack of shit.'

Tom shifted uncomfortably, his eyes remaining ahead but blinking rapidly.

Without warning, Effie jumped up and ran at Eames. The prefects rushed forwards, one of them catching her arm. She wrestled him off but the rest grabbed her. They dragged her back into her seat and held her arms behind the chair while she struggled against them.

'There is another way.' Eames raised his voice. 'Confess. Confess before it is too late. Are you the witches of St Olave's?'

Anna thought of Eleanor's screams as she'd delivered her own confession, could feel her helplessness all over again. The coven looked back at one another, fear souring the divisions between them now, yanking at the threads that bound them, testing if they were strong enough, or if one of them would – snap.

Manda raised her head, she took in a sharp breath and Anna prayed to the Goddess that Manda would hold, that they would all hold. *That I will hold.*

'Miss Everdell.' Eames rounded on her. 'Do you have anything you wish to say? Are you afraid of what Ms Fawkes might do to you if you come clean? We can protect you from her, you know.'

My friend.

My enemy.

My sister.

Effie had been lying to her, had been carrying out death magic behind her back. She couldn't trust her any more. Peter would tell her to turn Effie in now, to save her own skin.

'The only crime being committed here is by you,' Anna spat, hatred in her voice.

'Miss Fawkes, then . . .' Eames's eyes shifted to Effie.

'Fuck you,' Effie replied succinctly.

'It is decided, then.' Eames took the necklace from the flame and moved towards them – towards Rowan. 'Keep her down,' he commanded the prefects.

'No!' Anna cried. 'You don't need to test us all, test me! I'll—'

'No. Me.' Effie's voice rang over her, commanding as ever. 'I'm the ringleader after all, aren't I? Test me first and the rest are damned anyway.'

She managed to pull herself to her feet again. 'Otherwise I'm just going to keep trying to run away and make this whole thing much more of a struggle than it needs to be.'

Eames swivelled to Effie.

Effie pulled her sleeve up and pouted her lips at him. 'You know you want to, Inquisitor.'

'Effie! No!' Anna tried to get up from her seat but hands grabbed her, holding her down.

Without preamble or flourish, Eames took Effie's arm and with his gloved hand pressed the pendant into the soft, pale underside of her forearm. He watched curiously as it broke into her flesh, observing the outcome of his little experiment. It sizzled, whether from Effie's blood or her burning skin it was hard to tell.

Effie roared in agony and Anna felt it in her own skin, in her own body as if the pain was hers.

My friend.

My enemy.

My sister.

She wrenched through the hands holding her, springing towards Effie—

The door to the room flew open and Attis and Mr Ramsden barged through, the secretary behind them. 'I tried to stop them!' she said weakly.

Everything stopped.

Mr Ramsden surveyed the scene, his bulldog face shaking in confusion, in disbelief. 'What's going on?'

Effie was clutching her arm, her eyes wet with tears of pain. 'He burned me!' she raged. 'He fucking burned me!'

Anna's eyes were on Attis who she knew was in a different world – a blazing world where all that existed were him and Eames. She knew he would do something terrible.

Eames raised himself up. 'This is a private examination—'

Attis ran at him full pelt.

Anna cast the circle without thinking – a solid, invisible wall – and Attis rebounded against it, falling onto the floor as if he'd tripped. She was surprised herself it had worked – her magic rushing out from the terror inside of her, the terror of what would happen to him if he attacked Eames. She buckled down, holding the circle firm, knowing that Attis would feel it keeping him and his magic away. His eyes shot to hers, sparking with rage.

Mr Ramsden stepped forwards, his mouth moving, garbling, but it took a few moments for the words to follow. 'You have to stop this at once! This is – this is—' He stared at the burnt flesh of Effie's arm as if he couldn't quite believe it. 'Not allowed—'

'Your approval is not required,' Eames replied.

The prefects looked between Ramsden and the Inquisitor, caught between the old rules and the new.

There was a thudding noise and everyone turned.

Manda had slid off her chair and fallen to the floor. For a moment, everyone was too shocked to do anything. Then they all rushed towards her but the prefects got there first.

They turned Manda over – her face had emptied of colour but she appeared to be breathing. Thin, frail breaths.

'She's fainted,' one of them said.

'Take her to the nurse's office,' Eames instructed. 'And take the others to separate rooms. Mr Ramsden and I need to have a little chat.'

Anna's circle had faltered – Attis was no longer held back. He moved to Effie, throwing an arm around her and holding his body against her and the rest of the world. He turned to Ramsden, his face screwed into a rictus of fury. 'You did this. You let the devil in and now he's running the show, you fool!'

Eames had lost it.

Everyone had lost it.

Am I losing it?

Anna wished they hadn't separated them. She was held in one of the Ebury rooms, left with nothing but her circling thoughts. *Where is Effie? Is she OK? Where is Manda? Is she OK?* Her magic rolled in frothy, useless waves of fear through her. She wanted to use it, to break the door down, to find the others, but it would only put them at more risk. The locked door transported her back to Nana's vision of Eleanor, the feeling of powerlessness that had pervaded it, of suffering. The threads that connected them were pulling tighter.

Anna could feel the curse too as she sat on the floor. Stewing. Brooding. Trying not to let her thoughts turn against her sister, her emotions veering through disbelief, rage, betrayal and back to disbelief—

A poppet. Was it true? Had Manda and Effie been in possession of a poppet? *Why?* Had they been using Imagic on people? Manda's parents and Karim had been acting oddly for a long time . . . but then . . . *why the Language of the Dead?* That was used for one thing only – to commune with . . . to draw out spirits . . .

Anna didn't want the suspicions to form but they were already there, falling into place like a jigsaw puzzle made of twisted glass pieces, cutting her fingers as she tried to see the whole picture.

Effie and Manda's hushed whispers . . . Effie warning Manda . . . *threatening Manda?*

Effie was the one who had introduced them all to the Hel witches . . . she had known them already . . . had access to their knowledge, she was dating Azrael . . . *using Azrael? Working with him? What had she taken from him the other night? Spirit powder?*

Manda acting bizarrely, growing weaker, thinner, coughing, dizzy . . . how had Anna not seen it? Manda had Death Sickness. She was sure now. She remembered Azrael talking about it – *It's what can happen if you do not work with spirits safely. They can feed on your energy, drain you, rot you from the inside out . . .*

No. No.

Were Manda and Effie somehow involved in the death magic inside the school? The hysteria? Was the poppet part of the spell? Had they got caught up in it? Accidentally drawn the spirit here? Or had Effie been part of the bigger plot from the start, working with the Hel witches or ex-Hel witches? Had she somehow embroiled Manda in her plans?

No. It wasn't possible.

But Effie had sympathized with the idea of witches getting their revenge on the WIPS. And the hysteria spell had put their coven on the map. Turned the attention of the WIPS their way – London's attention their way – and no one loved attention more than Effie. *Setting the stage . . . all a game . . . it was always a game to Effie.*

No.

No.

No.

It couldn't be.

The secretary stepped into the room. Anna must have looked as terrible as she felt, because the secretary's face twinged with something like sympathy. 'You can leave now,' she said, handing over Anna's belongings. 'It's the end of the school day.'

Anna was surprised so many hours had passed. She stood up. 'Where are the others? Where's Effie? What's happened to Manda?'

'Miss Richardson is unwell. She's been taken home. Your other friends have been released too. Eames will expect you back in school tomorrow.'

Anna stared at her. 'When will this all end?'

The secretary pursed her lips. 'I don't know.'

'He burned Effie.'

'I am not privy to all of the Inquisitor's decisions and actions.' She tried to keep her face passive, but Anna could see it wasn't easy for her. How long had she had to wear that mask? Was she scared of him too? Could they find a way to get her to turn against Eames? To help them?

Anna shook her head. 'Why do you work for them?'

She sighed, long and slow. 'Because, Anna, I'm a single mum with two children. I need a job and this pays.' She looked away and opened the door wider. 'You're free to go.'

'I think you know that I'm not,' said Anna as she left.

She walked back to her locker. The corridor was busy but Anna couldn't see any of the coven. She took out her phone and checked it – a few panicked messages from Rowan asking where they all were and one from Manda saying she was home and OK, explaining nothing. Anna's dark suspicions flooded her again.

She spotted Darcey at her locker.

Anna went over to her. 'Can I speak to you?'

Through her instant frown, Darcey looked shocked that Anna had approached her. It had never happened before in all their time at school together. 'Are you insane?' Darcey spat.

'Perhaps,' said Anna, and apparently her response was enough to tip Darcey's hatred into intrigue.

'In there. Now.' Darcey jerked her head to an empty classroom.

A few jaws dropped as they walked into it together. Darcey's eyes moved over Anna with contempt. 'What?'

'Did you really see Effie and Manda with that doll?'

Darcey smiled, realizing what this was all about. 'I did. Oh.' She feigned sympathy, putting fingers to her lips. 'You didn't know. How pathetic.'

Anna breathed out despairingly. After years of bullying, she knew Darcey well. She was too gleeful to be lying.

'I warned you you couldn't trust Effie.'

'Shut up, Darcey.'

Darcey just laughed. 'Good luck, you're really going to need it.' She walked past Anna towards the door.

'Why do you do the things you do, Darcey?' said Anna. Darcey stopped and turned. Anna faced her, unflinching. 'Take pleasure in other people's pain.'

'You tried to destroy me, and now, I'm destroying all of you.'

'No.' Anna shook her head. 'This started before all that. Before Effie. From the moment I joined this school you wanted to ruin me. Why?'

Darcey did not reply. A look Anna had never seen passed over her face. She cast her head down, as if to stop Anna seeing it. 'You were so broken when you joined and . . . I saw myself.' Darcey's voice turned to a scratch, a whisper. 'I had a hard childhood, my parents were cruel, they used to—' Anna watched Darcey crumble, put her head in her hands, shaking—

Through her shock and confusion, for a brief moment Anna felt something in herself open towards Darcey, but then she saw that Darcey was shaking with laughter. Thick and putrid, it poured out of her.

'Oh wow, nobody. Were you actually feeling sorry for me then? You really think I was abused as a child?' Her laughter continued mirthlessly. 'This is it. This is why I had to crush you from the start, because you were always too soft. So hopeful. I've been trying to help you all this time. My parents have always been honest with me, taught me that the world doesn't care for such things, that it's a cruel, hard place. You either win or you lose. You can't do both and you can't win without beating others down. It's just how it works. Especially for women. It's harder for us so *we* have to be harder, more ruthless.'

Something about Darcey's speech made Anna uncommonly sad. 'You're a monster.'

Darcey shrugged. 'I'd rather be a monster than a loser. I've done my best. I've tried to teach you. I'm sure Effie will finish you off, but hey, maybe you'll surprise me, maybe you're the type to one day, just . . . snap. If you do, please take Effie down with you. Nothing would make me happier.'

'Oh, I wish I could,' said Anna, leaning towards her with a touch of menace. 'But if life's a game, Darcey, you should be worried, because Effie never loses.'

Darcey's smile faltered but only for a moment before it recalibrated, settled back into its ugly smugness.

Anna walked past her and left the room. Effie had messaged.

Meet in the sewing room. Now.

Anna didn't have her shadowrobe – it was in Attis's car. She tried his phone but the call didn't go through. She shouldn't go . . . but she couldn't not, not after everything that had just happened. Not without facing Effie.

She departed from school as if going home, walked quickly up the street and sneaked in through the back entrance, knowing it was stupid but a grim, cold, unthinking rage propelled her. She made it to the sewing room, opening the door to find Rowan and Attis. No Effie.

Attis moved towards Anna, wild-eyed. 'Are you OK? Have you seen her? Effie?'

'Yes. I'm fine. I haven't yet, not since . . .'

Attis looked on the edge of exploding, his fists clenched, his body a coiled spring, his face a rictus of fury and pain.

'She'll be here, Attis.' Rowan tried to calm him. 'She messaged us all.'

'I'll kill him,' he roared, his hands ringing the air. 'I'll kill Eames.'

'You can't. We need to go,' said Rowan. 'Run now. It's gone too far, he's gone too far, it's all gone too far . . . I have no idea what is going on any more.'

'Darcey just confirmed to me what Eames claimed,' said Anna. 'That she saw Effie and Manda with a poppet. A poppet marked with the Language of the Dead.' She turned to Attis. 'Do you know anything about this?'

He shook his head, as if he didn't care who had been found with what, only that Effie was OK.

'Rowan and I overheard Effie threatening Manda the other day.' It was all coming out now. 'And I saw Effie taking something from Azrael after the Well-Meet. Someone has been drawing a spirit to this school . . .'

Attis stopped his pacing now, turning to look at her, confusion and disbelief overtaking the grimace of his face. 'What are you saying, Anna?'

'I don't know!' she stammered, the words spilling out. 'Are – are Effie and Manda behind the hysteria here?'

'What?'

Anna spun around to find Effie in the doorway, her shirt rolled up, a large gel plaster on her arm. Anna flinched, feeling Effie's pain again wanting to run to her, but feeling Effie's anger too which was turning colder, harder by the moment.

Effie's eyes narrowed. 'What did you just say?'

Attis swept past Anna to Effie. He reached for the plaster, not touching it, his face crumpling. 'Are you OK?'

'No. It hurts like a bitch. I was forced to go to the nurse's office to get it seen to.'

Attis enfolded her in his arms, holding her head beneath his chin. 'I'm sorry I wasn't there.'

'My mum has some salve that clears burns right up . . .' Rowan's voice quaked. 'We can go to her now. We should go . . .'

'Eames has to pay for what he's done,' Effie growled.

Rowan stepped back. 'No, Effie. It's too late for revenge. You can explain everything to us, let's just go.'

'I don't think I need to,' said Effie, unfurling from Attis. 'My sister here already has everything worked out, it seems.'

Anna stood her ground as Effie moved towards her, as Attis and Rowan turned to look at her.

'Please, do carry on turning the coven against me, sis.'

Their eyes were locked on each other. Anna tried to see through Effie's gaze, to see what truly lay within, but it only pushed outwards, it would not let her in.

'Manda has Death Sickness, doesn't she?' Anna said – a statement, not a question.

Effie nodded. 'Yes.'

Rowan gasped.

'What have you been making her do?' Anna whispered.

Effie screwed her face up. 'Making her do?'

Anna tried to hold firm against Effie's contempt. 'We all know Manda is easily influenced by you and you're the one who dragged the Hel witches into our lives. The spell you tricked us all into casting last year spiralled out of control, maybe this has got too big too, bigger than you thought it would. Maybe you got in over your head with whoever you're working with—'

'The spell last year cast rumours, it didn't attack people en masse!'

'It ruined lives! And you never seemed to care . . .'

'Hey, both of you, come on—' Rowan attempted to intervene, but Effie put a hand up to her.

'Or maybe,' Effie stopped inches from Anna, 'you've finally turned as crazy as your aunt. I guess it was only a matter of time . . .'

Anna felt Effie's words like a knock to the ground, the ground opening up and swallowing her back into the welcoming arms of Aunt.

'Stop this.' Attis came between them. He stared at Anna, hard. 'Effie didn't cast the hysteria spell. I know who did—'

A noise in the corridor broke off his words. They all spun towards the door. *Manda?*

The handle turned. The door opened.

Peter and Tom stepped through.

They stared at them and Peter and Tom stared back, a mirror of shock. *Peter and Tom. Tom and Peter. It wasn't possible. It couldn't be happening.* Anna wanted to scream at herself. She had come here without her shadowrobe, they must have seen her, followed her . . .

All my fault.

Peter's eyes surveyed the room – taking it all in, searching out every shadow and secret: the altar, the candles, the mannequins. They came to rest on Anna, those clear blue eyes weighing her, finding her guilty.

'What are you doing here?' Attis bore towards them, fury and fear wrestling on his face.

Effie stepped in front, stopping him. 'Attis, they're here now, attacking them isn't going to help.'

Attis paced to the side. '*How* are they here?'

Peter raised his hands. 'Nobody move. Tom—' he jerked his head. 'call the Inquisitor now.'

But the door slammed shut behind Tom.

Effie tutted. 'I don't think so, boys. I don't know how you found us, but you won't be leaving.'

Finally, Effie was free to flex her magic and Anna could feel it bristling and stretching like a cat's back. She performed the freeze symbol with ease and Peter and Tom were suddenly held motionless, only their eyes able to move. Tom's had turned almost comically wide, like a mouse trapped in her claws. Peter's were still managing to translate all of his hatred and disgust.

'Effie, we can't keep them here.' Rowan's voice shook. 'There's no going back now, we're caught. We run. Fast.'

'As much as I'd like to see them pay.' Attis threw a dark glance to them. 'I agree.'

'Come on, people,' Effie rallied. 'What a lack of imagination we have in this room.' She walked a slow circle around Tom and Peter. 'We're witches, there's an abundance of things we can do to them. Perhaps we wipe their memories – I have no prior experience of memory magic and it could go very wrong but needs must. Or we could cast a spell of control – force them to be our slaves.' She drew closer to Peter, trailing her fingers down his chest. 'Or perhaps they'll keep quiet if I shrivel their balls to the size of peanuts.'

Anna knew she was toying with them, that the magic Effie was talking about was possible . . . but advanced, too dangerous, and they didn't have time.

Effie swivelled to Anna, as if an idea had struck her. 'Or perhaps, Anna, you could convince Peter not to turn us in seeing as he holds you in such high regard. Now, Peter, I know you're not the forgiving type, but, you see, sweet Anna here, it's not her fault she's afflicted with magic. She wasn't brought up with it and she's fought it to the bitter end. I lured her into all this. I was the corruptor.'

'Effie.' Attis pulled her away. 'What are you doing?'

Effie continued unabated. 'Attis, you can help change their minds too.' She faced Tom and Peter again. 'You see, we might be creatures of magic, but we haven't been casting the malefice spell in this school. We're wicked, but not entirely evil. Attis can explain.'

Attis paced, dragged a hand over his face. 'I don't see the point in telling *them*, but—' He stopped in front of Rowan and Anna. 'It's not Eames. It's his secretary.'

It took a moment for his words to sink in.

'The secretary . . .' Rowan gasped.

'That night we broke into Eames's office,' said Attis. 'Something bothered me but I couldn't work out what it was. Then after this morning, the burning—' He shot a savage look at Peter and Tom. 'I was held in the secretary's room for a time and I saw it, her tea cups. I'd noticed before they were stained a strange colour but it had been dark and she'd walked in on us, but today I could see it, they were yellow. Not enough to really be noticeable, but too yellow for ordinary tea, unless—'

'You'd been adding spirit powder to it . . .' said Anna.

'I managed to swipe a cup from her desk today. The residue is sulphurous. Not just that, but do you remember that night she came back to shred the invoice on her desk? I think it was because she'd signed the wrong name. Her name is Laura Seymour, but the name printed at the bottom of the invoice was Laura Wilmore. I think she signed her old name by accident.'

Anna remembered her introducing herself at the start of the school year before their first interview but Anna had been so terrified she hadn't taken the name in.

'Mór said it would be easy in the magical world to change your name and appearance,' said Rowan.

'Exactly,' said Attis. 'I think she's hidden her former identity but it slipped out by accident and she had to come back and shred the evidence just in case. I think she's the one who's been "working" in the Ebury wing late at night too, not Eames.'

Effie smiled and turned to Peter and Tom. 'I'm sure you're both confused, but basically spirit powder protects you if you're working with death magic, which is the magic that's been plaguing the school, and London too for that matter. But the person drawing it here is Eames's secretary.'

Effie loosened the grip of her magic just enough for them to speak.

'Bullshit,' Peter spat.

'I don't care who's casting what,' said Tom, his voice high-pitched. 'Just please don't shrivel my balls.'

Effie snorted. 'As always, Tom Kellman – more concerned about his groin than anything else.'

Anna was still reeling, still trying to make sense of everything. What was the poppet? Why had it had the Language of the Dead on it? If the secretary had cast the hysteria then she'd just wrongly accused her sister . . .

'I think it's time we go speak to Laura Wilmore,' said Effie.

'No way.' Attis shook his head.

'We have to,' said Anna grimly. 'It's only just gone six, she's probably still there.'

'We don't know what she's capable of,' Attis argued. 'She could turn the spell on us.'

'The hysteria just killed twenty people out in London!' Anna cried fiercely. 'We can't run knowing that we might be able to find a way to stop the spell if we speak to her.'

'Why would she tell us anything?'

'We can threaten her with exposure. Tell her that if she acts against us or hands us over to Eames or tries to cast the spell that we can blow her cover, hand her over to the magical world.'

'Now you're starting to talk like my sister,' said Effie, but there was no lightness in her voice. She did not look at Anna.

Attis put his head in his hands.

'Or we just tell the magical world what we know.' Rowan sounded desperate.

'It could be too late by then.' Effie nodded at Peter and Tom. 'These buffoons could go and alert Eames about everything we've said – the secretary could run.'

'I agree.' Anna nodded. 'We can't give up this opportunity.'

Rowan breathed out. 'I think I preferred it when you two were arguing.' She gestured her head at Peter and Tom. 'What about them?'

'They come with us.' Effie waved a hand and Peter and Tom were free. 'They learn the truth.'

Tom twisted a glance behind him. 'I don't want to know the truth. If I run for the door . . . are you going to turn me into something?'

'I don't need to, Tom,' Effie replied. 'You're already an ass.'

'Hey.' He turned back to her but there was no smirk on his face. It had long fled, replaced by something bewildered and scared. 'I tried today . . . when you kicked off in that room, everyone trying to wrestle you back into your seat . . . I messaged Attis. I was the one who alerted him to what was going on. I did what I could.'

Effie made a face at him. 'Thank you for sending a message, you're a real hero.'

'What was I meant to do?' Tom cried, his voice breaking. 'I didn't know . . . I didn't know Eames was going to do that . . . none of us did.' His head dropped to the floor.

Effie rounded on him. 'I'm sure you haven't enjoyed playing your role one bit. Are you going to run back to him? After what he did to me? After knowing what he's capable of? This is a moment of reckoning in your life, Tom. A chance to be the coward we all know and loathe, or to step up and be a man. What are you going to do?'

Tom lifted his head. 'I – I—'

'A coward then . . .' Effie made a scathing noise.

'Look. I'm not going to say anything, OK?' Tom raised shaking hands. 'I just want to get out of here and get as far away from all of you as possible. Just let me go and I'll step down as a prefect. I won't go near you again, no more stupid comments, no more harassing, no more anything.'

Effie turned back to the room. 'What do we think?'

'Let him go,' said Anna.

Attis moved towards Tom, backing him against the wall. 'If you say anything, I won't even need magic to break you.'

Tom looked terrified. 'Come on, man. I won't. I swear. I don't want any of you to get hurt.'

Attis moved back and Tom ran for the door.

'You better spend the rest of your life guarding your junk!' Effie yelled after him.

Attis exhaled, a charred sound. 'I'm not sure we should have let him go.'

'It's not him I'm concerned about,' Effie replied.

Peter hadn't moved. Anna turned to him. He stared at her – wounded, livid, *disgusted*. Surely there was no way she could convince him, not now. She put her hand out. He looked down at it, but then, to her surprise, he took it. They went to the far corner of the room away from the others. He threw her hand away.

'You're a witch,' his voice was toneless. A hard, terrible fact.

Anna shrugged vaguely. 'I am what I am, Peter, but we haven't been casting that spell—'

'It doesn't matter. You're still a witch. Capable of malefice.'

'I know you believe witches are some sort of abomination, but it's not true. I was born this way, it's just who I am.'

'You've lied to me this whole time.'

'How could I tell you the truth?' Anna cried. 'You joined up with Eames, I became enemy number one.'

'You could have told me before then.'

'Before then we were barely speaking, after what you did last year . . .'

Peter gritted his teeth and Anna reached for his hand again. She had to stop herself gripping it, too much rested on this moment, knowing if she couldn't convince him they were caught . . . or he was at the mercy of Effie. 'I didn't trust you then, but I do now,' she said, looking at him exactly how she imagined he'd want her to look at him – contrite, pleading, desperate. Green eyes entirely his to do with whatever he wanted. 'You've been the only one I can count on in all this. The only one I can turn to. My rock in this dark storm. And now you know the truth – that I'm part of the darkness, broken, impure . . .' She took a breath, widening her eyes. 'But I still need you. I've never needed you more.'

She looked down at his hand in hers, squeezing it, as if she would beg next.

She felt his grip on her hand tighten and she looked back up. His eyes remained distant. 'We go to the secretary's office and if she's responsible for the malefice then . . . I won't turn you in. For now.'

Anna could hardly believe she'd managed that much from him. 'What about the others?' she replied, too hastily.

'Or them,' he seethed. 'Not yet, anyway.'

Anna breathed out. 'Thank you. Thank you, Peter.'

'I told you, Anna. I'd do anything for us.' He stepped forwards, pulling her towards him roughly, leaning to whisper in her ear. 'Just never lie to me again.'

The whisper sank through her like a weight, tying a chain around her. She turned slowly back to the room, knowing she had somehow won and lost at the same time. 'Let's go and see the secretary.' She could not meet Attis's eyes.

Effie smiled without warmth. 'You see, we can all get along when we try.'

Attis strode out of the door, searching the doorframe with quiet fury. His eyes fell to the floor and he picked up a charging nail. 'One fell out,' he said, full of disbelief. His chimera must have fallen away, allowing Tom and Peter to see the door. He hammered it back into the frame, each angry blow of his hammer sending a jolt through Anna.

Attis ran quickly back to the car to fetch Anna's shadowrobe and then they set off. In Peter's defence he didn't lose it when the others disappeared into thin air. Anna threw her cloak over him and they walked side by side down the long corridors, Peter's breath harsh beside her as if he resented the magic aiding him.

The light was still on in the Ebury wing.

'Eames's car is gone,' said Attis. 'It's her.'

'Oh Mother Holle, please don't kill us,' Rowan pleaded as they made their way back up the stairs to the rooms that had been their cage only hours ago.

Attis opened the door quietly, slowly. Even so, the secretary jumped in her seat, her eyes darting over the open space before her, half of her hair falling out of the pen holding it up. They took off their cloaks and her mouth shook open. 'What on earth—'

Effie marched forwards. 'We know it's you. And before you try anything, think it through . . . there are four witches to one right now and with one press—' She held her phone up. 'I can send a message to one of the most connected people in the magical world, telling everyone you're behind the hysteria. They will come for you before you can say Ave fucking Satana.'

The secretary looked bewildered. 'I don't know what you're talking about.'

Attis picked up one of her tea mugs. 'We know you've been taking spirit powder in your tea. A little daily dose to keep you topped up, right? Sensible. Now is it Laura Seymour or Laura Wilmore?'

The secretary's already protruding eyes bulged further.

'If you leave,' said Anna. 'If you stop this spell, stop the others you're working with, bring it all to an end, we won't report you. But if you don't, we'll have no choice but to bring the whole magical world after you.'

The secretary stared at them all for another confused and scared moment – and then she began to laugh, head tipped back, teeth first. The crazed laughter of a person who'd gone so far beyond the end of their tether they'd started to fray. All of her hair fell out of its updo, hanging in fuzzy strands around her face. She pulled up her sleeve, waved her hand to uncover the chimera – revealing five Death Marks rotted into the flesh of her arm. 'Cross my heart and hope to die.'

Five. Not six. She never made it through Hel.

'You got me. A bunch of high school students have solved it all! Saved the day!' She laughed again, broken and bereft. 'If only you realized . . . all is already lost.'

'Please, stop this,' Anna pleaded.

The secretary looked up, her eyes sharper than Anna had ever seen them. 'Too late. Too late. The spell has gone too far – beyond us—'

'What do you mean?'

'We were hired by the WIPS – me and several other ex-Hel witches. They wanted us to carry out an unleashing spell and we did – at the

Tower of London itself. The centre of Hel witch magic,' she spat resentfully. 'I don't know what we dredged up that night, what we unleashed, but that kind of magic can't be put back into the box it came from. I was sent here, to help draw the spirit's energy to the school. And, oh, the WIPS liked the public's response to the hysteria in your school – such outrage – young people caught up in witchcraft! Children at risk! They wanted me to call it again and I did. But the third time, the swimming incident – the spirit did that itself. I never wanted anyone to die but . . . the spirit had gone beyond me by that point, drawn by the fear it created, feeding on it, and there's enough out there in London for it to feed again and again and again.' She fiddled with the pen on her desk, tapping it against the wood. *Tap. Tap. Tap.* 'Clever of them, really. It would have been easy enough to expose magic, spread videos and disinformation online, but that's easy to discredit too – the world is full of noise and it's hard these days to discern the lies from the truth. But fear. Now fear is a language we all speak. An instinct we can't outrun. The WIPS already have what they want: a captive, terrified audience. In the darkness, may chaos thrive.' Her voice had reached a crescendo, her eyes popping. 'You're simply too late.'

Anna tried to resist the despair of her words. 'Whatever the WIPS have planned in the future, the hysteria could kill people tomorrow. It has to stop.'

'You think I cast this spell for my own amusement?' she replied with a kind of weary pragmatism. 'I did it under the command of the WIPS and I told you – it can't be stopped. It will end . . . eventually.'

'You could go to the Underworld and stop it!'

The secretary tilted her head back up, an incredulous expression on her face. 'I'd be stupid to go against the orders of the WIPS and risk my life, but I'd be mad to go into the Underworld. I wouldn't just be risking my life but everything – my very *self*.' Her eyes travelled somewhere else briefly and Anna could feel the secretary's fear beneath her fraught exterior. A fear that lay deep inside her. 'Besides, the Hel witches would never let me go.'

'How can you live with yourself if you don't try?' said Anna.

The secretary returned to the room. 'Says the teenage girl who's never faced a shred of reality. You're looking for a simple story – good and evil – but life doesn't work that way, it's the powerful and the powerless. I made a decision which side to join. I needed this job. The WIPS pay well and their threats are concise. Am I proud of it? No. Do I have time for my pride? No. The WIPS are rising – work with them or be destroyed by them.'

Effie leant over her desk. 'You're a disgrace to witches.'

'I owe the magical world nothing.' The secretary's fingers moved to the Death Marks again, picking over them like they still hurt. 'It's never done anything for me. I gave years of my life to the Hel witches and when I couldn't pass all their *trials* I was all but discarded.' Her face crumpled into a toothy snarl. 'I didn't set out to do this, OK? The WIPS found *me*.'

'They recruited you into the Penitent . . .' said Rowan.

The secretary's head snapped to Rowan. 'How do you know about *that*?'

'Because we're not as young and naive as we look.'

'Perhaps not.' She smiled as cold as any Hel witch.

'Does Eames know?' Peter hissed, not hiding his revulsion for the woman before him. 'Does he know you've been directing the hysteria within the school?'

The secretary snorted. 'Of course not. He's a puppet. The WIPS have been shovelling him their strategies and methods, stringing this all out so that it gathers as much attention as possible while they consolidate their power. Eames doesn't even realize that the necklace around his neck *is* magic, it prevents malefice getting through. He's a jumped-up little prick, but he's the only thing protecting you all right now.'

'*How* is he protecting us?' Attis snarled.

'Because the WIPS don't care who gets thrown to them at the end of this, you're just another investigation to the big men upstairs, another chance to whip up chaos. But Eames believes in what he's doing. He wants to hand over the *true* witches.' She rolled her eyes. 'And he will—' Her pupils stilled, retreated. She chewed her lip as if she wasn't sure whether to say her next words.

'What is it?' Anna probed, sensing her reticence.

She looked at Anna. 'The WIPS are about to become an official governmental organization. It's all to be announced in the next few days and they want to show the public the results of everything they've been doing – wrap up several investigations, including your . . . The WIPS will be attending your school next week. Marcus Hopkins himself.'

Peter stepped forwards. 'What?'

The secretary ignored him. 'They want a big fanfare, to make an official announcement to the press, present their findings and those they believe responsible.'

'Marcus Hopkins is coming for us . . .' said Effie.

'They will take you,' the secretary stated.

Anna frowned. 'What do you mean?'

'Their first act as a government organization is going to be pushing through an emergency law allowing them to detain anyone suspected of witchcraft.'

Rowan inhaled sharply. Attis paced away, breathing heavily.

Even Effie's voice had lost its edge. 'Detain us where? How? What does that mean?'

'It means they can take you and hold you and after that—' The secretary shrugged, 'I don't know. I'm just a secretary.' She tied her hair back up with the pen. 'I'm not privy to the greater plans at work here, but mark my words, there *are* greater plans at work. The WIPS have cowan power and magical assistance. I suggest you run and hope they don't find you.'

'Wait, you'll just . . . let us go?' Rowan stuttered.

'You let me go – I'll let you go,' the secretary replied with business-like efficiency. 'So long as you tell nobody in the magical world about me. If you did . . . I'd have to tell the WIPS about you and we're all caught. As I said, I can't help with the spell, I couldn't stop it now even if I wanted to.'

Anna turned away – frustrated, defeated. How could you negotiate with someone who already believed everything was doomed?

'Fine,' Effie agreed. 'We keep our mouths shut and you keep yours shut, but we may require your help should it come to it. We'd hate to have to expose you . . .'

'And I, you.'

'No!' Anna cried. They hadn't come here to strike a deal, but to stop the hysteria. 'If you can't stop it you have to come clean to the magical world, you have to—'

'I don't have to do anything, Anna. Our positions are equally precarious. What about him?' She nodded at Peter threateningly. 'Why is Eames's little pet here?'

'He's with us,' said Anna.

'Are you sure about that?'

Attis went to speak but Effie raised her voice over him. 'He's under our control.'

'He better be,' the secretary threatened. 'Don't forget I can still draw the spirit here if needs be, I'd hate any deaths to be on your hands. Now go. I'm tired, I have paperwork to do and children to get home to.'

Anna went to speak again but the secretary raised a hand.

'Go before I change my mind.'

She turned back to her laptop, her face wan and lifeless in the office lighting.

They left, entirely bewildered. Anna had been searching for an enemy but had only found a beleaguered woman with nothing left to believe in.

They gathered at a safe distance from the school. Peter had not said a word during the entire walk and when Anna shrugged off their robe, he looked as if he might never speak again, his serious features locked into the deepest of frowns. His newfound beliefs in the WIPS had been shattered too.

'Told you so, Nowell,' said Effie, relishing it. 'You see? You're on the wrong side. We're the good witches here – witches of virtue, witches of impeccable character and shining morals. The bitch in there is the one you want, but, of course, if you out her to Eames, she'll out us . . . and we'll all be taken away.' She made a pointed glance at Anna. 'And it'll be all your fault.'

'Shut up, Effie.' Peter threw her a withering glance.

'I'm just saying.' She put her hands up. 'What are you going to do? Join us or damn us? Your daddy is already screwing my mummy – you could be part of the family . . .'

Peter's fingers curled.

'We can't let him go,' Attis thundered. 'He could run straight to Eames.'

'I'm not going to Eames,' Peter spat.

They stared at each other, eyes locked in a battle of wills, fists balled, rage and threat emanating off Attis in hot waves.

Peter stood his ground. 'I'm not going to Eames.'

'And why would we trust you?'

'I trust him,' said Anna, moving to stand beside Peter. Attis's eyes shifted to hers, his eyebrows rising with disbelief . . . and hurt. 'There isn't any choice,' Anna said to Attis. 'We're not going to kidnap him, are we?'

Attis moved away, kicking at the wall.

Peter turned to Anna, ignoring the others. 'I need to get home. Think everything through.' His eyes were still guarded as he looked over her, wary but processing, making sense of this new world he found himself in.

They watched him leave.

'Quite the evening.' Effie blew out a breath. 'There's still time for you to accuse me of casting more spells behind everyone's back if you want, sis?'

Anna had held it together all night but at the tone of Effie's voice, so full of contempt and buried hurt, she felt herself crumbling. She knew she'd lost it to the curse. In the back of her head, Aunt was laughing gleefully.

You were always my child.

'If the secretary cast the hysteria spell,' said Rowan, 'then what were you and Manda doing with that poppet?'

'Come and see for yourselves,' Effie replied forbiddingly.

PINS AND LOCKS

Only the Raven Tongued, who have travelled to Hel and learnt the language, may command a spirit and only if the name of the spirit is known. To have such power is a great and grave responsibility and only for those who have learnt in the darkness – that they are the light.

'Commanding', Hel Witch Initiation Stage Six

Mrs Richardson opened the door to Manda's house with a cheery smile and a surprising greeting. 'Hello, Effie! Lovely to see you again and you've brought some of Manda's other friends. Do come in.' She stepped to the side, her smile remaining in place.

A strange interaction considering Mrs Richardson wanted Manda to have nothing to do with any of them. The house wasn't as neat as Anna remembered. A few of the candles had burned down and not been replaced, the shoes were out of place – several discarded in the middle of the hallway. The carpet needed hoovering.

'She'll be glad of the company.' Mrs Richardson's eyes seemed fixed too, as if she were seeing them and not seeing them. 'Manda was sent home from school today unwell.' She was still smiling. 'Can I get any of you something from the kitchen?' She presented a hand down the hallway.

'We're fine, thanks, Mrs Richardson,' said Effie. 'Just going to see Manda.'

'Go ahead.' She watched them go up the stairs.

'Well, that was weird,' said Rowan, on the landing.

'Just wait.' Effie opened the door to Manda's room.

Anna gasped at the state of it. The room was nothing like it had been when she'd visited before, its order given way to chaos. Manda's creepy Victorian dolls were everywhere, but some desecrated, opened up or carved with symbols and words. There were other dolls, little fabric ones like the one at school, half made – thread, scissors and paraphernalia strewn about, shoe boxes lined up along the floor like a row of coffins . . .

Manda was lying in the bed, so still and small and frail that Anna suddenly didn't care what Manda had been doing, only if she was OK.

Manda began to stir, her eyes fluttering then flying open when she realized they were all there. She looked as if she wanted to sit up quickly, but struggled to do so, heaving herself up instead. They gathered around her.

'Manda, what's wrong?' Anna breathed.

'Do you have Death Sickness?' Rowan cried.

Manda looked over at Effie. 'Have you told them?'

'No, but I think the poppet and collapsing at school might have finally given you away.'

Manda screwed her face up as if she didn't want to remember it all. 'I still can't believe . . . how is your arm?'

'Hurts,' Effie replied, 'but you look worse than me.'

Manda lowered her eyes. 'You tell them.'

Effie shook her head and looked to Anna, Rowan and Attis. 'Manda has been combining death magic with Imagic – poppets – to control people around her.'

Manda's head fell into her hands. 'It's true.'

'MANDA?!' Rowan squealed then tried to calm herself. 'Death magic and poppets, that's like . . . that's like . . . combining henbane and hemlock, two poisons in one . . .'

'I know,' Manda responded quietly.

'How did this happen?' Rowan asked.

'Remember the night with the Hel witches?' Manda's gaze remained lowered.

'How could we forget?'

'When I was possessed, it was the single most thrilling moment of my life. I wasn't me. I was filled with something else, something powerful and compelling and . . . I've been holding back my whole life and I didn't want to any longer. I wanted to feel that way again. To live in that power. While you were all dancing I was finding everything out I could about death magic, reading their Books of the Dead, taking pictures of any spells I could find. I told myself I wouldn't use any of it, that it was just research but then, back home, I read one of the spells and couldn't get it out of my head. I'd been playing around with Imagic since our coven session on it, but I couldn't get it to work. But this spell showed how you could combine the two – poppets and spiritual energy.'

'Spiritual energy can enhance the power of any spell,' said Attis.

'Exactly and it was too tempting not to try. My life was so suffocating and I just wanted some small shred of control. I'd already drugged my parents with magic so it didn't seem like such a stretch to try out the spell on my mum. The opportunity arose – she cut her finger and I stole the plaster for her blood. Getting the hair and fingernail clippings was easier. But carving the symbols of the Language of the Dead into the doll . . . that was the hard part . . .' Manda's body seemed to shrink into the bed, into itself. 'I honestly didn't think it would work, but . . . it did. I cast the spell and Mum became more pliable. I could tell her what I was doing and she wouldn't question it. I could go out. I could meet you guys.' Her eyes expanded, doll-like themselves. 'It was—' she made a sound of exhilaration mixed with relief, 'for the first time in my life I was in control. I felt . . . fearless. I began to fashion my own fabric dolls, small and discreet, sewing the hair, blood and clippings inside. I've always been good at craft . . . and one thing led to another . . . .' Her eyes flashed to the line of shoe boxes on the floor. Anna saw then they had different names on them: Manda's parents' names. Karim. She recognized some of the names of the teachers in school.

'Go on,' Manda nodded. 'Have a look.'

Rowan opened the lids of the boxes with Manda's parents' names on. Fabric dolls – pins stuck into their eyes and ears.

'So they wouldn't see me any more,' Manda muttered. 'So they only heard what they wanted to hear.'

Rowan opened up the box marked KARIM. A pin in the heart. 'Compelled to want only me, obviously.'

Rowan took the lid off one of the teachers' boxes. Pins stuck into the mouth and hands. 'I could get the teachers to give me the grades I wanted, say whatever I needed . . . I'd stopped bothering to gather blood and fingernails by then, I found that just the link of hair was doing the job. I thought it was my power growing . . . but, of course, none of it was ever my power. It was the spirit . . . spirits . . . I don't know exactly what's been working through me. It didn't take me long to work out it was making me sick. I didn't have access to spirit powder and I'd taken some precautions at first . . . casting a circle, but I stopped bothering. I didn't care,' she said flatly. 'The only thing I cared about was keeping the spells going, making more poppets, keeping the feeling of power alive. I didn't know how to stop.' Her fingers spasmed and squeezed together as if she was barely holding on even now. 'Till Effie found out.'

'I think we all knew something was up,' said Effie, 'but I had a feeling it was something bad . . . I cornered Manda and she confessed.'

Manda shook her head at herself. 'In a twisted way I thought Effie would be on board . . .'

'Don't get me wrong,' Effie replied, 'I love dark magic but not if it's killing you, and it *was* killing you, Manda.'

'Funny,' said Manda, her voice as small as Anna had ever heard it. 'Because I'd never felt more alive.'

'Manda begged me not to tell any of you,' Effie continued. 'And I agreed on the condition that she stop.'

'I did try but I didn't know how . . . my whole life was only functioning by that point because of it and I couldn't go back. I don't think the spirits wanted me to give up. If anything I became more manic, more reckless—' She started to sob. 'I brought that poppet into school to see if I could force Ramsden to reinstate our exams somehow but Effie caught me with it. She forced me to drop it in that bin so no one would find it on me but Darcey, or one of her many minions, must have seen us through the door. And now I've ruined us all. Eames finding the poppet – I'm sorry – I'm sorry. I'll turn myself in . . . I will.'

'Like hell you will,' Effie snapped. 'We're a coven. We're all in.'

Anna lowered her own eyes with shame at Effie's words.

'But I'm a monster!' Manda wailed, with something of her old hypochondria.

Rowan rubbed her arm. 'You haven't been yourself. That's what death magic can do, it's why I'm so scared of it. Those kind of spirits can feed on the good in you, draw out the worst.'

'I hope so.' Manda's tears ran freely. 'Because if this is who I am . . . I'd rather let myself be consumed.'

'Manda, don't say that.' Anna swallowed. 'You seem already better.'

'I've started to feel more like myself again since the elixir.'

'I told Azrael what was going on,' Effie explained. 'He gave me an elixir to help with the Death Sickness, repel the spiritual energies feeding on her.' She gave Anna a brief but pointed look. 'But it will take time and determination.'

Manda nodded, looking unsure. 'I'll try – I will.' She looked up, with an edge of her old defiance. 'At least I've learnt one thing, from all this – my language.'

Rowan breathed in sharply. 'Death magic . . .?'

'No.' Manda managed a small slip of a smile.

'Oh thank the Goddess above.'

'Death magic has felt entirely consuming and wonderfully powerful, but it never felt like me. The poppets, however, with them it was like . . . like I knew exactly what I was doing, like something I'd buried had started to rise up in me again . . .' Her smile grew stronger, truer. 'Imagic is my language. I feel it.'

'Soul settling.' Rowan beamed. 'When you just know.'

'I think it's the only thing I know from all this mess.'

Anna stayed with Manda while the others packed up the dolls and death spell paraphernalia. Attis made a fire in the garden to burn any traces of the Language of the Dead away.

'I'm sorry, Anna,' Manda tried to apologize again.

'Please, don't apologize, we've all been losing our way,' said Anna, wrapped in her own thick layers of guilt as she thought of how she'd accused Effie and Manda of casting the hysteria spell only hours ago. Her self-recrimination worsened as she looked back at Manda, so frail and broken. How had she not seen how much pain her friend was in? She took Manda's hand. 'I'm sorry I wasn't there for you.'

'You tried. I've been pushing everyone away . . .' Manda clutched Anna's hand suddenly. 'What if I can't do it, Anna? What if I can't get through this? What if this magic I've been casting is stronger than I'll ever be and I get sucked back into it? Part of me wants it, even now . . .'

Anna could feel Manda's panic inside herself, yet the words rose to her lips as if she were speaking to herself. 'I don't think we can escape our darkness. I think . . . the more we run from it, the more we come to fear it. Perhaps, you need to listen to it instead, to work out why it led you here. *You* are stronger, Manda. Selene once told me that Hira is belief – your magic already believes in you. It's already shown you who you truly are.' Anna suddenly missed Selene desperately, and hated that they hadn't talked properly for weeks. Selene had tried but she'd been pushing her away too.

'You promise?' said Manda, desperation still in her eyes.

'A witch's promise.'

Manda sank back against the pillow. 'I know you understand more than anyone else. I just wanted to live up to my parents' expectations, become the person I'd always planned to be. Top grades. Top law school. Boyfriend. Be normal. For my parents to stop looking at me like . . . not just disappointed but *afraid*. As if they didn't know who I'd become. I just thought if I could try harder, become even more perfect . . . but the more I clutched onto my life the more it all fell apart and then I realized . . . why it's always been so hard . . . because it was never my life. I have no idea *what* my life is, but it took almost dying to realize – it isn't this.'

'A new start then.' Anna squeezed her hand. 'A blank page.'

'I have always liked a fresh blank page,' said Manda. 'There's nothing like new stationery.'

Anna smiled. 'I think some things about you will never change.'

Manda laughed but it turned into coughing. Anna handed her a handkerchief and saw with a jolt of fear that she was coughing up black. *Ectoplasm.*

Manda lay back down. 'If we survive this week, I have no idea what I want to do with my life . . . if I even want to be a lawyer. I know I need to break up with Karim. Oh Goddess, I've treated him so badly . . . I don't think I ever wanted to be with him. I'm not sure I've ever had feelings for any boy. I just wanted a boyfriend because I thought that's what I was meant to do, you know, break a man into loving you, marry him, produce children and then redirect all your energies into making their lives miserable instead of yours . . .'

Anna laughed and for a moment couldn't stop.

Manda snorted. 'I think I'm going to make a different plan.'

'I think that might be a good idea.'

Manda shook her head. 'How are you always so together?'

It was Anna's turn to look away now. 'Manda, I'm really not. I've been a total mess this year. I have no idea who I am any more since . . . Aunt died—' It hurt to say it, hurt to think it after Effie's words, confirming her worst fears: *You've finally turned as crazy as your aunt* . . .

'It's like without her, I'm nothing, just an imprint—'

'You're no imprint, Anna.'

'I've been trying to find a way out, but I think I've just been running too.'

'Maybe it's time to face your own darkness.' Manda raised her eyebrows over her wide, drained eyes.

'If it's not too late . . . I think I've messed everything up with Effie . . .'

'I'm sure you can work it out.' Manda fought a yawn. 'Effie's a nightmare but she never gave up on me once with all this.'

Anna lowered her head, the guilt dragging her down. 'I'll try. You sleep now.'

Once Manda had drifted off, Anna went back downstairs. Rowan was trying to speak some sense into Mr and Mrs Richardson who would apparently remain under Manda's magic until the spiritual energies had cleared. Anna saw Attis and Effie out in the garden. He was holding Effie as the fire burned behind them, their arms wrapped around one another. Entwined. The Lovers Card. Anna on the outside again. *The betrayer.* The one who'd let the curse get the better of her and she could feel it still boiling inside her – the jealousy, the bitterness, the pain of it. Perhaps, they were better off without her . . .

They met back at the bottom of the staircase.

'What are we going to do?' Rowan looked between them. 'Today changes everything. We know what Eames is capable of now. We know the secretary is behind the hysteria. And the WIPS are coming – coming to take us . . .' She wrung her hands. 'I'll tell Mum everything when I get home and she won't let us go back. It'll be done. We run tonight. Leave it all behind.'

'Manda isn't well enough to run tonight, you saw her,' said Effie quickly. 'And the WIPS aren't due till next week, there's still time.'

'For what?' Rowan cried, exasperated.

'To beat them at their own game. Things have changed, we may have people on our side now, people who are close to Eames . . .'

'Peter and Tom,' Attis spat. 'They're not going to help us! They put us at even more risk!'

'They won't tell,' said Effie. 'Tom was terrified and Peter's ours for the time being. Just a couple more days . . .' Effie pleaded, as if a plan were forming in her mind but she didn't have all the pieces yet. 'If I can't find a way then fine – we run. Manda will be stronger by then too and her parents less ... lobotomized. She can say goodbye properly.'

Anna knew that would tug at Rowan's heartstrings.

'But the hysteria could strike at our school at any moment,' Rowan stammered. 'It just killed people en masse, it could do it again.'

'It hasn't long struck St Olave's, we probably have a little time for the fear to reach breaking point again,' said Anna. 'If we're taken into hiding, there's nothing we can do to stop it.'

'Anna,' said Rowan gently, as if Anna *had* lost it. 'There *is* nothing we can do. You heard the secretary, they're not even controlling it any more, the spirit has taken over ...'

Anna grappled for a response. She knew logically Rowan was right but something was calling to her ... drawing her ... she knew it was time. *But time for what?* 'I'm not giving up yet,' she said, as stubbornly as Effie. 'I won't leave.'

Rowan looked at them as if she didn't know whether to cry or scream. She settled on cursing at the top of her voice: 'Mother bloody Holle! OK. OK. A couple of days. That's it. Enough time for Manda to get back on her feet and then I tell Mum *everything*.'

Attis shook his head, looking at Anna and Effie with sheer exasperation. 'Once Manda has recovered – we go. I'll watch her tonight. I'm not going to sleep anyway ...'

Anna glanced at him, wanting to say something, to alleviate some of his burden, but she stopped herself. She wasn't sure they were on speaking terms and what could she say that would make any of it any better? *I love you.* The words would only make it all worse.

Apparently, she and Effie weren't on speaking terms either. They took a cab back to Hackney in silence, a silence Anna could feel, rolling in seething waves towards her. Anna wanted to say something but she didn't know what she could say. Effie hadn't made anything easy, she never did, and Anna had grown tired of her tricks but ... Anna was the one who'd snapped – who'd let the curse get to her, distorting everything around her, inside of her. Breaking it all.

Back at the house, Effie went straight to her room, pretending as if Anna did not exist at all.

Anna could feel herself fracturing, like a piece of metal hammered too hard for too long. *I told you, my child, love and magic, they destroy*

everything in the end. Was it even Aunt speaking? Or simply her? Did
it matter any more?

Love and magic never destroyed everything. I did. Just like you, Aunt.

Anna went up the stairs but stopped at Selene's door, knocking on
it.

'Huh . . .' Selene's voice rose soft and muffled.

Anna opened the door. Selene was in bed – she sat up, her hair adrift
as if lost in a dream. 'You're back. Effie, too? What was wrong with
Manda?'

They'd messaged Selene to say they'd gone there for the evening, that
Manda wasn't feeling well.

'Nothing. Just a cold.' Anna paced into the room, stopping before
Selene's bed. 'I'm her, aren't I, Selene?' She held her head up defiantly
as if she were ready for the answer no matter how terrible it would be.
'I'm just like Aunt. Tell me the truth. No softening it, dancing around
it. Just the truth.'

Selene got out of bed, coming over to Anna. 'What's going on?'

'I thought I could escape it.' Anna's voice rose, oscillating. 'But I'm
right back where I started – I love Attis. I hate Effie. And I'm going
to destroy it all, just like Aunt. I've already started.'

Selene pulled Anna to the edge of the bed, sitting down beside her.
'Is that what you want me to say? That you're like her?'

'She's been with me all year, Selene. Haunting me. But maybe it was
never her.' Anna laughed desolately. 'Maybe it was me all along.'

'Anna—'

'You brought me up on stories of Marie, how she always drew
everyone's attention, how she was outgoing, boisterous, brave . . . how
she wasn't afraid to feel everything. She's Effie. And I'm Aunt. I always
was.'

The soft haze about Selene disappeared, replaced with a serious,
sorrowful expression Anna rarely saw. 'Well, that sounds incredibly tidy,
but I've always found if a story is black and white – it's not a true story.
The story of your aunt and Marie certainly wasn't so simple. You think
Marie was perfect? I guess that's my fault . . . I'm guilty of remembering
her with rose-tinted glasses, because it's easier that way and I am one
for the easier route in life.' She half smiled but there was little joy in
it, her eyes flicking upwards as if they were travelling back somewhere.
'I remember when we were at school, your mother found Vivienne's

diary. Viv had a crush on one of the teachers and, oh, it was full of daydreams and teenage angst. She was always a romantic at heart.'

'A romantic?' Anna hissed darkly, disbelievingly.

'Darling, creating a copy of your dead lover and keeping it locked away in the attic like a dream that never was . . . there's romance in that; dark, wretched, deranged romance, but romance still. Anyway, your mother took the diary and she was reading it out loud to me, in full dramatic swing, when Viv came in. We were caught red-handed and Viv was distraught . . . angry. She asked for it back but Marie turned it into a game, running away, jumping from bed to bed, reading from it, Viv shouting after her. It was mean, revealing her secrets like that.'

Anna had to admit it was hard to unite the image of the mother in her head with Selene's story.

'They saw things so differently, even then. Marie thought it a game – probably didn't understand why Vivienne was taking it all so seriously – and was feeling guilty at being caught, I imagine, while Vivienne saw nothing but Marie's cruelty, her own humiliation.'

'Effie plays games and I take everything too seriously,' said Anna. 'It's still us.'

'But your mother, she was quick to say sorry, to see her own faults, to admit she was wrong. Vivienne wouldn't hear of it. She was inflexible even then, convinced by her own righteousness. She refused to speak to your mother for over a month. I had to pass messages back and forth between them.' Selene laughed but it cut itself short. 'I worry, you see, I worry that Effie is like Vivienne sometimes, so . . . so set on her path and everything else be burned. Vivienne never questioned herself, her choices. She saw the world only her own way – and so she built walls around herself, lived in fear of herself. The very fact that you worry you're like your aunt, that you question yourself, is why you will never be like her. You face yourself, Anna, in a way Vivienne never could.' Selene brushed Anna's hair over her shoulder. 'And you have Marie's fire, matchstick . . . her warmth, her kindness, her heart. It's why you can't let your aunt go, because, despite everything she did to you, you loved her so much, so deeply. It is your love that haunts you, for fear is love turned inside out.'

'No.' Anna shook her head against it, the darkness opening up within her. *I won't look down.* 'If I ever loved her, it died the day I found out she killed my mother.'

'If only love were a simple story too,' Selene sighed. 'But it's not and I know that because I loved her too, Anna. Part of me still does.'

Anna realized she was crying, the tears rising up from the endless well inside her. 'I can't love her . . .'

Selene wiped one from her cheek. 'Your love is your greatest strength, Anna; don't fight it. You are far stronger than Vivienne – or me, for that matter.' Selene looked down at her fingers, fiddling with one. 'I was always too scared to bear the true weight of love.'

Anna looked up at her. 'You love Effie and me.'

'But that just *is*. It was the other kind of love I never had the courage for – that I ran from . . .' Selene looked unsure for a moment but then she stood up and went over to her jewellery box on her chest of drawers and took something out. She came back to sit by Anna on the bed and revealed the dull iron ring she'd taken from Aunt's house. 'This ring is a locking ring, created by the GoldiLocks witches.'

'I have no idea what that means.'

Selene laughed but it floated away sadly. 'Remember I told you I loved someone once? Well, I did, but it wasn't going to work out and I couldn't bear the pain of it. I wanted out. I wanted out of him, out of love. The GoldiLocks are the closest thing we have to lawyers in the magical world. They work with magical contracts, rings and keys – they can lock things away for good . . . even such things as love. And so that love I'd felt for him was locked away, inside this little thing.' She let it roll into the centre of her palm.

Anna looked down at the ring in shock, trying to imagine how such a dull and heavy thing could contain such a thing as Selene's love.

'But the contract for the spell required three blood signatures to seal it – my own, a GoldiLocks representative and a witness.' Selene closed her eyes, clutching the ring in her palm. 'I asked your aunt if she would be my witness, if she would give her magic to the spell, and she agreed. This was before she became a Binder, of course.'

'You didn't go to my mother?'

'I wanted to, but I couldn't face Marie. I knew she'd judge what I was doing, try to convince me out of it, tell me that it was better to hurt from love than to hide from it. Viv, however, understood such things, but it was a grave error. You see, as one of the signatories she had the power to undo the spell, to tear the wound open again. At the time, I never thought she'd use it against me, but that was before she began to change, before she became the Vivienne you knew.'

It dawned on Anna slowly and then all at once. 'You told me last year that she had something on you – that it was why you agreed to her plan, to raise Effie and I apart and bring us together at sixteen for the curse. It was this, wasn't it?'

Selene nodded. 'It was. I can't lie and tell you that I wasn't terrified of her undoing it – I'd become who I was on the back of that spell and I didn't know who I'd be if she unlocked it. But I had other reasons for going along with her plan too, or perhaps that's what I tell myself to help me sleep at night.' She smiled sadly. Selene always smiled through her sadness. 'I should have found another way. Anyway, now Vivienne is gone, she can't break the spell, but I fear this ring, still. This silly, ugly ring.'

She clasped her hand around it as if she didn't want to look at it any more. Anna tried to tally Selene's words with the powerful witch she knew, the witch who created potions of passion and longing and desire, potions of such colour they couldn't be contained. Selene was afraid of love. *Afraid.*

'But . . . you never want to fall in love?'

Selene shook her head with certainty. 'No. I tried it once and that was enough for me. I did love him, darling, I really did. He was a cowan. Married. Impossible situation. He broke it off with me just before Christmas which is why I can't stand the holiday still. Oh, but he was funny.' She smiled distantly. 'The belly-laugh kind of funny.'

Anna smiled too. 'What do you mean?'

'You know, the kind of person who can make you laugh from that deep place in your belly, the kind of laugh you can't stop once it's started. But love wasn't enough for me. I wanted it to be something it wasn't – something all-consuming. I wanted fireworks to go off in my soul every day, to burn like I'd flown too close to the sun – ecstasy, tragedy and nothing in between. But it was everything in between, it was complicated and confusing and hard, and it hurt all the time, and sometimes it was just . . . very ordinary. I'm Selene Fawkes. I don't *do* ordinary, darling.'

Anna laughed. 'That is true . . .'

'I can hear the *but* coming, Anna. I know you won't agree with my decision and that is because you're your mother's daughter, but it was *my* decision and it made me the woman I am today.'

Anna struggled to comprehend it all. *Had the decision taken away from who Selene was or had it made her?* Anna tried to imagine locking away her love for Attis, but she couldn't bear the thought of looking at his smile and feeling nothing. It would be worse than feeling too much, than feeling what she felt now.

'It's why I'm guarded over my love life, why who I date and how I date is my decision and my decision alone. I'm sorry if that's hurt you over Reiss.'

'I don't care who you date, Selene, I just want you to be careful. I don't trust Reiss.' *Nor his son . . .*

'I know.'

'Was that man you truly loved, was he . . . Attis's father?'

Selene nodded. 'My love was already locked away by then . . . when we made Attis, but I wanted it to be him.'

'Then you have a chance to love again, a different kind of love.'

Selene frowned. 'What's that?'

'To love Attis. You can't run from him forever. He's your son.'

Selene stilled. She didn't speak for a while, and when the words came, they were as soft as the tip of a paint brush, barely there. 'Don't you see, darling? If I let that in . . . even just a little, then I don't think I could have gone through with it, any of it. I wouldn't be able to live with myself.' She put a hand to her mouth, fingers shaking, tears quaking suddenly in her eyes, on the edge of release but not free. 'I told you, matchstick, I'm not as brave as you.'

'It's not too late.'

Anna felt Selene sag beside her, under the weight of the love she would not let herself feel.

'I want to be as brave as my mother . . .' Anna muttered.

Selene raised her chin to Anna, eyes of violet magnificence. 'You, Anna Everdell, are not your mother, or your aunt. And neither is Effie. They have both given each of you gifts but if you want to let your aunt go – you need to find your own way.

Anna stared back at Selene, seeing her now as she truly was and not as she'd imagined her for so much of her life – the fairy godmother of her dreams, come to rescue her. No. She was a beautiful clash of colours and contradictions; someone who needed saving too.

'Thanks, Selene. I'm glad you are exactly who you are.' Anna swallowed. 'And I'm so lucky to have you.'

Selene began to cry then.

THIMBLE

When a Hel witch marries another we do not call it heartknotting but bone-weaving, for a heart is easy to love, but to love the bones of another is a love that stands all tests of time.

Traditions and Customs, Books of the Dead: Tome 3576

You must go down to come back up,
Learn the truth where all forget . . .

Anna lay alone in the dark, Nana's riddle trickling through the deepest reaches of her mind. There was something about finally being lost that showed her which way she needed to go.

The mirrored book knows the way to the dead . . .

She put out her hand and the book of fairy tales flew to her, pages fluttering and releasing a black feather which danced in the air above her. She caught it and traced its black curve, sharp and soft, like the shadow of a laugh, like an arrow, like fear itself showing her the way.

It fell into place, light as snow.

Manda's poppets had reminded Anna of the basics of Imagic, how blood, hair and bone were required to link the poppet to your victim—

Three ways, three keys,
Can a man be owned:
Red, black, white,
Blood, hair and bone.

Anna opened the book to the fifth fairy tale: 'Trit-A-Trot'. The maiden who had to spin gold from straw; the strange man who came to her offering help in return for the black comb in her hair, one of her white teeth and the red heart of her firstborn. It was a key to the secrets of Imagic, wasn't it? The black comb for hair, the white tooth for bone, the red heart for blood. The three things required to cast an Imagic spell. And the final part – speaking the name of whoever it was you wished to control . . . Only when the girl knew Trit-A-Trot's true name did she take back power.

Then Bertie calling Eyevain by its other names including *Faen*. Anna turned to the third fairy tale: *The Ice Coffin*. Faen was one of the names of the seven brothers. Were their names codes for the sacred herbs of the Botanical language? The herbs of healing and eternal life? *Una, Wergulu, Maythen, Faen, Belene, Rugge and Springwort*.

The year before, the first fairy tale had helped Anna create her moon mirror. *Planetary*.

The second had held the secrets of earth, air, fire and water. *Elemental*.

She'd known the tales hid secret knowledge of spells, she just hadn't realized *which* spells, but now it was clear. They aligned with the seven original languages, the first seven spells of the Goddess, in their original order: Planetary. Elemental. Botanical. Verbal. Imagic. Symbolic. Emotional.

Which meant the fourth tale, 'The Seven Ravens', corresponded to Verbal. *Words*. The Language of the Dead – the first language ever to be written, created by the Goddess, to travel to the Underworld and speak with spirits. Could the tale show her how to travel there too? Was it . . . *a map to the Underworld?*

Anna snapped the book shut, terrified by her own deductions. The symbol on the front reflected the moonlight. A mirror. A tree above and a tree below. One gleaming with leaves and the other stripped to branch, to bone. *As above, so below.*

She stayed up until the moon rose high, grazing the edge of her window. She tried to think logically about it all but logic told her she was crazy. A loon beneath the moon. Her heart told her it was the only way left. The only path remaining. She'd read 'The Seven Ravens' so many times she knew it off by heart, as if the words were threaded into her own skin and she could feel them tugging . . .

No way out but through.

Anna knew what she had to do. She went downstairs and knocked on Effie's door, not hopeful Effie would be awake but a voice came back, harder than the knock. 'Who is it?'

'Anna.'

'Go away. I'm sleeping.'

'I need to speak to you.'

'Really? Oh, wait, I don't care.'

Anna opened the door anyway. Effie was alone in bed, her phone screen on. She lowered it and her face closed off, her eyes black and uncommunicative. 'What are you doing in here?'

'I need to talk to you. Can we go to the roof? It's important.'

'Going to accuse me of murder again? Ooo, or are you going to murder me? Push me off the roof so you can finish off the curse and have Attis.'

'I'm going to try to go to Hel,' said Anna.

Effie stared at her, a moon-slice of intrigue breaking through her eyes. 'You're joking.'

'Am I?'

A few minutes later they surfaced onto the roof together, the night drenching them in its sudden dark so that the boundaries between them didn't feel quite so immutable.

Still, Effie stood at a distance, folding her arms. 'So, you *have* finally lost it.'

Anna faced her. 'I know what I just said sounds mad. It *is* mad, but I've solved Nana's riddle and, basically, the book of fairy tales—'

Effie's eyes began to roll higher than the moon but Anna ploughed on.

'The seven fairy tales link to the seven original languages and their spells, which means the fourth fairy tale stands for Verbal, the first written language ever created, made by the Goddess to travel to the Underworld, to speak with spirits. I think the tale is a kind of guide to . . . navigating Hel.'

Effie flung a hand out. 'Let me get this straight, you're going into the mouth of Hel with nothing more than a fairy tale to guide you?'

Anna tried to think of something that sounded more convincing, but gave up. 'Well – yes – that's it. I can't explain it, I just know it. I know it like the way magic feels when you cast a spell, like you don't even understand what's happening but everything makes sense all at once. I know it like how we were drawn together before we even knew we were sisters. I know it like how the moon knows how to rise in the sky each night. I know it's been coming. The Underworld has been beckoning me.'

'This isn't helping your case.'

'I've been haunted all year, Effie! Half alive myself!' Anna cried, throwing away any reserve. 'Death and its ravens have been calling me, chasing me. I thought they were trying to destroy me, but I see now – they've been preparing me. Magic has been preparing me for this. The snows of Hel too . . . I've seen snow in my dreams, in the darkness . . . Think of the crystal ball with the medium. It's what she saw.' Anna knew she was talking too fast, making limited sense but she couldn't stop. 'The Underworld has been drawing me all this time. Nana's riddle knows it too – it wants me to go there. You told me to stop living in my aunt's shadow, well I'm not going to any more. I'm not going to let fear control me. I'm going to the place fear goes to die. And, anyway, there isn't a choice. You heard the secretary – the hysteria can't be stopped except by going to the source and no one else is going to go.'

'So you are?'

'A witch is only limited by her imagination.'

Effie smiled at that. 'And you think your imagination can encompass all of Hel?'

'I think I can do it and I have to do it – not just to stop the hysteria spell.' Anna paused with significance. 'The riddle: *You must go down to come back up, learn the truth where all forget* . . . I think it's referring to the Waters of the Dead, the River of Forgetting, that takes the memories of all who have died. Remember Mór said if you drink from it it will bring you the memory you seek. If I go to Hel, I can retrieve Eleanor's memories, I can discover the true story of the curse – how it began, how it was cast, how Attis was created. I think there's more to the story, another way to break us all free without him having to die or the curse having to kill one of us.'

Effie's face hardened, retreating from the moonlight. 'You sure about that? Feels to me like the cracks are already there . . .' Her implication was clear. 'After all, you already think I'm a mass murderer.'

'I don't think that – I – it wasn't that simple.' Anna moved towards her. 'I'm sorry, Effie, I'm sorry, I wasn't thinking straight, I was angry and suspicious and I leapt to stupid conclusions. You had the Hel witch connections – spending so much time with Azrael even though you don't seem to like him all that much – and you hate the WIPS and all the cowans who believe in their cause. I thought maybe you'd become caught up somehow in the hysteria spell as a way of retaliating against it all. I never thought you meant to kill people. Maybe the curse has got to me or maybe we just don't know each other at all. How could we? We've been sisters for less than a year.'

Effie's eyes stilled, shining with anger and other unknown emotions. 'You want to know me, *sis?* Well, here you go: I don't like cowans, but I don't want to see them die. I hate my enemies, but I protect my friends to the end. I've spent time with Azrael because he's useful for information . . . and I'm fucking lonely. Attis and I have been together my whole life – did you ever think how hard it might be for me not being able to turn to him when I need him, to have him when I want him? He was mine, Anna. Mine!'

Anna stepped back against her onslaught, feeling Effie's pain thrash against her.

'I need him,' said Effie, walking away, stopping in front of the empty tin drum where Attis's fire had long turned cold. She sat down on the edge of the sun lounger, smiling miserably like a clown with no tricks left. 'I know you had the world's worst childhood and all, but growing up with Selene wasn't easy. We were never still. Different countries, new schools, new people. She spoilt me, then ignored me, lavished me with attention, then disappeared. The summer.' Effie looked up to the sky. 'The summer was the only consistent thing in my life. She'd drop me off in Wales with Attis and it was like . . . home. Attis was my home. My only true friend. My first kiss. The first boy I slept with. The world could keep spinning and it didn't matter because we had each other. I was the first name on his lips and I always thought I'd be the last name too – and then . . . last year, the curse, you, discovering it had been a *lie*. When we went back to Wales this summer . . . it didn't even feel the same, like a part of him was already gone.' Her eyes met Anna's. 'Do you know what it's like to feel so lost you can barely breathe almost every second of the day?'

'I do,' Anna replied, coming to sit on the chair beside her. 'Like everything's broken.'

'No. I was *already* broken, that's the point. He held me together.'

'He loves you, Effie. He will always love you.'

Effie narrowed her eyes, a single tear unloosing. 'Is that what you want? Do you want him to love me?'

Anna held Effie's gaze. She could not hide the turmoil in her eyes, the turmoil inside of her. If they were going to do this together they had to show it all, bear it all. 'I know that whatever I feel, I don't want the curse to control me any more. I know I want to believe in us over it. I know I want you as my sister more than anything.'

Effie looked away. 'How it brings us together, even as it tears us apart . . .'

'It doesn't have to.' Anna grabbed her hand. 'We can overcome it.' Effie stared down at Anna's hand in hers. Anna wanted to feel their magic entwine, for Effie to call down her spider tattoo as she had done before—

But Effie took her hand back and shut her palm. 'Why have you told me about Hel?'

'Because I need your help. I need you to contact Azrael and see if he can get me to the senior Hel witches.'

'Why would they agree to meeting us again?'

'Because you're very convincing. Cajole. Exaggerate. Lie. Do what you have to do. I need to go tomorrow night.'

'OK.' Effie nodded. 'But only if I go too.'

Anna drew back. 'No. No – I – I thought you thought this whole thing was crazy?'

'When did crazy ever stop me doing something? I'm not letting my sister go alone into Hel. I'd never miss out on such fun.'

'You can't come.' A shrill note of panic entered Anna's voice. 'I know I just said all that but actually I have no idea what I'm doing.'

'I know.' Effie stood up, walking to the edge of the roof and turning around to lean against it. 'Hence, you need me. My street smarts. You grew up sewing embroideries, how are you going to survive the Underworld?'

'Effie, you can't, please—'

Effie put a hand up. 'This is non-negotiable. If you want my help to arrange this then either *we* go or neither of us goes.'

'If anything happened to you, it would be my fault.'

'This is my choice. It's our curse – we should end it together.'

Anna's insides tore in different directions. What if her plan *was* madness? What if she was luring her own sister to her death? What if it was merely the curse beckoning them there all along? She'd tried to be so certain in her uncertainty but it felt like she was walking an invisible tightrope over a ravine of unknown depths . . . and she was going to let her sister just follow her. But then . . . the thought of having Effie by her side, Effie's fearlessness in the face of the darkness. A part of her wanted her sister there too.

'You know you have no choice, so you may as well agree.' Effie shrugged, gazing out over London below, like a queen over her empire. She turned back to Anna, black hair flying about in the wind. 'Together.'

Anna smiled through her distress. 'Together.'

'Besides, everyone's always told me I should go to Hel. It's probably time I listened.'

Somehow, Anna made it through the next day of school. They didn't see Eames or Ramsden. There were rumours Ramsden had been sacked and Anna presumed them to be true. He'd stood up to Eames and that would not be tolerated. Anna and Effie spoke to no one of their plan, but there was one person Anna needed to speak to. She'd worked out the last line of Nana's riddle.

But heed his offer, hold tight your thread!

When she got home she dug out the card: JERRY TINKER. TRADER OF MAGICAL HOUSEHOLD WARES, FOR THE WITCH WITH TOO MUCH ON HER PLATE! The writing gleamed like slime and turned her stomach. Anna recalled the little ditty he'd sung to her: *Heed his offers, friend or foe, or else he'll sing: I told you so.* She'd not forgotten the moonthread – a thread of such light it could withstand any darkness. Where she was going, she was going to need it.

She dialled what looked like a nonsensical number. No one answered the call. She tried the number again and again and then threw the card down in frustration. How could she find Jerry Tinker now? Portobello Market wouldn't be on right now and she had no idea where else in London he could be.

While she tried to work out what to do, Anna went downstairs to meet Effie. Attis was down in his forge and Anna prayed he'd remain there. Effie was already dressed, all in white, as Anna had told her.

Effie rapped her hands against the kitchen counter. 'I should go. Azrael's waiting and we want to keep him sweet.' Azrael had managed to get them a meeting with the Hel witches but he wanted to meet with Effie first.

Anna nodded.

They stared at each other, half smiling, as if the idea of what they were going to do still felt like a joke, as if a smile could keep the fear away.

Selene came into the kitchen from upstairs. 'I'm going out to see Bertie, apparently there's new information—' She paused, looking between them. 'What are you two up to?'

Anna looked down. 'Just going to meet some friends for the evening.'

Selene frowned. 'You know I'm not one for rules, but I think I'd rather you both stay home for the time being.'

'We won't be late,' Effie replied, 'and we're always careful.'

Selene gave her a look. 'Could you please try to be careful for the first time in your life?' She forced a smile. 'How about I pick up some brownies from the bakery tonight? Entice you home early and we can have a decadent midnight snack before bed.'

'Sounds good,' Anna managed to say through the choke-hold of guilt. Where would they be at midnight? Would they ever return?

Effie threw a nod Selene's way, turning to leave, but stopped, swivelled around, walked to Selene and gave her a hug – brief and tight. Selene threw her arms out with a look of bafflement. Then she wrapped them around Effie and kissed her on the top of her head before Effie could pull away, which she did.

'Meet me later,' Effie said to Anna and left, not looking back.

Selene turned to Anna with renewed suspicion. 'Are you sure everything's OK? That wasn't like Effie . . .'

'Maybe she's coming around at last. Realizing she needs you.'

Selene's smile was real this time, tentative but real. 'Not as much as I need you two.' She looked flustered as she picked up her bag. 'I never thought I'd turn into one of those mums who worry, but here we are. Next I'll be getting wrinkles.'

'Never,' Anna declared.

'Thank you, darling, you're an excellent liar.'

Just after Selene had left, the doorbell rang, which was strange, because they didn't have a doorbell. Anna went into the hallway and looked out of the window. A squat, balding man wearing a scruffy suit was standing outside, carrying a black briefcase. *Jerry*. He'd come.

Now that he was here, Anna questioned what she was doing. She needed the moonthread, but at what cost? But she couldn't give up on the riddle, it had led her this far and Nana had not failed her. She had to trust in something. Besides, all stupid decisions paled in comparison with *going to Hel*. She opened the door.

'Zip!' Jerry raised a finger, a sly smile widening. 'You called! I thought I might be hearing from you again, Cindermaid . . .'

'Thank you for coming.'

He tipped an invisible hat. 'No trouble at all. I'm here for all witches, no matter the woes or warts they bear. Now, what can I get you?' He looked her up and down. 'Did you decide you wanted that figure-changing apron after all? Or I can do you—'

'No, Jerry. I require one thing only.'

'Ah! I see, a to-the-point customer. Is it one of my more *specialist* items, perhaps?'

'The moonthread,' said Anna directly, wanting to keep their encounter as brief as possible. She prayed he hadn't sold it already.

He made a low, wet clicking noise in his throat. 'I see, I see.' He opened his briefcase, reached deep into its black innards, his arm disappearing, and pulled out the spool of silver thread, so bright that everything else seemed to wither inconsequentially against it. 'No ordinary item,' he said, 'for no ordinary Cindermaid.'

Anna reached for it but he pulled his hand away. 'Now, how much did I say? Four hundred pounds?'

'You said three hundred.'

'Ah! But who can put a price on such an item? On such beauty, such magic . . .'

'I don't have that kind of money,' said Anna, fearing to speak her next words, 'so I'm going to have to take you up on your other offer.'

Jerry's murky eyes shone hungrily. 'A secret! Ah! Yes! I'm in the mood for a secret. It'll have to be a big one though. I sense a big one in you. It's been a long time since I've had something I can sink my teeth into.' He twisted a finger at her and wedged his foot against the door. 'And don't think you can trick me, I know when I'm being dealt an empty hand. So what is it?'

Anna looked at the moonthread in his hand. 'Its light never goes out no matter how dark?'

'Never. Now, your secret—'

'Actually, there is something else I might require. That bottomless thimble you showed me before. Can it hold liquid?'

'What strange requests you have for me . . . but yes.' He reached back into his briefcase, pulling out the thimble and a bottle of water. He took the lid off the bottle and poured the water into the thimble. The water disappeared into the thimble until the whole bottle was empty. Jerry tipped the thimble the other way and nothing came out. 'Stored in there until you need it.' This time when he tipped it out the water came running out, splashing all over their doorstep. He took a bow.

'Good. I'll take the moonthread and the thimble in return for my secret.'

Jerry gurgled a laugh. 'Now, now, two items equals two secrets.'

'That's my final offer.' Anna folded her arms. 'It's a very big secret, I think you'll want to hear it.'

His mouth slipped about, trying to contain its anger. He almost looked as if he was going to start stamping his feet. 'Hmm. A very sneaky Cindermaid.' Then he spat on his hand and put it out. 'Done.'

Anna grimaced, but spat on her own hand and met his, shaking firmly three times while trying to ignore the squelching sounds.

He leant in, ready.

Anna bent down to his ear, whispering her biggest secret. 'I'm a cursed witch.'

She could hear his lips slapping together again as if he were eating up her words. He pulled away, looking entirely satiated. 'Hmm. As good as I'd anticipated. What a dark little secret you have there, Cindermaid. Hmm. Yes. Dark indeed.'

Anna felt a rush of hollow fear at what she'd done, the risk she'd taken when cursed witches were going missing, but the risks ahead of her consumed everything else – she had to go into Hel, bind a spirit, and somehow get herself and her sister back out alive. He handed over the moonthread and thimble and she took them.

'Thank you.'

'No, thank you,' he said in a way that made her inwardly shudder and then he began to dance. 'When the tinker comes to call, share your secrets, warts and all! Heed his offers, friend or foe, or else he'll sing: I told you so—'

Anna closed the door on him.

She went back upstairs and took a quick, hot bath, scrubbing her hands but not quite able to scrub away the unease of what she'd done. She clothed herself in white just like the maiden in the fairy tale. White trousers, white jumper and a pair of trainers – light, agile, easy to run in. She laid her equipment out on her bed: a spool of thread. A thimble. Her mirror. Not the most formidable set of weapons considering where she was going.

She put her hand out to the wall, feeling dizzy. *Do I have any idea what I'm doing?*

Don't answer that.

She put the items into a small bag which she slung over her shoulder. She tied her hair back into a high ponytail and surveyed herself in the mirror. She hadn't spent a lot of time looking in mirrors over the past year and was surprised by how much older she looked – the year had taken its toll; the slow, ringing toll of Hel calling.

The day had almost faded beyond the window. Anna wanted to cling onto it, to the fragments of light on her walls. *What if I never see light again?* She put a fist to her stomach, almost doubling over with the fear of what she was about to do, not only for herself, but for Effie.

A sharp rap on her door startled her.

She dithered, fearing who it was.

'Anna, I know you're in there—'

She didn't want to open it. If there was one thing that could keep her from going to Hel – it was him.

'Anna—'

She opened the door a crack. 'Yep?'

'What's going on? Did I just hear you talking to someone? Who was it?'

'Er—'

'Peter?' Attis's face darkened.

'No. It wasn't Peter.'

He looked down at her, registering her odd outfit, the bag around her shoulder. 'Where are you going? You and Effie have been acting weird all day—'

'We're just going out. Effie's gone ahead.'

His brows knitted together. He knew as well as Anna that she and Effie were unlikely to be embarking on a friendly evening out. 'Effie told me she was seeing Azrael. What are you two planning? I didn't even think you were speaking.'

'It's best you don't know,' Anna whispered, but he stepped inside, eyes moving over her room.

'What's going on, Anna? I deserve to know.'

Anna stilled, trying to calm him. 'You're right. You do.' He came close, the smell of him blurring her thoughts and slicing open a clean line across her middle.

What if I never see him again?

She'd give up the light of day before that.

He was searching her now, not his usual, gentle inquiry but frantic and demanding. She drew back. 'We're going to the Underworld to stop the hysteria spell.'

He went still as if he hadn't quite heard her, then his expression curled like paper in flame, a furnace of outrage. 'WHAT? YOU'RE DOING WHAT? YOU AND EFFIE—' He shook his head. 'No. No way. That's not an option. That's an *insane* option. You can't go. I won't let you go.'

'We have to.'

'Nobody *has* to go to the Underworld!'

'I do.'

Anna told him then, explained it all as she had to Effie. Nana's riddle. The fairy tales. How death had been calling her. Then she told him the last bit, the bit she'd vowed to herself never to tell him – that she'd found his spell in the Bible. That it demanded his death. That she needed to go to Hel not only to stop the hysteria but the curse too. In Attis's defence, he listened. He listened with grey, turbulent eyes but when she'd finished, he closed them and spoke slowly, as if every word pained him. 'A fairy tale?'

'You told me that stories could be maps . . .'

'I chat a lot of bullshit when I'm trying to sound impressive!'

Anna held back a desperate laugh. 'But you were right. They can be. This one is.'

'How can you know? How will you navigate your way? How will you get back out again? Even if you get there, how will you bind a spirit?' His questions hammered like nails breaking against a wall.

'It won't all make sense . . . I don't think . . . until I'm there.' Anna spoke faster in response to the look on his face. 'I can't explain it, I just know that I'm connected to all this, to everything going on. That Hel has been calling me. Plenty of witches have travelled there and made it back out again.'

'After years of training!'

'I've had years of training! My life with Aunt was hell.' She tried to smile but he looked away. 'You don't have to understand it, Attis, you only have to trust me.'

His head shook as if it would never stop, his voice rough and broken. 'The whole year – you've spent the whole year telling me not to die and you're going to walk into the arms of death . . .'

'It's not the same.'

'*How* is this not the same?'

'Because I have no intention of dying. I can do this.' She stepped towards him. 'I know I can do this. This isn't giving up, it's the opposite.'

He looked up with a fresh challenge on his face. 'And if I kill myself now then I could end the curse. It would be over. Would you still go?'

'Yes.' Anna raised her head to him. 'I'm going first and foremost for the hysteria spell. And if you kill yourself now, all it will mean is I have no reason to come back—' Her voice caught.

His face tremored, as if he couldn't keep it together any more. 'Then, I'm coming.'

'No!' She tried not to scream. 'It isn't possible. Azrael has managed to get the Hel witches to agree to meet with Effie and me only. We're already pushing our luck, if we start asking for more people to come they're going to shut us down altogether. I can't risk it.'

'I'm not letting you two go alone.'

'And what if something happened to you in the Underworld? We could lose our only cure for the curse . . .'

His eyes narrowed. 'I thought you'd never let me die for the curse?'

'I won't.'

'Are you trying to Catch 22 me, Anna?'

'Maybe.'

'So I'm just expected to let the two people I care most about in the world . . . just leave?'

'Yes,' she said, pleading, but he stepped closer to her, backing her against the wall, beneath the might of him, beneath the hard slate of his eyes.

'I could stop you. I could make you stay.'

'I know—' She swallowed.

He looked down at her, hair falling about his face. 'Do you want me to?'

It was an unfair question. He was too close, so close she couldn't think straight. She felt acutely how unmatched they were – he was bigger, stronger, and though she'd held him with her circle before, she'd had the advantage of surprise – if their magic went head to head, she wasn't sure whose would win. And yet, it wasn't the threat of him that held her, but his proximity, the ache in her throat, the weakness in her limbs. He didn't need force, he could keep her there with a kiss.

'You told me you would never try to contain me,' she whispered.

He thumped his fist against the wall above her and moved away, lowering his head, his shoulders rounded in defeat.

She went over to him, putting a hand on one shoulder, drawing him back around. 'I'm sorry, Attis.'

'Don't be sorry, just come back.' He moved towards her as if he would grab her but his hands fell to his sides, his face just above hers. 'When do you need to leave?'

'In about ten minutes.'

'I need to tell you something before you go. I can't do it here.'

'OK . . .' Anna replied, as unsure as he looked.

He put out his hand. She took it.

They ran down the stairs together, Anna not knowing where they were going. He led her through the kitchen, out of the back door and into the garden. He turned to face her, and before she knew it, their garden and Mr Ramsden chewing on a plant were gone, replaced by the vastness that Attis had been holding back – a wildness that had upturned the clouds, twisted the trees, thrown boulders of rocks at the distant hills. It was evening in his chimera, a misty golden evening light still burning behind the hills as if a match had been lit beneath the ground. The air smelt of grass and the moment before rain. Anna felt the cracks in her heart break all over again. *Why bring her here? It had been hard enough to leave already.*

He took her hands now, softly, looking into her eyes, softer still. 'You were brave enough to tell me how you felt, but I've been a coward. I wasn't ready or I didn't want to be ready, but I am now.' His eyes moved over her face, *one dark, one light.* 'I love you, Anna Everdell.'

She wasn't sure if the words were real. If they were only a trick to make her stay. 'I thought . . . you hated me. After I accused Effie . . .'

He frowned. 'Hated you? No. No. Things have been complicated, confusing, but no, I could never—'

'But you love Effie . . .'

'Goddess-damn it, Anna! This isn't about Effie. This is about you. I loved you last year and I love you still. I thought, back then, that everything was simple. I thought making you fall for me would be easy, but it made everything impossible and ever since I've been lost and confused and an idiot seven times over. I've been trying to run back to who I used to be or to who I thought I was but you damn well won't let me and it's infuriating and utterly terrifying . . . but if you're facing Hel itself, I should at least be brave enough to tell you that I love you, because I do. I do. I do . . .'

He looked as if he were the one breaking now. Anna let his words sink in, trying not to fight them, trying to believe in them. She'd wished for them as much as she'd feared them and now there they were – rising above her into the sky like the stars he'd taught her to follow. There was a helpless, desperate look on his face. She tried to find her own words, but sense had fled her, her mind was an incoherent blur.

And so she looked down at their hands, focusing instead on the touch of their fingers, the exact shade of his warmth, a rough patch on his palm from working in the forge. She could feel his bones wrapped around her bones. Entwined but in motion – fingers moving over one another in tentative exploration. She could feel her entire body in that single, painful, all-encompassing touch.

The chimera seemed to pale against the realness of him. She looked up into his eyes. 'You love me?' She smiled.

He smiled back, the mists in his eyes clearing. 'Was it ever a question?'

She breathed in the simple joy of his words, pretending, just for a moment, that nothing else existed. Nothing but them and their world.

Then she separated her hands from his. 'Wait there. Did you compare loving me to having to journey into Hel?'

He laughed with sudden vigour. 'I'm merely pointing out the similarities.'

'You should try loving you then.'

'Touché.' His smile hitched. He stepped closer, the gold of the sky in his hair, in his eyes. 'Are you sure you have to go? I know several activities much more fun than travelling to the Underworld.' His eyes grazed over her lips.

Anna's stomach somersaulted, her body burning in response to that look. It took every last drop of her effort not to respond 'Attis . . .'

'I know.' He pushed himself away. 'We can't. We can't.' He shook his head as if to clear it. 'I haven't told you I love you for any reason other than to tell you. No agenda. Just a statement of fact. I don't want to come between you and Effie, it's why I've kept this in for so long.'

'You love Effie too,' said Anna.

He nodded. 'I always have.' His brow creased in confusion, as if he were seeing them both before him. 'I – it's different . . . I love Effie so much I was going to die for her, but loving you has made me want to live.'

Anna hardly dared to believe his words. 'You do?'

'I don't want to die, Anna. I intend to live.'

She stood back. 'You promise me Attis Lockerby, you promise me – you're not just saying it?'

'I swear by the moon.'

A faint moon appeared in the sky behind his head.

'No tricks.'

'I mean it, Anna.' He took her hands, the touch just as distracting as before, more so. 'I swear by the dark moon and the light, I've given up trying to die. I'm not leaving you, or Effie. I know you'll find a way to end the curse.'

Anna fixed him with a determined look. 'I will. I need to go.'

He nodded but did not let her go.

She pulled him in to her and he fell against her, his head resting on her shoulder. She ran a hand through the soft copper of his hair, feeling some of the heaviness he'd been carrying around lift at her touch.

'I'll come back,' she whispered, knowing if she did, she could never hold him like this again. He nodded and drew back, just a little. He kissed her on the cheek, soft as smoke, a painless flame that was gone almost as soon as it had been lit. The wilderness disappeared from view and they were back in the garden. Night had arrived, but where she was going would be darker.

'Go,' he said, his voice so low, so raw, she could barely hear it.

She pulled free of him, feeling parts of herself tearing.

'Anna,' he called. 'Take care of Effie, OK?'

'I will.' Her voice broke and she hurried inside, not looking back, his kiss burning like a brand.

BELOW

There is a Hel in each of us.

Hel Witch Proverb

Anna had never expected to find herself back on the Necropolis Railway, but here she was, stepping off the train with Effie and Azrael into the atemporal gloom of Raven Row. The station that should not exist but was clearly marked on the tube map in front of her, a faint symbol of a skull and crossbones etched into the wall above.

'I've done my best,' said Azrael. 'The Raven Tongued have summoned you.'

Effie snorted. 'Got to love a good summoning.'

Azrael blinked, expressionless. Anna sensed that Effie's hot and cold approach to their relationship might have started to prove wearing.

He led them from the station, down through the old tunnels and abandoned stairways, through the room of sleeping coffins, to the deep chill of the crossroads at the heart of the Hel witch headquarters. A small number of Hel witches were gathered around the grand table. There was no feast now, nothing but grave-faced looks at their approach, their eyes more remote than ever.

In the centre, was their ancient member from the Dumb Feast, sunken into his bones in his wheelchair, looking as if he hadn't moved position since then. Mór sat to one side, Felix the child on the other.

Mór stood up. 'Azrael insists you have urgent, imperative information for us.'

'Yes.' Anna nodded, stepping forwards. 'We wish to travel to Hel to end the hysteria spell ourselves.'

Beyond rippling with the slightest perturbations, Mór's face rarely changed expression, so to see it taken over by complete shock was something. Satisfying.

The other Hel witches' expressions varied between equal levels of shock, irritation, anger . . . some of them laughed.

'Unless any of you want to go for us?' Effie challenged. 'We're open to offers.'

That wiped the smirks from their faces.

Mór collected herself. 'Are you serious?'

'We are,' said Anna, holding Mór's eyes.

'You are the first non-Hel witches to ever request such a thing. It is simply not done.'

'We don't *want* to go. This isn't some magical jaunt, some whim. We're going to end the hysteria spell. The spirit must be bound or else more lives will be lost.

Mór arched her long neck. 'You know travelling to Hel involves decades of preparation – advanced purifying rituals, mental preparation and training, emotional strengthening. These are not games we play, they are essential, for Hel has no mercy on any soul.'

'I know,' Anna replied, just as severely. 'But Hel has been calling me and I think you know that, I think you've seen it. My magic has been carrying the shadow of death within it. I've had the raven dreams, the Language of the Dead has been whispering to me, the snows of Hel beckoning me.'

That set the Hel witches muttering again.

'You have nothing to lose, this is our choice, our risk. What do you say?'

There was the creak of a chair or the creak of a bone, Anna wasn't sure. The old man had moved. Looked up. His eyes white as a marble, seeing nothing, *seeing all*. His motion precipitated a pronounced response – a reverberation of gasps, a deep reverence spreading across the table. Mór stepped back.

Slowly, accompanied by further creaks and cracks, he raised his arm, an arthritic finger angling itself towards Anna. She had the sensation of what it might be like to look beneath the hood of the Grim Reaper. His mouth twitched. He had no lips, they had withered away, only a puckered line within his beard that looked as if it hadn't parted in centuries. Was he going to speak? Anna dared not breathe in case her breath dissolve him to dust. His mouth opened. She didn't know if she imagined the puff of dust that came out before his words.

'No,' he wheezed. He took a deep rattling, whistling breath, like a train arriving at a Necropolis platform. 'We do . . . not . . . interfere with the . . . concerns of the living.'

His finger dropped and his mouth sucked back into itself, his decree issued. Mór's fingers clasped together and she lowered her head.

'Easy for you to say when you're barely alive yourself!' Effie yelled.

'Effie,' Mór reprimanded. 'Eliphas has lived more lives than all of us put together. He is as wise as you are foolish and he has spoken.'

'You have to let us go!' Anna demanded. 'You have to!'

'We do not have to do anything. Azrael, please show our guests out.'

Anna knew she ought to feel relief as they wound back through the tunnels, but she didn't, she felt only a pounding frustration, a deep sense of emptiness from knowing they'd been denied their one chance to stop the events that had been put into motion. The concerns of the living were all she cared about. *Eliphas and all his wisdom be damned!*

'I told you it was unlikely,' said Azrael. 'I was surprised they even agreed to meet you. I think Mór secured it.'

'Well, it came to nothing, didn't it?' Effie seethed. 'Bloody Hel witches!'

Anna could hear them arguing ahead of her when a hand gripped her arm from the darkness.

She screamed. Mór stepped out and raised herself up to her full, precipitous height.

Effie spun around. 'What are you doing here?'

'I will take you,' Mór declared, her voice barely distinguishable from the darkness. 'I will assist you in your passage to the Underworld.'

'Really?' Anna thought about throwing her arms around Mór but withheld.

Azrael stared at Mór, confounded, repeating, 'Really?'

Effie was more suspicious. 'I thought Grandpa Death ran the show around here?'

'Then you haven't been listening. No one person is in charge here, for all are equal in the face of death.'

'Why have you sneaked up on us then?'

Mór pursed her lips, although there was a wry smile to them. 'I thought it prudent not to cause a stir. Now do you wish to go or have you changed your mind?' Her expression sobered.

'We do.' Anna nodded.

'Come then.'

Anna could hardly believe it as she, Effie and Azrael began after Mór, who led them further down the tunnel and through a side door.

'A shortcut to the entrance to the Underworld . . .' Mór elucidated.

'I've always been one for a shortcut,' Effie muttered.

Anna felt her own words turning to frost on her lips. She could feel it ahead. The entrance. Was it the deepening cold? The thickening darkness? The thinning of the air? As if all the superfluous life within it was being cut away, like fabric trimmed of its colour and design, leaving bare stitches you could almost see through. Anna felt less whole herself, as if she were being taken apart too – nothing left but threads of bone.

They went through a door and Anna knew they had arrived. The final tunnel of the crossroads. Its darkness moved, broken by the static of snow, never settling, never finding relief – everything bending and warping towards what lay ahead: *a tree*. Shadows were gathered around it. As they approached, the shadows became faces: a group of Hel witches, Yuki and Felix among them. The tree was white.

Not white. Bone.

Its trunk was so pale and smooth it looked almost translucent and yet there was a density to it – a gravity, a strength. It drew the snow and them towards it. Its branches were severe, its leaves black and its apples blacker still. It stood as still as if it had never known the wind, as ashen as if it had never felt sunlight.

Yuki ran to them and threw her arms around them, holding them both tightly. She pulled back. 'You are braver than the best of us.'

'Thank you, Yuki.' Anna squeezed her arm.

Effie looked around. 'But . . . where is the entrance? I thought you guys were the Gatekeepers. Isn't there some kind of gate? Is it in the tree? Beneath the tree?'

'There is no entrance,' Mór replied. 'The tree is symbolic. We carry out a ritual around it, a ritual that will help you let go of this world and travel to the world below; within.'

'I don't get it.'

'When you dream, where do you go? The Astral witches would tell you that you travel to another realm and yet the realm is also inseparable from you. Hel is the same. It is a place and not a place. It lies beyond us and within us. Your mind will find a way to make sense of it, but do not be fooled – it is real enough to hurt you, break you, you don't even have to die to be lost within it forever.'

'Wow. You should put that in the brochure,' Effie quipped, but her voice was faint.

'We will weave in wording from the unleashing spell into your ritual, asking that your journey take you to the spirit you seek – the spirit responsible for the hysteria. But as you enter Hel, set that intention in your mind too. You must learn the spirit's name to bind it. To know its name, you must speak the Language of the Dead. To learn the Language of the Dead, you must pass through Hel.'

Effie blew out a breath. 'That's a lot of hurdles.'

'The journey will be long and hard. If we sense it is all . . . going wrong, we can try to bring you back, but it doesn't always work. As you know, some return broken or not at all. Better to find your own way out.'

'Is that it?' Effie looked around at the Hel witches and back to Mór. 'Maybe a few more tips? Tell us *how* to get out? You have been after all, haven't you?'

Mór's eyes flickered like the snow. 'But my Hel would not be your Hel. My shadows are not your shadows. You will face seven trials of fear. Hel will try to break you apart, to unthread your very sense of self. You must find a way to keep yourself together.'

Anna tried to find the meaning in her words, but her mind was already so full of dread it was hard to think straight. The tree, though motionless, seemed to tear at the air around them, small incisions into another world. Was she ready? Hel had been calling her, but so had Aunt. Calling her home . . .

'We can go together?' Anna asked.

Mór nodded. 'As Effie informed us, you are sisters, joined by blood. It makes it easier for us to tie your journeys together, but we can't guarantee they will stay that way. You don't have to do this,' she added, suddenly.

'We do. For more reasons than one . . .'

Mór looked into Anna's eyes with a curiosity that did not need to know all the answers.

Anna did not look away. 'The Waters of the Dead. How can I get the memory I seek?'

Mór's lips tightened but she spoke. 'Before you gather the waters, simply state who and what it is you search for.'

'That's it?'

'That's it. It isn't finding the memory that's the hard part . . .' Mór gave her a meaningful look. 'Right. We will prepare the ritual.'

She turned to the others and they began their silent preparations.

Anna walked around the tree. Beneath her feet, extending from the trunk and embedded into the stone floor, were white circles and symbols – a bone-seal, marked with the Language of the Dead. She put a hand to the bark – it was ice cold. Effie ran her hands over it too, looking at Anna as if to say *what the hell are we doing?* Anna attempted to look brave.

Azrael came over, indicating where they should lie on the floor in front of the tree.

'Thanks, Azrael, for everything,' said Anna.

'How do you know I'm not just trying to get rid of Effie before she breaks up with me again?'

Anna froze but then saw the droll smile on his lips. It was the first joke she'd ever heard him make. Apparently he did have a sense of humour, it was just very dark. She found herself laughing at the gates of Hel.

Effie laughed too, giving him a kiss. 'Goodbye, Azrael.'

'Goodbye, Effie.'

Azrael retreated to join the other Hel witches who'd taken up positions in a circle around the tree. They held masks in their hands. Anna had seen such a mask before . . . a Helkappe. They were unsettling enough – long and narrow, half black, half white – but when they touched their faces . . .

'Mother fucking Holle . . .' Effie's voice turned faint.

The masks disappeared, and instead, half of their faces were stripped of flesh – one half living, one half dead. Mór turned to them and for some reason it wasn't as jarring as Anna had expected, seeing half of her skull, as if this were the real Mór, always somewhere between the two worlds.

'Thank you, Mór, for believing in us.'

'It is not my belief you need, it is your own.' She moved her eyes between them. 'Remember, in Hel you do not get lost – you lose yourself. Hold onto each other.'

They lay down. Anna reached out and took Effie's hand. She was surprised to find it was trembling. She squeezed it and they turned their heads to look at each other, lying on the floor in an unknown tunnel somewhere beneath London, or somewhere above the Underworld – it was hard to know.

Effie looked pale as the bone tree. She swallowed. 'You ready?'

'No,' Anna replied. 'You?'

'Fear is fun, remember? Let's die like there's no tomorrow.'

'This is why I need you here – for a terrifying pep talk.'

'I'm always here.'

They smiled briefly at each other and then Mór began to speak the Language of the Dead, slashing their smiles away.

The ritual began.

Anna wanted to scream but it was too late. The magic rose so suddenly and with such force that they were pinned to the ground. It was worse than all the death magic she'd ever felt put together, each word slicing through her, opening her up from the inside out. Everything was so still – the Hel witches, the tree above, her and Effie's frozen limbs, their hands still clasped together – but the world was moving, dissolving like the snow around them. They were dissolving, being sucked away to nothing—

And then falling.

Falling and falling, as if down an endless well.

Falling.

Falling through darkness.

Upwards or downwards?

Anna didn't know. She reached out, trying to hold onto something, but there was nothing there, no purchase, only a sense of frantic dread that she could fall forever. No way to stop.

Falling.

Falling.

Time disappearing.

Parts of her flying away like the pages of a book.

Falling.

Falling.

Nothing left to hold onto—

And then – an end.

The end of time? The end of the world? The end of herself? Anna couldn't separate any of these things.

She gulped for air, her body convulsing as if she were being born again. She couldn't feel anything – couldn't feel herself, she wasn't sure if she was there at all. She opened her eyes and saw someone else: *Effie*. Effie was beside her, her eyes closed but moving rapidly beneath their lids. *Still falling.*

Anna gripped Effie's hand and Effie jolted awake, screaming, her hand ripping free, her eyes a black explosion. Anna had never seen her look so terrified—

'Effie, I'm here,' Anna croaked.

Effie rolled her head, seeing Anna and not seeing her. 'Anna . . .' she whispered, like a question.

'Yes. It's me.' *I'm Anna.* The thought felt strange. 'I'm here.'

They sat up and Anna began to feel her body again, slowly, as if it were thawing, but it felt different too. No longer defined, as if its edges had been left open, frayed—

'Where is *here?*' Effie spluttered.

They were still by the bone tree, darkness all around, but as they slowly clambered to their feet, Anna began to perceive other shapes in the darkness. They were not where they had been. The shapes were sharp and ragged, ice white. More bone trees. Bleached trunks and black rotten tatters for leaves.

'The Bone Forest . . .' Anna whispered. Her voice did not travel – the air was too still for sound to move freely. There was no forest smell either, no smell at all; her breath took no form in the air; her hand left no shadow on the ground. She held it up to her face and her fingers were indistinct, hazy – no fingerprints at their tips. The light around them was strange. Not quite day, not quite night, but a senseless grey, speckled with snow – small flecks and flakes . . . not falling but suspended and swaying this way and that. It was hard to see through, hard to perceive anything, her senses were flattened by the strange world around them.

Snow caught in Effie's hair. 'Where do we go?'

'I don't know . . .' The maiden in the fairy tale had started in the Bone Forest too.

'I thought you knew what you were doing here?'

'I know we have to move,' said Anna, trying to sound confident. 'That we have to keep moving no matter what.'

Anna took out the moonthread. It was still bright, even more so here. She attached the spool to her belt and unwound it so the silver thread trailed and shimmered on the floor behind her and they set off. *One step at a time.* Their feet crunched against the dry, flaking ground, leaving no footprints either.

The forest did not let up, but seemed to grow denser, more tangled, more merciless – vast conifers with shivery needles; clusters of hazel with spiky, hazardous branches; knuckles of yew draped in black cassocks; fallen, hollow trunks of oak; thickets and brambles as gnarled as finger bones; and roots, everywhere roots, unsettling the earth beneath their feet, spreading out from trunks and decaying branches, thin as the fibres of bone. Everything shadowless. The snow ceaseless. A feeling of slow suffocation – this was not a place where things lived, but died. The feeling chasing Anna that if *they* slowed they would soon become as still and hollow as the trees around them.

Effie tripped on a root and a branch sliced at her leg – a shock of bright red blood.

Anna dropped beside her. 'Are you OK?'

'I don't know.' Effie inspected the cut. 'I can't really feel it.'

Anna checked it too – it didn't look too deep. 'Will you be OK to keep going?'

Effie nodded, eyeing the ruptured trunks around them. 'I'm not staying here.'

They walked on, more careful now, realizing that while the forest felt numb, it was fully capable of tearing them to pieces.

'How long do we keep going?' Effie asked.

Anna wasn't sure how to reply, time had lost all sense of meaning, but then, she spotted a bit of old concrete wall twisted into the trunk of a yew. She pointed at it and Effie's eyes widened. Next came a strip of old train track. Then, another scrap of wall. A used can of cola. A piece of scaffolding. Half a stone archway. A table littered with coffee cups. A stop sign. A building—

Through the forest, a city began to emerge forming like tissue around bone. The ground slowly hardened to concrete beneath their feet, still ruptured here and there by roots and trunks. A road stretched before them as buildings supplanted the towering conifers on either side. A red bus suddenly charged out of the trees ahead. They jumped out of the way onto a pavement. People began to appear, walking by in a blur of movement.

London.

It was London.

More people now, and cars, and buses, black taxi cabs. Anna recognized the stately buildings around them – white stone, grand and pillared, glossy with shopfronts. A large crossroads ahead, traffic lights pointing in all directions, flashing too quickly to make sense of. There were signs for the underground, staircases leading down on all four sides of the crossroads.

Effie spun around. 'Oxford Circus. It's Oxford Circus . . .'

It *was* Oxford Circus, but it wasn't. There were still bone trees scattered about, one breaking through the road, another engulfing the side of a building. It didn't feel quite like London either – the colours too flat, the sounds too muffled, as if it were only an imprint of the city, as if it could be torn away like a piece of tracing paper. Above them, the sky held two half-moons on either side: one black and one white.

The people looked real enough, each focused on their own preoccupations. A mother tugging a child along the pavement. A suited man gesticulating wildly as he talked on his phone. A woman pausing to peer in the shop window – though it was entirely empty save for an undressed mannequin staring back at her. A slow sea of people travelling down the stairs to the tube. A cloud of ravens appeared in the air above. They swept downward over the heads of the crowd and into the underground station.

'Now what?' Effie murmured.

Anna tried to think, to remember – in the fairy tale, the girl walking through the forest came to a clearing, a castle surrounded by . . . a moat. 'We head towards the river.' She pointed down Regent Street, which she knew went south towards the Thames.

Effie did not look convinced, but shrugged. They walked, heads down against the blizzard which flurried around and around, trapped between the imposing buildings on either side.

One step at a time.

Anna tried to keep her eyes ahead but it was hard . . . there were too many things that jarred and unsettled: the bone trees still strewn about; the way the window displays were all empty; the letters of the street signs jumbled and meaningless; the pigeons pecking around and around in circles. A horse-drawn carriage passed by . . . but the horse's face was stripped of flesh on one side, turning to reveal a majestic skull. And the people around them . . . now she could see . . . they weren't right either – they moved with purpose but their eyes betrayed them, eyes too still, too vacant.

A homeless man with a sign stretched out a hand towards her. A man in a red phone box watched them through the glass. They passed a greengrocer displaying stacks of moulding fruit. A pub crammed with people, faces pressed up against the windows. A girl skipped over the cracks in the pavement. Anna screamed soundlessly as a woman fell from the sky and landed in front of her. Anna ran towards her but the woman was already gone.

'Anna . . .' Effie pointed upwards. The same woman was standing on the ledge of the building above them. She fell again. Disappeared. Fell again. Disappeared. Fell again.

They watched wordlessly and then walked on, each step harder than the last.

One more step . . .

Anna was sure they should be at the river by now, but the streets seemed endless and all was lost in a haze of snow. They turned onto another street – white stone buildings, grand and pillared, glossy with shopfronts.

'Oxford Circus,' Effie stated, as they arrived back at the crossroads they had started at.

Anna spun about, the crowds more vigorous now, pushing past her to get down into the station. She struggled free of them. 'How? We were heading towards the river . . .'

A crying child tugged her mother along the pavement. A man gesticulated wildly as he talked on his phone. A woman turned into a shop and came back out again, turned around and went back in again. Anna looked more closely at the people going down into the underground – they were the same people coming up the stairs on the other side . . .

Everyone was stuck. Everyone was trapped.

'We keep going.' Anna tried to hold onto her own words, wondering if it was day or night – it was hard to tell, the light was too thin to be either and the half-moons seemed fixed in the sky. Time seemed to be trapped too, caught in little loops like the flurries of snow.

No matter how far they walked, the streets never seemed to lead them anywhere, the street signs no longer jumbled now but twisting into the Language of the Dead. Laughing at them. A homeless man stretched his hand towards them. A waiter dressed in black nodded their way. A man in a phone box slammed his hands against the window. A woman threw herself off a building again and again. A girl tried to skip over cracks in the pavement but the cracks had become too big. They passed back through Oxford Circus. Again and again. Always arriving back at the crossroads.

People were rushing down the stairs now, clambering, crushing. A woman stared at a mannequin in a shop window but her face had become as blank as it.

'We keep going . . .' Anna said. *Was that her voice?*

Effie's eyes stared back at her almost as lifeless as the people around them.

The suited man on his phone grabbed Anna's shoulders and shouted at her, though she could not hear what he was saying. It jolted her momentarily out of her apathy.

No.

They couldn't just keep going when going made no sense.

'We're lost, aren't we?' said Effie, vaguely.

Lost.

Anna tried to remember where she was, tried to get a grip but there was so little to hold onto. Hel was slippery as ice. *It's not real. It's not real.* White horses – half flesh, half skull – weaved through the traffic looking entirely nightmarishly real, their terrible jaws chomping as their heads tossed up and down. The crowds rushed, but they were hardly people any more, only shadows . . .

Anna looked up and the ravens darted through the sky again, a grim cloud of feathers. They flew down the steps into the underground. Disappearing.

Something gripped Anna – in the fairy tale the girl followed the raven through the woods to get to the castle. *You must go down to come back up . . .*

'We have to follow the ravens,' she cried.

'What?'

'WE HAVE TO FOLLOW THE RAVENS!'

'What . . . down there?' Effie turned to the entrance of the tube. Her features were barely discernible through the snow. 'The underground of the Underworld, is that a good idea?'

'Probably not.'

They stared at each other, stepping closer, and then with silent agreement they joined the crowd. They were quickly consumed, separated . . . Anna dragged along and jostled by the heaving mass of shadowy half-people as they rushed down the stairs. She felt a panicked sense of claustrophobia, knowing if she stumbled they would not stop, that they would trample right over her . . . and yet as she reached the bottom of the steps the people dissolved away. Only she and Effie remained, alone in Oxford Circus station. A clock displaying the time had two hands moving in opposite directions. The ticket barriers were open. It was still snowing.

A surge of ravens pummelled past them, flying over the barriers and down.

Anna looked at Effie and swallowed. 'Guess we're taking the train then.'

The escalators poured into darkness. Deadly quiet. They arrived at the platform but the timetable made no sense, flickering only with the letters of the Language of the Dead. There was a skull and crossbones on the wall, not faint now, but vivid, and a tube map beneath. Anna trailed her fingers along it – it was black and white, a tangle of lines, each looping back around and around; an inescapable knot.

'Should have taken the bus,' Effie muttered.

A deep rumbling noise rose from within the tunnel. A train crashed through, lights flickering manically, sparks flaring. The carriages were empty except one in which a sea of ravens raved, a writhing cloud, a fury of wings caught in the flashing lights.

The doors opened and Anna and Effie looked at each other. It was hard to get onto a train when you weren't sure if you'd ever get off it again. They stepped aboard and the doors screamed shut. The train took off at the same pace with which it had arrived, hurtling into the dark tunnel. They were torn apart by the jolting, careering motions. *Too fast. Much too fast.* Anna clung onto a pole. Effie held onto a seat, looking horrified and Anna realized why – they were now the only carriage on the track. No train. No driver. Getting faster. The lights flashed and Anna lost sight of Effie.

'Effie!' She spun around but the train veered around a bend and she was thrown to the floor. She scrambled to her feet. She couldn't hear anything except screams of metal, shrieks of ravens, laughter, laughter—

The lights flickered and her reflection in the windows was Aunt. Aunt all around, laughing, the darkness beyond moving too fast to comprehend. The train juddered and Anna was thrown again, her head slamming against the seats. There was the awareness of pain without really feeling it. She felt wetness run down her forehead over her eye. She crawled along the floor to the pole, curling around it, closing her eyes and saying her name over and over – *Anna. Anna. Anna*—

The train came to a sudden halt. The sound of doors opening.

Someone calling her.

'Anna! Anna!'

She unpeeled herself and scrabbled to her feet. Effie was on the platform, reaching a hand towards her. 'Quick!'

Their fingers interlocked. Effie yanked her off the train. She stared at Anna's face wildly. 'You're bleeding . . .'

'I fell . . .' Anna wiped blood from her eyes.

They stumbled to a bench and Effie checked Anna over. 'We could die here, couldn't we?' Effie stated, as if it were only just dawning on her. That this wasn't a game.

'We should go,' was all Anna could reply.

They ran out of the platform, up the escalators, into the station hall and back out into the grey air. Anna was desperately relieved to see they were no longer at Oxford Circus. Instead, ahead of them, lay the unmistakable outline of the Tower of London.

Like the girl in the fairy tale arriving at a great castle . . .

Anna walked to the fence. 'That's it. That's where we need to go.'

'The Tower of London?' Effie breathed out. Ravens were circling above. Around and around. 'I guess that adds up.'

'The source of the hysteria,' Anna whispered, things she didn't understand falling into place.

'What is *that?*' Effie pointed.

The Tower was surrounded, not by roads and gardens like in the London they knew, but by . . . blackness . . . so opaque it looked almost like rock, onyx. A faint glimmer on its surface gave it away.

'It's water . . .' said Anna, suddenly dry-mouthed. *A castle moat.*

They took the steps down towards the road and made for the Tower, the city deathly quiet, no people now, no traffic. Anna could see the river – the Thames running beneath Tower Bridge and alongside the Tower of London, but here, in Hel, it encircled the Tower too, cutting it off like an island, as it once would have been. A castle and its moat. The Tower rose jagged above the black waters – its thunderous assortment of walls and turrets more gargantuan, more brutal than its real world version. Its spires stabbed at a moon dark and a moon light, while ravens spun above, like they'd been trying to tell her all year this was exactly where she needed to go.

As they drew closer, Anna could see people gathered around the moat, shadowy figures. Many were drinking from it others were lolling beside it as if in a stupor, some staring into the water as if lost entirely.

'The River of the Dead,' said Anna. 'Flowing with the memories of all who have died . . .'

'Memory,' Effie repeated, as if the word were curious to her.

Anna understood. Memory felt different here too, hard to hold onto, as if their lives before were not quite real and yet painful to recall, like echoes with glass edges.

Anna. I am Anna Everdell.

They arrived at a single drawbridge. They crossed it and walked down the bank towards the moat and the figures – more appearing the closer they got. There was a feeling of hopelessness in the air. Anna's mouth felt parched.

Anna took out the thimble. 'Whatever you do, don't drink from the water, not here, not in Hel.' The maiden had not in the fairy tale, and she remembered Attis's story, of the raven sent by the Goddess who hadn't been able to stop drinking . . .

The black surface of the water was still and soundless as the dead. Anna knelt at the moat's edge between vaporous figures, trying to ignore them and their pervading despair. She had no reflection in the water and now she was close it was hard to tell if it was black or white. It was both – an unknowable darkness that glinted with bone – bones moving beneath its surface like ripples.

Bone remembers.

The dryness in Anna's mouth moved through her body. She felt as if she hadn't drunk for a hundred years, a feeling that if she just had one sip . . . everything would be OK. She could forget. Forget all of it. Forget the weight of *Anna*.

She spoke. 'I request the memories of Eleanor Everdell – the origin of our family curse and how its antidote spell was created.'

She dipped the thimble into the black waters, feeling no sense of whether it was warm or cold. *Just one sip . . .*

The waters were luminous with bone, entrancing, soft and supple. They promised sweet oblivion. She could hear the whispers of a thousand memories embroidered across time. The whispers beckoned her closer, closer—

She dropped the thimble into her bag but she did not move away. Instead she dipped her other hand into the river. The water came away clear in her palm. The thirst was overwhelming, a craving seizing her whole body.

Just . . .

One . . .

Sip . . .

She hadn't realized how close the water was to her lips when Effie batted her hand away. 'No!' The water spilt onto the grass. 'You can't—' Effie had moved closer and her eyes were on the water now too, listening, wanting—

Anna wrenched herself away from the river, looking again over the shadow-forms, nothing left of them but thirst and despair. 'Let's go. Now!' she cried to Effie.

They scrambled back up the slopes and ran through the open castle gates, leaning against the ancient stone walls and breathing hard.

They heard the pounding of feet and jangling of keys. A figure in a red coat appeared, gliding past them, holding a large set of keys, escorted by a circle of figures in uniform and the tall bearskin hats of the Tower Guards, arms swinging by their sides. They clanged the gates shut behind Anna and Effie and pulled heavy bars across the doors. The keys were inserted – the sound of locks turning.

'The Ceremony of the Keys . . .' Anna breathed out.

The men swivelled on black boots, their faces were shadowy and indiscernible beneath their hats. Anna and Effie hurried after them as they marched away from the door and down to the inner walls of the Tower complex. They followed them through the next gate and up towards the White Tower – the building at the heart of the castle. The

Guards finished their ceremony and then marched back from where they'd come. *Around and around.*

The White Tower looked monstrously tall before them, its towers high and forlorn as any fairy tale castle. The ravens circled above.

Anna locked eyes with Effie, recalling the fairy tale. 'Once we enter, you must not look back. Keep moving, don't stay anywhere too long. Don't look back. OK? Effie – OK?'

Effie nodded. Anna wished Effie would make a joke or say something inappropriate, but she seemed dazed by the Tower above them. They stepped through the doors together.

On the other side, Effie was gone.

Anna was standing alone in a long corridor lined with doors, the walls wood-panelled like St Olave's. She spun around, searching for Effie, screaming her name but it simply echoed back at her. *Where am I?*

Anna started down the corridor, trying the doors but they were all locked. She hammered on several. 'EFFIE! WHERE ARE YOU?'

There was no reply but Anna could hear something – faint sounds of laughter and cheering. She stopped, noticing light coming from beneath one of the doors ahead, flickering as if people were moving about within. She ran to it, the sounds of jubilation louder. She could smell things roasting and sweet fermenting berries. The maiden in the fairy tale had first arrived at . . . *a feast.*

Anna turned the handle and the door opened. The room was aglimmer with firelight. It reminded Anna of Demdike's manor room in his tarot tent, all drapes and handsome woods and dancing light. Only, instead of Demdike's desk, there was a table laid out with decadent food like the Hel witch feast, and at the end of the table sat . . . Attis. The fire made sweet caramel of his skin, and his eyes – as they looked up at her through his dark trails of hair – were so *real.* Inquisitive and mirthful, unguarded and open-ended; eyes dark and light and every shade that lived in between.

Anna ran towards him but stopped.

He smiled curiously and she felt the first rush of feeling she could remember for hours or days or however long she'd been in Hel, as if the sun had come out and burned away some of the grey listlessness.

'Anna.' It was his voice, low and playful, a flicker of mischief.

'Attis—'

He stood up. He was wearing his forge clothes, a white T-shirt and loose trousers. He put out his hands and she took them. They burned. 'I've been waiting for you for a long time,' he said, a little bit of soot on the end of his nose disarming her entirely.

'I have to go . . .'

'No.' His hands enclosed hers more tightly. 'Stay. We've got food to eat.'

He waved a hand over the table, picking up a raspberry. He held it to his own lips, playfully, then extended it to her mouth. It smelt sweet and overpowering – she'd forgotten what smell was, the seductive magic of it. She bit into the fruit and the taste was the red of dawn after a long night. His finger caught on the edge of her mouth. He tasted better.

He pulled her towards him. 'We have food to eat.'

'You said that already.'

'I'd rather not be talking.' His lips quirked, a crooked smile; an invitation.

Their gravities pulled them together as if there was no resisting it any more. Lips met hungrily. Raspberry and smoke. The warmth of the kiss waterfalling through her like one of his grounding symbols turned liquid, filling her body up so she could feel it again.

'We could lie down by the fire . . .' he suggested, voice a low gravel, raking at her desire.

'I have to go,' she repeated, uselessly.

He backed her against the wall, his body pushing against hers with threat and thrill. 'I could make you stay . . .'

He kissed her again and she let his lips find a path down her neck, his hands moving down her body—

She pushed him away.

His face fell, his brow gathering in pain that seeped through her defences. 'Anna, please—'

She reeled around him but he chased her to the fire.

'Anna, come on, don't leave.'

She darted this way and that but he blocked her path to the door.

'I need you. I need you here.'

His voice was made of temptation. *Don't listen. He's not real, not real . . .*

She drew herself up. 'I have to go, Attis.' She stepped forwards and he moved back. 'I have to go.'

'Anna—'

She pushed him against the wall now. 'Don't stop me.'

She moved her lips towards him to disarm him, but at the moment before the kiss, she darted from the room, his voice chasing after her, pleading, desperate. 'Anna, don't leave me here, alone . . . please—'

The door slammed shut and she leant against it trying to remember how to breathe.

Not real.

She wasn't sure how long she stood there listening to his pleas on the other side of the door, afraid what would happen if she left, more afraid what would happen if she went back in. Her body was dissolving again, disappearing at the edges.

She walked on – on and on down the corridor of doors – until another door showed light beneath it. She turned the handle and stepped through.

The light was so bright it took her eyes a moment to adjust. She was outside, in the vast cemetery Aunt had been buried in. Snow was layered on the ground, grave after grave splintering through it, like dark sails on a white ocean. As she walked through it, she could see the gravestones were inscribed with the Language of the Dead . . . but she could look now without flinching; she could almost sense the names beneath . . .

Then, two gravestones stood before her and these names she could read.

Marie Everdell.

Dominic Cruickshank.

Ahead, the light softened. A tree stirred in a breeze she couldn't feel. Grass extended beneath her feet, soft as a summer's day. It *was* a summer's day and she knew exactly where she was. Aunt's garden. Only it didn't belong to Aunt yet . . . it was still her parents' house and there they were – sitting beneath the sycamore tree laughing with one another, a baby in her mother's arms, exactly like the photograph Anna had stared at too many times.

Only nothing like it, because they were alive.

They turned to look at Anna and she knew those faces but she didn't know them at all. Her mother smiled and Anna had never imagined it quite that way. Selene had said it was a smile that could get anything it wanted and she could see why now – because it gave so much. There was so much heart in it, it left you utterly disarmed. Her dimples deepened – a natural extension – and her black fringe fell to her eyes, she flicked it out of the way as if by habit. Her father's dark hair was curlier than Anna had imagined. His eyes were brighter too; perhaps she'd thought of them as menacing for so long, but they were a frank green-blue, calm and wise.

'Anna, you're here!' Her mother patted the ground. 'Come and sit with us.'

Anna couldn't move. She'd never heard her mum's voice. The hues of it. Lower than she'd expected, soothing and warm, a little wry.

They were real, *so real*. Not shadows . . . not spirits but whole. That *was* the sound of her mother's voice. Hel knew such things, didn't it? After all, her mother's soul had passed through it. Was this some imprint of them? A captured echo?

The baby wriggled in her mother's arms and Marie made a gentle rocking motion as if she'd done it a hundred times before.

Anna sat down beside them.

'What would you like to know, my love?' her mother asked. 'We're here to tell you anything you wish.'

Anna could finally see the colour of her mother's eyes – not as dark as Effie's, not as green as hers – hazel, dappled with magic. Anna stared at them, not speaking, trying to take in all their details as if they might disappear at any moment, but they didn't. Her mother rocked the baby again. Anna looked at her newborn self, snuggled and dozy in her mother's arms.

'Anna?' her mother prompted gently.

Anna could feel the weight of a thousand questions – all the questions she'd asked herself late at night for so many years; all the details of her mother she'd craved to know for so long.

Anna sighed, not asking the questions she wanted to ask, but the question she must ask. 'How do I stop the curse?'

Her mother's smile tugged again, but this time sadly. 'You know as much as I do now, my love.'

Anna nodded. 'I have to go.'

'It's just, we've missed you,' said her father. 'Stay a little while and we can get to know you.'

Anna realized she was crying. 'I can't – I—'

She knew there was so much they could tell her, but she knew that if she stayed, she'd never have the strength to leave.

The baby had fallen asleep in her mother's arms.

She knelt down and hugged her father tightly, then her mother, trying to remember how they smelt.

The questions no longer seemed to matter because, right now, in the depths of Hel, she could *feel* them. Who they were. Her mother's open heart. Her father's kindness. How he'd never been a risk taker until he'd met her, how she liked the way he tempered her rashness. How she was stubborn but strong; how he loved learning but was quietly ambitious – wanted more, wanted to live beyond his books. How fiercely she loved the baby in her arms. How much they loved each other. Anna could feel who she would have been if none of it had ever happened. No deep scars and empty spaces, but lighter, freer, because she knew they were always there to come back to. So much love inside her she didn't know how to keep it all inside. She could feel a future of possibilities that had never even occurred to her.

'Please be careful,' her mother said. She'd begun to cry too.

'I love you both,' Anna replied, her heart pouring now through all those cracks, all the light she'd held back. 'And so does Effie and we're going to be fine. We're going to get through it all.'

'I know you will.' Marie nodded, strong and sure. 'We love you too, forever.'

One step at a time . . .

But moving away from them was the hardest step Anna had ever taken. She turned and walked through the garden and into her old house, wanting to look back but knowing she could not.

Inside, the house was dark. It no longer belonged to them. There was a staircase ahead of her – the staircase she'd walked every night in her dreams. She knew what came next in the fairy tale: the maiden had to face Mother Holle herself, Goddess of Hel, Queen of Darkness and Fear.

Anna already knew who was waiting for her. They'd been waiting all year.

Snow flurried down the staircase, raven calls echoed from somewhere above. Anna shook herself, turning to face it. Her heart would be hammering, rebelling, if she could feel it but there was no going back now. She began up the stairs.

Up and up it spiralled.

Up and up just like in her dreams.

Colder and colder.

The snow thicker.

The ravens calling.

Holding onto the walls and to herself.

Anna Everdell.

Anna Everdell.

Up and up and then—

A door ahead. The door to the third-floor room.

Anna could feel it, the secrets it held, things locked up too tightly, deeds so dark they'd bled through centuries. She did not want to open it, but the door was already open. It had been open the whole time. She put out a finger and pushed it wide. She stepped through and the world twisted like a piece of origami.

She was lying down, flat on her back in darkness. She tried to sit up but her head hit a wall. She reached out her hands and felt soft fabric. She knew where she was. She'd had this dream before, only now it was no dream.

A coffin.

'Welcome home, my child.' She felt Aunt's skeletal arms wrap around her from beneath.

Anna screamed so loudly all of Hel shook.

'The early bird catches the worm but the earliest worm escapes the bird.' Aunt snipped a thread beside her.

They were in their old living room. Dark outside. The room gloomy as Anna's memories of it. Aunt in her armchair. Anna on the sofa with a needle in her hand, stitching. The action was so familiar Anna barely noticed it, but she was startled to see what she was sewing: the Language of the Dead.

'Pay attention, child.' Aunt clicked her tongue and the needle pricked Anna's finger.

Anna felt no pain, the hurt went too deep for that. She watched the drop of blood spread over the fabric, covering it entirely. For a moment, she carried on sewing. Old habits die hard. *No.* She'd come too far to go back. She raised her head to Aunt.

'I don't know why you're looking at me like that.' Aunt slitted her eyes. 'You deserved it. You deserved all of it.'

Anna felt the waves of shame batter against her, but she was not that girl any more, she would not let them in. Anna dropped the needle. She picked up the fabric and tore it apart with her hands. Aunt's lips whitened, outrage pulling at her already too-tight face. 'WHAT do you think you're doing?'

'Leaving,' Anna stated, but when she tried to get up she felt pinpricks all over her body. She looked down and saw it was her flesh that was threaded now. The room was a web of threads, stitched through the walls, through the embroideries behind them, through the ceiling and carpet, stitched through her – every limb held in place, just like her dreams. She yanked her arm but it tugged uselessly.

Aunt's laugh rapped sharply. 'You really thought it was going to be that easy?'

Anna breathed out with futile rage. 'Let me go.'

'Tut. Tut. Tut.' A metronome began to tick somewhere. 'I can't. You know that. I'm never going to leave you, Anna.'

Anna tried to shake her head but it was held too still. 'No, no – let me go, please—'

'Please, please, pretty please . . .' Aunt mimicked her. 'You can't escape me. We're too alike, you and I.'

'I'm nothing like you,' Anna growled.

'Are you sure about that?'

They were in the third-floor room now. Anna realized she'd never truly left it.

She was lying on the bed, still held by threads. Aunt was standing at the end of the bed looking down at her, red hair unloosed. 'Wasn't I right about it all? Isn't the darkness coming? Aren't the shadows creeping? Aren't the fires lighting? The wind carries the sour tang of smoke already.' Aunt had never looked more alive.

Anna could smell what she spoke of, staining the darkness of Hel. She stared up at Aunt. 'You were right, Aunt, as always, but you couldn't be more wrong. You made me believe the world was made of fear but it's not. That was your fear, not mine.'

Aunt laughed dismissively. 'I didn't create the threats out there. I only tried to keep you safe from them.'

'You kept me suffocated! Trapped! Bound!' Anna spat. 'But I see now—' She stopped resisting. 'I see now that your Choke Knots were nothing but your love turned inside out. You didn't know how to love except in fear, never learning that love gives fear meaning. I won't be afraid like you.'

'You will be.' Aunt's voice echoed around her. 'The curse will see to that. Effie will make sure of it. That's if . . . she makes it out of here alive.'

Anna thought she could hear screaming in the distance – Effie's screams. 'What are you doing to her?' she yelled.

'Not me. Hel would never let a monster like her escape.'

'Is that why you're still here?'

Aunt roared at Anna's words, raging suddenly around the room. Throwing things. Tearing down the curtains. Ripping up the duvet so that feathers flew up around them. Pummelling her fists against the walls. Blood began to pour down the cracks she'd made. Aunt turned on Anna, bearing down on her, but then Aunt was the one on the bed and Anna was leaning over her, her hands wrapped around Aunt's throat. Aunt was laughing, gasping for breath and laughing, crying and raging, and laughing. 'Go on!' she spluttered. 'Go on! Do it, kill me. You know you want to. This is your last chance . . .'

Anna felt it again. The desire to squeeze. To make her stop. To make her go away forever. She lifted her hands away. 'No.' Anna's voice shook. 'I won't kill you, Aunt. I couldn't then – and I can't now, because . . . I love you. Despite everything you did to me, I love you. You've taught me that my love is stronger than anything else.'

Aunt screamed and the feathers swirled around them, a blizzard of pain and terror, and then they began to fall gently. They were sitting in Anna's old room, Aunt brushing Anna's hair.

'How alike we are,' Aunt said, softly now. 'Sixteen tomorrow. You must be ready for the year ahead.'

Aunt was no longer looking at Anna, but at herself in the mirror. She looked desperately afraid.

'It's time for you to go,' Anna whispered.

Aunt looked at Anna then, truly looked at her, perhaps for the first time ever. Not as an extension of herself, not as a reflection of her own sufferings, but as someone separate from herself. Aunt pulled the brush through Anna's hair one last time. 'It really is beautiful, this colour,' she murmured as she disappeared from the mirror.

Anna sat alone in her old room. The threads were still attached to her – white and thin as fibres of bone, like the roots of the trees in the Bone Forest . . . *not threads, but roots* . . . not holding her in place, but growing from her. They disappeared at the strange realization.

Free, at last.

Anna felt lighter, stronger . . . but the ravens were still calling, their sound feverish now. Urgent. She could almost understand it.

This way . . .

This way . . .

Anna walked out of her door and the staircase was there, the ravens above her. She took the final steps up to the top of the castle, not knowing what they would bring her to—

The room was small – stone-walled and circular with a small slit of window. A tower . . . *just like in the fairy tale.* In the centre, hanging from the ceiling, was a cage with a raven trapped inside. All of the noise, the racket, was coming from this one raven – throwing itself against the bars, wings beating madly, its caw shredding the air around them, turning all to raw fear. It beat against Anna, sharp and relentless, making it hard to think straight, to feel anything but dread.

Anna's eyes fell on Effie who was in the corner of the room, below the window, knees tucked up, arms clamped around herself. She looked as if she'd been that way for a while.

Anna rushed to her, dropping to the floor. 'Effie? Are you OK?'

Effie raised her head – her eyes were hollow. Anna tried to find her sister in them. Where had she been? What had she been through? 'Who's Effie?' Effie replied.

Anna choked back her panic, trying not to shake her. 'You're Effie. Effie Fawkes.'

'Who are you?'

'I'm . . .' Anna felt the panic shake her instead as she struggled to recall her own name. It was hard through the noise. *A . . . An . . . Anna Everdell.* 'I'm Anna,' she said, as if she could make it so. 'Anna. Your sister.'

'Anna.' Effie nodded vaguely. 'You're Anna.'

They stared at each other, holding onto what the other was seeing.

'Can you make it stop?' Effie's eyes flared with terror at the bird behind them. 'Make it stop.'

Anna rose unsteadily to her feet and turned to face the bird. Its sound hit her like a scream made of knives, flaying her, threatening to unravel her entirely—

Anna, you're Anna—

She took out her mirror and held it up like a shield and in the reflection she saw the truth – the raven was gone and inside the cage a shadow swirled, dark and formless, dense as a black hole.

She twisted back to Effie. 'It's the fear spirit. The Pied Piper. We have to let it out—'

Effie pulled herself up, clutching at the wall. 'WHAT?'

'We have to let it free.'

'No! You can't let it free! Aren't we – aren't we – meant to bind it . . . not release it!'

Anna looked back. The bird attacked the bars, its beak snapping viciously at her. She knew it didn't make sense, she didn't know why or how she knew it, but she did, deep inside herself – the unleashing spell had trapped it while drawing on its energy. The only way to stop the spell was to set it free.

'I have to—' she said, moving towards it, but Effie grabbed her arm and yanked her back.

'No! I won't let you kill us!'

Anna tried to break free, ducking from Effie's arms and running towards the cage. Effie dived for her leg and tripped her over. They scrabbled on the floor, fighting as the bird cawed rabidly, clawing at what was left of them.

Anna managed to get back to her feet but Effie gripped her from behind and threw her against the wall, Anna's head slamming against cold stone.

'Anna!' Effie ran to her.

Anna reached for her head. More blood. 'It's going to tear us apart, if we don't stop it,' she cried, gasping for breath. 'You have to trust me! EFFIE, TRUST ME!'

Effie stared at her, trembling and panting. A moment of pause and then she roared, 'DO IT! NOW! BEFORE I CHANGE MY MIND!'

Anna ran to the cage, holding the mirror up as if it could deflect the worst of its terror. Even so, the sound stripped away the last of her. Nothing left but bone and determination. She put her hand out and flicked the catch. It swung open.

The noise stopped.

The bird hopped to the door, turning its black eyes on Anna. It spoke—

Anna knew that birds could not speak, she knew what she was hearing was a raven's call, and yet she also knew it was the Language of the Dead. She understood it. The spirit had given her its name.

And then, cage and bird were gone and instead a shadow was standing motionless in the centre of the room. There was a vague human shape to it but only just – as if fear had twisted it far from what it had once been.

'The spell . . .' said Anna.

She turned and Effie was there, behind her. They stood together, facing the nameless shadow, speaking the Language of the Dead as if they'd always known it. They spoke the words of the unleashing spell – setting it free.

The shadow swirled, lifting into the air, forming the faint outline of a raven as it flew out through the window.

Anna didn't know how long she and Effie stood there, how long it took to find her voice. 'We go that way too . . .'

The window was bigger now, the light coming through it brighter, softer, almost like daylight, *true daylight*. They moved towards it but a voice called out from behind them.

'Anna.'

Then louder.

'Anna!'

It was Attis and his voice was desperate, despairing, all of its richness hammered hollow.

'Please! Don't leave me. I'm here alone . . . please . . . Anna . . .'

It wrapped around her so that she couldn't move.

'Please! Help me!'

Effie had frozen beside Anna too. 'Attis is calling me . . .'

Anna gripped Effie's hand. 'It's not him. We have to go—'

But Effie did not budge. Her eyes turned on Anna's and Anna could see straight through them. A void.

Anna shook her head, trying to drag Effie. 'Effie! No! It's not him. It's not him. Look – see—'

She held the mirror up and there was nothing behind them.

'Don't look back,' Anna begged. 'We can't look back. Not now. We have to jump.'

'I can't leave him.' Effie broke free of Anna's hand and spun away, looking back down the stairway, back into the darkness . . .

Everything collapsed.

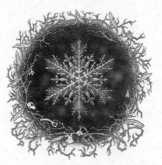

STILLNESS

May our flesh become rot.
May our breath become dust.
May our marrows return
To the oceans of life,
Until our bones are all
That are left of us.

Hel Witch Funeral Rite

Hel fell apart. Shadows rushed into the space it had left – black shapeless voids, as far as the eye could see and time could stretch. They circled Anna, reaching out, pawing and groping with numb, formless hands, taking all of her slowly until Anna was part of the darkness.

The True Darkness of Hel.

A darkness so complete there was nothing to compare it to. No well as deep. No night as black. No despair as absolute. It washed over her like an ocean, dissolving the last of her.

No way out.

Nowhere to go. Nowhere no longer existed. Hel was *everywhere*.

Somewhere, distantly, Anna could feel the moonthread beneath her fingers but the darkness had consumed it too. Its light had gone out.

She lay back. Finally, still. It didn't even hurt. The darkness was welcoming, easing all of the aches and pains away. She couldn't remember who she was, only that the journey had been hard, the life before that harder. The future would be no easier. But the darkness was soft and drifting and her bones were so cold. It was time to let go. What was her name again?

A . . . n . . . n . . . a . . .

A curious sound. She didn't know who it belonged to. It didn't matter any more. The silence wanted her to forget. To let go into the forever-ness.

A . . . . . . n . . . . . . n . . . . . . a . . . . . .

Letting go was so easy compared to everything else.

Nothing left but darkness and silence stretching on and on and on—

No need to feel anything any more.

Nothing.

Nothing.

Except—

A pinpoint of light above her – falling towards her.

A single snowflake in the endless dark.

She watched it fall towards her. Was it even falling? Or only part of the stillness? It seemed to hover above her and she could make out its shape – the articulation of its crystals, concise and clear, as if it were made of bone. A pattern. A pattern she knew.

Fear.

The pattern of fear.

A map of fear.

The sound of fear. A small sound in the vast silence as if it had been there all along. Notes delicate as a snowflake. A song the girl knew so deeply her soul stirred. Ripples in the darkness.

My song.

The melody grew like a seed opening, weaving with the darkness, with the fear she'd been holding back for so long. It flowed, filling up the waiting, empty spaces of the song, melting away its hard dark centre like morning frost.

My song.

The ending no longer mattered, only that she was playing. It spiralled around her bones putting her back together, and she felt it – the settling of her soul. Like coming undone.

My Hira is my song.

She knew the language of her magic. Its secret was in the song – spun with the pattern – the song of each of her emotions. A power so vast she could barely comprehend it. A power she needed now.

She drew all the fear inside her together, the darkness she'd been too afraid to face for so long, finding herself in the bottom of that well inside her.

My name is Anna Everdell.

She unleashed it, throwing out her circle – made of music, made of song. It pushed the darkness away, fragmenting its edges back to shadow, space opening up around her. But she needed more. She let her magic go – expanding outwards through the threads of her circle, the notes of her song. Transforming Hel. Turning the darkness into light.

She called out her name in the Language of the Dead.

It rang like the sound of a bell, the light spreading further, unbreakable, unconquerable until Anna saw her on the floor.

Effie.

Anna crawled to her, lifting Effie's hand. It was cold. Her eyes were empty.

'Effie—' Anna searched her face, drew Effie's hand to her cheek, tried to keep Hel at bay even while her heart broke. 'Effie, are you there? It's me, Anna.'

Too empty.

Anna let her magic pour into Effie, let all of herself pour into her.

'You are Effie Fawkes. Effie Fawkes.' Anna cradled her, half-frozen tears pouring down her cheeks. 'It's me. It's me. Your sister, Anna. Come back to me. I – I love you—'

The hand in Anna's pulsed.

'Effie!' Anna clutched her.

Something flickered in Effie's eyes, a wingbeat of life. Her lips moved, a fragment of sound. 'Anna.'

'Oh Goddess, yes. It's me. It's me.'

Effie gasped, breathing in. The light came back into her eyes. They held each other tightly, their magic joining together as if it was the most natural thing in the world . . . whatever world they were in.

Effie's eyes widened. 'Can you feel that?'

Anna nodded. The flow of their emotions pushing against Hel, turning it inside out.

Behind Effie's head Anna spotted a glimmer. The moonthread was bright and alive once more. 'It's time to go.'

'You don't have to tell me twice . . .'

Anna helped Effie to her feet. They began to move, Anna winding the thread back onto the spool, turning the shadows to light as they moved through them, retracing their steps, the thread pulling them onwards. Hel was formless now, or barely formed: vague outlines, dim impressions, but then . . . a staircase ahead. The moonthread led them up. Back into the ruined echo of the highest tower of the castle. Back to a window.

'We jump,' said Anna.

They peered out of the window, nothing lay below except darkness, no sense of how far or how deep the fall might be, if it would ever stop—

Effie looked at Anna. 'You sure about this?'

'A leap of faith.' Anna put out her hand.

Effie took it and they stepped up onto the ledge.

I won't look down.

I won't look down.

I won't look down . . .

Anna looked down and she was no longer afraid.

They jumped.

They flew.

Anna didn't know if the world was behind them or before them, if they were flying upwards or downwards, there was no sense of anything except Effie's hand in her own and a final rush of force as if the darkness had pleated tight and they were breaking through to the other side. She didn't remember reaching an end, only arriving.

She felt the floor beneath her, the texture of it so different to anything in Hel: real and solid and gritty and her bones hard against it. Her body was painful and cold where it lay, so cold it shook violently but Anna grew giddy at the sensation – the searing pain in her toes, the electric shivers in her chest, the icy air around her nostrils. The room smelt of dust and snow and rotting apples. She opened her eyes and, though they were deep below ground, the light was so rich and hued with colour that she had to close them again.

She opened them slowly and the shapes and shades slotted into place, dark and gloomy but perfect. How had she not realized how beautiful the world was before?

'It's the Hel rush,' Anna heard a voice say. A voice like cobwebs made of velvet. 'It will settle.'

Settle. Anna didn't want to settle. She could feel her body beating and roaring with life, a river undammed, a world undimmed. There was a hand in hers, thrumming with the same energy.

She turned her head and Effie was looking back at her.

They started to laugh, to squeal, to cry with delight.

A tall figure moved towards them tentatively – half skull, half flesh. She removed her mask and Mór's face was frightened. 'Are you . . . OK?'

Anna sat up, stretching her limbs, the movement both painful and wonderful. 'We are. We found our own way out.'

Mór shut her eyes, breathing out, slow and deep. 'We didn't know for sure – we were trying to bring you back but you both felt . . . beyond. Lost.'

'We were.' Anna looked at Effie. 'But we found each other.'

'Then . . . you have returned.' Mór tried not to sound astonished.

'Actually, Hel kicked us out,' said Effie.

Anna snorted.

Mór gave them a flat look.

Yuki and Azrael came forwards from the circle of Hel witches. 'I can't believe you made it, you actually made it!' Yuki cried.

'You are Initiated,' said Azrael, almost bowing before them.

'How long have we been gone?' Anna asked, the throbbing in her head growing by the second.

'An hour,' Mór replied.

'AN HOUR!' Anna and Effie exclaimed at the same time.

'It will not have felt like that in Hel. Time does not work in the same way there.'

It had felt like days, years, like Anna would never be the same person as before she went. How could such a thing be measured?

'Did you do it?' said Mór, her voice tense. 'Did you bind the spirit?'

'We did.' Anna nodded. 'It is done.'

Mór breathed in sharply. The Hel witches around them murmured. Anna shared another look with Effie and she knew they would never speak of what had passed in Hel, that there were no words that could capture it anyway. No words except . . . Anna could still feel the Language of the Dead on her tongue. Could still remember the sound of it – not nightmarish now – only words, but *not* words. She couldn't describe the language on this side of the Fabric, but knew if she needed to, she could still speak it – could draw its marrows up from inside her bones.

Mór pointed to their arms.

Effie and Anna looked down. There, on the skin above Anna's wrist, was a Death Mark. Effie had the same. The skin had given way – a scar of death. It wasn't a letter but a symbol that captured a concept with no direct translation, but it was something like – *through the shadows . . .*

'There you go,' said Effie. 'Matching tattoos.'

'I've never seen the same one form on two people before.' Mór peered with fascination, then looked back at them. 'You have passed through the shadows and out again. You speak the tongue of ravens now. Very few witches on this earth can say that. It is a great responsibility and you must carry it wisely.' Her eyes moved between them with the weight of death, a weight Anna had felt and understood now. 'Thank you.'

Anna and Effie nodded.

'Now, let us tend to your injuries. A shower may be necessary too.'

Anna and Effie looked down at themselves and at each other for the first time. They were covered in dirt – on their bodies, faces, beneath their fingernails, their clothes were ripped, their hair matted and wild. There was a cut on Effie's leg, Anna could feel dried blood on her own face, bruises on her body. Hel was real enough.

They emerged several hours later, clean and their cuts and bruises tended to. Mór had insisted they eat and drink, including an elixir to expel any lingering spiritual energies. Anna knew she should feel tired but she didn't. The Hel rush was still running through her and when they stepped outside, the world was overwhelming.

The city was made of glitter. So many kinds of light against the darkness, but all of it muffled by the slow fall of black feathers from the sky. They drifted down between the buildings, over the streets like silent rain, falling with eerie slowness.

Anna and Effie turned to each other, knowing it was somehow to do with what they'd just done. Mother Holle's touch.

People had stopped to look at them, confounded and entranced, some taking photos, others hurrying through it all, probably afraid of what it meant, wanting to get home.

Home.

Anna wanted to go home more than anything. There was the sudden sound of a car screeching through the traffic, overtaking a bus and swerving to a stop on the road in front of them. A battered Peugeot

206. Attis kicked the door open and didn't bother to shut it as he ran towards them. He bundled them into a hug, one under each arm, so tight that he could give Bertie a run for her money.

He pulled back and assessed them intently. 'Anna – your head . . . Effie, why are you limping?'

'Cut my leg.'

'I knew you shouldn't have gone! Any other injuries? Do you have all your limbs? Your faculties? Are your souls intact?'

'We're fine, but you should see Hel,' said Anna.

Attis managed a smile, shaking his head incredulously. He looked as if he hadn't taken a breath the whole time they'd been gone.

'We're back,' Effie reassured him. 'We're fine, mostly. And we did it.' She caught a black feather from the sky.

'I knew you would,' he said, looking at them rather than the sky, disbelief and pride in his eyes. 'Either that or someone's had a really big pillow fight.'

Anna could hardly believe it either. 'It's over,' she uttered.

'You are both now, officially, the most badass witches I know.'

'Were we not before?' Effie raised an eyebrow. 'Be careful how you answer – we can have you haunted, you know.'

'Spirits at our fingertips,' Anna confirmed.

Attis's eyes darted between them. 'Definitely both scarier now.'

They all laughed, the laughter of sheer and giddy relief. Anna could feel her magic still flowing from her, a song expanding outwards into the sounds of London: the low rumble of the buses, the splash of silver puddles, the buzz and blur of voices, the silence of the feathers . . .

A bus started beeping its horn angrily. Attis had parked in a bus lane.

'We'd better go,' he advised.

Back home, they went to the roof, both Anna and Effie still too full of life to sleep. They watched the feathers fall over London. It would cause a commotion in the news but the spell was over. The spirit was released. No more needless deaths at its hands.

Anna wished it was all over. But, of course, it was not. The secretary's words had stayed with her: *The WIPS already have what they want: a captive, terrified audience* . . .

Attis brought them some food, Anna not wanting to tell him they'd not long eaten. 'Thanks,' she said.

'I'm just glad you're back . . .' He smiled at her and it lingered, their eyes moving between each other's. She thought of their conversation before they'd left. Their hands entwined.

Effie was watching them from the other side of the roof. The curse wasn't over either, but Anna wouldn't let it have power over her any more. She moved away from Attis, just glad that they were all alive and with each other. That was enough.

Effie came over, poking her tongue out at Attis. 'We wouldn't have wanted to make your life easier by staying away.'

He wrinkled his nose back at her. 'Of course.'

They sat in the chairs, picking at the food, while Attis asked them questions, Anna and Effie managing to relay the gist of what had taken place without really saying what had happened at all. Just as there was no way to translate the Language of the Dead, there was no way to explain Hel – its secrets were not made of the same substance as the secrets on earth.

'So you have the waters,' he said.

Anna reached for her bag and pulled out the thimble. 'The memories of Eleanor Everdell.'

Attis smiled at her. 'I guess Nana's riddle came through in the end.'

Anna made a face at him. 'Did you just say something vaguely nice about Nana?'

'I wouldn't go that far.'

'She did send us into Hel, I'm not sure I trust the old bat yet,' Effie rumbled,

Attis looked to the sky. 'It's almost morning. What are we going to do tomorrow?'

Effie's eyes darted as if she were trying to work out all the possibilities of what might happen. 'We go to school,' she said. 'We see what the results of what we've done are. Ending their spell, crashing their plans, might be enough to redirect the attention of the WIPS, to stop them from coming.'

'I don't think it'll stop them forever,' said Attis.

'We can talk to the secretary. Get the inside track. If nothing's changed – we can still run tomorrow evening. One more day.'

'And the waters?' Attis tipped his head to the thimble.

'We drink them,' Anna replied.

He frowned. 'Is that wise tonight, after all you've been through?'

'We went through it for this.'

'I'm not being left on a cliffhanger,' said Effie.

'OK.' Attis stood up. He knew this was something they needed to do alone. 'I won't be far away.'

'We'll be fine, Attis.' Anna nodded at him.

He raised his hand, stoking the fire for them before he left.

Effie moved the chairs aside and Anna sat down by her on the floor, face to face, the fire flickering behind them. Anna had the thimble in her hand but, as they locked eyes, Anna wondered if Effie was thinking the same thing as her . . . of those final moments in Hel when their magic had joined together.

'I . . .' said Anna, not knowing how to put it into words. 'I'm not sure our mother's language was touch . . .'

Effie met her meaningful look with her own. 'I don't think so either.'

'Nor Aunt's . . .'

Effie shook her head.

'Did you—'

'Feel it? I did.' Effie's pupils seemed to pulse with excitement.

'Our language is Emotion.'

Anna knew it in her bones but saying it was another thing entirely. Like falling all over again – scary and exhilarating. Effie looked over-whelmed too, which Anna had not expected. She'd imagined Effie discovering her language would be a moment she seized, triumphed in, but Anna understood – it felt too big to seize at once, too delicate to grip. The settling of the soul.

For Anna, it had happened in that moment she'd seen the pattern of the snowflake. In it, she'd seen her fear, understood it, known how to use it. As the song had risen around her, she'd felt her other emotions too, each had their melody, their own open-ended patterns as the piano and spinning top had tried to show her. She'd been growing their roots this whole time. She didn't understand them, not yet, but she'd felt their power . . .

'The most powerful language there is.' Effie's voice glistened like a crown. 'I should have known.'

'It feels like only the beginning . . .'

'It is. From the ashes we rise.'

Anna thought of the snowdrop, its roots reaching all the way into Hel. It hadn't told them what their language would be, but where they would find it. Deep in the darkness. She met Effie's smile, sparks of magic leaping between their eyes. They began to laugh, giddy, astonished laughter, the laughter of sisters who have a secret that only belongs to them. Laughter on the edge of tears. Hel had made them even as it had broken them.

'So . . .' Effie took a breath. 'Shall we break the curse next?'

Anna reached for the thimble and held it up between them. 'A sip each?'

Effie nodded and Anna raised the thimble to her own lips. She remembered the rippling blackness of the waters, but there was no choice now – it was time to drink. She tipped it back, releasing the liquid within. She handed it to Effie who did the same. It tasted of nothing. Of oblivion.

Anna had felt a great deal of pain that night already but the pain she felt now was visceral; raw and animal. Not her body – *Eleanor's.* They were seeing the world, feeling the world through Eleanor—

Her body aches and groans, shakes with cold. Her belly is swollen and her heart torn up. She lies on a bed in a state of hopelessness, a bare room but for a table with a cup of water and Bible upon it, a barely simmering fire in the grate. It is night beyond the small window. The door is locked but she knows that someone is standing outside, keeping watch.

The last few weeks flash through her mind, shudder through her body. She's been locked up most of the time. Sometimes dragged for questioning into one of the other rooms. Forced to walk up and down incessantly until her legs give way. Not given enough food, not given enough sleep. Her body has been inspected, checked for the marks of a witch. Torture has been threatened . . . she knows they will go through with it, once she's given birth, they are only waiting. There've been men she knows – the local magistrate and others she grew up with – and men she doesn't know. Men in dark clothes and black boots. Her magic won't work. She's raged, she's cried, she's quaked with fear, but it's all given way to despair. Nobody cares what happens to her. But she cares what happens to the thing inside her – she puts a hand on her stomach. A fierce, protective love shoots through her. It is all that is keeping her breathing.

Another memory. A memory within a memory. She is young, climbing apple trees outside her family home, a farm, with her sister. Hannah is older and can climb higher. Hannah floats the apples down to her and she laughs at the magic and chases after them. They sleep in the same bed at night, sharing secrets, telling stories in entranced whispers. Stories about Black Annis, the witch who's said to haunt the surrounding woods.

Eleanor's belly tightens suddenly. She cries out but a movement behind her distracts her from her pain – the door opens and someone enters. At first she thinks it is the guard but then they step into view.

'Hannah . . .' Eleanor whispers.

Somebody else enters behind Hannah but they are hazy – an indistinct shadow.

'Who are you?' Eleanor asks the figure but it does not reply.

Hannah moves towards her. 'Eleanor.'

Eleanor's rage flickers back to life, but she is too weak to move. 'Why are you here? You've damned me to hell, sister!'

Hannah cocks her head. 'Let's not throw stones. You did steal my betrothed.'

'I was sixteen! Sixteen! Young and foolish!'

Another memory. Eleanor is kissing a man against the apple tree. She thinks his name in her head over and over . . . Henry Merkel. Henry Merkel. Henry Merkel. Her whole world, her whole life has been so small but he – he can change all that. He is to be wed to her sister but she wants him, needs him, and he wants her. His hands are on her. Envy burns beneath her skin – Hannah is already smarter, better at magic . . . why should she get to have him too?

Back in the cold room, Eleanor pushes the guilt away.

'Young and foolish you may have been,' says Hannah. 'But you kept him. You took him and left me with nothing. Rejected. Replaced. A laughing stock. No future. No prospects. I told you I'd come back. I told you I'd get my revenge . . .'

A memory. They are in their home. Hannah has Eleanor pinned against the wall, she is yelling, crying, the room swirling with objects, a whirlwind of Hannah's rage. Their mother is screaming. Eleanor fears her sister will kill her but Hannah pulls away. She tells Eleanor she will find Black Annis, learn the darkest magic there is to learn and return to destroy her. She vows it.

'You've had your revenge,' Eleanor croaks, weakening. 'What more can you do to me? I am already imprisoned for witchcraft. They will see me burn in the end. And you killed him. You took him from me—'

But it was worse than that. Eleanor looks back up at her sister, wondering how she'd done it. She hadn't just killed him. She'd made him love her . . .

'Are you remembering how he looked at me?' Hannah seems on the edge of laughter, of madness. 'The way he looked at me when I asked him to kill himself? How he did it willingly.'

Eleanor cries with pain, remembering that too – the love in his eyes as he'd looked at Hannah. She'd stolen him back before she took his life. 'You used magic!' Eleanor shrieks. 'That's not true love.'

'But it was. The truest. I told you I'd hone my magic . . . and I have. There is not a witch more powerful than me in the whole world.' For a moment Hannah is triumphant but it falters. She looks behind her, to the figure, and then back to Eleanor. 'I have one more act of vengeance in me, sister.' Her eyes move to Eleanor's swollen stomach.

Fear slices through Eleanor's hopelessness. She tries to get up but she can't. She's held to the bed by magic far stronger than hers. 'What are you going to do?' Her voice quakes.

The other figure comes forwards. It stands beside Hannah.

'Help me! Please!' Eleanor cries to it. 'Who are you? Why are you doing this?'

The figure takes Hannah's hand. Eleanor is screaming now, but she can't move. She can't do anything as Hannah places her other hand upon Eleanor's stomach.

'No! Please! Don't! Hannah, if you have any love left for me—'

But she is silenced.

Hannah raises her head and the words come out fast, an eruption of hatred held back—

'I curse you, sister! May our pain live on and on – one womb, one breath, sisters of blood, bound by love, so bound by death!'

The magic rips the world open. A tear through the Fabric.

Eleanor has never felt magic like it – magic beyond magic – an eclipse blocking out anything else. Her pain is beyond imaginable – she is being torn apart . . .

Eleanor wakes and they are gone. The fire has fizzled out. She puts a hand to her stomach. She knows what Hannah has done, knows it in her bones.

Her stomach squeezes tight. She roars as the contraction moves through her. Not now. Not now.

The pain is staggering but her love is stronger.

She climbs out of bed. To the fire. She throws another log on it, stokes it. Magic is still in the room. She can feel it around her, within her for the first time in so long. She must use it.

There is an old key in the drawer by her bed. She doesn't know what it is for, it doesn't open the door. She takes it, collapsing to the floor with another contraction. She screams inwardly, biting down on her teeth like an animal. She crawls to the fire, tearing the sharp edge of the key down her arm, releasing her blood. She drips it into her palm and puts her hand over the fire, the words of the spell pouring out of her before another contraction takes hold. Her voice shakes, but power flows through it. Power she has never known, born of her love.

She tips the blood onto the fire, contracting again as the fire roars and spits with magic. She lowers her head, panting and sweating. The fire goes out. In it lies a stone. Hot and red and gleaming. She picks it up. It's too hot to hold but she does. She drags herself back to the bed, clutching it tightly. The spell . . . she must write it down . . . she must hide it . . . she reaches for the Bible by her bedside—

The memory ended abruptly but Eleanor lingered. For a few moments, Anna could still feel her pain and desperation and love pouring through the broken seams of the memory, pulsing through Anna's veins. Effie looked dazed, a hand on her stomach as if she could feel Eleanor's suffering too. It took them a while to speak, sparks of sunrise threatening over the horizon.

'Hannah cast the curse,' said Anna. 'Like Nana said . . . a curse cannot be cast by just anyone, only one bound to the victim by love. Her own sister.'

'But someone else was there . . .' Effie hissed. 'Someone else helped to cast it.'

Anna nodded slowly, trying to hold onto all the details of the memory – the blurred figure in the background who'd stepped forth and held Hannah's hand. 'Do you think Eleanor could see them? Or was the figure only hazy for us?'

Effie narrowed her eyes. 'Maybe the memory's been tampered with.'

'Is that possible?'

'Someone removed the contents of the Everdell family history book. Someone who doesn't want the curse to be uncovered – or their identity.

And I've got a big fat guess who'd be powerful enough to do all that . . . Nana . . . . Black Annis! It tells us so in the memory . . . Hannah went off to find her and then she returns and casts the curse with a shadowy figure. Nana told us she didn't cast it, but what if she *helped* to cast it? A language loophole. A trick.'

'Why would Nana lead us all the way to this memory if it was about her?'

'Because she's enjoying the show – luring us deeper into the chaos of a curse we'll never solve.'

'We will,' Anna shot back. 'We have to. Nana, or whoever else this person is, could be the key – the other way we've been looking for. Attis wants to live and we have to make sure he does.'

Eleanor surged through Anna again, the love that had propelled her. Ferocious and brave. Pure and absolute. Releasing her blood . . . a stone condensing in the fire, dark red—

'The stone was formed of her blood . . .' Anna whispered with the realization. 'A curse can only be stopped by the blood of the one who cast the curse. Perhaps, because Eleanor and Hannah were sisters, Eleanor's blood would work too. She condensed it into a stone – the stone that created Attis four hundred years later. His blood is *her* blood.'

Effie looked up at Anna with a grimace. 'How could Hannah curse her sister like that? She'd already killed her husband—' Effie stopped, her eyes widening.

'What?'

Effie stood up. 'Hannah said she made Eleanor's husband love her before she killed him. *Love her.* And in Eleanor's confession . . . there were reports that a witch had been running around the town making men fall in love with her. People blamed Eleanor but it was Hannah.'

Anna walked after Effie.

Effie spun around to face her. 'The prophecy . . .'

Anna murmured it. '*When the Hunters rise again, a cursed witch will cast a love spell that will bring about the downfall of all . . .*'

Effie's eyes were so wide now they engulfed the sky, glinting with the red of dawn. 'Hannah claimed she was the most powerful witch in the world. What if she could cast the spell for love? What if the power of that spell runs in our family line? In us?'

Anna tried to take in her words.

'We just discovered our language is Emotional.' Effie did not relent, excited now. 'The spell for love would fall under the language of emotions, it could be our spell of power – our seed! Our *seed*.'

Anna's voice was faint. 'If so . . . it means the prophecy is about one of us – a cursed witch who can cast a love spell.'

'What are the chances? This isn't coincidence! This is fate! The hand of the Goddess herself pointing down at us!' Effie tipped her head back to the sky.

Anna couldn't deny that the stars had seemed to align, a constellation of foreboding – Effie only saw how they gleamed; Anna saw their shadows.

'*If* it is about one of us,' said Anna, 'then we're in even more danger than we thought. If the WIPS are hunting cursed witches because of the prophecy . . . this makes us the exact ones they want to find.'

Effie didn't seem to have heard her. She prowled to the rooftop edge. 'I always knew we were going to be powerful, but this . . . the spell for love is one of the original spells of the Goddess . . .'

'Selene says such magic is long lost.'

'Until now. It's in us, Anna. In *us*.'

Anna joined beside her, trying to bring her attention back to earth. 'We don't know that for sure. If the love spell is in our family line then, I admit, the prophecy certainly ticks several . . . highly concerning boxes. But we also don't know how prophecies work, if we can really believe in it, what it means, if it means anything at all. We can't lose sight of what matters – ending the curse. The sooner it is done the safer we are. If the Hunters find out about any of this then we are enemy number one. Perhaps going back to school is a bad idea . . .'

'We just went into Hel itself and you want to run?' Effie turned to her at last, her eyes full of plots in the making. 'Let's not underestimate ourselves. The prophecy suggests we are far more powerful than the Hunters.'

Anna wanted to argue with her sister but the guilt was still with her. She'd accused Effie of casting the hysteria spell and Effie had still come to Hel with her. Perhaps all of this would only work if they started believing in one another.

CONFESS

The last stage of Initiation comes to us all but for a Hel witch it is the culmi-
nation of a long journey and the beginning of a greater one. To tether our
thread, to keep our soul alive in the world of the dead. We live to die.

'Death', Hel Witch Initiation Stage Seven

Anna collapsed on her bed for a few hours before school. When her
alarm went off she felt awful. The Hel rush had started to fade and her
cuts and bruises stung and throbbed. At least the worst one was hidden
beneath her hair.

It felt strange, knowing that it might be her last day at St Olave's,
that she might never finish the year, graduate, leave for university.
Ending the hysteria had saved who knew how many lives but would
it really change the course of the WIPS? Would it really stop Eames?
It wasn't that Anna wanted to run – for Manda to leave her parents,
Rowan her family home – she just didn't believe the WIPS would give
up so easily.

The book of fairy tales and the feather were still scattered on the
floor. Anna picked the feather up. It felt lighter. Her fear wasn't gone
. . . it just didn't feel the same. She no longer felt suffocated and para-
lysed by it – like it had her cornered and trapped and buried six feet
under. It gleamed now, hammered into shape. Sharp as a knife she could
wield. Hard as bone. She knew its pattern. She'd sung its song. It was
part of her, not stronger than her. She wore the shadows of Hel now.
She went to the window and let the feather out, knowing it would not
return this time.

She unpacked her bag, taking out her mirror. Aunt was gone. Anna smiled at her new reflection. *Different. Free.*

She went down to Selene's room and knocked on the door. Selene was up and half dressed.

'What time did you two get back?' she asked, slipping on a dress from her wardrobe. 'I waited until I saw Attis. He told me he was going to pick you up but it was so late by then.'

'It was – er – a big night . . . Selene, I need to ask you something.'

Selene stopped in front of her, frowning. 'Yes, darling?'

'Was my mother's magical language Emotional?'

Selene's lips parted, a little gasp of breath. There was no hiding the truth from Anna now and Selene knew it. 'How did you—'

'Just a hunch,' said Anna quickly.

'No.' Selene's eyes narrowed with knowing. 'More than a hunch. You look . . . different. You know, don't you?'

'I do.'

Selene struggled through a series of expressions – surprise, confusion, pride – settling on a wistful smile. 'Oh, Anna.'

'My language is Emotional.' Anna stated it loud and clear. She could hardly believe it still.

'As was your mother's and your aunt's,' said Selene quietly.

'Why didn't you tell me?'

Selene took her hands. 'Oh, I wanted to, but it's a rare and powerful language, darling. I didn't want to give you false expectations in case yours didn't follow . . . although I thought it would. I could see it in you from the beginning . . . and Effie—' Her smile twinged. 'It was another reason why I kept it secret. You know what Effie is like . . . she wants it all and now, the world be damned. I didn't want her realizing yet that she's destined for the very power she craves.' Her hands tightened. 'Does she know too?'

'I don't think so.' Anna didn't want to lie to Selene but she didn't think it was her place to tell her. That was a moment for Effie and Selene, but Selene appeared terrified at the prospect. 'You shouldn't doubt Effie so much,' Anna said. 'You need to believe that she can handle things – the truth. I think it would help you get her back.'

'Perhaps you're right.' Selene nodded quietly. 'How did you find out your language? What happened last night?' She pulled Anna towards the bed but Anna resisted.

'I can't tell you now. I have to go. But I will. I'll tell you everything when I get home, I promise.'

For a moment, Selene did not release her. 'So much is happening at once . . .'

'Don't worry.' Anna pulled her hands free. 'We're stronger than you think.'

'That's what I'm afraid of . . .'

As they neared St Olave's, they could hear them already. The angry mob. Attis wound his window up, peering at the crowd outside the school gates. Spitting and snarling, calling for justice and punishment, waving placards not pitchforks, but the sentiment was the same.

Anna could hear their taunts as they stepped out of the car, several streets away.

'WITCHCRAFT IS A SIN!'

'SATAN'S WHORES!'

She raised her head, refusing to feel ashamed of the magic she carried any longer. They didn't deserve this. No one did.

'Let them rile themselves up,' Effie spat.

'Come on.' Attis ushered them through the back door. 'I'll see you later, Hel Queens.' He left them, heading towards the Boys' School.

Effie seemed as energized as she had the night before, but more on edge too. Had she even slept at all? They avoided the main corridor, splitting up and darting back towards the old toilets where they'd agreed to meet Rowan and Manda for a quick debrief before assembly. There was a lot they had to tell them and not much time.

Rowan was there already. 'We shouldn't all be here together,' she said.

'We know,' Anna agreed. 'We just have to tell you something. It's important, and safer in person.'

The door opened. Manda. She looked slightly better than when Anna had seen her last, but still too thin, too drained. Anna took her hand, drawing her into the room so she could at least lean against one of the sinks. 'How are you feeling?'

'Probably shouldn't be here.' Manda coughed. 'But school is making me and you know how I hate to miss a day, wouldn't look good on my record.' She managed a smile.

'There you go. Manda's back.' Rowan smiled weakly, then turned to Effie and Anna. 'We don't have long till assembly, what's going on?'

Anna took a breath. 'We ended the hysteria spell.'

'YOU WHA—'

'Rowan!' Anna put a finger to her lips.

'Sorry, but what? WHAT? Sorry. But *what*?'

Manda looked between them, troubled.

'It's a long story,' said Anna.

'We went to Hel. Learnt the Language of the Dead. Bound the spirit and jumped out of a tower.' Effie summed it up, enjoying their expressions as she finished.

'And I thought I'd gone insane,' Manda sputtered.

'You're joking,' Rowan whispered.

Anna pulled her sleeve up and removed the chimera hiding her Death Mark. It showed clear on her skin. Rowan and Manda recoiled from it.

Rowan put a hand to her mouth. 'The feathers over London . . .'

Anna nodded. 'Look, we'll tell you everything as soon as we can, but for now just know the spell is over. No more needless deaths. But we don't know what it could mean for us. We're hoping the WIPS already know that their plans have been hijacked and that it might set them back, give the magical world a chance to turn the situation around, maybe buy us time here. We're going to speak to the secretary.'

'I can't believe you guys did this.' Manda's mouth was still hanging open.

'I have so many questions. I don't think I've ever had so many questions, and that's saying something.' Rowan looked dazed. 'Can we at least hug?'

They met in the middle of the old toilets and held each other tightly.

'All in,' said Effie.

'All in,' they replied.

The bell rang for assembly and they sprang apart.

'We should go separately,' said Anna.

She left the toilets last. As she walked to assembly alone she prayed that Eames would not be there, that he would have been called away. But he was. He was on the stage. His prefects lined the room. Silence reigned and, even though the hysteria spell was over, the fear was still palpable. Anna moved slowly with her head down, trying not to alarm anyone. As she took her seat she began to scream at herself: *Why are we here? What are we doing? We should have gone already.* What if Eames had more tricks up his sleeve? More *tests*.

The Inquisitor began to speak. 'I just wanted to inform everyone that Mr Ramsden has taken leave. We are searching for a suitable replacement. I will not be staying much longer either. The investigation is due to be wrapped up early next week.'

So nothing had changed *yet*. Anna presumed the WIPS were still due next week. They would need to leave.

'Please,' Eames continued. 'If you have any lingering suspicions or knowledge that may inform my final decision then please do come forwards. Together, we can stop the spread and we will.' He raised his head. 'And to the witches among us now – this is your last chance. Confess now or face the consequences.'

The silence stretched out, reverberating like a string pulled too tight.

Then someone stood up.

It was so inconceivable that it took Anna a moment to take it in. *Effie.*

Effie was standing up.

She turned to face everyone, all of her restless energy condensed now, hardened into . . . fear. She was scared. Ripples of alarm spread out from her. Eames's eyes contracted, alert, but then she spoke and his face slackened with shock.

'I – I – I confess,' she said unsteadily. She lowered her head as if ashamed, her lips murmuring as if she were building up to saying more. Anna felt the world drop away. A sudden drenching cold, a hammer down her spine. She knew what was happening too late.

Too late.

Effie raised herself back up. 'I confess,' she said, simply, plainly. 'I confess.'

Eames looked exultant. It only lasted for a moment.

'I confess,' she continued. 'I confess. I confess. I confess.' She no longer appeared in control of herself. 'I confess – I confess – I confess – I confess—' Her eyes were disappearing, turning to holes out of which dread poured, thick and black as the river of Hel.

'I confess,' said the girl beside her.

'I confess,' another cried.

More joined in:

'I confess!'

'I confess!'

'I confess!'

There was no time – the hysteria spell was spreading too fast, with such force that Anna could barely breathe, let alone fight it.

'I confess!'

'I confess!'

'I confess!'

Everyone falling to its darkness. The clamour rising, as they all twisted inward to the desperate places inside of them – crying, jabbering, shrieking.

'I confess!'

'I confess!'

'I confess!'

The whole room now – hands rising to the ceiling, knees falling to the floor, voices shaking. Even Eames—

'I confess!'

Anna threw out her circle but she didn't have long – the spell was too powerful, the spirit too consuming. It would eat them all alive and feast on their bones.

'I confess!'

'I confess!'

'I confess!'

Screaming it at each other, raging at each other. They'd all tear each other apart before it was over.

Fear.

Anna could feel it breaking through her magic, filling her up. Too much – too dark – too deep—

Fear.

'I CONFESS!' The words erupted from her like a release, but a release that only dragged her deeper. 'I CONFESS! I CONFESS!'

The world went dark.

Fear.

She knew the spirit's name . . . its name . . .

'I CONFESS! I CONFESS!'

She grasped for it as her mind gave way to the spell, the Language of the Dead still on the tip of her tongue. Everyone was screaming. Dying—

Fear.

She would not let it take her.

The name of the spirit clawed and cawed its way up through her.

She screamed it aloud in the Language of the Dead.

She screamed its name and the words to bind it once more.

Anna fell to the floor, still spluttering. 'I confess . . . I confess . . . I confess . . .' but the energy was disappearing, sinking back through the Fabric. 'I confess . . .'

The screams around her faded, the words petering out.

Silence.

Anna lifted her head. People were alive . . . moving in a slow and lost daze . . . no one yet quite knowing where they were, what had happened. The dim memory of a word on their lips: *confess*.

One person did not move at all: *Effie*.

The centre of the blizzard.

Anna managed to stand up, limping towards her. She fell down beside her.

Effie was white and still, just like she'd been in Hel, only this wasn't Hel, this was the world where everything was black and white again; alive or dead. She wasn't breathing.

Anna heard herself cry out. 'She isn't breathing!' Her hands panicked over her. 'She isn't breathing!'

The room was stirring around her but all Anna could see was Effie. *Effie! Effie! What did you do? Why did you do this?*

No breath from her lips. Anna put a hand to her pulse but couldn't feel anything. She gave her magic to her but could feel no magic in return. Only emptiness.

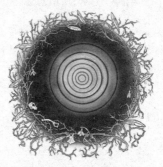

RUN

The raven knows itself.

Mór Nottambula, *Hel Witch and Raven Tongue*

'Someone call an ambulance!' Anna screamed.

But the room was moving too slowly. Everyone still lost, not yet able to break through the clutches of the spell. Eames watching dumbfounded from the stage.

Anna lifted her head from Effie. She tried to remember her first aid training. She locked her hands together on Effie's chest and pressed down. *Up and down. Up and down.*

Up and down. Please . . . please . . .

After what felt like too long, Effie's body convulsed.

Anna jerked back.

A guttural sound erupted from Effie's lips. A deep, wrenching sound. A choking sound. Her body sprang upright and the coughing reached a crescendo of inhuman noises, as if her throat were being torn open. Then Effie reached into her mouth and pulled out a long black feather.

She fell back down onto the floor, passed out cold, but breathing.

Suddenly more commotion. Peter and another prefect entered the room with Darcey, Corinne and Olivia. 'I found them!' he declared. 'I found them with these!' He lifted his hands up. He was holding dolls – poppets. 'They were trying to run.'

Darcey glared at the prefect holding her with affronted rage. 'Get off me!' she demanded. 'We were not running! We were locked in a class-room! This is ridiculous.'

The room was stirring more now. People returning to themselves. Did they remember what had just happened? Eames came down the steps from the stage, unsteadily, as if he'd forgotten how his legs worked. He turned to Peter, his voice a dry rasp. 'What is going on?'

'I caught them running away,' said Peter with certainty.

'WHAT?' Darcey screeched, her face contorting. 'THAT IS BULLSHIT! YOU CAN'T ACTUALLY BELIEVE THAT!' She spat at Eames, moving towards him as if she were going to shake him. She was quickly held back. 'THEY'RE THE WITCHES! THEY'RE THE FUCKING WHORE WITCHES!' She snarled and spat, looking to Anna and Effie, no longer able to hold in the fury and vitriol that was always simmering just beneath her surface.

'Take them to the Ebury wing,' Eames continued, as if he hadn't heard her. 'Take the others too.' He gestured to Anna and Effie, to a dazed Rowan and Manda. 'Nobody is leaving this school until I get to the bottom of *what* just happened.'

They carried Effie, unconscious, to the Ebury wing, Anna dragged after her, begging someone to call an ambulance. No one listened. They were dumped in the secretary's room and left, the door locked. The Coven of the Dark Moon and the Juicers.

'Effie.' Anna tried to rouse her. 'Effie!'

Rowan and Manda peered at her too.

Effie groaned, her eyes opening. They helped her to sit up.

'Effie? Are you OK?'

Darcey growled in their direction. 'What the fuck have you done?'

Corinne cowered against the wall. Olivia sat motionless.

'Nothing you don't deserve,' Effie croaked, the echo of a smile on her lips.

Darcey stood up. Anna had never seen her hair anything less than perfect, but now it was tearing free of her ponytail, her face a white muscle of outrage and indignation. 'I don't know how you've managed to – to twist this, but I will make sure Eames knows that you are responsible! My parents will never let this happen! You'll be punished! All of you punished!'

'Shut up, Darcey.' Effie flicked a hand towards her and Darcey's mouth snapped closed.

Darcey's eyes flared: confused – afraid – and then vindicated. She prised her mouth open. 'Malefice! I knew it. I knew you were witches, all of you. I was right! I was right!' She turned to Olivia and Corinne. 'Did you see that? I told you both, didn't I?' She laughed viciously. 'I knew it!'

'Shut up, Darcey!' Olivia snapped. 'You got us into this mess.'

Corinne joined Olivia's glare, though her eyes moved nervously to Effie.

Eames came into the room with several prefects and Darcey pivoted to them.

'Effie just did malefice!' she declared as if she were still in charge of the situation. 'In front of all of us!'

No one joined her tirade.

'TELL THEM OLIVIA! CORINNE! EFFIE JUST DID MAGIC!'

'Split them into different rooms,' Eames directed, as if Darcey were no more than a mild inconvenience, a fly he would swat later.

'No – no—' Darcey's face began to register what was truly happening. That the beast she'd fed was turning on her. That no one was safe. 'Inquisitor Eames.' She calmed her voice, adding polish to it. 'There's been some kind of misunderstanding – it's very clear who the witches in this room are—'

'I will be the decider of that, Ms Dulacey. Separate them.'

The prefects moved on them again.

Anna stood up, throwing her hands out. 'Effie's only just come around, she's still white as a sheet. Put me in with her, I can keep an eye, make sure she doesn't pass out again—' She looked past the prefects to Eames. 'You don't want someone dying on your hands now, do you? It'll distract from the end of the investigation.'

Eames nodded a vague assent and Effie and Anna were torn from Rowan and Manda and barrelled into one of the Ebury rooms to the sound of Darcey's incensed protestations.

Anna hadn't wanted to leave Effie after what had just happened but she also didn't want to be in the same room as her. Effie slumped down against the wall and Anna stood on the other side, barely able to look at her.

'What have you done?' Anna's voice was still shaking.

Effie levered her head up. 'I did what I had to do.'

They stared at each other across the gulf that had opened up between them.

'I'm trying to save us all,' said Effie. 'I acted decisively. I took a risk, one that I think will pay off.'

'A RISK?' Anna cried, then lowered her voice, its intensity sharpening. 'You almost just died! I thought . . .' She didn't want to go back to that moment. 'Jesus, Effie. You could have killed everyone in that room!'

'It needed to be convincing. A grand finale like no other.'

'That wasn't a grand finale! It was insanity! We went into Hel itself to *bind* that spirit, to put it away forever, and you – you – just used it, unleashed it all over again, like it was nothing!'

'I didn't *unleash* it. I commanded it. We have the power of the Language of the Dead and we're the only ones who know the spirit's Death Name, the only ones who have mastery over it. How could I not use that? Such power at our fingertips. It would be insanity *not* to use it.'

Anna stared down at her as if Effie were a stranger. After everything they'd been through . . . 'You never cared about saving lives, did you? It was only ever about the power.'

'I did this to save our lives, to save our coven!' Effie snarled, her anger building too. 'All in!'

'This wasn't to save us, this was to satisfy yourself. To win the game you so desperately wanted to win. If I hadn't – if I hadn't – you could have—'

'But I believed in you, sis.' Effie's voice twisted around her. 'I knew you'd be able to stop the spirit. You'd done it once – in Hel. I knew you wouldn't let me die—'

'It took everything I had—' Anna's voice broke. 'You didn't even tell me . . .'

'Because you'd never have let me go through with it. And it had to look real. We all had to go under the spell so there was no shred of doubt that we were *attacked*. Attacked by Darcey and her minions.' Effie's smile threatened again.

Anna could hear the protestors outside the gates. 'So that's your big plan, pin it all on the Juicers? Eames won't believe you.'

'Exactly, which is why Peter's help is so invaluable. He sent the Juicers fake messages from Eames requesting their presence in our form class-room this morning. No one was there, of course, but Peter locked the door temporarily, keeping them inside. Their absence from assembly would look suspicious enough, but then Peter finds poppets on them too . . . now that's just damning.' Her smile widened. 'He planted them, of course. I took some poppets from Manda's house when we were there, figured they'd be useful.'

'But – but they've already found a poppet on you and Manda in school . . .'

'Did they?' Effie countered. 'Darcey claimed to have seen us with a poppet and it was found in a bin. What if Darcey's been trying to frame us all along? Making up the allegations about us to start with? But then, in a final reckless attempt to eradicate us all, she and her friends cast malefice on the whole school. On us! I only just survived!' Effie's voice reached a dramatic crescendo. 'The feather was a nice touch, don't you think? Inspired by Manda's possession many moons ago.'

Anna shuddered at the memory of Effie coughing up the feather. 'Eames will see through it. Why would Darcey cast malefice on the whole school when she's already winning?'

'Because witches are emotional creatures.' Effie's eyes turned cold. 'At least Eames thinks so and he can't abide doubt. If it exists . . . he will question himself and we have Peter to persuade him. *You* know better than anyone how persuasive Peter can be. He's earnt Eames's trust and his father's relationship with the WIPS won't hurt.'

Anna saw Effie's mad plan falling into place. She shook her head. 'We can't let the Juicers take the blame for us – we don't know what will happen to them!'

'Why not?' Effie spat, merciless. 'They deserve it! Darcey deserves it above all. Anyway, they've got enough money to wangle their way out of the whole thing. They'll be fine.'

'We don't know that! We don't know what the WIPS are planning for those they take!'

'Exactly! Which is why it can't be us. We *are* witches. Cursed witches. It's them or us!' Effie's voice rose harshly. 'We win or we lose.'

'You sound like Darcey,' Anna muttered with disgust. 'Life's just a game . . .'

'She's not wrong. She just hasn't realized the rules have changed, that the game is much bigger than we thought.'

'This *isn't* a game!' Anna's fingers curled. She wanted to wipe the smile from Effie's lips. 'I'll tell Eames. I'll tell him the truth.'

'Come on,' said Effie, unfazed. 'You're really going to turn yourself in knowing what's at stake for us? And Eames won't just hand over us –

he'll hand over all of us.' She looked at Anna directly, slowing her words with significance. 'Attis, too. And he'll try to save us . . . will try to take the blame or use magic against them. What will they do to him then? It's them or us. Them or *him*. The Juicers can be damned to Hel for all I care.'

Anna flailed among Effie's words, trying to search through the tangle of them, the tangle of Effie. 'How much of you is even real? How much is a lie?'

'I'm not really sure,' Effie replied, holding Anna's eyes. 'I warned you not to trust me.'

'You said you wanted to be my sister.'

'I do. I'm keeping you from getting hurt.'

'That's not the same thing,' Anna spat.

'Don't you see? If we pull this off, we'll be free, no longer suspects of witchcraft. We can keep fighting the WIPS, but on our own terms. Help the magical world from a place of strength.'

'The saviour Effie?' Anna didn't buy it. 'It's power and attention you crave, and you suck everyone in – you sucked me in. No more. I'm done with your *games*. We don't even know if this will work—'

Effie lowered her eyes. 'Well, I need your help to finish it . . .'

'*What* does that mean?'

'It's just . . . Peter, you know what he's like. He's only going to help us on one condition . . .'

Anna stilled, a heaviness wrapping around her heart so tight it hurt to beat. Her voice came out a shadow of itself. 'No.'

Effie looked back up at her, eyes hard. 'I just risked my life to save this coven. We all have to play our part.'

'I'm not going to be the condition.' Anna shook her head. 'I can't . . .'

'It's not real. Just make him believe you love him, that you want to be with him, and he'll save us all.'

'For how long? We'll be in his debt, under his power for the fore-seeable. *I'll* be under his power. No. I can't do it. I can't. Effie—' Anna could see it then, the vast complexity of Effie's game. 'It was you, wasn't it? You're the one who led Peter to the sewing room. You – you pulled Attis's nail out of the wall and tipped them off so they'd find us . . . so Peter would find out . . .'

'That we're witches, the wicked and damned.' Effie laughed bleakly. 'If he was ever going to be of any real use to us, he had to know. It was a gamble, but I counted on his obsession with you. Peter is prepared to accept your magical defects in return for your love. Attis can't know of the plan, of course. If he knew you didn't want to be with Peter, he'd never let it happen. You'll have to convince them both.'

Anna looked at the girl across the room and had the feeling of barely knowing her at all. Or, perhaps, she knew her too well and hadn't wanted to see it. She stared until Effie was forced to meet her eyes. 'You couldn't just win, could you? You have to take home the prize. Attis. At the cost of me.'

'I told you, I'm broken without him!' Effie snarled but Anna could hear the fear in it. Effie couldn't hide it from her any more. 'I can't let you take him from me.'

'I thought you were the bravest person I'd ever met.' Anna shook her head, her words slow and cold. 'But I see through it now. You're not brave – you're bored. You're not made of courage – but chaos. You don't burn because you're alive – you burn because you're afraid of the darkness, because if you don't keep burning through everything you might actually have to face yourself.' Anna leant closer and the room seemed to contract around them. 'Don't forget, Effie, I've seen inside you – I've felt your Hel and I know what lurks there, the void, that missing space you're running from. You only got out of Hel because of me or you'd still be there.'

Anna saw the cracks in Effie's mask fracture, but Anna wasn't done.

'You don't know how to love, only to control, just like *our* aunt. And fear propels you, just like it propelled her. She's not dead – she's *you*.'

Effie stared at Anna, breathing hard, her mask cracking as her lip trembled, but then she threw her hands up. 'I guess it's decided then. I'm the evil sister and you're the good one. You really ought to watch out. It means I'm the killer in this little curse scenario of ours.'

'I never said you were evil. Just scared.'

Anna could feel Effie's fury now. 'Oh, don't pretend you're so perfect. You're the one who began our curse, *sister*. Not me.' Her words caught Anna off guard and Effie jumped at Anna's moment of weakness. 'Oh yes. The *kiss*. I know all about the kiss. I was painted as the great betrayer . . . the one who slept with Peter . . . but it was your little kiss with Attis that set the ball rolling last year. He told me about it over the summer.' Effie waved a hand as if it were nothing. 'And you've had plenty of opportunity to tell me about it too . . . but I guess you thought you'd keep it to yourself. Do you want to lecture me about trust now?'

Anna winced at the accusation, at the truth she'd held back. Effie had known. She'd known all along. 'I didn't want to hurt you—'

'Please, save me the sob story. I'm not blaming you, I'm just asking you to stop pretending you're better than me, because you're not and you hate it.'

'I'm not like you! I'm not tricking Attis into loving me. Don't you think he deserves more than that?'

'I know what's best for him, I've known him all my life!' Effie roared.

'But he's not that person any more, is he?' Anna replied, knowing what it would do to her. 'He's changed, because he loves me now.'

Effie's eyes expanded with hatred. She turned from Anna and did not reply. The sound of the protestors raged outside.

They did not speak for several hours and then – the door opened. Peter stepped through. He ignored Effie and knelt down by Anna. 'How are you doing?'

Anna pulled back from him, hating his simpering concern. Was it real? 'I'm fine, no thanks to you and Effie. I hear you two have been busy.'

Peter frowned, throwing a look of ire at Effie. 'I'm not doing this for her. I'm doing it for you, Anna.'

'Framing others, how very noble.'

'There's no other way.' Peter's voice turned hard. 'Eames has to have his witches and it's working. He's changing his mind. Helped by the fact the Juicers have turned on one another – Olivia and Corinne have given in to his offers of confession and are claiming Darcey forced them into everything.'

Effie laughed. 'Of course.'

'I thought you believed in what you were doing,' Anna whispered.

'I do.' Anger crept into Peter's tone. 'I believe malefice is wrong, that it must be controlled, but I know it's not something you've chosen, Anna, and I know you've never caused harm.' He reached for her hand. 'This is the only way I can save you, but it's not a done deal yet. Eames is still suspicious and . . . it would be easy to sway him back to all of you.' His grip tightened imperceptibly, but enough to make the threat clear. 'I need to know that you're on board with this, with *me*. That you want us to be together at the end of all this.'

His blue eyes, so steady and earnest. *A lie.* He knew exactly what he was asking, exactly what he was doing. He'd gone behind her back with Effie to make sure she had no choice in the matter.

Effie had turned away, but her warning was still going around in Anna's head. If they were taken by the WIPS, Attis wouldn't go easily or he'd try to direct it all onto himself. *What will they do to him then . . . ?*

She looked up at Peter. 'Of course.' Her voice was flat. *Did it even matter?* Peter just wanted her to play the game. 'Of course I want to be with you. The way you love me, in spite of what I am, in spite of my affliction. I'm forever in your debt.'

He pulled her closer. Ran a finger down her cheek, along the curve of her jaw. He tilted her face up and leant down to kiss her. Anna closed her eyes and tried to escape from every moment of it.

Peter pulled away, smiling. 'I'm glad you've made the right decision. Once this is all over, we can be together at last.'

He left. Anna and Effie stewed in the dark silence of the room, in the blood that ran through their veins. Anna knew now, no matter what happened, she would not be free. Effie's plan kept her trapped. Trapped by Peter. Trapped by the curse.

Perhaps Effie loved her, perhaps she didn't. Perhaps Effie was broken, or perhaps she relished what she'd done. Perhaps she truly believed she was stronger than the curse, while letting it destroy them. Anna didn't care any more. She didn't need to understand Effie, she didn't need to know her sister. She just wanted to get away from her. Forever.

'You think you've won,' Anna said, her voice emotionless, 'but you haven't. The curse is the only winner here.'

After a while, the noise began to escalate outside, the protestors speeding up their chants, excited. Anna and Effie went to separate windows and looked down. Vehicles were arriving – a row of cars, vans, driving up the hill towards the school . . .

The door to their room opened. The secretary slipped inside.

'What's going on?' Effie hissed.

The secretary, stone-faced, looked at them with disbelief. 'I don't know how you've done it, but Eames has informed the WIPS that Darcey and those other girls are responsible for all of it.'

'YES!' Effie's fist grasped the air.

'You're not off the hook yet.' The secretary looked to the door and back again. A nervous, rabbity twitch.

'What's happening outside?' said Anna with growing foreboding.

'Since Eames passed on his decision . . .' The secretary's eyes shifted. 'There's been a change of plan. The WIPS have decided to come today. Now. That's them outside, Hopkins and his Watchers.'

Anna moved towards her. 'What? No! Next week. They're not coming until next week.'

'They've brought it forwards.'

Anna stilled, trying to make sense of it through the shock.

Effie pushed past her. 'But they're coming for the others, right? Darcey, Corinne and Olivia?'

'Yes.' The secretary nodded. 'They will be paraded in front of the press: *the Witches of St Olave's*. Hopkins is due to give a speech. A great victory for the WIPS. But, behind closed doors.' She bit her lip. 'They've informed us that they're taking you both too. It is why everything has been speeded up.'

Anna and Effie stared at her, locked in place by her words.

Then Effie veered towards her, railing. 'What do you mean? Why? Why?!'

The secretary stepped back, speaking fast, hiss and spittle. 'Because they've been informed you're cursed witches . . .' Her eyes flashed over them with surprise. 'They're not going to let you get away now, and it sounds like it suits them to take you privately, behind the scenes. I think they're intending on taking your friends too.'

Anna was falling all over again. 'Who told them?'

Jerry! She knew . . . she knew she should never have told him . . .

'A new member of the Penitent. A witch called Lyanna Withering. She's just joined and apparently informed them at once.'

Worse. For a moment the panic threatened to overtake Anna – the kind of throat-tightening panic only a Binder could induce. *Mrs Withering.* Anna had known she'd never let them be. But joining the Hunters? The Hunters were everything the Binders feared. It made no sense . . . but then it did . . . *didn't it?* It made complete sense. She fell back against the wall. The Binders had never cared about protecting witches, only punishing them. What better way to do that, than to join the enemy? Would Aunt have joined them too? *Probably.*

'I've put my neck out on the line for you here,' the secretary said quickly, glancing at the door again. 'I didn't have to come in here and tell you. In return, make sure you stick to our deal. Keep quiet about me.'

Anna pulled herself back from the edge of terror. 'You have to help us get out.'

The secretary shook her head. 'Too late.'

'Get us out of here!' Effie threatened. 'Or we tell!'

'How can I? It would damn me anyway. There's surveillance, prefects everywhere . . . Hopkins has just arrived with his own security team. His Watchers are a different level entirely. You will never get past them.'

Effie pushed her against the wall. 'Get. Us. Out.'

'We have ended the hysteria spell.' Anna spoke up from behind them. 'Did you know it was over?'

The secretary looked past Effie to Anna, eyes bulging. 'No . . .'

'You were wrong about the Hel witches; they decided to help after all.'

The secretary's hand moved unconsciously to her wrist where her Death Marks lay. She blinked a few times. 'You're lying.'

'I'm not. They assisted us in travelling to Hel.'

'You?' The secretary snorted, a sharp, derisive sound.

Anna raised her head and spoke a word – in the Language of the Dead.

The secretary's eyes almost jumped from their sockets then, her face giving way to shock – alarm – then fear. She pulled away from Effie, staggering back, looking at them as if they'd transformed before her eyes: from misguided schoolgirls to dangerous witches. Her mouth trembled. 'It makes no difference now . . . the Hunters will still win.'

'It makes every difference.' Anna stepped towards her, dispensing her words slowly as a knife carving rot from fruit. 'We've stopped any more people from dying at your hands. You owe us, Laura Wilmore. You owe your own soul. Because we have been to Hel and I can tell you – our shadows are waiting for us all.'

The secretary blanched.

'Tell Peter,' Anna commanded. 'Tell him we need to get out. Now.'

The secretary wobbled to the door, cringing. 'I'll – I'll do what I can.' She slipped back out, the key turning in the lock.

Effie kicked the door after her. 'She's not going to help us! We need to get ourselves out of here!'

The sounds of the protestors grew louder outside. They ran back to the windows to find they'd let them in – the protestors had entered the gates, they were lining up outside the school, forming a crowd. A waiting, baying crowd. The press were readying themselves for the big announcement.

Anna caught a glimpse of Hopkins – even larger than he'd seemed on screen – smiling and chatting with someone; his laugh looked like a roar.

'We have to go!' Effie yelled.

'We can't just *go*!' Anna cried. 'There are prefects everywhere!'

'We're fucking witches! We use magic! We kept all of Hel at bay, I think we can handle some schoolboys.'

'But they're people, not spirits! We've never done magic like that on people!'

'We don't have a lot of choice!'

Noise drew their attention back to the window. The protestors' chants had turned wild. Darcey, Olivia and Corinne were being forced through the front doors. Held for all to see. Paraded. Humiliated. The crowd spat and snarled and looked as if they would eat them alive.

Effie growled with frustration. 'It should be over! We should be free!'

Anna ripped her gaze away from the look of terror on the Juicers' faces and locked eyes with Effie. 'It's your fault we're still here at all. We have to get Rowan and Manda and send word to Attis.'

'I never suggested leaving them!' Effie snapped back. 'Rowan and Manda are being held in one of the rooms; we deal with the prefects and get them. Find our phones and contact Attis.'

Anna tried to think of alternative options. There were none. She nodded.

They ran to the door, breathing hard as they stared at each other and, for the briefest of moments, Anna felt that spark of connection between them. But then she remembered – it was broken now. Effie moved her hand to the handle and with a burst of magic the lock clicked open. They stepped out.

Two prefects were standing in the room outside.

One of them went to shout but Anna made a knotting motion with her hands just like Aunt had used to. Their tongues locked in their mouths. Effie formed the freeze symbol and the prefects halted mid-motion, their eyes still rolling about.

Effie and Anna rushed to the other room and threw it open but there was no one inside.

'Quick,' Effie shouted, and they ran down the stairs to the next floor of the Ebury wing.

Four prefects now. The boys ran at them—

Effie spun around and froze two. Anna threw her hands up, forming the symbol Attis had made them practise over and over – freezing them just before they reached her. They wouldn't have long. Anna ducked past them and sprinted to one of the classroom doors. She burst it open and Rowan flew out.

'What's going on?'

'The WIPS ... the WIPS are here—' Anna tried to get the words out. 'They know Effie and I are cursed. They're coming for us. All of us.'

'Oh Goddess—' Rowan's face fell apart but she managed to point to a door. 'Manda's in there.'

Effie burst it open. Manda was lolling against the wall on the far side of the room. 'Manda!' Effie ran over to her, shaking her. 'Manda!'

She coughed, coming around.

'We have to go, Manda.'

Manda's head nodded up and down. 'OK ... OK—'

Anna and Rowan ran over and they helped her to her feet. 'The WIPS are coming for us.'

'What?' Manda stuttered.

Effie put Manda's arm around her shoulder and dragged her towards the door. 'No time to explain, just – we're going—'

But it was too late, the prefects they'd frozen upstairs bundled into the room, free already. The other prefects were stirring from their magical chains too. The Coven of the Dark Moon gathered in the centre, back to back. Encircled. Anna could feel the threads of their magic stitching together, tight bonds, knowing exactly what to do – they cast their circles, holding them back. She could see now just how terrified the boys looked, almost relieved that they couldn't get to them.

'To the door!' Effie ordered.

But another voice raked through the fray. 'Do not move.'

The voice that had lived beneath Anna's skin all year.

The Inquisitor lurched into the room placing himself between them and the exit, dead eyes darting, trying to contain the chaos around him. 'Nobody is leaving.'

Effie threw the freeze symbol at him – but it did nothing. His necklace sat heavy around his neck, protecting him from *malefice*. They would have to go through him.

'The WIPS are here,' Eames stated. 'There's nowhere to go. Better to accept your fate.'

'Not sure that's better for us,' Effie spat.

'Not my concern. My job is to hand you over and I will not fail.'

'But you already have, haven't you?' Effie accused. 'You chose the wrong witches.'

Eames's fury finally got the better of him. He charged towards her but at that moment the door flew open – Attis and Tom stepped through.

Eames knocked Effie off her feet, grappling with her. Attis tried to run towards her but chaos broke out – three prefects rounding on Attis and Tom. Rowan threw out the freeze symbol stopping another. Anna tried to hold off the rest but Eames had clambered on top of Effie, reaching for her throat—

Anna darted free and tackled Eames to the floor but he threw her off and staggered back to his feet. As Anna tried to clamber up, a knife flew past her face, curved upwards and sliced into the shoulder pad of Eames's black suit, pinning it, and him, to the wall. Attis's hits-any-target blade.

'I could have put it through your heart if I'd wanted,' Attis raged, blasting the prefects away and running at Eames. He pulled the knife out and held Eames against the wall instead – Eames's suit was torn, his combed hair scuffed upright, his Adam's apple oscillating. He struggled to get free but Attis held him tight, all of his wrath focused on him. He tried to rip Eames's necklace off but it would not come free – an unbreakable chain. 'Do you even know what this is?' Attis roared. 'Magic! You're wearing magic around your neck!'

'LIES!' Eames snarled.

Attis held the pendant tight in his fist. 'The very people you're working for – the people who claim to be protecting everyone – are using malefice.'

'LIES!' Eames yelled again, as if he would put his fingers in his ears.

Attis pressed the pendant against Eames's cheek. Anna realized Attis had been heating the metal up in his palm. It sizzled into Eames's skin. Burning flesh. Eames screamed, a high shriek, and Attis lowered his face to Eames's. 'I hope you remember exactly how it feels to be branded.'

'Let's go! Now!' Anna yelled.

Attis pushed Eames away. Eames clutched his cheek, sliding down the wall. They darted through the room, past frozen and writhing prefects. The hallway outside was still clear. They turned quickly into the stairwell.

'Fuck. Fuck. Fuck,' said Tom over and over again. 'What am I doing?'

'What *are* we doing?' Attis hollered.

'Peter . . . Peter is arranging transport for escape.' Tom looked at his phone, hands shaking.

Attis's face contorted. 'Peter—'

'There's a back door on the west side of the school, out onto Belvoir Street,' said Anna. 'Tell him to meet us there.'

'Fuck. Fuck. Fuck.'

'Shut up, Tom!' Effie shouted.

'Hey! I'm saving you right now!'

'Doesn't mean you can't shut up!'

'I can hear people coming!' Rowan cried.

'OK.' Tom nodded. 'Let's go – let's go.'

They fled down the stairway – Attis carrying Manda – down to the ground floor of the school. They darted from corridor to corridor, checking around every corner, until the side door was ahead of them. They stopped, trying to catch their breaths, Manda looking as if she might pass out.

Peter burst through the door. 'Stay inside!' he barked. 'The WIPS have just entered the main school and we won't have long until they circle the whole place. My father has agreed to help.'

Attis grabbed Peter. 'Why the hell is your father helping us?'

'Because I begged him,' Peter spat back. 'He'd do anything for me and I'm saving you. You don't have a lot of choice, do you?'

Attis growled, slamming Peter against the wall but letting him go.

'He's sending cars. They will arrive any minute. Anna is to go in one and the rest of you in the other.'

Attis spun back around. 'No. No way. We stick together.'

Peter held Attis's gaze confidently. 'There's not enough room.'

'Bullshit!' Attis towered over him.

'I'll go with Anna,' Rowan offered.

'No.' Peter's voice brooked no argument. 'It's been arranged. It's this way or no way, I'm afraid. Anna agrees.'

They all turned to her.

'Yes,' she said, not looking at Attis, forcing the words. 'It's all worked out.'

Peter nodded, victorious. 'Stay here. Don't move. I'll be back for you all in a moment.' He shut the door, leaving them in the corridor. Anna would be going with him. *Alone. Why alone?*

'Fuck. Fuck. Fuck,' said Tom again. 'Am I going on the run with witches? I can't believe I'm doing this – I – I—'

'Why *are* you doing this?' Rowan asked.

'Because, Peter – Peter—' He could barely speak. 'Peter said the WIPS were going to take you and – I – I don't think they're the good guys any more—'

'No shit, Sherlock,' Effie seethed.

'Anna.' Attis was beside her. She didn't look up at him. She couldn't. 'Can we talk?'

He took her arm and pulled her down the corridor away from the others, Effie's eyes following them.

'Attis, there's no time for this,' Anna cried. 'We have to go.'

'You can't go with him!'

'I want to,' she said but he looked as if he didn't buy it.

'You don't have to do this.'

She needed him to believe her. She met his eyes and almost broke – his were too full of confusion and pain. 'I trust Peter.' She blinked to keep the tears from her own eyes. 'You know he and I have grown close again and – and – yes, I love you, Attis, of course. It's fated. It's overpowering. It's our curse.' She made it sound inevitable, inconsequential. 'But I love Peter too. It's different with him, easier, safer . . .'

Attis shook his head, the maps of his eyes entirely lost. 'I don't understand.'

'You do, more than anyone. You love two people as well, don't you?' She held his gaze, fighting everything inside of her so that he wouldn't see. He couldn't see. Aunt had taught her to hide herself well. 'Don't contain me now.'

His arm fell away. 'Where's he taking you?'

She didn't know. 'We're all ending up in the same place. He's helping us escape, he's been on our side since he found out we were all witches.

He loves me. We need to trust him and we have to go.' She moved away.

'Anna—' She heard his voice, just the way it had sounded in Hel. Pleading, desperate, broken. Without its fire.

She didn't look back.

Effie was still staring but Anna did not look at her. She never wanted to look at her again.

Peter came through the door. 'It's time.' He grabbed Anna's arm, tight. 'Anna, you go in the car on the left. The rest of you the other. They'll take you somewhere safe.'

'You're not coming?' Anna frowned.

'I'll meet you later. I have to go back to Eames so he doesn't suspect I'm in on this. The school CCTV was deactivated half an hour ago, they'll think you all did it – messed with it. It'll allow me to slip back in. It's better I remain on the inside, for all of us.'

Attis fumed beneath his breath.

'Too late for me . . .' Tom muttered. 'Fuck.'

'Anna first,' Peter commanded. 'Go.'

Anna was thrust outside, into the daylight. She made for the car on the left. It was dark-windowed, anonymous.

Movement flickered to the side of her eyeline. Figures appeared around the building. Not prefects . . . but men, muscular and powerful, clad in black with silver necklaces swinging about their necks. Hopkins's Watchers. *Protected from magic.*

The door to Anna's car opened. Reiss Nowell was inside. 'GET IN, ANNA!' He reached for her—

But the figures were too close to the others – running towards them as they fled for the car. Tom careered into the front seat. Attis helped Manda in while Effie ran around the other side with Rowan.

Effie jumped in but Rowan – Rowan tripped and fell—

'No!' Anna went to run for her but Reiss grabbed her arm. 'INSIDE!'

As Rowan got up, one of the Watchers seized her. She cried out, struggling against him. Anna flailed against Reiss, turning to him, about to do magic when he hissed at her, 'Submit or I will instruct the other car to leave them all.'

Anna hesitated.

Effie had leapt back out of the car. Attis raced around the other side – but Rowan was dragged back as more Watchers charged around the corner. *Too many.*

'GO!' Rowan screamed. 'GO!'

Attis hesitated too.

Then, he grabbed Effie – a kicking and roaring Effie – and threw her in the car, jumping in after her as Reiss yanked Anna into their car.

The doors shut.

'NO!' Anna banged against the window. 'NO!

They raced off.

Anna watched Rowan through the back window. Surrounded.

It had all happened so fast.

Rowan.

All in.

All in—

One left behind.

Anna fell forwards unleashing a scream. A scream that could rip open Hel all over again. A scream made not of fear, but of love. Love – frayed, severed, torn in all directions.

Holding on by a thread, still.

The government welcome the WIPS in bold anti-malefice move

The Witchcraft Inquisitorial and Prevention Services will now operate as an official governmental organization. They will be working closely with various government departments to more effectively monitor and target incidents of malefice and to ensure the safety of the British public during this time of instability.

Halden Kramer, Head of Communications for WIPS, welcomes the move: 'We believe this partnership couldn't come soon enough. This collaboration is a significant step towards tackling the threats we all face. The government and our Prime Minister have listened to the cries of the people and responded with action, placing their faith in our expertise.'

WIPS Lead Inquisitor, Marcus Hopkins, adds: 'This month we have moved forward with several of our ongoing investigations, detaining a number of suspects of witchcraft. This step allows us to respond swiftly to neutralize any potential threats and prevent harm to the public while the investigations continue.

'Thanks to our efforts, we have seen a marked downturn in episodes of hysteria across the capital. And yet, the situation remains precarious. We are inundated with fresh suspicions of malefice on a daily basis. While witches remain among us, every citizen remains in danger.

'Developed in collaboration with the government, we will be launching a new app over the coming months, which will empower citizens to report suspected cases of witchcraft quickly and anonymously. Together, we can stop the spread.'

ACKNOWLEDGEMENTS

Writing *Shadowstitch* was such a different experience from *Threadneedle*. There was the pressure of a publishing deal, I had a newborn who didn't sleep, COVID had struck and I was going through my own personal struggles; my own shadows to be faced. Throughout the ups and downs – and sleepless nights – my husband, James, has been my anchor, helping me with the practical challenges of our busy lives but also believing in me throughout, even those days when I didn't believe in myself. I also have to thank his love of maps and knowledge of London's underground network, without which I wouldn't have been able to complete my London Necropolis Railway map. I think he was even more excited about it than I was.

I want to thank my family for everything. My parents, Elizabeth and James, who I really couldn't have written this book without. Not only their ongoing love and encouragement, but their tireless help and dedication that has made it possible for me to be both a mother and an author. For that I can never thank them enough. Rowan's family Christmas is a nod to my own Christmases at home and, yes, my mum does like big baubles.

To my sister, Ffion, for her early feedback on *Shadowstitch* and helping me understand TikTok, despite my struggle to 'not get weird' in almost every single video. My brother, Rhodri and his wife Lily, for buying a house with a small woods in the garden just so I can hang out there. I'm not sure this was their number one reason, but I'm taking it. And my brother's endless sarcasm which always keeps me on my comedic toes.

To my husband's parents, Anthea and Nick, who always have a welcoming, second home waiting for us in London whenever we need it and who have helped us copiously with childcare, allowing me to get out and about into the city when I need to. And James's sister and brother-in-law, Sophie and Owain, who are so generous with their time and on hand if we need help with anything.

To my Uncle Roger for championing *Threadneedle* everywhere he goes including being the first owner (and creator) of a *Threadneedle* t-shirt. And my Auntie Marion who has bought so many copies of my books I can't count.

To all of my friends who have spread the word of my books far and wide, displayed them proudly on their shelves, held book clubs for me and have even threatened to dress up as a needle and thread for various literary festivals. For always being there to laugh with. You all know who you are, my wild, cackling witches.

To the early readers of *Shadowstitch* – Jayne Ebury, Melissa Magment, Alison Palmer-Quinn and Katie Makey. Again, your notes have been vital in shaping *Shadowstitch* and your feedback gave me the confidence to believe in this book as much as *Threadneedle*.

To my agent, Alice Lutyens, for not panicking when I told her how long the book was and continuing to believe in and fight for this series every step of the way. And the wider team at Curtis Brown whose work has seen *Threadneedle* translated into many languages across the world.

To my incredible team at Harper Voyager – as well as the extended teams in the US, Canada and Australia – whose continued dedication, support and creativity have kept me inspired throughout. To my editors, Natasha Bardon and Melissa Frain, for going through the lengthy and complex process of editing *Shadowstitch*. You've made it shine. And to Kate Fogg for bringing the book together with all of its special details. A shout out to Robyn Watts for finding so many unique ways to bring my books to life, and Andrew Davis for providing me with yet another sensational cover.

To all of the bookshops and booksellers who have championed me from Waterstones, to Goldsboro, to my local independents. Getting to see my books in the windows across Wales and the rest of the UK has been a dream come true.

To all the readers, influencers, supporters – my threaders – your love for the series has made the journey so much fun. I always love hearing from you and still pinch myself that people are actually out there reading my words.

And to Serla Rusli, who penned my beautiful reader letter with her incredible handwriting.

Finally, to my nieces and nephews – Llio, Dylan and Eily – who remain my coolest fans. And my son, Taliesin, who made every practical step of writing this book difficult, but whose very existence in the world propels me to keep writing, keep inspiring, keep imagining. He also already believes I'm part witch so this is encouraging.